IS HE POPENJOY?

Anthony Trollope 1815-1882

Cover Painting:

"Too Early" by James Jacques Joseph Tissot, 1873.

Cover Design Copyright © 2009 by Vera Nazarian

ISBN-13: 978-1-60762-057-0
ISBN-10: 1-60762-057-X

First Publication: 1878
Edition transcribed from:
London: Chapman & Hall, 193, Piccadilly. 1879.
London: Bradbury, Agnew, & Co., Printers, Whitefriars

Reprint Trade Paperback Edition

October 2009

A Publication of
Norilana Books
P. O. Box 2188
Winnetka, CA 91396
www.norilana.com

Printed in the United States of America

Is He Popenjoy?

Norilana Books
Classics

www.norilana.com

Is He Popenjoy?

Anthony Trollope

Contents

Is He Popenjoy?

Chapter I.

Introductory.—Number One.

I would that it were possible so to tell a story that a reader should beforehand know every detail of it up to a certain point, or be so circumstanced that he might be supposed to know. In telling the little novelettes of our life, we commence our narrations with the presumption that these details are borne in mind, and though they be all forgotten, the stories come out intelligible at last. "You remember Mary Walker. Oh yes, you do;—that pretty girl, but such a queer temper! And how she was engaged to marry Harry Jones, and said she wouldn't at the church-door, till her father threatened her with bread and water; and how they have been living ever since as happy as two turtle-doves down in Devonshire,—till that scoundrel, Lieutenant Smith, went to Bideford! Smith has been found dead at the bottom of a saw-pit. Nobody's sorry for him. She's in a madhouse at Exeter; and Jones has disappeared, and couldn't have had more than thirty shillings in his pocket." This is quite as much as anybody ought to want to know previous to the unravelling of the tragedy of the Jones's. But such stories as those I have to tell cannot be written after that fashion. We novelists are constantly twitted with being long; and to the gentlemen who condescend to review us, and who take up our volumes with a view to business rather than pleasure, we must be infinite in length and tedium. But the story must be made intelligible from the beginning, or the real novel readers will not like it. The plan of jumping at once into the middle has been often tried, and sometimes seductively enough for a chapter or two; but the writer still has to hark back, and to begin again from the beginning,—not always very comfortably after the abnormal brightness of his few opening pages; and the reader who is then involved in some ancient family history, or long local explanation, feels himself to have been defrauded. It is as though one were asked to eat boiled mutton after woodcocks, caviar, or macaroni cheese. I hold that it is better to have the boiled mutton first, if boiled mutton there must be.

The story which I have to tell is something in its nature akin to that of poor Mrs. Jones, who was happy enough down in Devonshire till that wicked Lieutenant Smith came and persecuted her; not quite so tragic, perhaps, as it is stained neither by murder nor madness. But before I can hope to interest readers in the perplexed details of the life of a not unworthy lady, I must do more than remind them that they do know, or might have known, or should have known the antecedents of my personages. I must let them understand how it came to pass that so pretty, so pert, so gay, so good a girl as Mary Lovelace, without any great fault on her part, married a man so grim, so gaunt, so sombre, and so old as Lord George Germain. It will not suffice to say that she had done so. A hundred and twenty little incidents must be dribbled into the reader's intelligence, many of them, let me hope, in such manner that he shall himself be insensible to the process. But unless I make each one of them understood and appreciated by my ingenious, open-hearted, rapid reader,—by my reader who will always have his fingers impatiently ready to turn the page,—he will, I know, begin to masticate the real kernel of my story with infinite prejudices against Mary Lovelace.

Mary Lovelace was born in a country parsonage; but at the age of fourteen, when her life was in truth beginning, was transferred by her father to the deanery of Brotherton. Dean Lovelace had been a fortunate man in life. When a poor curate, a man of very humble origin, with none of what we commonly call Church interest, with nothing to recommend him but a handsome person, moderate education, and a quick intellect, he had married a lady with a considerable fortune, whose family had bought for him a living. Here he preached himself into fame. It is not at all to be implied from this that he had not deserved the fame he acquired. He had been active and resolute in his work, holding opinions which, if not peculiar, were at any rate advanced, and never being afraid of the opinions which he held. His bishop had not loved him, nor had he made himself dear to the bench of bishops generally. He had the reputation of having been in early life a sporting parson. He had written a book which had been characterised as tending to infidelity, and had more than once been invited to state dogmatically what was his own belief. He had never quite done so, and had then been made a dean. Brotherton, as all the world knows, is a most interesting little city, neither a Manchester nor a Salisbury; full of architectural excellencies, given to literature, and fond of hospitality. The Bishop of Brotherton,—who did not love the dean,—was not a general favourite, being strict, ascetic, and utterly hostile to all compromises. At first there were certain hostile passages between him and the new dean. But the Dean, who was and is urbanity itself, won the day, and soon became certainly the most popular man in Brotherton. His wife's fortune doubled his clerical income, and he lived in all respects as a dean ought to live. His wife had died very shortly after his promotion, and he had been left with one only daughter on whom to lavish his cares and his affection.

Now we must turn for a few lines to the family of Lord George Germain. Lord George was the brother of the Marquis of Brotherton, whose family residence was at Manor Cross, about nine miles from the city. The wealth of the family of the Germains was not equal to their rank, and the circumstances of the family were not made more comfortable by the peculiarities of the present marquis. He was an idle, self-indulgent, ill-conditioned man, who found that it suited his tastes better to live in Italy, where his means were ample, than on his own property, where he would have been comparatively a poor man. And he had a mother and four sisters, and a brother with whom he would hardly have known how to deal had he remained at Manor Cross. As it was, he allowed them to keep the house, while he simply took the revenue of the estate. With the marquis I do not know that it will be necessary to trouble the reader much at present. The old marchioness and her daughters lived always at Manor Cross in possession of a fine old house in which they could have entertained half the county, and a magnificent park,—which, however, was let for grazing up to the garden-gates,—and a modest income unequal to the splendour which should have been displayed by the inhabitants of Manor Cross.

And here also lived Lord George Germain, to whom at a very early period of his life had been entrusted the difficult task of living as the head of his family with little or no means for the purpose. When the old Marquis died,—very suddenly, and soon after the Dean's coming to Brotherton,—the widow had her jointure, some two thousand a year, out of the property, and the younger children had each a small settled sum. That the four ladies,—Sarah, Alice, Susanna, and Amelia,—should have sixteen thousand pounds among them, did not seem to be so very much amiss to those who knew how poor was the Germain family; but what was Lord George to do with four thousand pounds, and no means of earning a shilling? He had been at Eton, and had taken a degree at Oxford with credit, but had gone into no profession. There was a living in the family, and both father and mother had hoped that he would consent to take orders; but he had declined to do so, and there had seemed to be nothing for him but to come and live at Manor Cross. Then the old Marquis had died, and the elder brother, who had long been abroad, remained abroad. Lord George, who was the youngest of the family, and at that time about five-and-twenty, remained at Manor Cross, and became not only ostensibly but in very truth the managing head of the family.

He was a man whom no one could despise, and in whom few could find much to blame. In the first place he looked his poverty in the face, and told himself that he was a very poor man. His bread he might earn by looking after his mother and sisters, and he knew no other way in which he could do so. He was a just steward, spending nothing to gratify his own whims, acknowledging on all sides that he had nothing of his own, till some began to think that he was almost proud of his poverty. Among the ladies of the family, his mother and sisters, it was of course said that George must marry money. In such a position there is nothing else that the younger son of a marquis can do. But Lord George was a person somewhat difficult of instruction in such a matter. His mother was greatly afraid of him. Among his sisters Lady Sarah alone dared to say much to him; and even to her teaching on this subject he turned a very deaf ear. "Quite so, George," she said; "quite so. No man with a spark of spirit would marry a woman for her money,"—and she laid a great stress on the word "for,"—"but I do not see why a lady who has money should be less fit to be loved than one who has none. Miss Barm is a most charming young woman, of excellent manners, admirably educated, if not absolutely handsome, quite of distinguished appearance, and she has forty thousand pounds. We all liked her when she was here." But there came a very black frown upon Lord George's brow, and then even Lady Sarah did not dare to speak again in favour of Miss Barm.

Then there came a terrible blow. Lord George Germain was in love with his cousin, Miss De Baron! It would be long to tell, and perhaps unnecessary, how that young lady had made herself feared by the ladies of Manor Cross. Her father, a man of birth and fortune, but not perhaps with the best reputation in the world, had married a Germain of the last generation, and lived, when in the country, about twenty miles from Brotherton. He was a good deal on the turf, spent much of his time at card-playing clubs, and was generally known as a fast man. But he paid his way, had never put himself beyond the pale of society, and was, of course, a gentleman. As to Adelaide de Baron, no one doubted her dash, her wit, her grace, or her toilet. Some also gave her credit for beauty; but there were those who said that, though she would behave herself decently at Manor Cross and houses of that class, she could be loud elsewhere. Such was the lady whom Lord George loved, and it may be conceived that this passion was distressing to the ladies of Manor Cross. In the first place, Miss De Baron's fortune was doubtful and could not be large; and then—she certainly was not such a wife as Lady Brotherton and her daughters desired for the one male hope of the family.

But Lord George was very resolute, and for a time it seemed to them all that Miss de Baron,—of whom the reader will see much if he go through with our story,—was not unwilling to share the poverty of her noble lover. Of Lord George personally something must be said. He was a tall, handsome, dark-browed man, silent generally and almost gloomy, looking, as such men do, as though he were always revolving deep things in his mind, but revolving in truth things not very deep,—how far the money would go, and whether it would be possible to get a new pair of carriage-horses for his mother. Birth and culture had given to him a look of intellect greater than he possessed; but I would not have it thought that he traded on this or endeavoured to seem other than he was. He was simple, conscientious, absolutely truthful, full of prejudices, and weak-minded. Early in life he had been taught to entertain certain ideas as to religion by those with whom he had lived at college, and had therefore refused to become a clergyman. The bishop of the diocese had attacked him; but, though weak, he was obstinate. The Dean and he had become friends, and so he had learned to think himself in advance of the world. But yet he knew himself to be a backward, slow, unappreciative man. He was one who could bear reproach from no one else, but who never praised himself even to himself.

But we must return to his love, which is that which now concerns us. His mother and sisters altogether failed to persuade him. Week after week he went over to Baronscourt, and at last threw himself at Adelaide's feet. This was five years after his father's death, when he was already thirty years old. Miss De Baron, though never a favourite at Manor Cross, knew intimately the history of the family. The present marquis was over forty, and as yet unmarried;—but then Lord George was absolutely a pauper. In that way she might probably become a marchioness; but then of what use would life be to her, should she be doomed for the next twenty years to live simply as one of the ladies of Manor Cross? She consulted her father, but he seemed to be quite indifferent, merely reminding her that though he would be ready to do everything handsomely for her wedding, she would have no fortune till after his death. She consulted her glass, and told herself that, without self-praise, she must regard herself as the most beautiful woman of her own acquaintance. She consulted her heart, and found that in that direction she need not trouble herself. It would be very nice to be a marchioness, but she certainly was not in love with Lord George. He was handsome, no doubt—very handsome; but she was not sure that she cared much for men being handsome. She liked men that "had some go in them," who were perhaps a little fast, and who sympathised with her own desire for amusement. She could not bring herself to fall in love with Lord George. But then, the rank of a marquis is very high! She told Lord George that she must take time to consider.

When a young lady takes time to consider she has, as a rule, given way, Lord George felt it to be so, and was triumphant. The ladies at Manor Cross thought that they saw what was coming, and were despondent. The whole county declared that Lord George was about to marry Miss De Baron. The county feared that they would be very poor; but the recompence would come at last, as the present marquis was known not to be a marrying man. Lady Sarah was mute with despair. Lady Alice had declared that there was nothing for them but to make the best of it. Lady Susanna, who had high ideas of aristocratic duty, thought that George was forgetting himself. Lady Amelia, who had been snubbed by Miss De Baron, shut herself up and wept. The Marchioness took to her bed. Then, exactly at the same time, two things happened, both of which were felt to be of vital importance at Manor Cross. Miss De Baron wrote a most determined refusal to her lover, and old Mr. Tallowax died. Now old Mr. Tallowax had been Dean Lovelace's father-in-law, and had never had a child but she who had been the Dean's wife.

Lord George did in truth suffer dreadfully. There are men to whom such a disappointment as this causes enduring physical pain,—as though they had become suddenly affected with some acute and yet lasting disease. And there are men, too, who suffer the more because they cannot conceal the pain. Such a man was Lord George. He shut himself up for months at Manor Cross, and would see no one. At first it was his intention to try again, but very shortly after the letter to himself came one from Miss De Baron to Lady Alice, declaring that she was about to be married immediately to one Mr. Houghton; and that closed the matter. Mr. Houghton's history was well known to the Manor Cross family. He was a friend of Mr. De Baron, very rich, almost old enough to be the girl's father, and a great gambler. But he had a house in Berkeley Square, kept a stud of horses in Northamptonshire, and was much thought of at Newmarket. Adelaide De Baron explained to Lady Alice that the marriage had been made up by her father, whose advice she had thought it her duty to take. The news was told to Lord George, and then it was found expedient never to mention further the name of Miss De Baron within the walls of Manor Cross.

But the death of Mr. Tallowax was also very important. Of late the Dean of Brotherton had become very intimate at Manor Cross. For some years the ladies had been a little afraid of him, as they were by no means given to free opinions. But he made his way. They were decidedly high; the bishop was notoriously low; and thus, in a mild manner, without malignity on either side, Manor Cross and the Palace fell out. Their own excellent young clergyman was snubbed in reference to his church postures, and Lady Sarah was offended. But the Dean's manners were perfect. He never trod on any one's toes. He was rich, and as far as birth went, nobody,—but he knew how much was due to the rank of the Germains. In all matters he obliged them, and had lately made the deanery very pleasant to Lady Alice,—to whom a widowed canon at Brotherton was supposed to be partial. The interest between the deanery and Manor Cross was quite close; and now Mr. Tallowax had died leaving the greater part of his money to the Dean's daughter.

When a man suffers from disappointed love he requires consolation. Lady Sarah boldly declared her opinion,—in female conclave of course,—that one pretty girl is as good to a man as another, and might be a great deal better if she were at the same time better mannered and better dowered than the other. Mary Lovelace, when her grandfather died, was only seventeen. Lord George was at that time over thirty. But a man of thirty is still a young man, and a girl of seventeen may be a young woman. If the man be not more than fifteen years older than the woman the difference of age can hardly be regarded as an obstacle. And then Mary was much loved at Manor Cross. She had been a most engaging child, was clever, well-educated, very pretty, with a nice sparkling way, fond of pleasure no doubt, but not as yet instructed to be fast. And now she would have at once thirty thousand pounds, and in course of time would be her father's heiress.

All the ladies at Manor Cross put their heads together,—as did also Mr. Canon Holdenough, who, while these things had been going on, had been accepted by Lady Alice. They fooled Lord George to the top of his bent, smoothing him down softly amidst the pangs of his love, not suggesting Mary Lovelace at first, but still in all things acting in that direction. And they so far succeeded that within twelve months of the marriage of Adelaide De Baron to Mr. Houghton, when Mary Lovelace was not yet nineteen and Lord George was thirty-three, with some few grey hairs on his handsome head, Lord George did go over to the deanery and offer himself as a husband to Mary Lovelace.

Chapter II.

Introductory Number Two.

"What ought I to do, papa?" The proposition was in the first instance made to Mary through the Dean. Lord George had gone to the father, and the father with many protestations of personal goodwill, had declared that in such a matter he would not attempt to bias his daughter. "That the connection would be personally agreeable to myself, I need hardly say," said the Dean. "For myself, I have no objection to raise. But I must leave it to Mary. I can only say that you have my permission to address her." But the first appeal to Mary was made by her father himself, and was so made in conformity with his own advice. Lord George, when he left the deanery, had thus arranged it, but had been hardly conscious that the Dean had advised such an arrangement. And it may be confessed between ourselves,—between me and my readers, who in these introductory chapters may be supposed to be looking back together over past things,—that the Dean was from the first determined that Lord George should be his son-in-law. What son-in-law could he find that would redound more to his personal credit, or better advance his personal comfort. As to his daughter, where could a safer husband be found! And then she might in this way become a marchioness! His own father had kept livery stables at Bath. Her other grandfather had been a candlemaker in the Borough. "What ought I to do, papa?" Mary asked, when the proposition was first made to her. She of course admired the Germains, and appreciated, at perhaps more than its full value the notice she had received from them. She had thought Lord George to be the handsomest man she had ever seen. She had heard of his love for Miss De Baron, and had felt for him. She was not as yet old enough to know how dull was the house at Manor Cross, or how little of resource she might find in the companionship of such a man as Lord George. Of her own money she knew almost nothing. Not as yet had her fortune become as a carcase to the birds. And now, should she decide in Lord George's favour, would she be saved at any rate from that danger.

"You must consult your own feelings, my dear," said her father. She looked up to him in blank dismay. She had as yet no feelings.

"But, papa—"

"Of course, my darling, there is a great deal to be said in favour of such a marriage. The man himself is excellent,—in all respects excellent. I do not know that there is a young man of higher principles than Lord George in the whole county."

"He is hardly a young man, papa."

"Not a young man! He is thirty. I hope you do not call that old. I doubt whether men in his position of life should ever marry at an earlier age. He is not rich."

"Would that matter?"

"No; I think not. But of that you must judge. Of course with your fortune you would have a right to expect a richer match. But though he has not money, he has much that money gives. He lives in a large house with noble surroundings. The question is whether you can like him?"

"I don't know, papa." Every word she spoke she uttered hesitatingly. When she had asked whether "that would matter," she had hardly known what she was saying. The thing was so important to her, and yet so entirely mysterious and as yet unconsidered, that she could not collect her thoughts sufficiently for proper answers to her father's sensible but not too delicate inquiries. The only ideas that had really struck her were that he was grand and handsome, but very old.

"If you can love him I think you would be happy," said the Dean. "Of course you must look at it all round. He will probably live to be the Marquis of Brotherton. From all that I hear I do not think that his brother is likely to marry. In that case you would be the Marchioness of Brotherton, and the property, though not great, would then be handsome. In the meanwhile you would be Lady George Germain, and would live at Manor Cross. I should stipulate on your behalf that you should have a house of your own in town, for, at any rate, a portion of the year. Manor Cross is a fine place, but you would find it dull if you were to remain there always. A married woman too should always have some home of her own."

"You want me to do it, papa?"

"Certainly not. I want you to please yourself. If I find that you please yourself by accepting this man, I myself shall be better pleased than if you please yourself by rejecting him; but you shall never know that by my manner. I shall not put you on bread and water, and lock you up in the garret either if you accept him, or if you reject him." The Dean smiled as he said this, as all the world at Brotherton knew that he had never in his life even scolded his daughter.

"And you, papa?"

"I shall come and see you, and you will come and see me. I shall get on well enough. I have always known that you would leave me soon. I am prepared for that." There was something in this which grated on her feelings. She had, perhaps, taught herself to believe that she was indispensable to her father's happiness. Then after a pause he continued: "Of course you must be ready to see Lord George when he comes again, and you ought to remember, my dear, that marquises do not grow on every hedge."

With great care and cunning workmanship one may almost make a silk purse out of a sow's ear, but not quite. The care which Dean Lovelace had bestowed upon the operation in regard to himself had been very great, and the cunning workmanship was to be seen in every plait and every stitch. But still there was something left of the coarseness of the original material. Of all this poor Mary knew nothing at all; but yet she did not like being told of marquises and hedges where her heart was concerned. She had wanted,—had unconsciously wanted,—some touch of romance from her father to satisfy the condition in which she found herself. But there was no touch of romance there; and when she was left to herself to work the matter out in her own heart and in her own mind she was unsatisfied.

Two or three days after this Mary received notice that her lover was coming. The Dean had seen him and had absolutely fixed a time. To poor Mary this seemed to be most unromantic, most unpromising. And though she had thought of nothing else since she had first heard of Lord George's intention, though she had laid awake struggling to make up her mind, she had reached no conclusion. It had become quite clear to her that her father was anxious for the marriage, and there was much in it which recommended it to herself. The old elms of the park of Manor Cross were very tempting. She was not indifferent to being called My Lady. Though she had been slightly hurt when told that marquises did not grow on hedges, still she knew that it would be much to be a marchioness. And the man himself was good, and not only good but very handsome. There was a nobility about him beyond that of his family. Those prone to ridicule might perhaps have called him Werter-faced, but to Mary there was a sublimity in this. But then was she in love with him?

She was a sweet, innocent, ladylike, high-spirited, joyous creature. Those struggles of her father to get rid of the last porcine taint, though not quite successful as to himself, had succeeded thoroughly in regard to her. It comes at last with due care, and the due care had here been taken. She was so nice that middle-aged men wished themselves younger that they might make love to her, or older that they might be privileged to kiss her. Though keenly anxious for amusement, though over head and ears in love with sport and frolic, no unholy thought had ever polluted her mind. That men were men, and that she was a woman, had of course been considered by her. Oh, that it might some day be her privilege to love some man with all her heart and all her strength, some man who should be, at any rate to her, the very hero of heroes, the cynosure of her world! It was thus that she considered the matter. There could surely nothing be so glorious as being well in love. And the one to be thus worshipped must of course become her husband. Otherwise would her heart be broken, and perhaps his,—and all would be tragedy. But with tragedy she had no sympathy. The loved one must become her husband. But the pictures she had made to herself of him were not at all like Lord George Germain. He was to be fair, with laughing eyes, quick in repartee, always riding well to hounds. She had longed to hunt herself, but her father had objected. He must be sharp enough sometimes to others, though ever soft to her, with a silken moustache and a dimpled chin, and perhaps twenty-four years old. Lord George was dark, his eyes never laughed; he was silent generally, and never went out hunting at all. He was dignified, and tall, very handsome, no doubt,—and a lord. The grand question was that;—could she love him? Could she make another picture, and paint him as her hero? There were doubtless heroic points in the side wave of that coal-black lock,—coal-black where the few grey hairs had not yet shown themselves, in his great height, and solemn polished manners.

When her lover came, she could only remember that if she accepted him she would please everybody. The Dean had taken occasion to assure her that the ladies at Manor Cross would receive her with open arms. But on this occasion she did not accept him. She was very silent, hardly able to speak a word, and almost sinking out of sight when Lord George endeavoured to press his suit by taking her hand. But she contrived at last to make him the very answer that Adelaide De Baron had made. She must take time to think of it. But the answer came from her in a different spirit. She at any rate knew as soon as it was given that it was her destiny in life to become Lady George Germain. She did not say "Yes" at the moment, only because it is so hard for a girl to tell a man that she will marry him at the first asking! He made his second offer by letter, to which the Dean wrote the reply:—

> "My dear Lord George,
>
>   "My daughter is gratified by your affection, and flattered by your manner of showing it. A few plain words are perhaps the best. She will be happy to receive you as her future husband, whenever it may suit you to come to the deanery.
>
>   "Yours affectionately,
>
>   "HENRY LOVELACE."

Immediately upon this the conduct of Lord George was unexceptionable. He hurried over to Brotherton, and as he clasped his girl in his arms, he told her that he was the happiest man in England. Poor as he was he made her a handsome present, and besought her if she had any mercy, any charity, any love for him, to name an early day. Then came the four ladies from Manor Cross,—for Lady Alice had already become Lady Alice Holdenough,—and caressed her, and patted her, and petted her, and told her that she should be as welcome as flowers in May. Her father, too, congratulated her with more of enthusiasm, and more also of demonstrated feeling than she had ever before seen him evince. He had been very unwilling, he said, to express any strong opinion of his own. It had always been his desire that his girl should please herself. But now that the thing was settled he could assure her of his thorough satisfaction. It was all that he could have desired; and now he would be ready at any time to lay himself down, and be at rest. Had his girl married a spendthrift lord, even a duke devoted to pleasure and iniquity, it would have broken his heart. But he would now confess that the aristocracy of the county had charms for him; and he was not ashamed to rejoice that his child should be accepted within their pale. Then he brushed a real tear from his eyes, and Mary threw herself into his arms. The tear was real, and in all that he said there was not an insincere word. It was to him a very glory of glories that his child should be in the way of becoming the Marchioness of Brotherton. It was even a great glory that she should be Lady George Germain. The Dean never forgot the livery stable, and owned day and night that God had been very good to him.

It was soon settled that Mary was to be allowed three months for preparation, and that the marriage was to be solemnized in June. Of course she had much to do in preparing her wedding garments, but she had before her a much more difficult task than that at which she worked most sedulously. It was now the great business of her life to fall in love with Lord George. She must get rid of that fair young man with the silky moustache and the darling dimple. The sallow, the sublime, and the Werter-faced must be made to take the place of laughing eyes and pink cheeks. She did work very hard, and sometimes, as she thought, successfully. She came to a positive conclusion that he was the handsomest man she ever saw, and that she certainly liked the few grey hairs. That his manner was thoroughly noble no one could doubt. If he were seen merely walking down the street he would surely be taken for a great man. He was one of whom, as her husband, she could be always proud;—and that she felt to be a great thing. That he would not play lawn tennis, and that he did not care for riding were points in his character to be regretted. Indeed, though she made some tenderly cautious inquiries, she could not find what were his amusements. She herself was passionately fond of dancing, but he certainly did not dance. He talked to her, when he did talk, chiefly of his family, of his own poverty, of the goodness of his mother and sisters, and of the great regret which they all felt that they should have been deserted by the head of their family.

"He has now been away," said Lord George, "for ten years; but not improbably he may return soon, and then we shall have to leave Manor Cross."

"Leave Manor Cross!"

"Of course we must do so should he come home. The place belongs to him, and we are only there because it has not suited him to reside in England."

This he said with the utmost solemnity, and the statement had been produced by the answer which the Marquis had made to a letter announcing to him his brother's marriage. The Marquis had never been a good correspondent. To the ladies of the house he never wrote at all, though Lady Sarah favoured him with a periodical quarterly letter. To his agent, and less frequently to his brother, he would write curt, questions on business, never covering more than one side of a sheet of notepaper, and always signed "Yours, B." To these the inmates of Manor Cross had now become accustomed, and little was thought of them; but on this occasion he had written three or four complete sentences, which had been intended to have, and which did have, a plain meaning. He congratulated his brother, but begged Lord George to bear in mind that he himself might not improbably want Manor Cross for his own purpose before long. If Lord George thought it would be agreeable, Mr. Knox, the agent, might have instructions to buy Miss Lovelace a present. Of this latter offer Lord George took no notice; but the intimation concerning the house sat gravely on his mind.

The Dean did exactly as he had said with reference to the house in town. Of course it was necessary that there should be arrangements as to money between him and Lord George, in which he was very frank. Mary's money was all her own,—

giving her an income of nearly £1500 per annum. The Dean was quite of opinion that this should be left to Lord George's management, but he thought it right as Mary's father to stipulate that his daughter should have a home of her own. Then he suggested a small house in town, and expressed an opinion that his daughter should be allowed to live there six months in the year. The expense of such a sojourn might be in some degree shared by himself if Lord George would receive him for a month or so in the spring. And so the thing was settled, Lord George pledging himself that the house should be taken. The arrangement was distasteful to him in many ways, but it did not seem to be unreasonable, and he could not oppose it. Then came the letter from the Marquis. Lord George did not consider himself bound to speak of that letter to the Dean; but he communicated the threat to Mary. Mary thought nothing about it, except that her future brother-in-law must be a very strange man.

During all those three months she strove very hard to be in love, and sometimes she thought that she had succeeded. In her little way she studied the man's character, and did all she could to ingratiate herself with him. Walking seemed to be his chief relaxation, and she was always ready to walk with him. She tried to make herself believe that he was profoundly wise. And then, when she failed in other things, she fell back upon his beauty. Certainly she had never seen a handsomer face, either on a man's shoulders or in a picture. And so they were married.

Now I have finished my introduction,—having married my heroine to my hero,—and have, I hope, instructed my reader as to those hundred and twenty incidents, of which I spoke—not too tediously. If he will go back and examine, he will find that they are all there. But perhaps it will be better for us both that he should be in quiet possession of them without any such examination.

Chapter III.

Life At Manor Cross.

The married couple passed their honeymoon in Ireland, Lady Brotherton having a brother, an Irish peer, who lent them for a few months his house on the Blackwater. The marriage, of course, was celebrated in the cathedral, and equally of course, the officiating clergymen were the Dean and Canon Holdenough. On the day before the marriage Lord George was astonished to find how rich a man was his father-in-law.

"Mary's fortune is her own," he said; "but I should like to give her something. Perhaps I had better give it to you on her behalf."

Then he shuffled a cheque for a thousand pounds into Lord George's hands. He moreover gave his daughter a hundred pounds in notes on the morning of the wedding, and thus acted the part of the benevolent father and father-in-law to a miracle. It may be acknowledged here that the receipt of the money removed a heavy weight from Lord George's heart. He was himself so poor, and at the same time so scrupulous, that he had lacked funds sufficient for the usual brightness of a wedding tour. He would not take his mother's money, nor lessen his own small patrimony; but now it seemed that wealth was showered on him from the deanery.

Perhaps a sojourn in Ireland did as well as anything could towards assisting the young wife in her object of falling in love with her husband. He would hardly have been a sympathetic companion in Switzerland or Italy, as he did not care for lakes or mountains. But Ireland was new to him and new to her, and he was glad to have an opportunity of seeing something of a people as to whom so little is really known in England. And at Ballycondra, on the Blackwater, they were justified in feeling a certain interest in the welfare of the tenants around them. There was something to be done, and something of which they could talk. Lord George, who couldn't hunt, and wouldn't dance, and didn't care for mountains, could enquire with some zeal how much wages a peasant might earn, and what he would do with it when earned. It interested him to learn that whereas an English labourer will certainly eat and drink his wages from week to week,—so that he could not be trusted to pay any sum half-yearly,—an Irish peasant, though he be half starving, will save his money for the rent. And Mary, at his instance, also cared for these things. It was her gift, as with many women, to be able to care for everything. It was, perhaps, her misfortune that she was apt to care too much for many things. The honeymoon in Ireland answered its purpose, and Lady George, when she came back to Manor Cross, almost thought that she had succeeded. She was at any rate able to assure her father that she had been as happy as the day was long, and that he was absolutely—"perfect."

This assurance of perfection the Dean no doubt took at its proper value. He patted his daughter's cheek as she made it, and kissed her, and told her that he did not doubt but that with a little care she might make herself a happy woman. The house in town had already been taken under his auspices, but of course was not to be inhabited yet.

It was a very small but a very pretty little house, in a quaint little street called Munster Court, near Storey's Gate, with a couple of windows looking into St. James's Park. It was now September, and London for the present was out of the question. Indeed, it had been arranged that Lord George and his wife should remain at Manor Cross till after Christmas. But the house had to be furnished, and the Dean evinced his full understanding of the duties of a father-in-law in such an emergency. This, indeed, was so much the case that Lord George became a little uneasy. He had the greater part of the thousand pounds left, which he insisted on expending,—and thought that that should have sufficed. But the Dean explained in his most cordial manner,—and no man's manner could be more cordial than the Dean's,—that Mary's fortune from Mr. Tallowax had been unexpected, that having had but one child he intended to do well by her, and that, therefore, he could now assist in starting her well in life without doing himself a damage. The house in this way was decorated and furnished, and sundry journeys up to London served to brighten the autumn which might otherwise have been dull and tedious.

At this period of her life two things acting together, and both acting in opposition to her anticipations of life, surprised the young bride not a little. The one was her father's manner of conversation with her, and the other was her husband's. The Dean had never been a stern parent; but he had been a clergyman, and as a clergyman he had inculcated a certain strictness of life,—a very modified strictness, indeed, but something more rigid than might have come from him had he been a lawyer or a country gentleman. Mary had learned that he wished her to attend the cathedral services, and to interest herself respecting them, and she had always done so. He had explained to her that, although he kept a horse for her to ride, he, as the Dean of Brotherton, did not wish her to be seen in the hunting field. In her dress, her ornaments, her books, her parties, there had been always something to mark slightly her clerical belongings. She had never chafed against this because she loved her father and was naturally obedient; but she had felt something perhaps of a soft regret. Now her father, whom she saw very frequently, never spoke to her of any duties. How should her house be furnished? In what way would she lay herself out for London society? What enjoyments of life could she best secure? These seemed to be the matters on which he was most intent. It occurred to her that when speaking to her of the house in London he never once asked her what church she would attend; and that when she spoke with pleasure of being so near the Abbey, he paid little or no attention to her remark. And then, too, she felt, rather than perceived, that in his counsels to her he almost intimated that she must have a plan of life different from her husband's. There were no such instructions given, but it almost seemed as though this were implied. He took it for granted that her life was to be gay and bright, though he seemed to take it also for granted that Lord George did not wish to be gay and bright.

All this surprised her. But it did not perhaps surprise her so much as the serious view of life which her husband from day to day impressed upon her. That hero of her early dreams, that man with the light hair and the dimpled chin, whom she had not as yet quite forgotten, had never scolded her, had never spoken a serious word to her, and had always been ready to provide her with amusements that never palled. But Lord George made out a course of reading for her,—so much for the two hours after breakfast, so much for the hour before dressing,—so much for the evening; and also a table of results to be acquired in three months,—in six months,—and so much by the close of the first year; and even laid down the sum total of achievements to be produced by a dozen years of such work! Of course she determined to do as he would have her do. The great object of her life was to love him; and, of course, if she really loved him, she would comply with his wishes. She began her daily hour of Gibbon after breakfast with great zeal. But there was present to her an idea that if the Gibbon had come from her father, and the instigations to amuse herself from her husband, it would have been better.

These things surprised her; but there was another matter that vexed her. Before she had been six weeks at Manor Cross she found that the ladies set themselves up as her tutors. It was not the Marchioness who offended her so much as her three sisters-in-law. The one of the family whom she had always liked best had been also liked best by Mr. Holdenough, and had gone to live next door to her father in the Close. Lady Alice, though perhaps a little tiresome, was always gentle and good-natured. Her mother-in-law was too much in awe of her own eldest daughter ever to scold anyone. But Lady Sarah could be very severe; and Lady Susanna could be very stiff; and Lady Amelia always re-echoed what her elder sisters said.

Lady Sarah was by far the worst. She was forty years old, and looked as though she were fifty and wished to be thought sixty. That she was, in truth, very good, no one either at Manor Cross or in Brotherton or any of the parishes around ever doubted. She knew every poor woman on the estate, and had a finger in the making of almost every petticoat worn. She spent next to nothing on herself, giving away almost all her own little income. She went to church whatever was the weather. She was never idle and never wanted to be amused. The place in the carriage which would naturally have been hers she had always surrendered to one of her sisters when there had been five ladies at Manor Cross, and now she surrendered again to her brother's wife. She spent hours daily in the parish school. She was doctor and surgeon to the poor people,—never sparing herself. But she was harsh-looking, had a harsh voice, and was dictatorial. The poor people had become used to her and liked her ways. The women knew that her stitches never gave way, and the men had a wholesome confidence in her medicines, her plasters, and her cookery. But Lady George Germain did not see by what right she was to be made subject to her sister-in-law's jurisdiction.

Church matters did not go quite on all fours at Manor Cross. The ladies, as has before been said, were all high, the Marchioness being the least exigeant in that particular, and Lady Amelia the most so. Ritual, indeed, was the one point of interest in Lady Amelia's life. Among them there was assent enough for daily comfort; but Lord George was in this respect, and in this respect only, a trouble to them. He never declared himself openly, but it seemed to them that he did not care much about church at all. He would generally go of a Sunday morning; but there was a conviction that he did so chiefly to oblige his mother. Nothing was ever said of this. There was probably present to the ladies some feeling, not uncommon, that religion is not so necessary for men as for women. But Lady George was a woman.

And Lady George was also the daughter of a clergyman. There was now a double connexion between Manor Cross and the Close at Brotherton. Mr. Canon Holdenough, who was an older man than the Dean, and had been longer known in the diocese, was a most unexceptional clergyman, rather high, leaning towards the high and dry, very dignified, and quite as big a man in Brotherton as the Dean himself. The Dean was, indeed, the Dean; but Mr. Holdenough was uncle to a baronet, and the Holdenoughs had been Holdenoughs when the Conqueror came. And then he also had a private income of his own. Now all this gave to the ladies at Manor Cross a peculiar right to be great in church matters,—so that Lady Sarah was able to speak with much authority to Mary when she found that the bride, though a Dean's daughter, would only go to two services a week, and would shirk one of them if the weather gave the slightest colouring of excuse.

"You used to like the cathedral services," Lady Sarah said to her, one day, when Mary had declined to go to the parish church, to sing the praises of St. Processus.

"That was because they were cathedral services," said Mary.

"You mean to say that you attended the House of God because the music was good!" Mary had not thought the subject over sufficiently to be enabled to say that good music is supplied with the object of drawing large congregations, so she only shrugged her shoulders. "I, too, like good music, dear; but I do not think the want of it should keep me from church." Mary again shrugged her shoulders, remembering, as she did so, that her sister-in-law did not know one tune from another. Lady Alice was the only one of the family who had ever studied music.

"Even your papa goes on Saints' days," continued Lady Sarah, conveying a sneer against the Dean by that word "even."

"Papa is Dean. I suppose he has to go."

"He would not go to church, I suppose, unless he approved of going."

The subject then dropped. Lady George had not yet arrived at that sort of snarling home intimacy, which would have justified her in telling Lady Sarah that if she wanted a lesson at all, she would prefer to take it from her husband.

The poor women's petticoats was another source of trouble. Before the autumn was over,—by the end of October,—when Mary had been two months at Manor Cross, she had been got to acknowledge that ladies living in the country should employ a part of their time in making clothes for the poor people; and she very soon learned to regret the acknowledgment. She was quickly driven into a corner by an assertion from Lady Sarah that, such being the case, the time to be so employed should be defined. She had intended to make something,— perhaps an entire petticoat,—at some future time. But Lady Sarah was not going to put up with conduct such as that. Mary had acknowledged her duty. Did she mean to perform it, or to neglect it? She made one petticoat, and then gently appealed to her husband. Did not he think that petticoats could be bought cheaper than they could be made? He figured it out, and found that his wife could earn three-halfpence a day by two hours' work; and even Lady Sarah did not require from her more than two hours daily. Was it worth while that she should be made miserable for ninepence a week,—less than £2 a-year? Lady George figured it out also, and offered the exact sum, £1 19*s.*, to Lady Sarah, in order that she might be let off for the first twelve months. Then Lady Sarah was full of wrath. Was that the spirit in which offerings were to be made to the Lord? Mary was asked, with stern indignation, whether in bestowing the work of her hands upon the people, whether in the very fact that she was doing for the poor that which was distasteful to herself, she did not recognise the performance of a duty? Mary considered a while, and then said that she thought a petticoat was a petticoat, and that perhaps the one made by the regular petticoat-maker would be the best. She did not allude to the grand doctrine of the division of labour, nor did she hint that she might be doing more harm than good by interfering with regular trade, because she had not studied those matters. But that was the line of her argument. Lady Sarah told her that her heart in that matter was as hard as a nether millstone. The young wife, not liking this, withdrew; and again appealed to her husband. His mind was divided on the subject. He was clearly of opinion that the petticoat should be obtained in the cheapest market, but he doubted much about that three-halfpence in two hours. It might be that his wife could not do better at present; but experience would come, and in that case, she would be obtaining experience as well as earning three-halfpence. And, moreover, petticoats made at Manor Cross would, he thought, undoubtedly be better than any that could be bought. He came, however, to no final decision; and Mary, finding herself every morning sitting in a great petticoat conclave, hardly had an alternative but to join it.

It was not in any spirit of complaint that she spoke on the subject to her father as the winter came on. A certain old Miss Tallowax had come to the deanery, and it had been thought proper that Lady George should spend a day or two there. Miss Tallowax, also, had money of her own, and even still owned a share in the business; and the Dean had pointed out, both to Lord George and his wife, that it would be well that they should be civil to her. Lord George was to come on the last day, and dine and sleep at the deanery. On this occasion, when the Dean and his daughter were alone together, she said something in a playful way about the great petticoat contest.

"Don't you let those old ladies sit upon you," said the Dean. He smiled as he spoke, but his daughter well knew, from his tone, that he meant his advice to be taken seriously.

"Of course, papa, I should like to accommodate myself to them as much as I can."

"But you can't, my dear. Your manner of life can't be their manner, nor theirs yours. I should have thought George would see that."

"He didn't take their part, you know."

"Of course he didn't. As a married woman you are entitled to have your own way, unless he should wish it otherwise. I don't want to make this matter serious; but if it is pressed, tell them that you do not care to spend your time in that way. They cling to old fashions. That is natural enough; but it is absurd to suppose that they should make you as old-fashioned as themselves."

He had taken the matter up quite seriously, and had given his daughter advice evidently with the intention that she should profit by it. That which he had said as to her being a married woman struck her forcibly. No doubt these ladies at Manor Cross were her superiors in birth; but she was their brother's wife, and as a married woman had rights of her own. A little spirit of rebellion already began to kindle itself within her bosom; but in it there was nothing of mutiny against her husband. If he were to desire her to make petticoats all day, of course she would make them; but in this contest he had been, as it were, neutral, and had certainly given her no orders. She thought a good deal about it while at the deanery, and made up her mind that she would sit in the petticoat conclave no longer. It could not be her duty to pass her time in an employment in which a poor woman might with difficulty earn sixpence a day. Surely she might do better with her time than that, even though she should spend it all in reading Gibbon.

Chapter IV.

At The Deanery.

There was a dinner-party at the deanery during Miss Tallowax's sojourn at Brotherton. Mr. Canon Holdenough and Lady Alice were there. The bishop and his wife had been asked,—a ceremony which was gone through once a year,—but had been debarred from accepting the invitation by the presence of clerical guests at the palace. But his lordship's chaplain, Mr. Groschut, was present. Mr. Groschut also held an honorary prebendal stall, and was on of the chapter,—a thorn sometimes in the Dean's side. But appearances were well kept up at Brotherton, and no one was more anxious that things should be done in a seemly way than the Dean. Therefore, Mr. Groschut, who was a very low churchman and had once been a Jew, but who bore a very high character for theological erudition, was asked to the deanery. There was also one or two other clergymen there, with their wives, and Mr. and Mrs. Houghton. Mrs. Houghton, it will be remembered, was the beautiful woman who had refused to become the wife of Lord George Germain. Before taking this step, the Dean had been careful to learn whether his son-in-law would object to meet the Houghtons. Such objection would have been foolish, as the families had all known each other. Both Mr. De Baron, Mrs. Houghton's father, and Mr. Houghton himself, had been intimate with the late marquis, and had been friends of the present lord before he had quitted the country. A lady when she refuses a gentleman gives no cause of quarrel. All this the Dean understood; and as he himself had known both Mr. Houghton and Mr. De Baron ever since he came to Brotherton, he thought it better that there should be such a meeting. Lord George blushed up to the roots of his hair, and then said that he should be very glad to meet the gentleman and his wife.

The two young brides had known each other as girls, and now met with, at any rate, an appearance of friendship.

"My dear," said Mrs. Houghton, who was about four years the elder, "of course I know all about it, and so do you. You are an heiress, and could afford to please yourself. I had nothing of my own, and should have had to pass all my time at Manor Cross. Are you surprised?"

"Why should I be surprised?" said Lady George, who was, however, very much surprised at this address.

"Well, you know; he is the handsomest man in England. Everybody allows that; and, then, such a family—and such possibilities! I was very much flattered. Of course he had not seen you then, or only seen you as a child, or I shouldn't have had a chance. It is a great deal better as it is,—isn't it?"

"I think so, certainly."

"I am so glad to hear that you have a house in town. We go up about the first of April, when the hunting is over. Mr. Houghton does not ride much, but he hunts a great deal. We live in Berkeley Square, you know; and I do so hope we shall see ever so much of you."

"I'm sure I hope so too," said Lady George, who had never hitherto been very fond of Miss De Baron, and had entertained a vague idea that she ought to be a little afraid of Mrs. Houghton. But when her father's guest was so civil to her she did not know how to be other than civil in return.

"There is no reason why what has passed should make any awkwardness;—is there?"

"No," said Lady George, feeling that she almost blushed at the allusion to so delicate a subject.

"Of course not. Why should there? Lord George will soon get used to me, just as if nothing had happened; and I shall always be ever so fond of him,—in a way, you know. There shall be nothing to make you jealous."

"I'm not a bit afraid of that," said Lady George, almost too earnestly.

"You need not be, I'm sure. Not but what I do think he was at one time very—very much attached to me. But it couldn't be. And what's the good of thinking of such a thing when it can't be? I don't pretend to be very virtuous, and I like money. Now Mr. Houghton, at any rate, has got a large income. If I had had your fortune at my own command, I don't say what I might not have done."

Lady George almost felt that she ought to be offended by all this,—almost felt that she was disgusted; but, at the same time, she did not quite understand it. Her father had made a point of asking the Houghtons, and had told her that of course she would know the Houghtons up in town. She had an idea that she was very ignorant of the ways of life; but that now it would behove her, as a married woman, to learn those ways. Perhaps the free and easy mode of talking was the right thing. She did not like being told by another lady that that other lady would have married her own husband, only that he was a pauper; and the offence of all this seemed to be the greater because it was all so recent. She didn't like being told that she was not to be jealous, especially when she remembered that her husband had been desperately in love with the lady who told her so not many months ago. But she was not jealous, and was quite sure she never would be jealous; and, perhaps, it did not matter. All this had occurred in the drawing-room before dinner. Then Mr. Houghton came up to her, telling that he had been commissioned by the Dean to have the honour of taking her down to dinner. Having made his little speech, Mr. Houghton retired,—as gentlemen generally do retire when in that position.

"Be as nice as you can to him," said Mrs. Houghton. "He hasn't much to say for himself, but he isn't half a bad fellow; and a pretty woman like you can do what she likes with him."

Lady George, as she went down to dinner, assured herself that she had no slightest wish to take any unfair advantage of Mr. Houghton.

Lord George had taken down Miss Tallowax, the Dean having been very wise in this matter; and Miss Tallowax was in a seventh heaven of happiness. Miss Tallowax, though she had made no promises, was quite prepared to do great things for her noble connexions, if her noble connexions would treat her properly. She had already made half-a-dozen wills, and was quite ready to make another, if Lord George would be civil to her. The Dean was in his heart a little ashamed of his aunt; but he was man enough to be able to bear her eccentricities without showing his vexation, and sufficiently wise to know that more was to be won than lost by the relationship.

"The best woman in the world," he had said to Lord George beforehand, speaking of his aunt; "but, of course, you will remember that she was not brought up as a lady."

Lord George, with stately urbanity, had signified his intention of treating Miss Tallowax with every consideration.

"She has thirty thousand pounds at her own disposal," continued the Dean. "I have never said a word to her about money, but, upon my honour, I think she likes Mary better than any one else. It's worth bearing in mind, you know."

Lord George smiled again in a stately manner,—perhaps showing something of displeasure in his smile. But, nevertheless, he was well aware that it was worth his while to bear Miss Tallowax and her money in his mind.

"My lord," said Miss Tallowax, "I hope you will allow me to say how much honoured we all feel by Mary's proud position." Lord George bowed and smiled, and led the lady into the deanery dining-room. Words did not come easily to him, and he hardly knew how to answer the lady. "Of course, it's a great thing for people such as us," continued Miss Tallowax, "to be connected with the family of a Marquis." Again Lord George bowed. This was very bad, indeed,—a great deal worse than he had anticipated from the aunt of so courtly a man as his father-in-law, the Dean. The lady looked to be about sixty; very small, very healthy, with streaky red cheeks, small grey eyes, and a brown front. Then came upon him an idea, that it would be a very long time before the thirty thousand pounds, or any part of it, would come to him. And then there came to him another idea, that as he had married the Dean's daughter, it was his duty to behave well to the Dean's aunt, even though the money should never come to him. He therefore told Miss Tallowax that his mother hoped to have the pleasure of seeing her at Manor Cross before she left Brotherton. Miss Tallowax almost got out of her seat, as she curtseyed with her head and shoulders to this proposition.

The Dean was a very good man at the head of his own dinner-table, and the party went off pleasantly in spite of sundry attempts at clerical pugnacity made by Mr. Groschut. Every man and every beast has his own weapon. The wolf fights with his tooth, the bull with his horn, and Mr. Groschut always fought with his bishop,—so taught by inner instinct. The bishop, according to Mr. Groschut, was inclined to think that this and that might be done. That such a change might be advantageously made in reference to certain clerical meetings, and that the hilarity of the diocese might be enhanced by certain evangelical festivities. These remarks were generally addressed to Mr. Canon Holdenough, who made almost no reply to them. But the Dean was, on each occasion, prepared with some civil answer, which, while it was an answer, would still seem to change the conversation. It was a law in the Close that Bishop Barton should be never allowed to interfere with the affairs of

Brotherton Cathedral; and if not the bishop, certainly not the bishop's chaplain. Though the Canon and the Dean did not go altogether on all fours in reference to clerical affairs generally they were both agreed on this point. But the Chaplain, who knew the condition of affairs as well as they did, thought the law a bad law, and was determined to abolish it. "It certainly would be very pleasant, Mr. Holdenough, if we could have such a meeting within the confines of the Close. I don't mean to-day, and I don't mean to-morrow; but we might think of it. The bishop, who has the greatest love for the cathedral services, is very much of that mind."

"I do not know that I care very much for any out-of-door gatherings," said the Canon.

"But why out of doors?" asked the Chaplain.

"Whatever meeting there is to be in the Close, will, I hope, be held in the deanery," said the Dean; "but of all meetings, I must say that I like meetings such as this, the best. Germain, will you pass the bottle?" When they were alone together he always called his son-in-law, George; but in company he dropped the more familiar name.

Mr. De Baron, Mrs. Houghton's father, liked his joke. "Sporting men," he said, "always go to a meet, and clerical men to a meeting. What's the difference?"

"A good deal, if it is in the colour of the coat," said the Dean.

"The one is always under cover," said the Canon. "The other, I believe, is generally held out of doors."

"There is, I fancy, a considerable resemblance in the energy of those who are brought together," said the Chaplain.

"But clergymen ain't allowed to hunt, are they?" said Mr. Houghton, who, as usual, was a little in the dark as to the subject under consideration.

"What's to prevent them?" asked the Canon, who had never been out hunting in his life, and who certainly would have advised a young clergyman to abstain from the sport. But in asking the question, he was enabled to strike a sidelong blow at the objectionable chaplain, by seeming to question the bishop's authority.

"Their own conscience, I should hope," said the Chaplain, solemnly, thereby parrying the blow successfully.

"I am very glad, then," said Mr. Houghton, "that I didn't go into the Church." To be thought a real hunting man was the great object of Mr. Houghton's ambition.

"I am afraid you would hardly have suited us, Houghton," said the Dean. "Come, shall we go up to the ladies?"

In the drawing-room, after a little while, Lord George found himself seated next to Mrs. Houghton—Adelaide De Baron, as she had been when he had sighed in vain at her feet. How it had come to pass that he was sitting there he did not know, but he was quite sure that it had come to pass by no arrangement contrived by himself. He had looked at her once since he had been in the room, almost blushing as he did so, and had told himself that she was certainly very beautiful. He almost thought that she was more beautiful than his wife; but he knew,—he knew now,—that her beauty and her manners were not as well suited to him as those of the sweet creature whom he had married. And now he was once more seated close to her, and it was incumbent on him to speak to her. "I hope," she said, almost in a whisper, but still not seeming to whisper, "that we have both become very happy since we met last."

"I hope so, indeed," said he.

"There cannot, at least, be any doubt as to you, Lord George. I never knew a sweeter young girl than Mary Lovelace; so pretty, so innocent, and so enthusiastic. I am but a poor worldly creature compared to her."

"She is all that you say, Mrs. Houghton." Lord George also was displeased,—more thoroughly displeased than had been his wife. But he did not know how to show his displeasure; and though he felt it, he still felt, also, the old influence of the woman's beauty.

"I am so delighted to have heard that you have got a house in Munster Court. I hope that Lady George and I may be fast friends. Indeed, I won't call her Lady George; for she was Mary to me before we either of us thought of getting husbands for ourselves." This was not strictly true, but of that Lord George could know nothing. "And I do hope,—may I hope,—that you will call on me?"

"Certainly I will do so."

"It will add so much to the happiness of my life, if you will allow me to feel that all that has come and gone has not broken the friendship between us."

"Certainly not," said Lord George.

The lady had then said all that she had got to say, and changed her position as silently as she had occupied it. There was no abruptness of motion, and yet Lord George saw her talking to her husband at the other side of the room, almost while his own words were still sounding in his own ears. Then he watched her for the next few minutes. Certainly, she was very beautiful. There was no room for comparison, they were so unlike; otherwise, he would have been disposed to say that Adelaide was the more beautiful. But Adelaide certainly would not have suited the air of Manor Cross, or have associated well with Lady Sarah.

On the next day the Marchioness and Ladies Susannah and Amelia drove over to the deanery in great state, to call on Miss Tallowax, and to take Lady George back to Manor Cross. Miss Tallowax enjoyed the company of the Marchioness greatly. She had never seen a lady of that rank before. "Only think how I must feel," she said to her niece, that morning, "I, that never spoke to any one above a baronet's lady in my life."

"I don't think you'll find much difference," said Mary.

"You're used to it. You're one of them yourself. You're above a baronet's lady,—ain't you, my dear?"

"I have hardly looked into all that as yet, aunt." There must surely have been a little fib in this, or the Dean's daughter must have been very much unlike other young ladies.

"I suppose I ought to be afraid of you, my dear; only you are so nice and so pretty. And as for Lord George, he was quite condescending." Lady George knew that praise was intended, and therefore made no objection to the otherwise objectionable epithet.

The visit of the Marchioness was passed over with the less disturbance to Miss Tallowax because it was arranged that she was to be taken over to lunch at Manor Cross on the following day. Lord George had said a word, and Lady Sarah had consented, though, as a rule, Lady Sarah did not like the company of vulgar people. The peasants of the parish, down to the very poorest of the poor, were her daily companions. With them she would spend hours, feeling no inconvenience from their language or habits. But she did not like gentlefolk who were not gentle. In days now long gone by, she had only assented to the Dean, because holy orders are supposed to make a gentleman; for she would acknowledge a bishop to be as grand a nobleman as any, though he might have been born the son of a butcher. But nobility and gentry cannot travel backwards, and she had been in doubt about Miss Tallowax. But even with the Lady Sarah a feeling has made its way which teaches them to know that they must submit to some changes. The thing was to be regretted, but Lady Sarah knew that she was not strong enough to stand quite alone. "You know she is very rich," the Marchioness had said in a whisper; "and if Brotherton marries, your poor brother will want it so badly."

"That ought not to make any difference, mamma," said Lady Sarah. Whether it did make any difference or not, Lady Sarah herself probably hardly knew; but she did consent to the asking of Miss Tallowax to lunch at Manor Cross.

Chapter V.

Miss Tallowax Is Shown The House.

The Dean took his aunt over to Manor Cross in his brougham. The Dean's brougham was the neatest carriage in Brotherton, very much more so than the bishop's family carriage. It was, no doubt, generally to be seen with only one horse; and neither the bishop or Mrs. Barton ever stirred without two; but then one horse is enough for town work, and that one horse could lift his legs and make himself conspicuous in a manner of which the bishop's rather sorry jades knew nothing. On this occasion, as the journey was long, there were two horses—hired; but, nevertheless, the brougham looked very well as it came up the long Manor Cross avenue. Miss Tallowax became rather frightened as she drew near to the scene of her coming grandeur.

"Henry," she said to her nephew, "they will think so little of me."

"My dear aunt," replied the Dean, "in these days a lady who has plenty of money of her own can hold her head up anywhere. The dear old marchioness will think quite as much of you as you do of her."

What perhaps struck Miss Tallowax most at the first moment was the plainness of the ladies' dresses. She, herself, was rather gorgeous in a shot-silk gown and a fashionable bonnet crowded with flowers. She had been ashamed of the splendour of the article as she put it on, and yet had been ashamed also of her ordinary daily head gear. But when she saw the Marchioness, and especially when she saw Lady Sarah, who was altogether strange to her, she wished that she had come in her customary black gown. She had heard something about Lady Sarah from her niece, and had conceived an idea that Lady Sarah was the dragon of the family. But when she saw a little woman, looking almost as old as herself,—though in truth the one might have been the other's mother,—dressed in an old brown merino, with the slightest morsel of white collar to be seen round her neck, she began to hope that the dragon would not be very fierce.

"I hope you like Brotherton, Miss Tallowax," said Lady Sarah. "I think I have heard that you were here once before."

"I like Brotherton very much, my lady." Lady Sarah smiled as graciously as she knew how. "I came when they first made Henry dean, a long time ago now it seems. But he had not then the honour of knowing your mamma or the family."

"It wasn't long before we did know him," said the Marchioness. Then Miss Tallowax turned round and again curtseyed with her head and shoulders.

The Dean at this moment was not in the room, having been withdrawn from the ladies by his son-in-law at the front door; but as luncheon was announced, the two men came in. Lord George gave his arm to his wife's great aunt, and the Dean followed with the Marchioness.

"I really am a'most ashamed to walk out before her ladyship," said Miss Tallowax, with a slight attempt at laughing at her own ignorance.

But Lord George rarely laughed at anything, and certainly did not know how to treat pleasantly such a subject as this. "It's quite customary," he said very gravely.

The lunch was much more tremendous to Miss Tallowax than had been the dinner at the deanery. Though she was ignorant,—ignorant at any rate of the ways of such people as those with whom she was now consorting,—she was by no means a stupid old woman. She was soon able to perceive that in spite of the old merino gown, it was Lady Sarah's spirit that quelled them all. At first there was very little conversation. Lord George did not speak a word. The Marchioness never exerted herself. Poor Mary was cowed and unhappy. The Dean made one or two little efforts, but without much success. Lady Sarah was intent upon her mutton chop, which she finished to the last shred, turning it over and over in her plate so that it should be economically disposed of, looking at it very closely because she was short-sighted. But when the mutton chop had finally done its duty, she looked up from her plate and gave evident signs that she intended to take upon herself the weight of the conversation. All the subsequent ceremonies of the lunch itself, the little tarts and the jelly, and the custard pudding, she despised altogether, regarding them as wicked additions. One pudding after dinner she would have allowed, but nothing more of that sort. It might be all very well for parvenu millionaires to have two grand dinners a-day, but it could not be necessary that the Germains should live in that way, even when the Dean of Brotherton and his aunt came to lunch with them.

"I hope you like this part of the country, Miss Tallowax," she said, as soon as she had deposited her knife and fork over the bone.

"Manor Cross is quite splendid, my lady," said Miss Tallowax.

"It is an old house, and we shall have great pleasure in showing you what the people call the state rooms. We never use them. Of course you know the house belongs to my brother, and we only live here because it suits him to stay in Italy."

"That's the young Marquis, my lady?"

"Yes; my elder brother is Marquis of Brotherton, but I cannot say that he is very young. He is two years my senior, and ten years older than George."

"But I think he's not married yet?" asked Miss Tallowax.

The question was felt to be disagreeable by them all. Poor Mary could not keep herself from blushing, as she remembered how much to her might depend on this question of her brother-in-law's marriage. Lord George felt that the old lady was enquiring what chance there might be that her grand niece should ever become a marchioness. Old Lady Brotherton, who had always been anxious that her elder son should marry, felt uncomfortable, as did also the Dean, conscious that all there must be conscious how important must be the matter to him.

"No," said Lady Sarah, with stately gravity; "my elder brother is not yet married. If you would like to see the rooms, Miss Tallowax, I shall have pleasure in showing you the way."

The Dean had seen the rooms before, and remained with the old lady. Lord George, who thought very much of everything affecting his own family, joined the party, and Mary felt herself compelled to follow her husband and her aunt. The two younger sisters also accompanied Lady Sarah.

"This is the room in which Queen Elizabeth slept," said Lady Sarah, entering a large chamber on the ground floor, in which there was a four-post bedstead, almost as high as the ceiling, and looking as though no human body had profaned it for the last three centuries.

"Dear me," said Miss Tallowax, almost afraid to press such sacred boards with her feet. "Queen Elizabeth! Did she really now?"

"Some people say she never did actually come to Manor Cross at all," said the conscientious Lady Amelia; "but there is no doubt that the room was prepared for her."

"Laws!" said Miss Tallowax, who began to be less afraid of distant royalty now that a doubt was cast on its absolute presence.

"Examining the evidence as closely as we can," said Lady Sarah, with a savage glance at her sister, "I am inclined to think that she certainly did come. We know that she was at Brotherton in 1582, and there exists the letter in which Sir Humphrey Germaine, as he was then, is desired to prepare rooms for her. I myself have no doubt on the subject."

"After all it does not make much difference," said Mary.

"I think it makes all the difference in the world," said Lady Susanna. "That piece of furniture will always be sacred to me, because I believe it did once afford rest and sleep to the gracious majesty of England."

"It do make a difference, certainly," said Miss Tallowax, looking at the bed with all her eyes. "Does anybody ever go to bed here now?"

"Nobody, ever," said Lady Sarah. "Now we will go through to the great dining hall. That's the portrait of the first earl."

"Painted by Kneller," said Lady Amelia, proudly.

"Oh, indeed," said Miss Tallowax.

"There is some doubt as to that," said Lady Sarah. "I have found out that Sir Godfrey Kneller was only born in 1648, and as the first earl died a year or two after the restoration, I don't know that he could have done it."

"It was always said that it was painted by Kneller," said Lady Amelia.

"There has been a mistake, I fear," said Lady Sarah.

"Oh, indeed," said Miss Tallowax, looking up with intense admiration at a very ill-drawn old gentleman in armour. Then they entered the state dining-room or hall, and Miss Tallowax was informed that the room had not been used for any purpose whatever for very many years. "And such a beautiful room!" said Miss Tallowax, with much regret.

"The fact is, I believe, that the chimney smokes horribly," said Lord George.

"I never remember a fire here," said Lady Sarah. "In very cold weather we have a portable stove brought in, just to preserve the furniture. This is called the old ball room."

"Dear me!" ejaculated Miss Tallowax, looking round at the faded yellow hangings.

"We did have a ball here once," said Lady Amelia, "when Brotherton came of age. I can just remember it."

"Has it never been used since?" asked Mary.

"Never," said Lady Sarah. "Sometimes when it's rainy we walk up and down for exercise. It is a fine old house, but I often wish that it were smaller. I don't think people want rooms of this sort now as much as they used to do. Perhaps a time may come when my brother will make Manor Cross gay again, but it is not very gay now. I think that is all, Miss Tallowax."

"It's very fine;—very fine indeed," said Miss Tallowax, shivering. Then they all trooped back into the morning room which they used for their daily life.

The old lady when she had got back into the brougham with her nephew, the Dean, was able to express her mind freely. "I wouldn't live in that house, Henry, not if they was to give it me for nothing."

"They'd have to give you something to keep it up with."

"And not then, neither. Of course it's all very well having a bed that Queen Elizabeth slept in."

"Or didn't sleep in."

"I'd teach myself to believe she did. But dear me, that isn't everything. It nearly gave me the horrors to look at it. Room after room,—room after room,—and nobody living in any of them."

"People can't live in more than a certain number of rooms at once, aunt."

"Then what's the use of having them? And don't you think for the daughters of a Marchioness they are a little what you'd call—dowdy?"

"They don't go in for dress much."

"Why, my Jemima at home, when the dirty work is done, is twice smarter than Lady Sarah. And, Henry,—don't you think they're a little hard upon Mary?"

"Hard upon her;—how?" The Dean had listened to the old woman's previous criticisms with a smile; but now he was interested and turned sharply round to her. "How hard?"

"Moping her up there among themselves; and it seemed to me they snubbed her whenever she spoke." The Dean had not wanted his aunt's observation to make him feel this. The tone of every syllable addressed to his girl had caught his ear. He had been pleased to marry her into so good a family. He had been delighted to think that by means of his prosperity in the world his father's grand-daughter might probably become a peeress. But he certainly had not intended that even for such a reward as that his daughter should become submissive to the old maids at Manor Cross. Foreseeing something of this he had stipulated that she should have a house of her own in London; but half her time would probably be spent in the country, and with reference to that half of her time it would be necessary that she should be made to understand that as the wife of Lord George she was in no respect inferior to his sisters, and that in some respects she was their superior. "I don't see the good of living in a big house," continued Miss Tallowax, "if all the time everything is to be as dull as dull."

"They are older than she is, you know."

"Poor little dear! I always did say that young folk should have young folk about 'em. Of course it's a great thing for her to have a lord for her husband. But he looks a'most too old himself for such a pretty darling as your Mary."

"He's only thirty-three."

"It's in the looks, I suppose, because he's so grand. But it's that Lady Sarah puzzles me. It isn't in her looks, and yet she has it all her in own way. Well;—I liked going there, and I'm glad I've been; but I don't know as I shall ever want to go again." Then there was silence for some time; but as the brougham was driven into Brotherton Miss Tallowax spoke again. "I don't suppose an old woman like me can ever be of any use, and you'll always be at hand to look after her. But if ever she should want an outing, just to raise her spirits, old as I am, I think I could make it brighter for her than it is there." The Dean took her hand and pressed it, and then there was no more said.

When the brougham was driven away Lord George took his wife for a walk in the park. She was still struggling hard to be in love with him, never owning failure to herself, and sometimes assuring herself that she had succeeded altogether. Now, when he asked her to come with him, she put on her hat joyfully, and joined her hands over his arm as she walked away with him into the shrubbery.

"She's a wonderful old woman;—is not she, George?"

"Not very wonderful."

"Of course you think she's vulgar."

"I didn't say so."

"No; you're too good to say so, because she's papa's aunt. But she's very good. Don't you think she's very good?"

"I dare say she is. I don't know that I run into superlatives quite so much as you do."

"She has brought me such a handsome present. I could not show it you before them all just now, and it only came down from London this morning. She did not say a word about it before. Look here." Then she slipped her glove off and showed him a diamond ring.

"You should not wear that out of doors."

"I only put it on to show you. Wasn't it good of her? 'Young people of rank ought to wear nice things,' she said, as she gave it me. Wasn't it an odd thing for her to say? and yet I understood her." Lord George frowned, thinking that he also understood the old woman's words, and reminding himself that the ladies of rank at Manor Cross never did wear nice things. "Don't you think it was nice?"

"Of course she is entitled to make you a present if she pleases."

"It pleased me, George."

"I dare say, and as it doesn't displease me all is well. You, however, have quite sense enough to understand, that in this house more is thought of—of—of—" he would have said blood, but that he did not wish to hurt her,—"more is thought of personal good conduct than of rings and jewels."

"Rings and jewels, and—personal conduct may go together; mayn't they?"

"Of course they may."

"And very often do. You won't think my—personal conduct—will be injured because I wear my aunt's ring?"

When Lord George made his allusion to personal conduct one of her two hands dropped from his arm, and now, as she repeated the words, there was a little sting of sarcasm in her voice.

"I was intending to answer your aunt's opinion that young people ought to wear nice things. No doubt there is at present a great rage for rich ornaments and costly dress, and it was of these she was thinking when she spoke of nice things. When I spoke of personal conduct being more thought of here, I intended to imply that you had come into a family not given to rich ornaments and costly dress. My sisters feel that their portion in this world is assured to them without such outward badges, and wish that you should share the feeling."

This was a regular sermon, and to Mary's thinking was very disagreeable, and not at all deserved. Did her husband really mean to tell her that, because his sisters chose to dress themselves down in the country like dowdy old maids whom the world had deserted, she was to do the same up in London? The injustice of this on all sides struck home to her at the moment. They were old and she was young. They were plain; she was pretty. They were poor; she was rich. They didn't feel any wish to make themselves what she called "nice." She did feel a very strong wish in that direction. They were old maids; she was a young bride. And then what right had they to domineer over her, and to send word to her through her husband of their wishes as to her manner of dressing? She said nothing at the moment; but she became red, and began to feel that she had power within her to rebel at any rate against her sisters-in-law. There was silence for a moment or so, and then Lord George reverted to the subject.

"I hope you can sympathise with my sisters," he said. He had felt that the hand had been dropped, and had understood something of the reason.

She wished to rebel against them, but by no means wished to oppose him. She was aware, as though by instinct, that her life would be very bad indeed should she fail to sympathise with him. It was still the all-paramount desire of her heart to be in love with him. But she could not bring herself to say that she sympathised with them in this direct attack that was made on her own mode of thought.

"Of course, they are a little older than I am," she said, hoping to get out of the difficulty.

"And therefore, the more entitled to consideration. I think you will own that they must know what is, and what is not, becoming to a lady."

"Do you mean," said she, hardly able to choke a rising sob, "that they—have anything—to find fault with in me?"

"I have said nothing as to finding fault, Mary."

"Do they think that I do not dress as I ought to do?"

"Why should you ask such a question as that?"

"I don't know what else I am to understand, George. Of course I will do anything that you tell me. If you wish me to make any change, I will make it. But I hope they won't send me messages through you."

"I thought you would have been glad to know that they interested themselves about you." In answer to this Mary pouted, but her husband did not see the pout.

"Of course they are anxious that you should become one of them. We are a very united family. I do not speak now of my elder brother, who is in a great measure separated from us and is of a different nature. But my mother, my sisters, and I, have very many opinions in common. We live together, and have the same way of thinking. Our rank is high, and our means are small. But to me blood is much more than wealth. We acknowledge, however, that rank demands many sacrifices, and my sisters endeavour to make those sacrifices most conscientiously. A woman more thoroughly devoted to good works than Sarah I have never even read of. If you will believe this, you will understand what they mean, and what I mean, when we say that here at Manor Cross we think more of personal conduct than of rings and jewels. You wish, Mary, to be one of us; do you not?"

She paused for a moment, and then she answered, "I wish to be always one with you."

He almost wanted to be angry at this, but it was impossible. "To be one with me, dearest," he said, "you must be one, also, with them."

"I cannot love them as I do you, George. That, I am sure, is not the meaning of being married." Then she thought of it all steadily for a minute, and after that, made a further speech. "And I don't think I can quite dress like them. I'm sure you would not like it if I did."

As she said this she put her second hand back upon his arm.

He said nothing further on the subject till he had brought her back to the house, walking along by her side almost mute, not quite knowing whether he ought to be offended with her or to take her part. It was true that he would not have liked her to look like Lady Sarah, but he would have liked her to make some approach in that direction, sufficient to show submission. He was already beginning to fear the absence of all control which would befall his young wife in that London life to which, she was to be so soon introduced, and was meditating whether he could not induce one of his sisters to accompany them. As to Sarah he was almost hopeless. Amelia would be of little or no service, though she would be more likely to ingratiate herself with his wife than the others. Susanna was less strong than Sarah and less amiable than Amelia. And then, how would it be if Mary were to declare that she would rather begin the campaign without any of them?

The young wife, as soon as she found herself alone in her own bedroom, sat down and resolved that she would never allow herself to be domineered by her husband's sisters. She would be submissive to him in all things, but his authority should not be delegated to them.

Chapter VI.

Bad Tidings.

About the middle of October, there came a letter from the Marquis of Brotherton to his brother, which startled them all at Manor Cross very much indeed. In answering Lord George's communication as to the marriage, the Marquis had been mysterious and disagreeable;—but then he was always disagreeable and would on occasions take the trouble to be mysterious also. He had warned his brother that he might himself want the house at Manor Cross; but he had said the same thing frequently during his residence in Italy, being always careful to make his mother and sisters understand that they might have to take themselves away any day at a very short warning. But now the short warning had absolutely come, and had come in such a shape as to upset everything at Manor Cross, and to upset many things at the Brotherton Deanery. The letter was as follows:—

"My dear George,

"I am to be married to the Marchesa Luigi. Her name is Catarina Luigi, and she is a widow. As to her age, you can ask herself when you see her, if you dare. I haven't dared. I suppose her to be ten years younger than myself. I did not expect that it would be so, but she says now that she would like to live in England. Of course I've always meant to go back myself some day. I don't suppose we shall be there before May, but we must have the house got ready. My mother and the girls had better look out for a place as soon as they can. Tell my mother of course I will allow her the rent of Cross Hall, to which indeed she is entitled. I don't think she would care to live there, and neither she nor the girls would get on with my wife.

"Yours, B.

"I am waiting to know about getting the house painted and furnished."

When Lord George received this letter, he showed it first in privacy to his sister Sarah. As the reader will have understood, there had never been any close family affection between the present Marquis and his brothers and sisters; nor had he been a loving son to his mother. But the family at Manor Cross had always endeavoured to maintain a show of regard for the head of the family, and the old Marchioness would no doubt have been delighted had her eldest son come home and married an English wife. Lady Sarah, in performing what she had considered to be a family duty, had written regular despatches to her elder brother, telling him everything that happened about the place,— despatches which he, probably, never read. Now there had come a blow indeed. Lady Sarah read the letter, and then looked into her brother's face.

"Have you told Mary?" she asked.

"I have told no one."

"It concerns her as much as any of us. Of course, if he has married, it is right that he should have his house. We ought to wish that he should live hero."

"If he were different from what he is," said Lord George.

"If she is good it may be that he will become different. It is not the thing, but the manner in which he tells it to us! Did you ever hear her name before?"

"Never."

"What a way he has of mentioning her;—about her age," said Lady Sarah, infinitely shocked. "Well! Mamma must be told, of course. Why shouldn't we live at Cross Hall? I don't understand what he means about that. Cross Hall belongs to mamma for her life, as much as Manor Cross does to him for his."

Just outside the park gate, at the side of the park furthest away from Brotherton, and therefore placed very much out of the world, there stood a plain substantial house built in the days of Queen Anne, which had now for some generations been the habitation of the dowager of the Brotherton family. When the late marquis died, this had become for her life the property of the Marchioness; but had been ceded by her to her son, in return for the loan of the big house. The absentee Marquis had made with his mother the best bargain in his power, and had let the dower house, known as Cross Hall, to a sporting farmer. He now kindly offered to allow his mother to have the rent of her own house, signifying at the same time his wish that all his family should remove themselves out of his way.

"He wishes that we should take ourselves off," said Lord George, hoarsely.

"But I do not see why we are to give way to his wishes. George, where are we to go? Of what use can we be in a strange country? Wherever we are we shall be very poor, but our money will go further here than elsewhere. How are we to get up new interests in life? The land is his, but the poor people belong to us as much as to him. It is unreasonable."

"It is frightfully selfish."

"I for one am not prepared to obey him in this," said Lady Sarah. "Of course mamma will do as she pleases, but I do not see why we should go. He will never live here all the year through."

"He will be sick of it after a month. Will you read the letter to my mother?"

"I will tell her, George. She had better not see the letter, unless she makes a point of it. I will read it again, and then do you keep it. You should tell Mary at once. It is natural that she should have built hopes on the improbability of Brotherton's marriage."

Before noon on that day the news had been disseminated through the house. The old Marchioness, when she first heard of the Italian wife, went into hysterics, and then was partly comforted by reminding herself that all Italians were not necessarily bad. She asked after the letter repeatedly; and at last, when it was found to be impossible to explain to her otherwise what her eldest son meant about the houses, it was shown to her. Then she began to weep afresh.

"Why mayn't we live at Cross Hall, Sarah?" she said.

"Cross Hall belongs to you, mamma, and nothing can hinder you from living there."

"But Augustus says that we are to go away."

The Marchioness was the only one of the family who ever called the Marquis by his Christian name, and she did so only when she was much disturbed.

"No doubt he expresses a wish that we should do so?"

"Where are we to go to, and I at my age?"

"I think you should live at Cross Hall."

"But he says that we mayn't. We could never go on there if he wants us to go away."

"Why not, mamma? It is your house as much as this is his. If you will let him understand that when you leave this you mean to go there, he will probably say nothing more about it."

"Mr. Price is living there. I can't make Mr. Price go away directly the painter people come in here. They'll come to-morrow, perhaps, and what am I to do then?"

The matter was discussed throughout the whole day between Lady Sarah and her mother, the former bearing the old woman's plaintive weakness with the utmost patience, and almost succeeding, before the evening came, in inducing her mother to agree to rebel against the tyranny of her son. There were peculiar difficulties and peculiar hardships in the case. The Marquis could turn out all the women of his family at a day's notice. He had only to say to them, "Go!" and they must be gone. And he could be rid of them without even saying or writing another word. A host of tradesmen would come, and then of course they must go. But Mr. Price at Cross Hall must have a regular year's notice, and that notice could not now be given till Lady-day next.

"If the worst comes to the worst, mamma we will go and live in Brotherton for the time. Mr. Holdenough or the Dean would find some place for us." Then the old lady began to ask how Mary had borne the news; but as yet Lady Sarah had not been able to interest herself personally about Mary.

Lord George was surprised to find how little his wife was affected by the terrible thunderbolt which had fallen among them. On him the blow had been almost as terrible as on his mother. He had taken a house in town, at the instance of the Dean, and in consequence of a promise made before his marriage, which was sacred to him but which he regretted. He would have preferred himself to live the whole year through at Manor Cross. Though he had not very much to do there the place was never dull to him. He liked the association of the big house. He liked the sombre grandeur of the park. He liked the magistrates' bench, though he rarely spoke a word when he was there. And he liked the thorough economy of the life. But as to that house in town, though his wife's fortune would enable him to live there four or five months, he knew that he could not stretch the income so as to bear the expense of the entire year. And yet, what must he do now? If he could abandon the house in town, then he could join his mother as to some new country house. But he did not dare to suggest that the house in town should be abandoned. He was afraid of the Dean, and afraid, so to say, of his own promise. The thing had been stipulated, and he did not know how to go back from the stipulation.

"Going to leave Manor Cross," said Mary, when she was told. "Dear me; how odd. Where will they go to?"

It was evident to her husband from the tone of her voice that she regarded her own house in Munster Court, for it was her own, as her future residence,—as hers and his. In asking where "they" would live, she spoke of the other ladies of the family. He had expected that she would have shown some disappointment at the danger to her future position which this new marriage would produce. But in regard to that she was, he thought, either perfectly indifferent, or else a very good actor. In truth, she was almost indifferent. The idea that she might some day be Lady Brotherton had been something to her, but not much. Her happiness was not nearly as much disturbed by this marriage as it had been by the allusion made to her dress. She herself could hardly understand the terrible gloom which seemed during that evening and the whole of the next day to have fallen on the entire family.

"George, does it make you very unhappy?" she said, whispering to him on the morning of the second day.

"Not that my brother should marry," he said, "God forbid that I, as a younger brother, should wish to debar him from any tittle of what belongs to him. If he would marry well it ought to be a joy to us all."

"Is not this marrying well?"

"What, with a foreigner; with an Italian widow? And then there will, I fear, be great trouble in finding a comfortable home for my mother."

"Amelia says she can go to Cross Hall."

"Amelia does not know what she is talking of. It would be very long before they could get into Cross Hall, even if they can go there at all. It would have to be completely furnished, and there is no money to furnish it."

"Wouldn't your brother—?" Lord George shook his head. "Or papa." Lord George again shook his head—"What will they do?"

"If it were not for our house in London we might take a place in the country together," said Lord George.

All the various facts of the proposition now made to her flashed upon Mary's mind at once. Had it been suggested to her, when she was first asked to marry Lord George, that she should live permanently in a country house with his mother and sisters, in a house of which she would not be and could not be the mistress, she would certainly have rejected the offer. And now the tedium of such a life was plainer to her than it would have been then. But, under her father's auspices, a pleasant, gay little house in town had been taken for her, and she had been able to gild the dullness of Manor Cross with the brightness of her future prospects. For four or five months she would be her own mistress, and would be so in London. Her husband would be living on her money, but it would be the delight of her heart that he should be happy while doing so. And all this must be safe and wise, because it was to be done under the advice of her father. Now it was proposed to her that she should abandon all this and live in some smaller, poorer, duller country residence, in which she would be the least of the family instead of the mistress of her own house. She thought of it all for a moment, and then she answered him with a firm voice.

"If you wish to give up the house in London we will do so."

"It would distress you I fear." When we call on our friends to sacrifice themselves, we generally wish them also to declare that they like being sacrificed.

"I should be disappointed of course, George."

"And it would be unjust," said he.

"If you wish it I will not say a word against it."

On that afternoon he rode into Brotherton to tell the tidings to the Dean. Upon whatever they might among them decide, it was expedient that the Dean should be at once told of the marriage. Lord George, as he thought over it all on horseback, found difficulties on every side. He had promised

that his wife should live in town, and he could not go back from
that promise without injustice. He understood the nature of her
lately offered sacrifice, and felt that it would not liberate his
conscience. And then he was sure that the Dean would be loud
against any such arrangement. The money no doubt was Mary's
own money and, subject to certain settlement, was at Lord
George's immediate disposal; but he would be unable to endure
the Dean's reproaches. He would be unable also to endure his
own, unless—which was so very improbable—the Dean should
encourage him. But how were things to be arranged? Was he to
desert his mother and sisters in their difficulty? He was very
fond of his wife; but it had never yet occurred to him that the
daughter of Dean Lovelace could be as important to him as all
the ladies of the house of Germain. His brother purposed to
bring his wife to Manor Cross in May, when he would be up in
London. Where at that moment, and after what fashion, would
his mother and sisters be living?

The Dean showed his dismay at the marriage plainly
enough.

"That's very bad, George," he said; "very bad indeed!"

"Of course we don't like her being a foreigner."

"Of course you don't like his marrying at all. Why
should you? You all know enough of him to be sure that he
wouldn't marry the sort of woman you would approve."

"I don't know why my brother should not have married
any lady in England."

"At any rate he hasn't. He has married some Italian
widow, and it's a misfortune. Poor Mary!"

"I don't think Mary feels it at all."

"She will some day. Girls of her age don't feel that kind
of thing at first. So he is going to come over at once. What will
your mother do?"

"She has Cross Hall."

"That man Price is there. He will go out of course?"

"With notice he must go."

"He won't stand about that, if you don't interfere with his land and farm-yard. I know Price. He's not a bad fellow."

"But Brotherton does not want them to go there," said Lord George, almost in a whisper.

"Does not want your mother to live in her own house! Upon my word the Marquis is considerate to you all! He has said that plainly, has he? If I were Lady Brotherton I would not take the slightest heed of what he says. She is not dependent on him. In order that he may be relieved from the bore of being civil to his own family she is to be sent out about the world to look for a home in her old age! You must tell her not to listen for a minute to such a proposition."

Lord George, though he put great trust in his father-in-law, did not quite like hearing his brother spoken of so very freely by a man who was, after all, the son of a tradesman. It seemed to him as though the Dean made himself almost too intimate with the affairs at Manor Cross, and yet he was obliged to go on and tell the Dean everything.

"Even if Price went, there must be some delay in getting the house ready."

"The Marquis surely won't turn your mother out before the spring?"

"Tradesmen will have to come in. And then I don't quite know what we are to do as to the—expense of furnishing the new house. It will cost a couple of thousand pounds, and none of us have ready money." The Dean assumed a very serious face. "Every spoon and fork at Manor Cross, every towel and every sheet belongs to my brother."

"Was not the Cross House ever furnished?"

"Many years ago; in my grandmother's time. My father left money for the purpose, but it was given up to my sister Alice when she married Holdenough." He found himself explaining all the little intricacies of his family to the Dean, because it was necessary that he should hold council with some one. "I was thinking of a furnished house for them elsewhere."

"In London?"

"Certainly not there. My mother would not like it, nor would my sisters. I like the country very much the best myself."

"Not for the whole year?"

"I have never cared to be in London; but, of course, as for Mary and myself that is settled. You would not wish her to give up the house in Munster Court?"

"Certainly not. It would not be fair to her to ask her to live always under the wing of your mother and sisters. She would never learn to be a woman. She would always be in leading strings. Do you not feel that yourself?"

"I feel that beggars cannot be choosers. My mother's fortune is £2000 a year. As you know we have only 5000*l.* a piece. There is hardly income enough among us for a house in town and a house in the country."

The Dean paused a moment, and then replied that his daughter's welfare could not be made subordinate to that of the family generally. He then said that if any immediate sum of money were required he would lend it either to the dowager or to Lord George.

Lord George, as he rode home, was angry both with himself and with the Dean. There had been an authority in the Dean's voice which had grated upon his feelings; of course he intended to be as good as his word; but, nevertheless, his wife was his wife and subject to his will; and her fortune had been her own and had not come from the Dean. The Dean took too much upon himself. And yet, with all that, he had consulted the Dean about everything, and had confessed the family poverty. The thing, however, was quite certain to him; he could not get out of the house in town.

During the whole of that day Lady Sarah had been at work with her mother, instigating her to insist on her own rights, and at last she had succeeded.

"What would our life be, mamma," Lady Sarah had said, "if we were removed altogether into a new world. Here we are of some use. People know us, and give us credit for being what we are. We can live after our own fashion, and yet live in accordance with our rank. There is not a man or a woman or a child in the parish whom I do not know. There is not a house in which you would not see Amelia's and Susanna's work. We cannot begin all that over again."

"When I am gone, my dear, you must do so."

"Who can say how much may be done before that sad day shall come to us? He may have taken his Italian wife back again to Italy. Mamma, we ought not to run away from our duties." On the following morning it was settled among them that the dowager should insist on possession of her own house at Cross Hall, and a letter was written to the Marquis, congratulating him of course on his marriage, but informing him at the same time that the family would remain in the parish.

Some few days later Mr. Knox, the agent for the property, came down from London. He had received the orders of the Marquis, and would be prepared to put workmen into the house as soon as her ladyship would be ready to leave it. But he quite agreed that this could not be done at once. A beginning no doubt might be made while they were still there, but no painting should be commenced or buildings knocked down or put up till March. It was settled at the same time that on the first of March the family should leave the house.

"I hope my son won't be angry," the Marchioness said to Mr. Knox.

"If he be angry, my lady, he will be angry without a cause. But I never knew him to be very angry about anything."

"He always did like to have his own way, Mr. Knox," said the mindful mother.

Chapter VII.

"Cross Hall Gate."

While Mr. Knox was still in the country negotiations were opened with Mr. Price, the sporting farmer, who, like all sporting farmers, was in truth a very good fellow. He had never been liked by the ladies at Manor Cross, as having ways of his own which were not their ways. He did not go to church as often as they thought he ought to do; and, being a bachelor, stories were told about him which were probably very untrue. A bachelor may live in town without any inquiries as to any of the doings of his life; but if a man live forlorn and unmarried in a country house, he will certainly become the victim of calumny should any woman under sixty ever be seen about his place. It was said also of Mr. Price that sometimes, after hunting, men had been seen to go out of his yard in an uproarious condition. But I hardly think that old Sir Simon Bolt, the master of the hounds, could have liked him so well, or so often have entered his house, had there been much amiss there; and as to the fact of there always being a fox in Cross Hall Holt, which a certain little wood was called about half a mile of the house, no one even doubted that. But there had always been a prejudice against Price at the great house, and in this even Lord George had coincided.

But when Mr. Knox went to him and explained to him what was about to happen,—that the ladies would be forced, almost before the end of winter, to leave Manor Cross and make way for the Marquis, Mr. Price declared that he would clear out, bag and baggage, top-boots, spurs, and brandy-bottles, at a moment's notice. The Prices of the English world are not, as a rule, deficient in respect for the marquises and marchionesses. "The workmen can come in to-morrow," Price said, when he was told that some preparations would be necessary. "A bachelor can shake down anywhere, Mr. Knox." Now it happened that Cross Hall House was altogether distinct from the Cross Hall Farm, on which, indeed, there had been a separate farmhouse, now only used by labourers. But Mr. Price was a comfortable man, and, when the house had been vacant, had been able to afford himself the luxury of living there. So far the primary difficulties lessened themselves when they were well looked in the face. And yet things did not run altogether smoothly. The Marquis did not condescend to reply to his brother's letter; but he wrote what was for him a long letter to Mr. Knox, urging upon the agent the duty of turning his mother and sisters altogether out of the place. "We shall be a great deal better friends apart," he said. "If they remain there we shall see little or nothing of each other, and it will be very uncomfortable. If they will settle themselves elsewhere, I will furnish a house for them; but I don't want to have them at my elbow." Mr. Knox was of course bound to show this to Lord George, and Lord George was bound to consult Lady Sarah. Lady Sarah told her mother something of it, but not all; but she told it in such a way that the old lady consented to remain and to brave her eldest son. As for Lady Sarah herself, in spite of her true Christianity and real goodness, she did not altogether dislike the fight. Her brother was her brother, and the head of the family, and he had his privileges; but they too had their rights, and she was not disposed to submit herself to tyranny. Mr. Knox was therefore obliged to inform the Marquis in what softest language he could find applicable for the purpose that the ladies of the family had decided upon removing to the dower-house.

About a month after this there was a meet of the Brotherton Hunt, of which Sir Simon Bolt was the master, at Cross Hall Gate. The grandfather of the present Germains had in the early part of the century either established this special pack, or at any rate become the master of it. Previous to that the hunting probably had been somewhat precarious; but there had been, since his time, a regular Brotherton Hunt associated with a collar and button of its own,—a blue collar on a red coat, with B. H. on the buttons,—and the thing had been done well. They had four days a week, with an occasional bye, and 2500*l.* were subscribed annually. Sir Simon Bolt had been the master for the last fifteen years, and was so well known that no sporting pen and no sporting tongue in England ever called him more than Sir Simon. Cross Hall Gate, a well-loved meet, was the gate of the big park which opened out upon the road just opposite to Mr. Price's house. It was an old stone structure, with a complicated arch stretching across the gate itself, with a lodge on each side. It lay back in a semi-circle from the road, and was very imposing. In old days no doubt the gate was much used, as the direct traffic from London to Brotherton passed that way. But the railway had killed the road; and as the nearer road from the Manor Cross House to the town came out on the same road much nearer to Brotherton, the two lodges and all the grandeur were very much wasted. But it was a pretty site for a meet when the hounds were seated on their haunches inside the gate, or moving about slowly after the huntsman's horse, and when the horses and carriages were clustered about on the high road and inside the park. And it was a meet, too, much loved by the riding men. It was always presumed that Manor Cross itself was preserved for foxes, and the hounds were carefully run through the belt of woods. But half an hour did that, and then they went away to Price's Little Holt. On that side there were no more gentlemen's places; there was a gorse cover or two and sundry little spinnies; but the county was a country for foxes to run and men to ride; and with this before them, the members of the Brotherton Hunt were pleased to be summoned to Cross Hall Gate.

On such occasions Lord George was always there. He never hunted, and very rarely went to any other meet; but on these occasions he would appear mounted, in black, and would say a few civil words to Sir Simon, and would tell George Scruby, the huntsman, that he had heard that there was a fox among the laurels. George would touch his hat and say in his loud, deep voice, "Hope so, my lord," having no confidence whatever in a Manor Cross fox. Sir Simon would shake hands with him, make a suggestion about the weather, and then get away as soon as possible; for there was no sympathy and no common subject between the men. On this occasion Lady Amelia had driven down Lady Susanna in the pony-carriage, and Lady George was there, mounted, with her father the Dean, longing to be allowed to go away with the hounds but having been strictly forbidden by her husband to do so. Mr. Price was of course there, as was also Mr. Knox, the agent, who had a little shooting-box down in the country, and kept a horse, and did a little hunting.

There was good opportunity for talking as the hounds were leisurely taken through the loose belt of woods which were by courtesy called the Manor Cross coverts, and Mr. Price took the occasion of drawing a letter from his pocket and showing it to Mr. Knox.

"The Marquis has written to you!" said the agent in a tone of surprise, the wonder not being that the Marquis should write to Mr. Price, but that he should write to any one.

"Never did such a thing in his life before, and I wish he hadn't now."

Mr. Knox wished it also when he had read the letter. It expressed a very strong desire on the part of the Marquis that Mr. Price should keep the Cross Hall House, saying that it was proper that the house should go with the farm, and intimating the

Marquis's wish that Mr. Price should remain as his neighbour.
"If you can manage it, I'll make the farm pleasant and profitable
to you," said the Marquis.

"He don't say a word about her ladyship," said Price;
"but what he wants is just to get rid of 'em all, box and dice."

"That's about it, I suppose," said the agent.

"Then he's come to the wrong shop, that's what he has
done, Mr. Knox. I've three more year of my lease of the farm,
and after that, out I must go, I dare say."

"There's no knowing what may happen before that,
Price."

"If I was to go, I don't know that I need quite starve, Mr.
Knox."

"I don't suppose you will."

"I ain't no family, and I don't know as I'm just bound to
go by what a lord says, though he is my landlord. I don't know
as I don't think more of them ladies than I does of him.—him,
Mr. Knox."

And then Mr. Price used some very strong language
indeed. "What right has he to think as I'm going to do his dirty
work? You may tell him from me as he may do his own."

"You'll answer him, Price?"

"Not a line. I ain't got nothing to say to him. He knows
I'm a-going out of the house; and if he don't, you can tell him."

"Where are you going to?"

"Well, I was going to fit up a room or two in the old
farmhouse; and if I had anything like a lease, I wouldn't mind
spending three or four hundred pounds there. I was thinking of
talking to you about it, Mr. Knox."

"I can't renew the lease without his approval."

"You write and ask him, and mind you tell him that there
ain't no doubt at all as to any going out of Cross Hall after
Christmas. Then, if he'll make it fourteen years, I'll put the old
house up and not ask him for a shilling. As I'm a living sinner,
they're on a fox! Who'd have thought of that in the park? That's

the old vixen from the holt, as sure as my name's Price. Them cubs haven't travelled here yet."

So saying, he rode away, and Mr. Knox rode after him, and there was consternation throughout the hunt. It was so unaccustomed a thing to have to gallop across Manor Cross Park! But the hounds were in full cry, through the laurels, and into the shrubbery, and round the conservatory, close up to the house. Then she got into the kitchen-garden, and back again through the laurels. The butler and the gardener and the housemaid and the scullery-maid were all there to see. Even Lady Sarah came to the front door, looking very severe, and the old Marchioness gaped out of her own sitting-room window upstairs. Our friend Mary thought it excellent fun, for she was really able to ride to the hounds; and even Lady Amelia became excited as she flogged the pony along the road. Stupid old vixen, who ought to have known better! Price was quite right, for it was she, and the cubs in the holt were now finally emancipated from all maternal thraldom. She was killed ignominiously in the stokehole under the greenhouse,—she who had been the mother of four litters, and who had baffled the Brotherton hounds half a dozen times over the cream of the Brotherton country!

"I knew it," said Price in a melancholy tone, as he held up the head which the huntsman had just dissevered from the body. "She might 'a done better with herself than come to such a place as this for the last move."

"Is it all over?" asked Lady George.

"That one is pretty nearly all over, miss," said George Scruby, as he threw the fox to the hounds. "My Lady, I mean, begging your Ladyship's pardon." Some one had prompted him at the moment. "I'm very glad to see your Ladyship out, and I hope we'll show you something better before long."

But poor Mary's hunting was over. When George Scruby and Sir Simon and the hounds went off to the holt, she was obliged to remain with her husband and sisters-in-law.

While this was going on Mr. Knox had found time to say a word to Lord George about that letter from the Marquis. "I am afraid," he said, "your brother is very anxious that Price should remain at Cross Hall."

"Has he said anything more?"

"Not to me; but to Price he has."

"He has written to Price?"

"Yes, with his own hand, urging him to stay. I cannot but think it was very wrong." A look of deep displeasure came across Lord George's face. "I have thought it right to mention it, because it may be a question whether her Ladyship's health and happiness may not be best consulted by her leaving the neighbourhood."

"We have considered it all, Mr. Knox, and my mother is determined to stay. We are very much obliged to you. We feel that in doing your duty by my brother you are anxious to be courteous to us. The hounds have gone on; don't let me keep you."

Mr. Houghton was of course out. Unless the meets were very distant from his own place, he was always out. On this occasion his wife also was there. She had galloped across the park as quickly as anybody, and when the fox was being broken up in the grass before the hall-door, was sitting close to Lady George. "You are coming on?" she said in a whisper.

"I am afraid not," answered Mary.

"Oh, yes; do come. Slip away with me. Nobody'll see you. Get as far as the gate, and then you can see that covert drawn."

"I can't very well. The truth is, they don't want me to hunt."

"They! Who is they? 'They' don't want me to hunt. That is, Mr. Houghton doesn't. But I mean to get out of his way by riding a little forward. I don't see why that is not just as good as staying behind. Mr. Price is going to give me a lead. You know Mr. Price?"

"But he goes everywhere."

"And I mean to go everywhere. What's the good of half-doing it? Come along."

But Mary had not even thought of rebellion such as this—did not in her heart approve of it, and was angry with Mrs. Houghton. Nevertheless, when she saw the horsewoman gallop off across the grass towards the gate, she could not help thinking that she would have been just as well able to ride after Mr. Price as her old friend Adelaide de Baron. The Dean did go on, having intimated his purpose of riding on just to see Price's farm.

When the unwonted perturbation was over at Manor Cross Lord George was obliged to revert again to the tidings he had received from Mr. Knox. He could not keep it to himself. He felt himself obliged to tell it all to Lady Sarah.

"That he should write to such a man as Mr. Price, telling him of his anxiety to banish his own mother from her own house!"

"You did not see the letter?"

"No; but Knox did. They could not very well show such a letter to me; but Knox says that Price was very indignant, and swore that he would not even answer it."

"I suppose he can afford it, George? It would be very dreadful to ruin him."

"Price is a rich man. And after all, if Price were to do all that Brotherton desires him, he could only keep us out for a year or so. But don't you think you will all be very uncomfortable here. How will my mother feel if she isn't ever allowed to see him? And how will you feel if you find that you never want to see his wife?"

Lady Sarah sat silent for a few minutes before she answered him, and then declared for war. "It is very bad, George; very bad. I can foresee great unhappiness; especially the unhappiness which must come from constant condemnation of one whom we ought to wish to love and approve of before all others. But nothing can be so bad as running away. We ought not to allow anything to drive mamma from her own house, and us from our own duties. I don't think we ought to take any notice of Brotherton's letter to Mr. Price." It was thus decided between them that no further notice should be taken of the Marquis's letter to Mr. Price.

Chapter VIII.

Pugsby Brook.

There was great talking about the old vixen as they all trotted away to Cross Hall Holt;—how it was the same old fox that they hadn't killed in a certain run last January, and how one old farmer was quite sure that this very fox was the one which had taken them that celebrated run to Bamham Moor three years ago, and how she had been the mother of quite a Priam's progeny of cubs. And now that she should have been killed in a stokehole! While this was going on a young lady rode up along side of Mr. Price, and said a word to him with her sweetest smile.

"You remember your promise to me, Mr. Price?"

"Surely, Mrs. Houghton. Your nag can jump a few, no doubt."

"Beautifully. Mr. Houghton bought him from Lord Mountfencer. Lady Mountfencer couldn't ride him because he pulls a little. But he's a perfect hunter."

"We shall find him, Mrs. Houghton, to a moral; and do you stick to me. They generally go straight away to Thrupp's larches. You see the little wood. There's an old earth there, but that's stopped. There is only one fence between this and that, a biggish ditch, with a bit of a hedge on this side, but it's nothing to the horses when they're fresh."

"Mine's quite fresh."

"Then they mostly turn to the right for Pugsby; nothing but grass then for four miles a-head."

"And the jumping?"

"All fair. There's one bit of water,—Pugsby Brook,—that you ought to have as he'll be sure to cross it ever so much above the bridge. But, lord love you, Mrs. Houghton, that horse'll think nothing of the brook."

"Nothing at all, Mr. Price. I like brooks."

"I'm afraid he's not here, Price," said Sir Simon, trotting round the cover towards the whip, who was stationed at the further end.

"Well, Sir Simon, her as we killed came from the holt, you know," said the farmer, mindful of his reputation for foxes. "You can't eat your cake and have it too, can you, Sir Simon?"

"Ought to be able in a covert like this."

"Well, perhaps we shall. The best lying is down in that corner. I've seen a brace of cubs together there a score of times." Then there was one short low, dubious, bark, and then another a little more confirmed. "That's it, Sir Simon. There's your 'cake.'"

"Good hound, Blazer," cried Sir Simon, recognising the voice of his dog. And many of the pack recognised the well-known sound as plainly as the master, for you might hear the hounds rustling through the covert as they hurried up to certify to the scent which their old leader had found for them. The holt though thick was small and a fox had not much chance but by breaking. Once up the covert and once back again the animal went, and then Dick, the watchful whip, holding his hand up to his face, holloaed him away. "Gently, gentlemen," shouted Sir Simon, "let them settle. Now, Mr. Bottomley, if you'll only keep yourself a little steady, you'll find yourself the better for it at the finish." Mr. Bottomley was a young man from London, who was often addressed after this fashion, was always very unhappy for a few minutes, and then again forgot it in his excitement.

"Now, Mr. Price," said Mrs. Houghton in a fever of expectation. She had been dodging backwards and forwards trying to avoid her husband, and yet unwilling to leave the farmer's side.

"Wait a moment, ma'am; wait a moment. Now we're right; here to the left." So saying Mr. Price jumped over a low hedge, and Mrs. Houghton followed him, almost too closely. Mr. Houghton saw it, and didn't follow. He had made his way up, resolved to stop his wife, but she gave him the slip at the last moment. "Now through the gate, ma'am, and then on straight as an arrow for the little wood. I'll give you a lead over the ditch, but don't ride quite so close, ma'am." Then the farmer went away feeling perhaps that his best chance of keeping clear from his too loving friend was to make the pace so fast that she should not be able quite to catch him. But Lady Mountfencer's nag was fast too, was fast and had a will of his own. It was not without a cause that Lord Mountfencer had parted with so good a horse out of his stable. "Have a care, ma'am," said Price, as Mrs. Houghton canoned against him as they both landed over the big ditch; "have a care, or we shall come to grief together. Just see me over before you let him take his jump." It was very good advice, and is very often given; but both ladies and gentlemen, whose hands are a little doubtful, sometimes find themselves unable to follow it. But now they were at Thrupp's larches. George Scruby had led the way, as becomes a huntsman, and a score or more had followed him over the big fence. Price had been going a little to the left, and when they reached the wood was as forward as any one.

"He won't hang here, Sir Simon," said the farmer, as the master came up, "he never does."

"He's only a cub," said the master.

"The holt cubs this time of the year are nigh as strong as old foxes. Now for Pugsby."

Mrs. Houghton looked round, fearing every moment that her husband would come up. They had just crossed a road, and wherever there was a road there, she thought, he would certainly be.

"Can't we get round the other side, Mr. Price?" she said.

"You won't be any better nor here."

"But there's Mr. Houghton on the road," she whispered.

"Oh-h-h," ejaculated the farmer, just touching the end of his nose with his finger and moving gently on through the wood. "Never spoil sport," was the motto of his life, and to his thinking it was certainly sport that a young wife should ride to hounds in opposition to an old husband. Mrs. Houghton followed him, and as they got out on the other side, the fox was again away. "He ain't making for Pugsby's after all," said Price to George Scruby.

"He don't know that country yet," said the huntsman. "He'll be back in them Manor Cross woods. You'll see else."

The park of Manor Cross lay to the left of them, whereas Pugsby and the desirable grass country away to Bamham Moor were all to the right. Some men mindful of the big brook and knowing the whereabouts of the bridge, among whom was Mr. Houghton, kept very much to the right and were soon out of the run altogether. But the worst of it was that though they were not heading for their good country, still there was the brook, Pugsby brook, to be taken. Had the fox done as he ought to have done, and made for Pugsby itself, the leap would have been from grass to grass; but now it must be from plough to plough, if taken at all. It need hardly be said that the two things are very different. Sir Simon, when he saw how the land lay, took a lane leading down to the Brotherton road. If the fox was making for the park he must be right in that direction. It is not often that a master of hounds rides for glory, and Sir Simon had long since left all that to younger men. But there were still a dozen riders pressing on, and among them were the farmer and his devoted follower,— and a gentleman in black.

Let us give praise where praise is due, and acknowledge that young Bottomley was the first at the brook,—and the first over it. As soon as he was beyond Sir Simon's notice, he had scurried on across the plough, and being both light and indiscreet, had enjoyed the heartfelt pleasure of passing George Scruby. George, who hated Mr. Bottomley, grunted out his malediction, even though no one could hear him. "He'll soon be at the bottom of that," said George, meaning to imply in horsey phrase that the rider, if he rode over ploughed ground after that fashion, would soon come to the end of his steed's power. But Bottomley, if he could only be seen to jump the big brook before any one else, would have happiness enough for a month. To have done a thing that he could talk about was the charm that Bottomley found in hunting. Alas, though he rode gallantly at the brook and did get over it, there was not much to talk about; for, unfortunately, he left his horse behind him in the water. The poor beast going with a rush off the plough, came with her neck and shoulders against the opposite bank, and shot his rider well on to the dry land.

"That's about as good as a dead'un," said George, as he landed a yard or two to the right. This was ill-natured, and the horse in truth was not hurt. But a rider, at any rate a young rider, should not take a lead from a huntsman unless he is very sure of himself, of his horse, and of the run of the hounds. The next man over was the gentleman in black, who took it in a stand, and who really seemed to know what he was about. There were some who afterwards asserted that this was the Dean, but the Dean was never heard to boast of the performance.

Mrs. Houghton's horse was going very strong with her. More than once the farmer cautioned her to give him a pull over the plough. And she attempted to obey the order. But the horse was self-willed, and she was light; and in truth the heaviness of the ground would have been nothing to him had he been fairly well ridden. But she allowed him to rush with her through the mud. As she had never yet had an accident she knew nothing of fear, and she was beyond measure excited. She had been near enough to see that a man fell at the brook, and then she saw also that the huntsman got over, and also the gentleman in black. It seemed to her to be lovely. The tumble did not scare her at all, as others coming after the unfortunate one had succeeded. She was aware that there were three or four other men behind her, and she was determined that they should not pass her. They should see that she also could jump the river. She had not rid herself of her husband for nothing. Price, as he came near the water, knew that he had plenty to do, and knew also how very close to him the woman was. It was too late now to speak to her again, but he did not fear for his own horse if she would only give him room. He steadied the animal a yard or two from the margin as he came to the headland that ran down the side of the brook, and then took his leap.

But Mrs. Houghton rode us though the whole thing was to be accomplished by a rush, and her horse, true to the manner of horses, insisted on following in the direct track of the one who had led him so far. When he got to the bank he made his effort to jump high, but had got no footing for a fair spring. On he went, however, and struck Price's horse on the quarter so violently as to upset that animal, as well as himself.

Price, who was a thoroughly good horseman, was knocked off, but got on to the bank as Bottomley had done. The two animals were both in the brook, and when the farmer was able to look round, he saw that the lady was out of sight. He was in the water immediately himself, but before he made the plunge he had resolved that he never again would give a lady a lead till he knew whether she could ride.

Mr. Knox and Dick were soon on the spot, and Mrs. Houghton was extracted. "I'm blessed if she ain't dead," said the whip, pale as death himself. "H—sh!" said Mr. Knox; "she's not dead, but I'm afraid she's hurt." Price had come back through the water with the woman in his arms, and the two horses were still floundering about, unattended. "It's her shoulder, Mr.

Knox," said Price. "The horse has jammed her against the bank under water." During this time her head was drooping, and her eyes were closed, and she was apparently senseless. "Do you look to the horses, Dick. There ain't no reason why they should get their death of cold." By this time there were a dozen men round them, and Dick and others were able to attend to the ill-used nags. "Yes; it's her shoulder," continued Price. "That's out, any way. What the mischief will Mr. Houghton say to me when he comes up!"

There is always a doctor in the field,—sent there by some benignity of providence,—who always rides forward enough to be near to accidents, but never so forward as to be in front of them. It has been hinted that this arrangement is professional rather than providential; but the present writer, having given his mind to the investigation of the matter, is inclined to think that it arises from the general fitness of things. All public institutions have, or ought to have, their doctor, but in no institution is the doctor so invariably at hand, just when he is wanted, as in the hunting field. A very skilful young surgeon from Brotherton was on the spot almost as soon as the lady was out of the water, and declared that she had dislocated her shoulder.

What was to be done? Her hat had gone; she had been under the water; she was covered with mud; she was still senseless, and of course she could neither ride nor walk. There were ever so many suggestions. Price thought that she had better be taken back to Cross Hall, which was about a mile and a half distant. Mr. Knox, who knew the country, told them of a side gate in the Manor Cross wall, which made the great house nearer than Cross Hall. They could get her there in little over a mile. But how to get her there? They must find a door on which to carry her. First a hurdle was suggested, and then Dick was sent galloping up to the house for a carriage. In the meantime she was carried to a labourer's cottage by the roadside on a hurdle, and there the party was joined by Sir Simon and Mr. Houghton.

"It's all your fault," said the husband, coming up to Price as though he meant to strike him with his whip. "Part of it is no doubt, sir," said Price, looking his assailant full in the face, but almost sobbing as he spoke, "and I'm very unhappy about it." Then the husband went and hung over his wife, but his wife, when she saw him, found it convenient to faint again.

At about two o'clock the cortège with the carriage reached the great house. Sir Simon, after expressions of deep sorrow had, of course, gone on after his hounds. Mr. Knox, as belonging to Manor Cross, and Price, and, of course, the doctor, with Mr. Houghton and Mr. Houghton's groom, accompanied the carriage. When they got to the door all the ladies were there to receive them. "I don't think we want to see anything more of you," said Mr. Houghton to the farmer. The poor man turned round and went away home, alone, feeling himself to be thoroughly disgraced. "After all," he said to himself, "if you come to fault it was she nigh killed me, not me her. How was I to know she didn't know nothing about it!"

"Now, Mary, I think you'll own that I was right," Lord George said to his wife, as soon as the sufferer had been put quietly to bed.

"Ladies don't always break their arms," said Mary.

"It might have been you as well as Mrs. Houghton."

"As I didn't go, you need not scold me, George."

"But you were discontented because you were prevented," said he, determined to have the last word.

Chapter IX.

Mrs. Houghton.

Lady Sarah, who was generally regarded as the arbiter of the very slender hospitalities exercised at Manor Cross, was not at all well pleased at being forced to entertain Mrs. Houghton, whom she especially disliked; but, circumstanced as they were, there was no alternative. She had been put to bed with a dislocated arm, and had already suffered much in having it reduced, before the matter could be even discussed. And then it was of course felt that she could not be turned out of the house. She was not only generally hurt, but she was a cousin, also. "We must ask him, mamma," Lady Sarah said. The Marchioness whined piteously. Mr. Houghton's name had always been held in great displeasure by the ladies at Manor Cross. "I don't think we can help it. Mr. Sawyer"—Mr. Sawyer was the very clever young surgeon from Brotherton—"Mr. Sawyer says that she ought not to be removed for at any rate a week." The Marchioness groaned. But the evil became less than had been anticipated, by Mr. Houghton's refusal. At first, he seemed inclined to stay, but after he had seen his wife he declared that, as there was no danger, he would not intrude upon Lady Brotherton, but would, if permitted, ride over and see how his wife was progressing on the morrow. "That is a relief," said Lady Sarah to her mother; and yet Lady Sarah had been almost urgent in assuring Mr. Houghton that they would be delighted to have him.

In spite of her suffering, which must have been real, and her fainting, which had partly been so, Mrs. Houghton had had force enough to tell her husband that he would himself be inexpressibly bored by remaining at Manor Cross, and that his presence would inexpressibly bore "all those dowdy old women," as she called the ladies of the house. "Besides, what's the use?" she said; "I've got to lay here for a certain time. You would not be any good at nursing. You'd only kill yourself with ennui. I shall do well enough, and do you go on with your hunting." He had assented; but finding her to be well enough to express her opinion as to the desirability of his absence strongly, thought that she was well enough, also, to be rebuked for her late disobedience. He began, therefore, to say a word. "Oh! Jeffrey, are you going to scold me," she said, "while I am in such a state as this!" and then, again, she almost fainted. He knew that he was being ill-treated, but knowing, also, that he could not avoid it, he went away without a further word.

But she was quite cheerful that evening when Lady George came up to give her her dinner. She had begged that it might be so. She had known "dear Mary" so long, and was so warmly attached to her. "Dear Mary" did not dislike the occupation, which was soon found to comprise that of being head nurse to the invalid. She had never especially loved Adelaide De Baron, and had felt that there was something amiss in her conversation when they had met at the deanery; but she was brighter than the ladies at Manor Cross, was affectionate in her manner, and was at any rate young. There was an antiquity about every thing at Manor Cross, which was already crushing the spirit of the young bride.

"Dear me! this is nice," said Mrs. Houghton, disregarding, apparently altogether, the pain of her shoulder; "I declare, I shall begin to be glad of the accident!"

"You shouldn't say that."

"Why not, if I feel it? Doesn't it seem like a thing in a story that I should be brought to Lord George's house, and that he was my lover only quite the other day?" The idea had never occurred to Mary, and now that it was suggested to her, she did not like it. "I wonder when he'll come and see me. It would not make you jealous, I hope."

"Certainly not."

"No, indeed. I think he's quite as much in love with you as ever he was with me. And yet, he was very, very fond of me once. Isn't it odd that men should change so?"

"I suppose you are changed, too," said Mary,—hardly knowing what to say.

"Well,—yes,—no. I don't know that I'm changed at all. I never told Lord George that I loved him. And what's more, I never told Mr. Houghton so. I don't pretend to be very virtuous, and of course I married for an income. I like him very well, and I always mean to be good to him; that is, if he lets me have my own way. I'm not going to be scolded, and he need not think so."

"You oughtn't to have gone on to-day, ought you?"

"Why not? If my horse hadn't gone so very quick, and Mr. Price at that moment hadn't gone so very slow, I shouldn't have come to grief, and nobody would have known anything about it. Wouldn't you like to ride?"

"Yes; I should like it. But are not you exerting yourself too much?"

"I should die if I were made to lie here without speaking to any one. Just put the pillow a little under me. Now I'm all right. Who do you think was going as well as anybody yesterday? I saw him."

"Who was it?"

"The very Reverend the Dean of Brotherton, my dear."

"No!"

"But he was. I saw him jump the brook just before I fell into it. What will Mr. Groschut say?"

"I don't think papa cares much what Mr. Groschut says."

"And the Bishop?"

"I'm not sure that he cares very much for the Bishop either. But I am quite sure that he would not do anything that he thought to be wrong."

"A Dean never does, I suppose."

"My papa never does."

"Nor Lord George, I dare say," said Mrs. Houghton.

"I don't say anything about Lord George. I haven't known him quite so long."

"If you won't speak up for him, I will. I'm quite sure Lord George Germain never in his life did anything that he ought not to do. That's his fault. Don't you like men who do what they ought not to do?"

"No," said Mary, "I don't. Everybody always ought to do what they ought to do. And you ought to go to sleep, and so I shall go away." She knew that it was not all right,—that there was something fast, and also something vulgar, about this self-appointed friend of hers. But though Mrs. Houghton was fast, and though she was vulgar, she was a relief to the endless gloom of Manor Cross.

On the next day Mr. Houghton came, explaining to everybody that he had given up his day's hunting for the sake of his wife. But he could say but little, and could do nothing, and he did not remain long. "Don't stay away from the meet another day," his wife said to him; "I shan't get well any the sooner, and I don't like being a drag upon you." Then the husband went away, and did not come for the next two days. On the Sunday he came over in the afternoon and stayed for half-an-hour, and on the following Tuesday he appeared on his way to the meet in top boots and a red coat. He was, upon the whole, less troublesome to the Manor Cross people than might have been expected.

Mr. Price came every morning to enquire, and very gracious passages passed between him and the lady. On the Saturday she was up, sitting on a sofa in a dressing gown, and he was brought in to see her. "It was all my fault, Mr. Price," she said immediately. "I heard what Mr. Houghton said to you; I couldn't speak then, but I was so sorry."

"What a husband says, ma'am, at such a time, goes for nothing."

"What husbands say, Mr. Price, very often does go for nothing." He turned his hat in his hand, and smiled. "If it had not been so, all this wouldn't have happened, and I shouldn't have upset you into the water. But all the same, I hope you'll give me a lead another day, and I'll take great care not to come so close to you again." This pleased Mr. Price so much, that as he went home he swore to himself that if ever she asked him again, he would do just the same as he had done on the day of the accident.

When Price, the farmer, had seen her, of course it became Lord George's duty to pay her his compliments in person. At first he visited her in company with his wife and Lady Sarah, and the conversation was very stiff. Lady Sarah was potent enough to quell even Mrs. Houghton. But later in the afternoon Lord George came back again, his wife being in the room, and then there was a little more ease. "You can't think how it grieves me," she said, "to bring all this trouble upon you." She emphasised the word "you," as though to show him that she cared nothing for his mother and sisters.

"It is no trouble to me," said Lord George, bowing low. "I should say that it was a pleasure, were it not that your presence here is attended with so much pain to yourself."

"The pain is nothing," said Mrs. Houghton. "I have hardly thought of it. It is much more than compensated by the renewal of my intimacy with Lady George Germain." This she said with her very prettiest manner, and he told himself that she was, indeed, very pretty.

Lady George,—or Mary, as we will still call her, for simplicity, in spite of her promotion,—had become somewhat afraid of Mrs. Houghton; but now, seeing her husband's courtesy to her guest, understanding from his manner that he liked her society, began to thaw, and to think that she might allow herself to be intimate with the woman. It did not occur to her to be in any degree jealous,—not, at least, as yet. In her innocence she did not think it possible that her husband's heart should be untrue to her, nor did it occur to her that such a one as Mrs. Houghton could be preferred to herself. She thought that she knew herself to be better than Mrs. Houghton, and she certainly thought herself to be the better looking of the two.

Mrs. Houghton's beauty, such as it was, depended mainly on style; on a certain dash and manner which she had acquired, and which, to another woman, were not attractive. Mary knew that she, herself, was beautiful. She could not but know it. She had been brought up by all belonging to her with that belief; and so believing, had taught herself to acknowledge that no credit was due to herself on that score. Her beauty now belonged entirely to her husband. There was nothing more to be done with it, except to maintain her husband's love, and that, for the present, she did not in the least doubt. She had heard of married men falling in love with other people's wives, but she did not in the least bring home the fact to her own case.

In the course of that afternoon all the ladies of the family sat for a time with their guest. First came Lady Sarah and Lady Susanna. Mrs. Houghton, who saw very well how the land lay, rather snubbed Lady Sarah. She had nothing to fear from the dragon of the family. Lady Sarah, in spite of their cousinship, had called her Mrs. Houghton, and Mrs. Houghton, in return, called the other Lady Sarah. There was to be no intimacy, and she was only received there because of her dislocated shoulder. Let it be so. Lord George and his wife were coming up to town, and the intimacy should be there. She certainly would not wish to repeat her visit to Manor Cross.

"Some ladies do like hunting, and some don't," she said, in answer to a severe remark from Lady Sarah. "I am one of those who do, and I don't think an accident like that has anything to do with it."

"I can't say I think it an amusement fit for ladies," said Lady Sarah.

"I suppose ladies may do what clergymen do. The Dean jumped over the brook just before me." There was not much of an argument in this, but Mrs. Houghton knew that it would vex Lady Sarah, because of the alliance between the Dean and the Manor Cross family.

"She's a detestable young woman," Lady Sarah said to her mother, "and I can only hope that Mary won't see much of her up in town."

"I don't see how she can, after what there has been between her and George," said the innocent old lady. In spite, however, of this strongly expressed opinion, the old lady made her visit, taking Lady Amelia with her. "I hope, my dear, you find yourself getting better."

"So much better, Lady Brotherton! But I am so sorry to have given you all this trouble; but it has been very pleasant to me to be here, and to see Lord George and Mary together. I declare I think hers is the sweetest face I ever looked upon. And she is so much improved. That's what perfect happiness does. I do so like her."

"We love her very dearly," said the Marchioness.

"I am sure you do. And he is so proud of her!" Lady Sarah had said that the woman was detestable, and therefore the Marchioness felt that she ought to detest her. But, had it not been for Lady Sarah, she would have been rather pleased with her guest than otherwise. She did not remain very long, but promised that she would return on the next day.

On the following morning Mr. Houghton came again, staying only a few minutes; and while he was in his wife's sitting-room, both Lord George and Mary found them. As they were all leaving her together, she contrived to say a word to her old lover. "Don't desert me all the morning. Come and talk to me a bit. I am well now, though they won't let me move about." In obedience to this summons, he returned to her when his wife was called upon to attend to the ordinary cloak and petticoat conclave of the other ladies. In regard to these charitable meetings she had partly carried her own way. She had so far thrown off authority as to make it understood that she was not to be bound by the rules which her sisters-in-law had laid down for their own guidance. But her rebellion had not been complete, and she still gave them a certain number of weekly stitches. Lord George had said nothing of his purpose; but for a full hour before luncheon he was alone with Mrs. Houghton. If a gentleman may call on a lady in her house, surely he may, without scandal, pay her a visit in his own. That a married man should chat for an hour with another man's wife in a country house is not much. Where is the man and where the woman who has not done that, quite as a matter of course? And yet when Lord George knocked at the door there was a feeling on him that he was doing something in which he would not wish to be detected. "This is so good of you," she said. "Do sit down; and don't run away. Your mother and sisters have been here,—so nice of them, you know; but everybody treats me as though I oughtn't to open my mouth for above five minutes at a time. I feel as though I should like to jump the brook again immediately."

"Pray don't do that."

"Well, no; not quite yet. You don't like hunting, I'm afraid?"

"The truth is," said Lord George, "that I've never been able to afford to keep horses."

"Ah, that's a reason. Mr. Houghton, of course, is a rich man; but I don't know anything so little satisfactory in itself as being rich."

"It is comfortable."

"Oh yes, it is comfortable; but so unsatisfactory! Of course Mr. Houghton can keep any number of horses; but, what's the use, when he never rides to hounds? Better not have them at all, I think. I am very fond of hunting myself."

"I daresay I should have liked it had it come in my way early in life."

"You speak of yourself as if you were a hundred years old. I know your age exactly. You are just seventeen years younger than Mr. Houghton!" To this Lord George had no reply to make. Of course he had felt that when Miss De Baron had married Mr. Houghton she had married quite an old man. "I wonder whether you were much surprised when you heard that I was engaged to Mr. Houghton?"

"I was, rather."

"Because he is so old?"

"Not that altogether."

"I was surprised myself, and I knew that you would be. But what was I to do?"

"I think you have been very wise," said Lord George.

"Yes, but you think I have been heartless. I can see it in your eyes and hear it in your voice. Perhaps I was heartless;— but then I was bound to be wise. A man may have a profession before him. He may do anything. But what has a girl to think of? You say that money is comfortable."

"Certainly it is."

"How is she to get it, if she has not got it of her own, like dear Mary?"

"You do not think that I have blamed you."

"But even though you have not, yet I must excuse myself to you," she said with energy, bending forward from her sofa towards him. "Do you think that I do not know the difference?"

"What difference?"

"Ah, you shouldn't ask. I may hint at it, but you shouldn't ask. But it wouldn't have done, would it?" Lord George hardly understood what it was that wouldn't have done; but he knew that a reference was being made to his former love by the girl he had loved; and, upon the whole, he rather liked it. The flattery of such intrigues is generally pleasant to men, even when they cannot bring their minds about quick enough to understand all the little ins and outs of the woman's manoeuvres. "It is my very nature to be extravagant. Papa has brought me up like that. And yet I had nothing that I could call my own. I had no right to marry any one but a rich man. You said just now you couldn't afford to hunt."

"I never could."

"And I couldn't afford to have a heart. You said just now, too, that money is very comfortable. There was a time when I should have found it very, very comfortable to have had a fortune of my own."

"You have plenty now."

She wasn't angry with him, because she had already found out that it is the nature of men to be slow. And she wasn't angry with him, again, because, though he was slow, yet also was he evidently gratified. "Yes," she said, "I have plenty now. I have secured so much. I couldn't have done without a large income; but a large income doesn't make me happy. It's like eating and drinking. One has to eat and drink, but yet one doesn't care very much about it. Perhaps you don't regret hunting very much?"

"Yes I do, because it enables a man to know his neighbours."

"I know that I regret the thing I couldn't afford."

Then a glimmer of what she meant did come across him, and he blushed. "Things will not always turn out as they are wanted," he said. Then his conscience upbraided him, and he corrected himself. "But, God knows that I have no reason to complain. I have been fortunate."

"Yes, indeed."

"I sometimes think it is better to remember the good things we have than to regret those that are gone."

"That is excellent philosophy, Lord George. And therefore I go out hunting, and break my bones, and fall into rivers, and ride about with such men as Mr. Price. One has to make the best of it, hasn't one? But you, I see, have no regrets."

He paused for a moment, and then found himself driven to make some attempt at gallantry. "I didn't quite say that," he replied.

"You were able to re-establish yourself according to your own tastes. A man can always do so. I was obliged to take whatever came. I think that Mary is so nice."

"I think so too, I can assure you."

"You have been very fortunate to find such a girl; so innocent, so pure, so pretty, and with a fortune too. I wonder how much difference it would have made in your happiness if you had seen her before we had ever been acquainted. I suppose we should never have known each other then."

"Who can say?"

"No; no one can say. For myself, I own that I like it better as it is. I have something to remember that I can be proud of."

"And I something to be ashamed of."

"To be ashamed of!" she said, almost rising in anger.

"That you should have refused me!"

She had got it at last. She had made her fish rise to the fly. "Oh, no," she said; "there can be nothing of that. If I did not tell you plainly then, I tell you plainly now. I should have done very wrong to marry a poor man."

"I ought not to have asked you."

"I don't know how that may be," she said in a very low voice, looking down to the ground. "Some say that if a man loves he should declare his love, let the circumstances be what they may. I rather think that I agree with them. You at any rate knew that I felt greatly honoured, though the honour was out of my reach." Then there was a pause, during which he could find nothing to say. He was trapped by her flattery, but he did not wish to betray his wife by making love to the woman. He liked her words and her manner; but he was aware that she was a thing sacred as being another man's wife. "But it is all better as it is," she said with a laugh, "and Mary Lovelace is the happiest girl of her year. I am so glad you are coming to London, and do so hope you'll come and see me."

"Certainly I will."

"I mean to be such friends with Mary. There is no woman I like so much. And then circumstances have thrown us together, haven't they; and if she and I are friends, real friends, I shall feel that our friendship may be continued,—yours and mine. I don't mean that all this accident shall go for nothing. I wasn't quite clever enough to contrive it; but I am very glad of it, because it has brought us once more together, so that we may understand each other. Good-bye, Lord George. Don't let me keep you longer now. I wouldn't have Mary jealous, you know."

"I don't think there is the least fear of that," he said in real displeasure.

"Don't take me up seriously for my little joke," she said as she put out her left hand. He took it, and once more smiled, and then left her.

When she was alone there came a feeling on her that she had gone through some hard work with only moderate success; and also a feeling that the game was hardly worth the candle. She was not in the least in love with the man, or capable of being in love with any man. In a certain degree she was jealous, and felt that she owed Mary Lovelace a turn for having so speedily won her own rejected lover. But her jealousy was not strong enough for absolute malice. She had formed no plot against the happiness of the husband and wife when she came into the house; but the plot made itself, and she liked the excitement. He was heavy,—certainly heavy; but he was very handsome, and a lord; and then, too, it was much in her favour that he certainly had once loved her dearly.

Lord George, as he went down to lunch, felt himself to be almost guilty, and hardly did more than creep into the room where his wife and sisters were seated.

"Have you been with Mrs. Houghton?" asked Lady Sarah in a firm voice.

"Yes, I have been sitting with her for the last half hour," he replied; but he couldn't answer the question without hesitation in his manner. Mary, however, thought nothing about it.

Chapter X.

The Dean As A Sporting Man.

In Brotherton the Dean's performance in the run from Cross Hall Holt was almost as much talked of as Mrs. Houghton's accident. There had been rumours of things that he had done in the same line after taking orders, when a young man,—of runs that he had ridden, and even of visits which he had made to Newmarket and other wicked places. But, as far as Brotherton knew, there had been nothing of all this since the Dean had been a dean. Though he was constantly on horseback, he had never been known to do more than perhaps look at a meet, and it was understood through Brotherton generally that he had forbidden his daughter to hunt. But now, no sooner was his daughter married, and the necessity of setting an example to her at an end, than the Dean, with a rosette in his hat,—for so the story was told,—was after the hounds like a sporting farmer or a mere country gentleman! On the very next day Mr. Groschut told the whole story to the Bishop. But Mr. Groschut had not seen the performance, and the Bishop affected to disbelieve it. "I'm afraid, my lord," said the chaplain, "I'm afraid you'll find it's true." "If he rides after every pack of dogs in the county, I don't know that I can help it," said the Bishop. With this Mr. Groschut was by no means inclined to agree. A bishop is as much entitled to cause inquiries to be made into the moral conduct of a dean as of any country clergyman in his diocese. "Suppose he were to take to gambling on the turf," said Mr. Groschut, with much horror expressed in his tone and countenance. "But riding after a pack of dogs isn't gambling on the turf," said the Bishop, who, though he would have liked to possess the power of putting down the Dean, by no means relished the idea of being beaten in an attempt to do so.

And Mr. Canon Holdenough heard of it. "My dear," he said to his wife, "Manor Cross is coming out strong in the sporting way. Not only is Mrs. Houghton laid up there with a broken limb, but your brother's father-in-law took the brush on the same day."

"The Dean!" said Lady Alice.

"So they tell me."

"He was always so particular in not letting Mary ride over a single fence. He would hardly let her go to a meet on horseback."

"Many fathers do what they won't let their daughters do. The Dean has been always giving signs that he would like to break out a little."

"Can they do anything to him?"

"Oh dear no;—not if he was to hunt a pack of hounds himself, as far as I know."

"But I suppose it's wrong, Canon," said the clerical wife.

"Yes; I think it's wrong because it will scandalise. Everything that gives offence is wrong, unless it be something that is on other grounds expedient. If it be true we shall hear about it a good deal here, and it will not contribute to brotherly love and friendship among us clergymen."

There was another canon at Brotherton, one Dr. Pountner, a red-faced man, very fond of his dinner, a man of infinite pluck, and much attached to the Cathedral, towards the reparation of which he had contributed liberally. And, having an ear for music, he had done much to raise the character of the choir. Though Dr. Pountner's sermons were supposed to be the worst ever heard from the pulpit of the Cathedral, he was, on account of the above good deeds, the most popular clergyman in the city. "So I'm told you've been distinguishing yourself, Mr. Dean," said the Doctor, meeting our friend in the close.

"Have I done so lately, more than is usual with me?" asked the Dean, who had not hitherto heard of the rumour of his performances.

"I am told that you were so much ahead the other day in the hunting field, that you were unable to give assistance to the poor lady who broke her arm."

"Oh, that's it! If I do anything at all, though I may do it but once in a dozen years, I like to do it well, Dr. Pountner. I wish I thought that you could follow my example, and take a little exercise. It would be very good for you." The Doctor was a heavy man, and hardly walked much beyond the confines of the Close or his own garden. Though a bold man, he was not so ready as the Dean, and had no answer at hand. "Yes," continued our friend, "I did go a mile or two with them, and I enjoyed it amazingly. I wish with all my heart there was no prejudice against clergymen hunting."

"I think it would be an abominable practice," said Dr. Pountner, passing on.

The Dean himself would have thought nothing more about it had there not appeared a few lines on the subject in a weekly newspaper called the "Brotherton Church," which was held to be a pestilential little rag by all the Close. Deans, canons, and minor canons were all agreed as to this, Dr. Pountner hating the "Brotherton Church" quite as sincerely as did the Dean. The "Brotherton Church" was edited nominally by a certain Mr. Grease,—a very pious man who had long striven, but hitherto in vain, to get orders. But it was supposed by many that the paper was chiefly inspired by Mr. Groschut. It was always very laudatory of the Bishop. It had distinguished itself by its elaborate opposition to ritual. Its mission was to put down popery in the diocese of Brotherton. It always sneered at the Chapter generally, and very often said severe things of the Dean. On this occasion the paragraph was as follows; "There is a rumour current that Dean Lovelace was out with the Brotherton foxhounds last Wednesday, and that he rode with the pack all the day, leading the field. We do not believe this, but we hope that for the sake of the Cathedral and for his own sake, he will condescend to deny the report." On the next Saturday there was another paragraph, with a reply from the Dean; "We have received from the Dean of Brotherton the following startling letter, which we publish without comment. What our opinion on the subject may be our readers will understand.

"Deanery, November, 187—

"Sir,—You have been correctly informed that I was out with the Brotherton foxhounds on Wednesday week last. The other reports which you have published, and as to which after publication, you have asked for information, are unfortunately incorrect. I wish I could have done as well as my enemies accuse me of doing.

"I am, Sir,

"Your humble servant,

"HENRY LOVELACE.

"To the Editor of the 'Brotherton Church.'"

The Dean's friends were unanimous in blaming him for having taken any notice of the attack. The Bishop, who was at heart an honest man and a gentleman, regretted it. All the Chapter were somewhat ashamed of it. The Minor Canons were agreed that it was below the dignity of a dean. Dr. Pountner, who had not yet forgotten the allusion to his obesity, whispered in some clerical ear that nothing better could be expected out of a stable; and Canon Holdenough, who really liked the Dean in spite of certain differences of opinion, expostulated with him about it.

"I would have let it pass," said the Canon. "Why notice it at all?"

"Because I would not have any one suppose that I was afraid to notice it. Because I would not have it thought that I had gone out with the hounds and was ashamed of what I had done."

"Nobody who knows you would have thought that."

"I am proud to think that nobody who knows me would. I make as many mistakes as another, and am sorry for them afterwards. But I am never ashamed. I'll tell you what happened, not to justify my hunting, but to justify my letter. I was over at Manor Cross, and I went to the meet, because Mary went. I have not done such a thing before since I came to Brotherton, because there is,—what I will call a feeling against it. When I was there I rode a field or two with them, and I can tell you I enjoyed it."

"I daresay you did."

"Then, very soon after the fox broke, there was that brook at which Mrs. Houghton hurt herself. I happened to jump it, and the thing became talked about because of her accident. After that we came out on the Brotherton road, and I went back to Manor Cross. Do not suppose that I should have been ashamed of myself if I had gone on even half a dozen more fields."

"I'm sure you wouldn't."

"The thing in itself is not bad. Nevertheless,—thinking as the world around us does about hunting,—a clergyman in my position would be wrong to hunt often. But a man who can feel horror at such a thing as this is a prig in religion. If, as is more likely, a man affects horror, he is a hypocrite. I believe that most clergymen will agree with me in that; but there is no clergyman in the diocese of whose agreement I feel more certain than of yours."

"It is the letter, not the hunting, to which I object."

"There was an apparent cowardice in refraining from answering such an attack. I am aware, Canon, of a growing feeling of hostility to myself."

"Not in the Chapter?"

"In the diocese. And I know whence it comes, and I think I understand its cause. Let what will come of it I am not going to knock under. I want to quarrel with no man, and certainly with no clergyman,—but I am not going to be frightened out of my own manner of life or my own manner of thinking by fear of a quarrel."

"Nobody doubts your courage; but what is the use of fighting when there is nothing to win. Let that wretched newspaper alone. It is beneath you and me, Dean."

"Very much beneath us, and so is your butler beneath you. But if he asks you a question, you answer him. To tell the truth I would rather they should call me indiscreet than timid. If I did not feel that it would be really wrong and painful to my friends I would go out hunting three days next week, to let them know that I am not to be cowed."

There was a good deal said at Manor Cross about the newspaper correspondence, and some condemnation of the Dean expressed by the ladies, who thought that he had lowered himself by addressing a reply to the editor. In the heat of discussion a word or two was spoken by Lady Susanna,—who entertained special objections to all things low,—which made Mary very angry. "I think papa is at any rate a better judge than you can be," she said. Between sisters as sisters generally are, or even sisters-in-laws, this would not be much; but at Manor Cross it was felt to be misconduct. Mary was so much younger than they were! And then she was the grand-daughter of a tradesman! No doubt they all thought that they were willing to admit her among themselves on terms of equality; but then there was a feeling among them that she ought to repay this great goodness by a certain degree of humility and submission. From day to day the young wife strengthened herself in a resolution that she would not be humble and would not be submissive.

Lady Susanna, when she heard the words, drew herself up with an air of offended dignity. "Mary, dear," said Lady Sarah, "is not that a little unkind?"

"I think it is unkind to say that papa is indiscreet," said the Dean's daughter. "I wonder what you'd all think if I were to say a word against dear mamma." She had been specially instructed to call the Marchioness mamma.

"The Dean is not my father-in-law," said Lady Amelia, very proudly, as though in making the suggestion, she begged it to be understood that under no circumstances could such a connection have been possible.

"But he's my papa, and I shall stand up for him,—and I do say that he must know more about such things than any lady." Then Lady Susanna got up and marched majestically out of the room.

Lord George was told of this, and found himself obliged to speak to his wife. "I'm afraid there has been something between you and Susanna, dear."

"She abused papa, and I told her papa knew better than she did, and then she walked out of the room."

"I don't suppose she meant to—abuse the Dean."

"She called him names."

"She said he was indiscreet."

"That is calling him names."

"No, my dear, indiscreet is an epithet; and even were it a noun substantive, as a name must be, it could only be one name." It was certainly very hard to fall in love with a man who could talk about epithets so very soon after his marriage; but yet she would go on trying. "Dear George," she said, "don't you scold me. I will do anything you tell me, but I don't like them to say hard things of papa. You are not angry with me for taking papa's part, are you?"

He kissed her, and told her that he was not in the least angry with her; but, nevertheless, he went on to insinuate, that if she could bring herself to show something of submission to his sisters, it would make her own life happier and theirs and his. "I would do anything I could to make your life happy," she said.

Chapter XI.

Lord And Lady George Go Up To Town.

Time went on, and the day arranged for the migration to London came round. After much delicate fencing on one side and the other, this was fixed for the 31st January. The fencing took place between the Dean, acting on behalf of his daughter, and the ladies of the Manor Cross family generally. They, though they conceived themselves to have had many causes of displeasure with Mary, were not the less anxious to keep her at Manor Cross. They would all, at any moment, have gladly assented to an abandonment of the London house, and had taught themselves to look upon the London house as an allurement of Satan, most unwisely contrived and countenanced by the Dean. And there was no doubt that, as the Dean acted on behalf of his daughter, so did they act on behalf of their brother. He could not himself oppose the London house; but he disliked it and feared it, and now, at last, thoroughly repented himself of it. But it had been a stipulation made at the marriage; and the Dean's money had been spent. The Dean had been profuse with his money, and had shown himself to be a more wealthy man than any one at Manor Cross had suspected. Mary's fortune was no doubt her own; but the furniture had been in a great measure supplied by the Dean, and the Dean had paid the necessary premium on going into the house. Lord George felt it to be impossible to change his mind after all that had been done; but he had been quite willing to postpone the evil day as long as possible.

Lady Susanna was especially full of fears, and, it must be owned, especially inimical to all Mary's wishes. She was the one who had perhaps been most domineering to her brother's wife, and she was certainly the one whose domination Mary resisted with the most settled determination. There was a self-abnegation about Lady Sarah, a downright goodness, and at the same time an easily-handled magisterial authority, which commanded reverence. After three months of residence at Manor Cross, Mary was willing to acknowledge that Lady Sarah was more than a sister-in-law,—that her nature partook of divine omnipotence, and that it compelled respect, whether given willingly or unwillingly. But to none of the others would her spirit thus humble itself, and especially not to Lady Susanna. Therefore Lady Susanna was hostile, and therefore Lady Susanna was quite sure that Mary would fall into great trouble amidst the pleasures of the metropolis.

"After all," she said to her elder sister, "what is £1,500 a year to keep up a house in London?"

"It will only be for a few months," said Lady Sarah.

"Of course she must have a carriage, and then George will find himself altogether in the hands of the Dean. That is what I fear. The Dean has done very well with himself, but he is not a man whom I like to trust altogether."

"He is at any rate generous with his money."

"He is bound to be that, or he could not hold up his head at all. He has nothing else to depend on. Did you hear what Dr. Pountner said about him the other day? Since that affair with the newspaper, he has gone down very much in the Chapter. I am sure of that."

"I think you are a little hard upon him, Susanna."

"You must feel that he is very wrong about this house in London. Why is a man, because he's married, to be taken away from all his own pursuits? If she could not accommodate herself to his tastes, she should not have accepted him."

"Let us be just," said Lady Sarah.

"Certainly, let us be just," said Lady Amelia, who in these conversations seldom took much part, unless when called upon to support her eldest sister.

"Of course we should be just," said Lady Susanna.

"She did not accept him," said Lady Sarah, "till he had agreed to comply with the Dean's wish that they should spend part of their time in London."

"He was very weak," said Lady Susanna.

"I wish it could have been otherwise," continued Lady Sarah; "but we can hardly suppose that the tastes of a young girl from Brotherton should be the same as ours. I can understand that Mary should find Manor Cross dull."

"Dull!" exclaimed Lady Susanna.

"Dull!" ejaculated Lady Amelia, constrained on this occasion to differ even from her eldest sister. "I can't understand that she should find Manor Cross dull, particularly while she has her husband with her."

"The bargain, at any rate, was made," said Lady Sarah, "before the engagement was settled; and as the money is hers, I do not think we have a right to complain. I am very sorry that it should be so. Her character is very far from being formed, and his tastes are so completely fixed that nothing will change them."

"And then there's that Mrs. Houghton!" said Lady Susanna. Mrs. Houghton had of course left Manor Cross long since; but she had left a most unsatisfactory feeling behind her in the minds of all the Manor Cross ladies. This arose not only from their personal dislike, but from a suspicion, a most agonising suspicion, that their brother was more fond than he should have been of the lady's society. It must be understood that Mary herself knew nothing of this, and was altogether free from such suspicion. But the three sisters, and the Marchioness under their tuition, had decided that it would be very much better that Lord George should see no more of Mrs. Houghton. He was not, they thought, infatuated in such a fashion that he would run to London after her; but, when in London, he would certainly be thrown into her society. "I cannot bear to think of it," continued Lady Susanna. Lady Amelia shook her head. "I think, Sarah, you ought to speak to him seriously. No man has higher ideas of duty than he has; and if he be made to think of it, he will avoid her."

"I have spoken," replied Lady Sarah, almost in a whisper.

"Well!"

"Well!"

"Was he angry?"

"How did he bear it?"

"He was not angry, but he did not bear it very well. He told me that he certainly found her to be attractive, but that he thought he had power enough to keep himself free from any such fault as that. I asked him to promise me not to see her; but he declined to make a promise which he said he might not be able to keep."

"She is a horrid woman, and Mary. I am afraid, likes her," said Lady Susanna. "I know that evil will come of it."

Sundry scenes counter to this were enacted at the deanery. Mary was in the habit of getting herself taken over to Brotherton more frequently than the ladies liked; but it was impossible that they should openly oppose her visits to her father. On one occasion, early in January, she had got her husband to ride over with her, and was closeted with the Dean while he was away in the city. "Papa," she said, "I almost think that I'll give up the house in Munster Court."

"Give it up! Look here, Mary; you'll have no happiness in life unless you can make up your mind not to allow those old ladies at Manor Cross to sit upon you."

"It is not for their sake. He does not like it, and I would do anything for him."

"That is all very well; and I would be the last to advise you to oppose his wishes if I did not see that the effect would be to make him subject to his sisters' dominion as well as you. Would you like him to be always under their thumb?"

"No, papa; I shouldn't like that."

"It was because I foresaw all this that I stipulated so expressly as I did that you should have a house of your own. Every woman, when she marries, should be emancipated from other domestic control than that of her husband. From the nature of Lord George's family this would have been impossible at Manor Cross, and therefore I insisted on a house in town. I could do this the more freely because the wherewithal was to come from us, and not from them. Do not disturb what I have done."

"I will not go against you, of course, papa."

"And remember always that this is to be done as much for his sake as for yours. His position has been very peculiar. He has no property of his own, and he has lived there with his mother and sisters till the feminine influences of the house have almost domineered him. It is your duty to assist in freeing him from this." Looking at the matter in the light now presented to her, Mary began to think that her father was right. "With a husband there should at any rate be only one feminine influence," he added, laughing.

"I shall not over rule him, and I shall not try," said Mary, smiling.

"At any rate, do not let other women rule him. By degrees he will learn to enjoy London society, and so will you. You will spend half the year at Manor Cross or the deanery, and by degrees both he and you will be emancipated. For myself, I can conceive nothing more melancholy than would be his slavery and yours if you were to live throughout the year with those old women." Then, too, he said something to her of the satisfaction which she herself would receive from living in London, and told her that, for her, life itself had hardly as yet been commenced. She received her lessons with thankfulness and gratitude, but with something of wonder that he should so openly recommend to her a manner of life which she had hitherto been taught to regard as worldly.

After that no further hint was given to her that the house in London might yet be abandoned. When riding back with her husband, she had been clever enough to speak of the thing as a fixed certainty; and he had then known that he also must regard it as fixed. "You had better not say anything more about it," he said one day almost angrily to Lady Susanna, and then nothing more had been said about it—to him.

There were other causes of confusion,—of terrible confusion,—at Manor Cross, of confusion so great that from day to day the Marchioness would declare herself unable to go through the troubles before her. The workmen were already in the big house preparing for the demolition and reconstruction of everything as soon as she should be gone; and other workmen were already demolishing and reconstructing Cross Hall. The sadness of all this and the weight on the old lady's mind were increased by the fact that no member of the family had received so much even as a message from the Marquis himself since it had been decided that his wishes should not be obeyed. Over and over again the dowager attempted to give way, and suggested that they should all depart and be out of sight. It seemed to her that when a marquis is a marquis he ought to have his own way, though it be never so unreasonable. Was he not the head of the family? But Lady Sarah was resolved, and carried her point. Were they all to be pitched down in some strange corner, where they would be no better than other women, incapable of doing good or exercising influence, by the wish of one man who had never done any good anywhere, or used his own influence legitimately? Lady Sarah was no coward, and Lady Sarah stuck to Cross Hall, though in doing so she had very much to endure. "I won't go out, my Lady," said Price, "not till the day when her Ladyship is ready to come in. I can put up with things, and I'll see as all is done as your Ladyship wishes." Price, though he was a sporting farmer, and though men were in the habit of drinking cherry brandy at his house, and though naughty things had been said about him, had in these days become Lady Sarah's prime minister at Cross Hall, and was quite prepared in that capacity to carry on war against the Marquis.

When the day came for the departure of Mary and her husband, a melancholy feeling pervaded the whole household. A cook had been sent up from Brotherton who had lived at Manor Cross many years previously. Lord George took a man who had waited on himself lately at the old house, and Mary had her own maid who had come with her when she married. They had therefore been forced to look for but one strange servant. But this made the feeling the stronger that they would all be strange up in London. This was so strong with Lord George that it almost amounted to fear. He knew that he did not know how to live in London. He belonged to the Carlton, as became a conservative nobleman; but he very rarely entered it, and never felt himself at home when he was there. And Mary, though she had been quite resolved since the conversation with her father that she would be firm about her house, still was not without her own dread. She herself had no personal friends in town,—not one but Mrs. Houghton, as to whom she heard nothing but evil words from the ladies around her. There had been an attempt made to get one of the sisters to go up with them for the first month. Lady Sarah had positively refused, almost with indignation. Was it to be supposed that she would desert her mother at so trying a time? Lady Amelia was then asked, and with many regrets declined the invitation. She had not dared to use her own judgment, and Lady Sarah had not cordially advised her to go. Lady Sarah had thought that Lady Susanna would be the most useful. But Lady Susanna was not asked. There were a few words on the subject between Lord George and his wife. Mary, remembering her father's advice, had determined that she would not be sat upon, and had whispered to her husband that Susanna was always severe to her. When, therefore, the time came, they departed from Manor Cross without any protecting spirit.

There was something sad in this, even to Mary. She knew that she was taking her husband away from the life he liked, and that she, herself, was going to a life as to which she could not even guess, whether she would like it or not. But she had the satisfaction of feeling that she was at last going to begin to live as a married woman. Hitherto she had been treated as a child. If there was danger, there was, at any rate, the excitement which danger produces. "I am almost glad that we are going alone, George," she said. "It seems to me that we have never been alone yet."

He wished to be gracious and loving to her, and yet he was not disposed to admit anything which might seem to imply that he had become tired of living with his own family. "It is very nice, but—"

"But what, dear?"

"Of course I am anxious about my mother just at present."

"She is not to move for two months yet."

"No,—not to move; but there are so many things to be done."

"You can run down whenever you please?"

"That's expensive; but of course it must be done."

"Say that you'll like being with me alone." They had the compartment of the railway carriage all to themselves, and she, as she spoke, leaned against him, inviting him to caress her. "You don't think it a trouble, do you, having to come and live with me?" Of course he was conquered, and said, after his nature, what prettiest things he could to her, assuring her that he would sooner live with her than with any one in the world, and promising that he would always endeavour to make her happy. She knew that he was doing his best to be a loving husband, and she felt, therefore, that she was bound to be loyal in her endeavours to love him; but at the same time, at the very moment in which she was receiving his words with outward show of satisfied love, her imagination was picturing to her something else which would have been so immeasurably superior, if only it had been possible.

That evening they dined together, alone; and it was the first time that they had ever done so, except at an inn. Never before had been imposed on her the duty of seeing that his dinner was prepared for him. There certainly was very little of duty to perform in the matter, for he was a man indifferent as to what he ate, or what he drank. The plainness of the table at Manor Cross had surprised Mary, after the comparative luxury of the deanery. All her lessons at Manor Cross had gone to show that eating was not a delectation to be held in high esteem. But still she was careful that everything around him should be nice. The furniture was new, the glasses and crockery were new. Few, if any, of the articles used, had ever been handled before. All her bridal presents were there; and no doubt there was present to her mind the fact that everything in the house had in truth been given to him by her. If only she could make the things pleasant! If only he would allow himself to be taught that nice things are nice! She hovered around him, touching him every now and then with her light fingers, moving a lock of his hair, and then stooping over him and kissing his brow. It might still be that she would be able to galvanise him into that lover's vitality, of which she had dreamed. He never rebuffed her; he did not scorn her kisses, or fail to smile when his hair was moved; he answered every word she spoke to him carefully and courteously; he admired her pretty things when called upon to admire them. But through it all, she was quite aware that she had not galvanised him as yet.

Of course there were books. Every proper preparation had been made for rendering the little house pleasant. In the evening she took from her shelf a delicate little volume of poetry, something exquisitely bound, pretty to look at, and sweet to handle, and settled herself down to be happy in her own drawing-room. But she soon looked up from the troubles of Aurora Leigh to see what her husband was doing. He was comfortable in his chair, but was busy with the columns of the Brothershire Herald.

"Dear me, George, have you brought that musty old paper up here?"

"Why shouldn't I read the Herald here, as well as at Manor Cross?"

"Oh! yes, if you like it."

"Of course I want to know what is being done in the county." But when next she looked, the county had certainly faded from his mind, for he was fast asleep.

On that occasion she did not care very much for Aurora Leigh. Her mind was hardly tuned to poetry of that sort. The things around her were too important to allow her mind to indulge itself with foreign cares. And then she found herself looking at the watch. At Manor Cross ten o'clock every night brought all the servants into the drawing-room. First the butler would come and place the chairs, and then the maids, and then the coachman and footman would follow. Lord George read the prayers, and Mary had always thought them to be very tiring. But she now felt that it would almost be a relief if the butler would come in and place the chairs.

Chapter XII.

Miss Mildmay And Jack De Baron.

Lady George was not left long in her new house without visitors. Early on the day after her arrival, Mrs. Houghton came to her, and began at once, with great volubility, to explain how the land lay, and to suggest how it should be made to lie for the future. "I am so glad you have come. As soon, you know, as they positively forbade me to get on horseback again this winter, I made up my mind to come to town. What is there to keep me down there if I don't ride? I promised to obey if I was brought here,—and to disobey if I was left there. Mr. Houghton goes up and down, you know. It is hard upon him, poor old fellow. But then the other thing would be harder on me. He and papa are together somewhere now, arranging about the spring meetings. They have got their stables joined, and I know very well who will have the best of that. A man has to get up very early to see all round papa. But Mr. Houghton is so rich, it doesn't signify. And now, my dear, what are you going to do? and what is Lord George going to do? I am dying to see Lord George. I dare say you are getting a little tired of him by this time."

"Indeed, I'm not."

"You haven't picked up courage enough yet to say so; that's it, my dear. I've brought cards from Mr. Houghton, which means to say that though he is down somewhere at Newmarket in the flesh he is to be supposed to have called upon you and Lord George. And now we want you both to come and dine with us on Monday. I know Lord George is particular, and so I've brought a note. You can't have anything to do yet, and of course you'll come. Houghton will be back on Sunday, and goes down again on Tuesday morning. To hear him talk about it you'd think he was the keenest man in England across a country. Say that you'll come."

"I'll ask Lord George."

"Fiddle de dee. Lord George will be only too delighted to come and see me. I've got such a nice cousin to introduce to you; not one of the Germain sort, you know, who are all perhaps a little slow. This man is Jack De Baron, a nephew of papa's. He's in the Coldstreams, and I do think you'll like him. There's nothing on earth he can't do, from waltzing down to polo. And old Mildmay will be there, and Guss Mildmay, who is dying in love with Jack."

"And is Jack dying in love with Guss?"

"Oh! dear no; not a bit. You needn't be afraid. Jack De Baron has just £500 a year and his commission, and must, I should say, be over head and ears in debt. Miss Mildmay may perhaps have £5,000 for her fortune. Put this and that together, and you can hardly see anything comfortable in the way of matrimony, can you?"

"Then I fear your—Jack is mercenary."

"Mercenary;—of course he's mercenary. That is to say, he doesn't want to go to destruction quite at one leap. But he's awfully fond of falling in love, and when he is in love he'll do almost anything,—except marry."

"Then if I were you, I shouldn't ask—Guss to meet him."

"She can fight her own battles, and wouldn't thank me at all if I were to fight them for her after that fashion. There'll be

nobody else except Houghton's sister, Hetta. You never met
Hetta Houghton?"

"I've heard of her."

"I should think so. 'Not to know her,'—I forget the
words; but if you don't know Hetta Houghton, you're just
nowhere. She has lots of money, and lives all alone, and says
whatever comes uppermost, and does what she pleases. She goes
everywhere, and is up to everything. I always made up my mind
I wouldn't be an old maid, but I declare I envy Hetta Houghton.
But then she'd be nothing unless she had money. There'll be
eight of us, and at this time of the year we dine at half-past
seven, sharp. Can I take you anywhere? The carriage can come
back with you?"

"Thank you, no. I am going to pick Lord George up at
the Carlton at four."

"How nice! I wonder how long you'll go on picking up
Lord George at the Carlton."

She could only suppose, when her friend was gone, that
this was the right kind of thing. No doubt Lady Susanna had
warned her against Mrs. Houghton, but then she was not
disposed to take Lady Susanna's warnings on any subject. Her
father had known that she intended to know the woman; and her
father, though he had cautioned her very often as to the old
women at Manor Cross, as he called them, had never spoken a
word of caution to her as to Mrs. Houghton. And her husband
was well aware of the intended intimacy. She picked up her
husband, and rather liked being kept waiting a few minutes at
the club door in her brougham. Then they went together to look
at a new picture, which was being exhibited by gas-light in Bond
Street, and she began to feel that the pleasures of London were
delightful. "Don't you think those two old priests are
magnificent?" she said, pressing on his arm, in the obscurity of
the darkened chamber. "I don't know that I care much about old
priests," said Lord George.

"But the heads are so fine."

"I dare say. Sacerdotal pictures never please me. Didn't you say you wanted to go to Swann and Edgar's?" He would not sympathize with her about pictures, but perhaps she would be able to find out his taste at last.

He seemed quite well satisfied to dine with the Houghtons, and did, in fact, call at the house before that day came round. "I was in Berkeley Square this morning," he said one day, "but I didn't find any one."

"Nobody ever is at home, I suppose," she said. "Look here. There have been Lady Brabazon, and Mrs. Patmore Green, and Mrs. Montacute Jones. Who is Mrs. Montacute Jones?"

"I never heard of her."

"Dear me; how very odd. I dare say it was kind of her to come. And yesterday the Countess of Care called. Is not she some relative?"

"She is my mother's first cousin."

"And then there was dear old Miss Tallowax. And I wasn't at home to see one of them."

"No one I suppose ever is at home in London unless they fix a day for seeing people."

Lady George, having been specially asked to come "sharp" to her friend's dinner party, arrived with her husband exactly at the hour named, and found no one in the drawing-room. In a few minutes Mrs. Houghton hurried in, apologising. "It's all Mr. Houghton's fault indeed, Lord George. He was to have been in town yesterday, but would stay down and hunt to-day. Of course the train was late, and of course he was so tired that he couldn't dress without going to sleep first." As nobody else came for a quarter of an hour Mrs. Houghton had an opportunity of explaining some things. "Has Mrs. Montacute Jones called? I suppose you were out of your wits to find out who she was. She's a very old friend of papa's, and I asked her to call. She gives awfully swell parties, and has no end of money. She was one of the Montacutes of Montacute, and so she sticks her own name on to her husband's. He's alive, I believe, but he never shews. I think she keeps him somewhere down in Wales."

"How odd!"

"It is a little queer, but when you come to know her you'll find it will make no difference. She's the ugliest old woman in London, but I'd be as ugly as she is to have her diamonds."

"I wouldn't," said Mary.

"Your husband cares about your appearance," said Mrs. Houghton, turning her eyes upon Lord George. He simpered and looked pleased and did not seem to be at all disgusted by their friend's slang, and yet had she talked of "awfully swell" parties, he would, she was well aware, have rebuked her seriously.

Miss Houghton—Hetta Houghton—was the first to arrive, and she somewhat startled Mary by the gorgeous glories of her dress, though Mrs. Houghton afterwards averred that she wasn't "a patch upon Mrs. Montacute Jones." But Miss Houghton was a lady, and though over forty years of age, was still handsome.

"Been hunting to-day, has he?" she said. "Well, if he likes it, I shan't complain. But I thought he liked his ease too well to travel fifty miles up to town after riding about all day."

"Of course he's knocked up, and at his age it's quite absurd," said the young wife. "But Hetta, I want you to know my particular friend Lady George Germain. Lord George, if he'll allow me to say so, is a cousin, though I'm afraid we have to go back to Noah to make it out."

"Your great-grandmother was my great-grandmother's sister. That's not so very far off."

"When you get to grandmothers no fellow can understand it, can they, Mary?" Then came Mr. and Miss Mildmay. He was a gray-haired old gentleman, rather short and rather fat, and she looked to be just such another girl as Mrs. Houghton herself had been, though blessed with more regular beauty. She was certainly handsome, but she carried with her

that wearied air of being nearly worn out by the toil of searching
for a husband which comes upon some young women after the
fourth or fifth year of their labours. Fortune had been very hard
upon Augusta Mildmay. Early in her career she had fallen in
love, while abroad, with an Italian nobleman, and had
immediately been carried off home by her anxious parents. Then
in London she had fallen in love again with an English
nobleman, an eldest son, with wealth of his own. Nothing could
be more proper, and the young man had fallen also in love with
her. All her friends were beginning to hate her with virulence, so
lucky had she been! When on a sudden, the young lord told her
that the match would not please his father and mother, and that
therefore there must be an end of it. What was there to be done!
All London had talked of it; all London must know the utter
failure. Nothing more cruel, more barefaced, more unjust had
ever been perpetrated. A few years since all the Mildmays in
England, one after another, would have had a shot at the young
nobleman. But in these days there seems to be nothing for a girl
to do but to bear it and try again. So Augusta Mildmay bore it
and did try again; tried very often again. And now she was in
love with Jack De Baron. The worst of Guss Mildmay was that,
through it all, she had a heart and would like the young men,—
would like them, or perhaps dislike them, equally to her
disadvantage. Old gentlemen, such as was Mr. Houghton, had
been willing to condone all her faults, and all her loves, and to
take her as she was. But when the moment came, she would not
have her Houghton, and then she was in the market again. Now a
young woman entering the world cannot make a greater mistake
than not to know her own line, or, knowing it, not to stick to it.
Those who are thus weak are sure to fall between two stools. If a
girl chooses to have a heart, let her marry the man of her heart,
and take her mutton chops and bread and cheese, her stuff gown
and her six children, as they may come. But if she can decide
that such horrors are horrid to her, and that they must at any cost
be avoided, then let her take her Houghton when he comes, and

not hark back upon feelings and fancies, upon liking and loving, upon youth and age. If a girl has money and beauty too, of course she can pick and choose. Guss Mildmay had no money to speak of, but she had beauty enough to win either a working barrister or a rich old sinner. She was quite able to fall in love with the one and flirt with the other at the same time; but when the moment for decision came, she could not bring herself to put up with either. At present she was in real truth in love with Jack De Baron, and had brought herself to think that if Jack would ask her, she would risk everything. But were he to do so, which was not probable, she would immediately begin to calculate what could be done by Jack's moderate income and her own small fortune. She and Mrs. Houghton kissed each other affectionately, being at the present moment close in each other's confidences, and then she was introduced to Lady George. "Adelaide hasn't a chance," was Miss Mildmay's first thought as she looked at the young wife.

Then came Jack De Baron. Mary was much interested in seeing a man of whom she had heard so striking an account, and for the love of whom she had been told that a girl was almost dying. Of course all that was to be taken with many grains of salt; but still the fact of the love and the attractive excellence of the man had been impressed upon her. She declared to herself at once that his appearance was very much in his favour, and a fancy passed across her mind that he was somewhat like that ideal man of whom she herself had dreamed, ever so many years ago as it seemed to her now, before she had made up her mind that she would change her ideal and accept Lord George Germain. He was about the middle height, light haired, broad shouldered, with a pleasant smiling mouth and well formed nose; but above all, he had about him that pleasure-loving look, that appearance of taking things jauntily and of enjoying life, which she in her young girlhood had regarded as being absolutely essential to a pleasant lover. There are men whose very eyes glance business, whose every word imports care, who step as though their shoulders were weighed with thoughtfulness, who breathe solicitude, and who seem to think that all the things of life are too serious for smiles. Lord George was such a man, though he had in truth very little business to do. And then there are men who are always playfellows with their friends, who—even should misfortune be upon them,—still smile and make the best of it, who come across one like sunbeams, and who, even when tears are falling, produce the tints of a rainbow. Such a one Mary Lovelace had perhaps seen in her childhood and had then dreamed of him. Such a one was Jack De Baron, at any rate to the eye.

And such a one in truth he was. Of course the world had spoiled him. He was in the Guards. He was fond of pleasure. He was fairly well off in regard to all his own wants, for his cousin had simply imagined those debts with which ladies are apt to believe that young men of pleasure must be overwhelmed. He had gradually taught himself to think that his own luxuries and his own comforts should in his own estimation be paramount to everything. He was not naturally selfish, but his life had almost necessarily engendered selfishness. Marrying had come to be looked upon as an evil,—as had old age;—not of course an unavoidable evil, but one into which a man will probably fall sooner or later. To put off marriage as long as possible, and when it could no longer be put off to marry money was a part of his creed. In the meantime the great delight of his life came from women's society. He neither gambled nor drank. He hunted and fished, and shot deer and grouse, and occasionally drove a coach to Windsor. But little love affairs, flirtation, and intrigues, which were never intended to be guilty, but which now and again had brought him into some trouble, gave its charm to his life. On such occasions he would too, at times, be very badly in love, assuring himself sometimes with absolute heroism that he would never again see this married woman, or declaring to himself in moments of self-sacrificial grandness that he would at once marry that unmarried girl. And then, when he had escaped from

some especial trouble, he would take to his regiment for a
month, swearing to himself that for the next year he would see
no women besides his aunts and his grandmother. When making
this resolution he might have added his cousin Adelaide. They
were close friends, but between them there had never been the
slightest spark of a flirtation.

In spite of all his little troubles Captain De Baron was a
very popular man. There was a theory abroad about him that he
always behaved like a gentleman, and that his troubles were
misfortunes rather than faults. Ladies always liked him, and his
society was agreeable to men because he was neither selfish nor
loud. He talked only a little, but still enough not to be thought
dull. He never bragged or bullied or bounced. He didn't want to
shoot more deer or catch more salmon than another man. He
never cut a fellow down in the hunting-field. He never borrowed
money, but would sometimes lend it when a reason was given.
He was probably as ignorant as an owl of anything really
pertaining to literature, but he did not display his ignorance. He
was regarded by all who knew him as one of the most fortunate
of men. He regarded himself as being very far from blessed,
knowing that there must come a speedy end to the things which
he only half enjoyed, and feeling partly ashamed of himself in
that he had found for himself no better part.

"Jack," said Mrs. Houghton, "I can't blow you up for
being late, because Mr. Houghton has not yet condescended to
shew himself. Let me introduce you to Lady George Germain."
Then he smiled in his peculiar way, and Mary thought his face
the most beautiful she had ever seen. "Lord George Germain,—
who allows me to call him my cousin, though he isn't as near as
you are. My sister-in-law, you know." Jack shook hands with the
old lady in his most cordial manner. "I think you have seen Mr.
Mildmay before, and Miss Mildmay." Mary could not but look
at the greeting between the two, and she saw that Miss Mildmay
almost turned up her nose at him. She was quite sure that Mrs.
Houghton had been wrong about the love. There had surely only

been a pretence of love. But Mrs. Houghton had been right, and Mary had not yet learned to read correctly the signs which men and women hang out.

At last Mr. Houghton came down. "Upon my word," said his wife, "I wonder you ain't ashamed to shew yourself."

"Who says I'm not ashamed? I'm very much ashamed. But how can I help it if the trains won't keep their time? We were hunting all day to-day,—nothing very good, Lord George, but on the trot from eleven to four. That tires a fellow, you know. And the worst of it is I've got to do it again on Wednesday, Thursday, and Saturday."

"Is there a necessity?" asked Lord George.

"When a man begins that kind of thing he must go through with it. Hunting is like women. It's a jealous sport. Lady George, may I take you down to dinner? I am so sorry to have kept you waiting."

Chapter XIII.

More News From Italy.

Mr. Houghton took Lady George down to dinner; but Jack De Baron sat on his left hand. Next to him was Augusta Mildmay, who had been consigned to his care. Then came Lord George sitting opposite to his host at a round table, with Mrs. Houghton at his right hand. Mrs. Mildmay and Miss Hetta Houghton filled up the vacant places. To all this a great deal of attention had been given by the hostess. She had not wished to throw her cousin Jack and Miss Mildmay together. She would probably have said to a confidential friend that "there had been enough of all that." In her way she liked Guss Mildmay; but Guss was not good enough to marry her cousin. Guss herself must know that such a marriage was impossible. She had on an occasion said a word or two to Guss upon the subject. She had thought that a little flirtation between Jack and her other friend Lady George might put things right; and she had thought, too,— or perhaps felt rather than thought,—that Lord George had emancipated himself from the thraldom of his late love rather too quickly. Mary was a dear girl. She was quite prepared to make Mary her friend, being in truth somewhat sick of the ill-humours and disappointments of Guss Mildmay; but it might be as well that Mary should be a little checked in her triumph. She herself had been obliged to put up with old Mr. Houghton. She never for a moment told herself that she had done wrong; but of course she required compensation. When she was manoeuvring she never lost sight of her manoeuvres. She had had all this in her mind when she made up her little dinner-party. She had had it all in her mind when she arranged the seats. She didn't want to sit next to Jack herself, because Jack would have talked to her to the exclusion of Lord George, so she placed herself between Lord George and Mr. Mildmay. It had been necessary that Mr. Mildmay should take Miss Houghton down to dinner, and therefore she could not separate Guss from Jack De Baron. Anybody who understands dinner-parties will see it all at a glance. But she was convinced that Jack would devote himself to Lady George at his left hand; and so he did.

"Just come up to town, haven't you?" said Jack.

"Only last week."

"This is the nicest time in the year for London, unless you do a deal of hunting; then it's a grind."

"I never hunt at all; Lord George won't let me."

"I wish some one wouldn't let me. It would save me a deal of money, and a great deal of misery. It's all a delusion and a snare. You never get a run nowadays."

"Do you think so? I'd rather hunt than do anything."

"That's because you are not let to do it; the perversity of human nature, you know! The only thing I'm not allowed to do is to marry, and it's the only thing I care for."

"Who prevents it, Captain de Baron?"

"There's a new order come out from the Horse Guards yesterday. No one under a field officer is to marry unless he has got £2,000 a year."

"Marrying is cheaper than hunting."

"Of course, Lady George, you may buy your horses cheap or dear, and you may do the same with your wives. You may have a cheap wife who doesn't care for dress, and likes to sit at home and read good books."

"That's just what I do."

"But then they're apt to go wrong and get out of order."

"How do you mean? I shan't get out of order, I hope."

"The wheels become rusty, don't you think? and then they won't go as they ought. They scold and turn up their noses. What I want to find is perfect beauty, devoted affection, and £50,000."

"How modest you are."

In all this badinage there was not much to make a rival angry; but Miss Mildmay, who heard a word or two now and then, was angry. He was talking to a pretty woman about marriage and money, and of course that amounted to flirtation. Lord George, on her other hand, now and then said a word to her; but he was never given to saying many words, and his attention was nearly monopolised by his hostess. She had heard the last sentence, and determined to join the conversation.

"If you had the £50,000, Captain De Baron," she said, "I think you would manage to do without the beauty and the devoted affection."

"That's ill-natured, Miss Mildmay, though it may be true. Beggars can't be choosers. But you've known me a long time, and I think it's unkind that you should run me down with a new acquaintance. Suppose I was to say something bad of you."

"You can say whatever you please, Captain De Baron."

"There is nothing bad to say, of course, except that you are always down on a poor fellow in distress. Don't you think it's a grand thing to be good-natured, Lady George?"

"Indeed I do. It's almost better than being virtuous."

"Ten to one. I don't see the good of virtue myself. It always makes people stingy and cross and ill-mannered. I think one should always promise to do everything that is asked. Nobody would be fool enough to expect you to keep your word afterwards, and you'd give a lot of pleasure."

"I think promises ought to be kept, Captain De Baron."

"I can't agree to that. That's bondage, and it puts an embargo on the pleasant way of living that I like. I hate all kind of strictness, and duty, and self-denying, and that kind of thing. It's rubbish. Don't you think so?"

"I suppose one has to do one's duty."

"I don't see it. I never do mine."

"Suppose there were a battle to fight."

"I should get invalided at once. I made up my mind to that long ago. Fancy the trouble of it. And when they shoot you they don't shoot you dead, but knock half your face away, or something of that sort. Luckily we live in an island, and haven't much fighting to do. If we hadn't lived in an island I should never have gone into the army."

This was not flirting certainly. It was all sheer nonsense,—words without any meaning in them. But Mary liked it. She decidedly would not have liked it had it ever occurred to her that the man was flirting with her. It was the very childishness of the thing that pleased her,—the contrast to conversation at Manor Cross, where no childish word was ever spoken. And though she was by no means prepared to flirt with Captain De Baron, still she found in him something of the realisation of her dreams. There was the combination of manliness, playfulness, good looks, and good humour which she had pictured to herself. To sit well-dressed in a well-lighted room and have nonsense talked to her suited her better than a petticoat conclave. And she knew of no harm in it. Her father encouraged her to be gay, and altogether discouraged petticoat conclaves. So she smiled her sweetest on Captain De Baron, and replied to his nonsense with other nonsense, and was satisfied.

But Guss Mildmay was very much dissatisfied, both as to the amusement of the present moment and as to the conduct of Captain De Baron generally. She knew London life well, whereas Lady George did not know it at all; and she considered that this was flirtation. She may have been right in any accusation which she made in her heart against the man, but she was quite wrong in considering Lady George to be a flirt. She had, however, grievances of her own—great grievances. It was not only that the man was attentive to some one else, but that he was not attentive to her. He and she had had many passages in life together, and he owed it to her at any rate not to appear to neglect her. And then what a stick was that other man on the other side of her,—that young woman's husband! During the greater part of dinner she was sitting speechless,—not only loverless, but manless. It is not what one suffers that kills one, but what one knows that other people see that one suffers.

There was not very much conversation between Lord George and Mrs. Houghton at dinner. Perhaps she spoke as much to Mr. Mildmay as to him; for she was a good hostess, understanding and performing her duty. But what she did say to him she said very graciously, making allusions to further intimacy between herself and Mary, flattering his vanity by little speeches as to Manor Cross, always seeming to imply that she felt hourly the misfortune of having been forced to decline the honour of such an alliance as had been offered to her. He was, in truth, as innocent as his wife, except in this, that he would not have wished her to hear all that Mrs. Houghton said to him, whereas Mary would have had not the slightest objection to his hearing all the nonsense between her and Captain De Baron.

The ladies sat a long time after dinner, and when they went Mrs. Houghton asked her husband to come up in ten minutes. They did not remain much longer, but during those ten minutes Guss Mildmay said something of her wrongs to her friend, and Lady George heard some news from Miss Houghton. Miss Houghton had got Lady George on to a sofa, and was talking to her about Brotherton and Manor Cross. "So the Marquis is coming," she said. "I knew the Marquis years ago, when we used to be staying with the De Barons,—Adelaide's father and mother. She was alive then, and the Marquis used to come over there. So he has married?"

"Yes; an Italian."

"I did not think he would ever marry. It makes a difference to you;—does it not?"

"I don't think of such things."

"You will not like him, for he is the very opposite to Lord George."

"I don't know that I shall ever even see him. I don't think he wants to see any of us."

"I dare say not. He used to be very handsome, and very fond of ladies' society,—but, I think, the most selfish human being I ever knew in my life. That is a complaint that years do not cure. He and I were great friends once."

"Did you quarrel?"

"Oh, dear no. I had rather a large fortune of my own, and there was a time in which he was, perhaps, a little in want of money. But they had to build a town on his property in Staffordshire, and you see that did instead."

"Did instead!" said Lady George, altogether in the dark.

"There was suddenly a great increase to his income, and, of course, that altered his view. I am bound to say that he was very explicit. He could be so without suffering himself, or understanding that any one else would suffer. I tell you because you are one of the family, and would, no doubt, hear it all some day through Adelaide. I had a great escape."

"And he a great misfortune," said Mary civilly.

"I think he had, to tell you the truth. I am good-tempered, long-suffering, and have a certain grain of sagacity that might have been useful to him. Have you heard about this Italian lady?"

"Only that she is an Italian lady."

"He is about my age. If I remember rightly there is hardly a month or two between us. She is three or four years older."

"You knew her then?"

"I knew of her. I have been curious enough to enquire, which is, I dare say, more than any body has done at Manor Cross."

"And is she so old?"

"And a widow. They have been married, you know, over twelve months; nearly two years, I believe."

"Surely not; we heard of it only since our own marriage."

"Exactly; but the Marquis was always fond of a little mystery. It was the news of your marriage that made him hint at the possibility of such a thing; and he did not tell the fact till he had made up his mind to come home. I do not know that he has told all now."

"What else is there?"

"She has a baby,—a boy." Mary felt that the colour flew to her cheeks; but she knew that it did so, not from any disappointment of her own, not because these tidings were in truth a blow to her, but because others,—this lady, for instance,—would think that she suffered. "I am afraid it is so," said Miss Houghton.

"She may have twenty, for what I care," said Mary, recovering herself.

"I think Lord George ought to know."

"Of course I shall tell him what you told me. I am sorry that he is not nice, that's all. I should have liked a brother-in-law that I could have loved. And I wish he had married an English woman. I think English women are best for English men."

"I think so too. I am afraid you will none of you like the lady. She cannot speak a word of English. Of course you will use my name in telling Lord George. I heard it all from a friend of mine who is married to one of the Secretaries at the Embassy." Then the gentlemen came in, and Mary began to be in a hurry to get away that she might tell this news to her husband.

In the meantime Guss Mildmay made her complaints, deep but not loud. She and Mrs. Houghton had been very intimate as girls, knew each other's secrets, and understood each other's characters. "Why did you have him to such a party as this?" said Guss.

"I told you he was coming."

"But you didn't tell me about that young woman. You put him next to her on purpose to annoy me."

"That's nonsense. You know as well as I do that nothing can come of it. You must drop it, and you'd better do it at once. You don't want to be known as the girl who is dying for the love of a man she can't marry. That's not your métier."

"That's my own affair. If I choose to stick to him you, at least, ought not to cross me."

"But he won't stick to you. Of course he's my cousin, and I don't see why he's to be supposed never to say a word to anyone else, when it's quite understood that you're not going to have one another. What's the good of being a dog in the manger?"

"Adelaide, you never had any heart!"

"Of course not;—or, if I had, I knew how to get the better of so troublesome an appendage. I hate hearing about hearts. If he'd take you to-morrow you wouldn't marry him?"

"Yes, I would."

"I don't believe it. I don't think you'd be so wicked. Where would you live, and how? How long would it be before you hated each other? Hearts! As if hearts weren't just like anything else which either you can or you cannot afford yourself. Do you think I couldn't go and fall in love to-morrow, and think it the best fun in the world? Of course it's nice to have a fellow like Jack always ready to spoon, and sending one things, and riding with one, and all that. I don't know any young woman in London would like it better than I should. But I can't afford it, my dear, and so I don't do it."

"It seems to me you are going to do it with your old lover?"

"Dear Lord George! I swear it's only to bring Mary down a peg, because she is so proud of her nobleman. And then he is handsome! But, my dear, I've pleased myself. I have got a house over my head, and a carriage to sit in, and servants to wait on me, and I've settled myself. Do you do likewise, and you shall have your Lord George, or Jack De Baron, if he pleases;— only don't go too far with him."

"Adelaide," said the other, "I'm not good, but you're downright bad." Mrs. Houghton only laughed, as she got up from her seat to welcome the gentlemen as they entered the room.

Mary, as soon as the door of the brougham had been closed upon her, and her husband, began to tell her story. "What do you think Miss Houghton has told me?" Lord George, of course, could have no thoughts about it, and did not at first very much care what the story might have been. "She says that your brother was married ever so long ago!"

"I don't believe it," said Lord George, suddenly and angrily.

"A year before we were married, I mean."

"I don't believe it."

"And she says that they have a son."

"What!"

"That there is a baby,—a boy. She has heard it all from some friend of hers at Rome."

"It can't be true."

"She said that I had better tell you. Does it make you unhappy, George?" To this he made no immediate answer. "What can it matter whether he was married two months ago or two years? It does not make me unhappy;" as she said this, she locked herself close into his arm.

"Why should he deceive us? That would make me unhappy. If he had married in a proper way and had a family, here in England, of course I should have been glad. I should have been loyal to him as I am to the others. But if this be true, of course, it will make me unhappy. I do not believe it. It is some gossip."

"I could not but tell you."

"It is some jealousy. There was a time when they said that Brotherton meant to marry her."

"What difference could it make to her? Of course we all know that he is married. I hope it won't make you unhappy, George." But Lord George was unhappy, or at any rate, was moody, and would talk no more then on that subject, or any other. But in truth the matter rested on his mind all the night.

Chapter XIV.

"Are We To Call Him Popenjoy?"

The news which he had heard did afflict Lord George very much. A day or two after the dinner-party in Berkeley Square he found Mr. Knox, his brother's agent, and learned from him that Miss Houghton's story was substantially true. The Marquis had informed his man of business that an heir had been born to him, but had not communicated the fact to any one of the family! This omission, in such a family, was, to Lord George's thinking, so great a crime on the part of his brother, as to make him doubt whether he could ever again have fraternal relations with a man who so little knew his duty. When Mr. Knox showed him the letter his brow became very black. He did not often forget himself,—was not often so carried away by any feeling as to be in danger of doing so. But on this occasion even he was so moved as to be unable to control his words. "An Italian brat? Who is to say how it was born?"

"The Marquis, my Lord, would not do anything like that," said Mr. Knox, very seriously.

Then Lord George was ashamed of himself, and blushed up to the roots of his hair. He had hardly himself known what he had meant. But he mistrusted an Italian widow, because she was an Italian, and because she was a widow, and he mistrusted the whole connexion, because there had been in it none of that honourable openness which should, he thought, characterise all family doings in such a family as that of the Germains. "I don't know of what kind you mean," he said, shuffling, and knowing that he shuffled. "I don't suppose my brother would do anything really wrong. But it's a blot to the family—a terrible blot."

"She is a lady of good family,—a Marchese," said Mr. Knox.

"An Italian Marchese!" said Lord George, with that infinite contempt which an English nobleman has for foreign nobility not of the highest order.

He had learnt that Miss Houghton's story was true, and was certainly very unhappy. It was not at all that he had pictured to himself the glory of being himself the Marquis of Brotherton after his brother's death; nor was it only the disappointment which he felt as to any possible son of his own, though on that side he did feel the blow. The reflection which perplexed him most was the consciousness that he must quarrel with his brother, and that after such a quarrel he would become nobody in the world. And then, added to this, was the sense of family disgrace. He would have been quite content with his position had he been left master of the house at Manor Cross, even without any of his brother's income wherewith to maintain the house. But now he would only be his wife's husband, the Dean's son-in-law, living on their money, and compelled by circumstances to adapt himself to them. He almost thought that had he known that he would be turned out of Manor Cross, he would not have married. And then, in spite of his disclaimer to Mr. Knox, he was already suspicious of some foul practice. An heir to the title and property, to all the family honours of the Germains, had suddenly burst upon him, twelve months,—for aught that he knew, two or three years,—after the child's birth! Nobody had been informed when the child was born, or in what circumstances,—except that the mother was an Italian widow!

What evidence on which an Englishman might rely could possibly be forthcoming from such a country as Italy! Poor Lord George, who was himself as honest as the sun, was prepared to believe all evil things of people of whom he knew nothing! Should his brother die,—and his brother's health was bad,— what steps should he take? Would it be for him to accept this Italian brat as the heir to everything, or must he ruin himself by a pernicious lawsuit? Looking forward he saw nothing but family misery and disgrace, and he saw, also, inevitable difficulties with which he knew himself to be incapable to cope. "It is true," he said to his wife very gloomily, when he first met her after his interview with Mr. Knox.

"What Miss Houghton said? I felt sure it was true, directly she told me."

"I don't know why you should have felt sure, merely on her word, as to a thing so monstrous as this is. You don't seem to see that it concerns yourself."

"No; I don't. It doesn't concern me at all, except as it makes you unhappy." Then there was a pause for a moment, during which she crept close up to him, in a manner that had now become usual with her. "Why do you think I married you?" she said. He was too unhappy to answer her pleasantly,—too much touched by her sweetness to answer her unpleasantly; and so he said nothing. "Certainly not with any hope that I might become Marchioness of Brotherton. Whatever may have made me do such a thing, I can assure you that that had nothing to do with it."

"Can't you look forward? Don't you suppose that you may have a son?" Then she buried her face upon his shoulder. "And if so, would it not be better that a child so born should be the heir, than some Italian baby, of whom no one knows anything?"

"If you are unhappy, George, I shall be unhappy. But for myself I will not affect to care anything. I don't want to be a Marchioness. I only want to see you without a frown on your brow. To tell the truth, if you didn't mind it, I should care nothing about your brother and his doings. I would make a joke of this Marchese, who, Miss Houghton says, is a puckered-faced old woman. Miss Houghton seems to care a great deal more about it than I do."

"It cannot be a subject for a joke." He was almost angry at the idea of the wife of the head of the family being made a matter of laughter. That she should be reprobated, hated,—cursed, if necessary,—was within the limits of family dignity; but not that she should become a joke to those with whom she had unfortunately connected herself. When he had finished speaking to her she could not but feel that he was displeased, and could not but feel also the injustice of such displeasure. Of course she had her own little share in the general disappointments. But she had striven before him to make nothing of it, in order that he might be quite sure that she had married him—not with any idea of rank or wealth, but for himself alone. She had made light of the family misfortune, in order that he might be relieved. And yet he was angry with her! This was unreasonable. How much had she done for him! Was she not striving every hour of her life to love him, and, at any rate, to comfort him with the conviction that he was loved? Was she not constant in her assurance to herself that her whole life should be devoted to him? And yet he was surly to her simply because his brother had disgraced himself! When she was left alone she sat down and cried, and then consoled herself by remembering that her father was coming to her.

It had been arranged that the last days of February should be spent by Lord George with his mother and sisters at Cross Hall, and that the Dean should run up to town for a week. Lord George went down to Brotherton by a morning train, and the Dean came up on the same afternoon. But the going and coming were so fixed that the two men met at the deanery. Lord George had determined that he would speak fully to the Dean respecting his brother. He was always conscious of the Dean's low birth, remembering, with some slight discomfort, the stable-keeper and the tallow-chandler; and he was a little inclined to resent what he thought to be a disposition on the part of the Dean to domineer. But still the Dean was a practical, sagacious man, in whom he could trust; and the assistance of such a friend was necessary to him. Circumstances had bound him to the Dean, and he was a man not prone to bind himself to many men. He wanted and yet feared the confidence of friendship. He lunched with the Dean, and then told his story. "You know," he said, "that my brother is married?"

"Of course, we all heard that."

"He was married more than twelve months before he informed us that he was going to be married."

"No!"

"It was so."

"Do you mean, then, that he told you a falsehood?"

"His letter to me was very strange, though I did not think much of it at the time. He said, 'I am to be married'—naming no day."

"That certainly was—a falsehood, as, at that time, he was married."

"I do not know that harsh words will do any good."

"Nor I. But it is best, George, that you and I should be quite plain in our words to each other. Placed as he was, and as you were, he was bound to tell you of his marriage as soon as he knew it himself. You had waited till he was between forty and fifty, and, of course, he must feel that what you would do would depend materially upon what he did."

"It didn't at all."

"And then, having omitted to do his duty, he screens his fault by a—positive misstatement, when his intended return home makes further concealment impossible."

"All that, however, is of little moment," said Lord George, who could not but see that the Dean was already complaining that he had been left without information which he ought to have possessed when he was giving his daughter to a probable heir to the title. "There is more than that."

"What more?"

"He had a son born more than twelve months since."

"Who says so?" exclaimed the Dean, jumping up from his chair.

"I heard it first,—or rather Mary did,—in common conversation, from an old friend. I then learned the truth from Knox. Though he had told none of us, he had told Knox."

"And Knox has known it all through?"

"No, only lately. But he knows it now. Knox supposes that they are coming home so that the people about may be reconciled to the idea of his having an heir. There will be less trouble, he thinks, if the boy comes now, than if he were never heard of till he was ten or fifteen years old,—or perhaps till after my brother's death."

"There may be trouble enough still," said the Dean, almost with a gasp.

The Dean, it was clear, did not believe in the boy. Lord George remembered that he himself had expressed disbelief, and that Mr. Knox had almost rebuked him. "I have now told you all the facts," said Lord George, "and have told them as soon as I knew them."

"You are as true as the sun," said the Dean, putting his hand on his son-in-law's shoulder. "You will be honest. But you must not trust in the honesty of others. Poor Mary!"

"She does not feel it in the least;—will not even interest herself about it."

"She will feel it some day. She is no more than a child now. I feel it, George;—I feel it; and you ought to feel it."

"I feel his ill-treatment of myself."

"What—in not telling you? That is probably no more than a small part of a wide scheme. We must find out the truth of all this."

"I don't know what there is to find out," said Lord George, hoarsely.

"Nor do I; but I do feel that there must be something. Think of your brother's position and standing,—of his past life and his present character! This is no time now for being mealy-mouthed. When such a man as he appears suddenly with a foreign woman and a foreign child, and announces one as his wife and the other as his heir, having never reported the existence of one or of the other, it is time that some enquiry should be made. I, at any rate, shall make enquiry. I shall think myself bound to do so on behalf of Mary." Then they parted as confidential friends do part, but each with some feeling antagonistic to the other. The Dean, though he had from his heart acknowledged that Lord George was as honest as the sun, still felt himself to be aggrieved by the Germain family, and doubted whether his son-in-law would be urgent enough and constant in hostility to his own brother. He feared that Lord George would be weak, feeling; as regarded himself, that he would fight till he had spent his last penny, as long as there was a chance that, by fighting, a grandson of his own might be made Marquis of Brotherton. He, at any rate, understood his own heart in the matter, and knew what it was that he wanted. But Lord George, though he had found himself compelled to tell everything to the Dean, still dreaded the Dean. It was not in accordance with his principles that he should be leagued against his brother with such a man as Dean Lovelace, and he could see that the Dean was thinking of his own possible grandchildren, whereas he himself was thinking only of the family of Germain.

He found his mother and sister at the small house,—the house at which Farmer Price was living only a month or two since. No doubt it was the recognised dower house, but nevertheless there was still about it a flavour of Farmer Price. A considerable sum of money had been spent upon it, which had come from a sacrifice of a small part of the capital belonging to the three sisters, with an understanding that it should be repaid out of the old lady's income. But no one, except the old lady herself, anticipated such repayment. All this had created trouble and grief, and the family, which was never gay, was now more sombre than ever. When the further news was told to Lady Sarah it almost crushed her. "A child!" she said in a horror-stricken whisper, turning quite pale, and looking as though the crack of doom were coming at once. "Do you believe it?" Then her brother explained the grounds he had for believing it. "And that it was born in wedlock twelve months before the fact was announced to us." "It has never been announced to us," said Lord George.

"What are we to do? is my mother to be told? She ought to know at once; and yet how can we tell her? What shall you do about the Dean?"

"He knows."

"You told him?"

"Yes; I thought it best."

"Well,—perhaps. And yet it is terrible that any man so distant from us should have our secrets in his keeping."

"As Mary's father, I thought it right that he should know."

"I have always liked the Dean personally," said Lady Sarah. "There is a manliness about him which has recommended him, and having a full hand he knows how to open it. But he isn't—; he isn't quite—"

"No; he isn't quite—," said Lord George, also hesitating to pronounce the word which was understood by both of them.

"You must tell my mother, or I must. It will be wrong to withhold it. If you like, I will tell Susanna and Amelia."

"I think you had better tell my mother," said Lord George; "she will take it more easily from you. And then, if she breaks down, you can control her better." That Lady Sarah should have the doing of any difficult piece of work was almost a matter of course. She did tell the tale to her mother, and her mother did break down. The Marchioness, when she found that an Italian baby had been born twelve months before the time which she had been made to believe was the date of the marriage, took at once to her bed. What a mass of horrors was coming on them! Was she to go and see a woman who had had a baby under such circumstances? Or was her own eldest son, the very, very Marquis of Brotherton, to be there with his wife, and was she not to go and see them? Through it all her indignation against her son had not been hot as had been theirs against their brother. He was her eldest son,—the very Marquis,—and ought to be allowed to do almost anything he pleased. Had it not been impossible for her to rebel against Lady Sarah she would have obeyed her son in that matter of the house. And, even now, it was not against her son that her heart was bitter, but against the woman, who, being an Italian, and having been married, if married, without the knowledge of the family, presumed to say that her child was legitimate. Had her eldest son brought over with him to the halls of his ancestors an Italian mistress that would, of course, have been very bad, but it would not have been so bad as this. Nothing could be so bad as this. "Are we to call him Popenjoy?" she asked with a gurgling voice from amidst the bed clothes. Now the eldest son of the Marquis of Brotherton would, as a matter of course, be Lord Popenjoy, if legitimate. "Certainly we must," said Lady Sarah, authoritatively, "unless the marriage should be disproved."

"Poor dear little thing," said the Marchioness, beginning to feel some pity for the odious stranger as soon as she was told that he really was to be called Popenjoy. Then the Ladies Susanna and Amelia were informed, and the feeling became general throughout the household that the world must be near its end. What were they all to do when he should come? That was the great question. He had begun by declaring that he did not want to see any of them. He had endeavoured to drive them away from the neighbourhood, and had declared that neither his mother nor his sisters would "get on" with his wife. All the ladies at Cross Hall had a very strong opinion that this would turn out to be true, but still they could not bear to think that they should be living as it were next door to the head of the family, and never see him. A feeling began to creep over all of them, except Lady Sarah, that it would have been better for them to have obeyed the head of the family and gone elsewhere. But it was too late now. The decision had been made, and they must remain.

Lady Sarah, however, never gave way for a minute. "George," she said very solemnly, "I have thought a great deal about this, and I do not mean to let him trample upon us."

"It is all very sad," said Lord George.

"Yes, indeed. If I know myself, I think I should be the last person to attribute evil motives to my elder brother, or to stand in his way in aught that he might wish to do in regard to the family. I know all that is due to him. But there is a point beyond which even that feeling cannot carry me. He has disgraced himself." Lord George shook his head. "And he is doing all he can to bring disgrace upon us. It has always been my wish that he should marry."

"Of course, of course."

"It is always desirable that the eldest son should marry. The heir to the property then knows that he is the heir, and is brought up to understand his duties. Though he had married a foreigner, much as I should regret it, I should be prepared to receive her as a sister; it is for him to please himself; but in marrying a foreigner he is more specially bound to let it be known to all the world, and to have everything substantiated, than if he had married an English girl in her own parish church. As it is, we must call on her, because he says that she is his wife. But I shall tell him that he is acting very wrongly by us all, especially by you, and most especially by his own child, if he does not take care that such evidence of his marriage is forthcoming as shall satisfy all the world."

"He won't listen to you."

"I think I can make him, as far as that goes; at any rate I do not mean to be afraid of him. Nor must you."

"I hardly know whether I will even see him."

"Yes; you must see him. If we are to be expelled from the family house, let it be his doing, and not ours. We have to take care, George, that we do not make a single false step. We must be courteous to him, but above all we must not be afraid of him."

In the meantime the Dean went up to London, meaning to spend a week with his daughter in her new house. They had both intended that this should be a period of great joy to them. Plans had been made as to the theatres and one or two parties, which were almost as exciting to the Dean as to his daughter. It was quite understood by both of them that the Dean up in London was to be a man of pleasure, rather than a clergyman. He had no purpose of preaching either at St. Paul's or the Abbey. He was going to attend no Curates' Aid Society or Sons of the Clergy. He intended to forget Mr. Groschut, to ignore Dr. Pountney, and have a good time. That had been his intention, at least till he saw Lord George at the deanery. But now there were serious thoughts in his mind. When he arrived Mary had for the time got nearly rid of the incubus of the Italian Marchioness with her baby. She was all smiles as she kissed him. But he could not keep himself from the great subject.

"This is terrible news, my darling," he said at once.

"Do you think so, papa?"

"Certainly I do."

"I don't see why Lord Brotherton should not have a son and heir as well as anybody else."

"He is quite entitled to have a son and heir,—one may almost say more entitled than anyone else, seeing that he has got so much to leave to him,—but on that very account he is more bound than anyone else to let all the world feel sure that his declared son and heir is absolutely his son and heir."

"He couldn't be so vile as that, papa!"

"God forbid that I should say that he could. It may be that he considers himself married, though the marriage would not be valid here. Maybe he is married, and that yet the child is not legitimate." Mary could not but blush as her father spoke to her thus plainly. "All we do know is that he wrote to his own brother declaring that he was about to be married twelve months after the birth of the child whom he now expects us to recognise as the heir to the title. I for one am not prepared to accept his word without evidence, and I shall have no scruple in letting him know that such evidence will be wanted."

Chapter XV.

"Drop It."

For ten or twelve days after the little dinner in Berkeley Square Guss Mildmay bore her misfortunes without further spoken complaint. During all that time, though they were both in London, she never saw Jack De Baron, and she knew that in not seeing her he was neglecting her. But for so long she bore it. It is generally supposed that young ladies have to bear such sorrow without loud complaint; but Guss was more thoroughly emancipated than are some young ladies, and when moved was wont to speak her mind. At last, when she herself was only on foot with her father, she saw Jack De Baron riding with Lady George. It is quite true that she also saw, riding behind them, her perfidious friend, Mrs. Houghton, and a gentleman whom at that time she did not know to be Lady George's father. This was early in March, when equestrians in the park are not numerous. Guss stood for a moment looking at them, and Jack De Baron took off his hat. But Jack did not stop, and went on talking with that pleasant vivacity which she, poor girl, knew so well and valued so highly. Lady George liked it too, though she could hardly have given any reason for liking it, for, to tell the truth, there was not often much pith in Jack's conversation.

On the following morning Captain De Baron, who had lodgings in Charles Street close to the Guards' Club, had a letter brought to him before he was out of bed. The letter was from Guss Mildmay, and he knew the handwriting well. He had received many notes from her, though none so interesting on the whole as was this letter. Miss Mildmay's letter to Jack was as follows. It was written, certainly, with a swift pen, and, but that he knew her writing well, would in parts have been hardly legible.

"I think you are treating me very badly. I tell you openly and fairly. It is neither gentlemanlike or high spirited, as you know that I have no one to take my part but myself. If you mean to cut me, say so, and let me understand it at once. You have taken up now with that young married woman just because you know it will make me angry. I don't believe for a moment that you really care for such a baby-faced chit as that. I have met her too, and I know that she hasn't a word to say for herself. Do you mean to come and see me? I expect to hear from you, letting me know when you will come. I do not intend to be thrown over for her or anyone. I believe it is mostly Adelaide's doing, who doesn't like to think that you should really care for anyone. You know very well what my feelings are, and what sacrifice I am ready to make. And you know what you have told me of yourself. I shall be at home all this afternoon. Papa, of course, will go to his club at three. Aunt Julia has an afternoon meeting at the Institute for the distribution of prizes among the Rights-of-Women young men, and I have told her positively that I won't go. Nobody else will be admitted. Do come and at any rate let us have it out. This state of things will kill me,—though, of course, you don't mind that.

"G.

"I shall think you a coward if you don't come. Oh, Jack, do come."

She had begun like a lion, but had ended like a lamb; and such was the nature of every thought she had respecting him. She was full of indignation. She assured herself hourly that such treachery as his deserved death. She longed for a return of the old times,—thirty years since,—and for some old-fashioned brother, so that Jack might be shot at and have a pistol bullet in his heart. And yet she told herself as often that she could not live without him. Where should she find another Jack after her recklessness in letting all the world know that this man was her Jack? She hardly wanted to marry him, knowing full well the nature of the life which would then be before her. Jack had told her often that if forced to do that he must give up the army and go and live in—, he had named Dantzic as having the least alluring sound of any place he knew. To her it would be best that things should go on just as they were now till something should turn up. But that she should be enthralled and Jack free was not to be borne! She begrudged him no other pleasure. She was willing that he should hunt, gamble, eat, drink, smoke, and be ever so wicked, if that were his taste; but not that he should be seen making himself agreeable to another young woman. It might be that their position was unfortunate, but of that misfortune she had by far the heavier share. She could not eat, drink, smoke, gamble, hunt, and be generally wicked. Surely he might bear it if she could.

Jack, when he had read the letter, tossed it on to the counterpane, and rolled himself again in bed. It was not as yet much after nine, and he need not decide for an hour or two whether he would accept the invitation or not. But the letter bothered him and he could not sleep. She told him that if he did not come he would be a coward, and he felt that she had told him the truth. He did not want to see her,—not because he was tired of her, for in her softer humours she was always pleasant to him,—but because he had a clear insight into the misery of the whole connection. When the idea of marrying her suggested itself, he always regarded it as being tantamount to suicide. Were he to be persuaded to such a step he would simply be blowing his own brains out because someone else asked him to do so. He had explained all this to her at various times when suggesting Dantzic, and she had agreed with him. Then, at that point, his common sense had been better than hers, and his feeling really higher. "That being so," he had said, "it is certainly for your advantage that we should part." But this to her had been as though he were striving to break his own chains and was indifferent as to her misery. "I can take care of myself," she had answered him. But he knew that she could not take care of herself. Had she not been most unwise, most imprudent, she would have seen the wisdom of letting the intimacy of their acquaintance drop without any further explanation. But she was most unwise. Nevertheless, when she accused him of cowardice, must he not go?

He breakfasted uncomfortably, trying to put off the consideration, and then uncomfortably sauntered down to the Guard House, at St. James's. He had no intention of writing, and was therefore not compelled to make up his mind till the hour named for the appointment should actually have come. He thought for a while that he would write her a long letter, full of good sense; explaining to her that it was impossible that they should be useful to each other, and that he found himself compelled, by his regard for her, to recommend that their peculiar intimacy should be brought to an end. But he knew that such a letter would go for nothing with her,—that she would regard it simply as an excuse on his part. They two had tacitly agreed not to be bound by common sense,—not to be wise. Such tacit agreements are common enough between men, between women, and between men and women. What! a sermon from you! No indeed; not that. Jack felt all this,—felt that he could not preach without laying himself open to ridicule. When the time came he made up his mind that he must go. Of course it was very bad for her. The servants would all know it. Everybody would know it. She was throwing away every chance she had of doing well for herself. But what was he to do? She told him that he would be a coward, and he at any rate could not bear that.

Mr. Mildmay lived in a small house in Green Street, very near the Park, but still a modest, unassuming, cheap little house. Jack De Baron knew the way to it well, and was there not above a quarter-of-an-hour after the appointed time. "So aunt Ju has gone to the Rights of Women, has she?" he said, after his first greeting. He might have kissed her if he would, but he didn't. He had made up his mind about that. And so had she. She was ready for him, whether he should kiss her or not,—ready to accept either greeting, as though it was just that which she had expected.

"Oh, yes; she is going to make a speech herself."

"But why do they give prizes to young men?"

"Because the young men have stood up for the old women. Why don't you go and get a prize?"

"I had to be here instead."

"Had to be here, sir!"

"Yes, Guss; had to be here! Isn't that about it? When you tell me to come, and tell me that I am a coward if I don't come, of course I am here."

"And now you are here, what have you got to say for yourself?" This she attempted to say easily and jauntily.

"Not a word."

"Then I don't see what is the use of coming?"

"Nor I, either. What would you have me say?"

"I would have you,—I would have you—" And then there was something like a sob. It was quite real. "I would have you tell me—that you—love me."

"Have I not told you so a score of times; and what has come of it?"

"But is it true?"

"Come, Guss, this is simple folly. You know it is true; and you know, also, that there is no good whatever to be got from such truth."

"If you loved me, you would like—to—see me."

"No, I shouldn't;—no, I don't;—unless it could lead to something. There was a little fun to be had when we could spoon together,—when I hardly knew how to ask for it, and you hardly knew how to grant it; when it was a little shooting bud, and had to be nursed by smiles and pretty speeches. But there are only three things it can come to now. Two are impossible, and therefore there is the other."

"What are the three?"

"We might get married."

"Well?"

"One of the three I shall not tell you. And we might— make up our minds to forget it all. Do what the people call, part. That is what I suggest."

"So that you may spend your time in riding about with Lady George Germain."

"That is nonsense, Guss. Lady George Germain I have seen three times, and she talks only about her husband; a pretty little woman more absolutely in love I never came across."

"Pretty little fool!"

"Very likely. I have nothing to say against that. Only, when you have no heavier stone to throw against me than Lady George Germain, really you are badly off for weapons."

"I have stones enough, if I chose to throw them. Oh, Jack!"

"What more is there to be said?"

"Have you had enough of me already, Jack?"

"I should not have had half enough of you if either you or I had fifty thousand pounds."

"If I had them I would give them all to you."

"And I to you. That goes without telling. But as neither of us have got the money, what are we to do? I know what we had better not do. We had better not make each other unhappy by what people call recriminations."

"I don't suppose that anything I say can affect your happiness."

"Yes, it does; very much. It makes me think of deep rivers, and high columns; of express trains and prussic acid. Well as we have known each other, you have never found out how unfortunately soft I am."

"Very soft!"

"I am. This troubles me so that I ride over awfully big places, thinking that I might perhaps be lucky enough to break my neck."

"What must I feel, who have no way of amusing myself at all?"

"Drop it. I know it is a hard thing for me to say. I know it will sound heartless. But I am bound to say so. It is for your sake. I can't hurt myself. It does me no harm that everybody knows that I am philandering after you; but it is the very deuce for you." She was silent for a moment. Then he said again emphatically, "Drop it."

"I can't drop it," she said, through her tears.

"Then what are we to do?" As he asked this question, he approached her and put his arm round her waist. This he did in momentary vacillating mercy,—not because of the charm of the thing to himself, but through his own inability not to give her some token of affection.

"Marry," she said, in a whisper.

"And go and live at Dantzic for the rest of our lives!" He did not speak these words, but such was the exclamation which he at once made internally to himself. If he had resolved on anything, he had resolved that he would not marry her. One might sacrifice one's self, he had said to himself, if one could do her any good; but what's the use of sacrificing both. He withdrew his arm from her, and stood a yard apart from her, looking into her face.

"That would be so horrible to you!" she said.

"It would be horrible to have nothing to eat."

"We should have seven hundred and fifty pounds a year," said Guss, who had made her calculations very narrowly.

"Well, yes; and no doubt we could get enough to eat at such a place as Dantzic."

"Dantzic! you always laugh at me when I speak seriously."

"Or Lubeck, if you like it better; or Leipsig. I shouldn't care the least in the world where we went. I know a chap who lives in Minorca because he has not got any money. We might go to Minorca, only the mosquitoes would eat you up."

"Will you do it? I will if you will." They were standing now three yards apart, and Guss was looking terrible things. She did not endeavour to be soft, but had made up her mind as to the one step that must be taken. She would not lose him. They need not be married immediately. Something might turn up before any date was fixed for their marriage. If she could only bind him by an absolute promise that he would marry her some day! "I will, if you will," she said again, after waiting a second or two for his answer. Then he shook his head. "You will not, after all that you have said to me?" He shook his head again. "Then, Jack De Baron, you are perjured, and no gentleman."

"Dear Guss, I can bear that. It is not true, you know, as I have never made you any promise which I am not ready to keep; but still I can bear it."

"No promise! Have you not sworn that you loved me?"

"A thousand times."

"And what does that mean from a gentleman to a lady?"

"It ought to mean matrimony and all that kind of thing, but it never did mean it with us. You know how it all began."

"I know what it has come to, and that you owe it to me as a gentleman to let me decide whether I am able to encounter such a life or not. Though it were absolute destruction, you ought to face it if I bid you."

"If it were destruction for myself only—perhaps, yes. But though you have so little regard for my happiness, I still have some for yours. It is not to be done. You and I have had our little game, as I said before, and now we had better put the rackets down and go and rest ourselves."

"What rest? Oh, Jack,—what rest is there?"

"Try somebody else."

"Can you tell me to do that!"

"Certainly I can. Look at my cousin Adelaide."

"Your cousin Adelaide never cared for any human being in her life except herself. She had no punishment to suffer as I have. Oh, Jack! I do so love you." Then she rushed at him, and fell upon his bosom, and wept.

He knew that this would come, and he felt that, upon the whole, this was the worst part of the performance. He could bear her anger or her sullenness with fortitude, but her lachrymose caresses were insupportable. He held her, however, in his arms, and gazed at himself in the pier glass most uncomfortably over her shoulder. "Oh, Jack," she said, "oh, Jack,—what is to come next?" His face became somewhat more lugubrious than before, but he said not a word. "I cannot lose you altogether. There is no one else in the wide world that I care for. Papa thinks of nothing but his whist. Aunt Ju, with her 'Rights of Women,' is an old fool."

"Just so," said Jack, still holding her, and still looking very wretched.

"What shall I do if you leave me?"

"Pick up some one that has a little money. I know it sounds bad and mercenary, and all that, but in our way of life there is nothing else to be done. We can't marry like the ploughboy and milkmaid?"

"I could."

"And would be the first to find out your mistake afterwards. It's all very well saying that Adelaide hasn't got a heart. I dare say she has as much heart as you or me."

"As you;—as you."

"Very well. Of course you have a sort of pleasure in abusing me. But she has known what she could do, and what she could not. Every year as she grows older she will become more comfortable. Houghton is very good to her, and she has lots of money to spend. If that's heartlessness there's a good deal to be said for it." Then he gently disembarrassed himself of her arms, and placed her on a sofa.

"And this is to be the end?"

"Well,—I think so really." She thumped her hand upon the head of the sofa as a sign of her anger. "Of course we shall always be friends?"

"Never," she almost screamed.

"We'd better. People will talk less about it, you know."

"I don't care what people talk. If they knew the truth, no one would ever speak to you again."

"Good bye, Guss." She shook her head, as he had shaken his before. "Say a word to a fellow." Again she shook her head. He attempted to take her hand, but she withdrew it. Then he stood for perhaps a minute looking at her, but she did not move. "Good bye, Guss," he said again, and then he left the room.

When he got into the street he congratulated himself. He had undergone many such scenes before, but none which seemed so likely to bring the matter to an end. He was rather proud of his own conduct, thinking that he had been at the same time both tender and wise. He had not given way in the least, and had yet been explicit in assuring her of his affection. He felt now that he would go and hunt on the morrow without any desire to break his neck over the baron's fences. Surely the thing was done now for ever and ever! Then he thought how it would have been with him at this moment had he in any transient weakness told her that he would marry her. But he had been firm, and could now walk along with a light heart.

She, as soon as he had left her, got up, and taking the cushion off the sofa, threw it to the further end of the room. Having so relieved herself, she walked up to her own chamber.

Chapter XVI.

All Is Fish That Comes To His Net.

The Dean's week up in London during the absence of Lord George was gay enough; but through it all and over it all there was that cloud of seriousness which had been produced by the last news from Italy. He rode with his daughter, dined out in great state at Mrs. Montacute Jones's, talked to Mr. Houghton about Newmarket and the next Derby, had a little flirtation of his own with Hetta Houghton,—into which he contrived to introduce a few serious words about the Marquis,—and was merry enough; but, to his daughter's surprise, he never for a moment ceased to be impressed with the importance of the Italian woman and her baby. "What does it signify, papa?" she said.

"Not signify!"

"Of course it was to be expected that the Marquis should marry. Why should he not marry as well as his younger brother?"

"In the first place, he is very much older."

"As to that, men marry at any age. Look at Mr. Houghton." The Dean only smiled. "Do you know, papa, I don't think one ought to trouble about such things."

"That's nonsense, my dear. Men, and women too, ought to look after their own interests. It is the only way in which progress can be made in the world. Of course you are not to covet what belongs to others. You will make yourself very unhappy if you do. If Lord Brotherton's marriage were all fair and above board, nobody would say a word; but, as it has not been so, it will be our duty to find out the truth. If you should have a son, do not you think that you would turn every stone before you would have him defrauded of his rights?"

"I shouldn't think any one would defraud him."

"But if this child be—anything else than what he pretends to be, there will be fraud. The Germains, though they think as I do, are frightened and superstitious. They are afraid of this imbecile who is coming over; but they shall find that if they do not move in the matter, I will. I want nothing that belongs to another; but while I have a hand and tongue with which to protect myself, or a purse,—which is better than either,—no one shall take from me what belongs to me." All this seemed to Mary to be pagan teaching, and it surprised her much as coming from her father. But she was beginning to find out that she, as a married woman, was supposed to be now fit for other teaching than had been administered to her as a child. She had been cautioned in her father's house against the pomps and vanities of this wicked world, and could remember the paternal, almost divine expression of the Dean's face as the lesson was taught. But now it seemed to her that the pomps and vanities were spoken of in a very different way. The divine expression was altogether gone, and that which remained, though in looking at her it was always pleasant, was hardly paternal.

Miss Mildmay,—Aunt Ju as she was called,—and Guss Mildmay came and called, and as it happened the Dean was in the drawing-room when they came. They were known to be friends of Mrs. Houghton's who had been in Brothershire, and were therefore in some degree connected even with the Dean. Guss began at once about the new Marchioness and the baby;

and the Dean, though he did not of course speak to Guss Mildmay as he had done to his own daughter, still sneered at the mother and her child. In the meantime Aunt Ju was enlisting poor Mary. "I should be so proud if you would come with me to the Institute, Lady George."

"I am sure I should be delighted. But what Institute?"

"Don't you know?—in the Marylebone Road,—for relieving females from their disabilities."

"Do you mean Rights of Women? I don't think papa likes that," said Mary, looking round at her father.

"You haven't got to mind what papa likes and dislikes any more," said the Dean, laughing. "Whether you go in for the rights or the wrongs of women is past my caring for now. Lord George must look after that."

"I am sure Lord George could not object to your going to the Marylebone Institute," said Aunt Ju. "Lady Selina Protest is there every week, and Baroness Banmann, the delegate from Bavaria, is coming next Friday."

"You'd find the Disabilities awfully dull, Lady George," said Guss.

"Everybody is not so flighty as you are, my dear. Some people do sometimes think of serious things. And the Institute is not called the Disabilities."

"What is it all about?" said Mary.

"Only to empower women to take their own equal places in the world,—places equal to those occupied by men," said Aunt Ju eloquently. "Why should one-half of the world be ruled by the *ipse dixit* of the other?"

"Or fed by their labours?" said the Dean.

"That is just what we are not. There are 1,133,500 females in England—"

"You had better go and hear it all at the Disabilities, Lady George," said Guss. Lady George said that she would like to go for once, and so that matter was settled.

While Aunt Ju was pouring out the violence of her doctrine upon the Dean, whom she contrived to catch in a corner just before she left the house, Guss Mildmay had a little conversation on her own part with Lady George. "Captain De Baron," she said, "is an old friend of yours, I suppose." She, however, had known very well that Jack had never seen Lady George till within the last month.

"No, indeed; I never saw him till the other day."

"I thought you seemed to be intimate. And then the Houghtons and the De Barons and the Germains are all Brothershire people."

"I knew Mrs. Houghton's father, of course, a little; but I never saw Captain De Baron." This she said rather seriously, remembering what Mrs. Houghton had said to her of the love affair between this young lady and the Captain in question.

"I thought you seemed to know him the other night, and I saw you riding with him."

"He was with his cousin Adelaide,—not with us."

"I don't think he cares much for Adelaide. Do you like him?"

"Yes, I do; very much. He seems to be so gay."

"Yes, he is gay. He's a horrid flirt, you know."

"I didn't know; and what is more, I don't care."

"So many girls have said that about Captain De Baron; but they have cared afterwards."

"But I am not a girl, Miss Mildmay," said Mary, colouring, offended and resolved at once that she would have no intimacy and as little acquaintance as possible with Guss Mildmay.

"You are so much younger than so many of us that are girls," said Guss, thinking to get out of the little difficulty in that way. "And then it's all fish that comes to his net." She hardly knew what she was saying, but was anxious to raise some feeling that should prevent any increased intimacy between her own lover and Lady George. It was nothing to her whether or no she offended Lady George Germain. If she could do her work without sinning against good taste, well; but if not, then good taste must go to the wall. Good taste certainly had gone to the wall.

"Upon my word, I can hardly understand you!" Then Lady George turned away to her father. "Well, papa, has Miss Mildmay persuaded you to come to the Institute with me?"

"I am afraid I should hardly be admitted, after what I have just said."

"Indeed you shall be admitted, Mr. Dean," said the old woman. "We are quite of the Church's way of thinking, that no sinner is too hardened for repentance."

"I am afraid the day of grace has not come yet," said the Dean.

"Papa," said Lady George, as soon as her visitors were gone, "do you know I particularly dislike that younger Miss Mildmay."

"Is she worth being particularly disliked so rapidly?"

"She says nasty, impudent things. I can't quite explain what she said." And again Lady George blushed.

"People in society now do give themselves strange liberty;—women, I think, more than men. You shouldn't mind it."

"Not mind it?"

"Not mind it so as to worry yourself. If a pert young woman like that says anything to annoy you, put her down at the time, and then think no more about it. Of course you need not make a friend of her."

"That I certainly shall not do."

On the Sunday after this Lady George dined again with her father at Mr. Houghton's house, the dinner having been made up especially for the Dean. On this occasion the Mildmays were not there; but Captain De Baron was one of the guests. But then he was Mrs. Houghton's cousin, and had the run of the house on all occasions. Again, there was no great party; Mrs.

Montacute Jones was there, and Hetta,—Miss Houghton, that is, whom all the world called Hetta,—and Mrs. Houghton's father, who happened to be up in town. Again Lady George found herself sitting between her host and Jack De Baron, and again she thought that Jack was a very agreeable companion. The idea of being in any way afraid of him did not enter into her mind. Those horrid words which Guss Mildmay had said to her,—as to all being fish for his net,—had no effect of that nature. She assured herself that she knew herself too well to allow anything of that kind to influence her. That she, Lady George Germain, the daughter of the Dean of Brotherton, a married woman, should be afraid of any man, afraid of any too close intimacy! The idea was horrible and disgusting to her. So that when Jack proposed to join her and her father in the park on the next afternoon, she said that she would be delighted; and when he told her absurd stories of his regimental duties, and described his brother officers who probably did not exist as described by him, and then went on to hunting legends in Buckinghamshire, she laughed at everything he said and was very merry. "Don't you like Jack?" Mrs. Houghton said to her in the drawing-room.

"Yes, I do; very much. He's just what Jack ought to be."

"I don't know about that. I suppose Jack ought to go to church twice on Sundays, and give half what he has to the poor, just as well as John."

"Perhaps he does. But Jack is bound to be amusing, while John need not have a word to say for himself."

"You know he's my pet friend. We are almost like brother and sister, and therefore I need not be afraid of him."

"Afraid of him! Why should anybody be afraid of him?"

"I am sure you needn't. But Jack has done mischief in his time. Perhaps he's not the sort of man that would ever touch your fancy." Again Lady George blushed, but on this occasion she had nothing to say. She did not want to quarrel with Mrs. Houghton, and the suggestion that she could possibly love any other man than her husband had not now been made in so undisguised a manner as before.

"I thought he was engaged to Miss Mildmay," said Lady George.

"Oh, dear no; nothing of the kind. It is impossible, as neither of them has anything to speak of. When does Lord George come back?"

"To-morrow."

"Mind that he comes to see me soon. I do so long to hear what he'll say about his new sister-in-law. I had made up my mind that I should have to koto to you before long as a real live marchioness."

"You'll never have to do that."

"Not if this child is a real Lord Popenjoy. But I have my hopes still, my dear."

Soon after that Hetta Houghton reverted to the all important subject.

"You have found out that what I told you was true, Lady George."

"Oh yes,—all true."

"I wonder what the Dowager thinks about it."

"My husband is with his mother. She thinks, I suppose, just what we all think, that it would have been better if he had told everybody of his marriage sooner."

"A great deal better."

"I don't know whether, after all, it will make a great deal of difference. Lady Brotherton,—the Dowager I mean,—is so thoroughly English in all her ways that she never could have got on very well with an Italian daughter-in-law."

"The question is whether when a man springs a wife and family on his relations in that way, everything can be taken for granted. Suppose a man had been ever so many years in Kamptschatka, and had then come back with a Kamptschatkean female, calling her his wife, would everybody take it as all gospel?"

"I suppose so."

"Do you? I think not. In the first place it might be difficult for an Englishman to get himself married in that country according to English laws, and in the next, when there, he would hardly wish to do so."

"Italy is not Kamptschatka, Miss Houghton."

"Certainly not; and it isn't England. People are talking about it a great deal, and seem to think that the Italian lady oughtn't to have a walk over."

Miss Houghton had heard a good deal about races from her brother, and the phrase she had used was quite an everyday word to her. Lady George did not understand it, but felt that Miss Houghton was talking very freely about a very delicate matter. And she remembered at the same time what had been the aspirations of the lady's earlier life, and put down a good deal of what was said to personal jealousy. "Papa," she said, as she went home, "it seems to me that people here talk a great deal about one's private concerns."

"You mean about Lord Brotherton's marriage."

"That among other things."

"Of course they will talk about that. It is hardly to be considered private. And I don't know but what the more it is talked about the better for us. It is felt to be a public scandal, and that feeling may help us."

"Oh, papa, I wish you wouldn't think that we wanted any help."

"We want the truth, my dear, and we must have it."

On the next day they met Jack De Baron in the park. They had not been long together before the Dean saw an old friend on the footpath and stopped to speak to him. Mary would have stayed too, had not her horse displayed an inclination to go on, and that she had felt herself unwilling to make an effort in the matter. As she rode on with Captain De Baron she remembered all that had been said by Guss Mildmay and Mrs. Houghton, and remembered also her own decision that nothing of that kind could matter to her. It was an understood thing that ladies and gentlemen when riding should fall into this kind of intercourse. Her father was with her, and it would be absurd that she should be afraid to be a minute or two out of his sight. "I ought to have been hunting," said Jack; "but there was frost last night, and I do hate going down and being told that the ground is as hard as brickbats at the kennels, while men are ploughing all over the country. And now it's a delicious spring day."

"You didn't like getting up, Captain De Baron," she said.

"Perhaps there's something in that. Don't you think getting up is a mistake? My idea of a perfect world is one where nobody would ever have to get up."

"I shouldn't at all like always to lie in bed."

"But there might be some sort of arrangement to do away with the nuisance. See what a good time the dogs have."

"Now, Captain De Baron, would you like to be a dog?" This she said turning round and looking him full in the face.

"Your dog I would." At that moment, just over his horse's withers, she saw the face of Guss Mildmay who was leaning on her father's arm. Guss bowed to her, and she was obliged to return the salute. Jack De Baron turned his face to the path and seeing the lady raised his hat. "Are you two friends?" he asked.

"Not particularly."

"I wish you were. But, of course, I have no right to wish in such a matter as that." Lady George felt that she wished that Guss Mildmay had not seen her riding in the park on that day with Jack De Baron.

Chapter XVII.

The Disabilities.

It had been arranged that on Friday evening Lady George should call for Aunt Ju in Green Street, and that they should go together to the Institute in the Marylebone Road. The real and full name of the college, as some ladies delighted to call it, was, though somewhat lengthy, placarded in big letters on a long black board on the front of the building, and was as follows, "Rights of Women Institute; Established for the Relief of the Disabilities of Females." By friendly tongues to friendly ears "The College" or "the Institute" was the pleasant name used; but the irreverent public was apt to speak of the building generally as the "Female Disabilities." And the title was made even shorter. Omnibuses were desired to stop at the "Disabilities;" and it had become notorious that it was just a mile from King's Cross to the "Disabilities." There had been serious thoughts among those who were dominant in the Institute of taking down the big board and dropping the word. But then a change of a name implies such a confession of failure! It had on the whole been thought better to maintain the courage of the opinion which had first made the mistake. "So you're going to the Disabilities, are you?" Mrs. Houghton had said to Lady George.

"I'm to be taken by old Miss Mildmay."

"Oh, yes; Aunt Ju is a sort of first-class priestess among them. Don't let them bind you over to belong to them. Don't go in for it." Lady George had declared it to be very improbable that she should go in for it, but had adhered to her determination of visiting the Institute.

She called in Green Street fearing that she should see Guss Mildmay whom she had determined to keep at arm's distance as well as her friendship with Mrs. Houghton would permit; but Aunt Ju was ready for her in the passage. "I forgot to tell you that we ought to be a little early, as I have to take the chair. I daresay we shall do very well," she added, "if the man drives fast. But the thing is so important! One doesn't like to be flurried when one gets up to make the preliminary address." The only public meetings at which Mary had ever been present had appertained to certain lectures at Brotherton, at which her father or some other clerical dignity had presided, and she could not as yet understand that such a duty should be performed by a woman. She muttered something expressing a hope that all would go right. "I've got to introduce the Baroness, you know."

"Introduce the Baroness?"

"The Baroness Banmann. Haven't you seen the bill of the evening? The Baroness is going to address the meeting on the propriety of patronising female artists,—especially in regard to architecture. A combined college of female architects is to be established in Posen and Chicago, and why should we not have a branch in London, which is the centre of the world?"

"Would a woman have to build a house?" asked Lady George.

"She would draw the plans, and devise the proportions, and—and—do the æsthetic part of it. An architect doesn't carry bricks on his back, my dear."

"But he walks over planks, I suppose."

"And so could I walk over a plank; why not as well as a man? But you will hear what the Baroness says. The worst is that I am a little afraid of her English."

"She's a foreigner, of course. How will she manage?"

"Her English is perfect, but I am afraid of her pronunciation. However, we shall see." They had now arrived at the building, and Lady George followed the old lady in with the crowd. But when once inside the door they turned to a small passage on the left, which conducted those in authority to the august room preparatory to the platform. It is here that bashful speakers try to remember their first sentences, and that lecturers, proud of their prominence, receive the homage of the officers of the Institute. Aunt Ju, who on this occasion was second in glory, made her way in among the crowd and welcomed the Baroness, who had just arrived. The Baroness, was a very stout woman, about fifty, with a double chin, a considerable moustache, a low broad forehead, and bright, round, black eyes, very far apart. When introduced to Lady George, she declared that she had great honour in accepting the re-cog-nition. She had a stout roll of paper in her hand, and was dressed in a black stuff gown, with a cloth jacket buttoned up to neck, which hardly gave to her copious bust that appearance of manly firmness which the occasion almost required. But the virile collars budding out over it perhaps supplied what was wanting. Lady George looked at her to see if she was trembling. How, thought Lady George, would it have been with herself if she had been called upon to address a French audience in French! But as far as she could judge from experience, the Baroness was quite at her ease. Then she was introduced by Aunt Ju to Lady Selina Protest, who was a very little woman with spectacles,—of a most severe aspect. "I hope, Lady George, that you mean to put your shoulder to the wheel," said Lady Selina. "I am only here as a stranger," said Lady George. Lady Selina did not believe in strangers and passed on very severely. There was no time for further ceremonies, as a bald-headed old gentleman, who seemed to act as chief usher, informed Aunt Ju that it was time for her to take the Baroness on to the platform. Aunt Ju led the way, puffing a little, for she had been somewhat hurried on the stairs, and was not as yet quite used to the thing,—but still with a proudly prominent step. The Baroness waddled after her, apparently quite indifferent to the occasion. Then followed Lady Selina,— and Lady George, the bald-headed gentleman telling her where to place herself. She had never been on a platform before, and it seemed as though the crowd of people below was looking specially at her. As she sat down, at the right hand of the Baroness, who was of course at the right hand of the Chairwoman, the bald-headed gentleman introduced her to her other neighbour, Miss Doctor Olivia Q. Fleabody, from Vermont. There was so much of the name and it all sounded so strange to the ears of Lady George that she could remember very little of it, but she was conscious that her new acquaintance was a miss and a doctor. She looked timidly round, and saw what would have been a pretty face, had it not been marred by a pinched look of studious severity and a pair of glass spectacles of which the glasses shone in a disagreeable manner. There are spectacles which are so much more spectacles than other spectacles that they make the beholder feel that there is before him a pair of spectacles carrying a face, rather than a face carrying a pair of spectacles. So it was with the spectacles of Olivia Q. Fleabody. She was very thin, and the jacket and collars were quite successful. Sitting in the front row she displayed her feet,—and it may also be said her trousers, for the tunic which she wore came down hardly below the knees. Lady George's enquiring mind instantly began to ask itself what the lady had done with her petticoats. "This is a great occasion," said Dr. Fleabody, speaking almost out loud, and with a very strong nasal twang.

Lady George looked at the chair before she answered, feeling that she would not dare to speak a word if Aunt Ju were already on her legs; but Aunt Ju was taking advantage of the commotion which was still going on among those who were looking for seats to get her breath, and therefore she could whisper a reply. "I suppose it is," she said.

"If it were not that I have wedded myself in a peculiar manner to the prophylactick and therapeutick sciences, I would certainly now put my foot down firmly in the cause of architecture. I hope to have an opportunity of saying a few words on the subject myself before this interesting session shall have closed." Lady George looked at her again and thought that this enthusiastic hybrid who was addressing her could not be more than twenty-four years old.

But Aunt Ju was soon on her legs. It did not seem to Lady George that Aunt Ju enjoyed the moment now that it was come. She looked hot, and puffed once or twice before she spoke. But she had studied her few words so long, and had made so sure of them, that she could not go very far wrong. She assured her audience that the Baroness Banmann, whose name had only to be mentioned to be honoured both throughout Europe and America, had, at great personal inconvenience, come all the way from Bavaria to give them the advantage of her vast experience on the present occasion. Like a good chairwoman, she took none of the bread out of the Baroness's mouth—as we have occasionally known it to be done on such occasions—but confined herself to ecstatic praises of the German lady. All these the Baroness bore without a quiver, and when Aunt Ju sat down she stepped on to the rostrum of the evening amidst the plaudits of the room, with a confidence which to Lady George was miraculous. Then Aunt Ju took her seat, and was able for the next hour and a half to occupy her arm-chair with gratifying fainéant dignity.

The Baroness, to tell the truth, waddled rather than stepped to the rostrum. She swung herself heavily about as she went sideways; but it was manifest to all eyes that she was not in the least ashamed of her waddling. She undid her manuscript on the desk, and flattened it down all over with her great fat hand, rolling her head about as she looked around, and then gave a grunt before she began. During this time the audience was applauding her loudly, and it was evident that she did not intend to lose a breath of their incense by any hurry on her own part. At last the voices and the hands and the feet were silent. Then she gave a last roll to her head and a last pat to the papers, and began. "De manifest infairiority of de tyrant saix—."

Those first words, spoken in a very loud voice, came clearly home to Lady George's ear, though they were uttered with a most un-English accent. The Baroness paused before she completed her first sentence, and then there was renewed applause. Lady George could remark that the bald-headed old gentleman behind and a cadaverous youth who was near to him were particularly energetic in stamping on the ground. Indeed, it seemed that the men were specially charmed with this commencement of the Baroness's oration. It was so good that she repeated it with, perhaps, even a louder shout. "De manifest infairiority of de tyrant saix—." Lady George, with considerable trouble, was able to follow the first sentence or two, which went to assert that the inferiority of man to woman in all work was quite as conspicuous as his rapacity and tyranny in taking to himself all the wages. The Baroness, though addressing a mixed audience, seemed to have no hesitation in speaking of man generally as a foul worm who ought to be put down and kept under, and merely allowed to be the father of children. But after a minute or two Lady George found that she could not understand two words consecutively, although she was close to the lecturer. The Baroness, as she became heated, threw out her words quicker and more quickly, till it became almost impossible to know in what language they were spoken. By degrees our friend became aware that the subject of architecture had been reached, and then she caught a word or two as the Baroness declared that the science was "adaapted only to de æstetic and comprehensive intelligence of de famale mind." But the audience applauded throughout as though every word reached them; and when from time to time the Baroness wiped her brows with a very large handkerchief, they shook the building with their appreciation of her energy. Then came a loud rolling sentence, with the old words as an audible termination— "de manifest infairiority of de tyrant saix!" As she said this she waved her handkerchief in the air and almost threw herself over the desk. "She is very great to-night,—very great indeed," whispered Miss Doctor Olivia Q. Fleabody to Lady George. Lady George was afraid to ask her neighbour whether she understood one word out of ten that were being spoken.

Great as the Baroness was, Lady George became very tired of it all. The chair was hard and the room was full of dust, and she could not get up. It was worse than the longest and the worst sermon she had ever heard. It seemed to her at last that there was no reason why the Baroness should not go on for ever. The woman liked it, and the people applauded her. The poor victim had made up her mind that there was no hope of cessation, and in doing so was very nearly asleep, when, on a sudden, the Baroness had finished and had thrown herself violently back into her chair. "Baroness, believe me," said Dr. Fleabody, stretching across Lady George, "it is the greatest treat I ever had in my life." The Baroness hardly condescended to answer the compliment. She was at this moment so great a woman, at this moment so immeasurably the greatest human being at any rate in London, that it did not become her to acknowledge single compliments. She had worked hard and was very hot, but still she had sufficient presence of mind to remember her demeanour.

When the tumult was a little subsided, Lady Selina Protest got up to move a vote of thanks. She was sitting on the left-hand side of the Chair, and rose so silently that Lady George had at first thought that the affair was all over, and that they might go away. Alas, alas! there was more to be borne yet! Lady Selina spoke with a clear but low voice, and though she was quite audible, and an earl's sister, did not evoke any enthusiasm.

She declared that the thanks of every woman in England were due to the Baroness for her exertions, and of every man who wished to be regarded as the friend of women. But Lady Selina was very quiet, making no gestures, and was indeed somewhat flat. When she sat down no notice whatever was taken of her. Then very quickly, before Lady George had time to look about her, the Doctor was on her feet. It was her task to second the vote of thanks, but she was far too experienced an occupant of platforms to waste her precious occasion simply on so poor a task. She began by declaring that never in her life had a duty been assigned to her more consonant to her taste than that of seconding a vote of thanks to a woman so eminent, so humanitarian, and at the same time so essentially a female as the Baroness Banmann. Lady George, who knew nothing about speaking, felt at once that here was a speaker who could at any rate make herself audible and intelligible. Then the Doctor broke away into the general subject, with special allusions to the special matter of female architecture, and went on for twenty minutes without dropping a word. There was a moment in which she had almost made Lady George think that women ought to build houses. Her dislike to the American twang had vanished, and she was almost sorry when Miss Doctor Fleabody resumed her seat.

But it was after that,—after the Baroness had occupied another ten minutes in thanking the British public for the thanks that had been given to herself,—that the supreme emotion of the evening came to Lady George. Again she had thought, when the Baroness a second time rolled back to her chair, that the time for departure had come. Many in the hall, indeed, were already going, and she could not quite understand why no one on the platform had as yet moved. Then came that bald-headed old gentleman to her, to her very self, and suggested to her that she,—she, Lady George Germain, who the other day was Mary Lovelace, the Brotherton girl,—should stand up and make a speech! "There is to be a vote of thanks to Miss Mildmay as

Chairwoman," said the bald-headed old man, "and we hope, Lady George, that you will favour us with a few words."

Her heart utterly gave way and the blood flew into her cheeks, and she thoroughly repented of having come to this dreadful place. She knew that she could not do it, though the world were to depend upon it; but she did not know whether the bald-headed old gentleman might not have the right of insisting on it. And then all the people were looking at her as the horrible old man was pressing his request over her shoulder. "Oh," she said; "no, I can't. Pray don't. Indeed I can't,—and I won't." The idea had come upon her that it was necessary that she should be very absolute. The old man retired meekly, and himself made the speech in honour of Aunt Ju.

As they were going away Lady George found that she was to have the honour of conveying the Baroness to her lodgings in Conduit Street. This was all very well, as there was room for three in the brougham, and she was not ill-pleased to hear the ecstasies of Aunt Ju about the lecture. Aunt Ju declared that she had agreed with every word that had been uttered. Aunt Ju thought that the cause was flourishing. Aunt Ju was of opinion that women in England would before long be able to sit in Parliament and practice in the Law Courts. Aunt Ju was thoroughly in earnest; but the Baroness had expended her energy in the lecture, and was more inclined to talk about persons. Lady George was surprised to hear her say that this young man was a very handsome young man, and that old man a very nice old man. She was almost in love with Mr. Spuffin, the bald-headed gentleman usher; and when she was particular in asking whether Mr. Spuffin was married, Lady George could hardly think that this was the woman who had been so eloquent on the "infairiority of de tyrant saix."

But it was not till Aunt Ju had been dropped in Green Street, and the conversation fell upon Lady George herself, that the difficulty began. "You no speak?" asked the Baroness.

"What, in public! Not for the world!"

"You wrong dere. Noting so easy. Say just as you please, only say it vera loud. And alvays abuse somebody or someting. You s'ould try."

"I would sooner die," said Lady George. "Indeed, I should be dead before I could utter a word. Isn't it odd how that lady Doctor could speak like that."

"De American young woman! Dey have de impudence of—of—of everything you please; but it come to noting."

"But she spoke well."

"Dear me, no; noting at all. Dere was noting but vords, vords, vords. Tank you; here I am. Mind you come again, and you shall learn to speak."

Lady George, as she was driven home, was lost in her inability to understand it all. She had thought that the Doctor spoke the best of all, and now she was told that it was nothing. She did not yet understand that even people so great as female orators, so nobly humanitarian as the Baroness Banmann, can be jealous of the greatness of others.

Chapter XVIII.

Lord George Up In London.

Lord George returned to town the day after the lecture, and was not altogether pleased that his wife should have gone to the Disabilities. She thought, indeed, that he did not seem to be in a humour to be pleased with anything. His mind was thoroughly disturbed by the coming of his brother, and perplexed with the idea that something must be done though he knew not what. And he was pervaded by a feeling that in the present emergency it behoved him to watch his own steps, and more especially those of his wife. An anonymous letter had reached Lady Sarah, signed, "A Friend of the Family," in which it was stated that the Marquis of Brotherton had allied himself to the highest blood that Italy knew, marrying into a family that had been noble before English nobility had existed, whereas his brother had married the granddaughter of a stable-keeper and a tallow chandler. This letter had, of course, been shown to Lord George; and, though he and his sisters agreed in looking upon it as an emanation from their enemy, the new Marchioness, it still gave them to understand that she, if attacked, would be prepared to attack again. And Lord George was open to attack on the side indicated. He was, on the whole, satisfied with his wife. She was ladylike, soft, pretty, well-mannered, and good to him. But her grandfathers had been stable-keepers and tallow-chandlers. Therefore it was specially imperative that she should be kept from injurious influences. Lady Selina Protest and Aunt Ju, who were both well-born, might take liberties; but not so his wife. "I don't think that was a very nice place to go to, Mary."

"It wasn't nice at all, but it was very funny. I never saw such a vulgar creature as the Baroness, throwing herself about and wiping her face."

"Why should you go and see a vulgar creature throw herself about and wipe her face?"

"Why should anybody do it? One likes to see what is going on, I suppose. The woman's vulgarity could not hurt me, George."

"It could do you no good."

"Lady Selina Protest was there, and I went with Miss Mildmay."

"Two old maids who have gone crazy about Woman's Rights because nobody has married them. The whole thing is distasteful to me, and I hope you will not go there again."

"That I certainly shall not, because it is very dull," said Mary.

"I hope, also, that, independently of that, my request would be enough."

"Certainly it would, George; but I don't know why you should be so cross to me."

"I don't think that I have been cross; but I am anxious, specially anxious. There are reasons why I have to be very anxious in regard to you, and why you have to be yourself more particular than others."

"What reasons?" She asked this with a look of bewildered astonishment. He was not prepared to answer the question, and shuffled out of it, muttering some further words as to the peculiar difficulty of their position. Then he kissed her and left her, telling her that all would be well if she would be careful.

If she would be careful! All would be well if she would be careful! Why should there be need of more care on her part than on that of others? She knew that all this had reference in some way to that troublesome lady and troublesome baby who were about to be brought home; but she could not conceive how her conduct could be specially concerned. It was a sorrow to her that her husband should allow himself to be ruffled about the matter at all. It was a sorrow also that her father should do so. As to herself, she had an idea that if Providence chose to make her a Marchioness, Providence ought to be allowed to do it without any interference on her part. But it would be a double sorrow if she were told that she mustn't do this and mustn't do that because there was before her a dim prospect of being seated in a certain high place which was claimed and occupied by another person. And she was aware, too, that her husband had in very truth scolded her. The ladies at Manor Cross had scolded her before, but he had never done so. She had got away from Manor Cross, and had borne the scolding because the prospect of escape had been before her. But it would be very bad indeed if her husband should take to scold her. Then she thought that if Jack De Baron were married he would never scold his wife.

The Dean had not yet gone home, and in her discomfort she had recourse to him. She did not intend to complain of her husband to her father. Had any such idea occurred to her, she would have stamped it out at once, knowing that such a course would be both unloyal and unwise. But her father was so pleasant with her, so easy to be talked to, so easy to be understood, whereas her husband was almost mysterious,—at any rate, gloomy and dark. "Papa," she said, "what does George mean by saying that I ought to be more particular than other people?"

"Does he say so?"

"Yes; and he didn't like my going with that old woman to hear the other women. He says that I ought not to do it though anybody else might."

"I think you misunderstood him."

"No; I didn't, papa."

"Then you had better imagine that he was tired with his journey, or that his stomach was a little out of order. Don't fret about such things, and whatever you do, make the best of your husband."

"But how am I to know where I may go and where I mayn't? Am I to ask him everything first?"

"Don't be a child, whatever you do. You will soon find out what pleases him and what doesn't, and, if you manage well, what you do will please him. Whatever his manner may be, he is soft-hearted and affectionate."

"I know that, papa."

"If he says a cross word now and again just let it go by. You should not suppose that words always mean what they seem to mean. I knew a man who used to tell his wife ever so often that he wished she were dead."

"Good heavens, papa!"

"Whenever he said so she always put a little magnesia into his beer, and things went on as comfortably as possible. Never magnify things, even to yourself. I don't suppose Lord George wants magnesia as yet, but you will understand what I mean." She said that she did; but she had not, in truth, quite comprehended the lesson as yet, nor could her father as yet teach it to her in plainer language.

On that same afternoon Lord George called in Berkeley Square and saw Mrs. Houghton. At this time the whole circle of people who were in any way connected with the Germain family, or who, by the circumstances of their lives were brought within the pale of the Germain influence, were agog with the marriage of the Marquis. The newspapers had already announced the probable return of the Marquis and the coming of a new Marchioness and a new Lord Popenjoy. Occasion had been taken to give some details of the Germain family, and public allusion had even been made to the marriage of Lord

George. These are days in which, should your wife's grandfather have ever been insolvent, some newspaper, in its catering for the public, will think it proper to recall the fact. The Dean's parentage had been alluded to, and the late Tallowax will, and the Tallowax property generally. It had also been declared that the Marchesa Luigi,—now the present Marchioness,—had been born an Orsini; and also, in another paper, the other fact (?) that she had been divorced from her late husband. This had already been denied by Mr. Knox, who had received a telegram from Florence ordering such denial to be made. It may, therefore, be conceived that the Germains were at this moment the subject of much conversation, and it may be understood that Mrs. Houghton, who considered herself to be on very confidential terms with Lord George, should, as they were alone, ask a few questions and express a little sympathy. "How does the dear Marchioness like the new house?" she asked.

"It is tolerably comfortable."

"That Price is a darling, Lord George; I've known him ever so long. And, of course, it is the dower house."

"It was the suddenness that disturbed my mother."

"Of course; and then the whole of it must have gone against the grain with her. You bear it like an angel."

"For myself, I don't know that I have anything to bear."

"The whole thing is so dreadful. There are you and your dear wife,—everything just as it ought to be,—idolized by your mother, looked up to by the whole country, the very man whom we wish to see the head of such a family."

"Don't talk in that way, Mrs. Houghton."

"I know it is very distant; but still, I do feel near enough related to you all to be justified in being proud, and also to be justified in being ashamed. What will they do about calling upon her?"

"My brother will, of course, come to my mother first. Then Lady Sarah and one of her sisters will go over. After that he will bring his wife to Cross Hall if he pleases."

"I am so glad it is all settled; it is so much better. But you know, Lord George,—I must say it to you as I would to my own brother, because my regard for you is the same,—I shall never think that that woman is really his wife." Lord George frowned heavily, but did not speak. "And I shall never think that that child is really Lord Popenjoy."

Neither did Lord George in his heart of hearts believe that the Italian woman was a true Marchioness or the little child a true Lord Popenjoy; but he had confessed to himself that he had no adequate reason for such disbelief, and had perceived that it would become him to keep his opinion to himself. The Dean had been explicit with him, and that very explicitness had seemed to impose silence on himself. To his mother he had not whispered an idea of a suspicion. With his sisters he had been reticent, though he knew that Lady Sarah, at any rate, had her suspicions. But now an open expression of the accusation from so dear a friend as Mrs. Houghton,—from the Adelaide De Baron whom he had so dearly loved,—gratified him and almost tempted him into confidence. He had frowned at first, because his own family was to him so august that he could not but frown when anyone ventured to speak of it. Even crowned princes are driven to relax themselves on occasions, and Lord George Germain felt that he would almost like, just for once, to talk about his brothers and sisters as though they were Smiths and Joneses. "It is very hard to know what to think," he said.

Mrs. Houghton at once saw that the field was open to her. She had ventured a good deal, and, knowing the man, had felt the danger of doing so; but she was satisfied now that she might say almost anything. "But one is bound to think, isn't one? Don't you feel that? It is for the whole family that you have to act."

"What is to be done? I can't go and look up evidence."

"But a paid agent can. Think of Mary. Think of Mary's child,—if she should have one." As she said this she looked rather anxiously into his face, being desirous of receiving an answer to a question which she did not quite dare to ask.

"Of course there's all that," he said, not answering the question.

"I can only just remember him though papa knew him so well. But I suppose he has lived abroad till he has ceased to think and feel like an Englishman. Could anyone believe that a Marquis of Brotherton would have married a wife long enough ago to have a son over twelve months old, and never to have said a word about it to his brother or mother? I don't believe it."

"I don't know what to believe," said Lord George.

"And then to write in such a way about the house! Of course I hear it talked of by people who won't speak before you; but you ought to know."

"What do people say?"

"Everybody thinks that there is some fraud. There is old Mrs. Montacute Jones,—I don't know anybody who knows everything better than she does,—and she was saying that you would be driven by your duty to investigate the matter. 'I daresay he'd prefer to do nothing,' she said, 'but he must.' I felt that to be so true! Then Mr. Mildmay, who is so very quiet, said that there would be a lawsuit. Papa absolutely laughed at the idea of the boy being Lord Popenjoy, though he was always on good terms with your brother. Mr. Houghton says that nobody in society will give the child the name. Of course he's not very bright, but on matters like that he does know what he's talking about. When I hear all this I feel it a great deal, Lord George."

"I know what a friend you are."

"Indeed I am. I think very often what I might have been, but could not be; and though I am not jealous of the happiness and honours of another, I am anxious for your happiness and your honours." He was sitting near her, on a chair facing the fire, while she was leaning back on the sofa. He went on staring at the hot coals, flattered, in some sort elate, but very disturbed. The old feeling was coming back upon him. She was not as pretty as his wife,—but she was, he thought, more attractive, had more to say for herself, was more of a woman. She could pour herself into his heart and understand his feelings, whereas Mary did not sympathize with him at all in this great family trouble. But then Mary was, of course, his wife, and this woman was the wife of another man. He would be the last man in the world,—so he would have told himself could he have spoken to himself on the subject,—to bring disgrace on himself and misery on other people by declaring his love to another man's wife. He was the last man to do an injury to the girl whom he had made his own wife! But he liked being with his old love, and felt anxious to say a word to her that should have in it something just a little beyond the ordinary tenderness of friendship. The proper word, however, did not come to him at that moment. In such moments the proper word very often will not come. "You are not angry with me for saying so?" she asked.

"How can I be angry?"

"I don't think that there can have been such friendship, as there was between you and me, and that it should fade and die away, unless there be some quarrel. You have not quarrelled with me?"

"Quarrelled with you? Never!"

"And you did love me once?" She at any rate knew how to find the tender words that were required for her purpose.

"Indeed I did."

"It did not last very long; did it, Lord George?"

"It was you that—that—. It was you that stopped it."

"Yes, it was I that stopped it. Perhaps I found it easier to—stop than I had expected. But it was all for the best. It must have been stopped. What could our life have been? I was telling a friend to mine the other day, a lady, that there are people who cannot afford to wear hearts inside them. If I had jumped at your offer,—and there was a moment when I would have done so—"

"Was there?"

"Indeed there was, George." The "George" didn't mean quite as much as it might have meant between others, because they were cousins. "But, if I had, the joint home of us all must have been in Mr. Price's farm-house."

"It isn't a farm-house."

"You know what I mean. But I want you to believe that I thought of you quite as much as of myself,—more than of myself. I should at any rate have had brilliant hopes before me. I could understand what it would be to be the Marchioness of Brotherton. I could have borne much for years to think that at some future day I might hang on your arm in London salons as your wife. I had an ambition which now can never be gratified. I, too, can look on this picture and on that. But I had to decide for you as well as for myself, and I did decide that it was not for your welfare nor for your honour, nor for your happiness to marry a woman who could not help you in the world." She was now leaning forward and almost touching his arm. "I think sometimes that those most nearly concerned hardly know what a woman may have to endure because she is not selfish."

How could any man stand this? There are words which a man cannot resist from a woman even though he knows them to be false. Lord George, though he did not quite believe that all these words were sincere, did think that there was a touch of sincerity about them—an opinion which the reader probably will not share with Lord George. "Have you suffered?" he said, putting out his hand to her and taking hers.

"Suffered!" she exclaimed, drawing away her hand, and sitting bolt upright and shaking her head. "Do you think that I am a fool, not to know! Do you suppose that I am blind and deaf? When I said that I was one of those who could not afford to wear a heart, did you imagine that I had been able to get rid of the article? No, it is here still," and she put her hand upon her side. "It is here still, and very troublesome I find it. I suppose the time will come when it will die away. They say that every plant will fade if it be shut in from the light, and never opened to the rains of heaven."

"Alas! alas!" he said. "I did not know that you would feel like that."

"Of course I feel. I have had something to do with my life, and I have done this with it! Two men have honoured me with their choice, and out of the two I have chosen—Mr. Houghton. I comfort myself by telling myself that I did right;—and I did do right. But the comfort is not very comforting." Still he sat looking at the fire. He knew that it was open to him to get up and swear to her that she still had his heart. She could not be angry with him as she had said as much to himself. And he almost believed at the moment that it was so. He was quite alive to the attraction of the wickedness, though, having a conscience, he was aware that the wickedness should, if possible, be eschewed. There is no romance in loving one's own wife. The knowledge that it is a duty deadens the pleasure. "I did not mean to say all this," she exclaimed at last, sobbing.

"Adelaide!" he said.

"Do you love me? You may love me without anything wrong."

"Indeed I do." Then there was an embrace, and after that he hurried away, almost without another word.

Chapter XIX.

Rather "Boisterous."

"After all, he's very dreary!" It was this that Adelaide Houghton spoke to herself as soon as Lord George had left her. No doubt the whole work of the interview had fallen on to her shoulders. He had at last been talked into saying that he loved her, and had then run away frightened by the unusual importance and tragic signification of his own words. "After all, he's very dreary."

Mrs. Houghton wanted excitement. She probably did like Lord George as well as she liked any one. Undoubtedly she would have married him had he been able to maintain her as she liked to be maintained. But, as he had been unable, she had taken Mr. Houghton without a notion on her part of making even an attempt to love him. When she said that she could not afford to wear a heart,—and she had said so to various friends and acquaintances,—she did entertain an idea that circumstances had used her cruelly, that she had absolutely been forced to marry a stupid old man, and that therefore some little freedom was due to her as a compensation. Lord George was Lord George, and might, possibly, some day be a marquis. He was at any rate a handsome man, and he had owned allegiance to her before he had transferred his homage to that rich little chit Mary Lovelace. She was incapable of much passion, but she did feel that she owed it to herself to have some revenge on Mary Lovelace. The game as it stood had charms sufficient to induce her to go on with it; and yet,—after all, he was dreary.

Such was the lady's feeling when she was left alone; but Lord George went away from the meeting almost overcome by the excitement of the occasion. To him the matter was of such stirring moment that he could not go home, could not even go to his club. He was so moved by his various feelings, that he could only walk by himself and consider things. To her that final embrace had meant very little. What did it signify? He had taken her in his arms and kissed her forehead. It might have been her lips had he so pleased. But to him it had seemed to mean very much indeed. There was a luxury in it which almost intoxicated him, and a horror in it which almost quelled him. That she should so love him as to be actually subdued by her love could not but charm him. He had none of that strength which arms a man against flatterers;—none of that experience which strengthens a man against female cajolery. It was to him very serious and very solemn. There might, perhaps, have been exaggeration in her mode of describing her feelings, but there could be no doubt in this,—that he had held her in his arms and that she was another man's wife.

The wickedness of the thing was more wicked to him than the charm of it was charming. It was dreadful to him to think that he had done a thing of which he would have to be ashamed if the knowledge of it were brought to his wife's ears. That he should have to own himself to have been wrong to her would tear him to pieces! That he should lord it over her as a real husband, was necessary to his happiness, and how can a man be a real lord over a woman when he has had to confess his fault to her, and to beg her to forgive him? A wife's position with her husband may be almost improved by such asking for pardon. It will enhance his tenderness. But the man is so lowered that neither of them can ever forget the degradation. And, though it might never come to that, though this terrible passion might be concealed from her, still it was a grievance to him and a disgrace that he should have anything to conceal. It was a stain in his own eyes on his own nobility, a slur upon his escutcheon, a taint in his hitherto unslobbered honesty, and then the sin of it;—the sin of it! To him it already sat heavy on his conscience. In his ear, even now, sounded that commandment which he weekly prayed that he might be permitted to keep. While with her there was hardly left a remembrance of the kiss which he had imprinted on her brow, his lips were still burning with the fever. Should he make up his mind, now at once, that he would never, never see her again? Should he resolve that he would write to her a moving tragic letter,—not a love letter,—in which he would set forth the horrors of unhallowed love, and tell her that there must be a gulf between them, over which neither must pass till age should have tamed their passions! As he walked across the park he meditated what would be the fitting words for such a letter, and almost determined that it should be written. Did he not owe his first duty to his wife, and was he not bound for her sake to take such a step? Then, as he wandered alone in Kensington Gardens,—for it had taken him many steps, and occupied much time to think of it all,—there came upon him an idea that perhaps the lady would not receive the letter in the proper spirit. Some idea occurred to him of the ridicule which would befall him should the lady at last tell him that he had really exaggerated matters. And then the letter might be shown to others. He did love the lady. With grief and shame and a stricken conscience he owned to himself that he loved her. But he could not quite trust her. And so, as he walked down towards the Albert Memorial, he made up his mind that he would not write the letter. But he also made up his mind,—he thought that he made up his mind,—that he would go no more alone to Berkeley Square.

As he walked on he suddenly came upon his wife walking with Captain De Baron, and he was immediately struck by the idea that his wife ought not to be walking in Kensington Gardens with Captain De Baron. The idea was so strong as altogether to expel from his mind for the moment all remembrance of Mrs. Houghton. He had been unhappy before because he was conscious that he was illtreating his wife, but now he was almost more disturbed because it seemed to him to be possible that his wife was illtreating him. He had left her but a few minutes ago,—he thought of it now as being but a few minutes since,—telling her with almost his last word that she was specially bound, more bound than other women, to mind her own conduct,—and here she was walking in Kensington Gardens with a man whom all the world called Jack De Baron? As he approached them his brow became clouded, and she could see that it was so. She could not but fear that her companion would see it also. Lord George was thinking how to address them, and had already determined on tucking his wife under his own arm and carrying her off, before he saw that a very little way behind them the Dean was walking with—Adelaide Houghton herself. Though he had been more than an hour wandering about the park he could not understand that the lady whom he had left in her own house so recently, in apparently so great a state of agitation, should be there also, in her best bonnet and quite calm. He had no words immediately at command, but she was as voluble as ever. "Doesn't this seem odd?" she said. "Why, it is not ten minutes since you left me in Berkeley Square. I wonder what made you come here."

"What made you come?"

"Jack brought me here. If it were not for Jack I should never walk or ride or do anything, except sit in a stupid carriage. And just at the gate of the gardens we met the Dean and Lady George."

This was very simple and straightforward. There could be no doubt of the truth of it all. Lady George had come out with her father and nothing could be more as it ought to be. As to "Jack" and the lady he did not, at any rate as yet, feel himself justified in being angry at that arrangement. But nevertheless he was disturbed. His wife had been laughing when he first saw her, and Jack had been talking, and they had seemed to be very happy together. The Dean no doubt was there; but still the fact remained that Jack had been laughing and talking with his wife. He almost doubted whether his wife ought under any circumstances to laugh in Kensington Gardens. And then the Dean was so indiscreet! He, Lord George, could not of course forbid his wife to walk with her father;—but the Dean had no idea that any real looking after was necessary for anybody. He at once gave his arm to his wife, but in two minutes she had dropped it. They were on the steps of the Albert Memorial, and it was perhaps natural that she should do so. But he hovered close to her as they were looking at the figures, and was uneasy. "I think it's the prettiest thing in London," said the Dean, "one of the prettiest things in the world."

"Don't you find it very cold?" said Lord George, who did not at the present moment care very much for the fine arts.

"We have been walking quick," said Mrs. Houghton, "and have enjoyed it." The Dean with the two others had now passed round one of the corners. "I wonder," she went on, "I do wonder how it has come to pass that we should be brought together again so soon!"

"We both happened to come the same way," said Lord George, who was still thinking of his wife.

"Yes;—that must have been it. Though is it not a strange coincidence? My mind had been so flurried that I was glad to get out into the fresh air. When shall I see you again?" He couldn't bring himself to say—never. There would have been a mock-tragic element about the single word which even he felt. And yet, here on the steps of the monument, there was hardly an opportunity for him to explain at length the propriety of their both agreeing to be severed. "You wish to see me;—don't you?" she asked.

"I hardly know what to say."

"But you love me!" She was now close to him, and there was no one else near enough to interfere. She was pressing close up to him, and he was sadly ashamed of himself. And yet he did love her. He thought that she had never looked so well as at the present moment. "Say that you love me," she said, stamping her foot almost imperiously.

"You know I do, but—"

"But what."

"I had better come to you again and tell you all." The words were no sooner out of his mouth than he remembered that he had resolved that he would never go to her again. But yet, after what had passed, something must be done. He had also made up his mind that he wouldn't write. He had quite made up his mind about that. The words that are written remain. It would perhaps be better that he should go to her and tell her everything.

"Of course you will come again," she said. "What is it ails you? You are unhappy because she is here with my cousin Jack?" It was intolerable to him that any one should suspect him of jealousy. "Jack has a way of getting intimate with people, but it means nothing." It was dreadful to him that an allusion should be made to the possibility of anybody "meaning anything" with his wife.

Just at this moment Jack's voice was heard coming back round the corner, and also the laughter of the Dean. Captain De Baron had been describing the persons represented on the base of the monument, and had done so after some fashion of his own that had infinitely amused not only Lady George but her father also. "You ought to be appointed Guide to the Memorial," said the Dean.

"If Lady George will give me a testimonial no doubt I might get it, Dean," said Jack.

"I don't think you know anything about any of them," said Lady George. "I'm sure you've told me wrong about two. You're the last man in the world that ought to be a guide to anything."

"Will you come and be guide, and I'll just sweep the steps!"

Lord George heard the last words, and allowed himself to be annoyed at them, though he felt them to be innocent. He knew that his wife was having a game of pleasant play, like a child with a pleasant play-fellow. But then he was not satisfied that his wife should play like a child,—and certainly not with such a playfellow. He doubted whether his wife ought to allow playful intimacy from any man. Marriage was to him a very serious thing. Was he not prepared to give up a real passion because he had made this other woman his wife? In thinking over all this his mind was not very logical, but he did feel that he was justified in exacting particularly strict conduct from her because he was going to make Mrs. Houghton understand that they two, though they loved each other, must part. If he could sacrifice so much for his wife, surely she might sacrifice something for him.

They returned altogether to Hyde Park Corner and then they separated. Jack went away towards Berkeley Square with his cousin; the Dean got himself taken in a cab to his club; and Lord George walked his wife down Constitution Hill towards their own home. He felt it to be necessary that he should say something to his wife; but, at the same time, was specially anxious that he should give her no cause to suspect him of jealousy. Nor was he jealous, in the ordinary sense of the word. He did not suppose for a moment that his wife was in love with Jack De Baron, or Jack with his wife. But he did think that whereas she had very little to say to her own husband she had a great deal to say to Jack. And he was sensible, also, of a certain unbecomingness in such amusement on her part. She had to struggle upwards, so as to be able to sustain properly the position and dignity of Lady George Germain, and the possible dignity of the Marchioness of Brotherton. She ought not to want playfellows. If she would really have learned the names of all those artists on the base of the Memorial, as she might so easily have done, there would have been something in it. A lady ought to know, at any rate, the names of such men. But she had allowed this Jack to make a joke of it all, and had rather liked the joke. And the Dean had laughed loud,—more like the son of a stable-keeper than a Dean. Lord George was almost more angry with the Dean than with his wife. The Dean, when at Brotherton, did maintain a certain amount of dignity; but here, up in London, he seemed to be intent only on "having a good time," like some schoolboy out on a holiday.

"Were you not a little loud when you were on the steps of the Memorial?" he said.

"I hope not, George; not too loud."

"A lady should never be in the least loud, nor for the matter of that would a gentleman either if he knew what he was about."

She walked on a little way, leaning on his arm in silence, considering whether he meant anything by what he was saying, and how much he meant. She felt almost sure that he did mean something disagreeable, and that he was scolding her. "I don't quite know what you mean by loud, George? We were talking, and of course wanted to make each other hear. I believe with some people loud means—vulgar. I hope you didn't mean that."

He certainly would not tell his wife that she was vulgar. "There is," he said, "a manner of talking which leads people on to—to—being boisterous."

"Boisterous, George? Was I boisterous?"

"I think your father was a little."

She felt herself blush beneath her veil as she answered. "Of course if you tell me anything about myself, I will endeavour to do as you tell me; but, as for papa, I am sure he knows how to behave himself. I don't think he ought to be found fault with because he likes to amuse himself."

"And that Captain De Baron was very loud," said Lord George, conscious that though his ground might be weak in reference to the Dean, he could say what he pleased about Jack De Baron.

"Young men do laugh and talk, don't they, George?"

"What they do in their barracks, or when they are together, is nothing to you or me. What such a one may do when he is in company with my wife is very much to me, and ought to be very much to you."

"George," she said, again pausing for a moment, "do you mean to tell me that I have misbehaved myself? Because, if so, speak it out at once."

"My dear, that is a foolish question for you to ask. I have said nothing about misbehaviour, and you ought, at any rate, to wait till I have done so. I should be very sorry to use such a word, and do not think that I shall ever have occasion. But surely you will admit that there may be practices, and manners, and customs on which I am at liberty to speak to you. I am older than you."

"Husbands, of course, are older than their wives, but wives generally know what they are about quite as well as their husbands."

"Mary, that isn't the proper way to take what I say. You have a very peculiar place to fill in the world,—a place for which your early life could not give you the very fittest training."

"Then why did you put me there?"

"Because of my love, and also because I had no doubt whatever as to your becoming fit. There is a levity which is often pretty and becoming in a girl, in which a married woman in some ranks of life may, perhaps, innocently indulge, but which is not appropriate to higher positions."

"This is all because I laughed when Captain De Baron mispronounced the men's names. I don't know anything peculiar in my position. One would suppose that I was going to be made a sort of female bishop, or to sit all my life as a chairwoman, like that Miss Mildmay. Of course I laugh when things are said that make me laugh. And as for Captain De Baron, I think he is very nice. Papa likes him, and he is always at the Houghtons, and I cannot agree that he was loud and vulgar, or boisterous, because he made a few innocent jokes in Kensington Gardens."

He perceived now, for the first time since he had known her, that she had a temper of her own, which he might find some difficulty in controlling. She had endured gently enough his first allusions to herself, but had risen up in wrath against him from the moment in which he had spoken disparagingly of her father. At the moment he had nothing further to say. He had used what eloquence there was in him, what words he had collected together, and then walked home in silence. But his mind was full of the matter; and though he made no further allusion on that day, or for some subsequent days either to this conversation or to his wife's conduct in the park, he had it always in his mind. He must be the master, and in order that he might be master the Dean must be as little as possible in the house. And that intimacy with Jack De Baron must be crushed,—if only that she might be taught that he intended to be master.

Two or three days passed by, and during those two or three days he did not go to Berkeley Square.

Chapter XX.

Between Two Stools.

In the middle of the next week the Dean went back to Brotherton. Before starting he had an interview with Lord George which was not altogether pleasant; but otherwise he had thoroughly enjoyed his visit. On the day on which he started he asked his host what inquiries he intended to set on foot in reference to the validity of the Italian marriage and the legitimacy of the Italian baby. Now Lord George had himself in the first instance consulted the Dean on this very delicate subject, and was therefore not entitled to be angry at having it again mentioned; but nevertheless he resented the question as an interference. "I think," he replied, "that at present nothing had better be said upon the subject."

"I cannot agree with you there, George."

"Then I am afraid I must ask you to be silent without agreeing with me."

The Dean felt this to be intentionally uncivil. They two were in a boat together. The injury to be done, if there were an injury, would affect the wife as much as the husband. The baby which might some day be born, and which might be robbed of his inheritance, would be as much the grandchild of the Dean of

Brotherton as of the old Marquis. And then perhaps there was present to the Dean some unacknowledged feeling that he was paying and would have to pay for the boat. Much as he revered rank, he was not disposed to be snubbed by his son-in-law, because his son-in-law was a nobleman. "You mean to tell me that I am to hold my tongue," he said angrily.

"For the present I think we had both better do so."

"That may be, as regards any discussion of the matter with outsiders. I am not at all disposed to act apart from you on a subject of such importance to us both. If you tell me that you are advised this way or that, I should not, without very strong ground, put myself in opposition to that advice; but I do expect that you will let me know what is being done."

"Nothing is being done."

"And also that you will not finally determine on doing nothing without consulting me." Lord George drew himself up and bowed, but made no further reply; and then the two parted, the Dean resolving that he would be in town again before long, and Lord George reselving that the Dean should spend as little time as possible in his house. Now, there had been an undertaking, after a sort, made by the Dean,—a compact with his daughter contracted in a jocose fashion,—which in the existing circumstances was like to prove troublesome. There had been a question of expenditure when the house was furnished,— whether there should or should not be a carriage kept. Lord George had expressed an opinion that their joint means would not suffice to keep a carriage. Then the Dean had told his daughter that he would allow her £300 a-year for her own expenses, to include the brougham,—for it was to be no more than a brougham,—during the six months they would be in London, and that he would regard this as his subscription towards the household. Such a mode of being generous to his own child was pretty enough. Of course the Dean would be a welcome visitor. Equally, of course, a son-in-law may take any amount of money from a father-in-law as a portion of his wife's fortune. Lord George, though he had suffered some inward qualms, had found nothing in the arrangement to which he could object while his friendship with the deanery was close and pleasant. But now, as the Dean took his departure, and as Mary, while embracing her father, said something of his being soon back, Lord George remembered the compact with inward grief, and wished that there had been no brougham.

In the mean time he had not been to Berkeley Square; nor was he at all sure that he would go there. A distant day had been named, before that exciting interview in the square, on which the Houghtons were to dine in Munster Court. The Mildmays were also to be there, and Mrs. Montacute Jones, and old Lord Parachute, Lord George's uncle. That would be a party, and there would be no danger of a scene then. He had almost determined that, in spite of his promise, he would not go to Berkeley Square before the dinner. But Mrs. Houghton was not of the same mind. A promise on such a subject was a sacred thing, and therefore she wrote the following note to Lord George at his club. The secrecy which some correspondence requires certainly tends to make a club a convenient arrangement. "Why don't you come as you said you would? A." In olden times, fifteen or twenty years ago, when telegraph wires were still young, and messages were confined to diplomatic secrets, horse-racing, and the rise and fall of stocks, lovers used to indulge in rapturous expressions which would run over pages; but the pith and strength of laconic diction has now been taught to us by the self-sacrificing patriotism of the Post Office. We have all felt the vigour of telegrammatic expression, and, even when we do not trust the wire, we employ the force of wiry language. "Wilt thou be mine?—M. N.," is now the ordinary form of an offer of marriage by post; and the answer seldom goes beyond "Ever thine—P. Q." Adelaide Houghton's love-letter was very short, but it was short from judgment and with a settled purpose. She believed that a long epistle declaratory of her everlasting but unfortunate attachment would frighten him. These few words would say all that she had to say, and would say it safely. He certainly had promised that he would go to her, and, as a gentleman, he was bound to keep his word. He had mentioned no exact time, but it had been understood that the visit was to be made at once. He would not write to her. Heaven and earth! How would it be with him if Mr. Houghton were to find the smallest scrap from him indicating improper affection for Mrs. Houghton? He could not answer the note, and therefore he must go at once.

He went into a deserted corner of a drawing-room at his club, and there Seated himself for half an hour's meditation. How should he extricate himself from this dilemma? In what language should he address a young and beautiful woman devoted to him, but whose devotion he was bound to repudiate? He was not voluble in conversation, and he was himself aware of his own slowness. It was essential to him that he should prepare beforehand almost the very words for an occasion of such importance,—the very words and gestures and action. Would she not fly into his arms, or at least expect that he should open his own? That must be avoided. There must be no embracing. And then he must at once proceed to explain all the evils of this calamitous passion;—how he was the husband of another wife; how she was the wife of another husband; how they were bound by honour, by religion, and equally by prudence to remember the obligations they had incurred. He must beg her to be silent while he said all this, and then he would conclude by assuring her that she should always possess his steadiest friendship. The excogitation of this took long, partly because his mind was greatly exercised in the matter, and partly through a nervous desire to postpone the difficult moment. At last, however, he seized his hat and went away straight to Berkeley Square. Yes, Mrs. Houghton was at home. He had feared that there was but little chance that she should be out on the very day on which she knew that he would get her note. "Oh, so you have come at last," she said as soon as the drawing-room door was closed. She did not get up from her chair, and there was therefore no danger of that immediate embrace which he had felt that it would be almost equally dangerous to refuse or to accept.

"Yes," he said, "I have come."

"And now sit down and make yourself comfortable. It's very bad out of doors, isn't it?"

"Cold, but dry."

"With a wretched east wind. I know it, and I don't mean to stir out the whole day. So you may put your hat down, and not think of going for the next hour and a half." It was true that he had his hat still in his hand, and he deposited it forthwith on the floor, feeling that had he been master of the occasion, he would have got rid of it less awkwardly. "I shouldn't wonder if Mary were to be here by and by. There was a sort of engagement that she and Jack De Baron were to come and play bagatelle in the back drawing-room; but Jack never comes if he says he will, and I daresay she has forgotten all about it."

He found that his purpose was altogether upset. In the first place, he could hardly begin about her unfortunate passion when she received him just as though he were an ordinary acquaintance; and then the whole tenour of his mind was altered by this allusion to Jack De Baron. Had it come to this, that he could not get through a day without having Jack De Baron thrown at his head? He had from the first been averse to living in London; but this was much worse than he had expected. Was it to be endured that his wife should make appointments to play bagatelle with Jack De Baron by way of passing her time? "I had heard nothing about it," he said with gloomy, truthful significance. It was impossible for him to lie even by a glance of his eye or a tone of his voice. He told it all at once; how unwilling he was that his wife should come out on purpose to meet this man, and how little able he felt himself to prevent it.

"Of course dear Mary has to amuse herself," said the lady, answering the man's look rather than his words. "And why should she not?"

"I don't know that bagatelle is a very improving occupation."

"Or Jack a very improving companion, perhaps. But I can tell you, George, that there are more dangerous companions than poor Jack. And then, Mary, who is the sweetest, dearest young woman I know, is not impulsive in that way. She is such a very child. I don't suppose she understands what passion means. She has the gaiety of a lark, and the innocence. She is always soaring upwards, which is so beautiful."

"I don't know that there is much soaring upwards in bagatelle."

"Nor in Jack De Baron, perhaps. But we must take all that as we find it. Of course Mary will have to amuse herself. She will never live such a life as your sisters live at Manor Cross. The word that best describes her disposition is—gay. But she is not mischievous."

"I hope not."

"Nor is she—passionate. You know what I mean." He did know what she meant, and was lost in amazement at finding that one woman, in talking of another, never contemplated the idea that passion could exist in a wife for her husband. He was to regard himself as safe, not because his wife loved himself, but because it was not necessary to her nature to be in love with any one! "You need not be afraid," she went on to say. "I know Jack au fond. He tells me everything; and should there be anything to fear, I will let you know at once."

But what had all this to do with the momentous occasion which had brought him to Berkeley Square? He was almost beginning to be sore at heart because she had not thrown herself into his arms. There was no repetition of that "But you do love me?" which had been so very alarming but at the same time so very exciting on the steps of the Albert Memorial. And then there seemed to be a probability that the words which he had composed with so much care at his club would be altogether wasted. He owed it to himself to do or to say something, to allude in some way to his love and hers. He could not allow himself to be brought there in a flurry of excitement, and there to sit till it was time for him to go, just as though it were an ordinary morning visit. "You bade me come," he said, "and so I came."

"Yes, I did bid you come. I would always have you come."

"That can hardly be; can it?"

"My idea of a friend,—of a man friend, I mean, and a real friend—is some one to whom I can say everything, who will do everything for me, who will come if I bid him and will like to stay and talk to me just as long as I will let him; who will tell me everything, and as to whom I may be sure that he likes me better than anybody else in the world, though he perhaps doesn't tell me so above once a month. And then in return—"

"Well, what in return?"

"I should think a good deal about him, you know; but I shouldn't want always to be telling him that I was thinking about him. He ought to be contented with knowing how much he was to me. I suppose that would not suffice for you?"

Lord George was disposed to think that it would suffice, and that the whole matter was now being represented to him in a very different light than that in which he had hitherto regarded it. The word "friend" softened down so many asperities! With such a word in his mind he need not continually scare himself with the decalogue. All the pleasure might be there, and the horrors altogether omitted. There would, indeed, be no occasion for his eloquence; but he had already become conscious that at this interview his eloquence could not be used. She had given everything so different a turn! "Why not suffice for me?" he said. "Only this,—that all I did for my friend I should expect her to do for me."

"But that is unreasonable. Who doesn't see that in the world at large men have the best of it almost in everything. The husband is not only justified in being a tyrant, but becomes contemptible if he is not so. A man has his pocket full of money; a woman is supposed to take what he gives her. A man has all manner of amusements."

"What amusements have I?"

"You can come to me."

"Yes, I can do that."

"I cannot go to you. But when you come to me,—if I am to believe that I am really your friend,—then I am to be the tyrant of the moment. Is it not so? Do you think you would find me a hard tyrant? I own to you freely that there is nothing in the world I like so much as your society. Do I not earn by that a right to some obedience from you, to some special observance?"

All this was so different from what he had expected, and so much more pleasant! As far as he could look into it and think of it at the pressure of the moment he did not see any reason why it should not be as she proposed. There was clearly no need for those prepared words. There had been one embrace,—an embrace that was objectionable because, had either his wife seen it or Mr. Houghton, he would have been forced to own himself wrong; but that had come from sudden impulse, and need not be repeated. This that was now proposed to him was friendship, and not love. "You shall have all observance," he said with his sweetest smile.

"And as to obedience? But you are a man, and therefore must not be pressed too hard. And now I may tell you what is the only thing that can make me happy, and the absence of which would make me miserable."

"What thing?"

"Your society." He blushed up to his eyes as he heard this. "Now that, I think, is a very pretty speech, and I expect something equally pretty from you." He was much embarrassed, but was at the moment delivered from his embarrassment by the entrance of his wife. "Here she is," said Mrs. Houghton, getting up from her chair. "We have been just talking about you, my dear. If you have come for bagatelle, you must play with Lord George, for Jack De Baron isn't here."

"But I haven't come for bagatelle."

"So much the better, for I doubt whether Lord George would be very good at it. I have been made to play so much that I hate the very sound of the balls."

"I didn't expect to find you here," said Mary, turning to her husband.

"Nor I you, till Mrs. Houghton said that you were coming."

After that there was nothing of interest in their conversation. Jack did not come, and after a few minutes Lord George proposed to his wife that they should return home together. Of course she assented, and as soon as they were in the brougham made a little playful attack upon him. "You are becoming fond of Berkeley Square, I think."

"Mrs. Houghton is a friend of mine, and I am fond of my friends," he said, gravely.

"Oh, of course."

"You went there to play that game with Captain De Baron."

"No, I didn't. I did nothing of the kind."

"Were you not there by appointment?"

"I told her that I should probably call. We were to have gone to some shop together, only it seems she has changed her mind. Why do you tell me that I had gone there to play some game with Captain De Baron?"

"Bagatelle."

"Bagatelle, or anything else! It isn't true. I have played bagatelle with Captain de Baron, and I daresay I may again. Why shouldn't I?"

"And if so, would probably make some appointment to play with him."

"Why not?"

"That was all I said. What I suggested you had done is what you declare you will do."

"But I had done nothing of the kind. I know very well, from the tone of your voice, that you meant to scold me. You implied that I had done something wrong. If I had done it, it wouldn't be wrong, as far as I know. But your scolding me about it when I hadn't done it at all is very hard to bear."

"I didn't scold you."

"Yes you did, George. I understand your voice and your look. If you mean to forbid me to play bagatelle with Captain De Baron, or Captain anybody else, or to talk with Mr. This, or to laugh with Major That, tell me so at once. If I know what you want, I will do it. But I must say that I shall feel it very, very hard if I cannot take care of myself in such matters as that. If you are going to be jealous, I shall wish that I were dead."

Then she burst out crying; and he, though he would not quite own that he had been wrong, was forced to do so practically by little acts of immediate tenderness.

Chapter XXI.

The Marquis Comes Home.

Some little time after the middle of April, when the hunting was all over, and Mr. Price had sunk down into his summer insignificance, there came half a dozen telegrams to Manor Cross, from Italy, from Mr. Knox, and from a certain managing tradesman in London, to say that the Marquis was coming a fortnight sooner than he had expected. Everything was at sixes and sevens. Everything was in a ferment. Everybody about Manor Cross seemed to think that the world was coming to an end. But none of these telegrams were addressed to any of the Germain family, and the last people in the county who heard of this homeward rush of the Marquis were the ladies at Cross Hall, and they heard it from Lord George, upon whom Mr. Knox called in London; supposing, however, when he did call that Lord George had already received full information on the subject. Lord George's letter to Lady Sarah was full of dismay, full of horror. "As he has not taken the trouble to communicate his intentions to me, I shall not go down to receive him." "You will know how to deal with the matter, and will, I am sure, support our mother in this terrible trial." "I think that the child should, at any rate, at first be acknowledged by you all as Lord

Popenjoy." "We have to regard, in the first place, the honour of the family. No remissness on his part should induce us to forget for a moment what is due to the title, the property, and the name." The letter was very long, and was full of sententious instructions, such as the above. But the purport of it was to tell the ladies at Cross Hall that they must go through the first burden of receiving the Marquis without any assistance from himself.

The Dean heard of the reported arrival some days before the family did so. It was rumoured in Brotherton, and the rumour reached the deanery. But he thought that there was nothing that he could do on the spur of the moment. He perfectly understood the condition of Lord George's mind, and perceived that it would not be expedient for him to interfere quite on the first moment. As soon as the Marquis should have settled himself in the house, of course he would call; and when the Marquis had settled himself, and when the world had begun to recognise the fact that the Marquis, with his Italian Marchioness, and his little Italian, so-called Popenjoy, were living at Manor Cross, then,— if he saw his way,—the Dean would bestir himself.

And so the Marquis arrived. He reached the Brotherton station with his wife, a baby, a lady's maid, a nurse, a valet, a cook, and a courier, about three o'clock in the afternoon; and the whole crowd of them were carried off in their carriages to Manor Cross. A great many of the inhabitants of Brotherton were there to see, for this coming of the Marquis had been talked of far and wide. He himself took no notice of the gathering people,—was perhaps unaware that there was any gathering. He and his wife got into one carriage; the nurse, the lady's maid, and the baby into a second; the valet and courier, and cook into a third. The world of Brotherton saw them, and the world of Brotherton observed that the lady was very old and very ugly. Why on earth could he have married such a woman as that, and then have brought her home! That was the exclamation which was made by Brotherton in general.

It was soon ascertained by every one about Manor Cross that the Marchioness could not speak a word of English, nor could any of the newly imported servants do so with the exception of the courier, who was supposed to understand all languages. There was, therefore, an absolutely divided household. It had been thought better that the old family housekeeper, Mrs. Toff, should remain in possession. Through a long life she had been devoted to the old Marchioness and to the ladies of the family generally; but she would have been useless at their new home, and there was an idea that Manor Cross could not be maintained without her. It might also be expedient to have a friend in the enemy's camp. Other English servants had been provided,—a butler, two footmen, a coachman, and the necessary housemaids and kitchen maids. It had been stated that the Marquis would bring his own cook. There were, therefore, at once two parties, at the head of one of which was Mrs. Toff, and at the head of the other the courier,—who remained, none of the English people knew why.

For the first three days the Marchioness showed herself to no one. It was understood that the fatigues of the journey had oppressed her, and that she chose to confine herself to two or three rooms upstairs, which had been prepared for her. Mrs. Toff, strictly obeying orders which had come from Cross Hall, sent up her duty and begged to know whether she should wait upon my lady. My lady sent down word that she didn't want to see Mrs. Toff. These messages had to be filtered through the courier, who was specially odious to Mrs. Toff. His Lordship was almost as closely secluded as her Ladyship. He did, indeed, go out to the stables, wrapped up in furs, and found fault with everything he saw there. And he had himself driven round the park. But he did not get up on any of these days till noon, and took all his meals by himself. The English servants averred that during the whole of this time he never once saw the Marchioness or the baby; but then the English servants could not very well have known what he saw or what he did not see.

But this was very certain, that during those three days he did not go to Cross Hall, or see any one of his own family. Mrs. Toff in the gloaming of the evening, on the third day, hurried across the park to see—the young ladies as she still called them. Mrs. Toff thought that it was all very dreadful. She didn't know what was being done in those apartments. She had never set her eyes upon the baby. She didn't feel sure that there was any baby at all, though John,—John was one of the English servants,— had seen a bundle come into the house. Wouldn't it be natural and right that any real child should be carried out to take the air? "And then all manner of messes were," said Mrs. Toff, "prepared up in the closed room." Mrs. Toff didn't believe in anything, except that everything was going to perdition. The Marchioness was intent on asking after the health and appearance of her son, but Mrs. Toff declared that she hadn't been allowed to catch a sight of "my lord." Mrs. Toff's account was altogether very lachrymose. She spoke of the Marquis, of course, with the utmost respect. But she was sufficiently intimate with the ladies to treat the baby and its mother with all the scorn of an upturned nose. Nor was the name of Popenjoy once heard from her lips.

But what were the ladies to do? On the evening of the third day Lady Sarah wrote to her brother George, begging him to come down to them. "The matter was so serious, that he was," said Lady Sarah, "bound to lend the strength of his presence to his mother and sisters." But on the fourth morning Lady Sarah sent over a note to her brother, the Marquis.

"DEAR BROTHERTON,—We hope that you and your wife and little boy have arrived well, and have found things comfortable. Mamma is most anxious to see you,— as of course we all are. Will you not come over to us to-day. I dare say my sister-in-law may be too fatigued to come out as yet. I need not tell you that we are very anxious to see your little Popenjoy.

"Your affectionate Sister,

"SARAH GERMAIN."

It may be seen from this that the ladies contemplated peace, if peace were possible. But in truth the nature of the letter, though not the words, had been dictated by the Marchioness. She was intent upon seeing her son, and anxious to acknowledge her grandchild. Lady Sarah had felt her position to be very difficult, but had perceived that no temporary acceptance by them of the child would at all injure her brother George's claim, should Lord George set up a claim, and so, in deference to the old lady, the peaceful letter was sent off, with directions to the messenger to wait for an answer. The messenger came back with tidings that his Lordship was in bed. Then there was another consultation. The Marquis, though in bed, had of course read the letter. Had he felt at all as a son and a brother ought to feel, he would have sent some reply to such a message. It must be, they felt, that he intended to live there and utterly ignore his mother and sisters. What should they do then? How should they be able to live? The Marchioness surrendered herself to a paroxysm of weeping, bitterly blaming those who had not allowed her to go away and hide herself in some distant obscurity. Her son, her eldest son, had cast her off because she had disobeyed his orders! "His orders!" said Lady Sarah, in scorn, almost in wrath against her mother. "What right has he to give orders either to you or us? He has forgotten himself, and is only worthy to be forgotten." Just as she spoke the Manor Cross phaeton, with the Manor Cross ponies, was driven up to the door, and Lady Amelia, who went to the window, declared that Brotherton himself was in the carriage. "Oh, my son; my darling son," said the Marchioness, throwing up her arms.

It really was the Marquis. It seemed to the ladies to be a very long time indeed before he got into the room, so leisurely was he in divesting himself of his furs and comforters. During this time the Marchioness would have rushed into the hall had not Lady Sarah prevented her. The old lady was quite overcome with emotion, and prepared to lay at the feet of her eldest son, if he would only extend to her the slightest sign of affection. "So, here you all are," he said as he entered the room. "It isn't much of a house for you, but you would have it so." He was of course forced to kiss his mother, but the kiss was not very fervent in its nature. To each of his sisters he merely extended his hand. This Amelia received with empressement; for, after all, severe though he was, nevertheless he was the head of the family. Susanna measured the pressure which he gave, and returned back to him the exact weight. Lady Sarah made a little speech. "We are very glad to see you; Brotherton. You have been away a long time."

"A deuced long time."

"I hope your wife is well;—and the little boy. When will she wish that we should go and see her?" The Marchioness during this time had got possession of his left hand, and from her seat was gazing up into his face. He was a very handsome man, but pale, worn, thin, and apparently unhealthy. He was very like Lord George, but smaller in feature, and wanting full four inches of his brother's height. Lord George's hair was already becoming grey at the sides. That of the Marquis, who was ten years older, was perfectly black;—but his Lordship's valet had probably more to do with that than nature. He wore an exquisite moustache, but in other respects was close shaven. He was dressed with great care, and had fur even on the collar of his frock coat, so much did he fear the inclemency of his native climate.

"She doesn't speak a word of English, you know," he said, answering his sister's question.

"We might manage to get on in French," said Lady Sarah.

"She doesn't speak a word of French either. She never was out of Italy till now. You had better not trouble yourselves about her."

This was dreadful to them all. It was monstrous to them that there should be a Marchioness of Brotherton, a sister-in-law, living close to them, whom they were to acknowledge to be the reigning Marchioness, and that they should not be allowed to see her. It was not that they anticipated pleasure from her acquaintance. It was not that they were anxious to welcome such a new relation. This marriage, if it were a marriage, was a terrible blow to them. It would have been infinitely better for them all that, having such a wife, he should have kept her in Italy. But, as she was here in England, as she was to be acknowledged,—as far as they knew at present,—it was a fearful thing that she should be living close to them and not be seen by them. For some moments after his last announcement they were stricken dumb. He was standing with his back to the fire, looking at his boots. The Marchioness was the first to speak. "We may see Popenjoy!" she exclaimed through her sobs.

"I suppose he can be brought down,—if you care about it."

"Of course we care about it," said Lady Amelia.

"They tell me he is not strong, and I don't suppose they'll let him come out such weather as this. You'll have to wait. I don't think any body ought to stir out in this weather. It doesn't suit me, I know. Such an abominable place as it is I never saw in my life. There is not a room in the house that is not enough to make a man blow his brains out."

Lady Sarah could not stand this, nor did she think it right to put up with the insolence of his manner generally. "If so," she said, "it is a pity that you came away from Italy."

He turned sharply round and looked at her for an instant before he answered. And as he did so she remembered the peculiar tyranny of his eyes,—the tyranny to which, when a boy, he had ever endeavoured to make her subject, and all others around him. Others had become subject because he was the Lord Popenjoy of the day, and would be the future Marquis; but she, though recognising his right to be first in every thing, had ever rebelled against his usurpation of unauthorized power. He, too, remembered all this, and almost snarled at her with his eyes. "I suppose I might stay if I liked, or come back if I liked, without asking you," he said.

"Certainly."

"But you are the same as ever you were."

"Oh, Brotherton," said the Marchioness, "do not quarrel with us directly you have come back."

"You may be quite sure, mother, that I shall not take the trouble to quarrel with any one. It takes two for that work. If I wanted to quarrel with her or you, I have cause enough."

"I know of none," said Lady Sarah.

"I explained to you my wishes about this house, and you disregarded them altogether." The old lady looked up at her eldest daughter as though to say, "There,—that was your sin." "I knew what was better for you and better for me. It is impossible that there should be pleasant intercourse between you and my wife, and I recommended you to go elsewhere. If you had done so I would have taken care that you were comfortable." Again the Marchioness looked at Lady Sarah with bitter reproaches in her eyes.

"What interest in life would we have had in a distant home?" said Lady Sarah.

"Why not you as well as other people?"

"Because, unlike other people, we have become devoted to one spot. The property belongs to you."

"I hope so."

"But the obligations of the property have been, at any rate, as near to us as to you. Society, I suppose, may be found in a new place, but we do not care much for society."

"Then it would have been so much the easier."

"But it would have been impossible for us to find new duties."

"Nonsense," said the Marquis, "humbug; d——d trash."

"If you cannot speak otherwise than like that before your mother, Brotherton, I think you had better leave her," said Lady Sarah, bravely.

"Don't, Sarah,—don't!" said the Marchioness.

"It is trash and nonsense, and humbug. I told you that you were better away, and you determined to stay. I knew what was best for you, but you chose to be obstinate. I have not the slightest doubt as to who did it."

"We were all of the same mind," said Lady Susanna. "Alice said it would be quite cruel that mamma should be moved." Alice was now the wife of Canon Holdenough.

"It would have been very bad for us all to go away," said Lady Amelia.

"George was altogether against it," said Lady Susanna.

"And the Dean," said Lady Amelia, indiscreetly.

"The Dean!" exclaimed the Marquis. "Do you mean to say that that stable boy has been consulted about my affairs? I should have thought that not one of you would have spoken to George after he had disgraced himself by such a marriage."

"There was no need to consult any one," said Lady Sarah. "And we do not think George's marriage at all disgraceful."

"Mary is a very nice young person," said the Marchioness.

"I dare say. Whether she is nice or not is very little to me. She has got some fortune, and I suppose that was what he wanted. As you are all of you fixed here now, and seem to have spent a lot of money, I suppose you will have to remain. You have turned my tenant out—"

"Mr. Price was quite willing to go," said Lady Susanna.

"I dare say. I trust he may be as willing to give up the land when his lease is out. I have been told that he is a sporting friend of the Dean's. It seems to me that you have, all of you, got into a nice mess here by yourselves. All I want you to understand is that I cannot now trouble myself about you."

"You don't mean to give us up," said the afflicted mother. "You'll come and see me sometimes, won't you?"

"Certainly not, if I am to be insulted by my sister."

"I have insulted no one," said Lady Sarah, haughtily.

"It was no insult to tell me that I ought to have stayed in Italy, and not have come to my own house!"

"Sarah, you ought not to have said that," exclaimed the Marchioness.

"He complained that everything here was uncomfortable, and therefore I said it. He knows that I did not speak of his return in any other sense. Since he settled himself abroad there has not been a day on which I have not wished that he would come back to his own house and his own duties. If he will treat us properly, no one will treat him with higher consideration than I. But we have our own rights as well as he, and are as well able to guard them."

"Sarah can preach as well as ever," he said.

"Oh! my children,—oh! my children!" sobbed the old lady.

"I have had about enough of this. I knew what it would be when you wrote to me to come to you." Then he took up his hat, as though he were going.

"And am I to see nothing more of you?" asked his mother.

"I will come to you, mother,—once a-week if you wish it. Every Sunday afternoon will be as good a time as any other. But I will not come unless I am assured of the absence of Lady Sarah. I will not subject myself to her insolence, nor put myself in the way of being annoyed by a ballyragging quarrel."

"I and my sisters are always at Church on Sunday afternoons," said Lady Sarah.

In this way the matter was arranged, and then the Marquis took himself off. For some time after he left the room the Marchioness sat in silence, sobbing now and again, and then burying her face in her handkerchief. "I wish we had gone away when he told us," she said, at last.

"No, mamma," said her eldest daughter. "No,—certainly no. Even though all this is very miserable, it is not so bad as running away in order that we might be out of his way. No good can ever be got by yielding in what is wrong to any one. This is your house; and as yours it is ours."

"Oh, yes."

"And here we can do something to justify our lives. We have a work appointed to us which we are able to perform. What will his wife do for the people here? Why are we not to say our prayers in the Church which we all know and love? Why are we to leave Alice—and Mary? Why should he, because he is the eldest of us,—he, who for so many years has deserted the place,—why is he to tell us where to live, and where not to live. He is rich, and we are poor, but we have never been pensioners on his bounty. The park, I suppose, is now closed to us; but I am prepared to live here in defiance of him." This she said walking up and down the room as she spoke, and she said it with so much energy that she absolutely carried her sisters with her and again partly convinced her mother.

Chapter XXII.

The Marquis Among His Friends.

There was, of course, much perturbation of mind at Brotherton as to what should be done on this occasion of the Marquis's return. Mr. Knox had been consulted by persons in the town, and had given it as his opinion that nothing should be done. Some of the tradesmen and a few of the tenants living nearest to the town had suggested a triumphal entry,—green boughs, a bonfire, and fire works. This idea, however, did not prevail long. The Marquis of Brotherton was clearly not a man to be received with green boughs and bonfires. All that soon died away. But there remained what may be called the private difficulty. Many in Brotherton and around Brotherton had of course known the man when he was young, and could hardly bring themselves to take no notice of his return. One or two drove over and simply left their cards. The bishop asked to see him, and was told that he was out. Dr. Pountner did see him, catching him at his own hall door, but the interview was very short, and not particularly pleasant. "Dr. Pountner. Well; I do remember you, certainly. But we have all grown older, you know."

"I came," said the doctor, with a face redder than ever, "to pay my respects to your Lordship, and to leave my card on your wife."

"We are much obliged to you,—very much obliged. Unfortunately we are both invalids." Then the doctor, who had not got out of his carriage, was driven home again. The doctor had been a great many years at Brotherton, and had known the old Marquis well. "I don't know what you and Holdenough will make of him," the doctor said to the Dean. "I suppose you will both be driven into some communion with him. I shan't try it again."

The Dean and Canon Holdenough had been in consultation on the subject, and had agreed that they would each of them act as though the Marquis had been like any other gentleman, and his wife like any other newly married lady. They were both now connected with the family, and even bound to act on the presumption that there would be family friendship. The Dean went on his errand first, and the Dean was admitted into his sitting-room. This happened a day or two after the scene at Cross Hall. "I don't know that I should have troubled you so soon," said the Dean, "had not your brother married my daughter." The Dean had thought over the matter carefully, making up his mind how far he would be courteous to the man, and where he would make a stand if it were necessary that he should make a stand at all. And he had determined that he would ask after the new Lady Brotherton, and speak of the child as Lord Popenjoy, the presumption being that a man is married when he says so himself, and that his child is legitimate when declared to be so. His present acknowledgment would not bar any future proceedings.

"There has been a good deal of marrying and giving in marriage since I have been away," replied the Marquis.

"Yes, indeed. There has been your brother, your sister, and last, not least, yourself."

"I was not thinking of myself. I meant among you here. The church seems to carry everything before it."

It seemed to the Dean, who was sufficiently mindful of his daughter's fortune, and who knew to a penny what was the very liberal income of Canon Holdenough, that in these marriages the church had at least given as much as it had got. "The church holds its own," said the Dean, "and I hope that it always will. May I venture to express a hope that the Marchioness is well."

"Not very well."

"I am sorry for that. Shall I not have the pleasure of seeing her to-day?"

The Marquis looked as though he were almost astounded at the impudence of the proposition; but he replied to it by the excuse that he had made before. "Unless you speak Italian I'm afraid you would not get on very well with her."

"She will not find that I have the Tuscan tongue or the Roman mouth, but I have enough of the language to make myself perhaps intelligible to her ladyship."

"We will postpone it for the present, if you please, Mr. Dean."

There was an insolence declared in the man's manner and almost declared in his words, which made the Dean at once determine that he would never again ask after the new Marchioness, and that he would make no allusion whatever to the son. A man may say that his wife is too unwell to receive strangers without implying that the wish to see her should not have been expressed. The visitor bowed, and then the two men both sat silent for some moments. "You have not seen your brother since you have been back?" the Dean said at last.

"I have not seen him. I don't know where he is, or anything about him."

"They live in London,—in Munster Court."

"Very likely. He didn't consult me about his marriage, and I don't know anything about his concerns."

"He told you of it,—before it took place."

"Very likely,—though I do not exactly see how that concerns you and me."

"You must be aware that he is married to—my daughter."

"Quite so."

"That would, generally, be supposed to give a common interest."

"Ah! I dare say. You feel it so, no doubt. I am glad that you are satisfied by an alliance with my family. You are anxious for me to profess that it is reciprocal."

"I am anxious for nothing of the kind," said the Dean, jumping up from his chair. "I have nothing to get and nothing to lose by the alliance. The usual courtesies of life are pleasant to me."

"I wish that you would use them then on the present occasion by being a little quieter."

"Your brother has married a lady, and my daughter has married a gentleman."

"Yes; George is a great ass; in some respects the greatest ass I know; but he is a gentleman. Perhaps if you have anything else that you wish to say you will do me the honour of sitting down."

The Dean was so angry that he did not know how to contain himself. The Marquis had snubbed him for coming. He had then justified his visit by an allusion to the connection between them, and the Marquis had replied to this by hinting that though a Dean might think it a very fine thing to have his daughter married into the family of a Marquis, the Marquis probably would not look at it in the same light. And yet what was the truth? Whence had come the money which had made the marriage possible? In the bargain between them which party had had the best of it? He was conscious that it would not become him to allude to the money, but his feeling on the subject was very strong. "My lord," he said, "I do not know that there is anything to be gained by my sitting down again."

"Perhaps not. I dare say you know best."

"I came here intent on what I considered to be a courtesy due to your lordship. I am sorry that my visit has been mistaken."

"I don't see that there is anything to make a fuss about."

"It shall not be repeated, my lord." And so he left the room.

Why on earth had the man come back to England, bringing a foreign woman and an Italian brat home with him, if he intended to make the place too hot to hold him by insulting everybody around him? This was the first question the Dean asked himself, when he found himself outside the house. And what could the man hope to gain by such insolence? Instead of taking the road through the park back to Brotherton, he went on to Cross Hall. He was desirous of learning what were the impressions, and what the intentions, of the ladies there. Did this madman mean to quarrel with his mother and sisters as well as with his other neighbours? He did not as yet know what intercourse there had been between the two houses, since the Marquis had been at Manor Cross. And in going to Cross Hall in the midst of all these troubles, he was no doubt actuated in part by a determination to show himself to be one of the family. If they would accept his aid, no one would be more loyal than he to these ladies. But he would not be laid aside. If anything unjust were intended, if any fraud was to be executed, the person most to be injured would be that hitherto unborn grandson of his for whose advent he was so anxious. He had been very free with his money, but he meant to have his money's worth.

At Cross Hall he found Canon Holdenough's wife and the Canon. At the moment of his entrance old Lady Brotherton was talking to the clergyman, and Lady Alice was closeted in a corner with her sister Sarah. "I would advise you to go just as though you had heard nothing from us," Lady Sarah had said.

"Of course he would be readier to quarrel with me than with any one. For mamma's sake I would go away for a time if I had anywhere to go to."

"Come to us," Lady Alice had said. But Lady Sarah had declared that she would be as much in the way at Brotherton as at Cross Hall, and had then gone on to explain that it was Lady Alice's duty to call on her sister-in-law, and that she must do so,—facing the consequences whatever they might be. "Of course mamma could not go till he had been here," Lady Sarah added; "and now he has told mamma not to go at all. But that is nothing to you."

"I have just come from the house," said the Dean.

"Did you see him?" asked the old woman with awe.

"Yes; I saw him."

"Well!"

"I must say that he was not very civil to me, and that I suppose I have seen all of him that I shall see."

"It is only his manner," said her ladyship.

"An unfortunate manner, surely."

"Poor Brotherton!"

Then the Canon said a word. "Of course no one wants to trouble him. I can speak at least for myself. I do not,—certainly. I have requested her ladyship to ask him whether he would wish me to call or not. If he says that he does, I shall expect him to receive me cordially. If he does not—there's an end of it."

"I hope you won't all of you turn against him," said the Marchioness.

"Turn against him!" repeated the Dean. "I do not suppose that there is any one who would not be both kind and courteous to him, if he would accept kindness and courtesy. It grieves me to make you unhappy, Marchioness, but I am bound to let you know that he treated me very badly." From that moment the Marchioness made up her mind that the Dean was no friend of the family, and that he was, after all, vulgar and disagreeable. She undertook, however, to enquire from her son on next

Sunday whether he would wish to be called upon by his brother-in-law, the Canon.

On the following day Lady Alice went alone to Manor Cross,—being the first lady who had gone to the door since the new arrivals,—and asked for Lady Brotherton. The courier came to the door and said "not at home," in a foreign accent, just as the words might have been said to any chance caller in London. Then Lady Alice asked the man to tell her brother that she was there. "Not at home, miladi," said the man, in the same tone. At that moment Mrs. Toff came running through the long hall to the carriage door. The house was built round a quadrangle, and all the ground floor of the front and of one of the sides consisted of halls, passages, and a billiard-room. Mrs. Toff must have been watching very closely or she could hardly have known that Lady Alice was there. She came out and stood beside the carriage, and leaning in, whispered her fears and unhappinesses. "Oh! my lady, I'm afraid it's very bad. I haven't set eyes on the—the—his wife, my lady, yet; nor the little boy."

"Are they in now, Mrs. Toff?"

"Of course they're in. They never go out. He goes about all the afternoon in a dressing-gown, smoking bits of paper, and she lies in bed or gets up and doesn't do,—nothing at all, as far as I can see, Lady Alice. But as for being in, of course they're in; they're always in." Lady Alice, however, feeling that she had done her duty, and not wishing to take the place by storm, had herself driven back to Brotherton.

On the following Sunday afternoon the Marquis came, according to his promise, and found his mother alone. "The fact is, mother," he said, "you have got a regular church set around you during the last year or two, and I will have nothing to do with them. I never cared much for Brotherton Close, and now I like it less than ever." The Marchioness moaned and looked up into his face imploringly. She was anxious to say something in defence, at any rate, of her daughter's marriage, but specially anxious to say nothing that should not anger him. Of course he was unreasonable, but, according to her lights, he, being the Marquis, had a right to be unreasonable. "The Dean came to me the other day," continued he, "and I could see at a glance that he meant to be quite at home in the house, if I didn't put him down."

"You'll see Mr. Holdenough, won't you? Mr. Holdenough is a very gentlemanlike man, and the Holdenoughs were always quite county people. You used to like Alice."

"If you ask me, I think she has been a fool at her age to go and marry an old parson. As for receiving him, I shan't receive anybody,—in the way of entertaining them. I haven't come home for that purpose. My child will have to live here when he is a man."

"God bless him!" said the Marchioness.

"Or at any rate his property will be here. They tell me that it will be well that he should be used to this damnable climate early in life. He will have to go to school here, and all that. So I have brought him, though I hate the place."

"It is so nice to have you back, Brotherton."

"I don't know about its being nice. I don't find much niceness in it. Had I not got myself married I should never have come back. But it's as well that you all should know that there is an heir."

"God bless him!" said the Marchioness, again. "But don't you think that we ought to see him?"

"See him! Why?" He asked the question sharply, and looked at her with that savageness in his eyes which all the family remembered so well, and which she specially feared.

That question of the legitimacy of the boy had never been distinctly discussed at Cross Hall, and the suspicious hints on the subject which had passed between the sisters, the allusions to this and the other possibility which had escaped them, had been kept as far as possible from their mother. They had remarked among themselves that it was very odd that the marriage should have been concealed, and almost more than odd that an heir to the title should have been born without any announcement of such a birth. A dread of some evil mystery had filled their thoughts, and shown itself in their words and looks to each other. And, though they had been very anxious to keep this from their mother, something had crept through which had revealed a suspicion of the suspicion even to her. She, dear old lady, had resolved upon no line of conduct in the matter. She had conceived no project of rebelling against her eldest daughter, or of being untrue to her youngest son. But now that she was alone with her eldest son, with the real undoubted Marquis, with him who would certainly be to her more than all the world beside if he would only allow it, there did come into her head an idea that she would put him on his guard.

"Because,—because—"

"Because what? Speak out, mother."

"Because, perhaps they'll say that—that—"

"What will they say?"

"If they don't see him, they may think he isn't Popenjoy at all."

"Oh! they'll think that, will they? How will seeing help them?"

"It would be so nice to have him here, if it's only for a little," said the Marchioness.

"So that's it," he said, after a long pause. "That's George's game, and the Dean's; I can understand."

"No, no, no; not George," said the unhappy mother.

"And Sarah, I dare say, is in a boat with them. I don't wonder that they should choose to remain here and watch me."

"I am sure George has never thought of such a thing."

"George will think as his father-in-law bids him. George was never very good at thinking for himself. So you fancy they'll be more likely to accept the boy if they see him."

"Seeing is believing, Brotherton."

"There's something in that, to be sure. Perhaps they don't think I've got a wife at all, because they haven't seen her."

"Oh, yes; they believe that."

"How kind of them. Well, mother, you've let the cat out of the bag."

"Don't tell them that I said so."

"No; I won't tell. Nor am I very much surprised. I thought how it would be when I didn't announce it all in the old-fashioned way. It's lucky that I have the certificated proof of the date of my marriage, isn't it?"

"It's all right, of course. I never doubted it, Brotherton."

"But all the others did. I knew there was something up when George wasn't at home to meet me."

"He is coming." "He may stay away if he likes it. I don't want him. He won't have the courage to tell me up to my face that he doesn't intend to acknowledge my boy. He's too great a coward for that."

"I'm sure it's not George, Brotherton."

"Who is it, then?"

"Perhaps it's the Dean."

"D—— his impudence. How on earth among you could you let George marry the daughter of a low-bred ruffian like that,—a man that never ought to have been allowed to put his foot inside the house?"

"She had such a very nice fortune! And then he wanted to marry that scheming girl, Adelaide De Baron,—without a penny."

"The De Barons, at any rate, are gentlefolk. If the Dean meddles with me, he shall find that he has got the wrong sow by the ear. If he puts his foot in the park again I'll have him warned off as a trespasser."

"But you'll see Mr. Holdenough?"

"I don't want to see anybody. I mean to hold my own, and do as I please with my own, and live as I like, and toady no one. What can I have in common with an old parson like that?"

"You'll let me see Popenjoy, Brotherton?"

"Yes," he said, pausing a moment before he answered her. "He shall be brought here, and you shall see him. But mind, mother, I shall expect you to tell me all that you hear."

"Indeed, I will."

"You will not rebel against me, I suppose."

"Oh, no;—my son, my son!" Then she fell upon his neck, and he suffered it for a minute, thinking it wise to make sure of one ally in that house.

Chapter XXIII.

The Marquis Sees His Brother.

When Lord George was summoned down to Manor Cross,—or rather, to Cross Hall, he did not dare not to go. Lady Sarah had told him that it was his duty, and he could not deny the assertion. But he was very angry with his brother, and did not in the least wish to see him. Nor did he think that by seeing him he could in any degree render easier that horrible task which would, sooner or later, be imposed upon him, of testing the legitimacy of his brother's child. And there were other reasons which made him unwilling to leave London. He did not like to be away from his young wife. She was, of course, a matron now, and entitled to be left alone, according to the laws of the world; but then she was so childish, and so fond of playing bagatelle with Jack De Baron! He had never had occasion to find fault with her; not to say words to her which he himself would regard as fault-finding words though she had complained more than once of his scolding her. He would caution her, beg her to be grave, ask her to read heavy books, and try to impress her with the solemnity of married life. In this way he would quell her spirits for a few hours. Then she would burst out again, and there would be Jack De Baron and the bagatelle. In all these sorrows he solaced himself by asking advice from Mrs. Houghton. By degrees he told Mrs. Houghton almost everything. The reader may remember that there had been a moment in which he had resolved that he would not again go to Berkeley Square. But all that was very much altered now. He was there almost every day, and consulted the lady about every thing. She had induced him even to talk quite openly about this Italian boy, to express his suspicions, and to allude to most distressing duties which might be incumbent on him. She strenuously advised him to take nothing for granted. If the Marquisate was to be had by careful scrutiny she was quite of opinion that it should not be lost by careless confidence. This sort of friendship was very pleasant to him, and especially so, because he could tell himself that there was nothing wicked in it. No doubt her hand would be in his sometimes for a moment, and once or twice his arm had almost found its way round her waist. But these had been small deviations, which he had taken care to check. No doubt it had occurred to him, once or twice, that she had not been careful to check them. But this, when he thought of it maturely, he attributed to innocence.

It was at last, by her advice, that he begged that one of his sisters might come up to town, as a companion to Mary during his absence at Cross Hall. This counsel she had given to him after assuring him half-a-dozen times that there was nothing to fear. He had named Amelia, Mary having at once agreed to the arrangement, on condition that the younger of the three sisters should be invited. The letter was of course written to Lady Sarah. All such letters always were written to Lady Sarah. Lady Sarah had answered, saying, that Susanna would take the place destined for Amelia. Now Susanna, of all the Germain family, was the one whom Mary disliked the most. But there was no help for it. She thought it hard, but she was not strong enough in her own position to say that she would not have Susanna, because Susanna had not been asked. "I think Lady Susanna will be the best," said Lord George, "because she has so much strength of character."

"Strength of character! You speak as if you were going away for three years, and were leaving me in the midst of danger. You'll be back in five days, I suppose. I really think I could have got on without Susanna's—strength of character!" This was her revenge; but, all the same, Lady Susanna came.

"She is as good as gold," said Lord George, who was himself as weak as water. "She is as good as gold; but there is a young man comes here whom I don't care for her to see too often." This was what he said to Lady Susanna.

"Oh, indeed! Who is he?"

"Captain De Baron. You are not to suppose that she cares a straw about him."

"Oh, no; I am sure there can be nothing of that," said Lady Susanna, feeling herself to be as energetic as Cerberus, and as many-eyed as Argus.

"You must take care of yourself now, master Jack," Mrs. Houghton said to her cousin. "A duenna has been sent for."

"Duennas always go to sleep, don't they; and take tips; and are generally open to reason?"

"Oh, heavens! Fancy tipping Lady Susanna! I should think that she never slept in her life with both eyes at the same time, and that she thinks in her heart that every man who says a civil word ought to have his tongue cut out."

"I wonder how she'd take it if I were to say a civil word to herself?"

"You can try; but as far as Madame is concerned, you had better wait till Monsieur is back again."

Lord George, having left his wife in the hands of Lady Susanna, went down to Brotherton and on to Cross Hall. He arrived on the Saturday after that first Sunday visit paid by the Marquis to his mother. The early part of the past week had been very blank down in those parts. No further personal attempts had been made to intrude upon the Manor Cross mysteries. The Dean

had not been seen again, even at Cross Hall. Mr. Holdenough
had made no attempt after the reception,—or rather non-
reception,—awarded to his wife. Old Mr. De Baron had driven
over, and had seen the Marquis, but nothing more than that fact
was known at Cross Hall. He had been there for about an hour,
and as far as Mrs. Toff knew, the Marquis had been very civil to
him. But Mr. De Baron, though a cousin, was not by any means
one of the Germain party. Then, on Saturday there had been an
affair. Mrs. Toff had come to the Hall, boiling over with the
importance of her communication, and stating that she had
been—turned out of the house. She, who had presided over
everything material at Manor Cross for more than thirty years,
from the family pictures down to the kitchen utensils, had been
absolutely desired to—walk herself off. The message had been
given to her by that accursed Courier, and she had then insisted
on seeing the Marquis. "My Lord," she said, only laughed at her.
"'Mrs. Toff,' he had said, 'you are my mother's servant, and my
sisters'. You had better go and live with them.'" She had then
hinted at the shortness of the notice given her, upon which he
had offered her anything she chose to ask in the way of wages
and board wages. "But I wouldn't take a penny, my Lady; only
just what was due up to the very day." As Mrs. Toff was a great
deal too old a servant to be really turned away, and as she
merely migrated from Manor Cross to Cross Hall, she did not
injure herself much by refusing the offers made to her.

It must be held that the Marquis was justified in getting
rid of Mrs. Toff. Mrs. Toff was, in truth, a spy in his camp, and,
of course, his own people were soon aware of that fact. Her
almost daily journeys to Cross Hall were known, and it was
remembered, both by the Marquis and his wife, that this old
woman, who had never been allowed to see the child, but who
had known all the preceding generation as children, could not
but be an enemy. Of course it was patent to all the servants, and
to every one connected with the two houses, that there was war.
Of course, the Marquis, having an old woman acting spy in his

stronghold, got rid of her. But justice would shortly have required that the other old woman, who was acting spy in the other stronghold, should be turned out, also. But the Marchioness, who had promised to tell everything to her son, could not very well be offered wages and be made to go.

In the midst of the ferment occasioned by this last piece of work Lord George reached Cross Hall. He had driven through the park, that way being nearly as short as the high road, and had left word at the house that he would call on the following morning, immediately after morning church. This he did, in consequence of a resolution which he had made,—to act on his own judgment. A terrible crisis was coming, in which it would not be becoming that he should submit himself either to his eldest sister, or to the Dean. He had talked the matter over fully with Mrs. Houghton, and Mrs. Houghton had suggested that he should call on his way out to the Hall.

The ladies had at first to justify their request that he should come to them, and there was a difficulty in doing this, as he was received in presence of their mother. Lady Sarah had not probably told herself that the Marchioness was a spy, but she had perceived that it would not be wise to discuss everything openly in her mother's presence. "It is quite right that you should see him," said Lady Sarah.

"Quite right," said the old lady.

"Had he sent me even a message I should have been here, of course," said the brother. "He passed through London, and I would have met him there had he not kept everything concealed."

"He isn't like anybody else, you know. You mustn't quarrel with him. He is the head of the family. If we quarrel with him, what will become of us?"

"What will become of him if everybody falls off from him. That's what I am thinking of," said Lady Sarah.

Soon after this all the horrors that had taken place,— horrors which could not be entrusted to a letter,—were narrated him. The Marquis had insulted Dr. Pountner, he had not returned the Bishop's visit, he had treated the Dean with violent insolence, and he had refused to receive his brother-in-law, Mr. Holdenough, though the Holdenoughs had always moved in county society! He had declared that none of his relatives were to be introduced to his wife. He had not as yet allowed the so-called Popenjoy to be seen. He had said none of them were to trouble him at Manor Cross, and had explained his purpose, of only coming to the Hall when he knew that his sister Sarah was away. "I think he must be mad," said the younger brother.

"It is what comes of living in a godless country like Italy," said Lady Amelia.

"It is what comes of utterly disregarding duty," said Lady Sarah.

But what was to be done? The Marquis had declared his purpose of doing what he liked with his own, and certainly none of them could hinder him. If he chose to shut himself and his wife up at the big house, he must do so. It was very bad, but it was clear that they could not interfere with his eccentricities. How was anybody to interfere? Of course, there was present in the mind of each of them a feeling that this woman might not be his wife, or that the child might not be legitimate. But they did not like with open words among themselves to accuse their brother of so great a crime. "I don't see what there is to be done," said Lord George.

The Church was in the park, not very far from the house, but nearer to the gate leading to Brotherton. On that Sunday morning the Marchioness and her youngest daughter went there in the carriage, and in doing so, had to pass the front doors. The previous Sunday had been cold, and this was the first time that the Marchioness had seen Manor Cross since her son had been there. "Oh, dear! if I could only go in and see the dear child," she said.

"You know you can't, mamma," said Amelia.

"It is all Sarah's fault, because she would quarrel with him."

After Church the ladies returned in the carriage, and Lord George went to the house according to his appointment. He was shown into a small parlour, and in about half an hour's time luncheon was brought to him. He then asked whether his brother was coming. The servant went away, promising to enquire, but did not return. He was cross and would eat no lunch,—but after awhile rang the bell, loudly, and again asked the same question. The servant again went away and did not return. He had just made up his mind to leave the house and never to return to it, when the Courier, of whom he had heard, came to usher him into his brother's room. "You seem to be in a deuce of a hurry, George," said the Marquis, without getting out of his chair. "You forget that people don't get up at the same hour all the world over."

"It's half-past two now."

"Very likely; but I don't know that there is any law to make a man dress himself before that hour."

"The servant might have given me a message."

"Don't make a row now you are here, old fellow. When I found you were in the house I got down as fast as I could. I suppose your time isn't so very precious."

Lord George had come there determined not to quarrel if he could help it. He had very nearly quarrelled already. Every word that his brother said was in truth an insult,—being, as they were, the first words spoken after so long an interval. They were intended to be insolent, probably intended to drive him away. But if anything was to be gained by the interview he must not allow himself to be driven away. He had a duty to perform,—a great duty. He was the last man in England to suspect a fictitious heir,—would at any rate be the last to hint at such an iniquity without the strongest ground. Who is to be true to a brother if not a brother? Who is to support the honour of a great family if not its own scions? Who is to abstain from wasting the wealth and honour of another, if not he who has the nearest chance of possessing them? And yet who could be so manifestly bound as he to take care that no surreptitious head was imposed upon the family. This little child was either the real Popenjoy, a boy to be held by him as of all boys the most sacred, to the promotion of whose welfare all his own energies would be due,—or else a brat so abnormously distasteful and abominable as to demand from him an undying enmity, till the child's wicked pretensions should be laid at rest. There was something very serious in it, very tragic,—something which demanded that he should lay aside all common anger, and put up with many insults on behalf of the cause which he had in hand. "Of course I could wait," said he; "only I thought that perhaps the man would have told me."

"The fact is, George, we are rather a divided house here. Some of us talk Italian and some English. I am the only common interpreter in the house, and I find it a bore."

"I dare say it is troublesome."

"And what can I do for you now you are here?"

Do for him! Lord George didn't want his brother to do anything for him. "Live decently, like an English nobleman, and do not outrage your family." That would have been the only true answer he could have made to such a question. "I thought you would wish to see me after your return," he said.

"It's rather lately thought of; but, however, let that pass. So you've got a wife for yourself."

"As you have done also."

"Just so. I have got a wife too. Mine has come from one of the oldest and noblest families in Christendom."

"Mine is the granddaughter of a livery-stable keeper," said Lord George, with a touch of real grandeur; "and, thank God, I can be proud of her in any society in England."

"I dare say;—particularly as she had some money."

"Yes; she had money. I could hardly have married without. But when you see her I think you will not be ashamed of her as your sister-in-law."

"Ah! She lives in London and I am just at present down here."

"She is the daughter of the Dean of Brotherton."

"So I have heard. They used to make gentlemen Deans." After this there was a pause, Lord George finding it difficult to go on with the conversation without a quarrel. "To tell you the truth, George, I will not willingly see anything more of your Dean. He came here and insulted me. He got up and blustered about the room because I wouldn't thank him for the honour he had done our family by his alliance. If you please, George, we'll understand that the less said about the Dean the better. You see I haven't any of the money out of the stable-yard."

"My wife's money didn't come out of a stable-yard. It came from a wax-chandler's shop," said Lord George, jumping up, just as the Dean had done. There was something in the man's manner worse even than his words which he found it almost impossible to bear. But he seated himself again as his brother sat looking at him with a bitter smile upon his face. "I don't suppose," he said, "you can wish to annoy me."

"Certainly not. But I wish that the truth should be understood between us."

"Am I to be allowed to pay my respects to your wife?" said Lord George boldly.

"I think, you know, that we have gone so far apart in our marriages that there is nothing to be gained by it. Besides, you couldn't speak to her,—nor she to you."

"May I be permitted to see—Popenjoy?"

The Marquis paused a moment, and then rang the bell. "I don't know what good it will do you, but if he can be made fit he shall be brought down." The Courier entered the room and received certain orders in Italian. After that there was considerable delay, during which an Italian servant brought the Marquis a cup of chocolate and a cake. He pushed a newspaper over to his brother, and as he was drinking his chocolate, lighted a cigarette. In this way there was a delay of over an hour, and then there entered the room an Italian nurse with a little boy who seemed to Lord George to be nearly two years old. The child was carried in by the woman, but Lord George thought that he was big enough to have walked. He was dressed up with many ribbons, and was altogether as gay as apparel could make him. But he was an ugly, swarthy little boy, with great black eyes, small cheeks, and a high forehead,—very unlike such a Popenjoy as Lord George would have liked to have seen. Lord George got up and stood over him, and leaning down kissed the high forehead. "My poor little darling," he said.

"As for being poor," said the Marquis, "I hope not. As to being a darling, I should think it doubtful. If you've done with him, she can take him away, you know." Lord George had done with him, and so he was taken away. "Seeing is believing, you know," said the Marquis; "that's the only good of it." Lord George said to himself that in this case seeing was not believing.

At this moment the open carriage came round to the door. "If you like to get up behind," said the Marquis, "I can take you back to Cross Hall, as I am going to see my mother. Perhaps you'll remember that I wish to be alone with her." Lord George then expressed his preference for walking. "Just as you please. I want to say a word. Of course I took it very ill of you all when you insisted on keeping Cross Hall in opposition to my wishes. No doubt they acted on your advice."

"Partly so."

"Exactly; your's and Sarah's. You can't expect me to forget it, George;—that's all." Then he walked out of the room among the servants, giving his brother no opportunity for further reply.

Chapter XXIV.

The Marquis Goes Into Brotherton.

The poor dear old Marchioness must have had some feeling that she was regarded as a spy. She had promised to tell everything to her eldest son, and though she had really nothing to tell, though the Marquis did in truth know all that there was as yet to know, still there grew up at Cross Hall a sort of severance between the unhappy old lady and her children. This showed itself in no diminution of affectionate attention; in no intentional change of manner; but there was a reticence about the Marquis and Popenjoy which even she perceived, and there crept into her mind a feeling that Mrs. Toff was on her guard against her,—so that on two occasions she almost snubbed Mrs. Toff. "I never see'd him, my Lady; what more can I say?" said Mrs. Toff. "Toff, I don't believe you wanted to see your master's son and heir!" said the Marchioness. Then Mrs. Toff pursed up her lips, and compressed her nose, and half-closed her eyes, and the Marchioness was sure that Mrs. Toff did not believe in Popenjoy.

No one but Lord George had seen Popenjoy. To no eyes but his had the august baby been displayed. Of course many questions had been asked, especially by the old lady, but the answers to them had not been satisfactory. "Dark, is he?" asked the Marchioness. Lord George replied that the child was very swarthy. "Dear me! That isn't like the Germains. The Germains were never light, but they're not swarthy. Did he talk at all?" "Not a word." "Did he play about?" "Never was out of the nurse's arms." "Dear me! Was he like Brotherton?" "I don't think I am a judge of likenesses." "He's a healthy child?" "I can't say. He seemed to be a good deal done up with finery." Then the Marchioness declared that her younger son showed an unnatural indifference to the heir of the family. It was manifest that she intended to accept the new Popenjoy, and to ally herself with no party base enough to entertain any suspicion.

These examinations respecting the baby went on for the three first days of the week. It was Lord George's intention to return to town on the Saturday, and it seemed to them all to be necessary that something should be arranged before that. Lady Sarah thought that direct application should be made to her brother for proof of his marriage and for a copy of the register of the birth of his child. She quite admitted that he would resent such application with the bitterest enmity. But that she thought must be endured. She argued that nothing could be done more friendly to the child than this. If all was right the enquiry which circumstances certainly demanded would be made while he could not feel it. If no such proof were adduced now there would certainly be trouble, misery, and perhaps ruin in coming years. If the necessary evidence were forthcoming, then no one would wish to interfere further. There might be ill blood on their brother's part, but there would be none on theirs. Neither Lord George nor their younger sister gainsayed this altogether. Neither of them denied the necessity of enquiry. But they desired to temporise;—and then how was the enquiry to be made? Who was to bell the cat? And how should they go on when the Marquis refused to take any heed of them,—as, of course, he would do? Lady Sarah saw at once that they must employ a lawyer;—but what lawyer? Old Mr. Stokes, the family attorney, was the only lawyer they knew. But Mr. Stokes was Lord Brotherton's lawyer, and would hardly consent to be employed against his own client. Lady Sarah suggested that Mr. Stokes might be induced to explain to the Marquis that these enquiries should be made for his, the Marquis's, own benefit. But Lord George felt that this was impossible. It was evident that Lord George would be afraid to ask Mr. Stokes to undertake the work.

At last it came to be understood among them that they must have some friend to act with them. There could be no doubt who that friend should be. "As to interfering," said Lady Sarah, speaking of the Dean, "he will interfere, whether we ask him to or not. His daughter is as much affected as anybody, and if I understand him he is not the man to see any interest of his own injured by want of care." Lord George shook his head but yielded. He greatly disliked the idea of putting himself into the Dean's hands; of becoming a creature of the Dean's. He felt the Dean to be stronger than himself, endowed with higher spirit and more confident hopes. But he also felt that the Dean was—the son of a stable-keeper. Though he had professed to his brother that he could own the fact without shame, still he was ashamed. It was not the Dean's parentage that troubled him so much as a consciousness of some defect, perhaps only of the absence of some quality, which had been caused by that parentage. The man looked like a gentleman, but still there was a smell of the stable. Feeling this rather than knowing it Lord George resisted for awhile the idea of joining forces with the Dean; but when it was suggested to him as an alternative that he himself must go to Mr. Stokes and explain his suspicions in the lawyer's room, then he agreed that, as a first step, he would consult the Dean. The Dean, no doubt, would have his own lawyer, who would not care a fig for the Marquis.

It was thought by them at Cross Hall that the Dean would come over to them, knowing that his son-in-law was in the country; but the Dean did not come, probably waiting for the same compliment from Lord George. On the Friday Lord

George rode into Brotherton early, and was at the Deanery by eleven o'clock. "I thought I should see you," said the Dean, in his pleasantest manner. "Of course, I heard from Mary that you were down here. Well;—what do you think of it all?"

"It is not pleasant."

"If you mean your brother, I am bound to say, that he is very unpleasant. Of course you have seen him?"

"Yes; I have seen him."

"And her ladyship?"

"No. He said that as I do not speak Italian it would be no good."

"And he seemed to think," said the Dean, "that as I do speak Italian it would be dangerous. Nobody has seen her then?"

"Nobody."

"That promises well! And the little lord?"

"He was brought down to me."

"That was gracious! Well; what of him. Did he look like a Popenjoy?"

"He is a nasty little black thing."

"I shouldn't wonder."

"And looks——. Well, I don't want to abuse the poor child, and God knows, if he is what he pretends to be, I would do anything to serve him."

"That's just it, George," said the Dean, very seriously,— seriously, and with his kindest manner, being quite disposed to make himself agreeable to Lord George, if Lord George would be agreeable to him. "That's just it. If we were certified as to that, what would we not do for the child in spite of the father's brutality? There is no dishonesty on our side, George. You know of me, and I know of you, that if every tittle of the evidence of that child's birth were in the keeping of either of us, so that it could be destroyed on the moment, it should be made as public as the winds of heaven to-morrow, so that it was true evidence. If he be what he pretends to be, who would interfere with him? But if he be not?"

"Any suspicion of that kind is unworthy of us;—except on very strong ground."

"True. But if there be very strong ground, it is equally true that such suspicion is our duty. Look at the case. When was it that he told you that he was going to be married? About six months since, as far as my memory goes."

"He said, 'I am to be married.'"

"That is speaking in the future tense; and now he claims to have been married two or three years ago. Has he ever attempted to explain this?"

"He has not said a word about it. He is quite unwilling to talk about himself."

"I dare say. But a man in such circumstances must be made to talk about himself. You and I are so placed that if we did not make him talk about himself, we ought to be made to make him do so. He may be deceitful if he pleases. He may tell you and me fibs without end. And he may give us much trouble by doing so. Such trouble is the evil consequence of having liars in the world." Lord George winced at the rough word as applied by inference to his own brother. "But liars themselves are always troubled by their own lies. If he chooses to tell you that on a certain day he is about to be married, and afterwards springs a two-year old child upon you as legitimate, you are bound to think that there is some deceit. You cannot keep yourself from knowing that there is falsehood; and if falsehood, then probably fraud. Is it likely that a man with such privileges, and such property insured to a legitimate son, would allow the birth of such a child to be slurred over without due notice of it? You say that suspicion on our part without strong ground would be unworthy of us. I agree with you. But I ask you whether the grounds are not so strong as to force us to suspect. Come," he continued, as Lord George did not answer at once; "let us be open to each other, knowing as each does that the other means to do what is right. Do not you suspect?"

"I do," said Lord George.

"And so do I. And I mean to learn the truth."

"But how?"

"That is for us to consider; but of one thing I am quite sure. I am quite certain that we must not allow ourselves to be afraid of your brother. To speak the truth, as it must be spoken, he is a bully, George."

"I would rather you would not abuse him, sir."

"Speak ill of him I must. His character is bad, and I have to speak of it. He is a bully. He set himself to work to put me down when I did myself the honour to call on him, because he felt that my connexion with you would probably make me an enemy to him. I intend that he shall know that he cannot put me down. He is undoubtedly Lord Brotherton. He is the owner of a wide property. He has many privileges and much power, with which I cannot interfere. But there is a limit to them. If he have a legitimate son, those privileges will be that son's property, but he has to show to the world that that son is legitimate. When a man marries before all the world, in his own house, and a child is born to him as I may say openly, the proofs are there of themselves. No bringing up of evidence is necessary. The thing is simple, and there is no suspicion and no enquiry. But he has done the reverse of this, and now flatters himself that he can cow those who are concerned by a domineering manner. He must be made to feel that this will not prevail."

"Sarah thinks that he should be invited to produce the necessary certificates." Lord George, when he dropped his sister's title in speaking of her to the Dean, must have determined that very familiar intercourse with the Dean was a necessity.

"Lady Sarah is always right. That should be the first step. But will you invite him to do so? How shall the matter be broken to him?"

"She thinks a lawyer should do it."

"It must be done either by you or by a lawyer." Lord George looked very blank. "Of course, if the matter were left in my hands;—if I had to do it,—I should not do it personally. The question is, whether you might not in the first instance write to him?"

"He would not notice it."

"Very likely not. Then we must employ a lawyer."

The matter was altogether so distasteful to Lord George, that more than once during the interview he almost made up his mind that he would withdraw altogether from the work, and at any rate appear to take it for granted that the child was a real heir, an undoubted Popenjoy. But then, as often, the Dean showed him that he could not so withdraw himself. "You will be driven," said the Dean, "to express your belief, whatever it may be; and if you think that there has been foul play, you cannot deny that you think so." It was at last decided that Lord George should write a letter to his brother, giving all the grounds, not of his own suspicion, but which the world at large would have for suspecting; and earnestly imploring that proper evidence as to his brother's marriage and as to the child's birth, might be produced. Then, if this letter should not be attended to, a lawyer should be employed. The Dean named his own lawyer, Mr. Battle, of Lincoln's Inn Fields. Lord George having once yielded, found it convenient to yield throughout. Towards the end of the interview the Dean suggested that he would "throw a few words together," or, in other language, write the letter which his son-in-law would have to sign. This suggestion was also accepted by Lord George.

The two men were together for a couple of hours, and then, after lunch, went out together into the town. Each felt that he was now more closely bound to the other than ever. The Dean was thoroughly pleased that it should be so. He intended his son-in-law to be the Marquis, and being sanguine as well as pugnacious looked forward to seeing that time himself. Such a man as the Marquis would probably die early, whereas he himself was full of health. There was nothing he would not do to make Lord George's life pleasant, if only Lord George would be pleasant to him, and submissive. But Lord George himself was laden with many regrets. He had formed a conspiracy against the head of his own family, and his brother conspirator was the son of a stable-keeper. It might be also that he was conspiring against his own legitimate nephew; and if so, the conspiracy would of course fail, and he would be stigmatised for ever among the Germains as the most sordid and vile of the name.

The Dean's house was in the Close, joined on to the Cathedral, a covered stone pathway running between the two. The nearest way from the Deanery to the High Street was through the Cathedral, the transept of which could be entered by crossing the passage. The Dean and his son-in-law on this occasion went through the building to the west entrance, and there stood for a few minutes in the street while the Dean spoke to men who were engaged on certain repairs of the fabric. In doing this they all went out into the middle of the wide street in order that they might look up at the work which was being done. While they were there, suddenly an open carriage, with a postilion, came upon them unawares, and they had to retreat out of the way. As they did so they perceived that Lord Brotherton was in the carriage, enveloped in furs, and that a lady, more closely enveloped even than himself, was by his side. It was evident to them that he had recognised them. Indeed he had been in the act of raising his hand to greet his brother when he saw the Dean. They both bowed to him, while the Dean, who had the readier mind, raised his hat to the lady. But the Marquis steadily ignored them. "That's your sister-in-law," said the Dean.

"Perhaps so."

"There is no other lady here with whom he could be driving. I am pretty sure that it is the first time that either of them have been in Brotherton."

"I wonder whether he saw us."

"Of course he saw us. He cut me from fixed purpose, and you because I was with you. I shall not disturb him by any further recognition." Then they went on about their business, and in the afternoon, when the Dean had thrown his few words together, Lord George rode back to Cross Hall. "Let the letter be sent at once,—but date it from London." These were the last words the Dean said to him.

It was the Marquis and his wife. All Brotherton heard the news. She had absolutely called at a certain shop and the Marquis had condescended to be her interpreter. All Brotherton was now sure that there was a new Marchioness, a fact as to which a great part of Brotherton had hitherto entertained doubts. And it seemed that this act of condescension in stopping at a Brotherton shop was so much appreciated that all the former faults of the Marquis were to be condoned on that account. If only Popenjoy could be taken to a Brotherton pastrycook, and be got to eat a Brotherton bun, the Marquis would become the most popular man in the neighbourhood, and the undoubted progenitor of a long line of Marquises to come. A little kindness after continued cruelty will always win a dog's heart;—some say, also a woman's. It certainly seemed to be the way to win Brotherton.

Chapter XXV.

Lady Susanna In London.

In spite of the caution which he had received from his friend and cousin Mrs. Houghton, Jack De Baron did go to Munster Court during the absence of Lord George, and there did encounter Lady Susanna. And Mrs. Houghton herself, though she had given such excellent advice, accompanied him. She was of course anxious to see Lady Susanna, who had always especially disliked her; and Jack himself was desirous of making the acquaintance of a lady who had been, he was assured, sent up to town on purpose to protect the young wife from his wiles. Both Mrs. Houghton and Jack had become very intimate in Munster Court, and there was nothing strange in their dropping in together even before lunch. Jack was of course introduced to Lady Susanna. The two ladies grimaced at each other, each knowing the other's feeling towards herself. Mary having suspected that Lady Susanna had been sent for in reference to this special friend, determined on being specially gracious to Jack. She had already, since Lady Susanna's arrival, told that lady that she was able to manage her own little affairs. Lady Susanna had said an unfortunate word as to the unnecessary expense of four wax candles when they two were sitting alone in the drawing-room. Lady George had said that it was pretty. Lady Susanna had expostulated gravely, and then Lady George had spoken out. "Dear Susanna, do let me manage my own little affairs." Of course the words had rankled, and of course the love which the ladies bore to each other had not been increased. Lady George was now quite resolved to show dear Susanna that she was not afraid of her duenna.

"We thought we'd venture to see if you'd give us lunch," said Mrs. Houghton.

"Delightful!" exclaimed Lady George. "There's nothing to eat; but you won't mind that."

"Not in the least," said Jack. "I always think the best lunch in the world is a bit of the servants' dinner. It's always the best meat, and the best cooked and the hottest served."

There was plenty of lunch from whatsoever source it came, and the three young people were very merry. Perhaps they were a little noisy. Perhaps there was a little innocent slang in their conversation. Ladies do sometimes talk slang, and perhaps the slang was encouraged for the special edification of Lady Susanna. But slang was never talked at Manor Cross or Cross Hall, and was odious to Lady Susanna. When Lady George declared that some offending old lady ought to be "jumped upon," Lady Susanna winced visibly. When Jack told Lady George that "she was the woman to do it," Lady Susanna shivered almost audibly. "Is anything the matter?" asked Lady George, perhaps not quite innocently.

It seemed to Lady Susanna that these visitors were never going away, and yet this was the very man as to whom her brother had cautioned her! And what an odious man he was—in Lady Susanna's estimation! A puppy,—an absolute puppy! Good-looking, impudent, familiar, with a light visage, and continually smiling! All those little gifts which made him so pleasant to Lady George were stains and blemishes in the eyes of Lady Susanna. To her thinking, a man,—at any rate a gentleman,—should be tall, dark, grave, and given to silence rather than to much talk. This Jack chattered about everything, and hardly opened his mouth without speaking slang. About half-past three, when they had been chattering in the drawing-room for an hour, after having chattered over their lunch for a previous hour, Mrs. Houghton made a most alarming proposition. "Let us all go to Berkeley Square and play bagatelle."

"By all means," said Jack. "Lady George, you owe me two new hats already."

Playing bagatelle for new hats! Lady Susanna felt that if ever there could come a time in which interference would be necessary that time had come now. She had resolved that she would be patient; that she should not come down as an offended deity upon Lady George, unless some sufficient crisis should justify such action. But now surely, if ever, she must interpose. Playing at bagatelle with Jack De Baron for new hats, and she with the prospect before her of being Marchioness of Brotherton! "It's only one," said Lady George gaily, "and I daresay I'll win that back to-day. Will you come, Susanna?"

"Certainly not," said Lady Susanna, very grimly. They all looked at her, and Jack De Baron raised his eyebrows, and sat for a moment motionless. Lady Susanna knew that Jack De Baron was intending to ridicule her. Then she remembered that should this perverse young woman insist upon going to Mrs. Houghton's house with so objectionable a companion, her duty to her brother demanded that she also should go. "I mean," said Lady Susanna, "that I had rather not go."

"Why not?" asked Mary.

"I do not think that playing bagatelle for new hats is— is—the best employment in the world either for a lady or for a gentleman." The words were hardly out of her mouth before she herself felt that they were overstrained and more than even this occasion demanded.

"Then we will only play for gloves," said Mary. Mary was not a woman to bear with impunity such an assault as had been made on her.

"Perhaps you will not mind giving it up till George comes back," said Lord George's sister.

"I shall mind very much. I will go up and get ready. You can do as you please." So Mary left the room, and Lady Susanna followed her.

"She means to have her own way," said Jack, when he was alone with his cousin.

"She is not at all what I took her to be," said Mrs. Houghton. "The fact is, one cannot know what a girl is as long as a girl is a girl. It is only when she's married that she begins to speak out." Jack hardly agreed with this, thinking that some girls he had known had learned to speak out before they were married.

They all went out together to walk across the parks to Berkeley Square, orders being left that the brougham should follow them later in the afternoon. Lady Susanna had at last resolved that she also would go. The very fact of her entering Mrs. Houghton's house was disagreeable to her; but she felt that duty called her. And, after all, when they got to Berkeley Square no bagatelle was played at all. But the bagatelle would almost have been better than what occurred. A small parcel was lying on the table which was found to contain a pack of pictured cards made for the telling of fortunes, and which some acquaintance had sent to Mrs. Houghton. With these they began telling each other's fortunes, and it seemed to Lady Susanna that they were all as free with lovers and sweethearts as though the two ladies had been housemaids instead of being the wives of steady, well-born husbands. "That's a dark man, with evil designs, a wicked tongue, and no money," said Mrs. Houghton, as a combination of cards lay in Lady George's lap. "Jack, the lady with light hair is only flirting with you. She doesn't care for you one bit."

"I daresay not," said Jack.

"And yet she'll trouble you awfully. Lady Susanna, will you have your fortune told?"

"No," said Lady Susanna, very shortly.

This went on for an hour before the brougham came, during the latter half of which Lady Susanna sat without once opening her lips. If any play could have been childish, it was this play; but to her it was horrible. And then they all sat so near together, and that man was allowed to put cards into her brother's wife's hand and to take them out just as though they had been brother and sister, or playfellows all their days. And then, as they were going down to the brougham, the odious man got Lady George aside and whispered to her for two minutes. Lady Susanna did not hear a word of their whispers, but knew that they were devilish. And so she would have thought if she had heard them. "You're going to catch it, Lady George," Jack had said. "There's somebody else will catch something if she makes herself disagreeable," Lady George had answered. "I wish I could be invisible and hear it," had been Jack's last words.

"My dear Mary," said Lady Susanna, as soon as they were seated, "you are very young."

"That's a fault that will mend of itself."

"Too quickly, as you will soon find; but in the meantime, as you are a married woman, should you not be careful to guard against the indiscretions of youth?"

"Well, yes; I suppose I ought," said Mary, after a moment of mock consideration. "But then if I were unmarried I ought to do just the same. It's a kind of thing that is a matter of course without talking about it." She had firmly made up her mind that she would submit in no degree to Lady Susanna, and take from her no scolding. Indeed, she had come to a firm resolve long since that she would be scolded by no one but her husband—and by him as little as possible. Now she was angry with him because he had sent this woman to watch her, and was determined that he should know that, though she would submit to him, she would not submit to his sister. The moment for asserting herself had now come.

"A young married woman," said the duenna, "owes it to her husband to be peculiarly careful. She has his happiness and his honour in her hands."

"And he has hers. It seems to me that all these things are matters of course."

"They should be, certainly," said Lady Susanna, hardly knowing how to go on with her work; a little afraid of her companion, but still very intent. "But it will sometimes happen that a young person does not quite know what is right and what is wrong."

"And sometimes it happens that old people don't know. There was Major Jones had his wife taken away from him the other day by the Court because he was always beating her, and he was fifty. I read all about it in the papers. I think the old people are just as bad as the young."

Lady Susanna felt that her approaches were being cut off from her, and that she must rush at once against the citadel if she meant to take it. "Do you think that playing bagatelle is—nice?"

"Yes, I do;—very nice."

"Do you think George would like your playing with Captain De Baron?"

"Why not with Captain de Baron?" said Mary, turning round upon her assailant with absolute ferocity.

"I don't think he would like it. And then that fortune-telling! If you will believe me, Mary, it was very improper."

"I will not believe anything of the kind. Improper!—a joke about a lot of picture-cards!"

"It was all about love and lovers," said Lady Susanna, not quite knowing how to express herself, but still sure that she was right.

"Oh, what a mind you must have, Susanna, to pick wrong out of that! All about love and lovers! So are books and songs and plays at the theatre. I suppose you didn't understand that it was intended as a burlesque on fortune-telling?"

"And I am quite sure George wouldn't like the kind of slang you were talking with Captain De Baron at lunch."

"If George does not like anything he had better tell me so, and not depute you to do it for him. If he tells me to do anything I shall do it. If you tell me I shall pay no attention to it whatever. You are here as my guest, and not as my governess; and I think your interference very impertinent." This was strong language,—so strong that Lady Susanna found it impossible to continue the conversation at that moment. Nothing, indeed, was said between them during the whole afternoon, or at dinner, or in the evening,—till Lady Susanna had taken up her candlestick.

There had been that most clearly declared of all war which is shown by absolute silence. But Lady Susanna, as she was retiring to rest, thought it might be wise to make a little effort after peace. She did not at all mean to go back from what charges she had made. She had no idea of owning herself to be wrong. But perhaps she could throw a little oil upon the waters. "Of course," she said, "I should not have spoken as I have done but for my great love for George and my regard for you."

"As far as I am concerned, I think it a mistaken regard," said Mary. "Of course I shall tell George; but even to him I shall say that I will not endure any authority but his own."

"Will you hear me?"

"No, not on this subject. You have accused me of behaving improperly—with that man."

"I do think," began Lady Susanna, not knowing how to pick her words in this emergency, fearing to be too strong, and at the same time conscious that weakness would be folly—; "I do think that anything like—like—like flirting is so very bad!"

"Susanna," said Lady George, with a start as she heard the odious words, "as far as I can help it, I will never speak to you again." There certainly had been no oil thrown upon the waters as yet.

The next day was passed almost in absolute silence. It was the Friday, and each of them knew that Lord George would be home on the morrow. The interval was so short that nothing could be gained by writing to him. Each had her own story to tell, and each must wait till he should be there to hear it. Mary with a most distant civility went through her work of hostess. Lady Susanna made one or two little efforts to subdue her; but, failing, soon gave up the endeavour. In the afternoon Aunt Ju called with her niece, but their conversation did not lessen the breach. Then Lady Susanna went out alone in the brougham; but that had been arranged beforehand. They ate their dinner in silence, in silence read their books, and met in silence at the breakfast-table. At three o'clock Lord George came home, and then Mary, running downstairs, took him with her into the drawing-room. There was one embrace, and then she began. "George," she said, "you must never have Susanna here again."

"Why?" said he.

"She has insulted me. She has said things so nasty that I cannot repeat them, even to you. She has accused me to my face—of flirting. I won't bear it from her. If you said it, it would kill me; but of course you can say what you please. But she shall not scold me, and tell me that I am this and that because I am not as solemn as she is, George. Do you believe that I have ever— flirted?" She was so impetuous that he had been quite unable to stop her. "Did you mean that she should behave to me like that?"

"This is very bad," he said.

"What is very bad. Is it not bad that she should say such things to me as that? Are you going to take her part against me?"

"Dearest Mary, you seem to be excited."

"Of course I am excited. Would you wish me to have such things as that said to me, and not to be excited? You are not going to take part against me?"

"I have not heard her yet."

"Will you believe her against me? Will she be able to make you believe that I have—flirted? If so, then it is all over."

"What is all over?"

"Oh, George, why did you marry me, if you cannot trust me?"

"Who says that I do not trust you? I suppose the truth is you have been a little—flighty."

"Been what? I suppose you mean the same thing. I have talked and laughed, and been amused, if that means being flighty. She thinks it wicked to laugh, and calls it slang if every word doesn't come out of the grammar. You had better go and hear her, since you will say nothing more to me."

Lord George thought so too; but he stayed for a few moments in the dining-room, during which he stooped over his wife, who had thrown herself into an arm-chair, and kissed her. As he did so, she merely shook her head, but made no response to his caress. Then he slowly strode away, and went up stairs into the drawing-room.

What took place there need not be recorded at length. Lady Susanna did not try to be mischievous. She spoke much of Mary's youth, and expressed a strong opinion that Captain De Baron was not a fit companion for her. She was very urgent against the use of slang, and said almost harder things of Mrs. Houghton than she did of Jack. She never had meant to imply that Mary had allowed improper attentions from the gentleman, but that Mary, being young, had not known what attentions were proper and what improper. To Lady Susanna the whole matter was so serious that she altogether dropped the personal quarrel. "Of course, George," she said, "young people do not like to be told; but it has to be done. And I must say that Mary likes it as little as any person that I have ever known."

This multiplicity of troubles falling together on to the poor man's back almost crushed him. He had returned to town full of that terrible letter which he had pledged himself to write; but the letter was already driven out of his head for the time. It was essentially necessary that he should compose this domestic trouble, and of course he returned to his wife. Equally of course after a little time she prevailed. He had to tell her that he was sure that she never flirted. He had to say that she did not talk slang. He had to protest that the fortune-telling cards were absolutely innocent. Then she condescended to say that she would for the present be civil to Susanna, but even while saying that she protested that she would never again have her sister-in-law as a guest in the house. "You don't know, George, even yet, all that she said to me, or in what sort of way she behaved."

Chapter XXVI.

The Dean Returns To Town.

"Do you mean to say that you have any objection to my being acquainted with Captain De Baron?" This question Mary asked her husband on the Monday after his return. On that day Lady Susanna went back to Brothershire, having somewhat hurried her return in consequence of the uncomfortable state of things in Minister Court. They had all gone to church together on the intermediate Sunday, and Lady Susanna had done her best to conciliate her sister-in-law. But she was ignorant of the world, and did not know how bitter to a young married woman is such interference as that of which she had been guilty. She could not understand the amount of offence which was rankling in Mary's bosom. It had not consisted only in the words spoken, but her looks in the man's presence had conveyed the same accusation, so that it could be seen and understood by the man himself. Mary, with an effort, had gone on with her play, determined that no one should suppose her to be cowed by her grand sister-in-law; but through it all she had resolved always to look upon Lady Susanna as an enemy. She had already abandoned her threat of not speaking to her own guest; but nothing that Lady Susanna could say, nothing that

Lord George could say, softened her heart in the least. The woman had told her that she was a flirt, had declared that what she did and said was improper. The woman had come there as a spy, and the woman should never be her friend. In these circumstances Lord George found it impossible not to refer to the unfortunate subject again, and in doing so caused the above question to be asked. "Do you mean to say that you have any objection to my being acquainted with Captain De Baron?" She looked at him with so much eagerness in her eyes as she spoke that he knew that much at any rate of his present comfort might depend on the answer which he made.

He certainly did object to her being acquainted with Jack De Baron. He did not at all like Jack De Baron. In spite of what he had found himself obliged to say, in order that she might be comforted on his first arrival, he did not like slang, and he did not like fortune-telling cards or bagatelle. His sympathies in these matters were all with his sister. He did like spending his own time with Mrs. Houghton, but it was dreadful to him to think that his wife should be spending hers with Jack De Baron. Nevertheless he could not tell her so. "No," he said, "I have no particular objection."

"Of course if you had, I would never see him again. But it would be very dreadful. He would have to be told that you were—jealous."

"I am not in the least jealous," said he, angrily. "You should not use such a word."

"Certainly I should not have used it, but for the disturbance which your sister has caused. But after all that she has said, there must be some understanding. I like Captain De Baron very much, as I dare say you like other ladies. Why not?"

"I have never suspected anything."

"But Susanna did. Of course you don't like all this, George. I don't like it. I have been so miserable that I have almost cried my eyes out. But if people will make mischief, what is one to do? The only thing is not to have the mischief maker any more."

The worst of this was, to him, that she was so manifestly getting the better of him! When he had married her, not yet nine months since, she had been a little girl, altogether in his hands, not pretending to any self-action, and anxious to be guided in everything by him. His only fear had been that she might be too slow in learning that self-assertion which is necessary from a married woman to the world at large. But now she had made very great progress in the lesson, not only as regarded the world at large, but as regarded himself also. As for his family,—the grandeur of his family,—she clearly had no reverence for that. Lady Susanna, though generally held to be very awful, had been no more to her than any other Susan. He almost wished that he had told her that he did object to Jack De Baron. There would have been a scene, of course; and she, not improbably, might have told her father. That at present would have been doubly disagreeable, as it was incumbent upon him to stand well with the Dean, just at this time. There was this battle to be fought with his brother, and he felt that he could not fight it without the Dean!

Having given his sanction to Jack De Baron, he went away to his club to write his letter. This writing really amounted to no more than copying the Dean's words, which he had carried in his pocket ever since he had left the deanery, and the Dean's words were as follows:—

"Munster Court, *26th April, 187—.*

"MY DEAR BROTHERTON,—I am compelled to write to you under very disagreeable circumstances, and to do so on a subject which I would willingly avoid if a sense of duty would permit me to be silent.

"You will remember that you wrote to me in October last, telling me that you were about to be married. 'I am to be married to the Marchesa Luigi,' were your words. Up to that moment we had heard nothing of the lady or of any arrangement as to a marriage. When I told you of my own intended marriage a few months before that, you merely said in answer that you might probably soon want the house at Manor Cross yourself. It now seems that when you told us of your intended marriage you had already been married over two years, and that when I told you of mine you had a son over twelve months old,—a fact which I might certainly expect that you would communicate to me at such a time.

"I beg to assure you that I am now urged to write by no suspicions of my own; but I know that if things are left to go on as they are now, suspicions will arise at a future time. I write altogether in the interests of your son and heir; and for his sake I beseech you to put at once into the hands of your own lawyer absolute evidence of the date of your marriage, of its legality, and of the birth of your son. It will also be expedient that my lawyer shall see the evidence in your lawyer's hands. If you were to die as matters are now it would be imperative on me to take steps which would seem to be hostile to Popenjoy's interest. I think you must yourself feel that this would be so. And yet nothing would be further from my wish. If we were both to die, the difficulty would be still greater, as in that case proceedings would have to be taken by more distant members of the family.

"I trust you will believe me when I say that my only object is to have the matter satisfactorily settled.

Your affectionate brother,

"GEORGE GERMAIN."

When the Marquis received this letter he was not in the least astonished by it. Lord George had told his sister Sarah that it was to be written, and had even discussed with her the Dean's words. Lady Sarah had thought that as the Dean was a sagacious man, his exact words had better be used. And then Lady Amelia had been told, Lady Amelia having asked various questions on the subject. Lady Amelia had of course known that her brother would discuss the matter with the Dean, and had begged that she might not be treated as a stranger. Everything had not been told to Lady Amelia, nor had Lady Amelia told all that she had heard to her mother. But the Marchioness had known enough, and had communicated enough to her son to save him from any great astonishment when he got his brother's letter. Of course he had known that some steps would be taken.

He answered the letter at once.

> "MY DEAR BROTHER," he said,—"I don't think it necessary to let you know the reasons which induced me to keep my marriage private awhile. You rush at conclusions very fast in thinking that because a marriage is private, therefore it is illegal. I am glad that you have no suspicions of your own, and beg to assure you I don't care whether you have or not. Whenever you or anybody else may want to try the case, you or he or they will find that I have taken care that there is plenty of evidence. I didn't know that you had a lawyer. I only hope he won't run you into much expense in finding a mare's nest.
>
> "Yours truly,
>
> "B."

This was not in itself satisfactory; but such as it was, it did for a time make Lord George believe that Popenjoy was Popenjoy. It was certainly true of him that he wished Popenjoy to be Popenjoy. No personal longing for the title or property made him in his heart disloyal to his brother or his family. And then the trouble and expense and anxieties of such a contest were so terrible to his imagination, that he rejoiced when he thought that they might be avoided. But there was the Dean. The Dean must be satisfied as well as he, and he felt that the Dean would not be satisfied. According to agreement he sent a copy of his brother's letter down to the Dean, and added the assurance of his own belief that the marriage had been a marriage, that the heir was an heir, and that further steps would be useless. It need hardly be said that the Dean was not satisfied. Before dinner on the following day the Dean was in Minister Court. "Oh, papa," exclaimed Mary, "I am so glad to see you." Could it be anything about Captain De Baron that had brought him up? If so, of course she would tell him everything. "What brought you up so suddenly? Why didn't you write? George is at the club, I suppose." George was really in Berkeley Square at that moment. "Oh, yes; he will be home to dinner. Is there anything wrong at Manor Cross, papa?" Her father was so pleasant in his manner to her, that she perceived at once that he had not come up in reference to Captain De Baron. No complaint of her behaviour on that score had as yet reached him. "Where's your portmanteau, papa?"

"I've got a bed at the hotel in Suffolk Street. I shall only be here one night, or at the most two; and as I had to come suddenly I wouldn't trouble you."

"Oh, papa, that's very bad of you."

This she said with that genuine tone which begets confidence. The Dean was very anxious that his daughter should in truth be fond of his company. In the game which he intended to play her co-operation and her influence over her husband would be very necessary to him. She must be a Lovelace rather than a Germain till she should blaze forth as the presiding genius of the Germain family. That Lord George should become tired of him and a little afraid of him he knew could not be avoided; but to her he must, if possible, be a pleasant genius, never accompanied in her mind by ideas of parental severity or clerical heaviness. "I should weary you out if I came too often and came so suddenly," he said, laughing.

"But what has brought you, papa?"

"The Marquis, my dear, who, it seems to me, will, for some time to come, have a considerable influence on my doings."

"The Marquis!"

He had made up his mind that she should know everything. If her husband did not tell her, he would. "Yes, the Marquis. Perhaps I ought to say the Marchioness, only that I am unwilling to give that title to a lady who I think very probably has no right to it."

"Is all that coming up already?"

"The longer it is postponed the greater will be the trouble to all parties. It cannot be endured that a man in his position should tell us that his son is legitimate when that son was born more than a year before he had declared himself about to marry, and that he should then refuse to furnish us with any evidence."

"Have you asked him?" Mary, as she made the suggestion, was herself horror-stricken at the awfulness of the occasion.

"George has asked him."

"And what has the Marquis done?"

"Sent him back a jeering reply. He has a way of jeering which he thinks will carry everything before it. When I called upon him he jeered at me. But he'll have to learn that he cannot jeer you out of your rights."

"I wish you would not think about my rights, papa."

"Your rights will probably be the rights of some one else."

"I know, papa; but still—"

"It has to be done, and George quite agrees with me. The letter which he did write to his brother was arranged between us. Lady Sarah is quite of the same accord, and Lady Susanna—"

"Oh, papa, I do so hate Susanna." This she said with all her eloquence.

"I daresay she can make herself unpleasant."

"I have told George that she shall not come here again as a guest."

"What did she do?"

"I cannot bring myself to tell you what it was that she said. I told George, of course. She is a nasty evil-minded creature—suspecting everything."

"I hope there has been nothing disagreeable."

"It was very disagreeable, indeed, while George was away. Of course I did not care so much when he came back." The Dean, who had been almost frightened, was reassured when he learned that there had been no quarrel between the husband

and wife. Soon afterwards Lord George came in and was astonished to find that his letter had brought up the Dean so quickly. No discussion took place till after dinner, but then the Dean was very perspicuous, and at the same time very authoritative. It was in vain that Lord George asked what they could do, and declared that the evil troubles which must probably arise would all rest on his brother's head. "But we must prevent such troubles, let them rest where they will," said the Dean.

"I don't see what we can do."

"Nor do I, because we are not lawyers. A lawyer will tell us at once. It will probably be our duty to send a commissioner out to Italy to make enquiry."

"I shouldn't like to do that about my brother."

"Of course your brother should be told; or rather everything should be told to your brother's lawyer, so that he might be advised what steps he ought to take. We would do nothing secretly—nothing of which any one could say that we ought to be ashamed." The Dean proposed that they should both go to his attorney, Mr. Battle, on the following day; but this step seemed to Lord George to be such an absolute declaration of war that he begged for another day's delay; and it was at last arranged that he himself should on that intervening day call on Mr. Stokes, the Germain family lawyer. The Marquis, with one of his jeers, had told his brother that, being a younger brother, he was not entitled to have a lawyer. But in truth Lord George had had very much more to do with Mr. Stokes than the Marquis. All the concerns of the family had been managed by Mr. Stokes. The Marquis probably meant to insinuate that the family bill, which was made out perhaps once every three years, was charged against his account. Lord George did call on Mr. Stokes, and found Mr. Stokes very little disposed to give him any opinion. Mr. Stokes was an honest man who disliked trouble of this kind. He freely admitted that there was ground for enquiry, but did not think that he himself was the man who ought to make it. He would certainly communicate with the Marquis, should Lord George think it expedient to employ any other lawyer, and should that lawyer apply to him. In the meantime he thought that immediate enquiry would be a little precipitate. The Marquis might probably himself take steps to put the matter on a proper footing. He was civil, gracious, almost subservient; but he had no comfort to give and no advice to offer, and, like all attorneys, he was in favour of delay. "Of course, Lord George, you must remember that I am your brother's lawyer, and may in this matter be called upon to act as his confidential adviser." All this Lord George repeated that evening to the Dean, and the Dean merely said that it had been a matter of course.

Early on the next morning the Dean and Lord George went together to Mr. Battle's chambers. Lord George felt that he was being driven by his father-in-law; but he felt also that he could not help himself. Mr. Battle, who had chambers in Lincoln's Inn, was a very different man from Mr. Stokes, who carried on his business in a private house at the West End, who prepared wills and marriage settlements for gentlefolk, and who had, in fact, very little to do with law. Mr. Battle was an enterprising man with whom the Dean's first acquaintance had arisen through the Tallowaxes and the stable interests,—a very clever man, and perhaps a little sharp. But an attorney ought to be sharp, and it is not to be understood that Mr. Battle descended to sharp practice. But he was a solicitor with whom the old-fashioned Mr. Stokes's would not find themselves in accord. He was a handsome burly man, nearly sixty years of age, with grey hair and clean shorn face, with bright green eyes, and a well-formed nose and mouth,—a prepossessing man, till something restless about the eyes would at last catch the attention and a little change the judgment.

The Dean told him the whole story, and during the telling he sat looking very pleasant, with a smile on his face, rubbing his two hands together. All the points were made. The letter of the Marquis, in which he told his brother that he was to be married, was shown to him. The concealment of the birth of the boy till the father had made up his mind to come home was urged. The absurdity of his behaviour since he had been at home was described. The singularity of his conduct in allowing none of his family to become acquainted with his wife was pointed out. This was done by the Dean rather than by Lord George, and Lord George, as he heard it all, almost regarded the Dean as his enemy. At last he burst out in his own defence. "Of course you will understand, Mr. Battle, that our only object is to have the thing proved, so that hereafter there may be no trouble."

"Just so, my Lord."

"We do not want to oppose my brother, or to injure his child."

"We want to get at the truth," said the Dean.

"Just so."

"Where there is concealment there must be suspicion," urged the Dean.

"No doubt."

"But everything must be done quite openly," said Lord George. "I would not have a step taken without the knowledge of Mr. Stokes. If Mr. Stokes would do it himself on my brother's behalf it would be so much the better."

"That is hardly probable," said the Dean.

"Not at all probable," said Mr. Battle.

"I couldn't be a party to an adverse suit," said Lord George.

"There is no ground for any suit at all," said the lawyer. "We cannot bring an action against the Marquis because he chooses to call the lady he lives with a Marchioness, or because he calls an infant Lord Popenjoy. Your brother's conduct may be ill-judged. From what you tell me, I think it is. But it is not criminal."

"Then nothing need be done," said Lord George.

"A great deal may be done. Enquiry may be made now which might hereafter be impossible." Then he begged that he might have a week to consider the matter, and requested that the two gentlemen would call upon him again.

Chapter XXVII.

The Baroness Banmann Again.

A day or two after the meeting at Mr. Battle's office there came to Lord George a letter from that gentleman suggesting that, as the Dean had undertaken to come up to London again, and as he, Mr. Battle, might not be ready with his advice at the end of a week, that day fortnight might be fixed. To Lord George this delay was agreeable rather than otherwise, as he was not specially anxious for the return of his father-in-law, nor was he longing for action in this question as to his brother's heir. But the Dean, when the lawyer's letter reached him, was certain that Mr. Battle did not mean to lose the time simply in thinking over the matter. Some preliminary enquiry would now be made, even though no positive instructions had been given. He did not at all regret this, but was sure that Lord George would be very angry if he knew it. He wrote back to say that he would be in Munster Court on the evening before the day appointed.

It was now May, and London was bright with all the exotic gaiety of the season. The park was crowded with riders at one, and was almost impassable at six. Dress was outvying dress, and equipage equipage. Men and women, but principally

women, seemed to be intent on finding out new ways of
scattering money. Tradesmen no doubt knew much of defaulters,
and heads of families might find themselves pressed for means;
but to the outside west-end eye looking at the outside west-end
world it seemed as though wealth was unlimited and money a
drug. To those who had known the thing for years, to young
ladies who were now entering on their seventh or eighth
campaign, there was a feeling of business about it all which,
though it buoyed them up by its excitement, robbed amusement
of most of its pleasure. A ball cannot be very agreeable in which
you may not dance with the man you like and are not asked by
the man you want; at which you are forced to make a note that
that full-blown hope is futile, and that this little bud will surely
never come to flower. And then the toil of smiles, the pretence at
flirtation, the long-continued assumption of fictitious character,
the making of oneself bright to the bright, solemn to the solemn,
and romantic to the romantic, is work too hard for enjoyment.
But our heroine had no such work to do. She was very much
admired and could thoroughly enjoy the admiration. She had no
task to perform. She was not carrying out her profession by
midnight labours. Who shall say whether now and again a soft
impalpable regret,—a regret not recognised as such,—may not
have stolen across her mind, telling her that if she had seen all
this before she was married instead of afterwards, she might
have found a brighter lot for herself? If it were so, the only
enduring effect of such a feeling was a renewal of that oft-made
resolution that she would be in love with her husband. The ladies
whom she knew had generally their carriages and riding horses.
She had only a brougham, and had that kept for her by the
generosity of her father. The Dean, when coming to town, had
brought with him the horse which she used to ride, and wished
that it should remain. But Lord George, with a husband's
solicitude, and perhaps with something of a poor man's proper
dislike to expensive habits, had refused his permission. She
soon, too, learned to know the true sheen of diamonds, the

luxury of pearls, and the richness of rubies; whereas she herself wore only the little ornaments which had come from the deanery. And as she danced in spacious rooms and dined in noble halls, and was fêted on grand staircases, she remembered what a little place was the little house in Munster Court, and that she was to stay there only for a few weeks more before she was taken to the heavy dullness of Cross Hall. But still she always came back to that old resolution. She was so flattered, so courted, so petted and made much of, that she could not but feel that had all this world been opened to her sooner her destiny would probably have been different;—but then it might have been different, and very much less happy. She still told herself that she was sure that Lord George was all that he ought to be.

Two or three things did tease her certainly. She was very fond of balls, but she soon found that Lord George disliked them as much, and when present was always anxious to get home. She was a married woman, and it was open to her to go alone; but that she did not like, nor would he allow it. Sometimes she joined herself to other parties. Mrs. Houghton was always ready to be her companion, and old Mrs. Montacute Jones, who went everywhere, had taken a great liking to her. But there were two antagonistic forces, her husband and herself, and of course she had to yield to the stronger force. The thing might be managed occasionally,—and the occasion was no doubt much the pleasanter because it had to be so managed,—but there was always the feeling that these bright glimpses of Paradise, these entrances into Elysium, were not free to her as to other ladies. And then one day, or rather one night, there came a great sorrow,—a sorrow which robbed these terrestrial Paradises of half their brightness and more than half their joy. One evening he told her that he did not like her to waltz. "Why?" she innocently asked. They were in the brougham, going home, and she had been supremely happy at Mrs. Montacute Jones's house. Lord George said that he could hardly explain the reason. He made rather a long speech, in which he asked her whether she

was not aware that many married women did not waltz. "No,"
said she. "That is, of course, when they get old they don't." "I
am sure," said he, "that when I say I do not like it, that will be
enough." "Quite enough," she answered, "to prevent my doing
it, though not enough to satisfy me why it should not be done."
He said no more to her on the occasion, and so the matter was
considered to be settled. Then she remembered that her very last
waltz had been with Jack De Baron. Could it be that he was
jealous? She was well aware that she took great delight in
waltzing with Captain De Baron because he waltzed so well. But
now that pleasure was over, and for ever! Was it that her
husband disliked waltzing, or that he disliked Jack De Baron?

A few days after this Lady George was surprised by a
visit from the Baroness Banmann, the lady whom she had been
taken to hear at the Disabilities. Since that memorable evening
she had seen Aunt Ju more than once, and had asked how the
cause of the female architects was progressing; but she had
never again met the Baroness. Aunt Ju had apparently been
disturbed by these questions. She had made no further effort to
make Lady George a proselyte by renewed attendances at the
Rights of Women Institute, and had seemed almost anxious to
avoid the subject. As Lady George's acquaintance with the
Baroness had been owing altogether to Aunt Ju she was now
surprised that the German lady should call upon her.

The German lady began a story with great impetuosity,—
with so much impetuosity that poor Mary could not understand
half that was said to her. But she did learn that the Baroness had
in her own estimation been very ill-treated, and that the ill-
treatment had come mainly from the hands of Aunt Ju and Lady
Selina Protest. And it appeared at length that the Baroness
claimed to have been brought over from Bavaria with a promise
that she should have the exclusive privilege of using the hall of
the Disabilities on certain evenings, but that this privilege was
now denied to her. The Disabilities seemed to prefer her younger
rival, Miss Doctor Olivia Q. Fleabody, whom Mary now learned

to be a person of no good repute whatever, and by no means fit to address the masses of Marylebone. But what did the Baroness want of her? What with the female lecturer's lack of English pronunciation, what with her impetuosity, and with Mary's own innocence on the matter, it was some time before the younger lady did understand what the elder lady required. At last eight tickets were brought out of her pocket, on looking at which Mary began to understand that the Baroness had established a rival Disabilities, very near the other, in Lisson Grove; and then at last, but very gradually, she further understood that these were front-row tickets, and were supposed to be worth 2s. 6d. each. But it was not till after that, till further explanation had been made which must, she feared, have been very painful to the Baroness, that she began to perceive that she was expected to pay for the eight tickets on the moment. She had a sovereign in her pocket, and was quite willing to sacrifice it; but she hardly knew how to hand the coin bodily to a Baroness. When she did do so, the Baroness very well knew how to put it into her pocket. "You vill like to keep the entire eight?" asked the Baroness. Mary thought that four might perhaps suffice for her own wants;—whereupon the Baroness re-pocketed four, but of course did not return the change.

But even then the Baroness had not completed her task. Aunt Ju had evidently been false and treacherous, but might still be won back to loyal honesty. So much Mary gradually perceived to be the drift of the lady's mind. Lady Selina was hopeless. Lady Selina, whom the Baroness intended to drag before all the judges in England, would do nothing fair or honest; but Aunt Ju might yet be won. Would Lady George go with the Baroness to Aunt Ju? The servant had unfortunately just announced the brougham as being at the door. "Ah," said the Baroness, "it vould be ten minutes, and vould be my salvation." Lady George did not at all want to go to the house in Green Street. She had no great desire to push her acquaintance with Aunt Ju, she particularly disliked the younger Miss Mildmay, and she felt that she had no business to interfere in this matter. But there is nothing which requires so much experience to attain as the power of refusing. Almost before she had made up her mind whether she would refuse or not the Baroness was in the brougham with her, and the coachman had been desired to take them to Green Street. Throughout the whole distance the Baroness was voluble and unintelligible; but Lady George could hear the names of Selina Protest and Olivia Q. Fleabody through the thunder of the lady's loud complaints.

Yes, Miss Mildmay was at home. Lady George gave her name to the servant, and also especially requested that the Baroness Banmann might be first announced. She had thought it over in the brougham, and had determined that if possible it should appear that the Baroness had brought her. Twice she repeated the name to the servant. When they reached the drawing-room only the younger Miss Mildmay was present. She sent the servant to her aunt, and received her two visitors very demurely. With the Baroness, of whom probably she had heard quite enough, she had no sympathies; and with Lady George she had her own special ground of quarrel. Five or six very long minutes passed during which little or nothing was said. The Baroness did not wish to expend her eloquence on an unprofitable young lady, and Lady George could find no subject for small talk. At last the door was opened and the servant invited the Baroness to go downstairs. The Baroness had perhaps been unfortunate, for at this very time Lady Selina Protest was down in the dining-room discussing the affairs of the Institute with Aunt Ju. There was a little difficulty in making the lady understand what was required of her, but after a while she did follow the servant down to the dining-room.

Lady George, as soon as the door was closed, felt that the blood rushed to her face. She was conscious at the moment that Captain De Baron had been this girl's lover, and that there were some who said that it was because of her that he had deserted the girl. The girl had already said words to her on the subject which had been very hard to bear. She had constantly told herself that in this matter she was quite innocent,—that her friendship with Jack was simple, pure friendship, that she liked him because he laughed and talked and treated the world lightly; that she rarely saw him except in the presence of his cousin, and that everything was as it ought to be. And yet, when she found herself alone with this Miss Mildmay, she was suffused with blushes and uneasy. She felt that she ought to make some excuse for her visit. "I hope," she said, "that your aunt will understand that I brought the lady here only because she insisted on being brought." Miss Mildmay bowed. "She came to me, and I really couldn't quite understand what she had to say. But the brougham was there, and she would get into it. I am afraid there has been some quarrel."

"I don't think that matters at all," said Miss Mildmay.

"Only your aunt might think it so impertinent of me! She took me to that Institute once, you know."

"I don't know anything about the Institute. As for the German woman, she is an impostor; but it doesn't matter. There are three of them there now, and they can have it out together." Lady George didn't understand whether her companion meant to blame her for coming, but was quite sure, from the tone of the girl's voice and the look of her eyes, that she meant to be uncivil. "I am surprised," continued Miss Mildmay, "that you should come to this house at all."

"I hope your aunt will not think—"

"Never mind my aunt. The house is more my house than my aunt's. After what you have done to me—"

"What have I done to you?" She could not help asking the question, and yet she well knew the nature of the accusation. And she could not stop the rushing of the tell-tale blood.

Augusta Mildmay was blushing too, but the blush on her face consisted in two red spots beneath the eyes. The determination to say what she was going to say had come upon her suddenly. She had not thought that she was about to meet her rival. She had planned nothing; but now she was determined. "What have you done?" she said. "You know very well what you have done. Do you mean to tell me that you had never heard of anything between me and Captain De Baron? Will you dare to tell me that? Why don't you answer me, Lady George Germain?"

This was a question which she did not wish to answer, and one that did not at all appertain to herself—which did not require any answer for the clearing of herself; but yet it was now asked in such a manner that she could not save herself from answering it. "I think I did hear that you and he—knew each other."

"Knew each other! Don't be so mealy-mouthed. I don't mean to be mealy-mouthed, I can tell you. You knew all about it. Adelaide had told you. You knew that we were engaged."

"No," exclaimed Lady George; "she never told me that."

"She did. I know she did. She confessed to me that she had told you so."

"But what if she had?"

"Of course he is nothing to you," said the young lady with a sneer.

"Nothing at all;—nothing on earth. How dare you ask such a question? If Captain De Baron is engaged, I can't make him keep his engagements."

"You can make him break them."

"That is not true. I can make him do nothing of the kind. You have no right to talk to me in this way, Miss Mildmay."

"Then I shall do it without a right. You have come between me and all my happiness."

"You cannot know that I am a married woman," said Lady George, speaking half in innocence and half in anger, almost out of breath with confusion, "or you wouldn't speak like that."

"Psha!" exclaimed Miss Mildmay. "It is nothing to me whether you are married or single. I care nothing though you have twenty lovers if you do not interfere with me."

"It is a falsehood," said Lady George, who was now standing. "I have no lover. It is a wicked falsehood."

"I care nothing for wickedness or falseness either. Will you promise me if I hold my tongue that you will have nothing further to say to Captain De Baron?"

"No; I will promise nothing. I should be ashamed of myself to make such a promise."

"Then I shall go to Lord George. I do not want to make mischief, but I am not going to be treated in this way. How would you like it? When I tell you that the man is engaged to me why cannot you leave him alone?"

"I do leave him alone," said Mary, stamping her foot.

"You do everything you can to cheat me of him. I shall tell Lord George."

"You may tell whom you like," said Mary, rushing to the bell-handle and pulling it with all her might. "You have insulted me, and I will never speak to you again." Then she burst out crying, and hurried to the door. "Will you get me—my—carriage?" she said to the man through her sobs. As she descended the stairs she remembered that she had brought the German baroness with her, and that the German baroness would probably expect to be taken away again. But when she reached the hall the door of the dining-room burst open, and the German baroness appeared. It was evident that two scenes had been going on in the same house at the same moment. Through the door the Baroness came first, waving her hands above her head. Behind her was Aunt Ju, advancing with imploring gesture. And behind Aunt Ju might be seen Lady Selina Protest standing in mute dignity. "It is all a got up cheating and a fraud," said the Baroness: "and I vill have justice,—English justice." The servant was standing with the front door open, and the Baroness went straight into Lady George's brougham, as though it had been her own. "Oh, Lady George," said Aunt Ju, "what are you to do with her?" But Lady George was so taken up with her own trouble that she could hardly think of the other matter. She had to say something. "Perhaps I had better go with her. Good-bye." And then she followed the Baroness. "I did not tink dere was such robbery with ladies," said the Baroness. But the footman was asking for directions for the coachman. Whither was he to go? "I do not care," said the Baroness. Lady George asked her in a whisper whether she would be taken home. "Anywhere," said the Baroness. In the meantime the footman was still standing, and Aunt Ju could be seen in the hall through the open door of the house. During the whole time our poor Mary's heart was crushed by the accusations which had been made against her upstairs. "Home," said Mary in despair. To have the Baroness in Munster Court would be dreadful; but anything was better than standing in Green Street with the servant at the carriage window.

Then the Baroness began her story. Lady Selina Protest had utterly refused to do her justice, and Aunt Ju was weak enough to be domineered by Lady Selina. That, as far as Mary understood anything about it, was the gist of the story. But she did not try to understand anything about it. During the drive her mind was intent on forming some plan by which she might be able to get rid of her companion without asking her into her house. She had paid her sovereign, and surely the Baroness had no right to demand more of her. When she reached Munster Court her plan was in some sort framed. "And now, madam," she said, "where shall I tell my servant to take you?" The Baroness looked very suppliant. "If you vas not busy I should so like just one half-hour of conversation." Mary nearly yielded. For a moment she hesitated as though she were going to put up her hand and help the lady out. But then the memory of her own unhappiness steeled her heart, and the feeling grew strong within her that this nasty woman was imposing on her,—and she refused. "I am afraid, madam," she said, "that my time is altogether occupied." "Then let him take me to 10, Alexandrina

Row, Maida Vale," said the Baroness, throwing herself sulkily back into the carriage. Lady George gave the direction to the astounded coachman,—for Maida Vale was a long way off,—and succeeded in reaching her own drawing-room alone.

What was she to do? The only course in which there seemed to be safety was in telling all to her husband. If she did not, it would probably be told by the cruel lips of that odious woman. But yet, how was she to tell it? It was not as though everything in this matter was quite pleasant between her and him. Lady Susanna had accused her of flirting with the man, and that she had told to him. And in her heart of hearts she believed that the waltzing had been stopped because she had waltzed with Jack De Baron. Nothing could be more unjust, nothing more cruel; but still there were the facts. And then the sympathy between her and her husband was so imperfect. She was ever trying to be in love with him, but had never yet succeeded in telling even herself that she had succeeded.

Chapter XXVIII.

"What Matter If She Does?"

About noon on the day after the occurrences related in the last chapter Lady George owned to herself that she was a most unfortunate young woman. Her husband had gone out, and she had not as yet told him anything of what that odious Augusta Mildmay had said to her. She had made various little attempts but had not known how to go on with them. She had begun by giving him her history of the Baroness, and he had scolded her for giving the woman a sovereign and for taking the woman about London in her carriage. It is very difficult to ask in a fitting way for the sympathies and co-operation of one who is scolding you. And Mary in this matter wanted almost more than sympathy and co-operation. Nothing short of the fullest manifestation of affectionate confidence would suffice to comfort her; and, desiring this, she had been afraid to mention Captain De Baron's name. She thought of the waltzing, thought of Susanna, and was cowardly. So the time slipped away from her, and when he left her on the following morning her story had not been told. He was no sooner gone than she felt that if it were to be told at all it should have been told at once.

Was it possible that that venomous girl should really go to her husband with such a complaint? She knew well enough, or at any rate thought that she knew, that there had never been an engagement between the girl and Jack De Baron. She had heard it all over and over again from Adelaide Houghton, and had even herself been present at some joke on the subject between Adelaide and Jack. There was an idea that Jack was being pursued, and Mrs. Houghton had not scrupled to speak of it before him. Mary had not admired her friend's taste, and had on such occasions thought well of Jack because he had simply disowned any consciousness of such a state of things. But all this had made Mary sure that there was not and that there never had been any engagement; and yet the wretched woman, in her futile and frantic endeavours to force the man to marry her, was not ashamed to make so gross an attack as this!

If it hadn't been for Lady Susanna and those wretched fortune-telling cards, and that one last waltz, there would be nothing in it; but as it was, there might be so much! She had begun to fear that her husband's mind was suspicious,—that he was prone to believe that things were going badly. Before her marriage, when she had in truth known him not at all, her father had given her some counsels in his light airy way, which, however, had sunk deep into her mind and which she had endeavoured to follow to the letter. He had said not a word to her as to her conduct to other men. It would not be natural that a father should do so. But he had told her how to behave to her husband. Men, he had assured her, were to be won by such comforts as he described. A wife should provide that a man's dinner was such as he liked to eat, his bed such as he liked to lie on, his clothes arranged as he liked to wear them, and the household hours fixed to suit his convenience. She should learn and indulge his habits, should suit herself to him in external things of life, and could thus win from him a liking and a reverence which would wear better than the feeling generally called love, and would at last give the woman her proper influence. The Dean had meant to teach his child how she was to rule her husband, but of course had been too wise to speak of dominion. Mary, declaring to herself that the feeling generally called love should exist as well as the liking and the reverence, had laboured hard to win it all from her husband in accordance with her father's teaching; but it had seemed to her that her labour was wasted. Lord George did not in the least care what he ate. He evidently had no opinion at all about the bed; and as to his clothes, seemed to receive no accession of comfort by having one wife and her maid, instead of three sisters and their maid and old Mrs. Toff to look after them. He had no habits which she could indulge. She had looked about for the weak point in his armour, but had not found it. It seemed to her that she had no influence over him whatever. She was of course aware that they lived upon her fortune; but she was aware also that he knew that it was so, and that the consciousness made him unhappy. She could not, therefore, even endeavour to minister to his comfort by surrounding him with pretty things. All expenditure was grievous to him. The only matter in which she had failed to give way to any expressed wish had been in that important matter of their town residence; and, as to that, she had in fact had no power of yielding. It had been of such moment as to have been settled for her by previous contract. But, she had often thought, whether in her endeavour to force herself to be in love with him, she would not persistently demand that Munster Court should be abandoned, and that all the pleasures of her own life should be sacrificed.

Now, for a day or two, she heartily wished that she had done so. She liked her house; she liked her brougham; she liked the gaieties of her life; and in a certain way she liked Jack De Baron; but they were all to her as nothing when compared to her duty and her sense of the obligations which she owed to her husband. Playful and childish as she was, all this was very serious to her;—perhaps the more serious because she was playful and childish. She had not experience enough to know how small some things are, and how few are the evils which cannot be surmounted. It seemed to her that if Miss Mildmay were at this moment to bring the horrid charge against her, it might too probably lead to the crash of ruin and the horrors of despair. And yet, through it all, she had a proud feeling of her own innocence and a consciousness that she would speak out very loudly should her husband hint to her that he believed the accusation.

Her father would now be in London in a day or two, and on this occasion would again be staying in Munster Court. At last she made up her mind that she would tell everything to him. It was not, perhaps, the wisest resolution to which she could have come. A married woman should not usually teach herself to lean on her parents instead of her husband, and certainly not on her father. It is in this way that divided households are made. But she had no other real friend of whom she could ask a question. She liked Mrs. Houghton, but, as to such a matter as this, distrusted her altogether. She liked Miss Houghton, her friend's aunt, but did not know her well enough for such service as this. She had neither brother nor sister of her own, and her husband's brothers and sisters were certainly out of the question. Old Mrs. Montacute Jones had taken a great fancy to her, and she almost thought that she could have asked Mrs. Jones for advice; but she had no connection with Mrs. Jones, and did not dare to do it. Therefore she resolved to tell everything to her father.

On the evening before her father came to town there was another ball at Mrs. Montacute Jones's. This old lady, who had no one belonging to her but an invisible old husband, was the gayest of the gay among the gay people of London. On this occasion Mary was to have gone with Lady Brabazon, who was related to the Germains, and Lord George had arranged an escape for himself. They were to drive out together, and when she went to her ball he would go to bed. But in the course of the afternoon she told him that she was writing to Lady Brabazon to decline. "Why won't you go?" said he.

"I don't care about it."

"If you mean that you won't go without me, of course I will go."

"It isn't that exactly. Of course it is nicer if you go; though I wouldn't take you if you don't like it. But—"

"But what, dear?"

"I think I'd rather not to-night. I don't know that I am quite strong enough." Then he didn't say another word to press her,—only begging that she would not go to the dinner either if she were not well. But she was quite well, and she did go to the dinner.

Again she had meant to tell him why she would not go to Mrs. Jones's ball, but had been unable. Jack De Baron would be there, and would want to know why she would not waltz. And Adelaide Houghton would tease her about it, very likely before him. She had always waltzed with him, and could not now refuse without some reason. So she gave up her ball, sending word to say that she was not very well. "I shouldn't at all wonder if he has kept her at home because he's afraid of you," said Mrs. Houghton to her cousin.

Late in the following afternoon, before her husband had come home from his club, she told her father the whole story of her interview with Miss Mildmay. "What a tiger," he said, when he had heard it. "I have heard of women like that before, but I have never believed in them."

"You don't think she will tell him?"

"What matter if she does? What astonishes me most is that a woman should be so unwomanly as to fight for a man in such a way as that. It is the sort of thing that men used to do. 'You must give up your claim to that lady, or else you must fight me.' Now she comes forward and says that she will fight you."

"But, papa, I have no claim."

"Nor probably has she?"

"No; I'm sure she has not. But what does that matter? The horrid thing is that she should say all this to me. I told her that she couldn't know that I was married."

"She merely wanted to make herself disagreeable. If one comes across disagreeable people one has to bear with it. I suppose she was jealous. She had seen you dancing or perhaps talking with the man."

"Oh, yes."

"And in her anger she wanted to fly at some one."

"It is not her I care about, papa."

"What then?"

"If she were to tell George."

"What if she did? You do not mean to say that he would believe her? You do not think that he is jealous?"

She began to perceive that she could not get any available counsel from her father unless she could tell him everything. She must explain to him what evil Lady Susanna had already done; how her sister-in-law had acted as duenna, and had dared to express a suspicion about this very man. And she must tell him that Lord George had desired her not to waltz, and had done so, as she believed, because he had seen her waltzing with Jack De Baron. But all this seemed to her to be impossible. There was nothing which she would not be glad that he knew, if only he could be made to know it all truly. But she did not think that she could tell him what had really happened; and were she to do so, there would be horrid doubts on his mind. "You do not mean to say that he is given to that sort of thing?" asked the Dean, again with a look of anger.

"Oh no,—at least I hope not. Susanna did try to make mischief."

"The d—— she did," said the Dean. Mary almost jumped in her chair, she was so much startled by such a word from her father's mouth. "If he's fool enough to listen to that old cat, he'll make himself a miserable and a contemptible man. Did she say anything to him about this very man?"

"She said something very unpleasant to me, and of course I told George."

"Well?"

"He was all that was kind. He declared that he had no objection to make to Captain De Baron at all. I am sure there was no reason why he should."

"Tush!" exclaimed the Dean, as though any assurance or even any notice of the matter in that direction were quite unnecessary. "And there was an end of that?"

"I think he is a little inclined to be—to be—"

"To be what? You had better tell it all out, Mary."

"Perhaps what you would call strict. He told me not to waltz any more the other day."

"He's a fool," said the Dean angrily.

"Oh no, papa; don't say that. Of course he has a right to think as he likes, and of course I am bound to do as he says."

"He has no experience, no knowledge of the world. Perhaps one of the last things which a man learns is to understand innocence when he sees it." The word innocence was so pleasant to her that she put out her hand and touched his knee. "Take no notice of what that angry woman said to you. Above all, do not drop your acquaintance with this gentleman. You should be too proud to be influenced in any way by such scandal."

"But if she were to speak to George?"

"She will hardly dare. But if she does, that is no affair of yours. You can have nothing to do with it till he shall speak to you."

"You would not tell him?"

"No; I should not even think about it. She is below your notice. If it should be the case that she dares to speak to him, and that he should be weak enough to be moved by what such a creature can say to him, you will, I am sure, have dignity enough to hold your own with him. Tell him that you think too much of his honour as well of your own to make it necessary for him to trouble himself. But he will know that himself, and if he does speak to you, he will speak only in pity for her." All this he said slowly and seriously, looking as she had sometimes seen him look when preaching in the cathedral. And she believed him now as she always believed him then, and was in a great measure comforted.

But she could not but be surprised that her father should so absolutely refuse to entertain the idea that any intimacy between herself and Captain De Baron should be injurious. It gratified her that it should be so, but nevertheless she was surprised. She had endeavoured to examine the question by her own lights, but had failed in answering it. She knew well enough that she liked the man. She had discovered in him the realization of those early dreams. His society was in every respect pleasant to her. He was full of playfulness, and yet always gentle. He was not very clever, but clever enough. She had made the mistake in life,—or rather others had made it for her,—of taking herself too soon from her playthings and devoting herself to the stern reality of a husband. She understood something of this, and liked to think that she might amuse herself innocently with such a one as Jack De Baron. She was sure that she did not love him,—that there was no danger of her loving him; and she was quite confident also that he did not love her. But yet,—yet there had been a doubt on her mind. Innocent as it all was, there might be cause of offence to her husband. It was this thought that had made her sometimes long to be taken away from London and be immured amidst the dullness of Cross Hall. But of such dangers and of such fears her father saw nothing. Her father simply bade her to maintain her own dignity and have her own way. Perhaps her father was right.

On the next day the Dean and his son-in-law went, according to appointment, to Mr. Battle. Mr. Battle received them with his usual bland courtesy, and listened attentively to whatever the two gentlemen had to say. Lawyers who know their business always allow their clients to run out their stories even when knowing that the words so spoken are wasted words. It is the quickest way of arriving at their desired result. Lord George had a good deal to say, because his mind was full of the conviction that he would not for worlds put an obstacle in the way of his brother's heir, if he could be made sure that the child was the heir. He wished for such certainty, and cursed the heavy chance that had laid so grievous a duty on his shoulders.

When he had done, Mr. Battle began. "I think, Lord George, that I have learned most of the particulars."

Lord George started back in his chair. "What particulars?" said the Dean.

"The Marchioness's late husband,—for she doubtless is his Lordship's wife,—was a lunatic."

"A lunatic!" said Lord George.

"We do not quite know when he died, but we believe it was about a month or two before the date at which his Lordship wrote home to say that he was about to be married."

"Then that child cannot be Lord Popenjoy," said the Dean with exultation.

"That's going a little too fast, Mr. Dean. There may have been a divorce."

"There is no such thing in Roman Catholic countries," said the Dean. "Certainly not in Italy."

"I do not quite know," said the lawyer. "Of course we are as yet very much in the dark. I should not wonder if we found that there had been two marriages. All this is what we have got to find out. The lady certainly lived in great intimacy with your brother before her first husband died."

"How do you know anything about it?" asked Lord George.

"I happened to have heard the name of the Marchese Luigi, and I knew where to apply for information."

"We did not mean that any inquiry should be made so suddenly," said Lord George angrily.

"It was for the best," said the Dean.

"Certainly for the best," said the unruffled lawyer. "I would now recommend that I may be commissioned to send out my own confidential clerk to learn all the circumstances of the case; and that I should inform Mr. Stokes that I am going to do so, on your instructions, Lord George." Lord George shivered. "I think we should even offer to give his Lordship time to send an agent with my clerk if he pleases to do so, or to send one separately at the same time, or to take any other step that he may please. It is clearly your duty, my Lord, to have the inquiry made."

"Your manifest duty," said the Dean, unable to restrain his triumph.

Lord George pleaded for delay, and before he left the lawyer's chambers almost quarrelled with his father-in-law; but before he did leave them he had given the necessary instructions.

Chapter XXIX.

Mr. Houghton Wants A Glass Of Sherry.

Lord George, when he got out of the lawyer's office with his father-in-law, expressed himself as being very angry at what had been done. While discussing the matter within, in the presence of Mr. Battle, he had been unable to withstand the united energies of the Dean and the lawyer, but, nevertheless, even while he had yielded, he had felt that he was being driven.

"I don't think he was at all justified in making any inquiry," he said, as soon as he found himself in the Square.

"My dear George," replied the Dean, "the quicker this can be done the better."

"An agent should only act in accordance with his instructions."

"Without disputing that, my dear fellow, I cannot but say that I am glad to have learned so much."

"And I am very sorry."

"We both mean the same thing, George."

"I don't think we do," said Lord George, who was determined to be angry.

"You are sorry that it should be so,—and so am I." The triumph which had sat in the Dean's eye when he heard the news in the lawyer's chambers almost belied this latter assertion. "But I certainly am glad to be on the track as soon as possible, if there is a track which it is our duty to follow."

"I didn't like that man at all," said Lord George.

"I neither like him nor dislike him; but I believe him to be honest, and I know him to be clever. He will find out the truth for us."

"And when it turns out that Brotherton was legally married to the woman, what will the world think of me then?"

"The world will think that you have done your duty. There can be no question about it, George. Whether it be agreeable or disagreeable, it must be done. Could you have brought yourself to have thrown the burden of doing this upon your own child, perhaps some five-and-twenty years hence, when it may be done so much easier now by yourself."

"I have no child," said Lord George.

"But you will have." The Dean, as he said this, could not keep himself from looking too closely into his son-in-law's face. He was most anxious for the birth of that grandson who was to be made a Marquis by his own energies.

"God knows. Who can say?"

"At any rate there is that child at Manor Cross. If he be not the legitimate heir, is it not better for him that the matter should be settled now than when he may have lived twenty years in expectation of the title and property?" The Dean said much more than this, urging the propriety of what had been done, but he did not succeed in quieting Lord George's mind.

That same day the Dean told the whole story to his daughter, perhaps in his eagerness adding something to what he had heard from the lawyer. "Divorces in Roman Catholic countries," he said, "are quite impossible. I believe they are never granted, except for State purposes. There may be some new civil law, but I don't think it; and then, if the man was an acknowledged lunatic, it must have been impossible."

"But how could the Marquis be so foolish, papa?"

"Ah, that is what we do not understand. But it will come out. You may be sure it will all come out. Why did he come home to England and bring them with him? And why just at this time? Why did he not communicate his first marriage; and if not that, why the second? He probably did not intend at first to put his child forward as Lord Popenjoy, but has become subsequently bold. The woman, perhaps, has gradually learned the facts and insisted on making the claim for her child. She may gradually have become stronger than he. He may have thought that by coming here and declaring the boy to be his heir, he would put down suspicion by the very boldness of his assertion. Who can say? But these are the facts, and they are sufficient to justify us in demanding that everything shall be brought to light." Then for the first time, he asked her what immediate hope there was that Lord George might have an heir. She tried to laugh, then blushed; then wept a tear or two, and muttered something which he failed to hear. "There is time enough for all that, Mary," he said, with his pleasantest smile, and then left her.

Lord George did not return home till late in the afternoon. He went first to Mrs. Houghton's house, and told her nearly everything. But he told it in such a way as to make her understand that his strongest feeling at the present moment was one of anger against the Dean.

"Of course, George," she said, for she always called him George now,—"The Dean will try to have it all his own way."

"I am almost sorry that I ever mentioned my brother's name to him."

"She, I suppose, is ambitious," said Mrs. Houghton. 'She,' was intended to signify Mary.

"No. To do Mary justice, it is not her fault. I don't think she cares for it."

"I dare say she would like to be a Marchioness as well as any one else. I know I should."

"You might have been," he said, looking tenderly into her face.

"I wonder how I should have borne all this. You say that she is indifferent. I should have been so anxious on your behalf,—to see you installed in your rights!"

"I have no rights. There is my brother."

"Yes; but as the heir. She has none of the feeling about you that I have, George." Then she put out her hand to him, which he took and held. "I begin to think that I was wrong. I begin to know that I was wrong. We could have lived at any rate."

"It is too late," he said, still holding her hand.

"Yes,—it is too late. I wonder whether you will ever understand the sort of struggle which I had to go through, and the feeling of duty which overcame me at last. Where should we have lived?"

"At Cross Hall, I suppose."

"And if there had been children, how should we have brought them up?" She did not blush as she asked the question, but he did. "And yet I wish that I had been braver. I think I should have suited you better than she."

"She is as good as gold," he said, moved by a certain loyalty which, though it was not sufficient absolutely to protect her from wrong, was too strong to endure to hear her reproached.

"Do not tell me of her goodness," said Mrs. Houghton, jumping up from her seat. "I do not want to hear of her goodness. Tell me of my goodness. Does she love you as I do? Does she make you the hero of her thoughts? She has no idea of any hero. She would think more of Jack De Baron whirling round the room with her than of your position in the world, or of his, or even of her own." He winced visibly when he heard Jack De Baron's name. "You need not be afraid," she continued, "for though she is, as you say, as good as gold, she knows nothing about love. She took you when you came because it suited the ambition of the Dean,—as she would have taken anything else that he provided for her."

"I believe she loves me," he said, having in his heart of hearts, at the moment, much more solicitude in regard to his absent wife than to the woman who was close to his feet and was flattering him to the top of his bent.

"And her love, such as it is, is sufficient for you?"

"She is my wife."

"Yes; because I allowed it; because I thought it wrong to subject your future life to the poverty which I should have brought with me. Do you think there was no sacrifice then?"

"But, Adelaide;—it is so."

"Yes, it is so. But what does it all mean? The time is gone by when men, or women either, were too qualmish and too queasy to admit the truth even to themselves. Of course you are married, and so am I; but marriage does not alter the heart. I did not cease to love you because I would not marry you. You could not cease to love me merely because I refused you. When I acknowledged to myself that Mr. Houghton's income was necessary to me, I did not become enamoured of him. Nor I suppose did you when you found the same as to Miss Lovelace's money."

Upon this he also jumped up from his seat, and stood before her. "I will not have even you say that I married my wife for her money."

"How was it then, George? I am not blaming you for doing what I did as well as you."

"I should blame myself. I should feel myself to be degraded."

"Why so? It seems to me that I am bolder than you. I can look the cruelties of the world in the face, and declare openly how I will meet them. I did marry Mr. Houghton for his money, and of course he knew it. Is it to be supposed that he or any human being could have thought that I married him for love? I make his house comfortable for him as far as I can, and am civil to his friends, and look my best at his table. I hope he is satisfied with his bargain; but I cannot do more. I cannot wear him in my heart. Nor, George, do I believe that you in your heart can ever wear Mary Lovelace!" But he did,—only that he thought that he had space there for two, and that in giving habitation to this second love he was adding at any rate to the excitements of his life. "Tell me, George," said the woman, laying her hand upon his breast, "is it she or I that have a home there?"

"I will not say that I do not love my wife," he said.

"No; you are afraid. The formalities of the world are so much more to you than to me! Sit down, George. Oh, George!" Then she was on her knees at his feet, hiding her face upon her hands, while his arms were almost necessarily thrown over her and embracing her. The lady was convulsed with sobs, and he was thinking how it would be with him and her should the door be opened and some pair of eyes see them as they were. But her ears were sharp in spite of her sobs. There was the fall of a foot on the stairs which she heard long before it reached him, and, in a moment, she was in her chair. He looked at her, and there was no trace of a tear. "It's Houghton," she said, putting her finger up to her mouth with almost a comic gesture. There was a smile in her eyes, and a little mockery of fear in the trembling of her hand and the motion of her lips. To him it seemed to be tragic enough. He had to assume to this gentleman whom he had been injuring a cordial friendly manner,—and thus to lie to him. He had to make pretences, and at a moment's notice to feign himself something very different from what he was. Had the man come a little more quickly, had the husband caught him with the wife at his knees, nothing could have saved him and his own wife from utter misery. So he felt it to be, and the feeling almost overwhelmed him. His heart palpitated with emotion as the wronged husband's hand was on the door. She, the while, was as thoroughly composed as a stage heroine. But she had flattered him and pretended to love him, and it did not occur to him that he ought to be angry with her. "Who would ever think of seeing you at this time of day?" said Mrs. Houghton.

"Well, no; I'm going back to the club in a few minutes. I had to come up to Piccadilly to have my hair cut!"

"Your hair cut!"

"Honour bright! Nothing upsets me so much as having my hair cut. I'm going to ring for a glass of sherry. By the bye, Lord George, a good many of them are talking at the club about young Popenjoy."

"What are they saying?" Lord George felt that he must open his mouth, but did not wish to talk to this man, and especially did not wish to talk about his own affairs.

"Of course I know nothing about it; but surely the way Brotherton has come back is very odd. I used to be very fond of your brother, you know. There was nobody her father used to swear by so much as him. But, by George, I don't know what to make of it now. Nobody has seen the Marchioness!"

"I have not seen her," said Lord George; "but she is there all the same for that."

"Nobody doubts that she's there. She's there, safe enough. And the boy is there too. We're all quite sure of that. But you know the Marquis of Brotherton is somebody."

"I hope so," said Lord George.

"And when he brings his wife home people will expect,—will expect to know something about it;—eh?" All this was said with an intention of taking Lord George's part in a question which was already becoming one of interest to the public. It was hinted here and there that there was "a screw loose" about this young Popenjoy, who had just been brought from Italy, and that Lord George would have to look to it. Of course they who were connected with Brothershire were more prone to talk of it than others, and Mr. Houghton, who had heard and said a good deal about it, thought that he was only being civil to Lord George in seeming to take part against the Marquis.

But Lord George felt it to be matter of offence that any outsider should venture to talk about his family. "If people would only confine themselves to subjects with which they are acquainted, it would be very much better," he said;—and then almost immediately took his leave.

"That's all regular nonsense, you know," Mr. Houghton said as soon as he was alone with his wife. "Of course people are talking about it. Your father says that Brotherton must be mad."

"That's no reason why you should come and tell Lord George what people say. You never have any tact."

"Of course I'm wrong; I always am," said the husband, swallowing his glass of sherry and then taking his departure.

Lord George was now in a very uneasy state of mind. He intended to be cautious,—had intended even to be virtuous and self-denying; and yet, in spite of his intentions, he had fallen into such a condition of things with Mr. Houghton's wife, that were the truth to be known, he would be open to most injurious proceedings. To him the love affair with another man's wife was more embarrassing even than pleasant. Its charm did not suffice to lighten for him the burden of the wickedness. He had certain inklings of complaint in his own mind against his own wife, but he felt that his own hands should be perfectly clean before he could deal with those inklings magisterially and maritally. How would he look were she to turn upon him and ask him as to his own conduct with Adelaide Houghton? And then into what a sea of trouble had he not already fallen in this matter of his brother's marriage? His first immediate duty was that of writing to his elder sister, and he expressed himself to her in strong language. After telling her all that he had heard from the lawyer, he spoke of himself and of the Dean. "It will make me very unhappy," he wrote. "Do you remember what Hamlet says:

'O, cursed spite,
That ever I was born to set it right!'

"I feel like that altogether. I want to get nothing by it. No man ever less begrudged to his elder brother than I do all that belongs to him. Though he has himself treated me badly, I would support him in anything for the sake of the family. At this moment I most heartily wish that the child may be Lord Popenjoy. The matter will destroy all my happiness perhaps for the next ten years;—perhaps for ever. And I cannot but think that the Dean has interfered in a most unjustifiable manner. He drives me on, so that I almost feel that I shall be forced to quarrel with him. With him it is manifestly personal ambition, and not duty." There was much more of it in the same strain, but at the same time an acknowledgment that he had now instructed the Dean's lawyer to make the inquiry.

Lady Sarah's answer was perhaps more judicious; and as it was shorter it shall be given entire.

"Cross Hall, May 10, 187—.

"MY DEAR GEORGE,—Of course it is a sad thing to us all that this terrible inquiry should be forced upon us;— and more grievous to you than to us, as you must take the active part in it. But this is a manifest duty, and duties are seldom altogether pleasant. All that you say as to yourself,—which I know to be absolutely true,—must at any rate make your conscience clear in the matter. It is not for your sake nor for our sake that this is to be done, but for the sake of the family at large, and to prevent the necessity of future lawsuits which would be ruinous to the property. If the child be legitimate, let that, in God's name, be proclaimed so loud that no one shall hereafter be able to cast a doubt upon the fact. To us it must be matter of deepest sorrow that our brother's child and the future head of our family should have been born under circumstances which, at the best, must still be disgraceful. But, although that is so, it will be equally our duty to acknowledge his rights to the full, if they be his rights. Though the son of the widow of a lunatic foreigner, still if the law says that he is Brotherton's heir, it is for us to render the difficulties in his way as light as possible. But that we may do so, we must know what he is.

"Of course you find the Dean to be pushing and perhaps a little vulgar. No doubt with him the chief feeling is one of personal ambition. But in his way he is wise, and I do not know that in this matter he has done anything which had better have been left undone. He believes that the child is not legitimate;—and so in my heart do I.

"You must remember that my dear mother is altogether on Brotherton's side. The feeling that there should be an heir is so much to her, and the certainty that the boy is at any rate her grandson, that she cannot endure that a doubt should be expressed. Of course this does not tend to make our life pleasant down here. Poor dear mamma! Of course we do all we can to comfort her.

"Your affectionate sister,

"SARAH GERMAIN."

Chapter XXX.

The Dean Is Very Busy.

A week had passed away and nothing had as yet been heard from the Marquis, nor had Mr. Battle's confidential clerk as yet taken his departure for Italy, when Mrs. Montacute Jones called one day in Munster Court. Lady George had not seen her new old friend since the night of the ball to which she had not gone, but had received more than one note respecting her absence on that occasion, and various other little matters. Why did not Lady George come and lunch; and why did not Lady George come and drive? Lady George was a little afraid that there was a conspiracy about her in reference to Captain De Baron, and that Mrs. Montacute Jones was one of the conspirators. If so Adelaide Houghton was certainly another. It had been very pleasant. When she examined herself about this man, as she endeavoured to do, she declared that it had been as innocent as pleasant. She did not really believe that either Adelaide Houghton or Mrs. Montacute Jones had intended to do mischief. Mischief, such as the alienation of her own affections from her husband, she regarded as quite out of the question. She would not even admit to herself that it was possible that she should fall into such a pit as that. But there were other dangers;

and those friends of hers would indeed be dangerous if they brought her into any society that made her husband jealous. Therefore, though she liked Mrs. Montacute Jones very much, she had avoided the old lady lately, knowing that something would be said about Jack De Baron, and not quite confident as to her own answers.

And now Mrs. Montacute Jones had come to her. "My dear Lady George," she said, "where on earth have you been? Are you going to cut me? If so, tell me at once."

"Oh, Mrs. Jones," said Lady George, kissing her, "how can you ask such a question?"

"Because you know it requires two to play at that game, and I'm not going to be cut." Mrs. Montacute Jones was a stout built but very short old lady, with grey hair curled in precise rolls down her face, with streaky cheeks, giving her a look of extreme good health, and very bright grey eyes. She was always admirably dressed, so well dressed that her enemies accused her of spending enormous sums on her toilet. She was very old,— some people said eighty, adding probably not more than ten years to her age,—very enthusiastic, particularly in reference to her friends; very fond of gaiety, and very charitable. "Why didn't you come to my ball?"

"Lord George doesn't care about balls," said Mary, laughing.

"Come, come! Don't try and humbug me. It had been all arranged that you should come when he went to bed. Hadn't it now?"

"Something had been said about it."

"A good deal had been said about it, and he had agreed. Are you going to tell me that he won't go out with you, and yet dislikes your going out without him? Is he such a Bluebeard as that?"

"He's not a Bluebeard at all, Mrs. Jones."

"I hope not. There has been something about that German Baroness;—hasn't there?"

"Oh dear no."

"I heard that there was. She came and took you and the brougham all about London. And there was a row with Lady Selina. I heard of it."

"But that had nothing to do with my going to your party."

"Well, no; why should it? She's a nasty woman, that Baroness Banmann. If we can't get on here in England without German Baronesses and American she doctors, we are in a bad way. You shouldn't have let them drag you into that lot. Women's rights! Women are quite able to hold their own without such trash as that. I'm told she's in debt everywhere, and can't pay a shilling. I hope they'll lock her up."

"She is nothing to me, Mrs. Jones."

"I hope not. What was it then? I know there was something. He doesn't object to Captain De Baron; does he?"

"Object to him! Why should he object to Captain De Baron?"

"I don't know why. Men do take such fancies into their heads. You are not going to give up dancing;—are you?"

"Not altogether. I'm not sure that I care for it very much."

"Oh, Lady George; where do you expect to go to?" Mary could not keep herself from laughing, though she was at the same time almost inclined to be angry with the old lady's interference. "I should have said that I didn't know a young person in the world fonder of dancing than you are. Perhaps he objects to it."

"He doesn't like my waltzing," said Mary, with a blush. On former occasions she had almost made up her mind to confide her troubles to this old woman, and now the occasion seemed so suitable that she could not keep herself from telling so much as that.

"Oh!" said Mrs. Montacute Jones. "That's it! I knew there was something. My dear, he's a goose, and you ought to tell him so."

"Couldn't you tell him," said Mary, laughing.

"Would do it in half a minute, and think nothing of it!"

"Pray, don't. He wouldn't like it at all."

"My dear, you shouldn't be afraid of him. I'm not going to preach up rebellion against husbands. I'm the last woman in London to do that. I know the comfort of a quiet house as well as any one, and that two people can't get along easy together unless there is a good deal of give and take. But it doesn't do to give up everything. What does he say about it?"

"He says he doesn't like it."

"What would he say if you told him you didn't like his going to his club."

"He wouldn't go."

"Nonsense! It's being a dog in the manger, because he doesn't care for it himself. I should have it out with him,—nicely and pleasantly. Just tell him that you're fond of it, and ask him to change his mind. I can't bear anybody interfering to put down the innocent pleasures of young people. A man like that just opens his mouth and speaks a word, and takes away the whole pleasure of a young woman's season! You've got my card for the 10th of June?"

"Oh yes,—I've got it."

"And I shall expect you to come. It's only going to be a small affair. Get him to bring you if you can, and you do as I bid you. Just have it out with him,—nicely and quietly. Nobody hates a row so much as I do, but people oughtn't to be trampled on."

All this had considerable effect upon Lady George. She quite agreed with Mrs. Jones that people ought not to be trampled on. Her father had never trampled on her. From him there had been very little positive ordering as to what she might and what she might not do. And yet she had been only a child when living with her father. Now she was a married woman, and the mistress of her own house. She was quite sure that were she to ask her father, the Dean would say that such a prohibition as this was absurd. Of course she could not ask her father. She would not appeal from her husband to him. But it was a hardship, and she almost made up her mind that she would request him to revoke the order.

Then she was very much troubled by a long letter from the Baroness Banmann. The Baroness was going to bring an action jointly against Lady Selina Protest and Miss Mildmay, whom the reader will know as Aunt Ju; and informed Lady George that she was to be summoned as a witness. This was for a while a grievous affliction to her. "I know nothing about it," she said to her husband, "I only just went there once because Miss Mildmay asked me."

"It was a very foolish thing for her to do."

"And I was foolish, perhaps; but what can I say about it? I don't know anything."

"You shouldn't have bought those other tickets."

"How could I refuse when the woman asked for such a trifle?"

"Then you took her to Miss Mildmay's."

"She would get into the brougham, and I couldn't get rid of her. Hadn't I better write and tell her that I know nothing about it?" But to this Lord George objected, requesting her altogether to hold her peace on the subject, and never even to speak about it to anyone. He was not good humoured with her, and this was clearly no occasion for asking him about the waltzing. Indeed, just at present he rarely was in a good humour, being much troubled in his mind on the great Popenjoy question.

At this time the Dean was constantly up in town, running backwards and forwards between London and Brotherton, prosecuting his enquiry and spending a good deal of his time at Mr. Battle's offices. In doing all this he by no means acted in perfect concert with Lord George, nor did he often stay or even dine at the house in Munster Court. There had been no quarrel, but he found that Lord George was not cordial with him, and therefore placed himself at the hotel in Suffolk Street. "Why doesn't papa come here as he is in town?" Mary said to her husband.

"I don't know why he comes to town at all," replied her husband.

"I suppose he comes because he has business, or because he likes it. I shouldn't think of asking why he comes; but as he is here, I wish he wouldn't stay at a nasty dull hotel after all that was arranged."

"You may be sure he knows what he likes best," said Lord George sulkily. That allusion to "an arrangement" had not served to put him in a good humour.

Mary had known well why her father was so much in London, and had in truth known also why he did not come to Munster Court. She could perceive that her father and husband were drifting into unfriendly relations, and greatly regretted it. In her heart she took her father's part. She was not keen as he was in this matter of the little Popenjoy, being restrained by a feeling that it would not become her to be over anxious for her own elevation or for the fall of others; but she had always sympathised with her father in everything, and therefore she sympathised with him in this. And then there was gradually growing upon her a conviction that her father was the stronger man of the two, the more reasonable, and certainly the kinder. She had thoroughly understood when the house was furnished, very much at the Dean's expense, that he was to be a joint occupant in it when it might suit him to be in London. He himself had thought less about this, having rather submitted to the suggestion as an excuse for his own liberality than contemplated any such final arrangement. But Lord George remembered it. The house would certainly be open to him should he choose to come;—but Lord George would not press it.

Mr. Stokes had thought it proper to go in person to Manor Cross, in order that he might receive instructions from the Marquis. "Upon my word, Mr. Stokes," said the Marquis, "only that I would not seem to be uncourteous to you I should feel disposed to say that this interview can do no good."

"It is a very serious matter, my Lord."

"It is a very serious annoyance, certainly, that my own brother and sisters should turn against me, and give me all this trouble because I have chosen to marry a foreigner. It is simply an instance of that pigheaded English blindness which makes us think that everything outside our own country is or ought to be given up to the devil. My sisters are very religious, and, I daresay, very good women. But they are quite willing to think that I and my wife ought to be damned because we talk Italian, and that my son ought to be disinherited because he was not baptised in an English church. They have got this stupid story into their heads, and they must do as they please about it. I will have no hand in it. I will take care that there shall be no difficulty in my son's way when I die."

"That will be right, of course, my Lord."

"I know where all this comes from. My brother, who is an idiot, has married the daughter of a vulgar clergyman, who thinks in his ignorance that he can make his grandson, if he has one, an English nobleman. He'll spend his money and he'll burn his fingers, and I don't care how much money he spends or how much he burns his hands. I don't suppose his purse is so very long but that he may come to the bottom of it." This was nearly all that passed between Mr. Stokes and the Marquis. Mr. Stokes then went back to town and gave Mr. Battle to understand that nothing was to be done on their side.

The Dean was very anxious that the confidential clerk should be dispatched, and at one time almost thought that he would go himself. "Better not, Mr. Dean. Everybody would know," said Mr. Battle.

"And I should intend everybody to know," said the Dean. "Do you suppose that I am doing anything that I'm ashamed of."

"But being a dignitary—" began Mr. Battle.

"What has that to do with it? A dignitary, as you call it, is not to see his child robbed of her rights. I only want to find the truth, and I should never take shame to myself in looking for that by honest means." But Mr. Battle prevailed, persuading the Dean that the confidential clerk, even though he confined himself to honest means, would reach his point more certainly than a Dean of the Church of England.

But still there was delay. Mr. Stokes did not take his journey down to Brotherton quite as quickly as he perhaps might have done, and then there was a prolonged correspondence carried on through an English lawyer settled at Leghorn. But at last the man was sent. "I think we know this," said Mr. Battle to the Dean on the day before the man started, "there were certainly two marriages. One of them took place as much as five years ago, and the other after his lordship had written to his brother."

"Then the first marriage must have been nothing," said the Dean.

"It does not follow. It may have been a legal marriage, although the parties chose to confirm it by a second ceremony."

"But when did the man Luigi die?"

"And where and how? That is what we have got to find out. I shouldn't wonder if we found that he had been for years a lunatic."

Almost all this the Dean communicated to Lord George, being determined that his son-in-law should be seen to act in co-operation with him. They met occasionally in Mr. Battle's chambers, and sometimes by appointment in Munster Court. "It is essentially necessary that you should know what is being done," said the Dean to his son-in-law. Lord George fretted and fumed, and expressed an opinion that as the matter had been put into a lawyer's hands it had better be left there. But the Dean had very much his own way.

Chapter XXXI.

The Marquis Migrates To London.

Soon after Mr. Stokes' visit there was a great disturbance at Manor Cross, whether caused or not by that event no one was able to say. The Marquis and all the family were about to proceed to London. The news first reached Cross Hall through Mrs. Toff, who still kept up friendly relations with a portion of the English establishment at the great house. There probably was no idea of maintaining a secret on the subject. The Marquis and his wife, with Lord Popenjoy and the servants, could not have had themselves carried up to town without the knowledge of all Brotherton, nor was there any adequate reason for supposing that secrecy was desired. Nevertheless Mrs. Toff made a great deal of the matter, and the ladies at Cross Hall were not without a certain perturbed interest as though in a mystery. It was first told to Lady Sarah, for Mrs. Toff was quite aware of the position of things, and knew that the old Marchioness herself was not to be regarded as being on their side. "Yes, my Lady, it's quite true," said Mrs. Toff. "The horses is ordered for next Friday." This was said on the previous Saturday, so that considerable time was allowed for the elucidation of the mystery. "And the things is already being packed, and her Ladyship,—that is, if she is her

Ladyship,—is taking every dress and every rag as she brought with her."

"Where are they going to, Toff?—Not to the Square?" Now the Marquis of Brotherton had an old family house in Cavendish Square, which, however, had been shut up for the last ten or fifteen years, but was still known as the family house by all the adherents of the family.

"No, my Lady. I did hear from one of the servants that they are going to Scumberg's Hotel, in Albemarle Street."

Then Lady Sarah told the news to her mother. The poor old lady felt that she was ill-used. She had been at any rate true to her eldest son, had always taken his part during his absence by scolding her daughters whenever an allusion was made to the family at Manor Cross, and had almost worshipped him when he would come to her on Sunday. And now he was going off to London without saying a word to her of the journey. "I don't believe that Toff knows anything about it," she said. "Toff is a nasty, meddling creature, and I wish she had not come here at all." The management of the Marchioness under these circumstances was very difficult, but Lady Sarah was a woman who allowed no difficulty to crush her. She did not expect the world to be very easy. She went on with her constant needle, trying to comfort her mother as she worked. At this time the Marchioness had almost brought herself to quarrel with her younger son, and would say very hard things about him and about the Dean. She had more than once said that Mary was a "nasty sly thing," and had expressed herself as greatly aggrieved by that marriage. All this came of course from the Marquis, and was known by her daughters to come from the Marquis; and yet the Marchioness had never as yet been allowed to see either her daughter-in-law or Popenjoy.

On the following day her son came to her when the three sisters were at church in the afternoon. On these occasions he would stay for a quarter of an hour, and would occupy the greater part of the time in abusing the Dean and Lord George.

But on this day she could not refrain from asking him a question. "Are you going up to London, Brotherton?"

"What makes you ask?"

"Because they tell me so. Sarah says that the servants are talking about it."

"I wish Sarah had something to do better than listening to the servants?"

"But you are going?"

"If you want to know, I believe we shall go up to town for a few days. Popenjoy ought to see a dentist, and I want to do a few things. Why the deuce shouldn't I go up to London as well as any one else?"

"Of course, if you wish it."

"To tell you the truth, I don't much wish anything, except to get out of this cursed country again."

"Don't say that, Brotherton. You are an Englishman."

"I am ashamed to say I am. I wish with all my heart that I had been born a Chinese or a Red Indian." This he said, not in furtherance of any peculiar cosmopolitan proclivities, but because the saying of it would vex his mother. "What am I to think of the country, when the moment I get here I am hounded by all my own family because I choose to live after my own fashion and not after theirs?"

"I haven't hounded you."

"No. You might possibly get more by being on good terms with me than bad. And so might they if they knew it. I'll be even with Master George before I've done with him; and I'll be even with that parson, too, who still smells of the stables. I'll lead him a dance that will about ruin him. And as for his daughter—"

"It wasn't I got up the marriage, Brotherton."

"I don't care who got it up. But I can have enquiries made as well as another person. I am not very fond of spies; but if other people use spies, so can I too. That young woman is no better than she ought to be. The Dean, I daresay, knows it; but he shall know that I know it. And Master George shall know what I think about it. As there is to be war, he shall know what it is to have war. She has got a lover of her own already, and everybody who knows them is talking about it."

"Oh, Brotherton!"

"And she is going in for women's rights! George has made a nice thing of it for himself. He has to live on the Dean's money, so that he doesn't dare to call his soul his own. And yet he's fool enough to send a lawyer to me to tell me that my wife is a ——, and my son a ——!" He made use of very plain language, so that the poor old woman was horrified and aghast and dumbfounded. And as he spoke the words there was a rage in his eyes worse than anything she had seen before. He was standing with his back to the fire, which was burning though the weather was warm, and the tails of his coat were hanging over his arms as he kept his hands in his pockets. He was generally quiescent in his moods, and apt to express his anger in sarcasm rather than in outspoken language; but now he was so much moved that he was unable not to give vent to his feelings. As the Marchioness looked at him, shaking with fear, there came into her distracted mind some vague idea of Cain and Abel, though had she collected her thoughts she would have been far from telling herself that her eldest son was Cain. "He thinks," continued the Marquis, "that because I have lived abroad I shan't mind that sort of thing. I wonder how he'll feel when I tell him the truth about his wife. I mean to do it;—and what the Dean will think when I use a little plain language about his daughter. I mean to do that too. I shan't mince matters. I suppose you have heard of Captain De Baron, mother?"

Now the Marchioness unfortunately had heard of Captain De Baron. Lady Susanna had brought the tidings down to Cross Hall. Had Lady Susanna really believed that her sister-in-law was wickedly entertaining a lover, there would have been some reticence in her mode of alluding to so dreadful a subject. The secret would have been confided to Lady Sarah in awful conclave, and some solemn warning would have been conveyed to Lord George, with a prayer that he would lose no time in withdrawing the unfortunate young woman from evil influences. But Lady Susanna had entertained no such fear. Mary was young, and foolish, and fond of pleasure. Hard as was this woman in her manner, and disagreeable as she made herself, yet she could, after a fashion, sympathise with the young wife. She had spoken of Captain De Baron with disapprobation certainly, but had not spoken of him as a fatal danger. And she had spoken also of the Baroness Banmann and Mary's folly in going to the Institute. The old Marchioness had heard of these things, and now, when she heard further of them from her son, she almost believed all that he told her. "Don't be hard upon poor George," she said.

"I give as I get, mother. I'm not one of those who return good for evil. Had he left me alone, I should have left him alone. As it is, I rather think I shall be hard upon poor George. Do you suppose that all Brotherton hasn't heard already what they are doing;—that there is a man or a woman in the county who doesn't know that my own brother is questioning the legitimacy of my own son? And then you ask me not to be hard."

"It isn't my doing, Brotherton."

"But those three girls have their hand in it. That's what they call charity! That's what they go to church for!"

All this made the poor old Marchioness very ill. Before her son left her she was almost prostrate; and yet, to the end, he did not spare her. But as he left he said one word which apparently was intended to comfort her. "Perhaps Popenjoy had better be brought here for you to see before he is taken up to town." There had been a promise made before that the child should be brought to the hall to bless his grandmother. On this occasion she had been too much horrified and overcome by what had been said to urge her request; but when the proposition was renewed by him of course she assented.

Popenjoy's visit to Cross Hall was arranged with a good deal of state, and was made on the following Tuesday. On the Monday there came a message to say that the child should be brought up at twelve on the following day. The Marquis was not coming himself, and the child would of course be inspected by all the ladies. At noon they were assembled in the drawing-room; but they were kept there waiting for half an hour, during which the Marchioness repeatedly expressed her conviction that now, at the last moment, she was to be robbed of the one great desire of her heart. "He won't let him come because he's so angry with George," she said, sobbing.

"He wouldn't have sent a message yesterday, mother," said Lady Amelia, "if he hadn't meant to send him."

"You are all so very unkind to him," ejaculated the Marchioness.

But at half-past twelve the cortège appeared. The child was brought up in a perambulator which had at first been pushed by the under-nurse, an Italian, and accompanied by the upper-nurse, who was of course an Italian also. With them had been sent one of the Englishmen to show the way. Perhaps the two women had been somewhat ill-treated, as no true idea of the distance had been conveyed to them; and though they had now been some weeks at Manor Cross, they had never been half so far from the house. Of course the labour of the perambulator had soon fallen to the man; but the two nurses, who had been forced to walk a mile, had thought that they would never come to the end of their journey. When they did arrive they were full of plaints, which, however, no one could understand. But Popenjoy was at last brought into the hall.

"My darling," said the Marchioness, putting out both her arms. But Popenjoy, though a darling, screamed frightfully beneath his heap of clothes.

"You had better let him come into the room, mamma," said Lady Susanna. Then the nurse carried him in, and one or two of his outer garments were taken from him.

"Dear me, how black he is!" said Lady Susanna.

The Marchioness turned upon her daughter in great anger. "The Germains were always dark," she said. "You're dark yourself,—quite as black as he is. My darling!"

She made another attempt to take the boy; but the nurse with voluble eloquence explained something which of course none of them understood. The purport of her speech was an assurance that "Tavo," as she most unceremoniously called the child whom no Germain thought of naming otherwise than as Popenjoy, never would go to any "foreigner." The nurse therefore held him up to be looked at for two minutes while he still screamed, and then put him back into his covering raiments. "He is very black," said Lady Sarah severely.

"So are some people's hearts," said the Marchioness with a vigour for which her daughters had hardly given her credit. This, however, was borne without a murmur by the three sisters.

On the Friday the whole family, including all the Italian servants, migrated to London, and it certainly was the case that the lady took with her all her clothes and everything that she had brought with her. Toff had been quite right, there. And when it came to be known by the younger ladies at Cross Hall that Toff had been right, they argued from the fact that their brother had concealed something of the truth when saying that he intended to go up to London only for a few days. There had been three separate carriages, and Toff was almost sure that the Italian lady had carried off more than she had brought with her, so exuberant had been the luggage. It was not long before Toff effected an entrance into the house, and brought away a report that very many things were missing. "The two little gilt cream-jugs is gone," she said to Lady Sarah, "and the minitshur with the pearl settings out of the yellow drawing-room!" Lady Sarah explained that as these things were the property of her brother, he or his wife might of course take them away if so pleased. "She's got 'em unbeknownst to my Lord, my Lady," said Toff, shaking her head. "I could only just scurry through with half an eye; but when I comes to look there will be more, I warrant you, my Lady."

The Marquis had expressed so much vehement dislike of everything about his English home, and it had become so generally understood that his Italian wife hated the place, that everybody agreed that they would not come back. Why should they? What did they get by living there? The lady had not been outside the house a dozen times, and only twice beyond the park gate. The Marquis took no share in any county or any country pursuit. He went to no man's house and received no visitors. He would not see the tenants when they came to him, and had not even returned a visit except Mr. De Baron's. Why had he come there at all? That was the question which all the Brothershire people asked of each other, and which no one could answer. Mr. Price suggested that it was just devilry,—to make everybody unhappy. Mrs. Toff thought that it was the woman's doing,— because she wanted to steal silver mugs, miniatures, and such like treasures. Mr. Waddy, the vicar of the parish, said that it was "a trial," having probably some idea in his own mind that the Marquis had been sent home by Providence as a sort of precious blister which would purify all concerned in him by counter irritation. The old Marchioness still conceived that it had been brought about that a grandmother might take delight in the presence of her grandchild. Dr. Pountner said that it was impudence. But the Dean was of opinion that it had been deliberately planned with the view of passing off a supposititious child upon the property and title. The Dean, however, kept his opinion very much to himself.

Of course tidings of the migration were sent to Munster Court. Lady Sarah wrote to her brother, and the Dean wrote to his daughter. "What shall you do, George? Shall you go and see him?"

"I don't know what I shall do?"

"Ought I to go?"

"Certainly not. You could only call on her, and she has not even seen my mother and sisters. When I was there he would not introduce me to her, though he sent for the child. I suppose I had better go. I do not want to quarrel with him if I can help it."

"You have offered to do everything together with him, if only he would let you."

"I must say that your father has driven me on in a manner which Brotherton would be sure to resent."

"Papa has done everything from a sense of duty, George."

"Perhaps so. I don't know how that is. It is very hard sometimes to divide a sense of duty from one's own interest. But it has made me very miserable,—very wretched, indeed."

"Oh George; is it my fault?"

"No; not your fault. If there is one thing worse to me than another, it is the feeling of being divided from my own family. Brotherton has behaved badly to me."

"Very badly."

"And yet I would give anything to be on good terms with him. I think I shall go and call. He is at an hotel in Albemarle Street. I have done nothing to deserve ill of him, if he knew all."

It should, of course, be understood that Lord George did not at all know the state of his brother's mind towards him, except as it had been exhibited at that one interview which had taken place between them at Manor Cross. He was aware that in every conversation which he had had with the lawyers,—both with Mr. Battle and Mr. Stokes,—he had invariably expressed himself as desirous of establishing the legitimacy of the boy's birth. If Mr. Stokes had repeated to his brother what he had said, and had done him the justice of explaining that in all that he did he was simply desirous of performing his duty to the family, surely his brother would not be angry with him! At any rate it would not suit him to be afraid of his brother, and he went to the hotel. After being kept waiting in the hall for about ten minutes, the Italian courier came down to him. The Marquis at the present moment was not dressed, and Lord George did not like being kept waiting. Would Lord George call at three o'clock on the following day. Lord George said that he would, and was again at Scumberg's Hotel at three o'clock on the next afternoon.

Chapter XXXII.

Lord George Is Troubled.

This was a day of no little importance to Lord George; so much so, that one or two circumstances which occurred before he saw his brother at the hotel must be explained. On that day there had come to him from the Dean a letter written in the Dean's best humour. When the house had been taken in Munster Court there had been a certain understanding, hardly quite a fixed assurance, that it was to be occupied up to the end of June, and that then Lord George and his wife should go into Brothershire. There had been a feeling ever since the marriage that while Mary preferred London, Lord George was wedded to the country. They had on the whole behaved well to each other in the matter. The husband, though he feared that his wife was surrounded by dangers, and was well aware that he himself was dallying on the brink of a terrible pitfall, would not urge a retreat before the time that had been named. And she, though she had ever before her eyes the fear of the dullness of Cross Hall, would not ask to have the time postponed. It was now the end of May, and a certain early day in July had been fixed for their retreat from London. Lord George had, with a good grace, promised to spend a few days at the deanery before he went to Cross Hall, and had given Mary permission to remain there for some little time afterwards. Now there had come a letter from the Dean full of smiles and pleasantness about this visit. There were tidings in it about Mary's horse, which was still kept at the deanery, and comfortable assurances of sweetest welcome. Not a word had been said in this letter about the terrible family matter. Lord George, though he was at the present moment not disposed to think in the most kindly manner of his father-in-law, appreciated this, and had read the letter aloud to his wife at the breakfast table with pleasant approbation. As he left the house to go to his brother, he told her that she had better answer her father's letter, and had explained to her where she would find it in his dressing room.

But on the previous afternoon he had received at his club another letter, the nature of which was not so agreeable. This letter had not been pleasant even to himself, and certainly was not adapted to give pleasure to his wife. After receiving it he had kept it in the close custody of his breast-pocket; and when, as he left the house, he sent his wife to find that which had come from her father, he certainly thought that this prior letter was at the moment secure from all eyes within the sanctuary of his coat. But it was otherwise. With that negligence to which husbands are so specially subject, he had made the Dean's letter safe next to his bosom, but had left the other epistle unguarded. He had not only left it unguarded, but had absolutely so put his wife on the track of it that it was impossible that she should not read it.

Mary found the letter and did read it before she left her husband's dressing room,—and the letter was as follows:—

"Dearest George;—" When she read the epithet, which she and she only was entitled to use, she paused for a moment and all the blood rushed up into her face. She had known the handwriting instantly, and at the first shock she put the paper down upon the table. For a second there was a feeling prompting her to read no further. But it was only for a second. Of course she would read it. It certainly never would have occurred to her to search her husband's clothes for letters. Up to this moment she had never examined a document of his except at his bidding or in compliance with his wish. She had suspected nothing, found nothing, had entertained not even any curiosity about her husband's affairs. But now must she not read this letter to which he himself had directed her? Dearest George! And that in the handwriting of her friend,—her friend!—Adelaide Houghton;— in the handwriting of the woman to whom her husband had been attached before he had known herself! Of course she read the letter.

"DEAREST GEORGE,—

"I break my heart when you don't come to me; for heaven's sake be here to-morrow. Two, three, four, five, six, seven—I shall be here any hour till you come. I don't dare to tell the man that I am not at home to anybody else, but you must take your chance. Nobody ever does come till after three or after six. He never comes home till half-past seven. Oh me! what is to become of me when you go out of town? There is nothing to live for, nothing;—only you. Anything that you write is quite safe. Say that you love me. A."

The letter had grieved him when he got it,—as had other letters before that. And yet it flattered him, and the assurance of the woman's love had in it a certain candied sweetness which prevented him from destroying the paper instantly, as he ought to have done. Could his wife have read all his mind in the matter her anger would have been somewhat mollified. In spite of the candied sweetness he hated the correspondence. It had been the woman's doing and not his. It is so hard for a man to be a Joseph! The Potiphar's wife of the moment has probably had some encouragement,—and after that Joseph can hardly flee unless he be very stout indeed. This Joseph would have fled, though after a certain fashion he liked the woman, had he been able to assure himself that the fault had in no degree been his. But looking back, he thought that he had encouraged her, and did not know how to fly. Of all this Mary knew nothing. She only knew that old Mr. Houghton's wife, who professed to be her dear friend, had written a most foul love-letter to her husband, and that her husband had preserved it carefully, and had then through manifest mistake delivered it over into her hands.

She read it twice, and then stood motionless for a few minutes thinking what she would do. Her first idea was that she would tell her father. But that she soon abandoned. She was grievously offended with her husband; but, as she thought of it, she became aware that she did not wish to bring on him any anger but her own. Then she thought that she would start immediately for Berkeley Square, and say what she had to say to Mrs. Houghton. As this idea presented itself to her, she felt that she could say a good deal. But how would that serve her? Intense as was her hatred at present against Adelaide, Adelaide was nothing to her in comparison with her husband. For a moment she almost thought that she would fly after him, knowing, as she did, that he had gone to see his brother at Scumberg's Hotel. But at last she resolved that she would do nothing and say nothing till he should have perceived that she had read the letter. She would leave it open on his dressing-table so that he might know immediately on his return what had been done. Then it occurred to her that the servants might see the letter if she exposed it. So she kept it in her pocket, and determined that when she heard his knock at the door she would step into his room, and place the letter ready for his eyes. After that she spent the whole day in thinking of it, and read the odious words over and over again till they were fixed in her memory. "Say that you love me!" Wretched viper; ill-conditioned traitor! Could it be that he, her husband, loved this woman better than her? Did not all the world know that the woman was plain and affected, and vulgar, and odious? "Dearest George!" The woman could not have used such language without his sanction. Oh;—what should she do? Would it not be necessary that she should go back and live with her father? Then she thought of Jack De Baron. They called Jack De Baron wild; but he would not have been guilty of wickedness such as this. She clung, however, to the resolution of putting the letter ready for her husband, so that he should know that she had read it before they met.

In the meantime Lord George, ignorant as yet of the storm which was brewing at home, was shown into his brother's sitting-room. When he entered he found there, with his brother, a lady whom he could recognise without difficulty as his sister-in-law. She was a tall, dark woman, as he thought very plain, but with large bright eyes and very black hair. She was ill-dressed, in a morning wrapper, and looked to him to be at least as old as her husband. The Marquis said something to her in Italian which served as an introduction, but of which Lord George could not understand a word. She curtseyed and Lord George put out his hand. "It is perhaps as well that you should make her acquaintance," said the Marquis. Then he again spoke in Italian, and after a minute or two the lady withdrew. It occurred to Lord George afterwards that the interview had certainly been arranged. Had his brother not wished him to see the lady, the lady could have been kept in the background here as well as at Manor Cross. "It's uncommon civil of you to come," said the Marquis as soon as the door was closed. "What can I do for you?"

"I did not like that you should be in London without my seeing you."

"I daresay not. I daresay not. I was very much obliged to you, you know, for sending that lawyer down to me."

"I did not send him."

"And particularly obliged to you for introducing that other lawyer into our family affairs."

"I would have done nothing of the kind if I could have helped it. If you will believe me, Brotherton, my only object is to have all this so firmly settled that there may not be need of further enquiry at a future time."

"When I am dead?"

"When we may both be dead."

"You have ten years advantage of me. Your own chance isn't bad."

"If you will believe me—"

"But suppose I don't believe you! Suppose I think that in saying all that you are lying like the very devil!" Lord George jumped in his chair, almost as though he had been shot. "My dear fellow, what's the good of this humbug? You think you've got a chance. I don't believe you were quick enough to see it yourself, but your father-in-law has put you up to it. He is not quite such an ass as you are; but even he is ass enough to fancy that because I, an Englishman, have married an Italian lady, therefore the marriage may, very likely, be good for nothing."

"We only want proof."

"Does anybody ever come to you and ask you for proofs of your marriage with that very nice young woman, the Dean's daughter?"

"Anybody may find them at Brotherton."

"No doubt. And I can put my hand on the proofs of my marriage when I want to do so. In the meantime I doubt whether you can learn anything to your own advantage by coming here."

"I didn't want to learn anything."

"If you would look after your own wife a little closer, I fancy it would be a better employment for you. She is at present probably amusing herself with Captain De Baron."

"That is calumny," said Lord George, rising from his chair.

"No doubt. Any imputation coming from me is calumny. But you can make imputations as heavy and as hard as you please—and all in the way of honour. I've no doubt you'll find her with Captain De Baron if you'll go and look."

"I should find her doing nothing that she ought not to do," said the husband, turning round for his hat and gloves.

"Or perhaps making a speech at the Rights of Women Institute on behalf of that German baroness who, I'm told, is in gaol. But, George, don't you take it too much to heart. You've got the money. When a man goes into a stable for his wife, he can't expect much in the way of conduct or manners. If he gets the money he ought to be contented." He had to hear it all to the last bitter word before he could escape from the room and make his way out into the street.

It was at this time about four o'clock, and in his agony of mind he had turned down towards Piccadilly before he could think what he would do with himself for the moment. Then he remembered that Berkeley Square was close to him on the other side, and that he had been summoned there about this hour. To give him his due, it should be owned that he had no great desire to visit Berkeley Square in his present condition of feeling. Since the receipt of that letter,—which was now awaiting him at home,—he had told himself half a dozen times that he must and would play the part of Joseph. He had so resolved when she had first spoken to him of her passion, now some months ago; and then his resolution had broken down merely because he had not at the moment thought any great step to be necessary. But now it was clear that some great step was necessary. He must make her know that it did not suit him to be called "dearest George" by her, or to be told to declare that he loved her. And this accusation against his wife, made in such coarse and brutal language by his brother, softened his heart to her. Why, oh why, had he allowed himself to be brought up to a place he hated as he had always hated London! Of course Jack De Baron made him unhappy, though he was at the present moment prepared to swear that his wife was as innocent as any woman in London.

But now, as he was so near, and as his decision must be declared in person, he might as well go to Berkeley Square. As he descended Hay Hill he put his hand into his pocket for the lady's letter, and pulled out that from the Dean which he had intended to leave with his wife. In an instant he knew what he had done. He remembered it all, even to the way in which he had made the mistake with the two letters. There could be no doubt but that he had given Adelaide Houghton's letter into his wife's hands, and that she had read it. At the bottom of Hill Street, near the stables, he stopped suddenly and put his hand up to his head. What should he do now? He certainly could not pay his visit in Berkeley Square. He could not go and tell Mrs. Houghton that he loved her, and certainly would not have strength to tell her that he did not love her while suffering such agony as this. Of course he must see his wife. Of course he must,—if I may use the slang phrase,—of course he must "have it out with her," after some fashion, and the sooner the better. So he turned his stops homewards across the Green Park. But, in going homewards, he did not walk very fast.

What would she do? How would she take it? Of course women daily forgive such offences; and he might probably, after the burst of the storm was over, succeed in making her believe that he did in truth love her and did not love the other woman. In his present mood he was able to assure himself most confidently that such was the truth. He could tell himself now that he never wished to see Adelaide Houghton again. But, before anything of this could be achieved, he would have to own himself a sinner before her. He would have, as it were, to grovel at her feet. Hitherto, in all his intercourse with her, he had been masterful and marital. He had managed up to this point so to live as to have kept in all respects the upper hand. He had never yet been found out even in a mistake or an indiscretion. He had never given her an opening for the mildest finding of fault. She, no doubt, was young, and practice had not come to her. But, as a natural consequence of this, Lord George had hitherto felt that an almost divine superiority was demanded from him. That sense of divine superiority must now pass away.

I do not know whether a husband's comfort is ever perfect till some family peccadilloes have been conclusively proved against him. I am sure that a wife's temper to him is sweetened by such evidence of human imperfection. A woman will often take delight in being angry; will sometimes wrap herself warm in prolonged sullenness; will frequently revel in complaint;—but she enjoys forgiving better than aught else. She never feels that all the due privileges of her life have been accorded to her, till her husband shall have laid himself open to the caresses of a pardon. Then, and not till then, he is her equal; and equality is necessary for comfortable love. But the man, till he be well used to it, does not like to be pardoned. He has assumed divine superiority, and is bound to maintain it. Then, at last, he comes home some night with a little too much wine, or he cannot pay the weekly bills because he has lost too much money at cards, or he has got into trouble at his office and is in doubt for a fortnight about his place, or perhaps a letter from a lady falls into wrong hands. Then he has to tell himself that he has been "found out." The feeling is at first very uncomfortable; but it is, I think, a step almost necessary in reaching true matrimonial comfort. Hunting men say that hard rain settles the ground. A good scold with a "kiss and be friends" after it, perhaps, does the same.

Now Lord George had been found out. He was quite sure of that. And he had to undergo all that was unpleasant without sufficient experience to tell him that those clouds too would pass away quickly. He still walked homewards across St. James's Park, never stopping, but dragging himself along slowly, and when he came to his own door he let himself in very silently. She did not expect him so soon, and when he entered the drawing-room was startled to see him. She had not as yet put the letter, as she had intended, on his dressing-table, but still had it in her pocket; nor had it occurred to her that he would as yet have known the truth. She looked at him when he entered, but did not at first utter a word. "Mary," he said.

"Well; is anything the matter?"

It was possible that she had not found the letter,—possible, though very improbable. But he had brought his mind so firmly to the point of owning what was to be owned and defending what might be defended, that he hardly wished for escape in that direction. At any rate, he was not prepared to avail himself of it. "Did you find the letter?" he asked.

"I found a letter."

"Well!"

"Of course I am sorry to have intruded upon so private a correspondence. There it is." And she threw the letter to him. "Oh, George!"

He picked up the letter, which had fallen to the ground, and, tearing it into bits, threw the fragments into the grate. "What do you believe about it, Mary?"

"Believe!"

"Do you think that I love any one as I love you?"

"You cannot love me at all,—unless that wicked, wretched creature is a liar."

"Have I ever lied to you? You will believe me?"

"I do not know."

"I love no one in the world but you."

Even that almost sufficed for her. She already longed to have her arms round his neck and to tell him that it was all forgiven;—that he at least was forgiven. During the whole morning she had been thinking of the angry words she would say to him, and of the still more angry words which she would speak of that wicked, wicked viper. The former were already forgotten; but she was not as yet inclined to refrain as to Mrs. Houghton. "Oh, George, how could you bear such a woman as that;—that you should let her write to you in such language? Have you been to her?"

"What, to-day?"

"Yes, to-day."

"Certainly not. I have just come from my brother."

"You will never go into the house again! You will promise that!"

Here was made the first direct attack upon his divine superiority! Was he, at his wife's instance, to give a pledge that he would not go into a certain house under any circumstances? This was the process of bringing his nose down to the ground which he had feared. Here was the first attempt made by his wife to put her foot on his neck. "I think that I had better tell you all that I can tell," he said.

"I only want to know that you hate her," said Mary.

"I neither hate her nor love her. I did—love her—once. You knew that."

"I never could understand it. I never did believe that you really could have loved her." Then she began to sob. "I shouldn't—ever—have taken you—if—I had."

"But from the moment when I first knew you it was all changed with me." As he said this he put out his arms to her, and she came to him. "There has never been a moment since in which you have not had all my heart."

"But why—why—why—," she sobbed, meaning to ask how it could have come to pass that the wicked viper could, in those circumstances, have written such a letter as that which had fallen into her hands.

The question certainly was not unnatural. But it was a question very difficult to answer. No man likes to say that a woman has pestered him with unwelcome love, and certainly Lord George was not the man to make such a boast. "Dearest Mary," he said, "on my honour as a gentleman I am true to you."

Then she was satisfied and turned her face to him and covered him with kisses. I think that morning did more than any day had done since their marriage to bring about the completion of her desire to be in love with her husband. Her heart was so softened towards him that she would not even press a question that would pain him. She had intended sternly to exact from him a pledge that he would not again enter the house in Berkeley

Square, but she let even that pass by because she would not annoy him. She gathered herself up close to him on the sofa, and drawing his arm over her shoulder, sobbed and laughed, stroking him with her hands as she crouched against his shoulder. But yet, every now and then, there came forth from, her some violent ebullition against Mrs. Houghton. "Nasty creature! wicked, wicked beast! Oh, George, she is so ugly!" And yet before this little affair, she had been quite content that Adelaide Houghton should be her intimate friend.

It had been nearly five when Lord George reached the house, and he had to sit enduring his wife's caresses, and listening to devotion to himself and her abuses of Mrs. Houghton till past six. Then it struck him that a walk by himself would be good for him. They were to dine out, but not till eight, and there would still be time. When he proposed it, she acceded at once. Of course she must go and dress, and equally of course he would not, could not go to Berkeley Square now. She thoroughly believed that he was true to her, but yet she feared the wiles of that nasty woman. They would go to the country soon, and then the wicked viper would not be near them.

Lord George walked across to Pall Mall, looked at an evening paper at his club, and then walked back again. Of course it had been his object to have a cool half hour in which to think it all over,—all that had passed between him and his wife, and also what had passed between him and his brother. That his wife was the dearest, sweetest woman in the world he was quite sure. He was more than satisfied with her conduct to him. She had exacted from him very little penitence:—had not required to put her foot in any disagreeable way upon his neck. No doubt she felt that his divine superiority had been vanquished, but she had uttered no word of triumph. With all that he was content. But what was he to do with Mrs. Houghton, as to whom he had sworn a dozen times within the last hour that she was quite indifferent to him. He now repeated the assertion to himself, and felt himself to be sure of the fact. But still he was her lover. He had allowed her so to regard him, and something must be done. She would write to him letters daily if he did not stop it; and every such letter not shown to his wife would be a new treason against her. This was a great trouble. And then, through it all, those terrible words which his brother had spoken to him about Captain De Baron rung in his ears. This afternoon had certainly afforded no occasion to him to say a word about Captain De Baron to his wife. When detected in his own sin he could not allude to possible delinquencies on the other side. Nor did he think that there was any delinquency. But Cæsar said that Cæsar's wife should be above suspicion, and in that matter every man is a Cæsar to himself. Lady Susanna had spoken about this Captain, and Adelaide Houghton had said an ill-natured word or two, and he himself had seen them walking together. Now his brother had told him that Captain De Baron was his wife's lover. He did not at all like Captain De Baron.

Chapter XXXIII.

Captain De Baron.

Of course as the next day or two passed by, the condition of Mrs. Houghton was discussed between Lord George and his wife. The affair could not be passed over without further speech. "I am quite contented with you," he said; "more than contented. But I suppose she does not feel herself contented with Mr. Houghton."

"Then why did she marry him?"

"Ah;—why indeed."

"A woman ought to be contented with her husband. But at any rate what right can she have to disturb other people? I suppose you never wrote her a love-letter."

"Never, certainly;—since her marriage." This indeed was true. The lady had frequently written to him, but he had warily kept his hands from pen and ink and had answered her letters by going to her.

"And yet she could persevere! Women can do such mean things! I would sooner have broken my heart and died than have asked a man to say that he loved me. I don't suppose you have much to be proud of. I daresay she has half a dozen others. You won't see her again?"

"I think I may be driven to do so. I do not wish to have to write to her, and yet I must make her understand that all this is to be over."

"She'll understand that fast enough when she does not see you. It would have served her right to have sent that letter to her husband."

"That would have been cruel, Mary."

"I didn't do it. I thought of doing it, and wouldn't do it. But it would have served her right. I suppose she was always writing."

"She had written, but not quite like that," said Lord George. He was not altogether comfortable during this conversation.

"She writes lots of such letters no doubt. You do then mean to go there again?"

"I think so. Of course I do not look upon her as being so utterly a castaway as you do."

"I believe her to be a heartless, vile, intriguing woman, who married an old man without caring a straw for him, and who doesn't care how miserable she makes other people. And I think she is very—very ugly. She paints frightfully. Anybody can see it. And as for false hair,—why, it's nearly all false." Lady George certainly did not paint, and had not a shred of false hair about her. "Oh, George, if you do go, do be firm! You will be firm;—will you not?"

"I shall go simply that this annoyance may be at an end."

"Of course you will tell her that I will never speak to her again. How could I? You would not wish it;—would you?" In answer to this there was nothing for him to say. He would have wished that a certain amount of half friendly intercourse should be carried on; but he could not ask her to do this. After a time he might perhaps be able to press on her the advantage of avoiding a scandal, but as yet he could not do even that. He had achieved more than he had a right to expect in obtaining her permission to call once more in Berkeley Square himself. After that they would soon be going down to Brotherton, and when they were there things might be allowed to settle themselves. Then she asked him another question. "You don't object to my going to Mrs. Jones' party on Thursday?"

The question was very sudden, so that he was almost startled. "It is a dance, I suppose."

"Oh yes, a dance of course."

"No;—I have no objection."

She had meant to ask him to reconsider his verdict against round dances, but she could hardly do so at this moment. She could not take advantage of her present strength to extract from him a privilege which under other circumstances he had denied to her. Were she to do so it would be as much as to declare that she meant to waltz because he had amused himself with Mrs. Houghton. Her mind was not at all that way given. But she did entertain an idea that something more of freedom should be awarded to her because her husband had given her cause of offence and had been forgiven. While he was still strong with that divine superiority which she had attributed to him, she had almost acknowledged to herself that he had a right to demand that she should be dull and decorous. But now that she had found him to be in the receipt of clandestine love-letters, it did seem that she might allow herself a little liberty. She had forgiven him freely. She had really believed that in spite of the letter she herself was the woman he loved. She had said something to herself about men amusing themselves, and had told herself that though no woman could have written such a letter as that without disgracing herself altogether, a man might receive it and even keep it in his pocket without meaning very much harm. But the accident must, she thought, be held to absolve her from some part of the strictness of her obedience. She almost thought that she would waltz at Mrs. Jones's ball; perhaps not with Captain De Baron; perhaps not with much energy or with full enjoyment; but still sufficiently to disenthral herself. If possible she would say a word to her husband first. They were both going to a rather crowded affair at Lady Brabazon's before the night of Mrs. Jones's party. They had agreed that they would do little more than shew themselves there. He was obliged to go to this special place and he hated staying. But even at Lady Brabazon's she might find an opportunity of saying what she wished to say.

On that day she took him out in her brougham, and on her return home was alone all the afternoon till about five; and then who should come to her but Captain De Baron. No doubt they two had become very intimate. She could not at all have defined her reasons for liking him. She was quite sure of one thing,—she was not in the least in love with him. But he was always gay, always good humoured, always had plenty to say. He was the source of all the fun that ever came in her way; and fun was very dear to her. He was nice-looking and manly, and gentle withal. Why should she not have her friend? He would not write abominable letters and ask her to say that she loved him! And yet she was aware that there was a danger. She knew that her husband was a little jealous. She knew that Augusta Mildmay was frightfully jealous. That odious creature Mrs. Houghton had made ever so many nasty little allusions to her and Jack. When his name was announced she almost wished that he had not come; but yet she received him very pleasantly. He immediately began about the Baroness Banmann. The Baroness had on the previous evening made her way on to the platform at the Disabilities when Dr. Fleabody was lecturing, and Lady Selina was presiding and had, to use Jack's own words, "Kicked up the most delightful bobbery that had ever been witnessed! She bundled poor old Lady Selina out of the chair."

"Nonsense!"

"So I am told;—took the chair by the back and hoisted her out."

"Didn't they send for the police?"

"I suppose they did at last; but the American doctor was too many for her. The Baroness strove to address the meeting; but Olivia Q. Fleabody has become a favourite, and carried the day. I am told that at last the bald-headed old gentleman took the Baroness home in a cab. I'd have given a five-pound note to be there. I think I must go some night and hear the Doctor."

"I wouldn't go again for anything."

"You women are all so jealous of each other. Poor Lady Selina! I'm told she was very much shaken."

"How did you hear it all?"

"From Aunt Ju," said the Captain. "Aunt Ju was there, of course. The Baroness tried to fly into Aunt Ju's arms, but Aunt Ju seems to have retired."

Then the quarrel must have been made up between Captain De Baron and Miss Mildmay. That was the idea which at once came into Mary's head. He could hardly have seen Aunt Ju without seeing her niece at the same time. Perhaps it was all settled. Perhaps, after all, they would be married. It would be a pity, because she was not half nice enough for him. And then Mary doubted whether Captain Dc Baron as a married man would be nearly so pleasant as in his present condition. "I hope Miss Mildmay is none the worse," she said.

"A little shaken in her nerves."

"Was—Augusta Mildmay there?"

"Oh dear no. It is quite out of her line. She is not at all disposed to lay aside the feeblenesses of her sex and go into one of the learned professions. By the bye, I am afraid you and she are not very good friends."

"What makes you say that, Captain De Baron?"

"But are you?"

"I don't know why you should enquire."

"It is natural to wish that one's own friends should be friends."

"Has Miss Mildmay said—anything about—me?"

"Not a word;—nor you about her. And, therefore, I know that something is wrong."

"The last time I saw her I did not think that Miss Mildmay was very happy," said Mary, in a low voice.

"Did she complain to you?" Mary had no answer ready for this question. She could not tell a lie easily, nor could she acknowledge the complaint which the lady had made, and had made so loudly. "I suppose she did complain," he said, "and I suppose I know the nature of her complaint."

"I cannot tell;—though, of course, it was nothing to me."

"It is very much to me, though. I wish, Lady George, you could bring yourself to tell me the truth." He paused, but she did not speak. "If it were as I fear, you must know how much I am implicated. I would not for the world that you should think I am behaving badly."

"You should not permit her to think so, Captain De Baron."

"She doesn't think so. She can't think so. I am not going to say a word against her. She and I have been dear friends, and there is no one,—hardly any one,—for whom I have a greater regard. But I do protest to you, Lady George, that I have never spoken an untrue word to Augusta Mildmay in my life."

"I have not accused you."

"But has she? Of course it is a kind of thing that a man cannot talk about without great difficulty."

"Is it not a thing that a man should not talk about at all?"

"That is severe, Lady George;—much more severe than I should have expected from your usual good nature. Had you told me that nothing had been said to you, there would have been an end of it. But I cannot bear to think that you should have been told that I had behaved badly, and that I should be unable to vindicate myself."

"Have you not been engaged to marry Miss Mildmay?"

"Never."

"Then why did you allow yourself to become so—so much to her?"

"Because I liked her. Because we were thrown together. Because the chances of things would have it so. Don't you know that that kind of thing is occurring every day? Of course, if a man were made up of wisdom and prudence and virtue and self-denial, this kind of thing wouldn't occur. But I don't think the world would be pleasanter if men were like that. Adelaide Houghton is Miss Mildmay's most intimate friend, and Adelaide has always known that I couldn't marry." As soon as Mrs. Houghton's name was mentioned a dark frown came across Lady George's brow. Captain De Baron saw it, but did not as yet know anything of its true cause.

"Of course I am not going to judge between you," said Lady George, very gravely.

"But I want you to judge me. I want you of all the world to feel that I have not been a liar and a blackguard."

"Captain De Baron! how can you use such language?"

"Because I feel this very acutely. I do believe that Miss Mildmay has accused me to you. I do not wish to say a word against her. I would do anything in the world to protect her from the ill words of others. But I cannot bear that your mind should be poisoned against me. Will you believe me when I tell you that I have never said a word to Miss Mildmay which could possibly be taken as an offer of marriage?"

"I had rather give no opinion."

"Will you ask Adelaide?"

"No; certainly not." This she said with so much vehemence that he was thoroughly startled. "Mrs. Houghton is not among the number of my acquaintances."

"Why not? What is the matter?"

"I can give no explanation, and I had rather that no questions should be asked. But so it is."

"Has she offended Lord George?"

"Oh dear no; that is to say I cannot tell you anything more about it. You will never see me in Berkeley Square again. And now, pray say no more about it."

"Poor Adelaide. Well; it does seem terrible that there should be such misunderstandings. She knows nothing about it. I was with her this morning, and she was speaking of you with the greatest affection." Mary struggled hard to appear indifferent to all this, but struggled in vain. She could not restrain herself from displaying her feeling. "May I not ask any further questions?"

"No, Captain De Baron."

"Nor hope that I may be a peacemaker between you?"

"Certainly not. I wish you wouldn't talk about it any more."

"I certainly will not if it offends you. I would not offend you for all the world. When you came up to town, Lady George, a few months ago, there were three or four of us that soon became such excellent friends! And now it seems that everything has gone wrong. I hope we need not quarrel—you and I?"

"I know no reason why we should."

"I have liked you so much. I am sure you have known that. Sometimes one does come across a person that one really likes; but it is so seldom."

"I try to like everybody," she said.

"I don't do that. I fear that at first starting I try to dislike everybody. I think it is natural to hate people the first time you see them."

"Did you hate me?" she asked, laughing.

"Oh, horribly,—for two minutes. Then you laughed, or cried, or sneezed, or did something in a manner that I liked, and I saw at once that you were the most charming human being in the world."

When a young man tells a young woman that she is the most charming human being in the world, he is certainly using peculiar language. In most cases the young man would be supposed to be making love to the young woman. Mary, however, knew very well that Captain De Baron was not making love to her. There seemed to be an understanding that all manner of things should be said between them, and that yet they should mean nothing. But, nevertheless, she felt that the language which this man had used to her would be offensive to her husband if he knew that it had been used when they two were alone together.

Had it been said before a room-full of people it would not have mattered. And yet she could not rebuke him. She could not even look displeased. She had believed all that he had said to her about Augusta Mildmay, and was glad to believe it. She liked him so much, that she would have spoken to him as to a brother of the nature of her quarrel with Mrs. Houghton, only that, even to a brother, she would not have mentioned her husband's folly. When he spoke of her crying, or laughing, or sneezing, she liked the little attempt at drollery. She liked to know that he had found her charming. Where is the woman who does not wish to charm, and is not proud to think that she has succeeded with those whom she most likes? She could not rebuke him. She could not even avoid letting him see that she was pleased. "You have a dozen human beings in the world who are the most delightful," she said, "and another dozen who are the most odious."

"Quite a dozen who are the most odious, but only one, Lady George, who is the most delightful." He had hardly said this when the door opened and Lord George entered the room. Lord George was not a clever hypocrite. If he disliked a person he soon showed his dislike in his manner. It was very clear to both of them on the present occasion that he did not like the presence of Captain De Baron. He looked very gloomy,—almost angry, and after speaking hardly more than a single word to his wife's guest, he stood silent and awkward, leaning against the mantel-piece. "What do you think Captain De Baron tells me?" Mary said, trying, but not very successfully, to speak with natural ease.

"I don't in the least know."

"There has been such a scene at the Women's Institute! That Baroness made a dreadful attack on poor Lady Selina Protest."

"She and the American female doctor were talking against each other from the same platform, at the same time," said De Baron.

"Very disgraceful!" said Lord George. "But then the whole thing is disgraceful, and always was. I should think Lord Plausible must be thoroughly ashamed of his sister." Lady Selina was sister to the Earl of Plausible, but, as all the world knew, was not on speaking terms with her brother.

"I suppose that unfortunate German lady will be put in prison," said Lady George.

"I only trust she may never be able to put her foot into your house again."

Then there was a pause. He was apparently so cross that conversation seemed to be impossible. The Captain would have gone away at once had he been able to escape suddenly. But there are times when it is very hard to get out of a room, at which a sudden retreat would imply a conviction that something was wrong. It seemed to him that for her sake he was bound to remain a few minutes longer. "When do you go down to Brothershire?" he asked.

"About the 7th of July," said Mary.

"Or probably earlier," said Lord George;—at which his wife looked up at him, but without making any remark.

"I shall be down at my cousin's place some day in August," De Baron said. Lord George frowned more heavily than ever. "Mr. De Baron is going to have a large gathering of people about the end of the month."

"Oh, indeed," said Mary.

"The Houghtons will be there." Then Mary also frowned. "And I have an idea that your brother, Lord George, has half promised to be one of the party."

"I know nothing at all about it."

"My cousin was up in town yesterday with the Houghtons. Good-bye, Lady George; I shan't be at Lady Brabazon's, because she has forgotten to invite me, but I suppose I shall see you at Mrs. Montacute Jones'?"

"I shall certainly be at Mrs. Montacute Jones'," said Mary, trying to speak cheerfully.

The bell was rang and the door was closed, and then the husband and wife were together. "A dreadful communication has just been made to me," said Lord George in his most solemn and funereal voice;—"a most dreadful communication!"

Chapter XXXIV.

A Dreadful Communication.

"A most dreadful communication!" There was something in Lord George's voice as he uttered these words which so frightened his wife that she became at the moment quite pale. She was sure, almost sure from his countenance that the dreadful communication had some reference to herself. Had any great calamity happened in regard to his own family he would not have looked at her as he was now looking. And yet she could not imagine what might be the nature of the communication. "Has anything happened at Manor Cross?" she asked.

"It is not about Manor Cross."

"Or your brother?"

"It is not about my brother; it does not in any way concern my family. It is about you."

"About me! Oh, George! do not look at me like that. What is it?"

He was very slow in the telling of the story; slow even in beginning to tell it; indeed, he hardly knew how to begin. "You know Miss Augusta Mildmay?" he asked.

Then she understood it all. She might have told him that he could spare himself all further trouble in telling, only that to do so would hardly have suited her purpose; therefore she had to listen to the story, very slowly told. Miss Augusta Mildmay had written to him begging him to come to her. He, very much astonished at such a request, had nevertheless obeyed it; and Augusta Mildmay had assured him that his wife, by wicked wiles and lures, was interfering between her and her affianced lover Captain De Baron. Mary sat patiently till she had heard it all,—sat almost without speaking a word; but there was a stern look on her face which he had never seen there before. Still he went on with his determined purpose. "These are the kind of things which are being repeated of you," he said at last. "Susanna made the same complaint. And it had reached Brotherton's ears. He spoke to me of it in frightfully strong language. And now this young lady tells me that you are destroying her happiness."

"Well!"

"You can't suppose that I can hear all this without uneasiness."

"Do you believe it?"

"I do not know what to believe. I am driven mad."

"If you believe it, George, if you believe a word of it, I will go away from you. I will go back to papa. I will not stay with you to be doubted."

"That is nonsense."

"It shall not be nonsense. I will not live to hear myself accused by my husband as to another man. Wicked young woman! Oh, what women are and what they can do! She has never been engaged to Captain De Baron."

"What is that to you or me?"

"Nothing, if you had not told me that I stood in her way."

"It is not her engagement, or her hopes, whether ill or well founded, or his treachery to a lady, that concerns you and me, Mary; but that she should send for me and tell me to my face that you are the cause of her unhappiness. Why should she pitch upon you?"

"How can I say? Because she is very wicked."

"And why should Susanna feel herself obliged to caution me as to this Captain De Baron? She had no motive. She is not wicked."

"I don't know that."

"And why should my brother tell me that all the world is speaking of your conduct with this very man?"

"Because he is your bitterest enemy. George, do you believe it?"

"And why, when I come home with all this heavy on my heart, do I find this very man closeted with you?"

"Closeted with me!"

"You were alone with him."

"Alone with him! Of course I am alone with anyone who calls. Would you like me to tell the servant that Captain De Baron is to be excluded,—so that all the world might know that you are jealous?"

"He must be excluded."

"Then you must do it. But it will be unnecessary. As you believe all this, I will tell my father everything and will go back to him. I will not live here, George, to be so suspected that the very servants have to be told that I am not to be allowed to see one special man."

"No; you will go down into the country with me."

"I will not stay in the same house with you," she said, jumping up from her seat, "unless you tell me that you suspect me of nothing—not even of an impropriety. You may lock me up, but you cannot hinder me from writing to my father."

"I trust you will do nothing of the kind."

"Not tell him! Who then is to be my friend if you turn against me? Am I to be all alone among a set of people who think nothing but ill of me?"

"I am to be your friend."

"But you think ill of me."

"I have not said so, Mary."

"Then say at once that you think no ill, and do not threaten me that I am to be taken into the country for protection. And when you tell me of the bold-faced villany of that young woman, speak of her with the disgust that she deserves; and say that your sister Susanna is suspicious and given to evil thoughts; and declare your brother to be a wicked slanderer if he has said a word against the honour of your wife. Then I shall know that you think no ill of me; and then I shall know that I may lean upon you as my real friend."

Her eyes flashed fire as she spoke, and he was silenced for the moment by an impetuosity and a passion which he had not at all expected. He was not quite disposed to yield to her, to assure her of his conviction that those to whom she alluded were all wrong, and that she was all right; but yet he was beginning to wish for peace. That Captain De Baron was a pestilential young man whose very business it was to bring unhappiness into families, he did believe; and he feared also that his wife had allowed herself to fall into an indiscreet intimacy with this destroyer of women's characters. Then there was that feeling of Cæsar's wife strong within his bosom, which he could, perhaps, have more fully explained to her but for that unfortunate letter from Mrs. Houghton. Any fault, however, of that kind on his part was, in his estimation, nothing to a fault on the part of his wife. She, when once assured that he was indifferent about Mrs. Houghton, would find no cause for unhappiness in the matter. But what would all the world be to him if his wife were talked about commonly in connection with another man? That she should not absolutely be a castaway would not save him from a perpetual agony which he would find to be altogether unendurable. He was, he was sure, quite right as to that theory about Cæsar's wife, even though, from the unfortunate position of circumstances, he could not dilate upon it at the present moment. "I think," he said, after a pause, "that you will allow that you had better drop this gentleman's acquaintance."

"I will allow nothing of the kind, George. I will allow nothing that can imply the slightest stain upon my name or upon your honour. Captain De Baron is my friend. I like him very much. A great many people know how intimate we are. They shall never be taught to suppose that there was anything wrong in that intimacy. They shall never, at any rate, be taught so by anything that I will do. I will admit nothing. I will do nothing myself to show that I am ashamed. Of course you can take me into the country; of course you can lock me up if you like; of course you can tell all your friends that I have misbehaved myself; you can listen to calumny against me from everybody; but if you do I will have one friend to protect me, and I will tell papa everything." Then she walked away to the door as though she were leaving the room.

"Stop a moment," he said. Then she stood with her hand still on the lock, as though intending to stay merely till he should have spoken some last word to her. He was greatly surprised by her strength and resolution, and now hardly knew what more to say to her. He could not beg her pardon for his suspicion; he could not tell her that she was right; and yet he found it impossible to assert that she was wrong. "I do not think that passion will do any good," he said.

"I do not know what will do any good. I know what I feel."

"It will do good if you will allow me to advise you."

"What is your advice?"

"To come down to the country as soon as possible, and to avoid, as far as possible, seeing Captain De Baron before you go."

"That would be running away from Captain De Baron. I am to meet him at Mrs. Montacute Jones' ball."

"Send an excuse to Mrs. Montacute Jones."

"You may do so, George, if you like. I will not. If I am told by you that I am not to meet this man, of course I shall obey you; but I shall consider myself to have been insulted,—to have been insulted by you." As she said this his brow became very black. "Yes, by you. You ought to defend me from these people who tell stories about me, and not accuse me yourself. I cannot and will not live with you if you think evil of me." Then she opened the door, and slowly left the room. He would have said more had he known what to say. But her words came more fluently than his, and he was dumbfounded by her volubility; yet he was as much convinced as ever that it was his duty to save her from the ill repute which would fall upon her from further intimacy with this Captain. He could, of course, take her into the country to-morrow, if he chose to do so; but he could not hinder her from writing to the Dean; he could not debar her from pen and ink and the use of the post-office; nor could he very well forbid her to see her father.

Of course if she did complain to the Dean she would tell the Dean everything. So he told himself. Now, when a man assumes the divine superiority of an all-governing husband his own hands should be quite clean. Lord George's hands were by no means clean. It was not, perhaps, his own fault that they were dirty. He was able at any rate to tell himself that the fault had not been his. But there was that undoubted love-letter from Mrs. Houghton. If the Dean were to question him about that he could not lie. And though he would assure himself that the fault had all been with the lady, he could not excuse himself by that argument in discussing the matter with the Dean. He was in such trouble that he feared to drive his wife to retaliation; and yet he must do his duty. His honour and her honour must be his first consideration. If she would only promise him not willingly to see Captain De Baron there should be an end of it, and he would allow her to stay the allotted time in London; but if she would not do this he thought that he must face the Dean and all his terrors.

But he hardly knew his wife—was hardly aware of the nature of her feelings. When she spoke of appealing to her father, no idea crossed her mind of complaining of her husband's infidelity. She would seek protection for herself, and would be loud enough in protesting against the slanderous tongues of those who had injured her. She would wage war to the knife against the Marquis, and against Lady Susanna, and against Augusta Mildmay, and would call upon her father to assist her in that warfare; but she would not condescend to allude to a circumstance which, if it were an offence against her, she had pardoned, but as to which, in her heart of hearts, she believed her husband to be, if not innocent, at least not very guilty. She despised Adelaide Houghton too much to think that her husband had really loved such a woman, and was too confident in herself to doubt his love for many minutes. She could hate Adelaide Houghton for making the attempt, and yet could believe that the attempt had been futile.

Nevertheless when she was alone she thought much of Mrs. Houghton's letter. Throughout her interview with her husband she had thought of it, but had determined from the very first that she would not cast it in his teeth. She would do nothing ungenerous. But was it not singular that he should be able to upbraid her for her conduct, for conduct in which there had been no trespass, knowing as he must have known, feeling as he must have felt, that every word of that letter was dwelling in her memory! He had, at any rate, intended that the abominable correspondence should be clandestine. He must have been sadly weak, to make the least of it, to have admitted such a correspondence. "Pray tell me that you love me!" That had been the language addressed to him only a few days since by a married lady to whom he had once made an offer of marriage; and yet he could now come and trample on her as though his marital superiority had all the divinity of snow-white purity. This was absolute tyranny. But yet in complaining to her father of his tyranny she would say nothing of Adelaide Houghton. Of the accusations made against herself she would certainly tell her father, unless they were withdrawn as far as her own husband could withdraw them. For an hour after leaving him her passion still sustained her. Was this to be her reward for all her endeavours to become a loving wife?

They were engaged to dine that evening with a certain Mrs. Patmore Green, who had herself been a Germain, and who had been first cousin to the late marquis. Mary came down dressed into the drawing room at the proper time, not having spoken another word to her husband, and there she found him also dressed. She had schooled herself to show no sign either of anger or regret, and as she entered the room said some indifferent words about the brougham. He still looked as dark as a thunder-cloud, but he rang the bell and asked the servant a question. The brougham was there, and away they went to Mrs. Patmore Green's. She spoke half-a-dozen words on the way, but he hardly answered her. She knew that he would not do so, being aware that it was not within his power to rise above the feelings of the moment. But she exerted herself so that he might know that she did not mean to display her ill-humour at Mrs. Patmore Green's house.

Lady Brabazon, whose sister had married a Germain, was there, and a Colonel Ansley, who was a nephew of Lady Brotherton's; so that the party was very much a Germain party. All these people had been a good deal exercised of late on the great Popenjoy question. So immense is the power of possession that the Marquis, on his arrival in town, had been asked to all the Germain houses in spite of his sins, and had been visited with considerable family affection and regard; for was he not the head of them all? But he had not received these offers graciously, and now the current of Germain opinion was running against him. Of the general propriety of Lord George's conduct ever since his birth there had never been a doubt, and the Greens and Brabazons and Ansleys were gradually coming round to the opinion that he was right to make enquiries as to the little Popenjoy's antecedents. They had all taken kindly to Mary, though they were, perhaps, beginning to think that she was a little too frivolous, too fond of pleasure for Lord George. Mrs.

Patmore Green, who was the wife of a very rich man, and the mother of a very large family, and altogether a very worthy woman, almost at once began to whisper to Mary—"Well, my dear, what news from Italy?"

"I never hear anything about it, Mrs. Green," said Mary, with a laugh.

"And yet the Dean is so eager, Lady George!"

"I won't let papa talk to me about it. Lord Brotherton is quite welcome to his wife and his son, and everything else for me—only I do wish he would have remained away."

"I think we all wish that, my dear."

Mr. Patmore Green, and Colonel Ansley, and Lady Brabazon all spoke a word or two in the course of the evening to Lord George on the same subject, but he would only shake his head and say nothing. At that time this affair of his wife's was nearer to him and more burdensome to him than even the Popenjoy question. He could not rid himself of this new trouble even for a moment. He was still thinking of it when all the enquiries about Popenjoy were being made. What did it matter to him how that matter should be settled, if all the happiness of his life were to be dispelled by this terrible domestic affliction. "I am afraid this quarrel with his brother will be too much for Lord George," said Mr. Patmore Green to his wife, when the company were gone. "He was not able to say a word the whole evening."

"And I never knew her to be more pleasant," said Mrs. Patmore Green. "She doesn't seem to care about it the least in the world." The husband and wife did not speak a word to each other as they went home in the brougham. Mary had done her duty by sustaining herself in public, but was not willing to let him think that she had as yet forgiven the cruelty of his suspicions.

Chapter XXXV.

"I Deny It."

During the whole of that night Lord George lay suffering from his troubles, and his wife lay thinking about them. Though the matter affected her future life almost more materially than his, she had the better courage to maintain her, and a more sustained conviction. It might be that she would have to leave her home and go back to the deanery, and in that there would be utter ruin to her happiness. Let the result, however, be as it would, she could never own herself to have been one tittle astray, and she was quite sure that her father would support her in that position. The old *'ruat coelum'* feeling was strong within her. She would do anything she could for her husband short of admitting, by any faintest concession, that she had been wrong in reference to Captain De Baron. She would talk to him, coax him, implore him, reason with him, forgive him, love him, and caress him. She would try to be gentle with him this coming morning. But if he were obdurate in blaming her, she would stand on her own innocence and fight to the last gasp. He was supported by no such spirit of pugnacity. He felt it to be his duty to withdraw his wife from the evil influence of this man's attractions, but felt, at the same time, that he might possibly lack the strength to do so. And then, what is the good of withdrawing a wife, if the wife thinks that she ought not to be withdrawn? There are sins as to which there is no satisfaction in visiting the results with penalties. The sin is in the mind, or in the heart, and is complete in its enormity, even though there be no result. He was miserable because she had not at once acknowledged that she never ought to see this man again, as soon as she had heard the horrors which her husband had told her. "George," she said to him at breakfast, the next morning, "do not let us go on in this way together."

"In what way?"

"Not speaking to each other,—condemning each other."

"I have not condemned you, and I don't know why you should condemn me."

"Because I think that you suspect me without a cause."

"I only tell you what people say!"

"If people told me bad things of you, George,—that you were this or that, or the other, should I believe them?"

"A woman's name is everything."

"Then do you protect my name. But I deny it. Her name should be as nothing when compared with her conduct. I don't like to be evil spoken of, but I can bear that, or anything else, if you do not think evil of me,—you and papa." This reference to her father brought back the black cloud which her previous words had tended to dispel. "Tell me that you do not suspect me."

"I never said that I suspected you of anything."

"Say that you are sure that in regard to this man I never said, or did, or thought anything that was wrong. Come, George, have I not a right to expect that from you?" She had come round the table and was standing over him, touching his shoulder.

"Even then it would be better that you should go away from him."

"No!"

"I say that it would be better, Mary."

"And I say that it would be worse,—much worse. What? Will you bid your wife make so much of any man as to run away from him? Will you let the world say that you think that I cannot be safe in his company? I will not consent to that, George. The running away shall not be mine. Of course you can take me away, if you please, but I shall feel—"

"Well!"

"You know what I shall feel. I told you last night."

"What do you want me to do?" he asked, after a pause.

"Nothing."

"I am to hear these stories and not even to tell you that I have heard them?"

"I did not say that, George. I suppose it is better that you should tell me. But I think you should say at the same time that you know them to be false." Even though they were false, there was that doctrine of Cæsar's wife which she would not understand! "I think I should be told, and then left to regulate my own ways accordingly." This was mutinously imperious, and yet he did not quite know how to convince her of her mutiny. Through it all he was cowed by the remembrance of that love-letter, which, of course, was in her mind, but which she was either too generous or too wise to mention. He almost began to think that it was wisdom rather than generosity, feeling himself to be more cowed by her reticence than he would have been by her speech.

"You imagine, then, that a husband should never interfere."

"Not to protect a wife from that from which she is bound to protect herself. If he has to do so, she is not the worth the trouble, and he had better get rid of her. It is like preventing a man from drinking by locking up the wine."

"That has to be done sometimes."

"It sha'n't be done to me, George. You must either trust me, or we must part."

"I do trust you," he said, at last.

"Then let there be an end of all this trouble. Tell Susanna that you trust me. For your brother and that disappointed young woman I care nothing. But if I am to spend my time at Cross Hall, whatever they may think, I should not wish them to believe that you thought evil of me. And, George, don't suppose that because I say that I will not run away from Captain De Baron, all this will go for nothing with me. I will not avoid Captain De Baron, but I will be careful to give no cause for ill-natured words." Then she put her arm round his neck, and kissed him, and had conquered him.

When he went away from the house he had another great trouble before him. He had not seen Mrs. Houghton as yet, since his wife had found that love-letter; but she had written to him often. She had sent notes to his club almost wild with love and anger,—with that affectation of love and anger which some women know how to assume, and which so few men know how to withstand. It was not taken to be quite real, even by Lord George; and yet he could not withstand it. Mrs. Houghton, who understood the world thoroughly, had become quite convinced that Lady George had quarrelled with her. The two women had been very intimate ever since Lady George had been in town, and now for the last few days they had not seen each other. Mrs. Houghton had called twice, and had been refused. Then she had written, and had received no answer. She knew then that Mary had discovered something, and, of course, attributed her lover's absence to the wife's influence. But it did not occur to her that she should, on this account, give up her intercourse with Lord George. Scenes, quarrels, reconciliations, troubles, recriminations, jealousies, resolves, petty triumphs, and the general upsetting of the happiness of other people,—these were to her the sweets of what she called a passion. To give it all up because her lover's wife had found her out, and because her lover was in trouble, would be to abandon her love just when it was producing the desired fruit. She wrote short letters and long letters, angry letters, and most affectionate letters to Lord

George at his club, entreating him to come to her, and almost driving him out of his wits. He had, from the first, determined that he would go to her. He had even received his wife's sanction for doing so; but, knowing how difficult it would be to conduct such an interview, had, hitherto, put off the evil hour. But now a day and an hour had been fixed, and the day and the hour had come. The hour had very nearly come. When he left his house there was still time for him to sit for awhile at his club, and think what he would say to this woman.

He wished to do what was right. There was not a man in England less likely to have intended to amuse himself with a second love within twelve months of his marriage than Lord George Germain. He had never been a Lothario,—had never thought himself to be gifted in that way. In the first years of his manhood, when he had been shut up at Manor Cross, looking after his mother's limited means, with a full conviction that it was his duty to sacrifice himself to her convenience, he had been apt to tell himself that he was one of those men who have to go through life without marrying—or loving. Though strikingly handsome, he had never known himself to be handsome. He had never thought himself to be clever, or bright, or agreeable. High birth had been given to him, and a sense of honour. Of those gifts he had been well aware and proud enough, but had taken credit to himself for nothing else. Then had come that startling episode of his life in which he had fallen in love with Adelaide De Baron, and then the fact of his marriage with Mary Lovelace. Looking back at it now, he could hardly understand how it had happened that he had either fallen in love or married. He certainly was not now the least in love with Mrs. Houghton. And, though he did love his wife dearly, though the more he saw of her the more he admired her, yet his marriage had not made him happy. He had to live on her money, which galled him, and to be assisted by the Dean's money, which was wormwood to him. And he found himself to be driven whither he did not wish to go, and to be brought into perils from which his experience did not suffice to extricate him. He already repented the step he had taken in regard to his brother, knowing that it was the Dean who had done it, and not he himself. Had he not married, he might well have left the battle to be fought in after years,—when his brother should be dead, and very probably he himself also.

He was aware that he must be very firm with Mrs. Houghton. Come what might he must give her to understand quite clearly that all love-making must be over between them. The horrors of such a condition of things had been made much clearer to him than before by his own anxiety in reference to Captain De Baron. But he knew himself to be too soft-hearted for such firmness. If he could send some one else, how much better it would be! But, alas! this was a piece of work which no deputy could do for him. Nor could a letter serve as a deputy. Let him write as carefully as he might, he must say things which would condemn him utterly were they to find their way into Mr. Houghton's hands. One terrible letter had gone astray, and why not another?

She had told him to be in Berkeley Square at two, and he was there very punctually. He would at the moment have given much to find the house full of people; but she was quite alone. He had thought that she would receive him with a storm of tears, but when he entered she was radiant with smiles. Then he remembered how on a former occasion she had deceived him, making him believe that all her lures to him meant little or nothing just when he had determined to repudiate them because he had feared that they meant so much. He must not allow himself to be won in that way again. He must be firm, even though she smiled. "What is all this about?" she said in an affected whisper as soon as the door was closed. He looked very grave and shook his head. "'Thou canst not say I did it. Never shake thy gory locks at me.' That wife of yours has found out something, and has found it out from you, my Lord."

"Yes, indeed."

"What has she found out?"

"She read a letter to me which you sent to the club."

"Then I think it very indecent behaviour on her part. Does she search her husband's correspondence? I don't condescend to do that sort of thing."

"It was my fault. I put it into her hand by mistake. But that does not matter."

"Not matter! It matters very much to me, I think. Not that I care. She cannot hurt me. But, George, was not that careless— very careless; so careless as to be—unkind?"

"Of course it was careless."

"And ought you not to think more of me than that? Have you not done me an injury, sir, when you owed me all solicitude and every possible precaution?" This was not to be denied. If he chose to receive such letters, he was bound at any rate to keep them secret. "But men are so foolish—so little thoughtful! What did she say, George?"

"She behaved like an angel."

"Of course. Wives in such circumstances always do. Just a few drops of anger, and then a deluge of forgiveness. That was it, was it not?"

"Something like it."

"Of course. It happens every day,—because men are so stupid, but at the same time so necessary. But what did she say of me I Was she angel on my side of the house as well as yours?"

"Of course she was angry."

"It did not occur to her that she had been the interloper, and had taken you away from me?"

"That was not so. You had married."

"Psha! Married! Of course I had married. Everybody marries. You had married; but I did not suppose that for that reason you would forget me altogether. People must marry as circumstances suit. It is no good going back to that old story. Why did you not come to me sooner, and tell me of this tragedy I Why did you leave me to run after her and write to her?"

"I have been very unhappy."

"So you ought to be. But things are never so bad in the wearing as in the anticipation. I don't suppose she'll go about destroying my name and doing me a mischief?"

"Never."

"Because if she did, you know, I could retaliate."

"What do you mean by that, Mrs. Houghton?"

"Nothing that need disturb you, Lord George. Do not look such daggers at me. But women have to be forbearing to each other. She is your wife, and you may be sure I shall never say a nasty word about her,—unless she makes herself very objectionable to me."

"Nobody can say nasty things about her."

"That is all right, then. And now what have you to say to me about myself? I am not going to be gloomy because a little misfortune has happened. It is not my philosophy to cry after spilt milk."

"I will sit down a minute," he said; for hitherto he had been standing.

"Certainly; and I will sit opposite to you,—for ten minutes if you wish it. I see that there is something to be said. What is it?"

"All that has passed between you and me for the last month or two must be forgotten."

"Oh, that is it!"

"I will not make her miserable, nor will I bear a burden upon my own conscience."

"Your conscience! What a speech for a man to make to a woman! And how about my conscience? And then one thing further. You say that it must be all forgotten?"

"Yes, indeed."

"Can you forget it?"

"I can strive to do so. By forgetting, one means laying it aside. We remember chiefly those things which we try to remember."

"And you will not try to remember me—in the least? You will lay me aside—like an old garment? Because this—angel—has come across a scrawl which you were too careless either to burn or to lock up! You will tell yourself to forget me, as you would a servant that you had dismissed,—much more easily than you would a dog? Is that so?"

"I did not say that I could do it easily."

"You shall not do it at all. I will not be forgotten. Did you ever love me, sir?"

"Certainly I did. You know that I did."

"When? How long since? Have you ever sworn that you loved me since this—angel—has been your wife?" Looking back as well as he could, he rather thought that he never had sworn that he loved her in these latter days. She had often bidden him to do so; but as far as he could recollect at the moment, he had escaped the absolute utterance of the oath by some subterfuge. But doubtless he had done that which had been tantamount to swearing; and, at any rate, he could not now say that he had never sworn. "Now you come to tell me that it must all be forgotten! Was it she taught you that word?"

"If you upbraid me I will go away."

"Go, sir,—if you dare. You first betray me to your wife by your egregious folly, and then tell me that you will leave me because I have a word to say for myself. Oh, George, I expected more tenderness than that from you."

"There is no use in being tender. It can only produce misery and destruction."

"Well; of all the cold-blooded speeches I ever heard, that is the worst. After all that has passed between us, you do not scruple to tell me that you cannot even express tenderness for me, lest it should bring you into trouble! Men have felt that before, I do not doubt; but I hardly think any man was ever hard enough to make such a speech. I wonder whether Captain De Baron is so considerate."

"What do you mean by that?"

"You come here and talk to me about your angel, and then tell me that you cannot show me even the slightest tenderness, lest it should make you miserable,—and you expect me to hold my tongue."

"I don't know why you should mention Captain De Baron."

"I'll tell you why, Lord George. There are five or six of us playing this little comedy. Mr. Houghton and I are married, but we have not very much to say to each other. It is the same with you and Mary."

"I deny it."

"I daresay; but at the same time you know it to be true. She consoles herself with Captain De Baron. With whom Mr. Houghton consoles himself I have never taken the trouble to enquire. I hope someone is good-natured to him, poor old soul. Then, as to you and me,—you used, I think, to get consolation here. But such comforts cost trouble, and you hate trouble." As she said this, she wound her arm inside his; and he, angry as he was with her for speaking as she had done of his wife, could not push her from him roughly. "Is not that how it is, George?"

"No?"

"Then I don't think you understand the play as well as I do."

"No! I deny it all."

"All?"

"Everything about Mary. It's a slander to mention that man's name in connection with her,—a calumny which I will not endure."

"How is it, then, if they mention mine in connection with you?"

"I am saying nothing about that."

"But I suppose you think of it. I am hardly of less importance to myself than Lady George is to herself. I did think I was not of less importance to you."

"Nobody ever was or ever can be of so much importance to me as my wife, and I will be on good terms with no one who speaks evil of her."

"They may say what they like of me?"

"Mr. Houghton must look to that."

"It is no business of yours, George?"

He paused a moment, and then found the courage to answer her. "No—none," he said. Had she confined herself to her own assumed wrongs, her own pretended affection,—had she contented herself with quarrelling with him for his carelessness, and had then called upon him for some renewed expression of love,—he would hardly have been strong enough to withstand her. But she could not keep her tongue from speaking evil of his wife. From the moment in which he had called Mary an angel, it was necessary to her comfort to malign the angel. She did not quite know the man, or the nature of men generally. A man, if his mind be given that way, may perhaps with safety whisper into a woman's ear that her husband is untrue to her. Such an accusation may serve his purpose. But the woman, on her side, should hold her peace about the man's wife. A man must be very degraded indeed if his wife be not holy to him. Lord George had been driving his wife almost mad during the last twenty-four hours by implied accusations, and yet she was to him the very holy of holies. All the Popenjoy question was as nothing to him in comparison with the sanctity of her name. And now, weak as he was, incapable as he would have been, under any other condition of mind, of extricating himself from the meshes which this woman was spinning for him, he was enabled to make an immediate and most salutary plunge by the genuine anger she had produced. "No, none," he said.

"Oh, very well. The angel is everything to you, and I am nothing?"

"Yes; my wife is everything to me."

"How dared you, then, come here and talk to me of love? Do you think I will stand this,—that I will endure to be treated in

this way? Angel, indeed! I tell you that she cares more for Jack
De Baron's little finger than for your whole body. She is never
happy unless he is with her. I don't think very much of my
cousin Jack, but to her he is a god."

"It is false."

"Very well. It is nothing to me; but you can hardly
expect, my Lord, that I should hear from you such pleasant
truths as you have just told me, and not give you back what I
believe to be truth in return."

"Have I spoken evil of any one? But I will not stay here,
Mrs. Houghton, to make recriminations. You have spoken most
cruelly of a woman who never injured you, who has always been
your firm friend. It is my duty to protect her, and I shall always
do so in all circumstances. Good morning." Then he went before
she could say another word to him. He would perhaps have been
justified had he been a little proud of the manner in which he had
carried himself through this interview; but he entertained no
such feeling. To the lady he had just left he feared that he had
been rough and almost cruel. She was not to him the mass of
whipped cream turned sour which she may perhaps be to the
reader. Though he had been stirred to anger, he had been
indignant with circumstances rather than with Mrs. Houghton.
But in truth the renewed accusation against his wife made him so
wretched that there was no room in his breast for pride. He had
been told that she liked Jack De Baron's little finger better than
his whole body, and had been so told by one who knew both his
wife and Jack De Baron. Of course there had been spite and
malice and every possible evil passion at work. But then
everybody was saying the same thing. Even though there were
not a word of truth in it, such a rumour alone would suffice to
break his heart. How was he to stop cruel tongues, especially the
tongue of this woman, who would now be his bitterest enemy? If
such things were repeated by all connected with him, how would
he be able to reconcile his own family to his wife? There was
nothing which he valued now but the respect which he held in

his own family and that which his wife might hold. And in his own mind he could not quite acquit her. She would not be made to understand that she might injure his honour and destroy his happiness even though she committed no great fault. To take her away with a strong hand seemed to be his duty. But then there was the Dean, who would most certainly take her part,—and he was afraid of the Dean.

Chapter XXXVI.

Popenjoy Is Popenjoy.

Then came Lady Brabazon's party. Lord George said nothing further to his wife about Jack De Baron for some days after that storm in Berkeley Square,—nor did she to him. She was quite contented that matters should remain as they now were. She had vindicated herself, and if he made no further accusation, she was willing to be appeased. He was by no means contented;—but as a day had been fixed for them to leave London, and that day was now but a month absent, he hardly knew how to insist upon an alteration of their plans. If he did so he must declare war against the Dean, and, for a time, against his wife also. He postponed, therefore, any decision, and allowed matters to go on as they were. Mary was no doubt triumphant in her spirit. She had conquered him for a time, and felt that it was so. But she was, on that account, more tender and observant to him than ever. She even offered to give up Lady Brabazon's party, altogether. She did not much care for Lady Brabazon's party, and was willing to make a sacrifice that was perhaps no sacrifice. But to this he did not assent. He declared himself to be quite ready for Lady Brabazon's party, and to Lady Brabazon's party they went. As she was on the staircase she asked him a question. "Do you mind my having a waltz to-night?" He could not bring himself for the moment to be stern enough to refuse. He knew that the pernicious man would not be there. He was quite sure that the question was not asked in reference to the pernicious man. He did not understand, as he should have done, that a claim was being made for general emancipation, and he muttered something which was intended to imply assent. Soon afterwards she took two or three turns with a stout middle-aged gentleman, a Count somebody, who was connected with the German embassy. Nothing on earth could have been more harmless or apparently uninteresting. Then she signified to him that she had done her duty to Lady Brabazon and was quite ready to go home. "I'm not particularly bored," he said; "don't mind me." "But I am," she whispered, laughing, "and as I know you don't care about it, you might as well take me away." So he took her home. They were not there above half-an-hour, but she had carried her point about the waltzing.

On the next day the Dean came to town to attend a meeting at Mr. Battle's chambers by appointment. Lord George met him there, of course, as they were at any rate supposed to act in strict concert; but on these days the Dean did not stay in Munster Court when in London.

He would always visit his daughter, but would endeavour to do so in her husband's absence, and was unwilling even to dine there. "We shall be better friends down at Brotherton," he said to her. "He is always angry with me after discussing this affair of his brother's; and I am not quite sure that he likes seeing me here." This he had said on a previous occasion, and now the two men met in Lincoln's-Inn-Fields, not having even gone there together.

At this meeting the lawyer told them a strange story, and one which to the Dean was most unsatisfactory,—one which he resolutely determined to disbelieve. "The Marquis," said Mr. Battle, "had certainly gone through two marriage ceremonies with the Italian lady, one before the death and one after the death of her first reputed husband. And as certainly the so-called Popenjoy had been born before the second ceremony." So much the Dean believed very easily, and the information tallied altogether with his own views. If this was so, the so-called Popenjoy could not be a real Popenjoy, and his daughter would be Marchioness of Brotherton when this wicked ape of a marquis should die; and her son, should she have one, would be the future marquis. But then there came the remainder of the lawyer's story. Mr. Battle was inclined, from all that he had learned, to believe that the Marchioness had never really been married at all to the man whose name she had first borne, and that the second marriage had been celebrated merely to save appearances.

"What appearances!" exclaimed the Dean. Mr. Battle shrugged his shoulders. Lord George sat in gloomy silence. "I don't believe a word of it," said the Dean.

Then the lawyer went on with his story. This lady had been betrothed early in life to the Marchese Luigi; but the man had become insane—partially insane and by fits and starts. For some reason, not as yet understood, which might probably never be understood, the lady's family had thought it expedient that the lady should bear the name of the man to whom she was to be married. She had done so for some years and had been in possession of some income belonging to him. But Mr. Battle was of opinion that she had never been Luigi's wife. Further enquiries might possibly be made, and might add to further results. But they would be very expensive. A good deal of money had already been spent. "What did Lord George wish?"

"I think we have done enough," said Lord George, slowly,—thinking also that he had been already constrained to do much too much.

"It must be followed out to the end," said the Dean. "What! Here is a woman who professed for years to be a man's wife, who bore his name, who was believed by everybody to have been his wife—"

"I did not say that, Mr. Dean," interrupted the lawyer.

"Who lived on the man's revenues as his wife, and even bore his title, and now in such an emergency as this we are to take a cock and bull story as gospel. Remember, Mr. Battle, what is at stake."

"Very much is at stake, Mr. Dean, and therefore these enquiries have been made,—at a very great expense. But our own evidence as far as it goes is all against us. The Luigi family say that there was no marriage. Her family say that there was, but cannot prove it. The child may die, you know."

"Why should he die?" asked Lord George.

"I am trying the matter all round, you know. I am told the poor child is in ill health. One has got to look at probabilities. Of course you do not abandon a right by not prosecuting it now."

"It would be a cruelty to the boy to let him be brought up as Lord Popenjoy and afterwards dispossessed," said the Dean.

"You, gentlemen, must decide," said the lawyer. "I only say that I do not recommend further steps."

"I will do nothing further," said Lord George. "In the first place I cannot afford it."

"We will manage that between us," said the Dean. "We need not trouble Mr. Battle with that. Mr. Battle will not fear but that all expenses will be paid."

"Not in the least," said Mr. Battle, smiling.

"I do not at all believe the story," said the Dean. "It does not sound like truth. If I spent my last shilling in sifting the matter to the bottom, I would go on with it. Though I were obliged to leave England for twelve months myself, I would do it. A man is bound to ascertain his own rights."

"I will have nothing more to do with it," said Lord George, rising from his chair. "As much has been done as duty required; perhaps more. Mr. Battle, good morning. If we could know as soon as possible what this unfortunate affair has cost, I shall be obliged." He asked his father-in-law to accompany him, but the Dean said that he would speak a word or two further to Mr. Battle and remained.

At his club Lord George was much surprised to find a note from his brother. The note was as follows:—

> "Would you mind coming to me here to-morrow or the next day at 3.
>
> "B. Scumberg's Hotel, Tuesday."

This to Lord George was very strange indeed. He could not but remember all the circumstances of his former visit to his brother,—how he had been insulted, how his wife had been vilified, how his brother had heaped scorn on him. At first he thought that he was bound to refuse to do as he was asked. But why should his brother ask him? And his brother was his brother,—the head of his family. He decided at last that he would go, and left a note himself at Scumberg's Hotel that evening, saying that he would be there on the morrow.

He was very much perplexed in spirit as he thought of the coming interview. He went to the Dean's club and to the Dean's hotel, hoping to find the Dean, and thinking that as he had consented to act with the Dean against his brother, he was bound in honour to let the Dean know of the new phase in the affair. But he did not find his father-in-law. The Dean returned to Brotherton on the following morning, and therefore knew nothing of this meeting till some days after it had taken place. The language which the Marquis had used to his brother they were last together had been such as to render any friendly intercourse almost impossible. And then the mingled bitterness, frivolity, and wickedness of his brother, made every tone of the man's voice and every glance of his eye distasteful to Lord George. Lord George was always honest, was generally serious, and never malicious. There could be no greater contrast than that which had been produced between the brothers, either by difference of disposition from their birth, or by the varied circumstances of a residence on an Italian lake and one at Manor Cross. The Marquis thought his brother to be a fool, and did not scruple to say so on all occasions. Lord George felt that his brother was a knave, but would not have so called him on any consideration. The Marquis in sending for his brother hoped that even after all that had passed, he might make use of Lord George. Lord George in going to his brother, hoped that even after all that had passed he might be of use to the Marquis.

When he was shown into the sitting-room at the hotel, the Marchioness was again there. She, no doubt, had been tutored. She got up at once and shook hands with her brother-in-law, smiling graciously. It must have been a comfort to both of them that they spoke no common language, as they could hardly have had many thoughts to interchange with each other.

"I wonder why the deuce you never learned Italian," said the Marquis.

"We never were taught," said Lord George.

"No;—nobody in England ever is taught anything but Latin and Greek,—with this singular result, that after ten or a dozen years of learning not one in twenty knows a word of either language. That is our English idea of education. In after life a little French may be picked up, from necessity; but it is French of the very worst kind. My wonder is that Englishman can hold their own in the world at all."

"They do," said Lord George,—to whom all this was ear-piercing blasphemy. The national conviction that an Englishman could thrash three foreigners, and if necessary eat them, was strong with him.

"Yes; there is a ludicrous strength even in their pig-headedness. But I always think that Frenchmen, Italians, and Prussians must in dealing with us, be filled with infinite disgust. They must ever be saying, 'pig, pig, pig,' beneath their breath, at every turn."

"They don't dare to say it out loud," said Lord George.

"They are too courteous, my dear fellow." Then he said a few words to his wife in Italian, upon which she left the room, again shaking hands with her brother-in-law, and again smiling.

Then the Marquis rushed at once into the middle of his affairs.

"Don't you think George that you are an infernal fool to quarrel with me."

"You have quarrelled with me. I haven't quarrelled with you."

"Oh no;—not at all! When you send lawyer's clerks all over Italy to try to prove my boy to be a bastard, and that is not quarrelling with me! When you accuse my wife of bigamy that is not quarrelling with me! When you conspire to make my house in the country too hot to hold me, that is not quarrelling with me!"

"How have I conspired? with whom have I conspired?"

"When I explained my wishes about the house at Cross Hall, why did you encourage those foolish old maids to run counter to me. You must have understood pretty well that it would not suit either of us to be near the other, and yet you chose to stick up for legal rights."

"We thought it better for my mother."

"My mother would have consented to anything that I proposed. Do you think I don't know how the land lies? Well; what have you learned in Italy?" Lord George was silent. "Of course, I know. I'm not such a fool as not to keep my ears and eyes open. As far as your enquiries have gone yet, are you justified in calling Popenjoy a bastard?"

"I have never called him so;—never. I have always declared my belief and my wishes to be in his favour."

"Then why the d—— have you made all this rumpus?"

"Because it was necessary to be sure. When a man marries the same wife twice over—"

"Have you never heard of that being done before? Are you so ignorant as not to know that there are a hundred little reasons which may make that expedient? You have made your enquiries now and what is the result?"

Lord George paused a moment before he replied, and then answered with absolute honesty. "It is all very odd to me. That may be my English prejudice. But I do think that your boy is legitimate."

"You are satisfied as to that?"

He paused again, meditating his reply. He did not wish to be untrue to the Dean, but then he was very anxious to be true to his brother. He remembered that in the Dean's presence he had told the lawyer that he would have nothing to do with further enquiries. He had asked for the lawyer's bill, thereby withdrawing from the investigation. "Yes," he said slowly; "I am satisfied."

"And you mean to do nothing further?"

Again he was very slow, remembering how necessary it would be that he should tell all this to the Dean, and how full of wrath the Dean would be. "No; I do not mean to do anything further."

"I may take that as your settled purpose?"

There was another pause, and then he spoke, "Yes; you may."

"Then, George, let us try and forget what has passed. It cannot pay for you and me to quarrel. I shall not stay in England very long. I don't like it. It was necessary that the people about should know that I had a wife and son, and so I brought him and her to this comfortless country. I shall return before the winter, and for anything that I care you may all go back to Manor Cross."

"I don't think my mother would like that."

"Why shouldn't she like it? I suppose I was to be allowed to have my own house when I wanted it? I hope there was no offence in that, even to that dragon Sarah? At any rate, you may as well look after the property; and if they won't live there, you can. But there's one question I want to ask you."

"Well?"

"What do you think of your precious father-in-law; and what do you think that I must think of him? Will you not admit that for a vulgar, impudent brute, he is about as bad as even England can supply?" Of course Lord George had nothing to say in answer to this. "He is going on with this tom-foolery, I believe?"

"You mean the enquiry?"

"Yes; I mean the enquiry whether my son and your nephew is a bastard. I know he put you up to it. Am I right in saying that he has not abandoned it?"

"I think you are right."

"Then by heaven I'll ruin him. He may have a little money, but I don't think his purse is quite so long as mine. I'll lead him such a dance that he shall wish he had never heard the name of Germain. I'll make his deanery too hot to hold him. Now, George, as between you and me this shall be all passed over. That poor child is not strong, and after all you may probably be my heir. I shall never live in England, and you are welcome to the house. I can be very bitter, but I can forgive; and as far as you are concerned I do forgive. But I expect you to drop your precious father-in-law." Lord George was again silent. He could not say that he would drop the Dean; but at this moment he was not sufficiently fond of the Dean to rise up in his stirrups and fight a battle for him. "You understand me," continued the Marquis, "I don't want any assurance from you. He is determined to prosecute an enquiry adverse to the honour of your family, and in opposition to your settled convictions. I don't think that after that you can doubt about your duty. Come and see me again before long; won't you?" Lord George said that he would come again before long, and then departed.

As he walked home his mind was sorely perplexed and divided. He had made up his mind to take no further share in the Popenjoy investigation, and must have been right to declare as much to his brother. His conscience was clear as to that. And then there were many reasons which induced him to feel coldly about the Dean. His own wife had threatened him with her father. And the Dean was always driving him. And he hated the Dean's money. He felt that the Dean was not quite all that a gentleman should be. But, nevertheless, it behoved him above all things to be honest and straightforward with the Dean.

There had been something in his interview with his brother to please him, but it had not been all delightful.

Chapter XXXVII.

Preparations For The Ball.

How was he to keep faith with the Dean? This was Lord George's first trouble after his reconciliation with his brother. The Dean was back at the deanery, and Lord George mistrusted his own power of writing such a letter as would be satisfactory on so abstruse a matter. He knew that he should fail in making a good story, even face to face, and that his letter would be worse than spoken words. In intellect he was much inferior to the Dean, and was only too conscious of his own inferiority. In this condition of mind he told his story to his wife. She had never even seen the Marquis, and had never quite believed in those ogre qualities which had caused so many groans to Lady Sarah and Lady Susanna. When, therefore, her husband told her that he had made his peace with his brother she was inclined to rejoice. "And Popenjoy is Popenjoy," she said smiling.

"I believe he is, with all my heart."

"And that is to be an end of it, George? You know that I have never been eager for any grandeur."

"I know it. You have behaved beautifully all along."

"Oh; I won't boast. Perhaps I ought to have been more ambitious for you. But I hate quarrels, and I shouldn't like to have claimed anything which did not really belong to us. It is all over now."

"I can't answer for your father."

"But you and papa are all one."

"Your father is very steadfast. He does not know yet that I have seen my brother. I think you might write to him. He ought to know what has taken place. Perhaps he would come up again if he heard that I had been with my brother."

"Shall I ask him to come here?"

"Certainly. Why should he not come here? There is his room. He can always come if he pleases." So the matter was left, and Mary wrote her letter. It was not very lucid;—but it could hardly have been lucid, the writer knowing so few of the details. "George has become friends with his brother," she said, "and wishes me to tell you. He says that Popenjoy is Popenjoy, and I am very glad. It was such a trouble. George thinks you will come up to town when you hear, and begs you will come here. Do come, papa! It makes me quite wretched when you go to that horrid hotel. There is such a lot of quarrelling, and it almost seems as if you were going to quarrel with us when you don't come here. Pray, papa, never, never do that. If I thought you and George weren't friends it would break my heart. Your room is always ready for you, and if you'll say what day you'll be here I will get a few people to meet you." The letter was much more occupied with her desire to see her father than with that momentous question on which her father was so zealously intent. Popenjoy is Popenjoy! It was very easy to assert so much. Lord George would no doubt give way readily, because he disliked the trouble of the contest. But it was not so with the Dean. "He is no more Popenjoy than I am Popenjoy," said the Dean to himself when he read the letter. Yes; he must go up to town again. He must know what had really taken place between the two brothers. That was essential, and he did not doubt but

that he should get the exact truth from Lord George. But he
would not go to Munster Court. There was already a difference
of opinion between him and his son-in-law sufficient to make
such a sojourn disagreeable. If not disagreeable to himself, he
knew that it would be so to Lord George. He was sorry to vex
Mary, but Mary's interests were more at his heart than her
happiness. It was now the business of his life to make her a
Marchioness, and that business he would follow whether he
made himself, her, and others happy or unhappy. He wrote to
her, bidding her tell her husband that he would again be in
London on a day which he named, but adding that for the present
he would prefer going to the hotel. "I cannot help it," said Lord
George moodily. "I have done all I could to make him welcome
here. If he chooses to stand off and be stiff he must do so."

At this time Lord George had many things to vex him.
Every day he received at his club a letter from Mrs. Houghton,
and each letter was a little dagger. He was abused by every
epithet, every innuendo, and every accusation familiar to the
tongues and pens of the irritated female mind. A stranger reading
them would have imagined that he had used all the arts of a
Lothario to entrap the unguarded affections of the writer, and
then, when successful, had first neglected the lady and
afterwards betrayed her. And with every stab so given there was
a command expressed that he should come instantly to Berkeley
Square in order that he might receive other and worse gashes at
the better convenience of the assailant. But as Mrs. Bond's
ducks would certainly not have come out of the pond had they
fully understood the nature of that lady's invitation, so neither
did Lord George go to Berkeley Square in obedience to these
commands. Then there came a letter which to him was no longer
a little dagger, but a great sword,—a sword making a wound so
wide that his life-blood seemed to flow. There was no accusation
of betrayal in this letter. It was simply the broken-hearted
wailings of a woman whose love was too strong for her. Had he
not taught her to regard him as the only man in the world whose

presence was worth having? Had he not so wound himself into every recess of her heart as to make life without seeing him insupportable? Could it be possible that, after having done all this, he had no regard for her? Was he so hard, so cruel, such adamant as to deny her at least a farewell? As for herself, she was now beyond all fear of consequences. She was ready to die if it were necessary,—ready to lose all the luxuries of her husband's position rather than never see him again. She had a heart! She was inclined to doubt whether any one among her acquaintances was so burdened. Why, oh why, had she thought so steadfastly of his material interests when he used to kneel at her feet and ask her to be his bride, before he had ever seen Mary Lovelace? Then this long epistle was brought to an end. *"Come to me to-morrow, A. H. Destroy this the moment you have read it."* The last behest he did obey. He would put no second letter from this woman in his wife's way. He tore the paper into minute fragments, and deposited the portions in different places. That was easily done; but what should be done as to the other behest? If he went to Berkeley Square again, would he be able to leave it triumphantly as he had done on his last visit? That he did not wish to see her for his own sake he was quite certain. But he thought it incumbent on him to go yet once again. He did not altogether believe all that story as to her tortured heart. Looking back at what had passed between them since he had first thought himself to be in love with her, he could not remember such a depth of love-making on his part as that which she described. In the ordinary way he had proposed to her, and had, in the ordinary way, been rejected. Since that, and since his marriage, surely the protestations of affection had come almost exclusively from the lady! He thought that it was so, and yet was hardly sure. If he had got such a hold on her affections as she described, certainly, then, he owed to her some reparation. But as he remembered her great head of false hair and her paint, and called to mind his wife's description of her, he almost protested to himself that she was deceiving him;—he almost read her rightly. Nevertheless, he would go once more. He would go and tell her sternly that the thing must come to an end, and that no more letters were to be written.

He did go and found Jack De Baron there, and heard Jack discourse enthusiastically about Mrs. Montacute Jones's ball, which was to be celebrated in two or three days from the present time. Then Mrs. Houghton was very careful to ask some question in Lord George's presence as to some special figure-dance which was being got up for the occasion. It was a dance newly introduced from Moldavia, and was the most ravishing thing in the way of dancing that had ever yet found its way into this country. Nobody had yet seen it, and it was being kept a profound secret,—to be displayed only at Mrs. Montacute Jones's party. It was practised in secret in her back drawing room by the eight performers, with the assistance of a couple of most trustworthy hired musicians, whom that liberal old lady, Mrs. Montacute Jones, supplied,—so that the rehearsals might make the performers perfect for the grand night. This was the story as told with great interest by Mrs. Houghton, who seemed for the occasion almost to have recovered from her heart complaint. That, however, was necessarily kept in abeyance during Jack's presence. Jack, though he had been enthusiastic about Mrs. Jones and her ball before Lord George's arrival, and though he had continued to talk freely up to a certain point, suddenly became reticent as to the great Moldavian dance. But Mrs. Houghton would not be reticent. She declared the four couple who had been selected as performers to be the happy, fortunate ones of the season. Mrs. Montacute Jones was a nasty old woman for not having asked her. Of course there was a difficulty, but there might have been two sets. "And Jack is such a false loon," she said to Lord George, "that he won't show me one of the figures."

"Are you going to dance it?" asked Lord George.

"I fancy I'm to be one of the team."

"He is to dance with Mary," said Mrs. Houghton. Then Lord George thought that he understood the young man's reticence, and he was once again very wretched. There came that cloud upon his brow which never sat there without being visible to all who were in the company. No man told the tale of his own feelings so plainly as he did. And Mrs. Houghton, though declaring herself to be ignorant of the figure, had described the dance as a farrago of polkas, waltzes, and galops, so that the thing might be supposed to be a fast rapturous whirl from the beginning to the end. And his wife was going through this indecent exhibition at Mrs. Montacute Jones' ball with Captain de Baron after all that he had said!

"You are quite wrong in your ideas about the dance," said Jack to his cousin. "It is the quietest thing out,—almost as grave as a minuet. It's very pretty, but people here will find it too slow." It may be doubted whether he did much good by this explanation. Lord George thought that he was lying, though he had almost thought before that Mrs. Houghton was lying on the other side. But it was true at any rate that after all that had passed a special arrangement had been made for his wife to dance with Jack De Baron. And then his wife had been called by implication, "One of the team."

Jack got up to go, but before he left the room Aunt Ju was there, and then that sinful old woman Mrs. Montacute Jones herself. "My dear," she said in answer to a question from Mrs. Houghton about the dance, "I am not going to tell anybody anything about it. I don't know why it should have been talked of. Four couple of good looking young people are going to amuse themselves, and I have no doubt that those who look on will be very much gratified." Oh, that his wife, that Lady Mary Germain, should be talked of as one of "four couple of good looking young people," and that she should be about to dance with Jack De Baron, in order that strangers might be gratified by looking at her!

It was manifest that nothing special could be said to Mrs. Houghton on that occasion, as one person came after another. She looked all the while perfectly disembarrassed. Nobody could have imagined that she was in the presence of the man whose love was all the world to her. When he got up to take his leave she parted from him as though he were no more to her than he ought to have been. And indeed he too had for the time been freed from the flurry of his affair with Mrs. Houghton by the other flurry occasioned by the Moldavian dance. The new dance was called, he had been told, the Kappa-kappa. There was something in the name suggestive of another dance of which he had heard,—and he was very unhappy.

He found the Dean in Munster Court when he reached his own house. The first word that his wife spoke to him was about the ball. "George, papa is going with me on Friday to Mrs. Montacute Jones'."

"I hope he will like it," said Lord George.

"I wish you would come."

"Why should I go? I have already said that I would not."

"As for the invitation that does not signify in the least. Do come just about twelve o'clock. We've got up such a dance, and I should like you to come and see it."

"Who is we?"

"Well;—the parties are not quite arranged yet. I think I'm to dance with Count Costi. Something depends on colours of dress and other matters. The gentlemen are all to be in some kind of uniform. We have rehearsed it, and in rehearsing we have done it all round, one with the other."

"Why didn't you tell me before?"

"We weren't to tell till it was settled."

"I mean to go and see it," said the Dean. "I delight in anything of that kind."

Mary was so perfectly easy in the matter, so free from doubt, so disembarrassed, that he was for the moment tranquillised. She had said that she was to dance, not with that pernicious Captain, but with a foreign Count. He did not like foreign Counts, but at the present moment he preferred any one to Jack De Baron. He did not for a moment doubt her truth. And she had been true,—though Jack De Baron and Mrs. Houghton had been true also. When Mary had been last at Mrs. Jones' house the matter had not been quite settled, and in her absence Jack had foolishly, if not wrongly, carried his point with the old lady. It had been decided that the performers were to go through their work in the fashion that might best achieve the desired effect;—that they were not to dance exactly with whom they pleased, but were to have their parts assigned them as actors on a stage. Jack no doubt had been led by his own private wishes in securing Mary as his partner, but of that contrivance on his part she had been ignorant when she gave her programme of the affair to her husband. "Won't you come in and see it?" she said again.

"I am not very fond of those things. Perhaps I may come in for a few minutes."

"I am fond of them," said the Dean. "I think any innocent thing that makes life joyous and pretty is good."

"That is rather begging the question," said Lord George, as he left the room.

Mary had not known what her husband meant by begging the question, but the Dean had of course understood him. "I hope he is not going to become ascetic," he said. "I hope at least that he will not insist that you should be so."

"It is not his nature to be very gay," she answered.

On the next day, in the morning, was the last rehearsal, and then Mary learned what was her destiny. She regretted it, but could not remonstrate. Jack's uniform was red. The Count's dress was blue and gold. Her dress was white, and she was told that the white and red must go together. There was nothing more to be said. She could not plead that her husband was afraid of Jack De Baron. Nor certainly would she admit to herself that she was in the least afraid of him herself. But for her husband's foolish jealousy she would infinitely have preferred the arrangement as now made,—just as a little girl prefers as a playmate a handsome boy whom she has long known, to some ill-visaged stranger with whom she has never quarrelled and never again made friends. But when she saw her husband she found herself unable to tell him of the change which had been made. She was not actor enough to be able to mention Jack De Baron's name to him with tranquility.

On the next morning,—the morning of the important day,—she heard casually from Mrs. Jones that Lord George had been at Mrs. Houghton's house. She had quite understood from her husband that he intended to see that evil woman again after the discovery and reading of the letter. He had himself told her that he intended it; and she, if she had not actually assented, had made no protest against his doing so. But that visit, represented as being one final necessary visit, had, she was well aware, been made some time since. She had not asked him what had taken place. She had been unwilling to show any doubt by such a question. The evil woman's name had never been on her tongue since the day on which the letter had been read. But now, when she heard that he was there again, so soon, as a friend joining in general conversation in the evil woman's house, the matter did touch her. Could it be that he was deceiving her after all, and that he loved the woman? Did he really like that helmet, that paint and that affected laugh? And had he lied to her,—deceived her with a premeditated story which must have been full of lies? She could hardly bring herself to believe this; and yet, why, why, why should he be there? The visit of which he had spoken had been one intended to put an end to all close friendship,—one in which he was to tell the woman that though the scandal of an outward quarrel might be avoided, he and she were to meet no more. And yet he was there. For aught she knew, he might be there every day! She did know that Mrs. Montacute Jones had found him there. Then he could come home to her and talk of the impropriety of dancing! He could do such thinks as this, and yet be angry with her because she liked the society of Captain De Baron!

Certainly she would dance with Captain De Baron. Let him come and see her dancing with him; and then, if he dared to upbraid her, she would ask him why he continued his intimacy in Berkeley Square. In her anger she almost began to think that a quarrel was necessary. Was it not manifest that he was deceiving her about that woman? The more she thought of it the more wretched she became; but on that day she said nothing of it to him. They dined together, the Dean dining with them. He was perturbed and gloomy, the Dean having assured them that he did not mean to allow the Popenjoy question to rest. "I stand in no awe of your brother," the Dean had said to him. This had angered Lord George, and he had refused to discuss the matter any further.

At nine Lady George went up to dress, and at half-past ten she started with her father. At that time her husband had left the house and had said not a word further as to his intention of going to Mrs. Jones' house. "Do you think he will come?" she said to the Dean.

"Upon my word I don't know. He seems to me to be in an ill-humour with all the world."

"Don't quarrel with him, papa."

"I do not mean to do so. I never mean to quarrel with anyone, and least of all with him. But I must do what I conceive to be my duty whether he likes it or not."

Chapter XXXVIII.

The Kappa-Kappa.

Mrs. Montacute Jones' house in Grosvenor Place was very large and very gorgeous. On this occasion it was very gorgeous indeed. The party had grown in dimensions. The new Moldavian dance had become the topic of general discourse. Everybody wanted to see the Kappa-kappa. Count Costi, Lord Giblet, young Sir Harry Tripletoe, and, no doubt, Jack De Baron also, had talked a good deal about it at the clubs. It had been intended to be a secret, and the ladies, probably, had been more reticent. Lady Florence Fitzflorence had just mentioned it to her nineteen specially intimate friends. Madame Gigi, the young wife of the old Bohemian minister, had spoken of it only to the diplomatic set; Miss Patmore Green had been as silent as death, except in her own rather large family, and Lady George had hardly told anybody, except her father. But, nevertheless, the secret had escaped, and great efforts had been made to secure invitations. "I can get you to the Duchess of Albury's in July if you can manage it for me," one young lady said to Jack De Baron.

"Utterly impossible!" said Jack, to whom the offered bribe was not especially attractive. "There won't be standing room in the cellars. I went down on my knees to Mrs. Montacute Jones for a very old friend, and she simply asked me whether I was mad." This was, of course, romance; but, nevertheless, the crowd was great, and the anxiety to see the Kappa-kappa universal.

By eleven the dancing had commenced. Everything had been arranged in the strictest manner. Whatever dance might be going on was to be brought to a summary close at twelve o'clock, and then the Kappa-kappa was to be commenced. It had been found that the dance occupied exactly forty minutes. When it was over the doors of the banquetting hall would be opened. The Kappa-kappaites would then march into supper, and the world at large would follow them.

Lady George, when she first entered the room, found a seat near the hostess, and sat herself down, meaning to wait for the important moment. She was a little flurried as she thought of various things. There was the evil woman before her, already dancing. The evil woman had nodded at her, and had then quickly turned away, determined not to see that her greeting was rejected; and there was Augusta Mildmay absolutely dancing with Jack De Baron, and looking as though she enjoyed the fun. But to Mary there was something terrible in it all. She had been so desirous to be happy,—to be gay,—to amuse herself, and yet to be innocent. Her father's somewhat epicurean doctrines had filled her mind completely. And what had hitherto come of it? Her husband mistrusted her; and she at this moment certainly mistrusted him most grievously. Could she fail to mistrust him? And she, absolutely conscious of purity, had been so grievously suspected! As she looked round on the dresses and diamonds, and heard the thick hum of voices, and saw on all sides the pretence of cordiality, as she watched the altogether unhidden flirtations of one girl, and the despondent frown of another, she began to ask herself whether her father had not been wrong when he insisted that she should be taken to London. Would she not have been more safe and therefore more happy even down at

Cross Hall, with her two virtuous sisters-in-law? What would become of her should she quarrel with her husband, and how should she not quarrel with him if he would suspect her, and would frequent the house of that evil woman?

Then Jack De Baron came up to her, talking to her father. The Dean liked the young man, who had always something to say for himself, whose manners were lively, and who, to tell the truth, was more than ordinarily civil to Lady George's father. Whether Jack would have put himself out of the way to describe the Kappa-kappa to any other dignitary of the Church may be doubted, but he had explained it all very graciously to the Dean. "So it seems that, after all, you are to dance with Captain De Baron," said the Dean.

"Yes; isn't it hard upon me? I was to have stood up with a real French Count, who has real diamond buttons, and now I am to be put off with a mere British Captain, because my white frock is supposed to suit his red coat!"

"And who has the Count?"

"That odiously fortunate Lady Florence;—and she has diamonds of her own! I think they should have divided the diamonds. Madame Gigi has the Lord. Between ourselves, papa,"—and as she said this she whispered, and both her father and Jack bent over to hear her—"we are rather afraid of our Lord; ain't we, Captain De Baron? There has been ever so much to manage, as we none of us quite wanted the Lord. Madame Gigi talks very little English, so we were able to put him off upon her."

"And does the Lord talk French?"

"That doesn't signify as Giblet never talks at all," said Jack.

"Why did you have him?"

"To tell you the truth, among us all there is rather a hope that he will propose to Miss Patmore Green. Dear Mrs. Montacute Jones is very clever at these things, and saw at a glance that nothing would be so likely to make him do it as seeing Madeline Green dancing with Tripletoe. No fellow ever did dance so well as Tripletoe, or looked half so languishing. You see, Dean, there are a good many in's and out's in these matters, and they have to be approached carefully." The Dean was amused, and his daughter would have been happy, but for the double care which sat heavy at her heart. Then Jack suggested to her that she might as well stand up for a square dance. All the other Kappa-kappaites had danced or were dancing. The one thing on which she was firmly determined was that she would not be afraid of Captain De Baron. Whatever she did now she did immediately under her father's eye. She made no reply, but got up and put her hand on the Captain's arm without spoken assent, as a woman will do when she is intimate with a man.

"Upon my word, for a very young creature I never saw such impudence as that woman's," said a certain Miss Punter to Augusta Mildmay. Miss Punter was a great friend of Augusta Mildmay, and was watching her friend's broken heart with intense interest.

"It is disgusting," said Augusta.

"She doesn't seem to mind the least who sees it. She must mean to leave Lord George altogether, or she would never go on like that. De Baron wouldn't be such a fool as to go off with her?"

"Men are fools enough for anything," said the broken-hearted one. While this was going on Mary danced her square dance complaisantly; and her proud father, looking on, thought that she was by far the prettiest woman in the room.

Before the quadrille was over a gong was struck, and the music stopped suddenly. It was twelve o'clock, and the Kappa-kappa was to be danced. It is hard in most amusements to compel men and women into disagreeable punctuality; but the stopping of music will bring a dance to a sudden end. There were some who grumbled, and one or two declared that they would not even stay to look at the Kappa-kappa. But Mrs.

Montacute Jones was a great autocrat; and in five minutes' time the four couples were arranged, with ample space, in spite of the pressing crowd.

It must be acknowledged that Jack De Baron had given no correct idea of the dance when he said that it was like a minuet; but it must be remembered also that Lady George had not been a party to that deceit. The figure was certainly a lively figure. There was much waltzing to quick time, the glory of which seemed to consist in going backwards, and in the interweaving of the couples without striking each other, as is done in skating. They were all very perfect, except poor Lord Giblet, who once or twice nearly fell into trouble. During the performance they all changed partners more than once, but each lady came back to her own after very short intervals. All those who were not envious declared it to be very pretty and prophesied great future success for the Kappa-kappa. Those who were very wise and very discreet hinted that it might become a romp when danced without all the preparation which had been given to it on the present occasion. It certainly became faster as it progressed, and it was evident that considerable skill and considerable physical power were necessary for its completion. "It would be a deal too stagey for my girls," said Mrs. Conway Smith, whose "girls" had, during the last ten years, gone through every phase of flirtation invented in these latter times. Perhaps it did savour a little too much of ballet practice; perhaps it was true that with less care there might have been inconveniences. Faster it grew and faster; but still they had all done it before, and done it with absolute accuracy. It was now near the end. Each lady had waltzed a turn with each gentleman. Lady George had been passed on from the Count to Sir Harry, and from Sir Harry to Lord Giblet. After her turn it was his lordship's duty to deliver her up to her partner, with whom she would make a final turn round the dancing space; and then the Kappa-kappa would have been danced. But alas! as Lord Giblet was doing this he lost his head and came against the Count and Madame Gigi. Lady

George was almost thrown to the ground, but was caught by the Captain, who had just parted with Lady Florence to Sir Harry. But poor Mary had been almost on the floor, and could hardly have been saved without something approaching to the violence of an embrace.

Lord George had come into the room very shortly after the Kappa-kappa had been commenced, but had not at once been able to get near the dancers. Gradually he worked his way through the throng, and when he first saw the performers could not tell who was his wife's partner. She was then waltzing backwards with Count Costi; and he, though he hated waltzing, and considered the sin to be greatly aggravated by the backward movement, and though he hated Counts, was still somewhat pacified. He had heard since he was in the room how the partners were arranged, and had thought that his wife had deceived him. The first glance was reassuring. But Mary soon returned to her real partner; and he slowly ascertained that she was in very truth waltzing with Captain De Baron. He stood there, a little behind the first row of spectators, never for a moment seen by his wife, but able himself to see everything, with a brow becoming every moment blacker and blacker. To him the exhibition was in every respect objectionable. The brightness of the apparel of the dancers was in itself offensive to him. The approach that had been made to the garishness of a theatrical performance made the whole thing, in his eyes, unfit for modest society. But that his wife should be one of the performers, that she should be gazed at by a crowd as she tripped about, and that, after all that had been said, she should be tripping in the arms of Captain De Baron, was almost more than he could endure. Close to him, but a little behind, stood the Dean, thoroughly enjoying all that he saw. It was to him a delight that there should be such a dance to be seen in a lady's drawing-room, and that he should be there to see it. It was to him an additional delight that his daughter should have been selected as one of the dancers. These people were all persons of rank and fashion, and his girl was among them quite as their equal,—his girl, who some day should be Marchioness of Brotherton. And it gratified him thoroughly to think that she enjoyed it,—that she did it well,—that she could dance so that standers-by took pleasure in seeing her dancing. His mind in the matter was altogether antagonistic to that of his son-in-law.

Then came the little accident. The Dean, with a momentary impulse, put up his hand, and then smiled well pleased when he saw how well the matter had been rectified by the Captain's activity. But it was not so with Lord George. He pressed forward into the circle with so determined a movement that nothing could arrest him till he had his wife by the arm. Everybody, of course, was staring at him. The dancers were astounded. Mary apparently thought less of it than the others, for she spoke to him with a smile. "It is all right, George; I was not in the least hurt."

"It is disgraceful!" said he, in a loud voice; "come away."

"Oh, yes," she said; "I think we had finished. It was nobody's fault."

"Come away; I will have no more of this."

"Is there anything wrong?" asked the Dean, with an air of innocent surprise.

The offended husband was almost beside himself with passion. Though he knew that he was surrounded by those who would mock him he could not restrain himself. Though he was conscious at the moment that it was his special duty to shield his wife, he could not restrain his feelings. The outrage was too much for him. "There is very much the matter," he said, aloud; "let her come away with me." Then he took her under his arm, and attempted to lead her away to the door.

Mrs. Montacute Jones had, of course, seen it all, and was soon with him. "Pray, do not take her away, Lord George," she said.

"Madam, I must be allowed to do so," he replied, still pressing on. "I would prefer to do so."

"Wait till her carriage is here."

"We will wait below. Good-night, good-night." And so he went out of the room with his wife on his arm, followed by the Dean. Since she had perceived that he was angry with her, and that he had displayed his anger in public Mary had not spoken a word. She had pressed him to come and see the dance, not without a purpose in her mind. She meant to get rid of the thraldom to which he had subjected her when desiring her not to waltz, and had done so in part when she obtained his direct sanction at Lady Brabazon's. No doubt she had felt that as he took liberties as to his own life, as he received love-letters from an odious woman, he was less entitled to unqualified obedience than he might have been had his hands been perfectly clean. There had been a little spirit of rebellion engendered in her by his misconduct; but she had determined to do nothing in secret. She had asked his leave to waltz at Lady Brabazon's, and had herself persuaded him to come to Mrs. Montacute Jones'. Perhaps she would hardly have dared to do so had she known that Captain De Baron was to be her partner. While dancing she had been unaware of her husband's presence, and had not thought of him. When he had first come to her she had in truth imagined that he had been frightened by her narrow escape from falling. But when he bade her come away with that frown on his face, and with that awful voice, then she knew it all. She had no alternative but to take his arm, and to "come away." She had not courage enough,—I had better perhaps say impudence enough,—to pretend to speak to him or to anyone near him with ease. All eyes were upon her, and she felt them; all tongues would be talking of her, and she already heard the ill-natured words. Her own husband had brought all this upon her,—her own husband, whose love-letter from another woman she had so lately seen, and so readily forgiven! It was her own husband who had so cruelly, so causelessly subjected her to shame in public, which could never be washed out or forgotten! And who would sympathise with her? There was no one now but her father. He would stand by her; he would be good to her; but her husband by his own doing had wilfully disgraced her.

Not a word was spoken till they were in the cloak-room, and then Lord George stalked out to find the brougham, or any cab that might take them away from the house. Then for the first time the Dean whispered a word to her. "Say as little as you can to him to-night, but keep up your courage."

"Oh, papa!"

"I understand it all. I will be with you immediately after breakfast."

"You will not leave me here alone?"

"Certainly not,—nor till you are in your carriage. But listen to what I am telling you. Say as little as you can till I am with you. Tell him that you are unwell to-night, and that you must sleep before you talk to him."

"Ah! you don't know, papa."

"I know that I will have the thing put on a right footing." Then Lord George came back, having found a cab. He gave his arm to his wife and took her away, without saying a word to the Dean. At the door of the cab the Dean bade them both good-night. "God bless you, my child," he said.

"Good-night; you'll come to-morrow?"

"Certainly." Then the door was shut, and the husband and wife were driven away.

Of course this little episode contributed much to the amusement of Mrs. Montacute Jones's guests. The Kappa-kappa had been a very pretty exhibition, but it had not been nearly so exciting as that of the jealous husband. Captain De Baron, who remained, was, of course, a hero. As he could not take his partner into supper, he was honoured by the hand of Mrs. Montacute Jones herself. "I wouldn't have had that happen for a thousand pounds," said the old lady.

"Nor I for ten," said Jack.

"Has there been any reason for it?"

"None in the least. I can't explain of what nature is my intimacy with Lady George, but it has been more like that of children than grown people."

"I know. When grown people play at being children, it is apt to be dangerous."

"But we had no idea of the kind. I may be wicked enough. I say nothing about that. But she is as pure as snow. Mrs. Jones, I could no more dare to press her hand than I would to fly at the sun. Of course I like her."

"And she likes you."

"I hope so,—in that sort of way. But it is shocking that such a scene should come from such a cause."

"Some men, Captain De Baron, don't like having their handsome young wives liked by handsome young officers. It's very absurd, I grant."

Mrs. Jones and Captain De Baron did really grieve at what had been done, but to others, the tragedy coming after the comedy had not been painful. "What will be the end of it?" said Miss Patmore Green to Sir Harry.

"I am afraid they won't let her dance it any more," said Sir Harry, who was intent solely on the glories of the Kappa-kappa. "We shall hardly get any one to do it so well."

"There'll be something worse than that, I'm afraid," said Miss Green.

Count Costi suggested to Lady Florence that there would certainly be a duel. "We never fight here in England, Count."

"Ah! dat is bad. A gentleman come and make himself vera disagreeable. If he most fight perhaps he would hold his tong. I tink we do things better in Paris and Vienna." Lord Giblet volunteered his opinion to Madame Gigi that it was very disgraceful. Madame Gigi simply shrugged her shoulders, and opened her eyes. She was able to congratulate herself on being able to manage her own husband better than that.

Chapter XXXIX.

Rebellion.

Lady George never forgot that slow journey home in the cab,—for in truth it was very slow. It seemed to her that she would never reach her own house. "Mary," he said, as soon as they were seated, "you have made me a miserable man." The cab rumbled and growled frightfully, and he felt himself unable to attack her with dignity while they were progressing. "But I will postpone what I have to say till we have reached home."

"I have done nothing wrong," said Mary, very stoutly.

"You had better say nothing more till we are at home." After that not a word more was said, but the journey was very long.

At the door of the house Lord George gave his hand to help her out of the cab, and then marched before her through the passage into the dining-room. It was evident that he was determined to make his harangue on that night. But she was the first to speak. "George," she said, "I have suffered very much, and am very tired. If you please, I will go to bed."

"You have disgraced me," he said.

"No; it is you that have disgraced me and put me to shame before everybody,—for nothing, for nothing. I have done nothing of which I am ashamed." She looked up into his face, and he could see that she was full of passion, and by no means in a mood to submit to his reproaches. She, too, could frown, and was frowning now. Her nostrils were dilated, and her eyes were bright with anger. He could see how it was with her; and though he was determined to be master, he hardly knew how he was to make good his masterdom.

"You had better listen to me," he said.

"Not to-night. I am too ill, too thoroughly wretched. Anything you have got to say of course I will listen to,—but not now." Then she walked to the door.

"Mary!" She paused with her hand on the lock. "I trust that you do not wish to contest the authority which I have over you?"

"I do not know; I cannot say. If your authority calls upon me to own that I have done anything wrong, I shall certainly contest it. And if I have not, I think—I think you will express your sorrow for the injury you have done me to-night." Then she left the room before he had made up his mind how he would continue his address. He was quite sure that he was right. Had he not desired her not to waltz? At that moment he quite forgot the casual permission he had barely given at Lady Brabazon's, and which had been intended to apply to that night only. Had he not specially warned her against this Captain De Baron, and told her that his name and hers were suffering from her intimacy with the man? And then, had she not deceived him directly by naming another person as her partner in that odious dance? The very fact that she had so deceived him was proof to him that she had known that she ought not to dance with Captain De Baron, and that she had a vicious pleasure in doing so which she had been determined to gratify even in opposition to his express orders. As he stalked up and down the room in his wrath, he forgot as much as he remembered. It had been represented to him that this odious romp had been no more than a minuet; but he did not bear in mind that his wife had been no party to that misrepresentation. And he forgot, too, that he himself had been present as a spectator at her express request. And when his wrath was at the fullest he almost forgot those letters from Adelaide Houghton! But he did not forget that all Mrs. Montacute Jones' world had seen him as in his offended marital majesty he took his wife out from amidst the crowd, declaring his indignation and his jealousy to all who were there assembled. He might have been wrong there. As he thought of it all he confessed to himself as much as that. But the injury done had been done to himself rather than to her. Of course they must leave London now, and leave it for ever. She must go with him whither he might choose to take her. Perhaps Manor Cross might serve for their lives' seclusion, as the Marquis would not live there. But Manor Cross was near the deanery, and he must sever his wife from her father. He was now very hostile to the Dean, who had looked on and seen his abasement, and had smiled. But, through it all, there never came to him for a moment any idea of a permanent quarrel with his wife. It might, he thought, be long before there was permanent comfort between them. Obedience, absolute obedience, must come before that could be reached. But of the bond which bound them together he was far too sensible to dream of separation. Nor, in his heart, did he think her guilty of anything but foolish, headstrong indiscretion,—of that and latterly of dissimulation. It was not that Cæsar had been wronged, but that his wife had enabled idle tongues to suggest a wrong to Cæsar.

He did not see her again that night, betaking himself at a very late hour to his own dressing-room. On the next morning at an early hour he was awake thinking. He must not allow her to suppose for a moment that he was afraid of her. He went into her room a few minutes before their usual breakfast hour, and found her, nearly dressed, with her maid. "I shall be down directly, George," she said in her usual voice. As he could not bid the woman go away, he descended and waited for her in the parlour. When she entered the room she instantly rang the bell and contrived to keep the man in the room while she was making the tea. But he would not sit down. How is a man to scold his wife properly with toast and butter on a plate before him? "Will you not have your tea?" she asked—oh, so gently.

"Put it down," he said. According to her custom, she got up and brought it round to his place. When they were alone she would kiss his forehead as she did so; but now the servant was just closing the door, and there was no kiss.

"Do come to your breakfast, George," she said.

"I cannot eat my breakfast while all this is on my mind. I must speak of it. We must leave London at once."

"In a week or two."

"At once. After last night, there must be no more going to parties." She lifted her cup to her lips and sat quite silent. She would hear a little more before she answered him. "You must feel yourself that for some time to come, perhaps for some years, privacy will be the best for us."

"I feel nothing of the kind, George."

"Could you go and face those people after what happened last night?"

"Certainly I could, and should think it my duty to do so to-night, if it were possible. No doubt you have made it difficult, but I would do it."

"I was forced to make it difficult. There was nothing for me to do but to take you away."

"Because you were angry, you were satisfied to disgrace me before all the people there. What has been done cannot be helped. I must bear it. I cannot stop people from talking and thinking evil. But I will never say that I think evil of myself by hiding myself. I don't know what you mean by privacy. I want no privacy."

"Why did you dance with that man?"

"Because it was so arranged."

"You had told me it was some one else?"

"Do you mean to accuse me of a falsehood, George? First one arrangement had been made, and then another."

"I had been told before how it was to be."

"Who told you? I can only answer for myself."

"And why did you waltz?"

"Because you had withdrawn your foolish objection. Why should I not dance like other people? Papa does not think it wrong?"

"Your father has nothing to do with it."

"If you ill-treat me, George, papa must have something to do with it. Do you think he will see me disgraced before a room full of people, as you did yesterday, and hold his tongue? Of course you are my husband, but he is still my father; and if I want protection he will protect me."

"I will protect you," said Lord George, stamping his foot upon the floor.

"Yes; by burying me somewhere. That is what you say you mean to do. And why? Because you get some silly nonsense into your head, and then make yourself and me ridiculous in public. If you think I am what you seem to suspect, you had better let papa have me back again,—though that is so horrible that I can hardly bring myself to think of it. If you do not think so, surely you should beg my pardon for the affront you put on me last night."

This was a way in which he had certainly not looked at the matter. Beg her pardon! He, as a husband, beg a wife's pardon under any circumstances! And beg her pardon for having carried her away from a house in which she had manifestly disobeyed him. No, indeed. But then he was quite as strongly opposed to that other idea of sending her back to her father, as a man might send a wife who had disgraced herself. Anything would be better than that. If she would only acknowledge that she had been indiscreet, they would go down together into Brothershire, and all might be comfortable. Though she was angry with him, obstinate and rebellious, yet his heart was softened to her because she did not throw the woman's love-letter in his teeth. He had felt that here would be his great difficulty, but his difficulty now arose rather from the generosity which kept her silent on the subject. "What I did," he said, "I did to protect you."

"Such protection was an insult." Then she left the room before he had tasted his tea or his toast. She had heard her father's knock, and knew that she would find him in the drawing-room. She had made up her mind how she would tell the story to him; but when she was with him he would have no story told at all. He declared that he knew everything, and spoke as though there could be no doubt as to the heinousness, or rather, absurdity, of Lord George's conduct. "It is very sad,—very sad, indeed," he said; "one hardly knows what one ought to do."

"He wants to go down—to Cross Hall."

"That is out of the question. You must stay out your time here and then come to me, as you arranged. He must get out of it by saying that he was frightened by thinking that you had fallen."

"It was not that, papa."

"Of course it was not; but how else is he to escape from his own folly?"

"You do not think that I have been—wrong—with Captain De Baron?"

"I! God bless you, my child. I think that you have been wrong! He cannot think so either. Has he accused you?"

Then she told him, as nearly as she could, all that had passed between them, including the expression of his desire that she should not waltz, and his subsequent permission given at Lady Brabazon's. "Pish!" he ejaculated. "I hate these attempted restrictions. It is like a woman telling her husband not to smoke. What a fool a man must be not to see that he is preparing misery for himself by laying embargoes on the recreations of his nearest companion!" Then he spoke of what he himself would do. "I must see him, and if he will not hear reason you must go with me to the Deanery without him."

"Don't separate us, papa."

"God forbid that there should be any permanent separation. If he be obstinate, it may be well that you should be away from him for a week or two. Why can't a man wash his dirty linen at home, if he has any to wash. His, at any rate, did not come to him with you."

Then there was a very stormy scene in the dining-room between the two men. The Dean, whose words were infinitely more ready and available than those of his opponent, said very much the most, and by the fierce indignation of his disclaimers, almost prevented the husband from dwelling on the wife's indiscretion. "I did not think it possible that such a man as you could have behaved so cruelly to such a girl."

"I was not cruel; I acted for the best."

"You degraded yourself, and her too."

"I degraded no one," said Lord George.

"It is hard to think what may now best be done to cure the wound which she has been made to suffer. I must insist on this,—that she must not be taken from town before the day fixed for her departure."

"I think of going to-morrow," said Lord George, gloomily.

"Then you must go alone, and I must remain with her."

"Certainly not;—certainly not."

"She will not go. She shall not be made to run away. Though everything have to be told in the public prints, I will not submit to that. I suppose you do not dare to tell me that you suspect her of any evil?"

"She has been indiscreet."

"Suppose I granted that,—which I don't,—is she to be ground into dust in this way for indiscretion? Have not you been indiscreet?" Lord George made no direct answer to this question, fearing that the Dean had heard the story of the love-letter; but of that matter the Dean had heard nothing. "In all your dealings with her, can you tax yourself with no deviation from wisdom?"

"What a man does is different. No conduct of mine can blemish her name."

"But it may destroy her happiness,—and if you go on in this way it will do so."

During the whole of that day the matter was discussed. Lord George obstinately insisted on taking his wife down to Cross Hall, if not on the next day, then on the day after. But the Dean, and with the Dean the young wife, positively refused to accede to this arrangement. The Dean had his things brought from the inn to the house in Munster Court, and though he did not absolutely declare that he had come there for his daughter's protection, it was clear that this was intended. In such an emergency Lord George knew not what to do. Though the quarrel was already very bitter, he could not quite tell his father-in-law to leave the house; and then there was always present to his mind a feeling that the Dean had a right to be there in accordance with the pecuniary arrangement made. The Dean would have been welcome to the use of the house and all that was in it, if only Mary would have consented to be taken at once down to Cross Hall. But being under her father's wing, she would not consent. She pleaded that by going at once, or running away as she called it, she would own that she had done something wrong, and she was earnest in declaring that nothing should wring such a confession from her. Everybody, she said, knew that she was to stay in London to the end of June. Everybody knew that she was then to go to the Deanery. It was not to be borne that people should say that her plans had been altered because she had danced the Kappa-kappa with Captain De Baron. She must see her friends before she went, or else her friends would know that she had been carried into banishment. In answer to this, Lord George declared that he, as husband, was paramount. This Mary did not deny, but, paramount as the authority was, she would not, in this instance, be governed by it.

It was a miserable day to them all. Many callers came, asking after Lady George, presuming that her speedy departure from the ball had been caused by her accident. No one was admitted, and all were told that she had not been much hurt. There were two or three stormy scenes between the Dean and his son-in-law, in one of which Lord George asked the Dean whether he conceived it to be compatible with his duty as a clergyman of the Church of England to induce a wife to disobey her husband. In answer to this, the Dean said that in such a matter the duty of a Church dignitary was the same as that of any other gentleman, and that he, as a gentleman, and also as a dignitary, meant to stand by his daughter. She refused to pack up, or to have her things packed. When he came to look into himself, he found that he had not power to bid the servants do it in opposition to their mistress. That the power of a husband was paramount he was well aware, but he did not exactly see his way to the exercise of it. At last he decided that he, at any rate, would go down to Cross Hall. If the Dean chose to create a separation between his daughter and her husband, he must bear the responsibility.

On the following day he did go down to Cross Hall, leaving his wife and her father in Munster Court without any definite plans.

Chapter XL.

As To Bluebeard.

When Lord George left his own house alone he was very wretched, and his wife, whom he left behind him, was as wretched as himself. Of course the matter had not decided itself in this way without very much absolute quarrelling between them. Lord George had insisted, had stamped his foot, and had even talked of force. Mary, prompted by her father, had protested that she would not run away from the evil tongues of people who would be much more bitter in her absence than they would dare to be if she remained among them. He, when he found that his threat of forcible abduction was altogether vain, had to make up his mind whether he also would remain. But both the Dean and his wife had begged that he would do so, and he would not even seem to act in obedience to them. So he went, groaning much in spirit, puzzled to think what story he should tell to his mother and sisters, terribly anxious as to the future, and in spirit repentant for the rashness of his conduct at the ball. Before he was twenty miles out of London he was thinking with infinite regret of his love for his wife, already realising the misery of living without her, almost stirred to get out at the next station and return by the first train to Munster Court. In this hour of his sorrow there came upon him a feeling of great hatred for Mrs. Houghton. He almost believed that she had for her own vile purposes excited Captain De Baron to make love to his wife. And then, in regard to that woman, his wife had behaved so well! Surely something was due to so much generosity. And then, when she had been angry with him, she had been more beautiful than ever. What a change had those few months in London made in her! She had lost her childish little timidities, and had bloomed forth a beautiful woman. He had no doubt as to her increased loveliness, and had been proud to think that all had acknowledged it. But as to the childish timidity, perhaps he would have preferred that it should not have been so quickly or so entirely banished. Even at Brotherton he hankered to return to London; but, had he done so, the Brotherton world would have known it. He put himself into a carriage instead, and had himself driven through the park to Cross Hall.

All this occurred on the day but one subsequent to the ball, and he had by the previous post informed Lady Sarah that he was coming. But in that letter he had said that he would bring his wife with him, and on his immediate arrival had to answer questions as to her unexpected absence. "Her father was very unwilling that she should come," he said.

"But I thought he was at the hotel," said Lady Sarah.

"He is in Munster Court, now. To tell the truth I am not best pleased that it should be so; but at the last moment I did not like to contradict her. I hate London and everything in it. She likes it, and as there was a kind of bargain made I could not well depart from it."

"And you have left her alone with her father in London," said Lady Susanna, with a tone of pretended dismay.

"How can she be alone if her father is with her," answered Lord George, who did not stand in awe of Lady Susanna as he did of Lady Sarah. Nothing further at the moment was said, but all the sisters felt that there was something wrong.

"I don't think it at all right that Mary should be left with the Dean," said the old lady to her second daughter. But the old lady was specially prejudiced against the Dean as being her eldest son's great enemy. Before the day was over Lord George wrote a long letter to his wife,—full of affection indeed, but still more full of covert reproaches. He did not absolutely scold her; but he told her that there could be no happiness between a wife and a husband unless the wife would obey, and he implored her to come to him with as little delay as possible. If she would only come, all should be right between them.

Mary, when her husband was really gone, was much frightened at her own firmness. That doctrine of obedience to her husband had been accepted by her in full. When disposed to run counter to the ladies at Manor Cross, she always had declared to herself that they bore no authority delegated from "George," and that she would obey "George," and no one but George. She had told him more than once, half-playfully, that if he wanted anything done, he must tell her himself. And this, though he understood it to contain rebellion against the Germains generally, had a pleasant flavour with him as acknowledging so completely his own power. She had said to her father, and unfortunately to Mrs. Houghton when Mrs. Houghton was her friend, that she was not going to do what all the Germain women told her; but she had always spoken of her husband's wishes as absolutely imperative. Now she was in open mutiny against her husband, and, as she thought of it, it seemed to her to be almost impossible that peace should be restored between them.

"I think I will go down very soon," she said to her father, after she had received her husband's letter.

"What do you call very soon?"

"In a day or two."

"Do not do anything of the kind. Stay here till the appointed time comes. It is only a fortnight now. I have made arrangements at Brotherton, so that I can be with you till then.

After that come down to me. Of course your husband will come over to you at the deanery."

"But if he shouldn't come?"

"Then he would be behaving very wickedly. But, of course, he will come. He is not a man to be obstinate in that fashion."

"I do not know that, papa."

"But I do. You had better take my advice in this matter. Of course I do not want to foster a quarrel between you and your husband."

"Pray,—pray don't let there be a quarrel."

"Of course not. But the other night he lost his head, and treated you badly. You and I are quite willing to forgive and forget all that. Any man may do a foolish thing, and men are to be judged by general results rather than single acts."

"He is very kind to me—generally."

"Just so; and I am not angry with him in the least. But after what occurred it would be wrong that you should go away at once. You felt it yourself at the moment."

"But anything would be better than quarrelling, papa."

"Almost anything would be better than a lasting quarrel with your husband; but the best way to avoid that is to show him that you know how to be firm in such an emergency as this." She was, of course, compelled by her father's presence and her father's strength to remain in town, but she did so longing every hour to pack up and be off to Cross Hall. She had very often doubted whether she could love her husband as a husband ought to be loved, but now, in her present trouble, she felt sure of her own heart. She had never been really on bad terms with him before since their marriage, and the very fact of their separation increased her tenderness to him in a wonderful degree. She answered his letter with Language full of love and promises and submission, loaded with little phrases of feminine worship, merely adding that papa thought she had better stay in town till the end of the month. There was not a word of reproach in it.

She did not allude to his harsh conduct at the ball, nor did she write the name of Mrs. Houghton.

Her father was very urgent with her to see all her friends, to keep any engagements previously made, to be seen at the play, and to let all the world know by her conduct that she was not oppressed by what had taken place. There was some intention of having the Kappa-kappa danced again, as far as possible by the same people. Lord Giblet was to retire in favour of some more expert performer, but the others were supposed to be all worthy of an encore. But of course there arose a question as to Lady George. There could be no doubt that Lord George had disapproved very strongly of the Kappa-kappa. The matter got to the Dean's ears, and the Dean counselled his daughter to join the party yet again. "What would he say, papa?" The Dean was of opinion that in such case Lord George would say and do much less than he had said and done before. According to his views, Lord George must be taught that his wife had her privileges as well as he his. This fresh difficulty dissolved itself because the second performance was fixed for a day after that on which it had been long known that Lady George was to leave London; and even the Dean did not propose that she should remain in town after that date with a direct view to the Kappa-kappa.

She was astonished at the zeal with which he insisted that she should go out into the gay world. He almost ridiculed her when she spoke of economy in her dress, and seemed to think that it was her duty to be a woman of fashion. He still spoke to her from time to time of the Popenjoy question, always asserting his conviction that, whatever the Marquis might think, even if he were himself deceived through ignorance of the law, the child would be at last held to be illegitimate. "They tell me, too," he said, "that his life is not worth a year's purchase."

"Poor little boy!"

"Of course, if he had been born as the son of the Marquis of Brotherton ought to be born, nobody would wish him anything but good."

"I don't wish him anything but good," said Mary.

"But as it is," continued the Dean, apparently not observing his daughter's remark, "everybody must feel that it would be better for the family that he should be out of the way. Nobody can think that such a child can live to do honour to the British peerage."

"He might be well brought up."

"He wouldn't be well brought up. He has an Italian mother and Italian belongings, and everything around him as bad as it can be. But the question at last is one of right. He was clearly born when his mother was reputed to be the wife, not of his father, but of another man. That cock-and-bull story which we have heard may be true. It is possible. But I could not rest in my bed if I did not persevere in ascertaining the truth." The Dean did persevere, and was very constant in his visits to Mr. Battle's office. At this time Miss Tallowax came up to town, and she also stayed for a day or two in Munster Court. What passed between the Dean and his aunt on the subject Mary, of course, did not hear; but she soon found that Miss Tallowax was as eager as her father, and she learned that Miss Tallowax had declared that the inquiry should not languish from want of funds. Miss Tallowax was quite alive to the glory of the Brotherton connection.

As the month drew to an end Mary, of course, called on all her London friends. Her father was always eager to know whom she saw, and whether any allusion was made by any of them to the scene at the ball. But there was one person, who had been a friend, on whom she did not call, and this omission was observed by the Dean. "Don't you ever see Mrs. Houghton now?" he asked.

"No, papa," said Mary, with prompt decision.

"Why not?"

"I don't like her."

"Why don't you like her? You used to be friends. Have you quarrelled?"

"Yes; I have quarrelled with her."

"What did she do?" Mary was silent. "Is it a secret?"

"Yes, papa; it is a secret. I would rather you would not ask. But she is a nasty vile creature, and I will never speak to her again."

"That is strong language, Mary."

"It is. And now that I have said that, pray don't talk about her any more."

The Dean was discreet, and did not talk about Mrs. Houghton any more; but he set his mind to work to guess, and guessed something near the truth. Of course he knew that his son-in-law had professed at one time to love this lady when she had been Miss De Baron, and he had been able to see that subsequently to that they had been intimate friends. "I don't think, my dear," he said, laughing, "that you can be jealous of her attractions."

"I am not in the least jealous of her, papa. I don't know anyone that I think so ugly. She is a nasty made-up thing. But pray don't talk about her anymore." Then the Dean almost knew that Mary had discovered something, and was too noble to tell a story against her husband.

The day but one before she was to leave town Mrs. Montacute Jones came to her. She had seen her kind old friend once or twice since the catastrophe at the ball, but always in the presence of other persons. Now they were alone together. "Well, my dear," said Mrs. Jones, "I hope you have enjoyed your short season. We have all been very fond of you."

"You have been very kind to me, Mrs. Jones."

"I do my best to make young people pleasant, my dear. You ought to have liked it all, for I don't know anybody who has been so much admired. His Royal Highness said the other night that you were the handsomest woman in London."

"His Royal Highness is an old fool," said Mary, laughing.

"He is generally thought to be a very good judge in that matter. You are going to keep the house, are you not?"

"Oh, yes; I think there is a lease."

"I am glad of that. It is a nice little house, and I should be sorry to think that you are not coming back."

"We are always to live here half the year, I believe," said Mary. "That was agreed when we married, and that's why I go away now."

"Lord George, I suppose, likes the country best?"

"I think he does. I don't, Mrs. Jones."

"They are both very well in their way, my dear. I am a wicked old woman, who like to have everything gay. I never go out of town till everything is over, and I never come up till everything begins. We have a nice place down in Scotland, and you must come and see me there some autumn. And then we go to Rome. It's a pleasant way of living, though we have to move about so much."

"It must cost a great deal of money?"

"Well, yes. One can't drive four-in-hand so cheap as a pair. Mr. Jones has a large income." This was the first direct intimation Mary had ever received that there was a Mr. Jones. "But we weren't always rich. When I was your age I hadn't nearly so nice a house as you. Indeed, I hadn't a house at all, for I wasn't married, and was thinking whether I would take or reject a young barrister of the name of Smith, who had nothing a year to support me on. You see I never got among the aristocratic names, as you have done."

"I don't care a bit about that."

"But I do. I like Germains, and Talbots, and Howards, and so does everybody else, only so many people tell lies about it. I like having lords in my drawing-room. They look handsomer and talk better than other men. That's my experience.

And you are pretty nearly sure with them that you won't find you have got somebody quite wrong."

"I know a lord," said Mary, "who isn't very right. That is, I don't know him, for I never saw him."

"You mean your wicked brother-in-law. I should like to know him of all things. He'd be quite an attraction. I suppose he knows how to behave like a gentleman?"

"I'm not so sure of that. He was very rough to papa."

"Ah;—yes. I think we can understand that, my dear. Your father hasn't made himself exactly pleasant to the Marquis. Not that I say he's wrong. I think it was a pity, because everybody says that the little Lord Popenjoy will die. You were talking of me and my glories, but long before you are my age you will be much more glorious. You will make a charming Marchioness."

"I never think about it, Mrs. Jones; and I wish papa didn't. Why shouldn't the little boy live? I could be quite happy enough as I am if people would only be good to me and let me alone."

"Have I distressed you?" asked the old woman.

"Oh, dear no;—not you."

"You mean what happened at my house the other night?"

"I didn't mean anything particular, Mrs. Jones. But I do think that people sometimes are very ill-natured."

"I think, you know, that was Lord George's doing. He shouldn't have taken you off so suddenly. It wasn't your fault that the stupid man tripped. I suppose he doesn't like Captain De Baron?"

"Don't talk about it, Mrs. Jones."

"Only that I know the world so well that what I say might, perhaps, be of use. Of course I know that he has gone out of town."

"Yes, he has gone."

"I was so glad that you didn't go with him. People will talk, you know, and it did look as though he were a sort of

Bluebeard. Bluebeards, my dear, must be put down. There may
be most well-intentioned Bluebeards, who have no chambers of
horrors, no secrets,"—Mary thought of the letter from Mrs.
Houghton, of which nobody knew but herself,—"who never cut
off anybody's heads, but still interfere dreadfully with the
comfort of a household. Lord George is very nearly all that a
man ought to be."

"He is the best man in the world," said Mary.

"I am sure you think so. But he shouldn't be jealous, and
above all he shouldn't show that he's jealous. You were bound, I
think, to stay behind and show the world that you had nothing to
fear. I suppose the Dean counselled it?"

"Yes;—he did."

"Fathers of married daughters shouldn't often interfere,
but there I think he was right. It is much better for Lord George
himself that it should be so. There is nothing so damaging to a
young woman as to have it supposed she has had to be
withdrawn from the influence of a young man."

"It would be wicked of anybody to think so," said Mary,
sobbing.

"But they must have thought so if you hadn't remained.
You may be sure, my dear, that your father was quite right. I am
sorry that you cannot make one in the dance again, because we
shall have changed Lord Giblet for Lord Augustus Grandison,
and I am sure it will be done very well. But of course I couldn't
ask you to stay for it. As your departure was fixed beforehand
you ought not to stay for it. But that is very different from being
taken away in a jiffey, like some young man who is spending
more than he ought to spend, and is hurried off suddenly nobody
knows where."

Mary, when Mrs. Jones had left the house, found that
upon the whole she was thankful to her friend for what had been
said. It pained her to hear her husband described as a jealous
Bluebeard; but the fact of his jealousy had been so apparent, that
in any conversation on the matter intended to be useful so much

had to be acknowledged. She, however, had taken the strong course of trusting to her father rather than to her husband, and she was glad to find that her conduct and her father's conduct were approved by so competent a judge as Mrs. Montacute Jones. And throughout the whole interview there had been an air of kindness which Mary had well understood. The old lady had intended to be useful, and her intentions were accepted.

On the next morning, soon after breakfast, the Dean received a note which puzzled him much, and for an hour or two left him in doubt as to what he would do respecting it,—whether he would comply with, or refuse to comply with, the request made in it. At first he said nothing of the letter to his daughter. He had, as she was aware, intended to go to Lincoln's Inn early in the day, but he sat thinking over something, instead of leaving the house, till at last he went to Mary and put the letter into her hands. "That," said he, "is one of the most unexpected communications I ever had in my life, and one which it is most difficult to answer. Just read it." The letter, which was very short, was as follows:—

"The Marquis of Brotherton presents his compliments to the Dean of Brotherton, and begs to say that he thinks that some good might now be done by a personal interview. Perhaps the Dean will not object to call on the Marquis here at some hour after two o'clock to-morrow.

"Scumberg's Hotel,

"Albemarle Street.

"29th June, 187—."

"But we go to-morrow," said Mary.

"Ah;—he means to-day. The note was written last night. I have been thinking about it, and I think I shall go."

"Have you written to him?"

"There is no need. A man who sends to me a summons to come to him so immediately as that has no right to expect an answer. He does not mean anything honest."

"Then why do you go?"

"I don't choose to appear to be afraid to meet him. Everything that I do is done above board. I rather imagine that he doesn't expect me to come; but I will not let him have to say that he had asked me and that I had refused. I shall go."

"Oh, papa, what will he say to you?"

"I don't think he can eat me, my dear; nor will he dare even to murder me. I daresay he would if he could."

And so it was decided; and at the hour appointed the Dean sallied forth to keep the appointment.

Chapter XLI.

Scumberg's.

The Dean as he walked across the park towards Albemarle Street had many misgivings. He did not at all believe that the Marquis entertained friendly relations in regard to him, or even such neutral relations as would admit of the ordinary courtesies of civilized life. He made up his mind that he would be insulted,—unless indeed he should be so cowed as to give way to the Marquis. But, that he himself thought to be impossible. The more he reflected about it, the more assured he became that the Marquis had not expected him to obey the summons. It was possible that something might be gained on the other side by his refusal to see the elder brother of his son-in-law. He might, by refusing, leave it open to his enemies to say that he had rejected an overture to peace, and he now regarded as his enemies almost the entire Germain family. His own son-in-law would in future, he thought, be as much opposed to him as the head of the family. The old Marchioness, he knew, sincerely believed in Popenjoy. And the daughters, though they had at first been very strong in their aversion to the foreign mother and the foreign boy, were now averse to him also, on other grounds. Of course Lord George would complain of his wife at Cross Hall.

Of course the story of the Kappa-kappa would be told in a manner that would horrify those three ladies. The husband would of course be indignant at his wife's disobedience in not having left London when ordered by him to do so. He had promised not to foster a quarrel between Mary and Lord George, but he thought it by no means improbable that circumstances would for a time render it expedient that his daughter should live at the deanery, while Lord George remained at Cross Hall. As to nothing was he more fully resolved than this,—that he would not allow the slightest blame to be attributed to his daughter, without repudiating and resenting the imputation. Any word against her conduct, should such word reach his ears even through herself, he would resent, and it would go hard with him, but he would exceed such accusations by recriminations. He would let them know, that if they intended to fight, he also could fight. He had never uttered a word as to his own liberality in regard to money, but he had thought of it much. Theirs was the rank, and the rank was a great thing in his eyes; but his was at present the wealth; and wealth, he thought was as powerful as rank. He was determined that his daughter should be a Marchioness, and in pursuit of that object he was willing to spend his money;—but he intended to let those among whom he spent it know that he was not to be set on one side, as a mere parson out of the country, who happened to have a good income of his own.

It was in this spirit,—a spirit of absolute pugnacity,—that he asked for the Marquis at Scumberg's hotel. Yes;—the Marquis was at home, and the servant would see if his master could be seen. "I fancy that I have an appointment with him," said the Dean, as he gave his card. "I am rather hurried, and if he can't see me perhaps you'll let me know at once." The man soon returned, and with much condescension told the Dean that his lordship would see him. "That is kind, as his lordship told me to come," said the Dean to himself, but still loud enough for the servant to hear him. "His Lordship will be with you in a few minutes," said the man, as he shut the door of the sitting room.

"I shall be gone if he's not here in a very few minutes," said the Dean, unable to restrain himself.

And he very nearly did go before the Marquis came to him. He had already walked to the rug with the object of ringing the bell, and had then decided on giving the lord two minutes more, resolving also that he would speak his mind to the lord about this delay, should the lord make his appearance before the two minutes were over. The time had just expired when his lordship did make his appearance. He came shuffling into the room after a servant, who walked before him with the pretence of carrying books and a box of papers. It had all been arranged, the Marquis knowing that he would secure the first word by having his own servant in the room. "I am very much obliged to you for coming, Mr. Dean," he said. "Pray sit down. I should have been here to receive you if you had sent me a line."

"I only got your note this morning," said the Dean angrily.

"I thought that perhaps you might have sent a message. It doesn't signify in the least. I never go out till after this, but had you named a time I should have been here to receive you. That will do, John,—shut the door. Very cold,—don't you think it."

"I have walked, my lord, and am warm."

"I never walk,—never could walk. I don't know why it is, but my legs won't walk."

"Perhaps you never tried."

"Yes, I have. They wanted to make me walk in Switzerland twenty years ago, but I broke down after the first mile. George used to walk like the very d——. You see more of him now than I do. Does he go on walking?"

"He is an active man."

"Just that. He ought to have been a country letter-carrier. He would have been as punctual as the sun, and has quite all the necessary intellect."

"You sent for me, Lord Brotherton—"

"Yes; yes. I had something that I thought I might as well say to you, though, upon my word, I almost forget what it was."

"Then I may as well take my leave."

"Don't do that. You see, Mr. Dean, belonging to the church militant as you do, you are so heroically pugnacious! You must like fighting very much."

"When I have anything which I conceive it to be my duty to fight for, I think I do."

"Things are generally best got without fighting. You want to make your grandson Marquis of Brotherton."

"I want to ensure to my grandson anything that may be honestly and truly his own."

"You must first catch a grandson."

It was on his lips to say that certainly no heir should be caught on his side of the family after the fashion that had been practised by his lordship in catching the present pseudo-Popenjoy; but he was restrained by a feeling of delicacy in regard to his own daughter. "My lord," he said, "I am not here to discuss any such contingency."

"But you don't scruple to discuss my contingency, and that in the most public manner. It has suited me, or at any rate it has been my chance, to marry a foreigner. Because you don't understand Italian fashions you don't scruple to say that she is not my wife."

"I have never said so."

"And to declare that my son is not my son."

"I have never said that."

"And to set a dozen attorneys to work to prove that my heir is a bastard."

"We heard of your marriage, my lord, as having been fixed for a certain date,—a date long subsequent to that of the birth of your son. What were we to think?"

"As if that hadn't been explained to you, and to all the world, a dozen times over. Did you never hear of a second marriage being solemnized in England to satisfy certain scruples? You have sent out and made your inquiries, and what have they come to? I know all about it."

"As far as I am concerned you are quite welcome to know everything."

"I dare say;—even though I should be stung to death by the knowledge. Of course I understand. You think that I have no feeling at all."

"Not much as to duty to your family, certainly," said the Dean, stoutly.

"Exactly. Because I stand a little in the way of your new ambition, I am the Devil himself. And yet you and those who have abetted you think it odd that I haven't received you with open arms. My boy is as much to me as ever was your daughter to you."

"Perhaps so, my lord. The question is not whether he is beloved, but whether he is Lord Popenjoy."

"He is Lord Popenjoy. He is a poor weakling, and I doubt whether he may enjoy the triumph long, but he is Lord Popenjoy. You must know it yourself, Dean."

"I know nothing of the kind," said the Dean, furiously.

"Then you must be a very self-willed man. When this began George was joined with you in the unnatural inquiry. He at any rate has been convinced."

"It may be he has submitted himself to his brother's influence."

"Not in the least. George is not very clever, but he has at any rate had wit enough to submit to the influence of his own legal adviser,—or rather to the influence of your legal adviser. Your own man, Mr. Battle, is convinced. You are going on with this in opposition even to him. What the devil is it you want? I am not dead, and may outlive at any rate you. Your girl hasn't got a child, and doesn't seem likely to have one. You happen to have married her into a noble family, and now, upon my word, it seems to me that you are a little off your head with downright pride."

"Was it for this you sent for me?"

"Well;—yes it was. I thought it might be as well to argue it out. It isn't likely that there should be much love between us, but we needn't cut each other's throats. It is costing us both a d——d lot of money; but I should think that my purse must be longer than yours."

"We will try it, my lord."

"You intend to go on with this persecution then?"

"The Countess Luigi was presumably a married woman when she bore that name, and I look upon it as a sacred duty to ascertain whether she was so or not."

"Sacred!" said the Marquis, with a sneer.

"Yes;—sacred. There can be no more sacred duty than that which a father owes to his child."

"Ah!" Then the Marquis paused and looked at the Dean before he went on speaking. He looked so long that the Dean was preparing to take his hat in his hand ready for a start. He showed that he was going to move, and then the Marquis went on speaking. "Sacred! Ah!—and such a child!"

"She is one of whom I am proud as a father, and you should be proud as a sister-in-law."

"Oh, of course. So I am. The Germains were never so honoured before. As for her birth I care nothing about that. Had she behaved herself, I should have thought nothing of the stable."

"What do you dare to say?" said the Dean, jumping from his seat.

The Marquis sat leaning back in his arm-chair, perfectly motionless. There was a smile,—almost a pleasant smile on his face. But there was a very devil in his eye, and the Dean, who stood some six feet removed from him, saw the devil plainly. "I live a solitary life here, Mr. Dean," said the Marquis, "but even I have heard of her."

"What have you heard?"

"All London have heard of her,—this future Marchioness, whose ambition is to drive my son from his title and estates. A sacred duty, Mr. Dean, to put a coronet on the head of that young ——!" The word which we have not dared to print was distinctly spoken,—more distinctly, more loudly, more incisively, than any word which had yet fallen from the man's lips. It was evident that the lord had prepared the word, and had sent for the father that the father might hear the word applied to his own daughter,—unless indeed he should first acknowledge himself to have lost his case. So far the interview had been carried out very much in accordance with the preparations as arranged by the Marquis; but, as to what followed, the Marquis had hardly made his calculations correctly.

A clergyman's coat used to save him from fighting in fighting days; and even in these days, in which broils and personal encounters are held to be generally disreputable, it saves the wearer from certain remote dangers to which other men are liable. And the reverse of this is also true. It would probably be hard to extract a first blow from the whole bench of bishops. And deans as a rule are more sedentary, more quiescent, more given to sufferance even than bishops. The normal Dean is a goodly, sleek, bookish man, who would hardly strike a blow under any provocation. The Marquis, perhaps, had been aware of this. He had, perhaps, fancied that he was as good a man as the Dean who was at least ten years his senior. He had not at any rate anticipated such speedy violence as followed the utterance of the abominable word.

The Dean, as I have said, had been standing about six feet from the easy chair in which the Marquis was lolling when the word was spoken. He had already taken his hat in his hand and had thought of some means of showing his indignation as he left the room. Now his first impulse was to rid himself of his hat, which he did by pitching it along the floor. And then in an instant he was at the lord's throat. The lord had expected it so little that up to the last he made no preparation for defence. The

Dean had got him by his cravat and shirt-collar before he had begun to expect such usage as this. Then he simply gurgled out some ejaculated oath, uttered half in surprise and half in prayer. Prayer certainly was now of no use. Had five hundred feet of rock been there the Marquis would have gone down it, though the Dean had gone with him. Fire flashed from the clergyman's eyes, and his teeth were set fast and his very nostrils were almost ablaze. His daughter! The holy spot of his life! The one being in whom he believed with all his heart and with all his strength!

The Dean was fifty years of age, but no one had ever taken him for an old man. They who at home at Brotherton would watch his motions, how he walked and how he rode on horseback, how he would vault his gates when in the fields, and scamper across the country like a schoolboy, were wont to say that he was unclerical. Perhaps Canons Pountner and Holdenough, with Mr. Groschut, the bishop's chaplain, envied him something of his juvenile elasticity. But I think that none of them had given him credit for such strength as he now displayed. The Marquis, in spite of what feeble efforts he made, was dragged up out of his chair and made to stand, or rather to totter, on his legs. He made a clutch at the bell-rope, which to aid his luxurious ease had been brought close to his hand as he sat, but failed, as the Dean shook him hither and thither. Then he was dragged on to the middle of the rug, feeling by this time that he was going to be throttled. He attempted to throw himself down, and would have done so but that the Dean with his left hand prevented him from falling. He made one vigorous struggle to free himself, striving as he did so to call for assistance. But the Dean having got his victim's back to the fireplace, and having the poor wretch now fully at his command, threw the man with all his strength into the empty grate. The Marquis fell like a heap within the fender, with his back against the top bar and his head driven further back against the bricks and iron. There for a second or two he lay like a dead mass.

Less than a minute had done it all, and for so long a time the Dean's ungoverned fury had held its fire. What were consequences to him with that word as applied to his child ringing in his ears? How should he moderate his wrath under such outrage as that? Was it not as though beast had met beast in the forest between whom nothing but internecine fight to the end was possible? But when that minute was over, and he saw what he had done,—when the man, tumbled, dishevelled, all alump and already bloody, was lying before him,—then he remembered who he was himself and what it was that he had done. He was Dean Lovelace, who had already made for himself more than enough of clerical enmity; and this other man was the Marquis of Brotherton, whom he had perhaps killed in his wrath, with no witness by to say a word as to the provocation he had received.

The Marquis groaned and impotently moved an arm as though to raise himself. At any rate, he was not dead as yet. With a desire to do what was right now, the Dean rang the bell violently, and then stooped down to extricate his foe. He had succeeded in raising the man and in seating him on the floor with his head against the arm-chair before the servant came. Had he wished to conceal anything, he could without much increased effort have dragged the Marquis up into his chair; but he was anxious now simply that all the truth should be known. It seemed to him still that no one knowing the real truth would think that he had done wrong. His child! His daughter! His sweetly innocent daughter! The man soon rushed into the room, for the ringing of the bell had been very violent. "Send for a doctor," said the Dean, "and send the landlord up."

"Has my lord had a fit?" said the man, advancing into the room. He was the servant, not of the hotel, but of the Marquis himself.

"Do as I bid you;—get a doctor and send up the landlord immediately. It is not a fit, but his lordship has been much hurt. I knocked him down." The Dean made the last statement slowly and firmly, under a feeling at the moment that it became him to leave nothing concealed, even with a servant.

"He has murdered me," groaned the Marquis. The injured one could speak at least, and there was comfort in that. The servant rushed back to the regions below, and the tidings were soon spread through the house. Resident landlord there was none. There never are resident landlords in London hotels. Scumberg was a young family of joint heirs and heiresses, named Tomkins, who lived at Hastings, and the house was managed by Mrs. Walker. Mrs. Walker was soon in the room, with a German deputy manager kept to maintain the foreign Scumberg connection, and with them sundry waiters and the head chambermaid. Mrs. Walker made a direct attack upon the Dean, which was considerably weakened by accusations from the lips of the Marquis himself. Had he remained speechless for a while the horrors of the Dean's conduct would have been greatly aggravated. "My good woman," said the Dean, "wait till some official is here. You cannot understand. And get a little warm water and wash his lordship's head."

"He has broken my back," said his lordship. "Oh, oh, oh."

"I am glad to hear you speak, Lord Brotherton," said the Dean. "I think you will repent having used such a word as that to my daughter." It would be necessary now that everybody should understand everything; but how terrible would it be for the father even to say that such a name had been applied to his child!

First there came two policemen, then a surgeon, and then a sergeant. "I will do anything that you suggest, Mr. Constable," said the Dean, "though I hope it may not be necessary that I should remain in custody. I am the Dean of Brotherton." The sergeant made a sign of putting his finger up to his cap. "This, man, as you know, is the Marquis of Brotherton." The sergeant bowed to the groaning nobleman. "My daughter is married to his brother. There have been family quarrels, and he just now applied a name to his own sister-in-law, to my child,—which I will not utter because there are women here. Fouler slander never came from a man's mouth. I took him from his chair and threw him beneath the grate. Now you know it all. Were it to do again, I would do it again."

"She is a——," said the imprudent prostrate Marquis. The sergeant, the doctor who was now present, and Mrs. Walker suddenly became the Dean's friends. The Marquis was declared to be much shaken, to have a cut head, and to be very badly bruised about the muscles of the back. But a man who could so speak of his sister-in-law deserved to have his head cut and his muscles bruised. Nevertheless the matter was too serious to be passed over without notice. The doctor could not say that the unfortunate nobleman had received no permanent injury;—and the sergeant had not an opportunity of dealing with deans and marquises every day of his life. The doctor remained with his august patient and had him put to bed, while the Dean and the sergeant together went off in a cab to the police-office which lies in the little crowded streets between the crooked part of Regent Street and Piccadilly. Here depositions were taken and forms filled, and the Dean was allowed to depart with an understanding that he was to be forthcoming immediately when wanted. He suggested that it had been his intention to go down to Brotherton on the following day, but the Superintendent of Police recommended him to abandon that idea. The superintendent thought that the Dean had better make arrangements to stay in London till the end of the week.

Chapter XLII.

"Not Go!"

The Dean had a great deal to think of as he walked home a little too late for his daughter's usual dinner hour. What should he tell her;—and what should he do as to communicating or not communicating tidings of the day's work to Lord George? Of course everybody must know what had been done sooner or later. He would have had no objection to that,—providing the truth could be told accurately,—except as to the mention of his daughter's name in the same sentence with that abominable word. But the word would surely be known, and the facts would not be told with accuracy unless he told them himself. His only, but his fully sufficient defence was in the word. But who would know the tone? Who would understand the look of the man's eye and the smile on his mouth? Who could be made to conceive, as the Dean himself had conceived, the aggravated injury of the premeditated slander? He would certainly write and tell Lord George everything. But to his daughter he thought that he would tell as little as possible. Might God in his mercy save her ears, her sacred feelings, her pure heart from the wound of that word! He felt that she was dearer to him than ever she had been,—that he would give up deanery and everything if he could save her by doing so. But he felt that if she were to be sacrificed in the contest, he would give up deanery and everything in avenging her.

But something must be told to her. He at any rate must remain in town, and it would be very desirable that she should stay with him. If she went alone she would at once be taken to Cross Hall; and he could understand that the recent occurrence would not add to the serenity of her life there. The name that had been applied to her, together with the late folly of which her husband had been guilty, would give those Manor Cross dragons,—as the Dean was apt in his own thoughts to call the Ladies Germain—a tremendous hold over her. And should she be once at Cross Hall he would hardly be able to get her back to the deanery.

He hurried up to dress as soon as he reached the house, with a word of apology as to being late, and then found her in the drawing room.

"Papa," she said, "I do like Mrs. Montacute Jones."

"So do I, my dear, because she is good-humoured."

"But she is so good-natured also! She has been here again to-day and wants me and George to go down to Scotland in August. I should so like it."

"What will George say?"

"Of course he won't go; and of course I shan't. But that doesn't make it the less good-natured. She wishes all her set to think that what happened the other night doesn't mean anything."

"I'm afraid he won't consent."

"I know he won't. He wouldn't know what to do with himself. He hates a house full of people. And now tell me what the Marquis said." But dinner was announced, and the Dean was not forced to answer this question immediately.

"Now, papa," she said again, as soon as the coffee was brought and the servant was gone, "do tell me what my most noble brother-in-law wanted to say to you?"

That he certainly would not tell. "Your brother-in-law, my dear, behaved about as badly as a man could behave."

"Oh, dear! I am so sorry!"

"We have to be sorry,—both of us. And your husband will be sorry." He was so serious that she hardly knew how to speak to him. "I cannot tell you everything; but he insulted me, and I was forced to—strike him."

"Strike him! Oh, papa!"

"Bear with me, Mary. In all things I think well of you, and do you try to think well of me."

"Dear papa! I will. I do. I always did."

"Anything he might have said of myself I could have borne. He could have applied no epithet to me which, I think, could even have ruffled me. But he spoke evil of you." While he was sitting there he made up his mind that he would tell her as much as that, though he had before almost resolved that he would not speak to her of herself. But she must hear something of the truth, and better that she should hear it from his than from other lips. She turned very pale, but did not immediately make any reply. "Then I was full of wrath," he continued. "I did not even attempt to control myself; but I took him by the throat and flung him violently to the ground. He fell upon the grate, and it may be that he has been hurt. Had the fall killed him he would have deserved it. He had courage to wound a father in his tenderest part, only because that father was a clergyman. His belief in a black coat will, I think, be a little weakened by what occurred to-day."

"What will be done?" she asked, whispering.

"Heaven only knows. But I can't go out of town to-morrow. I shall write to George to-night and tell him everything that has occurred, and shall beg that you may be allowed to stay with me for the few days that will be necessary."

"Of course I will not leave you."

"It is not that. But I do not want you to go to Cross Hall quite at present. If you went without me they would not let you come to the deanery. Of course there will be a great commotion at Cross Hall. Of course they will condemn me. Many will condemn me, as it will be impossible to make the world believe the exact truth."

"I will never condemn you," she said. Then she came over and threw herself on her knees at his feet, and embraced him. "But, papa, what did the man say of me?"

"Not what he believed;—but what he thought would give me the greatest anguish. Never mind. Do not ask any more questions. You also had better write to your husband, and you can tell him fully all that I have told you. If you will write to-night I will do so also, and I will take care that they shall have our letters to-morrow afternoon. We must send a message to say that we shall not be at the deanery to-morrow." The two letters to Lord George were both written that night, and were both very long. They told the same story, though in a different tone. The Dean was by no means apologetic, but was very full and very true. When he came to the odious word he could not write it, but he made it very clear without writing. Would not the husband feel as he the father had felt in regard to his young wife, the sweet pure girl of whose love and possession he ought to be so proud? How would any brother be forgiven who had assailed such a treasure as this;—much less such a brother as this Marquis? Perhaps Lord George might think it right to come up. The Dean would of course ask at the hotel on the following day, and would go to the police office. He believed, he said, that no permanent injury had been done. Then came, perhaps, the pith of his letter. He trusted that Lord George would agree with him in thinking that Mary had better remain with him in town during the two or three days of his necessarily prolonged sojourn. This was put in the form of a request; but was put in a manner intended to show that the request if not granted would be enforced. The Dean was fully determined that Mary should not at once go down to Cross Hall.

Her letter was supplicatory, spasmodic, full of sorrow, and full of love. She was quite sure that her dear papa would have done nothing that he ought not to have done; but yet she was very sorry for the Marquis, because of his mother and sisters, and because of her dear, dear George. Could he not run up to them and hear all about it from papa? If the Marquis had said ill-natured things of her it was very cruel, because nobody loved her husband better than she loved her dear, dear George,— and so on. The letters were then sent under cover to the housekeeper at the deanery, with orders to send them on by private messenger to Cross Hall.

On the following day the Dean went to Scumberg's, but could not learn much there. The Marquis had been very bad, and had had one and another doctor with him almost continually; but Mrs. Walker could not take upon herself to say that "it was dangerous." She thought it was "in'ard." Mrs. Walkers always do think that it is "in'ard" when there is nothing palpable outward. At any rate his lordship had not been out of bed and had taken nothing but tapioca and brandy. There was very little more than this to be learned at the police court. The case might be serious, but the superintendent hoped otherwise. The superintendent did not think that the Dean should go down quite to-morrow. The morrow was Friday; but he suggested Saturday as possible, Monday as almost certain. It may be as well to say here that the Dean did not call at the police court again, and heard nothing further from the officers of the law respecting the occurrence at Scumberg's. On the Friday he called again at Scumberg's, and the Marquis was still in bed. His "in'ards" had not ceased to be matter of anxiety to Mrs. Walker; but the surgeon, whom the Dean now saw, declared that the muscles of the nobleman's back were more deserving of sympathy. The surgeon, with a gravity that almost indicated offence, expressed his opinion that the Marquis's back had received an injury which—which might be—very injurious.

Lord George when he received the letters was thrown into a state of mind that almost distracted him. During the last week or two the animosity felt at Cross Hall against the Marquis had been greatly weakened. A feeling had come upon the family that after all Popenjoy was Popenjoy; and that, although the natal circumstances of such a Popenjoy were doubtless unfortunate for the family generally, still, as an injury had been done to the Marquis by the suspicion, those circumstances ought now to be in a measure forgiven. The Marquis was the head of the family, and a family will forgive much to its head when that head is a Marquis. As we know the Dowager had been in his favour from the first, Lord George had lately given way and had undergone a certain amount of reconciliation with his brother. Lady Amelia had seceded to her mother, as had also Mrs. Toff, the old housekeeper. Lady Susanna was wavering, having had her mind biased by the objectionable conduct of the Dean and his daughter. Lady Sarah was more stanch. Lady Sarah had never yet given way; she never did give way; and, in her very heart, she was the best friend that Mary had among the ladies of the family. But when her brother gave up the contest she felt that further immediate action was impossible. Things were in this state at Cross Hall when Lord George received the two letters. He did not wish to think well of the Dean just at present, and was horrified at the idea of a clergyman knocking a Marquis into the fire-place. But the word indicated was very plain, and that word had been applied to his own wife. Or, perhaps, no such word had really been used. Perhaps the Dean had craftily saved himself from an absolute lie, and in his attempt to defend the violence of his conduct had brought an accusation against the Marquis, which was in its essence, untrue. Lord George was quite alive to the duty of defending his wife; but in doing so he was no longer anxious to maintain affectionate terms with his wife's father. She had been very foolish. All the world had admitted as much. He had seen it with his own eyes at that wretched ball. She had suffered her name to be joined with that of a stranger in a manner derogatory to her husband's honour. It was hardly surprising that his brother should have spoken of her conduct in disparaging terms;—but he did not believe that his brother had used that special term. Personal violence;—blows and struggling, and that on the part of a Dean of the Church of England, and violence such as this seemed to have been,—violence that might have killed the man attacked, seemed to him to be in any case unpardonable. He certainly could not live on terms of friendship with the Dean immediately after such a deed. His wife must be taken away and secluded, and purified by a long course of Germain asceticism.

But what must he do now at once? He felt that it was his duty to hurry up to London, but he could not bring himself to live in the same house with the Dean. His wife must be taken away from her father. However bad may have been the language used by the Marquis, however indefensible, he could not allow himself even to seem to keep up affectionate relations with the man who had half slaughtered his brother. He too thought of what the world would say, he too felt that such an affair, after having become known to the police, would be soon known to every one else. But what must he do at once? He had not as yet made up his mind as to this when he took his place at the Brotherton Railway Station on the morning after he had received the letters.

But on reaching the station in London he had so far made up his mind as to have his portmanteau taken to the hotel close at hand, and then to go to Munster Court. He had hoped to find his wife alone; but on his arrival the Dean was there also. "Oh, George," she said, "I am so glad you have come; where are your things?" He explained that he had no things, that he had come up only for a short time, and had left his luggage at the station. "But you will stay here to-night?" asked Mary, in despair.

Lord George hesitated, and the Dean at once saw how it was. "You will not go back to Brotherton to-day," he said. Now, at this moment the Dean had to settle in his mind the great question whether it would be best for his girl that she should be separated from her husband or from her father. In giving him his due it must be acknowledged that he considered only what might in truth be best for her. If she were now taken away from him there would be no prospect of recovery. After all that had passed, after Lord George's submission to his brother, the Dean was sure that he would be held in abhorrence by the whole Germain family. Mary would be secluded and trodden on, and reduced to pale submission by all the dragons till her life would be miserable. Lord George himself would be prone enough to domineer in such circumstances. And then that ill word which had been spoken, and which could only be effectually burned out of the thoughts of people by a front to the world at the same time innocent and bold, would stick to her for ever if she were carried away into obscurity.

But the Dean knew as well as others know how great is the evil of a separation, and how specially detrimental such a step would be to a young wife. Than a permanent separation anything would be better; better even that she should be secluded and maligned, and even, for a while, trodden under foot. Were such separation to take place his girl would have been altogether sacrificed, and her life's happiness brought to shipwreck. But then a permanent separation was not probable. She had done nothing wrong. The husband and wife did in truth love each other dearly. The Marquis would be soon gone, and then Lord George would return to his old habits of thought and his old allegiance. Upon the whole the Dean thought it best that his present influence should be used in taking his daughter to the deanery.

"I should like to return quite early to-morrow," said Lord George, very gravely, "unless my brother's condition should make it impossible."

"I trust you won't find your brother much the worse for what has happened," said the Dean.

"But you will sleep here to-night," repeated Mary.

"I will come for you the first thing in the morning," said Lord George in the same funereal voice.

"But why;—why?"

"I shall probably have to be a good deal with my brother during the afternoon. But I will be here again in the afternoon. You can be at home at five, and you can get your things ready for going to-morrow."

"Won't you dine here?"

"I think not."

Then there was silence for a minute. Mary was completely astounded. Lord George wished to say nothing further in the presence of his father-in-law. The Dean was thinking how he would begin to use his influence. "I trust you will not take Mary away to-morrow."

"Oh;—certainly."

"I trust not. I must ask you to hear me say a few words about this."

"I must insist on her coming with me to-morrow, even though I should have to return to London myself afterwards."

"Mary," said her father, "leave us for a moment." Then Mary retired, with a very saddened air. "Do you understand, George, what it was that your brother said to me?"

"I suppose so," he answered, hoarsely.

"Then, no doubt, I may take it for granted that you approve of the violence of my resentment? To me as a clergyman, and as a man past middle life, the position was very trying. But had I been an Archbishop, tottering on the grave with years, I must have endeavoured to do the same." This he said with great energy. "Tell me, George, that you think that I was right."

But George had not heard the word, had not seen the man's face. And then, though he would have gone to a desert island with his wife, had such exile been necessary for her protection, he did believe that she had misconducted herself. Had he not seen her whirling round the room with that man after she had been warned against him. "It cannot be right to murder a man," he said at last.

"You do not thank me then for vindicating your honour and your wife's innocence?"

"I do not think that that was the way. The way is to take her home."

"Yes;—to her old home,—to the deanery for a while; so that the world, which will no doubt hear the malignant epithet applied to her by your wicked brother, may know that both her husband and her father support her. You had promised to come to the deanery."

"We cannot do that now."

"Do you mean that after what has passed you will take your brother's part?"

"I will take my wife to Cross Hall," he said, leaving the room and following Mary up to her chamber.

"What am I to do, papa?" she said when she came down about half-an-hour afterwards. Lord George had then started to Scumberg's, saying that he would come to Munster Court again before dinner, but telling her plainly that he would not sit down to dine with her father, "He has determined to quarrel with you."

"It will only be for a time, dearest."

"But what shall I do?"

Now came the peril of the answer. He was sure, almost sure, that she would in this emergency rely rather upon him than on her husband, if he were firm; but should he be firm as against the husband, how great would be his responsibility! "I think, my dear," he said, at last, "that you should go with me to Brotherton."

"But he will not let me."

"I think that you should insist on his promise."

"Don't make us quarrel, papa."

"Certainly not. Anything would be better than a permanent quarrel. But, after what has been said, after the foul lies that have been told, I think that you should assert your purpose of staying for awhile with your father. Were you now to go to Cross Hall there would be no limit to their tyranny." He left her without a word more, and calling at Scumberg's Hotel was told that the Marquis could not move.

At that moment Lord George was with his brother, and the Marquis could talk though he could not move. "A precious family you've married into, George," he said, almost as soon as his brother was in the room. Then he gave his own version of the affair, leaving his brother in doubt as to the exact language that had been used. "He ought to have been a coal-heaver instead of a clergyman," said the Marquis.

"Of course he would be angry," said Lord George.

"Nothing astonishes me so much," said the Marquis, "as the way in which you fellows here think you may say whatever comes into your head about my wife, because she is an Italian, and you seem to be quite surprised if I object; yet you rage like wild beasts if the compliment is returned. Why am I to think better of your wife than you of mine?"

"I have said nothing against your wife, Brotherton."

"By ——, I think you have said a great deal,—and with much less reason than I have. What did you do yourself when you found her struggling in that fellow's arms at the old woman's party?" Some good-natured friend had told the Marquis the whole story of the Kappa-kappa. "You can't be deaf to what all the world is saying of her." This was wormwood to the wretched husband, and yet he could not answer with angry, self-reliant indignation, while his brother was lying almost motionless before him.

Lord George found that he could do nothing at Scumberg's Hotel. He was assured that his brother was not in danger, and that the chief injury done was to the muscles of his back, which bruised and lacerated as they were, would gradually recover such elasticity as they had ever possessed. But other words were said and other hints expressed, all of which tended to increase his animosity against the Dean, and almost to engender anger against his wife. To himself, personally, except in regard to his wife, his brother had not been ungracious. The Marquis intended to return to Italy as soon as he could. He hated England and everything in it. Manor Cross would very soon be at Lord George's disposal, "though I do hope," said the Marquis, "that the lady who has condescended to make me her brother-in-law, will never reign paramount there." By degrees there crept on Lord George's mind a feeling that his brother looked to a permanent separation,—something like a repudiation. Over and over again he spoke of Mary as though she had disgraced herself utterly; and when Lord George defended his wife, the lord only smiled and sneered.

The effect upon Lord George was to make him very imperious as he walked back to Munster Court. He could not repudiate his wife, but he would take her away with a very high hand. Crossing the Green Park, at the back of Arlington Street, whom should he meet but Mrs. Houghton with her cousin Jack. He raised his hat, but could not stop a moment. Mrs. Houghton made an attempt to arrest him,—but he escaped without a word and went on very quickly. His wife had behaved generously about Mrs. Houghton. The sight of the woman brought that truth to his mind. He was aware of that. But no generosity on the part of the wife, no love, no temper, no virtue, no piety can be accepted by Cæsar as weighing a grain in counterpoise against even suspicion.

He found his wife and asked her whether her things were being packed. "I cannot go to-morrow," she said.

"Not go?"

"No, George;—not to Cross Hall. I will go to the deanery. You promised to go to the deanery."

"I will not go to the deanery. I will go to Cross Hall." There was an hour of it, but during the entire hour, the young wife persisted obstinately that she would not be taken to Cross Hall. "She had," she said, "been very badly treated by her husband's family." "Not by me," shouted the husband. She went on to say that nothing could now really put her right but the joint love of her father and her husband. Were she at Cross Hall her father could do nothing for her. She would not go to Cross Hall. Nothing short of policemen should take her to Cross Hall to-morrow.

Chapter XLIII.

Real Love.

"He is looking awfully cut up," Mrs. Houghton said to her cousin.

"He is one of the most infernal fools that ever I came across in my life," said Jack.

"I don't see that he is a fool at all,—any more than all men are fools. There isn't one among you is ever able to keep his little troubles to himself. You are not a bit wiser than the rest of them yourself."

"I haven't got any troubles,—of that sort."

"You haven't a wife,—but you'll be forced into having one before long. And when you like another man's wife you can't keep all the world from knowing it."

"All the world may know everything that has taken place between me and Lady George," said Jack. "Of course I like her."

"I should say, rather."

"And so do you."

"No, I don't, sir. I don't like her at all. She is a foolish, meaningless little creature, with nothing to recommend her but a pretty colour. And she has cut me because her husband will come and pour out his sorrow into my ears. For his sake I used to be good to her."

"I think she is the sweetest human being I ever came across in my life," said Jack, enthusiastically.

"Everybody in London knows that you think so,—and that you have told her your thoughts."

"Nobody in London knows anything of the kind. I never said a word to her that her husband mightn't have heard."

"Jack!"

"I never did."

"I wonder you are not ashamed to confess such simplicity, even to me."

"I am not a bit ashamed of that, though I am ashamed of having in some sort contributed to do her an injury. Of course I love her."

"Rather,—as I said before."

"Of course you intended that I should."

"I intended that you should amuse yourself. As long as you are good to me, I shall be good to you."

"My dear Adelaide, nobody can be so grateful as I am. But in this matter the thing hasn't gone quite as you intended. You say that she is meaningless."

"Vapid, flabby, childish, and innocent as a baby."

"Innocent I am sure she is. Vapid and flabby she certainly is not. She is full of fun, and is quite as witty as a woman should be."

"You always liked fools, Jack."

"Then how did I come to be so very fond of you." In answer to this she merely made a grimace at him. "I hadn't known her three days," continued he, "before I began to feel how impossible it would be to say anything to her that ought not to be said."

"That is just like the world all over," said Mrs. Houghton. "When a man really falls in love with a woman he always makes her such a goddess that he doesn't dare to speak to her. The effect is that women are obliged to put up with men who ain't in love with them,—either that, or vouchsafe to tell their own little story,—when, lo, they are goddesses no longer."

"I dare say it's very ridiculous," said Jack, in a mooning despondent way. "I dare say I'm not the man I ought to be after the advantages I have had in such friends as you and others."

"If you try to be severe to me, I'll quarrel with you."

"Not severe at all. I'm quite in earnest. A man, and a woman too, have to choose which kind of role shall be played. There is innocence and purity, combined with going to church and seeing that the children's faces are washed. The game is rather slow, but it lasts a long time, and leads to great capacity for digesting your dinner in old age. You and I haven't gone in for that."

"Do you mean to say that I am not innocent?"

"Then there is the Devil with all his works,—which I own are, for the most part, pleasant works to me. I have always had a liking for the Devil."

"Jack!"

"Of all the saints going he is certainly the most popular. It is pleasant to ignore the Commandments and enjoy the full liberty of a debauched conscience. But there are attendant evils. It costs money and wears out the constitution."

"I should have thought that you had never felt the latter evil."

"The money goes first, no doubt. This, however, must surely be clear. A man should make up his mind and not shilly-shally between the two."

"I should have thought you had made up your mind very absolutely."

"I thought so, too, Adelaide, till I knew Lady George Germain. I'll tell you what I feel about her now. If I could have any hope that he would die I would put myself into some reformatory to fit myself to be her second husband."

"Good heavens!"

"That is one idea that I have. Another is to cut his throat, and take my chance with the widow. She is simply the only woman I ever saw that I have liked all round."

"You come and tell me this, knowing what I think of her."

"Why shouldn't I tell you? You don't want me to make love to you?"

"But a woman never cares to hear all these praises of another."

"It was you began it, and if I do speak of her I shall tell the truth. There is a freshness as of uncut flowers about her."

"Psha! Worms and grubs!"

"And when she laughs one dreams of a chaste Venus."

"My heavens, Jack! You should publish all that!"

"The dimples on her cheeks are so alluring that I would give my commission to touch them once with my finger. When I first knew her I thought that the time would come when I might touch them. Now I feel that I would not commit such an outrage to save myself from being cashiered."

"Shall I tell you what you ought to do?"

"Hang myself."

"Just say to her all that you have said to me. You would soon find that her dimples are not more holy than another's."

"You think so."

"Of course I think so. The only thing that puzzles me is that you, Jack De Baron, should be led away to such idolatry. Why should she be different from others? Her father is a money-loving, selfish old reprobate, who was born in a stable. She married the first man that was brought to her, and has never cared for him because he does not laugh, and dance, and enjoy himself after her fashion. I don't suppose she is capable of caring very much for anybody, but she likes you better than any one else. Have you seen her since the row at Mrs. Jones's?"

"No."

"You have not been, then?"

"No."

"Why not?"

"Because I don't think she would wish to see me," said Jack. "All that affair must have troubled her."

"I don't know how that is. She has been in town ever since, and he certainly went down to Brotherton. He has come up, I suppose, in consequence of this row between the Dean and his brother. I wonder what really did happen?"

"They say that there was a scuffle and that the parson had very much the best of it. The police were sent for, and all that kind of thing. I suppose the Marquis said something very rough to him."

"Or he to the Marquis, which is rather more likely. Well,—good-day, Jack." They were now at the house-door in Berkeley Square. "Don't come in, because Houghton will be here." Then the door was opened. "But take my advice, and go and call in Munster Court at once. And, believe me, when you have found out what one woman is, you have found out what most women are. There are no such great differences."

It was then six o'clock, and he knew that in Munster Court they did not dine till near eight. There was still time with a friend so intimate as he was for what is styled a morning call. The words which his cousin had spoken had not turned him,—had not convinced him. Were he again tempted to speak his real mind about this woman,—as he had spoken in very truth his real mind,—he would still express the same opinion. She was to him like a running stream to a man who had long bathed in stagnant waters. But the hideous doctrines which his cousin had preached to him were not without their effect. If she were as other women,—meaning such women as Adelaide Houghton,—or if she were not, why should he not find out the truth? He was well aware that she liked him. She had not scrupled to show him that by many signs. Why should he scruple to say a word that might show him how the wind blew? Then he remembered a few words which he had spoken, but which had been taken so innocently, that they, though they had been meant to be mischievous, had become innocent themselves. Even things impure became pure by contact with her. He was sure, quite sure, that that well-known pupil of Satan, his cousin, was altogether wrong in her judgment. He knew that Adelaide Houghton could not recognise, and could not appreciate, a pure woman. But still,—still it is so poor a thing to miss your plum because you do not dare to shake the tree! It is especially so, if you are known as a professional stealer of plums!

When he got into Piccadilly, he put himself into a cab, and had himself driven to the corner of Munster Court. It was a little street, gloomy to look at, with dingy doors and small houses, but with windows looking into St. James's Park. There was no way through it, so that he who entered it must either make his way into some house, or come back. He walked up to the door, and then taking out his watch, saw that it was half-past six. It was almost too late for calling. And then this thing that he intended to do required more thought than he had given it. Would it not be well for him that there should be something holy, even to him, in spite of that Devil's advocate who had been so powerful with him. So he turned, and walking slowly back towards Parliament Street, got into another cab, and was taken to his club. "It has come out," said Major M'Mickmack to him, immediately on his entrance, "that when the Dean went to see Brotherton at the hotel, Brotherton called Lady George all the bad names he could put his tongue to."

"I dare say. He is blackguard enough for anything," said De Baron.

"Then the old Dean took his lordship in his arms, and pitched him bang into the fireplace. I had it all from the police myself."

"I always liked the Dean."

"They say he is as strong as Hercules," continued M'Mickmack. "But he is to lose his deanery."

"Gammon!"

"You just ask any of the fellows that know. Fancy a clergyman pitching a Marquis into the fire!"

"Fancy a father not doing so if the Marquis spoke ill of his daughter," said Jack De Baron.

Chapter XLIV.

What The Brotherton Clergymen Said About It.

Had Jack knocked at the door and asked for Lady George he certainly would not have seen her. She was enduring at that moment, with almost silent obstinacy, the fierce anger of her indignant husband. "She was sure that it would be bad for her to go to Cross Hall at present, or anywhere among the Germains, while such things were said of her as the Marquis had said." Could Lord George have declared that the Marquis was at war with the family as he had been at war some weeks since, this argument would have fallen to the ground. But he could not do so, and it seemed to be admitted that by going to Cross Hall she was to take part against her father, and so far to take part with the Marquis, who had maligned her. This became her strong point, and as Lord George was not strong in argument, he allowed her to make the most of it. "Surely you wouldn't let me go anywhere," she said, "where such names as that are believed against me?" She had not heard the name, nor had he, and they were in the dark;—but she pleaded her cause well, and appealed again and again to her husband's promise to take her to the deanery. His stronghold was that of marital authority,—authority unbounded, legitimate, and not to be questioned. "But if you commanded me to quarrel with papa?" she asked.

"I have commanded nothing of the kind."

"But if you did?"

"Then you must quarrel with him."

"I couldn't,—and I wouldn't," said she, burying her face upon the arm of the sofa.

At any rate on the next morning she didn't go, nor, indeed, did he come to fetch her, so convinced had he been of the persistency of her obstinacy. But he told her as he left her that if she separated herself from him now, then the separation must be lasting. Her father, however, foreseeing this threat, had told her just the reverse. "He is an obstinate man," the Dean had said, "but he is good and conscientious, and he loves you."

"I hope he loves me."

"I am sure he does. He is not a fickle man. At present he has put himself into his brother's hands, and we must wait till the tide turns. He will learn by degrees to know how unjust he has been."

So it came to pass that Lord George went down to Cross Hall in the morning and that Mary accompanied her father to the deanery the same afternoon. The Dean had already learned that it would be well that he should face his clerical enemies as soon as possible. He had already received a letter worded in friendly terms from the Bishop, asking him whether he would not wish to make some statement as to the occurrence at Scumberg's Hotel which might be made known to the clergymen of the Cathedral. He had replied by saying that he wished to make no such statement, but that on his return to Brotherton he would be very willing to tell the Bishop the whole story if the Bishop wished to hear it. He had been conscious of Mr. Groschut's hand even among the civil phrases which had come from the Bishop himself. "In such a matter," he said in his reply, "I am amenable to the laws of the land, and am not, as I take it, amenable to any other authority." Then he went on to say that for his own satisfaction he should be very glad to tell the story to the Bishop.

The story as it reached Brotherton had, no doubt, given rise to a great deal of scandal and a great deal of amusement. Pountner and Holdenough were to some extent ashamed of their bellicose Dean. There is something ill-mannered, ungentlemanlike, what we now call rowdy, in personal encounters, even among laymen,—and this is of course aggravated when the assailant is a clergyman. And these canons, though they kept up pleasant, social relations with the Dean, were not ill-disposed to make use of so excellent a weapon against a man, who, though coming from a lower order than themselves, was never disposed in any way to yield to them. But the two canons were gentlemen, and as gentlemen were gracious. Though they liked to have the Dean on the hip, they did not want to hurt him sorely when they had gotten him there. They would be contented with certain sly allusions, and only half-expressed triumphs. But Mr. Groschut was confirmed in his opinion that the Dean was altogether unfit for his position,— which, for the interests of the Church, should be filled by some such man as Mr. Groschut himself, by some God-fearing clergyman, not known as a hard rider across country and as a bruiser with his fists. There had been an article in the "Brotherton Church Gazette," in which an anxious hope was expressed that some explanation would be given of the very incredible tidings which had unfortunately reached Brotherton. Then Mr. Groschut had spoken a word in season to the Bishop. Of course he said it could not be true; but would it not be well that the Dean should be invited to make his own statement? It was Mr. Groschut who had himself used the word "incredible" in the article. Mr. Groschut, in speaking to the Bishop, said that the tidings must be untrue. And yet he believed and rejoiced in believing every word of them. He was a pious man, and did not know that he was lying. He was an anxious Christian, and did not know that he was doing his best to injure an enemy behind his back. He hated the Dean;—but he thought that he loved him. He was sure that the Dean would go to some unpleasant place, and gloried in the certainty; but he thought that he was most anxious for the salvation of the Dean's soul. "I think your Lordship owes it to him to offer him the opportunity," said Mr. Groschut.

The Bishop, too, was what we call a severe man;—but his severity was used chiefly against himself. He was severe in his principles; but, knowing the world better than his chaplain, was aware how much latitude it was necessary that he should allow in dealing with men. And in his heart of hearts he had a liking for the Dean. Whenever there were any tiffs the Dean could take a blow and give a blow, and then think no more about it. This, which was a virtue in the eyes of the Bishop, was no virtue at all to Mr. Groschut, who hated to be hit himself and wished to think that his own blows were fatal. In urging the matter with the bishop, Mr. Groschut expressed an opinion that, if this story were unfortunately true, the Dean should cease to be Dean. He thought that the Dean must see this himself. "I am given to understand that he was absolutely in custody of the police," said Mr. Groschut. The Bishop was annoyed by his chaplain; but still he wrote the letter.

On the very morning of his arrival in Brotherton the Dean went to the palace. "Well, my lord," said the Dean, "you have heard this cock and bull story."

"I have heard a story," said the Bishop. He was an old man, very tall and very thin, looking as though he had crushed out of himself all taste for the pomps and vanities of this wicked world, but singularly urbane in his manner, with an old-fashioned politeness. He smiled as he invited the Dean to a seat, and then expressed a hope that nobody had been much hurt. "Very serious injuries have been spoken of here, but I know well how rumour magnifies these things."

"Had I killed him, my lord, I should have been neither more nor less to blame than I am now, for I certainly endeavoured to do my worst to him." The Bishop's face assumed a look of pain and wonder. "When I had the miscreant in my hands I did not pause to measure the weight of my indignation. He told me, me a father, that my child was ———." He had risen from his chair, and as he pronounced the word, stood looking into the Bishop's eyes. "If there be purity on earth, sweet feminine modesty, playfulness devoid of guile, absolute freedom from any stain of leprosy, they are to be found with my girl."

"Yes! yes; I am sure of that."

"She is my worldly treasure. I have none other. I desire none other. I had wounded this man by certain steps which I have taken in reference to his family;—and then, that he might wound me in return, he did not scruple, to use that word to his own sister-in-law, to my daughter. Was that a time to consider whether a clergyman may be justified in putting out his strength? No; my lord. Old as you are you would have attempted it yourself. I took him up and smote him, and it is not my fault if he is not a cripple for life." The Bishop gazed at him speechlessly, but felt quite sure that it was not in his power to rebuke his fellow clergyman. "Now, my lord," continued the Dean, "you have heard the story. I tell it to you, and I shall tell it to no one else. I tell it you, not because you are the bishop of this diocese, and I, the Dean of this Cathedral,—and as such I am in such a matter by no means subject to your lordship's authority;—but, because of all my neighbours you are the most respected, and I would wish that the truth should be known to some one." Then he ceased, neither enjoining secrecy, or expressing any wish that the story should be correctly told to others.

"He must be a cruel man," said the Bishop.

"No, my lord;—he is no man at all. He is a degraded animal unfortunately placed almost above penalties by his wealth and rank. I am glad to think that he has at last encountered some little punishment, though I could wish that the use of the scourge had fallen into other hands than mine." Then he took his leave, and as he went the Bishop was very gracious to him.

"I am almost inclined to think he was justified," said the Bishop to Mr. Groschut.

"Justified, my lord! The Dean;—in striking the Marquis of Brotherton, and then falling into the hands of the police!"

"I know nothing about the police."

"May I ask your lordship what was his account of the transaction."

"I cannot give it you. I simply say that I think that he was justified." Then Mr. Groschut expressed his opinion to Mrs. Groschut that the Bishop was getting old,—very old indeed. Mr. Groschut was almost afraid that no good could be done in the diocese till a firmer and a younger man sat in the seat.

The main facts of the story came to the knowledge of the canons, though I doubt whether the Bishop ever told all that was told to him. Some few hard words were said. Canon Pountner made a remark in the Dean's hearing about the Church militant, which drew forth from the Dean an allusion to the rites of Bacchus, which the canon only half understood. And Dr. Holdenough asked the Dean whether there had not been some little trouble between him and the Marquis. "I am afraid you have been a little hard upon my noble brother-in-law," said the Doctor. To which the Dean replied that the Doctor should teach his noble brother-in-law better manners. But, upon the whole, the Dean held his own well, and was as carefully waited upon to his seat by the vergers as though there had been no scene at Scumberg's Hotel.

For a time no doubt there was a hope on the part of Mr. Groschut and his adherents that there would be some further police interference;—that the Marquis would bring an action, or that the magistrates would demand some inquiry. But nothing was done. The Marquis endured his bruised back at any rate in silence. But there came tidings to Brotherton that his lordship would not again be seen at Manor Cross that year. The house had been kept up as though for him, and he had certainly declared his purpose of returning when he left the place. He had indeed spoken of living there almost to the end of autumn. But early in July it became known that when he left Scumberg's Hotel, he would go abroad;—and before the middle of July it was intimated to Lady Alice, and through her to all Brotherton, that the Dowager with her daughters and Lord George were going back to the old house.

In the meantime Lady George was still at the deanery, and Lord George at Cross Hall, and to the eyes of the world the husband had been separated from his wife. His anger was certainly very deep, especially against his wife's father. The fact that his commands had been twice,—nay as he said thrice,—disobeyed rankled in his mind. He had ordered her not to waltz, and she had waltzed with, as Lord George thought, the most objectionable man in all London. He had ordered her to leave town with him immediately after Mrs. Jones's ball, and she had remained in town. He had ordered her now to leave her father and to cleave to him; but she had cleft to her father and had deserted him. What husband can do other than repudiate his wife under such circumstances as these! He was moody, gloomy, silent, never speaking of her, never going into Brotherton lest by chance he should see her; but always thinking of her,—and always, always longing for her company.

She talked of him daily to her father, and was constant in her prayer that they should not be made to quarrel. Having so long doubted whether she could ever love him, she now could not understand the strength of her own feeling. "Papa, mightn't I write to him," she said. But her father thought that she should not herself take the first step at any rate till the Marquis was gone. It was she who had in fact been injured, and the overture should come from the other side. Then at last, in a low whisper, hiding her face, she told her father a great secret,—adding with a voice a little raised, "Now, papa, I must write to him."

"My darling, my dearest," said the Dean, leaning over and kissing her with more than his usual demonstration of love.

"I may write now."

"Yes, dear, you should certainly tell him that." Then the Dean went out and walked round the deanery garden, and the cathedral cloisters, and the close, assuring himself that after a very little while the real Lord Popenjoy would be his own grandson.

Chapter XLV.

Lady George At The Deanery.

It took Mary a long long morning,—not altogether an unhappy morning,—to write her letter to her husband. She was forced to make many attempts before she could tell the great news in a fitting way, and even when the telling was done she was very far from being satisfied with the manner of it. There should have been no necessity that such tidings should be told by letter. It was cruel, very cruel, that such a moment should not have been made happy to her by his joy. The whisper made to her father should have been made to him,—but that things had gone so untowardly with her. And then, in her present circumstances, she could not devote her letter to the one event. She must refer to the said subject of their separation. "Dear, dearest George, pray do not think of quarrelling with me," she said twice over in her letter. The letter did get itself finished at last, and the groom was sent over with it on horseback.

What answer would he make to her? Would he be very happy? would he be happy enough to forgive her at once and come and stay with her at the deanery? or would the importance of the moment make him more imperious than ever in commanding that she should go with him to Cross Hall. If he did command her now she thought that she must go. Then she sat meditating what would be the circumstances of her life there,— how absolutely she would be trodden upon; how powerless she would be to resist those Dorcas conclaves after her mutiny and subsequent submission! Though she could not quite guess, she could nearly guess what bad things had been said of her; and the ladies at Cross Hall were, as she understood, now in amity with him who had said them. They had believed evil of her, and of course, therefore, in going to Cross Hall, she would go to it as to a reformatory. But the deanery would be to her a paradise if only her husband would but come to her there. It was not only that she was mistress of everything, including her own time, but that her father's infinite tenderness made all things soft and sweet to her. She hated to be scolded, and the slightest roughness of word or tone seemed to her to convey a rebuke. But he was never rough. She loved to be caressed by those who were dear and near and close to her, and his manner was always caressing. She often loved, if the truth is to be spoken, to be idle, and to spend hours with an unread book in her hand under the shade of the deanery trees, and among the flowers of the deanery garden. The Dean never questioned her as to those idle hours. But at Cross Hall not a half-hour would be allowed to pass without enquiry as to its purpose. At Cross Hall there would be no novels,—except those of Miss Edgeworth, which were sickening to her. She might have all Mudie down to the deanery if she chose to ask for it. At Cross Hall she would be driven out with the Dowager, Lady Susanna, and Lady Amelia, for two hours daily, and would have to get out of the carriage at every cottage she came to. At the deanery there was a pair of ponies, and it was her great delight to drive her father about the roads outside the city. She sometimes thought that a long sojourn at Cross Hall would kill her. Would he not be kind to her now, and loving, and would he not come and stay with her for one or two happy weeks in her father's house? If so, how dearly she would love him; how good she would be to him; how she would strive to gratify him in all his whims! Then she thought of Adelaide Houghton and the letter; and she thought also of those subsequent visits to Berkeley Square. But still she did not in the least believe that he cared for Adelaide Houghton. It was impossible that he should like a painted, unreal, helmeted creature, who smelt of oils, and was never unaffected for a moment. At any rate she would never, never throw Adelaide Houghton in his teeth. If she had been imprudent, so had he; and she would teach him how small errors ought to be forgiven. But would he come to her, or would he only write? Surely he would come to her now when there was matter of such vital moment to be discussed between them! Surely there would be little directions to her given, which should be obeyed,—oh, with such care, if he would be good to her.

That pernicious groom must have ridden home along the road nearly as quick as the Dean's cob would carry him for the express purpose of saying that there was no message. When he had been about ten minutes in the Cross Hall kitchen, he was told that there was no message, and had trotted off with most unnecessary speed. Mary was with her father when word was brought to him, saying that there was no message. "Oh, papa, he doesn't care!" she said.

"He will be sure to write," said the Dean, "and he would not allow himself to write in a hurry."

"But why doesn't he come?"

"He ought to come."

"Oh, papa;—if he doesn't care, I shall die."

"Men always care very much."

"But if he has made up his mind to quarrel with me for ever, then he won't care. Why didn't he send his love?"

"He wouldn't do that by the groom."

"I'd send him mine by a chimney-sweep if there were nobody else." Then the door was opened, and in half a second she was in her husband's arms. "Oh, George, my darling, my own, I am so happy. I thought you would come. Oh, my dear!"

Then the Dean crept out without a word, and the husband and the wife were together for hours.

"Do you think she is well," said Lord George to the Dean in the course of the afternoon.

"Well? why shouldn't she be well!"

"In this condition I take it one never quite knows."

"I should say there isn't a young woman in England in better general health. I never knew her to be ill in my life since she had the measles."

"I thought she seemed flushed."

"No doubt,—at seeing you."

"I suppose she ought to see the doctor."

"See a fiddlestick. If she's not fretted she won't want a doctor till the time comes when the doctor will be with her whether she wants him or not. There's nothing so bad as coddling. Everybody knows that now. The great thing is to make her happy."

There came a cloud across Lord George's brow as this was said,—a cloud which he could not control, though, as he had hurried across the park on horseback, he had made up his mind to be happy and good-humoured. He certainly had cared very much. He had spoken no word on the subject to anyone, but he had been very much disappointed when he had been married twelve months and no hope of an heir had as yet been vouchsafed to him. When his brother had alluded to the matter, he had rebuked even his brother. He had never ventured to ask a question even of his wife. But he had been himself aware of his own bitter disappointment. The reading of his wife's letter had given him a feeling of joy keener than any he had before felt. For a moment he had been almost triumphant. Of course he would go to her. That distasteful Popenjoy up in London was sick and ailing; and after all this might be the true Popenjoy who, in coming days, would re-establish the glory of the family. But, at any rate, she was his wife, and the bairn would be his bairn. He had been made a happy man, and had determined to enjoy to the full the first blush of his happiness. But when he was told that she was not to be fretted, that she was to be made especially happy, and was so told by her father, he did not quite clearly see his way for the future. Did this mean that he was to give up everything, that he was to confess tacitly that he had been wrong in even asking his wife to go with him to Cross Hall, and that he was to be reconciled in all things to the Dean? He was quite ready to take his wife back, to abstain from accusations against her, to let her be one of the family, but he was as eager as ever to repudiate the Dean. To the eyes of his mother the Dean was now the most horrible of human beings, and her eldest born the dearest of sons. After all that he had endured he was again going to let her live at the old family house, and all those doubts about Popenjoy had, she thought, been fully satisfied. The Marquis to her thinking was now almost a model Marquis, and this dear son, this excellent head of the family, had been nearly murdered by the truculent Dean. Of course the Dean was spoken of at Cross Hall in very bitter terms, and of course those terms made impression on Lord George. In the first moments of his paternal anxiety he had been willing to encounter the Dean in order that he might see his wife; but he did not like to be told by the Dean that his wife ought to be made happy. "I don't know what there is to make her unhappy," he said, "if she will do her duty."

"That she has always done," said the Dean, "both before her marriage and since."

"I suppose she will come home now," said Lord George.

"I hardly know what home means. Your own home I take it is in Munster Court."

"My own home is at Manor Cross," said Lord George, proudly.

"While that is the residence of Lord Brotherton it is absolutely impossible that she should go there. Would you take her to the house of a man who has scurrilously maligned her as he has done?"

"He is not there or likely to be there. Of course she would come to Cross Hall first."

"Do you think that would be wise? You were speaking just now with anxiety as to her condition."

"Of course I am anxious."

"You ought to be at any rate. Do you think, that as she is now she should be subjected to the cold kindnesses of the ladies of your family?"

"What right have you to call their kindness cold?"

"Ask yourself. You hear what they say. I do not. You must know exactly what has been the effect in your mother's house of the scene between me and your brother at that hotel. I spurned him from me with violence because he had maligned your wife. I may expect you to forgive me."

"It was very unfortunate."

"I may feel sure that you as a man must exonerate me from blame in that matter, but I cannot expect your mother to see it in the same light. I ask you whether they do not regard her as wayward and unmanageable?"

He paused for a reply; and Lord George found himself obliged to say something. "She should come and show that she is not wayward or unmanageable."

"But she would be so to them. Without meaning it they would torment her, and she would be miserable. Do you not know that it would be so?" He almost seemed to yield. "If you wish her to be happy, come here for a while. If you will stay here with us for a month, so that this stupid idea of a quarrel shall be wiped out of people's minds, I will undertake that she shall then go to Cross Hall. To Manor Cross she cannot go while the Marquis is its ostensible master."

Lord George was very far from being prepared to yield in this way. He had thought that his wife in her present condition would have been sure to obey him, and had even ventured to hope that the Dean would make no further objection. "I don't think that this is the place for her," he said. "Wherever I am she should be with me."

"Then come here, and it will be all right," said the Dean.

"I don't think that I can do that."

"If you are anxious for her health you will." A few minutes ago the Dean had been very stout in his assurances that everything was well with his daughter, but he was by no means unwilling to take advantage of her interesting situation to forward his own views. "I certainly cannot say that she ought to go to Cross Hall at present. She would be wretched there. Ask yourself."

"Why should she be wretched?"

"Ask yourself. You had promised her that you would come here. Does not the very fact of your declining to keep that promise declare that you are dissatisfied with her conduct, and with mine?" Lord George was dissatisfied with his wife's conduct and with the Dean's, but at the present moment did not wish to say so. "I maintain that her conduct is altogether irreproachable; and as for my own, I feel that I am entitled to your warmest thanks for what I have done. I must desire you to understand that we will neither of us submit to blame."

Nothing had been arranged when Lord George left the deanery. The husband could not bring himself to say a harsh word to his wife. When she begged him to promise that he would come over to the deanery, he shook his head. Then she shed a tear, but as she did it she kissed him, and he could not answer her love by any rough word. So he rode back to Cross Hall, feeling that the difficulties of his position were almost insuperable.

On the next morning Mr. Price came to him. Mr. Price was the farmer who had formerly lived at Cross Hall, who had given his house up to the Dowager, and who had in consequence been told that he must quit the land at the expiration of his present term. "So, my lord, his lordship ain't going to stay very long after all," said Mr. Price.

"I don't quite know as yet," said Lord George.

"I have had Mr. Knox with me this morning, saying that I may go back to the Hall whenever I please. He took me so much by surprise, I didn't know what I was doing."

"My mother is still there, Mr. Price."

"In course she is, my lord. But Mr. Knox was saying that she is going to move back at once to the old house. It's very kind of his lordship, I'm sure, to let bygones be bygones." Lord George could only say that nothing was as yet settled, but that Mr. Price would be, of course, welcome to Cross Hall, should the family go back to Manor Cross.

This took place about the 10th of June, and for a fortnight after that no change took place in any of their circumstances. Lady Alice Holdenough called upon Lady George, and, with her husband, dined at the deanery; but Mary saw nothing else of any of the ladies of the family. No letter came from either of her sisters-in-law congratulating her as to her new hopes, and the Manor Cross carriage never stopped at the Dean's door. The sisters came to see Lady Alice, who lived also in the Close, but they never even asked for Lady George. All this made the Dean very angry, so that he declared that his daughter should under no circumstances be the first to give way. As she had not offended, she should never be driven to ask for pardon. During this time Lord George more than once saw his wife, but he had no further interview with the Dean.

Chapter XLVI.

Lady Sarah's Mission.

Towards the end of June the family at Cross Hall were in great perturbation. In the first place it had been now settled that they were to go back to the great house early in July. This might have been a source of unalloyed gratification. The old Marchioness had been made very unhappy by the change to Cross Hall, and had persisted in calling her new home a wretched farmhouse. Both Lady Susanna and Lady Amelia were quite alive to the advantages of the great mansion. Lord George had felt that his position in the county had been very much injured by recent events. This might partly have come from his residence in London; but had, no doubt, been chiefly owing to the loss of influence arising from the late migration. He was glad enough to go back again. But Lady Sarah was strongly opposed to the new movement. "I don't think that mamma should be made liable to be turned out again," she had said to her brother and sisters.

"But mamma is particularly anxious to go," Amelia had replied.

"You can't expect mamma to think correctly about Brotherton," said Lady Sarah. "He is vicious and fickle, and I do not like to feel that any of us should be in his power." But Lady Sarah, who had never been on good terms with her elder brother, was overruled, and everybody knew that in July the family was to return to Manor Cross.

Then there came tidings from London,—unauthorised tidings, and, one may say, undignified tidings,—but still tidings which were received with interest. Mrs. Toff had connections with Scumberg's, and heard through these connections that things at Scumberg's were not going on in a happy way. Mrs. Toff's correspondent declared that the Marquis had hardly been out of his bed since he had been knocked into the fireplace. Mrs. Toff, who had never loved the Dean and had never approved of that alliance, perhaps made the most of this. But the report, which was first made to the Dowager herself, caused very great uneasiness. The old lady said that she must go up to London herself to nurse her son. Then a letter was written by Lady Amelia to her brother, asking for true information. This was the answer which Lady Amelia received;—

"DEAR A.,—I'm pretty well, thank you. Don't trouble yourselves. Yours, B."

"I'm sure he's dying," said the Marchioness, "and he's too noble-hearted to speak of his sufferings." Nevertheless she felt that she did not dare to go up to Scumberg's just at present.

Then there came further tidings. Mrs. Toff was told that the Italian Marchioness had gone away, and had taken Popenjoy with her. There was not anything necessarily singular in this. When a gentleman is going abroad with his family, he and his family need not as a matter of course travel together. Lord Brotherton had declared his purpose of returning to Italy, and there could be no reason why his wife, with the nurses and the august Popenjoy, should not go before him. It was just such an arrangement as such a man as Lord Brotherton would certainly make. But Mrs. Toff was sure that there was more in it than this.

The Italian Marchioness had gone off very suddenly. There had been no grand packing up;—but there had been some very angry words. And Popenjoy, when he was taken away, was supposed to be in a very poor condition of health. All this created renewed doubts in the mind of Lord George, or rather, perhaps, renewed hopes. Perhaps, after all, Popenjoy was not Popenjoy. And even if he were, it seemed that everyone concurred in thinking that the poor boy would die. Surely the Marquis would not have allowed a sick child to be carried away by an indiscreet Italian mother if he cared much for the sick child. But then Lord George had no real knowledge of these transactions. All this had come through Mrs. Toff, and he was hardly able to rely upon Mrs. Toff. Could he have communicated with the Dean, the Dean would soon have found out the truth. The Dean would have flown up to London and have known all about it in a couple of hours; but Lord George was not active and clever as the Dean.

Then he wrote a letter to his brother;—as follows;—

"MY DEAR BROTHERTON,—We have heard through Mr. Knox that you wish us to move to Manor Cross at once, and we are preparing to do so. It is very kind of you to let us have the house, as Cross Hall is not all that my mother likes, and as there would hardly be room for us should my wife have children. I ought perhaps to have told you sooner that she is in the family way. We hear too that you are thinking of starting for Italy very soon, and that the Marchioness and Popenjoy have already gone. Would it suit you to tell us something of your future plans? It is not that I want to be inquisitive, but that I should like to know with reference to your comfort and our own whether you think that you will be back at Manor Cross next year. Of course we should be very sorry to be in your way, but we should not like to give up Cross Hall till we know that it will not be wanted again.

"I hope you are getting better. I could of course come up to town at a moment's notice, if you wished to see me.

"Yours affectionately,

"GEORGE GERMAIN."

There was nothing in this letter which ought to have made any brother angry, but the answer which came to it certainly implied that the Marquis had received it with dudgeon.

"MY DEAR GEORGE," the Marquis said,

"I can give you no guarantee that I shall not want Manor Cross again, and you ought not to expect it. If you and the family go there of course I must have rent for Cross Hall. I don't suppose I shall ever recover altogether from the injury that cursed brute did me.

"Yours, 'B.'

"As to your coming family of course I can say nothing. You won't expect me to be very full of joy. Nevertheless, for the honour of the family, I hope it is all right."

There was a brutality about this which for a time made the expectant father almost mad. He tore the letter at once into fragments, so that he might be ready with an answer if asked to show it to his sisters. Lady Sarah had known of his writing, and did ask as to her brother's answer. "Of course he told me nothing," said Lord George. "He is not like any other brother that ever lived."

"May I see his letter?"

"I have destroyed it. It was not fit to be seen. He will not say whether he means to come back next year or not."

"I would not stir, if it were for me to determine," said Lady Sarah. "Nobody ever ought to live in another person's house as long as he has one of his own;—and of all men certainly not in Brotherton's." Nevertheless, the migration went on, and early in July the Marchioness was once more in possession of her own room at Manor Cross, and Mrs. Toff was once again in the ascendant.

But what was to be done about Mary? Had Popenjoy been reported to enjoy robust health, and had Mary been as Mary was a month or two since, the Marchioness and Lady

Susanna would have been contented that the present separation should have been permanent. They would at any rate have taken no steps to put an end to it which would not have implied abject submission on Mary's part. But now things were so altered! If this Popenjoy should die, and if Mary should have a son, Mary's position would be one which they could not afford to overlook. Though Mary should be living in absolute rebellion with that horrid Dean, still her Popenjoy would in course of time be the Popenjoy, and nothing that any Germain could do would stand in her way. Her Popenjoy would be Popenjoy as soon as the present Marquis should die, and the family estates would all in due time be his! Her position had been becoming daily more honourable as these rumours were received. Everyone at Manor Cross, down to the boy in the kitchen, felt that her dignity had been immeasurably increased. Her child should now certainly be born at Manor Cross,—though the deanery would have been quite good enough had the present Popenjoy been robust. Something must be done. The Marchioness was clear that Mary should be taken into favour and made much of,—even hinted that she should not be asked to make shirts and petticoats,—if only she could be separated from the pestilential Dean. She spoke in private to her son, who declared that nothing would separate Mary from her father. "I don't think I could entertain him after what he did to Brotherton," said the Marchioness, bursting into tears.

There were great consultations at Manor Cross, in which the wisdom of Lady Sarah and Lady Susanna, and sometimes the good offices of Lady Alice Holdenough were taxed to the utmost. Lady Sarah had since the beginning of these latter troubles been Mary's best friend, though neither Mary nor the Dean had known of her good services. She had pretty nearly understood the full horror of the accusation brought by the Marquis, and had in her heart acquitted the Dean. Though she was hard she was very just. She believed no worse evil of Mary than that she had waltzed when her husband had wished her not

IS HE POPENJOY? 473

to do so. To Lady Sarah all waltzing was an abomination, and disobedience to legitimate authority was abominable also. But then Mary had been taken to London, and had been thrown into temptation, and was very young. Lady Sarah knew that her own life was colourless, and was contented. But she could understand that women differently situated should not like a colourless existence. She had seen Adelaide Houghton and her sister-in-law together, and had known that her brother's lot had fallen in much the better place, and, to her, any separation between those whom God had bound together was shocking and wicked. Lady Susanna was louder and less just. She did not believe that Mary had done anything to merit expulsion from the family; but she did think that her return to it should be accompanied by sackcloth and ashes. Mary had been pert to her, and she was not prone to forgive. Lady Alice had no opinion,—could say nothing about it; but would be happy if, by her services, she could assuage matters.

"Does she ever talk of him," Lady Susanna asked.

"Not to me; I don't think she dares. But whenever he goes there she is delighted to see him."

"He has not been for the last ten days," said Lady Sarah.

"I don't think he will ever go again,—unless it be to fetch her," said Lady Susanna. "I don't see how he can keep on going there, when she won't do as he bids her. I never heard of such a thing! Why should she choose to live with her father when she is his wife? I can't understand it at all."

"There has been some provocation," said Lady Sarah.

"What provocation? I don't know of any. Just to please her fancy, George had to take a house in London, and live there against his own wishes."

"It was natural that she should go to the deanery for a few days; but when she was there no one went to see her."

"Why did she not come here first?" said Lady Susanna. "Why did she take upon herself to say where she would go, instead of leaving it to her husband. Of course it was the Dean.

How can any man be expected to endure that his wife should be governed by her father instead of by himself? I think George has been very forbearing."

"You have hardly told the whole story," said Lady Sarah. "Nor do I wish to tell it. Things were said which never should have been spoken. If you will have me, Alice, I will go to Brotherton for a day or two, and I will then go and see her."

And so it was arranged. No one in the house was told of the new plan, Lady Susanna having with difficulty been brought to promise silence. Lady Sarah's visit was of course announced, and that alone created great surprise, as Lady Sarah very rarely left home. The Marchioness had two or three floods of tears over it, and suggested that the carriage would be wanted for the entire day. This evil, however, was altogether escaped, as Lady Alice had a carriage of her own. "I'm sure I don't know who is to look after Mrs. Green," said the Marchioness. Mrs. Green was an old woman of ninety who was supported by Germain charity and was visited almost daily by Lady Sarah. But Lady Amelia promised that she would undertake Mrs. Green. "Of course I'm nobody," said the Marchioness. Mrs. Toff and all who knew the family were sure that the Marchioness would, in truth, enjoy her temporary freedom from her elder daughter's control.

Whatever might have been Lord George's suspicion, he said nothing about it. It had not been by agreement with him that the ladies of the family had abstained from calling on his wife. He had expressed himself in very angry terms as to the Dean's misconduct in keeping her in Brotherton, and in his wrath had said more than once that he would never speak to the Dean again. He had not asked any one to go there; but neither had he asked them not to do so. In certain of his moods he was indignant with his sisters for their treatment of his wife; and then again he would say to himself that it was impossible that they should go into the Dean's house after what the Dean had done. Now, when he heard that his eldest sister was going to the Close, he said not a word.

On the day of her arrival Lady Sarah knocked at the deanery door alone. Up to this moment she had never put her foot in the house. Before the marriage she had known the Dean but slightly, and the visiting to be done by the family very rarely fell to her share. The streets of Brotherton were almost strange to her, so little was she given to leave the sphere of her own duties. In the hall, at the door of his study, she met the Dean. He was so surprised that he hardly knew how to greet her. "I am come to call upon Mary," said Lady Sarah, very brusquely.

"Better late than never," said the Dean, with a smile.

"I hope so," said Lady Sarah, very solemnly. "I hope that I am not doing that which ought not to be done. May I see her?"

"Of course you can see her. I dare say she will be delighted. Is your carriage here?"

"I am staying with my sister. Shall I go upstairs?"

Mary was in the garden, and Lady Sarah was alone for a few minutes in the drawing-room. Of course she thought that this time was spent in conference by the father and daughter; but the Dean did not even see his child. He was anxious enough himself that the quarrel should be brought to an end, if only that end could be reached by some steps to be taken first by the other side. Mary, as she entered the room, was almost frightened, for Lady Sarah had certainly been the greatest of the bugbears when she was living at Manor Cross, "I am come to congratulate you," said Lady Sarah, putting her hand out straight before her.

Better late than never. Mary did not say so, as her father had done, but only thought it. "Thank you," she said, in a very low voice. "Has any one else come?"

"No,—no one else. I am with Alice, and as I have very very much to say, I have come alone. Oh! Mary,—dear Mary, is not this sad?" Mary was not at all disposed to yield, or to acknowledge that the sadness was, in any degree, her fault, but she remembered, at the moment, that Lady Sarah had never called her "dear Mary" before. "Don't you wish that you were back with George?"

"Of course I do. How can I wish anything else?"

"Why don't you go back to him?"

"Let him come here and fetch me, and be friends with papa. He promised that he would come and stay here. Is he well, Sarah?"

"Yes; he is well."

"Quite well? Give him my love,—my best love. Tell him that in spite of everything I love him better than all the world."

"I am sure you do."

"Yes;—of course I do. I could be so happy now if he would come to me."

"You can go to him. I will take you if you wish it."

"You don't understand," said Mary.

"What don't I understand?"

"About papa."

"Will he not let you go to your husband?"

"I suppose he would let me go;—but if I were gone what would become of him?"

Lady Sarah did not, in truth, understand this. "When he gave you to be married," she said, "of course he knew that you must go away from him and live with your husband. A father does not expect a married daughter to stay in his own house."

"But he expects to be able to go to hers. He does not expect to be quarrelled with by everybody. If I were to go to Manor Cross, papa couldn't even come and see me."

"I think he could."

"You don't know papa if you fancy he would go into any house in which he was not welcome. Of course I know that you have all quarrelled with him. You think because he beat the Marquis up in London that he oughtn't ever to be spoken to again. But I love him for what he did more dearly than ever. He did it for my sake. He was defending me, and defending George. I have done nothing wrong. If it is only for George's sake, I will never admit that I have deserved to be treated in this way. None of you have come to see me before, since I came back from London, and now George doesn't come."

"We should all have been kind to you if you had come to us first."

"Yes; and then I should never have been allowed to be here at all. Let George come and stay here, if it is only for two days, and be kind to papa, and then I will go with him to Manor Cross."

Lady Sarah was much surprised by the courage and persistence of the young wife's plea. The girl had become a woman, and was altered even in appearance. She certainly looked older, but then she was certainly much more beautiful than before. She was dressed, not richly, but with care, and looked like a woman of high family. Lady Sarah, who never changed either the colour or the material of her brown morning gown, liked to look at her, telling herself that should it ever be this woman's fate to be Marchioness of Brotherton, she would not in appearance disgrace the position. "I hope you can understand that we are very anxious about you," she said.

"I don't know."

"You might know, then. Your baby will be a Germain."

"Ah,—yes,—for that! You can't think I am happy without George. I am longing all day long, from morning to night, that he will come back to me. But after all that has happened, I must do what papa advises. If I were just to go to Manor Cross now, and allow myself to be carried there alone, you would all feel that I had been—forgiven. Isn't that true?"

"You would be very welcome."

"Susanna would forgive me, and your mother. And I should be like a girl who has been punished, and who is expected to remember ever so long that she has been naughty. I won't be forgiven, except by George,—and he has nothing to forgive. You would all think me wicked if I were there, because I would not live in your ways."

"We should not think you wicked, Mary."

"Yes, you would. You thought me wicked before."

"Don't you believe we love you, Mary?"

She considered a moment before she made a reply, but then made it very clearly: "No," she said, "I don't think you do. George loves me. Oh, I hope he loves me."

"You may be quite sure of that. And I love you."

"Yes;—just as you love all people, because the Bible tells you. That is not enough."

"I will love you like a sister, Mary, if you will come back to us."

She liked being asked. She was longing to be once more with her husband. She desired of all things to be able to talk to him of her coming hopes. There was something in the tone of Lady Sarah's voice, different from the tones of old, which had its effect. She would promise to go if only some slightest concession could be made, which should imply that neither she nor her father had given just cause of offence. And she did feel,—she was always feeling,—that her husband ought to remember that she had never brought counter-charges against him. She had told no one of Mrs. Houghton's letter. She was far too proud to give the slightest hint that she too had her grievance. But surely he should remember it. "I should like to go," she said.

"Then come back with me to-morrow." Lady Sarah had come only on this business, and if the business were completed there would be no legitimate reason for her prolonged sojourn at Brotherton.

"Would George come here for one night."

"Surely, Mary, you would not drive a bargain with your husband."

"But papa!"

"Your father can only be anxious for your happiness."

"Therefore I must be anxious for his. I can't say that I'll go without asking him."

"Then ask him and come in and see me at Alice's house this afternoon. And tell your father that I say you shall be received with all affection."

Mary made no promise that she would do even this as Lady Sarah took her leave; but she did at once consult her father. "Of course you can go if you like it, dearest."

"But you!"

"Never mind me. I am thinking only of you. They will be different to you now that they think you will be the mother of the heir."

"Would you take me, and stay there, for one night?"

"I don't think I could do that, dear. I do not consider that I have been exactly asked."

"But if they will ask you?"

"I cannot ask to be asked. To tell the truth I am not at all anxious to be entertained at Manor Cross. They would always be thinking of that fireplace into which the Marquis fell."

The difficulty was very great and Mary could not see her way through it. She did not go to Dr. Holdenough's house that afternoon, but wrote a very short note to Lady Sarah begging that George might come over and talk to her.

Chapter XLVII.

"That Young Fellow In There."

A day or two after this Lord George did call at the deanery, but stayed there only for a minute or two, and on that occasion did not even speak of Mary's return to Manor Cross. He was considerably flurried, and showed his wife the letter which had caused his excitement. It was from his brother, and like most of the Marquis's letters was very short.

"I think you had better come up and see me. I'm not very well. B." That was the entire letter, and he was now on his way to London.

"Do you think it is much, George?"

"He would not write like that unless he were really ill. He has never recovered from the results of that—accident."

Then it occurred to Mary that if the Marquis were to die, and Popenjoy were to die, she would at once be the Marchioness of Brotherton, and that people would say that her father had raised her to the title by—killing the late lord. And it would be so. There was something so horrible in this that she trembled as she thought of it. "Oh, George!"

"It is very—very sad."

"It was his fault; wasn't it? I would give all the world that he were well; but it was his fault." Lord George was silent. "Oh, George, dear George, acknowledge that. Was it not so? Do you not think so? Could papa stand by and hear him call me such names as that? Could you have done so?"

"A man should not be killed for an angry word."

"Papa did not mean to kill him!"

"I can never be reconciled to the man who has taken the life of my brother."

"Do you love your brother better than me?"

"You and your father are not one."

"If this is to be said of him I will always be one with papa. He did it for my sake and for yours. If they send him to prison I will go with him. George, tell the truth about it."

"I always tell the truth," he said angrily.

"Did he not do right to protect his girl's name? I will never leave him now; never. If everybody is against him, I will never leave him."

No good was to be got from the interview. Whatever progress Lady Sarah may have made was altogether undone by the husband's sympathy for his injured brother. Mary declared to herself that if there must be two sides, if there must be a real quarrel, she could never be happy again, but that she certainly would not now desert her father. Then she was left alone. Ah, what would happen if the man were to die. Would any woman ever have risen to high rank in so miserable a manner! In her tumult of feelings she told her father everything, and was astonished by his equanimity. "It may be so," he said, "and if so, there will be considerable inconvenience."

"Inconvenience, papa!"

"There will be a coroner's inquest, and perhaps some kind of trial. But when the truth comes out no English jury will condemn me."

"Who will tell the truth, papa?"

The Dean knew it all, and was well aware that there would be no one to tell the truth on his behalf,—no one to tell it in such guise that a jury would be entitled to accept the telling as evidence. A verdict of manslaughter with punishment, at the discretion of the judge, would be the probable result. But the Dean did not choose to add to his daughter's discomfort by explaining this. "The chances are that this wretched man is dying. No doubt his health is bad. How should the health of such a man be good? But had he been so hurt as to die from it, the doctor would have found something out long since. He may be dying, but he is not dying from what I did to him." The Dean was disturbed, but in his perturbation he remembered that if the man were to die there would be nothing but that little alien Popenjoy between his daughter and the title.

Lord George hurried up to town, and took a room for himself at an hotel in Jermyn Street. He would not go to Scumberg's, as he did not wish to mix his private life with that of his brother. That afternoon he went across, and was told that his brother would see him at three o'clock the next day. Then he interrogated Mrs. Walker as to his brother's condition. Mrs. Walker knew nothing about it, except that the Marquis lay in bed during the most of his time, and that Dr. Pullbody was there every day. Now Dr. Pullbody was an eminent physician, and had the Marquis been dying from an injury in his back an eminent surgeon would have been required. Lord George dined at his club on a mutton chop and a half a pint of sherry, and then found himself terribly dull. What could he do with himself? Whither could he betake himself? So he walked across Piccadilly and went to the old house in Berkeley Square.

He had certainly become very sick of the woman there. He had discussed the matter with himself and had found out that he did not care one straw for the woman. He had acknowledged to himself that she was a flirt, a mass of affectation, and a liar. And yet he went to her house. She would be soft to him and would flatter him, and the woman would trouble herself to do so.

She would make him welcome, and in spite of his manifest neglect would try, for the hour, to make him comfortable.

He was shown up into the drawing-room and there he found Jack De Baron, Guss Mildmay;—and Mr. Houghton, fast asleep. The host was wakened up to bid him welcome, but was soon slumbering again. De Baron and Guss Mildmay had been playing bagatelle,—or flirting in the back drawing-room, and after a word or two returned to their game. "Ill is he?" said Mrs. Houghton, speaking of the Marquis, "I suppose he has never recovered from that terrible blow."

"I have not seen him yet, but I am told that Dr. Pullbody is with him."

"What a tragedy,—if anything should happen! She has gone away; has she not."

"I do not know. I did not ask."

"I think she has gone, and that she has taken the child with her; a poor puny thing. I made Houghton go there to enquire, and he saw the child. I hear from my father that we are to congratulate you."

"Things are too sad for congratulation."

"It is horrible; is it not? And Mary is with her father."

"Yes, she's at the deanery."

"Is that right?—when all this is going on?"

"I don't think anything is right," he said, gloomily.

"Has she—quarrelled with you, George?" At the sound of his Christian name from the wife's lips he looked round at the sleeping husband. He was quite sure that Mr. Houghton would not like to hear his wife call him George. "He sleeps like a church," said Mrs. Houghton, in a low voice. The two were sitting close together and Mr. Houghton's arm-chair was at a considerable distance. The occasional knocking of the balls, and the continued sound of voices was to be heard from the other room. "If you have separated from her I think you ought to tell me."

"I saw her to-day as I came through."

"But she does not go to Manor Cross?"

"She has been at the deanery since she went down."

Of course this woman knew of the quarrel which had taken place in London. Of course she had been aware that Lady George had stayed behind in opposition to her husband's wishes. Of course she had learned every detail as to the Kappa-kappa. She took it for granted that Mary was in love with Jack De Baron, and thought it quite natural that she should be so. "She never understood you as I should have done, George," whispered the lady. Lord George again looked at the sleeping man, who grunted and moved, "He would hardly hear a pistol go off."

"Shouldn't I?" said the sleeping man, rubbing away the flies from his nose. Lord George wished himself back at his club.

"Come out into the balcony," said Mrs. Houghton. She led the way and he was obliged to follow her. There was a balcony to this house surrounded with full-grown shrubs, so that they who stood there could hardly be seen from the road below. "He never knows what any one is saying." As she spoke she came close up to her visitor. "At any rate he has the merit of never troubling me or himself by any jealousies."

"I should be very sorry to give him cause," said Lord George.

"What's that you say?" Poor Lord George had simply been awkward, having intended no severity. "Have you given him no cause?"

"I meant that I should be sorry to trouble him."

"Ah—h! That is a different thing. If husbands would only be complaisant, how much nicer it would be for everybody." Then there was a pause. "You do love me, George?" There was a beautiful moon that was bright through the green foliage, and there was a smell of sweet exotics, and the garden of the Square was mysteriously pretty as it lay below them in the moonlight. He stood silent, making no immediate answer to this appeal. He was in truth plucking up his courage for a great effort. "Say that you love me. After all that is passed you must love me." Still he was silent. "George, will you not speak?"

"Yes; I will speak."

"Well, sir!"

"I do not love you."

"What! But you are laughing at me. You have some scheme or some plot going on."

"I have nothing going on. It is better to say it. I love my wife."

"Psha! love her;—yes, as you would a doll or any pretty plaything. I loved her too till she took it into her stupid head to quarrel with me. I don't grudge her such love as that. She is a child."

It occurred to Lord George at the moment that his wife had certainly more than an infantine will of her own. "You don't know her," he said.

"And now, after all, you tell me to my face that you do not love me! Why have you sworn so often that you did?" He hadn't sworn it often. He had never sworn it at all since she had rejected him. He had been induced to admit a passion in the most meagre terms. "Do you own yourself to be false?" she asked.

"I am true to my wife."

"Your wife! One would think you were the curate of the parish. And is that to be all?"

"Yes, Mrs. Houghton; that had better be all."

"Then why did you come here? Why are you here now?" She had not expected such courage from him, and almost thought more of him now than she had ever thought before. "How dare you come to this house at all?"

"Perhaps I should not have come."

"And I am nothing to you?" she asked in her most plaintive accents. "After all those scenes at Manor Cross you can think of me with indifference?" There had been no scenes, and as she spoke he shook his head, intending to disclaim them.

"Then go!" How was he to go? Was he to wake Mr. Houghton? Was he to disturb that other loving couple? Was he to say no word of farewell to her? "Oh, stay," she added, "and unsay it all—unsay it all and give no reason, and it shall be as though it were never said." Then she seized him by the arm and looked passionately up into his eyes. Mr. Houghton moved restlessly in his chair and coughed aloud. "He'll be off again in half a moment," said Mrs. Houghton. Then he was silent, and she was silent, looking at him. And he heard a word or two come clearly from the back drawing-room. "You will, Jack; won't you, dear Jack?"

The ridicule of the thing touched even him. "I think I had better go," he said.

"Then go!"

"Good-night, Mrs. Houghton."

"I will not say good-night. I will never speak to you again. You are not worth speaking to. You are false. I knew that men could be false, but not so false as you. Even that young fellow in there has some heart. He loves your—darling wife, and will be true to his love." She was a very devil in her wickedness. He started as though he had been stung, and rushed inside for his hat. "Halloa, Germain, are you going?" said the man of the house, rousing himself for the moment.

"Yes, I am going. Where did I leave my hat?"

"You put it on the piano," said Mrs. Houghton in her mildest voice, standing at the window. Then he seized his hat and went off. "What a very stupid man he is," she said, as she entered the room.

"A very good sort of fellow," said Mr. Houghton.

"He's a gentleman all round," said Jack De Baron. Jack knew pretty well how the land lay and could guess what had occurred.

"I am not so sure of that," said the lady. "If he were a gentleman as you say all round, he would not be so much afraid of his elder brother. He has come up to town now merely because Brotherton sent to him, and when he went to Scumberg's the Marquis would not see him. He is just like his sisters,—priggish, punctilious and timid."

"He has said something nasty to you," remarked her husband, "or you would not speak of him like that."

She had certainly said something very nasty to him. As he returned to his club he kept on repeating to himself her last words;—"He loves your darling wife." Into what a mass of trouble had he not fallen through the Dean's determination that his daughter should live in London! He was told on all sides that this man was in love with his wife, and he knew,—he had so much evidence for knowing,—that his wife liked the man. And now he was separated from his wife, and she could go whither her father chose to take her. For aught that he could do she might be made to live within the reach of this young scoundrel. No doubt his wife would come back if he would agree to take her back on her own terms. She would again belong to him if he would agree to take the Dean along with her. But taking the Dean would be to put himself into the Dean's leading strings. The Dean was strong and imperious; and then the Dean was rich. But anything would be better than losing his wife. Faulty as he thought her to be, she was sweet as no one else was sweet. When alone with him she would seem to make every word of his a law. Her caresses were full of bliss to him. When he kissed her her face would glow with pleasure. Her voice was music to him; her least touch was joy. There was a freshness about the very things which she wore which pervaded his senses. There was a homeliness about her beauty which made her more lovely in her own room than when dressed for balls and parties. And yet he had heard it said that when dressed she was declared to be the most lovely woman that had come to London that season. And now she was about to become the mother of his child. He was thoroughly in love with his wife. And yet he was told that his wife was "Jack De Baron's darling!"

Chapter XLVIII.

The Marquis Makes A Proposition.

The next morning was very weary with him, as he had nothing to do till three o'clock. He was most anxious to know whether his sister-in-law had in truth left London, but he had no means of finding out. He could not ask questions on such a subject from Mrs. Walker and her satellites; and he felt that it would be difficult to ask even his brother. He was aware that his brother had behaved to him badly, and he had determined not to be over courteous,—unless, indeed, he should find his brother to be dangerously ill. But above all things he would avoid all semblance of inquisitiveness which might seem to have a reference to the condition of his own unborn child. He walked up and down St. James' Park thinking of all this, looking up once at the windows of the house which had brought so much trouble on him, that house of his which had hardly been his own, but not caring to knock at the door and enter it. He lunched in solitude at his club, and exactly at three o'clock presented himself at Scumberg's door. The Marquis's servant was soon with him, and then again he found himself alone in that dreary sitting-room. How wretched must his brother be, living there from day to day without a friend, or, as far as he was aware, without a companion!

He was there full twenty minutes, walking about the room in exasperated ill-humour, when at last the door was opened and his brother was brought in between two men-servants. He was not actually carried, but was so supported as to appear to be unable to walk. Lord George asked some questions, but received no immediate answers. The Marquis was at the moment thinking too much of himself and of the men who were ministering to him to pay any attention to his brother. Then by degrees he was fixed in his place, and after what seemed to be interminable delay the two men went away. "Ugh!" ejaculated the Marquis.

"I am glad to see that you can at any rate leave your room," said Lord George.

"Then let me tell you that it takes deuced little to make you glad."

The beginning was not auspicious, and further progress in conversation seemed to be difficult. "They told me yesterday that Dr. Pullbody was attending you."

"He has this moment left me. I don't in the least believe in him. Your London doctors are such conceited asses that you can't speak to them? Because they can make more money than their brethren in other countries they think that they know everything, and that nobody else knows anything. It is just the same with the English in every branch of life. The Archbishop of Canterbury is the greatest priest going, because he has the greatest income, and the Lord Chancellor the greatest lawyer. All you fellows here are flunkies from top to bottom."

Lord George certainly had not come up to town merely to hear the great dignitaries of his country abused. But he was comforted somewhat as he reflected that a dying man would hardly turn his mind to such an occupation. When a sick man criticises his doctor severely he is seldom in a very bad way. "Have you had anybody else with you, Brotherton?"

"One is quite enough. But I had another. A fellow named Bolton was here, a baronet, I believe, who told me I ought to walk a mile in Hyde Park every day. When I told him I couldn't he said I didn't know till I tried. I handed him a five-pound note, upon which he hauled out three pounds nineteen shillings change and walked off in a huff. I didn't send for him any more."

"Sir James Bolton has a great reputation."

"No doubt. I daresay he could cut off my leg if I asked him, and would then have handed out two pounds eighteen with the same indifference."

"I suppose your back is better?"

"No, it isn't,—not a bit. It gets worse and worse."

"What does Dr. Pullbody say?"

"Nothing that anybody can understand. By George! he takes my money freely enough. He tells me to eat beefsteaks and drink port-wine. I'd sooner die at once. I told him so, or something a little stronger, I believe, and he almost jumped out of his shoes."

"He doesn't think there is any—danger?"

"He doesn't know anything about it. I wish I could have your father-in-law in a room by ourselves, with a couple of loaded revolvers. I'd make better work of it than he did."

"God forbid!"

"I daresay he won't give me the chance. He thinks he has done a plucky thing because he's as strong as a brewer's horse. I call that downright cowardice."

"It depends on how it began, Brotherton."

"Of course there had been words between us. Things always begin in that way."

"You must have driven him very hard."

"Are you going to take his part? Because, if so, there may as well be an end of it. I thought you had found him out and had separated yourself from him. You can't think that he is a gentleman?"

"He is a very liberal man."

"You mean to sell yourself, then, for the money that was made in his father's stables?"

"I have not sold myself at all. I haven't spoken to him for the last month."

"So I understood; therefore I sent for you. You are all back at Manor Cross now?"

"Yes;—we are there."

"You wrote me a letter which I didn't think quite the right thing. But, however, I don't mind telling you that you can have the house if we can come to terms about it."

"What terms?"

"You can have the house and the park, and Cross Hall Farm, too, if you'll pledge yourself that the Dean shall never enter your house again, and that you will never enter his house or speak to him. You shall do pretty nearly as you please at Manor Cross. In that event I shall live abroad, or here in London if I come to England. I think that's a fair offer, and I don't suppose that you yourself can be very fond of the man." Lord George sat perfectly silent while the Marquis waited for a reply. "After what has passed," continued he, "you can't suppose that I should choose that he should be entertained in my dining-room."

"You said the same about my wife before."

"Yes, I did; but a man may separate himself from his father-in-law when he can't very readily get rid of his wife. I never saw your wife."

"No;—and therefore cannot know what she is."

"I don't in the least want to know what she is. You and I, George, haven't been very lucky in our marriages."

"I have."

"Do you think so? You see I speak more frankly of myself. But I am not speaking of your wife. Your wife's father has been a blister to me ever since I came back to this country, and you must make up your mind whether you will take his part or mine. You know what he did, and what he induced you to do about Popenjoy. You know the reports that he has spread abroad.

And you know what happened in this room. I expect you to throw him off altogether." Lord George had thrown the Dean off altogether. For reasons of his own he had come to the conclusion that the less he had to do with the Dean the better for himself; but he certainly could give no such pledge as this now demanded from him. "You won't make me this promise?" said the Marquis.

"No; I can't do that."

"Then you'll have to turn out of Manor Cross," said the Marquis, smiling.

"You do not mean that my mother must be turned out?"

"You and my mother, I suppose, will live together?"

"It does not follow. I will pay you rent for Cross Hall."

"You shall do no such thing. I will not let Cross Hall to any friend of the Dean's."

"You cannot turn your mother out immediately after telling her to go there?"

"It will be you who turn her out,—not I. I have made you a very liberal offer," said the Marquis.

"I will have nothing to do with it," said Lord George. "In any house in which I act as master I will be the judge who shall be entertained and who not."

"The first guests you will ask, no doubt, will be the Dean of Brotherton and Captain De Baron." This was so unbearable that he at once made a rush at the door. "You'll find, my friend," said the Marquis, "that you'll have to get rid of the Dean and of the Dean's daughter as well." Then Lord George swore to himself as he left the room that he would never willingly be in his brother's company again.

He was rushing down the stairs, thinking about his wife, swearing to himself that all this was calumny, yet confessing to himself that there must have been terrible indiscretion to make the calumny so general, when he was met on the landing by Mrs. Walker in her best silk gown. "Please, my lord, might I take the liberty of asking for one word in my own room?" Lord George followed her and heard the one word. "Please, my lord, what are we to do with the Marquis?"

"Do with him!"

"About his going."

"Why should he go? He pays his bills, I suppose?"

"Oh yes, my lord; the Marquis pays his bills. There ain't no difficulty there, my lord. He's not quite himself."

"You mean in health?"

"Yes, my lord;—in health. He don't give himself,—not a chance. He's out every night,—in his brougham."

"I thought he was almost confined to his room?"

"Out every night, my lord,—and that Courier with him on the box. When we gave him to understand that all manner of people couldn't be allowed to come here, we thought he'd go."

"The Marchioness has gone?"

"Oh yes;—and the poor little boy. It was bad enough when they was here, because things were so uncomfortable; but now—. I wish something could be done, my lord." Lord George could only assure her that it was out of his power to do anything. He had no control over his brother, and did not even mean to come and see him again. "Dearie me!" said Mrs. Walker; "he's a very owdacious nobleman, I fear,—is the Marquis."

All this was very bad. Lord George had learned, indeed, that the Marchioness and Popenjoy were gone, and was able to surmise that the parting had not been pleasant. His brother would probably soon follow them. But what was he to do himself! He could not, in consequence of such a warning, drag his mother and sisters back to Cross Hall, into which house Mr. Price, the farmer, had already moved himself. Nor could he very well leave his mother without explaining to her why he did so. Would it be right that he should take such a threat, uttered as that had been, as a notice to quit the house? He certainly would not live in his brother's house in opposition to his brother. But how was he to obey the orders of such a madman?

When he reached Brotherton he went at once to the deanery and was very glad to find his wife without her father. He did not as yet wish to renew his friendly relations with the Dean, although he had refused to pledge himself to a quarrel. He still thought it to be his duty to take his wife away from her father, and to cause her to expiate those calumnies as to De Baron by some ascetic mode of life. She had been, since his last visit, in a state of nervous anxiety about the Marquis. "How is he, George?" she asked at once.

"I don't know how he is. I think he's mad."

"Mad?"

"He's leading a wretched life."

"But his back? Is he;—is he—? I am afraid that papa is so unhappy about it! He won't say anything, but I know he is unhappy."

"You may tell your father from me that as far as I can judge his illness, if he is ill, has nothing to do with that."

"Oh, George, you have made me so happy."

"I wish I could be happy myself. I sometimes think that we had better go and live abroad."

"Abroad! You and I?"

"Yes. I suppose you would go with me?"

"Of course I would. But your mother?"

"I know there is all manner of trouble about it." He could not tell her of his brother's threat about the house, nor could he, after that threat, again bid her come to Manor Cross. As there was nothing more to be said he soon left her, and went to the house which he had again been forbidden to call his home.

But he told his sister everything. "I was afraid," she said, "that we should be wrong in coming here."

"It is no use going back to that now."

"Not the least. What ought we to do? It will break mamma's heart to be turned out again."

"I suppose we must ask Mr. Knox."

"It is unreasonable;—monstrous! Mr. Price has got all his furniture back again into the Hall! It is terrible that any man should have so much power to do evil."

"I could not pledge myself about the Dean, Sarah."

"Certainly not. Nothing could be more wicked than his asking you. Of course, you will not tell mamma."

"Not yet."

"I should take no notice of it whatever. If he means to turn us out of the house let him write to you, or send word by Mr. Knox. Out every night in London! What does he do?" Lord George shook his head. "I don't think he goes into society." Lord George could only shake his head again. There are so many kinds of society! "They said he was coming down to Mr. De Baron's in August."

"I heard that too. I don't know whether he'll come now. To see him brought in between two servants you'd think that he couldn't move."

"But they told you he goes out every night?"

"I've no doubt that is true."

"I don't understand it all," said Lady Sarah. "What is he to gain by pretending. And so they used to quarrel."

"I tell you what the woman told me."

"I've no doubt it's true. And she has gone and taken Popenjoy? Did he say anything about Popenjoy?"

"Not a word," said Lord George.

"It's quite possible that the Dean may have been right all through. What terrible mischief a man may do when he throws all idea of duty to the winds! If I were you, George, I should just go on as though I had not seen him at all."

That was the decision to which Lord George came, but in that he was soon shaken by a letter which he received from Mr. Knox. "I think if you were to go up to London and see your brother it would have a good effect," said Mr. Knox. In fact Mr. Knox's letter contained little more than a petition that Lord

George would pay another visit to the Marquis. To this request, after consultation with his sister, he gave a positive refusal.

"MY DEAR MR. KNOX," he said,

"I saw my brother less than a week ago, and the meeting was so unsatisfactory in every respect that I do not wish to repeat it. If he has anything to say to me as to the occupation of the house he had better say it through you. I think, however, that my brother should be told that though I may be subject to his freaks, we cannot allow that my mother should be annoyed by them.

"Faithfully yours,

"GEORGE GERMAIN."

At the end of another week Mr. Knox came in person. The Marquis was willing that his mother should live at Manor Cross,—and his sisters. But he had,—so he said,—been insulted by his brother, and must insist that Lord George should leave the house. If this order were not obeyed he should at once put the letting of the place into the hands of a house agent. Then Mr. Knox went on to explain that he was to take back to the Marquis a definite reply. "When people are dependent on me I choose that they shall be dependent," the Marquis had said.

Now, after a prolonged consultation to which Lady Susanna was admitted,—so serious was the thing to be considered,—it was found to be necessary to explain the matter to the Marchioness. Some step clearly must be taken. They must all go, or Lord George must go. Cross Hall was occupied, and Mr. Price was going to be married on the strength of his occupation. A lease had been executed to Mr. Price, which the Dowager herself had been called upon to sign. "Mamma will never be made to understand it," said Lady Susanna.

"No one can understand it," said Lord George. Lord George insisted that the ladies should continue to live at the large house, insinuating that, for himself, he would take some wretched residence in the most miserable corner of the globe, which he could find.

The Marchioness was told and really fell into a very bad way. She literally could not understand it, and aggravated matters by appearing to think that her younger son had been wanting in respect to his elder brother. And it was all that nasty Dean! And Mary must have behaved very badly or Brotherton would not have been so severe! "Mamma," said Lady Sarah, moved beyond her wont, "you ought not to think such things. George has been true to you all his life, and Mary has done nothing. It is all Brotherton's fault. When did he ever behave well? If we are to be miserable, let us at any rate tell the truth about it." Then the Marchioness was put to bed and remained there for two days.

At last the Dean heard of it,—first through Lady Alice, and then directly from Lady Sarah, who took the news to the deanery. Upon which he wrote the following letter to his son-in-law;—

"MY DEAR GEORGE,—I think your brother is not quite sane. I never thought that he was. Since I have had the pleasure of knowing you, especially since I have been connected with the family, he has been the cause of all the troubles that have befallen it. It is to be regretted that you should ever have moved back to Manor Cross, because his temper is so uncertain, and his motives so unchristian!

"I think I understand your position now, and will therefore not refer to it further than to say, that when not in London I hope you will make the deanery your home. You have your own house in town, and when here will be close to your mother and sisters. Anything I can do to make this a comfortable residence for you shall be done; and it will surely go for something with you, that a compliance with this request on your part will make another person the happiest woman in the world.

"In such an emergency as this am I not justified in saying that any little causes of displeasure that may have existed between you and me should now be forgotten? If you will think of them they really amount to nothing. For you I have the esteem of a friend and the affection of a father-in-law. A more devoted wife than my daughter does not live. Be a man and come to us, and let us make much of you.

"She knows I am writing, and sends her love; but I have not told her of the subject lest she should be wild with hope.

"Affectionately yours,

"HENRY LOVELACE."

The letter as he read it moved him to tears, but when he had finished the reading he told himself that it was impossible. There was one phrase in the letter which went sorely against the grain with him. The Dean told him to be a man. Did the Dean mean to imply that his conduct hitherto had been unmanly?

Chapter XLIX.

"Wouldn't You Come Here—For A Week?"

Lord George Germain was very much troubled by the nobility of the Dean's offer. He felt sure that he could not accept it, but he felt at the same time that it would be almost as difficult to decline to accept it. What else was he to do? where was he to go? how was he now to exercise authority over his wife? With what face could he call upon her to leave her father's house, when he had no house of his own to which to take her? There was, no doubt, the house in London, but that was her house, and peculiarly disagreeable to him. He might go abroad; but then what would become of his mother and sisters? He had trained himself to think that his presence was necessary to the very existence of the family; and his mother, though she ill-treated him, was quite of the same opinion. There would be a declaration of a break up made to all the world if he were to take himself far away from Manor Cross. In his difficulty, of course he consulted Lady Sarah. What other counsellor was possible to him?

He was very fair with his sister, trying to explain everything to her—everything, with one or two exceptions. Of course he said nothing of the Houghton correspondence, nor did he give exactly a true account of the scene at Mrs. Montacute Jones' ball; but he succeeded in making Lady Sarah understand that though he accused his wife of nothing, he felt it to be incumbent on him to make her completely subject to his own authority. "No doubt she was wrong to waltz after what you told her," said Lady Sarah.

"Very wrong."

"But it was simply high spirits, I suppose."

"I don't think she understands how circumspect a young married woman ought to be," said the anxious husband. "She does not see how very much such high spirits may injure me. It enables an enemy to say such terrible things."

"Why should she have an enemy, George?" Then Lord George merely whispered his brother's name. "Why should Brotherton care to be her enemy?"

"Because of the Dean."

"She should not suffer for that. Of course, George, Mary and I are very different. She is young and I am old. She has been brought up to the pleasures of life, which I disregard, perhaps because they never came in my way. She is beautiful and soft,—a woman such as men like to have near them. I never was such a one. I see the perils and pitfalls in her way; but I fancy that I am prone to exaggerate them, because I cannot sympathise with her yearnings. I often condemn her frivolity, but at the same time I condemn my own severity. I think she is true of heart,—a loving woman. And she is at any rate your wife."

"You don't suppose that I wish to be rid of her?"

"Certainly not; but in keeping her close to you you must remember that she has a nature of her own. She cannot feel as you do in all things any more than you feel as she does."

"One must give way to the other."

"Each must give way to the other if there is to be any happiness."

"You don't mean to say she ought to waltz, or dance stage dances?"

"Let all that go for the present. She won't want to dance much for a time now, and when she has a baby in her arms she will be more apt to look at things with your eyes. If I were you I should accept the Dean's offer."

There was a certain amount of comfort in this, but there was more pain. His wife had defied him, and it was necessary to his dignity that she should be brought to submission before she was received into his full grace. And the Dean had encouraged her in those acts of defiance. They had, of course, come from him. She had been more her father's daughter than her husband's wife, and his pride could not endure that it should be so. Everything had gone against him. Hitherto he had been able to desire her to leave her father and to join him in his own home. Now he had no home to which to take her. He had endeavoured to do his duty,—always excepting that disagreeable episode with Mrs. Houghton,—and this was the fruit of it. He had tried to serve his brother, because his brother was Marquis of Brotherton, and his brother had used him like an enemy. His mother treated him, with steady injustice. And now his sister told him that he was to yield to the Dean! He could not bring himself to yield to the Dean. At last he answered the Dean's letter as follows;—

"My Dear Dean,—

"Your offer is very kind, but I do not think that I can accept it just at present. No doubt I am very much troubled by my brother's conduct. I have endeavoured to do my duty by him, and have met with but a poor return. What arrangements I shall ultimately make as to a home for myself and Mary, I cannot yet say. When anything is settled I shall, of course, let her know at once. It will always be, at any rate, one of my chief objects to make her comfortable, but I think that this should be done under my roof and not under yours. I hope to be able to see her in a day or two, when perhaps I shall have been able to settle upon something.

"Yours always affectionately,

"G. Germain."

Then, upon reading this over and feeling that it was cold and almost heartless, he added a postscript. "I do feel your offer to be very generous, but I think you will understand the reasons which make it impossible that I should accept it." The Dean as he read this declared to himself that he knew the reasons very well. The reasons were not far to search. The man was pigheaded, foolish, and obstinately proud. So the Dean thought. As far as he himself was concerned Lord George's presence in the house would not be a comfort to him. Lord George had never been a pleasant companion to him. But he would have put up with worse than Lord George for the sake of his daughter.

On the very next day Lord George rode into Brotherton and went direct to the deanery. Having left his horse at the inn he met the Dean in the Close, coming out of a side door of the Cathedral close to the deanery gate. "I thought I would come in to see Mary," he said.

"Mary will be delighted."

"I did not believe that I should be able to come so soon when I wrote yesterday."

"I hope you are going to tell her that you have thought better of my little plan."

"Well;—no; I don't think I can do that. I think she must come to me first, sir."

"But where!"

"I have not yet quite made up my mind. Of course there is a difficulty. My brother's conduct has been so very strange."

"Your brother is a madman, George."

"It is very easy to say so, but that does not make it any better. Though he be ever so mad the house is his own. If he chooses to turn me out of it he can. I have told Mr. Knox that I would leave it within a month,—for my mother's sake; but that as I had gone there at his express instance, I could not move sooner. I think I was justified in that."

"I don't see why you should go at all."

"He would let the place."

"Or, if you do go, why you should not come here. But, of course, you know your own business best. How d'ye do, Mr. Groschut? I hope the Bishop is better this morning."

At this moment, just as they were entering the deanery gate, the Bishop's chaplain had appeared. He had been very studious in spreading a report, which he had no doubt believed to be true, that all the Germain family, including Lord George, had altogether repudiated the Dean, whose daughter, according to his story, was left upon her father's hands because she would not be received at Manor Cross. For Mr. Groschut had also heard of Jack De Baron, and had been cut to the soul by the wickedness of the Kappa-kappa. The general iniquity of Mary's life in London had been heavy on him. Brotherton, upon the whole, had pardoned the Dean for knocking the Marquis into the fireplace, having heard something of the true story with more or less correctness. But the Chaplain's morals were sterner than those of Brotherton at large, and he was still of opinion that the Dean was a child of wrath, and poor Mary, therefore, a grandchild. Now, when he saw the Dean and his son-in-law apparently on friendly terms, the spirit of righteousness was vexed within him as he acknowledged this to be another sign that the Dean was escaping from that punishment which alone could be of service to him in this world. "His Lordship is better this morning. I hope, my Lord, I have the pleasure of seeing your Lordship quite well." Then Mr. Groschut passed on.

"I'm not quite sure," said the Dean, as he opened his own door, "whether any good is ever done by converting a Jew."

"But St. Paul was a converted Jew," said Lord George.

"Well—yes; in those early days Christians were only to be had by converting Jews or Pagans; and in those days they did actually become Christians. But the Groschuts are a mistake."

Then he called to Mary, and in a few minutes she was in her husband's arms on the staircase. The Dean did not follow them, but went into his own room on the ground floor; and Lord George did not see him again on that day.

Lord George remained with his wife nearly all the afternoon, going out with her into the town as she did some little shopping, and being seen with her in the market-place and Close. It must be owned of Mary that she was proud thus to be seen with him again, and that in buying her ribbons and gloves she referred to him, smiling as he said this, and pouting and pretending to differ as he said that, with greater urgency than she would have done had there been no breach between them. It had been terrible to her to think that there should be a quarrel,— terrible to her that the world should think so. There was a gratification to her in feeling that even the shopkeepers should see her and her husband together. And when she met Canon Pountner and stopped a moment in the street while that worthy divine shook hands with her husband, that was an additional pleasure to her. The last few weeks had been heavy to her in spite of her father's affectionate care,—heavy with a feeling of disgrace from which no well-minded young married woman can quite escape, when she is separated from her husband. She had endeavoured to do right. She thought she was doing right. But it was so sad! She was fond of pleasure, whereas he was little given to any amusement; but no pleasures could be pleasant to her now unless they were in some sort countenanced by him. She had never said such a word to a human being, but since that dancing of the Kappa-kappa she had sworn to herself a thousand times that she would never waltz again. And she hourly yearned for his company, having quite got over that first difficulty of her married life, that doubt whether she could ever learn to love her husband. During much of this day she was actually happy in spite of the great sorrow which still weighed so heavily upon them both.

And he liked it also in his way. He thought that he had never seen her looking more lovely. He was sure that she had never been more gracious to him. The touch of her hand was pleasant to his arm, and even he had sufficient spirit of fun about him to enjoy something of the mirth of her little grimaces. When he told her what her father had said about Mr. Groschut, even he laughed at her face of assumed disgust. "Papa doesn't hate him half as much as I do," she said. "Papa always does forgive at last, but I never can forgive Mr. Groschut."

"What has the poor man done?"

"He is so nasty! Don't you see that his face always shines. Any man with a shiny face ought to be hated." This was very well to give as a reason, but Mary entertained a very correct idea as to Mr. Groschut's opinion of herself.

Not a word had been said between the husband and wife as to the great question of residence till they had returned to the deanery after their walk. Then Lord George found himself unable to conceal from her the offer which the Dean had made. "Oh, George,—why don't you come?"

"It would not be—fitting."

"Fitting! Why not fitting? I think it would fit admirably. I know it would fit me." Then she leaned over him and took his hand and kissed it.

"It was very good of your father."

"I am sure he meant to be good."

"It was very good of your father," Lord George repeated,—"very good indeed; but it cannot be. A married woman should live in her husband's house and not in her father's."

Mary gazed into his face with a perplexed look, not quite understanding the whole question, but still with a clear idea as to a part of it. All that might be very true, but if a husband didn't happen to have a house then might not the wife's father's house be a convenience? They had indeed a house, provided no doubt with her money, but not the less now belonging to her husband, in which she would be very willing to live if he pleased it,—the house in Munster Court. It was her husband that made objection to their own house. It was her husband who wished to live near Manor Cross, not having a roof of his own under which to do so. Were not these circumstances which ought to have made the deanery a convenience to him? "Then what will you do?" she asked.

"I cannot say as yet." He had become again gloomy and black-browed.

"Wouldn't you come here—for a week?"

"I think not, my dear."

"Not when you know how happy it would make me to have you with me once again. I do so long to be telling you everything." Then she leant against him and embraced him, and implored him to grant her this favour. But he would not yield. He had told himself that the Dean had interfered between him and his wife, and that he must at any rate go through the ceremony of taking his wife away from her father. Let it be accorded to him that he had done that, and then perhaps he might visit the deanery. As for her, she would have gone with him anywhere now, having fully established her right to visit her father after leaving London.

There was nothing further settled, and very little more said, when Lord George left the deanery and started back to Manor Cross. But with Mary there had been left a certain comfort. The shopkeepers and Dr. Pountner had seen her with her husband, and Mr. Groschut had met Lord George at the deanery door.

Chapter L.

Rudham Park.

Lord George had undertaken to leave Manor Cross by the middle of August, but when the first week of that month had passed away he had not as yet made up his mind what he would do with himself. Mr. Knox had told him that should he remain with his mother the Marquis would not, as Mr. Knox thought, take further notice of the matter; but on such terms as these he could not consent to live in his brother's house.

On a certain day early in August Lord George had gone with a return ticket to a town but a few miles distant from Brotherton to sit on a committee for the distribution of coals and blankets, and in the afternoon got into a railway carriage on his way home. How great was his consternation when, on taking his seat, he found that his brother was seated alongside of him! There was one other old gentleman in the carriage, and the three passengers were all facing the engine. On two of the seats opposite were spread out the Marquis's travelling paraphernalia,—his French novel, at which he had not looked, his dressing bag, the box in which his luncheon had been packed, and his wine flask. There was a small basket of strawberries, should he be inclined to eat fruit, and an early peach out of a hothouse, with some flowers. "God Almighty, George;—is that you?" he said. "Where the devil have you been?"

"I've been to Grumby."

"And what are the people doing at Grumby?"

"Much the same as usual. It was the coal and blanket account."

"Oh!—the coal and blanket account! I hope you liked it." Then he folded himself afresh in his cloaks, ate a strawberry, and looked as though he had taken sufficient notice of his brother.

But the matter was very important to Lord George. Nothing ever seemed to be of importance to the Marquis. It might be very probable that the Marquis, with half-a-dozen servants behind him, should drive up to the door at Manor Cross without having given an hour's notice of his intention. It seemed to be too probable to Lord George that such would be the case now. For what other reason could he be there? And then there was his back. Though they had quarrelled he was bound to ask after his brother's back. When last they two had met, the Marquis had been almost carried into the room by two men. "I hope you find yourself better than when I last saw you," he said, after a pause of five minutes.

"I've not much to boast of. I can just travel, and that's all."

"And how is—Popenjoy?"

"Upon my word I can't tell you. He has never seemed to be very well when I've seen him."

"I hope the accounts have been better," said Lord George, with solicitude.

"Coal and blanket accounts!" suggested the Marquis. And then the conversation was again brought to an end for five minutes.

But it was essential that Lord George should know whither his brother was going. If to Manor Cross, then, thought Lord George, he himself would stay at an inn at Brotherton.

Anything, even the deanery, would be better than sitting at table with his brother, with the insults of their last interview unappeased. At the end of five minutes he plucked up his courage, and asked his brother another question. "Are you going to the house, Brotherton?"

"The house! What house? I'm going to a house, I hope."

"I mean to Manor Cross."

"Not if I know it. There is no house in this part of the country in which I should be less likely to show my face." Then there was not another word said till they reached the Brotherton Station, and there the Marquis, who was sitting next the door, requested his brother to leave the carriage first. "Get out, will you?" he said. "I must wait for somebody to come and take these things. And don't trample on me more than you can help." This last request had apparently been made, because Lord George was unable to step across him without treading on the cloak.

"I will say good-bye, then," said Lord George, turning round on the platform for a moment.

"Ta, ta," said the Marquis, as he gave his attention to the servant who was collecting the fruit, and the flowers, and the flask. Lord George then passed on out of the station, and saw no more of his brother.

"Of course he is going to Rudham," said Lady Susanna, when she heard the story. Rudham Park was the seat of Mr. De Baron, Mrs. Houghton's father, and tidings had reached Manor Cross long since that the Marquis had promised to go there in the autumn. No doubt other circumstances had seemed to make it improbable that the promise should be kept. Popenjoy had gone away ill,—as many said, in a dying condition. Then the Marquis had been thrown into a fireplace, and report had said that his back had been all but broken. It had certainly been generally thought that the Marquis would go nowhere after that affair in the fireplace, till he returned to Italy. But Lady Susanna was, in truth, right. His Lordship was on his way to Rudham Park.

Mr. De Baron, of Rudham Park, though a much older man than the Marquis, had been the Marquis's friend,—when the Marquis came of age, being then the Popenjoy of those days and a fast young man known as such about England. Mr. De Baron, who was a neighbour, had taken him by the hand. Mr. De Baron had put him in the way of buying and training race-horses, and had, perhaps, been godfather to his pleasures in other matters. Rudham Park had never been loved at Manor Cross by others than the present Lord, and for that reason, perhaps, was dearer to him. He had promised to go there soon after his return to England, and was now keeping his promise. On his arrival there the Marquis found a houseful of people. There were Mr. and Mrs. Houghton, and Lord Giblet, who, having engaged himself rashly to Miss Patmore Green, had rushed out of town sooner than usual that he might devise in retirement some means of escaping from his position; and, to Lord Giblet's horror, there was Mrs. Montacute Jones, who, he well knew, would, if possible, keep him to the collar. There was also Aunt Julia, with her niece Guss, and of course, there was Jack De Baron. The Marquis was rather glad to meet Jack, as to whom he had some hope that he might be induced to run away with Lord George's wife, and thus free the Germain family from that little annoyance. But the guest who surprised the Marquis the most, was the Baroness Banmann, whose name and occupation he did not at first learn very distinctly.

"All right again, my lord?" asked Mr. De Baron, as he welcomed his noble guest.

"Upon my word I'm not, then. That coal-heaving brute of a parson pretty nearly did for me."

"A terrible outrage it was."

"Outrage! I should think so. There's nothing so bad as a clerical bully. What was I to do with him? Of course he was the stronger. I don't pretend to be a Samson. One doesn't expect that kind of thing among gentlemen?"

"No, indeed."

"I wish I could have him somewhere with a pair of foils with the buttons off. His black coat shouldn't save his intestines. I don't know what the devil the country is come to, when such a fellow as that is admitted into people's houses."

"You won't meet him here, Brotherton."

"I wish I might. I think I'd manage to be even with him before he got away. Who's the Baroness you have got?"

"I don't know much about her. My daughter Adelaide,— Mrs. Houghton, you know,—has brought her down. There's been some row among the women up in London. This is one of the prophets, and I think she is brought here to spite Lady Selina Protest who has taken an American prophetess by the hand. She won't annoy you, I hope?"

"Not in the least. I like strange wild beasts. And so that is Captain De Baron, of whom I have heard?"

"That is my nephew, Jack. He has a small fortune of his own, which he is spending fast. As long as it lasts one has to be civil to him."

"I am delighted to meet him. Don't they say he is sweet on a certain young woman?"

"A dozen, I believe."

"Ah,—but one I know something of."

"I don't think there is anything in that, Brotherton;—I don't, indeed, or I shouldn't have brought him here."

"I do, though. And as to not bringing him here, why shouldn't you bring him? If she don't go off with him, she will with somebody else, and the sooner the better, according to my ideas." This was a matter upon which Mr. De Baron was not prepared to dilate, and he therefore changed the subject.

"My dear Lord Giblet, it is such a pleasure to me to meet you here," old Mrs. Jones said to that young nobleman. "When I was told you were to be at Rudham, it determined me at once." This was true, for there was no more persistent friend living than old Mrs. Jones, though it might be doubted whether, on this occasion, Lord Giblet was the friend on whose behalf she had come to Rudham.

"It's very nice, isn't it?" said Lord Giblet, gasping.

"Hadn't we a pleasant time of it with our little parties in Grosvenor Place?"

"Never liked anything so much in life; only I don't think that fellow Jack De Baron, dances so much better than other people, after all?"

"Who says he does? But I'll tell you who dances well. Olivia Green was charming in the Kappa-kappa. Don't you think so?"

"Uncommon pretty." Lord Giblet was quite willing to be understood to admire Miss Patmore Green, though he thought it hard that people should hurry him on into matrimony.

"The most graceful girl I ever saw in my life, certainly," said Mrs. Montacute Jones. "His Royal Highness, when he heard of the engagement, said that you were the happiest man in London."

Lord Giblet could not satisfy himself by declaring that H.R.H. was an old fool, as poor Mary had done on a certain occasion,—but at the present moment he did not feel at all loyal to the Royal Family generally. Nor did he, in the least, know how to answer Mrs. Jones. She had declared the engagement as a fact, and he did not quite dare to deny it altogether. He had, in an unguarded moment, when the weather had been warm and the champagne cool, said a word with so definite a meaning that the lady had been justified in not allowing it to pass by as idle. The lady had accepted him, and on the following morning he had found the lock of hair and the little stud which she had given him, and had feverish reminiscences of a kiss. But surely he was not a bird to be caught with so small a grain of salt as that! He had not as yet seen Mr. Patmore Green, having escaped from London at once. He had answered a note from Olivia, which had called him "dearest Charlie" by a counter note, in which he had called her "dear O," and had signed himself "ever yours, G," promising to meet her up the river. But of course he had not gone up the river! The rest of the season might certainly be done without assistance from him. He knew that he would be pursued. He could not hope not to be pursued. But he had not thought that Mrs. Montacute Jones would be so quick upon him. It was impossible that H.R.H should have heard of any engagement as yet. What a nasty, false, wicked old woman she was! He blushed, red as a rose, and stammered out that he "didn't know." He was only four-and-twenty, and perhaps he didn't know.

"I never saw a girl so much in love in my life," continued Mrs. Jones. "I know her just as well as if she were my own, and she speaks to me as she doesn't dare to speak to you at present. Though she is barely twenty-one, she has been very much sought after already, and the very day she marries she has ten thousand pounds in her own hands. That isn't a large fortune, and of course you don't want a large fortune, but it isn't every girl can pay such a sum straight into her husband's bank the moment she marries!"

"No, indeed," said Lord Giblet. He was still determined that nothing should induce him to marry Miss Green; but nevertheless, behind that resolution there was a feeling, that if anything should bring about the marriage, such a sum of ready money would be a consolation. His father, the Earl of Jopling, though a very rich man, kept him a little close, and ten thousand pounds would be nice. But then, perhaps the old woman was lying.

"Now I'll tell you what I want you to do," said Mrs. Jones, who was resolved that if the game were not landed it should not be her fault. "We go from here to Killancodlem next week. You must come and join us."

"I've got to go and grouse at Stranbracket's," said Lord Giblet, happy in an excuse.

"It couldn't be better. They're both within eight miles of Dunkeld." If so, then ropes shouldn't take him to Stranbracket's that year. "Of course you'll come. It's the prettiest place in

Perth, though I say it, as oughtn't. And she will be there. If you really want to know a girl, see her in a country house."

But he didn't really want to know the girl. She was very nice, and he liked her uncommonly, but he didn't want to know anything more about her. By George! Was a man to be persecuted this way, because he had once spooned a girl a little too fiercely? As he thought of this he almost plucked up his courage sufficiently to tell Mrs. Jones that she had better pick out some other young man for deportation to Killancodlem. "I should like it ever so," he said.

"I'll take care that you shall like it, Lord Giblet. I think I may boast that when I put my wits to work I can make my house agreeable. I'm very fond of young people, but there's no one I love as I do Olivia Green. There isn't a young woman in London has so much to be loved for. Of course you'll come. What day shall we name?"

"I don't think I could name a day."

"Let us say the 27th. That will give you nearly a week at the grouse first. Be with us to dinner on the 27th."

"Well,—perhaps I will."

"Of course you will. I shall write to Olivia to-night, and I daresay you will do so also."

Lord Giblet, when he was let to go, tried to suck consolation from the £10,000. Though he was still resolved, he almost believed that Mrs. Montacute Jones would conquer him. Write to Olivia to-night! Lying, false old woman! Of course she knew that there was hardly a lady in England to whom it was so little likely that he should write as to Miss Patmore Green. How could an old woman, with one foot in the grave, be so wicked? And why should she persecute him? What had he done to her? Olivia Green was not her daughter, or even her niece. "So you are going to Killancodlem?" Mrs. Houghton said to him that afternoon.

"She has asked me," said Lord Giblet.

"It's simply the most comfortable house in all Scotland, and they tell me some of the best deer-stalking. Everybody likes to get to Killancodlem. Don't you love old Mrs. Jones?"

"Charming old woman!"

"And such a friend! If she once takes to you she never drops you."

"Sticks like wax, I should say."

"Quite like wax, Lord Giblet. And when she makes up her mind to do a thing she always does it. It's quite wonderful; but she never gets beaten."

"Doesn't she now?"

"Never. She hasn't asked us to Killancodlem yet, but I hope she will." A manly resolution now roused itself in Lord Giblet's bosom that he would be the person to beat Mrs. Jones at last. But yet he doubted. If he were asked the question by anyone having a right to ask he could not deny that he had proposed to marry Miss Patmore Green.

"So you've come down to singe your wings again?" said Mrs. Houghton to her cousin Jack.

"My wings have been burned clean away already, and, in point of fact, I am not half so near to Lady George here as I was in London."

"It's only ten miles."

"If it were five it would be the same. We're not in the same set down in Barsetshire."

"I suppose you can have yourself taken to Brotherton if you please?"

"Yes,—I can call at the deanery; but I shouldn't know what to say when I got there."

"You've become very mealy-mouthed of a sudden."

"Not with you, my sweet cousin. With you I can discuss the devil and all his works as freely as ever; but with Lady George, at her father's house, I think I should be dumb. In truth, I haven't got anything to say to her."

"I thought you had."

"I know you think so; but I haven't. It is quite on the card that I may ride over some day, as I would to see my sister."

"Your sister!"

"And that I shall make eager enquiries after her horse, her pet dog, and her husband."

"You will be wrong there, for she has quarrelled with her husband altogether."

"I hope not."

"They are not living together, and never even see each other. He's at Manor Cross, and she's at the deanery. She's a divinity to you, but Lord George seems to have found her so human that he's tired of her already."

"Then it must be his own fault."

"Or perhaps yours, Jack. You don't suppose a husband goes through a little scene like that at Mrs. Jones' without feeling it?"

"He made an ass of himself, and a man generally feels that afterwards," said Jack.

"The truth is, they're tired of each other. There isn't very much in Lord George, but there is something. He is slow, but there is a certain manliness at the bottom of it. But there isn't very much in her!"

"That's all you know about it."

"Perhaps you may know her better, but I never could find anything. You confess to being in love, and of course a lover is blind. But where you are most wrong is in supposing that she is something so much better than other women. She flirted with you so frankly that she made you think her a goddess."

"She never flirted with me in her life."

"Exactly;—because flirting is bad, and she being a goddess cannot do evil. I wish you'd take her in your arms and kiss her."

"I shouldn't dare."

"No;—and therefore you're not in the way to learn that she's a woman just the same as other women. Will Mrs. Jones succeed with that stupid young man?"

"With Giblet? I hope so. It can't make any difference to him whether it's this one or another, and I do like Mrs. Jones."

"Would they let me have just a little lecture in the dining-room?" asked the Baroness of her friend, Aunt Ju. There had been certain changes among the Disabilities up in London. Lady Selina Protest had taken Dr. Olivia Q. Fleabody altogether by the hand, and had appointed her chief professor at the Institute, perhaps without sufficient authority. Aunt Ju had been cast into the shade, and had consequently been driven to throw herself into the arms of the Baroness. At present there was a terrible feud in which Aunt Ju was being much worsted. For the Baroness was an old Man of the Sea, and having got herself on to Aunt Ju's shoulders could not be shaken off. In the meantime Dr. Fleabody was filling the Institute, reaping a golden harvest, and breaking the heart of the poor Baroness, who had fallen into much trouble and was now altogether penniless.

"I'm afraid not," said Aunt Ju. "I'm afraid we can't do that."

"Perhaps de Marquis would like it?"

"I hardly think so."

"He did say a word to me, and I tink he would like it. He vant to understand."

"My dear Baroness, I'm sure the Marquis of Brotherton does not care about it in the least. He is quite in the dark on such subjects—quite benighted." What was the use, thought the Baroness, of bringing her down to a house in which people were so benighted that she could not be allowed to open her mouth or carry on her profession. Had she not been enticed over from her own country in order that she might open her mouth, and preach her doctrine, and become a great and a wealthy woman? There was a fraud in this enforced silence which cut her to the very quick. "I tink I shall try," she said, separating herself in her wrath from her friend.

Chapter LI.

Guss Mildmay's Success.

The treatment which the Marquis received at Rudham did not certainly imply any feeling that he had disgraced himself by what he had done either at Manor Cross or up in London. Perhaps the ladies there did not know as much of his habits as did Mrs. Walker at Scumberg's. Perhaps the feeling was strong that Popenjoy was Popenjoy, and that therefore the Marquis had been injured. If a child be born in British purple,—true purple, though it may have been stained by circumstances,—that purple is very sacred. Perhaps it was thought that under no circumstances should a Marquis be knocked into the fireplace by a clergyman. There was still a good deal of mystery, both as to Popenjoy and as to the fireplace, and the Marquis was the hero of these mysteries. Everyone at Rudham was anxious to sit by his side and to be allowed to talk to him. When he abused the Dean, which he did freely, those who heard him assented to all he said. The Baroness Banmann held up her hands in horror when she heard the tale, and declared the Church to be one grand bêtise. Mrs. Houghton, who was very attentive to the Marquis and whom the Marquis liked, was pertinacious in her enquiries after Popenjoy, and cruelly sarcastic upon the Dean. "Think what was his bringing up," said Mrs. Houghton.

"In a stable," said the Marquis.

"I always felt it to be a great pity that Lord George should have made that match;—not but what she is a good creature in her way."

"She is no better than she should be," said the Marquis. Then Mrs. Houghton found herself able to insinuate that perhaps, after all, Mary was not a good creature, even in her own way. But the Marquis's chief friend was Jack De Baron. He talked to Jack about races and billiards, and women; but though he did not refrain from abusing the Dean, he said no word to Jack against Mary. If it might be that the Dean should receive his punishment in that direction he would do nothing to prevent it. "They tell me she's a beautiful woman. I have never seen her myself," said the Marquis.

"She is very beautiful," said Jack.

"Why the devil she should have married George, I can't think. She doesn't care for him the least."

"Don't you think she does?"

"I'm sure she don't. I suppose her pestilent father thought it was the nearest way to a coronet. I don't know why men should marry at all. They always get into trouble by it."

"Somebody must have children," suggested Jack.

"I don't see the necessity. It's nothing to me what comes of the property after I'm gone. What is it, Madam?" They were sitting out on the lawn after lunch and Jack and the Marquis were both smoking. As they were talking the Baroness had come up to them and made her little proposition. "What! a lecture! If Mr. De Baron pleases, of course. I never listen to lectures myself,—except from my wife."

"Ah! dat is vat I vant to prevent."

"I have prevented it already by sending her to Italy. Oh, rights of women! Very interesting; but I don't think I'm well enough myself. Here is Captain De Baron, a young man as strong as a horse, and very fond of women. He'll sit it out."

"I beg your pardon; what is it?" Then the Baroness, with rapid words, told her own sad story. She had been deluded, defrauded, and ruined by those wicked females, Lady Selina Protest and Dr. Fleabody. The Marquis was a nobleman whom all England, nay, all Europe, delighted to honour. Could not the Marquis do something for her? She was rapid and eloquent, but not always intelligible. "What is it she wants?" asked the Marquis, turning to Jack.

"Pecuniary assistance, I think, my Lord."

"Yah, yah. I have been bamboozled of everything, my Lord Marquis."

"Oh, my G—, De Baron shouldn't have let me in for this. Would you mind telling my fellow to give her a ten-pound note?" Jack said that he would not mind; and the Baroness stuck to him pertinaciously, not leaving his side a moment till she had got the money. Of course there was no lecture. The Baroness was made to understand that visitors at a country house in England could not be made to endure such an infliction; but she succeeded in levying a contribution from Mrs. Montacute Jones, and there were rumours afloat that she got a sovereign out of Mr. Houghton.

Lord Giblet had come with the intention of staying a week, but, the day after the attack made upon him by Mrs. Montacute Jones, news arrived which made it absolutely necessary that he should go to Castle Gossling at once. "We shall be so sorry to miss you," said Mrs. Montacute Jones, whom he tried to avoid in making his general adieux, but who was a great deal too clever not to catch him.

"My father wants to see me about the property, you know."

"Of course. There must be a great deal to do between you." Everybody who knew the affairs of the family was aware that the old Earl never thought of consulting his son; and Mrs. Montacute Jones knew everything.

"Ever so much; therefore I must be off at once. My fellow is packing my things now; and there is a train in an hour's time."

"Did you hear from Olivia this morning?"

"Not to-day."

"I hope you are as proud as you ought to be of having such a sweet girl belonging to you." Nasty old woman! What right had she to say these things? "I told Mrs. Green that you were here, and that you were coming to meet Olivia on the 27th."

"What did she say?"

"She thinks you ought to see Mr. Green as you go through London. He is the easiest, most good-natured man in the world. Don't you think you might as well speak to him?" Who was Mrs. Montacute Jones that she should talk to him in this way? "I would send a telegram if I were you, to say I would be there to-night."

"Perhaps it would be best," said Lord Giblet.

"Oh, certainly. Now mind, we expect you to dinner on the 27th. Is there anybody else you'd specially like me to ask?"

"Nobody in particular, thank ye."

"Isn't Jack De Baron a friend of yours?"

"Yes,—I like Jack pretty well. He thinks a great deal of himself, you know."

"All the young men do that now. At any rate I'll ask Jack to meet you." Unfortunately for Lord Giblet Jack appeared in sight at this very moment. "Captain De Baron, Lord Giblet has been good enough to say that he'll come to my little place at Killancodlem on the 27th. Can you meet him there?"

"Delighted, Mrs. Jones. Who ever refuses to go to Killancodlem?"

"It isn't Killancodlem and its little comforts that are bringing his lordship. We shall be delighted to see him; but he is coming to see——. Well I suppose it's no secret now, Lord Giblet?" Jack bowed his congratulations, and Lord Giblet again blushed as red as a rose.

Detestable old woman! Whither should he take himself? In what furthest part of the Rocky Mountains should he spend the coming autumn? If neither Mr. nor Mrs. Green called upon him for an explanation, what possible right could this abominable old harpy have to prey upon him? Just at the end of a cotillion he had said one word! He knew men who had done ten times as much and had not been as severely handled. And he was sure that Jack De Baron had had something to do with it. Jack had been hand in hand with Mrs. Jones at the making up of the Kappa-kappa. But as he went to the station he reflected that Olivia Green was a very nice girl. If those ten thousand pounds were true they would be a great comfort to him. His mother was always bothering him to get married. If he could bring himself to accept this as his fate he would be saved a deal of trouble. Spooning at Killancodlem, after all, would not be bad fun. He almost told himself that he would marry Miss Green, were it not that he was determined not to be dictated to by that old harridan.

Many people came and went at Rudham Park, but among those who did not go was Guss Mildmay. Aunt Julia, who had become thoroughly ashamed of the Baroness, had wished to take her departure on the third day; but Guss had managed to stop her. "What's the good of coming to a house for three days? You said you meant to stay a week. They know what she is now, and the harm's done. It was your own fault for bringing her. I don't see why I'm to be thrown over because you've made a mistake about a vulgar old woman. We've nowhere to go to till November, and now we are out of town for heaven's sake let us stay as long as we can." In this way Guss carried her point, watching her opportunity for a little conversation with her former lover.

At last the opportunity came. It was not that Jack had avoided her, but that it was necessary that she should be sure of having half-an-hour alone with him. At last she made the opportunity, calling upon him to walk with her one Sunday morning when all other folk were in church—or, perhaps, in bed. "No; I won't go to church," she had said to Aunt Ju. "What is the use of your asking 'why not?' I won't go. They are quite accustomed at Rudham to people not going to church. I always go in a stiff house, but I won't go here. When you are at Rome you should do as the Romans do. I don't suppose there'll be half-a-dozen there out of the whole party." Aunt Ju went to church as a matter of course, and the opportunity of walking in the grounds with Jack was accomplished. "Are you going to Killancodlem?" she said.

"I suppose I shall, for a few days."

"Have you got anything to say before you go?"

"Nothing particular."

"Of course I don't mean to me."

"I've nothing particular to say to anybody just at present. Since I've been here that wretched old Marquis has been my chief fate. It's quite a pleasure to hear him abuse the Dean."

"And the Dean's daughter?"

"He has not much good to say about her either."

"I'm not surprised at that, Jack. And what do you say to him about the Dean's daughter?"

"Very little, Guss."

"And what are you going to say to me about her?"

"Nothing at all, Guss."

"She's all the world to you, I suppose?"

"What's the use of your saying that? In one sense she's nothing to me. My belief is that the only man she'll ever care a pin about is her husband. At any rate she does not care a straw for me."

"Nor you for her?"

"Well;—Yes I do. She's one of my pet friends. There's nobody I like being with better."

"And if she were not married?"

"God knows what might have happened. I might have asked her to have me, because she has got money of her own. What's the use of coming back to the old thing, Guss?"

"Money, money, money!"

"Nothing more unfair was ever said to anyone. Have I given any signs of selling myself for money? Have I been a fortune hunter? No one has ever found me guilty of so much prudence. All I say is that having found out the way to go to the devil myself, I won't take any young woman I like with me there by marrying her. Heavens and earth! I can fancy myself returned from a wedding tour with some charmer, like you, without a shilling at my banker's, and beginning life at lodgings, somewhere down at Chelsea. Have you no imagination? Can't you see what it would be? Can't you fancy the stuffy sitting room with the horsehair chairs, and the hashed mutton, and the cradle in the corner before long?"

"No I can't," said Guss.

"I can;—two cradles, and very little of the hashed mutton; and my lady wife with no one to pin her dress for her but the maid of all work with black fingers."

"It wouldn't be like that."

"It very soon would, if I were to marry a girl without a fortune. And I know myself. I'm a very good fellow while the sun shines, but I couldn't stand hardship. I shouldn't come home to the hashed mutton. I should dine at the club, even though I had to borrow the money. I should come to hate the cradle and its occupant, and the mother of its occupant. I should take to drink, and should blow my brains out just as the second cradle came. I can see it all as plain as a pikestaff. I often lay awake the whole night and look at it. You and I, Guss, have made a mistake from the beginning. Being poor people we have lived as though we were rich."

"I have never done so."

"Oh yes, you have. Instead of dining out in Fitzroy Square and drinking tea in Tavistock Place, you have gone to balls in Grosvenor Square and been presented at Court."

"It wasn't my fault."

"It has been so, and therefore you should have made up your mind to marry a rich man."

"Who was it asked me to love him?"

"Say that I did if you please. Upon my word I forget how it began, but say that it was my fault. Of course it was my fault. Are you going to blow me up for that? I see a girl, and first I like her, and then I love her, and then I tell her so;—or else she finds it out without my telling. Was that a sin you can't forgive?"

"I never said it was a sin."

"I don't mind being a worm, but I won't be trodden upon overmuch. Was there ever a moment in which you thought that I thought of marrying you?"

"A great many, Jack."

"Did I ever say so?"

"Never. I'll do you justice there. You have been very cautious."

"Of course you can be severe, and of course I am bound to bear it. I have been cautious,—for your sake!"

"Oh, Jack!"

"For your sake. When I first saw how it was going to be,—how it might be between you and me,—I took care to say outright that I couldn't marry unless a girl had money."

"There will be something—when papa dies."

"The most healthy middle-aged gentleman in London! There might be half a dozen cradles, Guss, before that day. If it will do you good, you shall say I'm the greatest rascal walking."

"That will do me no good."

"But I don't know that I can give you any other privilege."

Then there was a long pause during which they were sauntering together under an old oak tree in the park. "Do you love me, Jack?" she then asked, standing close up to him.

"God bless my soul! That's going back to the beginning."

"You are heartless,—absolutely heartless. It has come to that with you that any real idea of love is out of the question."

"I can't afford it, my dear."

"But is there no such thing as love that you can't help? Can you drop a girl out of your heart altogether simply because she has got no money? I suppose you did love me once?" Here Jack scratched his head. "You did love me once?" she said, persevering with her question.

"Of course I did," said Jack, who had no objection to making assurances of the past.

"And you don't now?"

"Whoever said so? What's the good of talking about it?"

"Do you think you owe me nothing?"

"What's the good of owing, if a man can't pay his debts?"

"You will own nothing then?"

"Yes, I will. If anyone left me twenty thousand pounds to-morrow, then I should owe you something."

"What would you owe me?"

"Half of it."

"And how would you pay me?" He thought a while before he made his answer. He knew that in that case he would not wish to pay the debt in the only way in which it would be payable. "You mean then that you would—marry me?"

"I shouldn't be afraid of the hashed mutton and cradles."

"In that case you—would marry me?"

"A man has no right to take so much on himself as to say that."

"Psha!"

"I suppose I should. I should make a devilish bad husband even then."

"Why should you be worse than others?"

"I don't know. Perhaps I was made worse. I can't fancy myself doing any duty well. If I had a wife of my own I should be sure to fall in love with somebody else's."

"Lady George for instance."

"No;—not Lady George. It would not be with somebody whom I had learned to think the very best woman in all the world. I am very bad, but I'm just not bad enough to make love to her. Or rather I am very foolish, but just not foolish enough to think that I could win her."

"I suppose she's just the same as others, Jack."

"She's not just the same to me. But I'd rather not talk about her, Guss. I'm going to Killancodlem in a day or two, and I shall leave this to-morrow!"

"To-morrow!"

"Well; yes; to-morrow. I must be a day or two in town, and there is not much doing here. I'm tired of the old Marquis who is the most illnatured brute I ever came across in my life, and there's no more fun to be made of the Baroness. I'm not sure but that she has the best of the fun. I didn't think there was an old woman in the world could get a five pound note out of me; but she had."

"How could you be so foolish?"

"How indeed! You'll go back to London?"

"I suppose so;—unless I drown myself."

"Don't do that, Guss?"

"I often think it will be best. You don't know what my life is,—how wretched. And you made it so."

"Is that fair, Guss?"

"Quite fair! Quite true! You have made it miserable. You know you have. Of course you know it."

"Can I help it now?"

"Yes you can. I can be patient if you will say that it shall be some day. I could put up with anything if you would let me hope. When you have got that twenty thousand pounds—?"

"But I shall never have it."

"If you do,—will you marry me then? Will you promise me that you will never marry anybody else?"

"I never shall."

"But will you promise me? If you will not say so much as that to me you must be false indeed. When you have the twenty thousand pounds will you marry me?"

"Oh, certainly."

"And you can laugh about such a matter when I am pouring out my very soul to you? You can make a joke of it when it is all my life to me! Jack, if you will say that it shall happen some day,—some day,—I will be happy. If you won't,—I can only die. It may be play to you, but it's death to me." He looked at her, and saw that she was quite in earnest. She was not weeping, but there was a drawn, heavy look about her face which, in truth, touched his heart. Whatever might be his faults he was not a cruel man. He had defended himself without any scruples of conscience when she had seemed to attack him, but now he did not know how to refuse her request. It amounted to so little! "I don't suppose it will ever take place, but I think I ought to allow myself to consider myself as engaged to you," she said.

"As it is you are free to marry anyone else," he replied.

"I don't care for such freedom. I don't want it. I couldn't marry a man whom I didn't love."

"Nobody knows what that they can do till they're tried."

"Do you suppose, sir, I've never been tried? But I can't bring myself to laugh now, Jack. Don't joke now. Heaven knows when we may see each other again. You will promise me that, Jack?"

"Yes;—if you wish it." And so at last she had got a promise from him! She said nothing more to fix it, fearing that in doing so she might lose it; but she threw herself into his arms and buried her face upon his bosom.

Afterwards, when she was leaving him, she was very solemn in her manner to him. "I will say good-bye now, Jack, for I shall hardly see you again to speak to. You do love me?"

"You know I do."

"I am so true to you! I have always been true to you. God bless you, Jack. Write me a line sometimes." Then he escaped, having brought her back to the garden among the flowers, and he wandered away by himself across the park. At last he had engaged himself. He knew that it was so, and he knew that she would tell all her friends. Adelaide Houghton would know, and would, of course, congratulate him. There never could be a marriage. That would, of course, be out of the question. But, instead of being the Jack De Baron of old, at any rate free as air, he would be the young man engaged to marry Augusta Mildmay. And then he could hardly now refuse to answer the letters which she would be sure to write to him, at least twice a week. There had been a previous period of letter-writing, but that had died a natural death through utter neglect on his part. But now—. It might be as well that he should take advantage of the new law and exchange into an Indian regiment.

But, even in his present condition, his mind was not wholly occupied with Augusta Mildmay. The evil words which had been spoken to him of Mary had not been altogether fruitless. His cousin Adelaide had told him over and over again that Lady George was as other women,—by which his cousin had intended to say that Lady George was the same as herself. Augusta Mildmay had spoken of his Phoenix in the same strain. The Marquis had declared her to be utterly worthless. It was not that he wished to think of her as they thought, or that he could be brought so to think; but these suggestions, coming as they did from those who knew how much he liked the woman, amounted to ridicule aimed against the purity of his worship. They told him,—almost told him,—that he was afraid to speak of love to

Lady George. Indeed he was afraid, and within his own breast he was in some sort proud of his fear. But, nevertheless, he was touched by their ridicule. He and Mary had certainly been dear friends. Certainly that friendship had given great umbrage to her husband. Was he bound to keep away from her because of her husband's anger? He knew that they two were not living together. He knew that the Dean would at any rate welcome him. And he knew, too, that there was no human being he wished to see again so much as Lady George. He had no purpose as to anything that he would say to her, but he was resolved that he would see her. If then some word warmer than any he had yet spoken should fall from him, he would gather from her answer what her feelings were towards him. In going back to London on the morrow he must pass by Brotherton, and he would make his arrangements so as to remain there for an hour or two.

Chapter LII.

Another Lover.

The party at Rudham Park had hardly been a success,—nor was it much improved in wit or gaiety when Mrs. Montacute Jones, Lord Giblet, and Jack de Baron had gone away, and Canon Holdenough and his wife, with Mr. Groschut, had come in their places. This black influx, as Lord Brotherton called it, had all been due to consideration for his Lordship. Mr. De Baron thought that his guest would like to see, at any rate, one of his own family, and Lady Alice Holdenough was the only one whom he could meet. As to Mr. Groschut, he was the Dean's bitterest enemy, and would, therefore, it was thought, be welcome. The Bishop had been asked, as Mr. De Baron was one who found it expedient to make sacrifices to respectability; but, as was well known, the Bishop never went anywhere except to clerical houses. Mr. Groschut, who was a younger man, knew that it behoved him to be all things to all men, and that he could not be efficacious among sinners unless he would allow himself to be seen in their paths. Care was, of course, taken that Lady Alice should find herself alone with her brother. It was probably expected that the Marquis would be regarded as less of an ogre in the country if it were known that he had had communication with one of the family without quarrelling with her. "So you're come here," he said.

"I didn't know that people so pious would enter De Baron's doors."

"Mr. De Baron is a very old friend of the Canon's. I hope he isn't very wicked, and I'm afraid we are not very pious."

"If you don't object, of course I don't. So they've all gone back to the old house?"

"Mamma is there."

"And George?" he asked in a sharp tone.

"And George,—at present."

"George is, I think, the biggest fool I ever came across in my life. He is so cowed by that man whose daughter he has married that he doesn't know how to call his soul his own."

"I don't think that, Brotherton. He never goes to the deanery to stay there."

"Then what makes him quarrel with me? He ought to know which side his bread is buttered."

"He had a great deal of money with her, you know."

"If he thinks his bread is buttered on that side, let him stick to that side and say so. I will regard none of my family as on friendly terms with me who associate with the Dean of Brotherton or his daughter after what took place up in London." Lady Alice felt this to be a distinct threat to herself, but she allowed it to pass by without notice. She was quite sure that the Canon would not quarrel with the Dean out of deference to his brother-in-law. "The fact is they should all have gone away as I told them, and especially when George had married the girl and got her money. It don't make much difference to me, but it will make a deal to him."

"How is Popenjoy, Brotherton?" asked Lady Alice, anxious to change the conversation.

"I don't know anything about him."

"What!"

"He has gone back to Italy with his mother. How can I tell? Ask the Dean. I don't doubt that he knows all about him. He has people following them about, and watching every mouthful they eat."

"I think he has given all that up."

"Not he. He'll have to, unless he means to spend more money than I think he has got."

"George is quite satisfied about Popenjoy now," said Lady Alice.

"I fancy George didn't like the expense. But he began it, and I'll never forgive him. I fancy it was he and Sarah between them. They'll find that they will have had the worst of it. The poor little beggar hadn't much life in him. Why couldn't they wait?"

"Is it so bad as that, Brotherton?"

"They tell me he is not a young Hercules. Oh yes;—you can give my love to my mother. Tell her that if I don't see her it is all George's fault. I am not going to the house while he's there." To the Canon he hardly spoke a word, nor was the Canon very anxious to talk to him. But it became known throughout the country that the Marquis had met his sister at Rudham Park, and the general effect was supposed to be good.

"I shall go back to-morrow, De Baron," he said to his host that same afternoon. This was the day on which Jack had gone to Brotherton.

"We shall be sorry to lose you. I'm afraid it has been rather dull."

"Not more dull than usual. Everything is dull after a certain time of life unless a man has made some fixed line for himself. Some men can eat and drink a great deal, but I haven't got stomach for that. Some men play cards; but I didn't begin early enough to win money, and I don't like losing it. The sort of things that a man does care for die away from him, and of course it becomes dull."

"I wonder you don't have a few horses in training."

"I hate horses, and I hate being cheated."

"They don't cheat me," said Mr. De Baron.

"Ah;—very likely. They would me. I think I made a mistake, De Baron, in not staying at home and looking after the property."

"It's not too late, now."

"Yes, it is. I could not do it. I could not remember the tenants' names, and I don't care about game. I can't throw myself into a litter of young foxes, or get into a fury of passion about pheasants' eggs. It's all beastly nonsense, but if a fellow could only bring himself to care about it that wouldn't matter. I don't care about anything."

"You read."

"No, I don't. I pretend to read—a little. If they had left me alone I think I should have had myself bled to death in a warm bath. But I won't now. That man's daughter shan't be Lady Brotherton if I can help it. I have rather liked being here on the whole, though why the d—— you should have a Germain impostor in your house, and a poor clergyman, I can't make out."

"He's the Deputy Bishop of the diocese."

"But why have the Bishop himself unless he happen to be a friend? Does your daughter like her marriage?"

"I hope so. She does not complain."

"He's an awful ass,—and always was. I remember when you used always to finish up your books by making him bet as you pleased."

"He always won."

"And now you've made him marry your daughter. Perhaps he has won there. I like her. If my wife would die and he would die, we might get up another match and cut out Lord George after all." This speculation was too deep even for Mr. De Baron, who laughed and shuffled himself about, and got out of the room.

"Wouldn't you have liked to be a marchioness," he said, some hours afterwards, to Mrs. Houghton. She was in the habit of sitting by him and talking to him late in the evening, while he was sipping his curaçoa and soda water, and had become accustomed to hear odd things from him. He liked her because he could say what he pleased to her, and she would laugh and listen, and show no offence. But this last question was very odd. Of course she thought that it referred to the old overtures made to her by Lord George; but in that case, had she married Lord George, she could only have been made a marchioness by his own death,—by that and by the death of the little Popenjoy of whom she had heard so much.

"If it had come in my way fairly," she said with an arch smile.

"I don't mean that you should have murdered anybody. Suppose you had married me?"

"You never asked me, my lord."

"You were only eight or nine years old when I saw you last."

"Isn't it a pity you didn't get yourself engaged to me then? Such things have been done."

"If the coast were clear I wonder whether you'd take me now."

"The coast isn't clear, Lord Brotherton."

"No, by George. I wish it were, and so do you too, if you'd dare to say so."

"You think I should be sure to take you."

"I think you would. I should ask you at any rate. I'm not so old by ten years as Houghton."

"Your age would not be the stumbling block."

"What then?"

"I didn't say there would be any. I don't say that there would not. It's a kind of thing that a woman doesn't think of."

"It's just the kind of thing that women do think of."

"Then they don't talk about it, Lord Brotherton. Your brother you know did want me to marry him."

"What, George? Before Houghton?"

"Certainly;—before I had thought of Mr. Houghton."

"Why the deuce did you refuse him? Why did you let him take that little ——" He did not fill up the blank, but Mrs. Houghton quite understood that she was to suppose everything that was bad. "I never heard of this before."

"It wasn't for me to tell you."

"What an ass you were."

"Perhaps so. What should we have lived upon? Papa would not have given us an income."

"I could."

"But you wouldn't. You didn't know me then."

"Perhaps you'd have been just as keen as she is to rob my boy of his name. And so George wanted to marry you! Was he very much in love?"

"I was bound to suppose so, my lord."

"And you didn't care for him!"

"I didn't say that. But I certainly did not care to set up housekeeping without a house or without the money to get one. Was I wrong?"

"I suppose a fellow ought to have money when he wants to marry. Well, my dear, there is no knowing what may come yet. Won't it be odd, if after all, you should be Marchioness of Brotherton some day? After that won't you give me a kiss before you say good-night."

"I would have done if you had been my brother-in-law,—or, perhaps, if the people were not all moving about in the next room. Good-night, Marquis."

"Good-night. Perhaps you'll regret some day that you haven't done what I asked."

"I might regret it more if I did." Then she took herself off, enquiring in her own mind whether it might still be possible that she should ever preside in the drawing-room at Manor

Cross. Had he not been very much in love with her, surely he would not have talked to her like that.

"I think I'll say good-bye to you, De Baron," the Marquis said to his host, that night.

"You won't be going early."

"No;—I never do anything early. But I don't like a fuss just as I am going. I'll get down and drive away to catch some train. My man will manage it all."

"You go to London?"

"I shall be in Italy within a week. I hate Italy, but I think I hate England worse. If I believed in heaven and thought I were going there, what a hurry I should be in to die."

"Let us know how Popenjoy is."

"You'll be sure to know whether he is dead or alive. There's nothing else to tell. I never write letters except to Knox, and very few to him. Good-night."

When the Marquis was in his room, his courier, or the man so called, came to undress him. "Have you heard anything to-day?" he asked in Italian. The man said that he had heard. A letter had reached him that afternoon from London. The letter had declared that little Popenjoy was sinking. "That will do Bonni," he said. "I will get into bed by myself." Then he sat down and thought of himself, and his life, and his prospects,— and of the prospects of his enemies.

Chapter LIII.

Poor Popenjoy!

On the following morning the party at Rudham Park were assembled at breakfast between ten and eleven. It was understood that the Marquis was gone,—or going. The Mildmays were still there with the Baroness, and the Houghtons, and the black influx from the cathedral town. A few other new comers had arrived on the previous day. Mr. Groschut, who was sitting next to the Canon, had declared his opinion that, after all, the Marquis of Brotherton was a very affable nobleman. "He's civil enough," said the Canon, "when people do just what he wants."

"A man of his rank and position of course expects to have some deference paid to him."

"A man of his rank and position should be very careful of the rights of others, Mr. Groschut."

"I'm afraid his brother did make himself troublesome. You're one of the family, Canon, and therefore, of course, know all about it."

"I know nothing at all about it, Mr. Groschut."

"But it must be acknowledged that the Dean behaved very badly. Violence!—personal violence! And from a clergyman,—to a man of his rank!"

"You probably don't know what took place in that room. I'm sure I don't. But I'd rather trust the Dean than the Marquis any day. The Dean's a man!"

"But is he a clergyman?"

"Of course he is; and a father. If he had been very much in the wrong we should have heard more about it through the police."

"I cannot absolve a clergyman for using personal violence," said Mr. Groschut, very grandly. "He should have borne anything sooner than degrade his sacred calling." Mr. Groschut had hoped to extract from the Canon some expression adverse to the Dean, and to be able to assure himself that he had enrolled a new ally.

"Poor dear little fellow!" aunt Ju was saying to Mrs. Holdenough. Of course she was talking of Popenjoy. "And you never saw him?"

"No; I never saw him."

"I am told he was a lovely child."

"Very dark, I fancy."

"And all those—those doubts? They're all over now?"

"I never knew much about it, Miss Mildmay. I never inquired into it. For myself, I always took it for granted that he was Popenjoy. I think one always does take things for granted till somebody proves that it is not so."

"The Dean, I take it, has given it up altogether," said Mrs. Houghton to old Lady Brabazon, who had come down especially to meet her nephew, the Marquis, but who had hardly dared to speak a word to him on the previous evening, and was now told that he was gone. Lady Brabazon for a week or two had been quite sure that Popenjoy was not Popenjoy, being at that time under the influence of a very strong letter from Lady Sarah. But, since that, a general idea had come to prevail that the

Dean was wrong-headed, and Lady Brabazon had given in her adhesion to Popenjoy. She had gone so far as to call at Scumberg's, and to leave a box of bonbons.

"I hope so, Mrs. Houghton; I do hope so. Quarrels are such dreadful things in families. Brotherton isn't, perhaps, all that he might have been."

"Not a bad fellow, though, after all."

"By no means, Mrs. Houghton, and quite what he ought to be in appearance. I always thought that George was very foolish."

"Lord George is foolish—sometimes."

"Very stubborn, you know, and pigheaded. And as for the Dean,—is was great interference on his part, very great interference. I won't say that I like foreigners myself. I should be very sorry if Brabazon were to marry a foreigner. But if he chooses to do so I don't see why he is to be told that his heir isn't his heir. They say she is a very worthy woman, and devoted to him." At this moment the butler came in and whispered a word to Mr. De Baron, who immediately got up from his chair. "So my nephew hasn't gone," said Lady Brabazon. "That was a message from him. I heard his name."

Her ears had been correct. The summons which Mr. De Baron obeyed had come from the Marquis. He went upstairs at once, and found Lord Brotherton sitting in his dressing-gown, with a cup of chocolate before him, and a bit of paper in his hand. He did not say a word, but handed the paper, which was a telegram, to Mr. De Baron. As the message was in Italian, and as Mr. De Baron did not read the language, he was at a loss. "Ah! you don't understand it," said the Marquis. "Give it me. It's all over with little Popenjoy."

"Dead!" said Mr. De Baron.

"Yes. He has got away from all his troubles,—lucky dog! He'll never have to think what he'll do with himself. They'd almost told me that it must be so, before he went."

"I grieve for you greatly, Brotherton."

"There's no use in that, old fellow. I'm sorry to be a bother to you, but I thought it best to tell you. I don't understand much about what people call grief. I can't say that I was particularly fond of him, or that I shall personally miss him. They hardly ever brought him to me, and when they did, it bothered me. And yet, somehow it pinches me;—it pinches me."

"Of course it does."

"It will be such a triumph to the Dean, and George. That's about the worst of it. But they haven't got it yet. Though I should be the most miserable dog on earth I'll go on living as long as I can keep my body and soul together. I'll have another son yet, if one is to be had for love or money. They shall have trouble enough before they find themselves at Manor Cross."

"The Dean'll be dead before that time;—and so shall I," said Mr. De Baron.

"Poor little boy! You never saw him. They didn't bring him in when you were over at Manor Cross?"

"No;—I didn't see him."

"They weren't very proud of showing him. He wasn't much to look at. Upon my soul I don't know whether he was legitimate or not, according to English fashions." Mr. De Baron stared. "They had something to stand upon, but,—damn it,— they went about it in such a dirty way! It don't matter now, you know, but you needn't repeat all this."

"Not a word," said Mr. De Baron, wondering why such a communication should have been made to him.

"And there was plenty of ground for a good fight. I hardly know whether she had been married or not. I never could quite find out." Again Mr. De Baron stared. "It's all over now."

"But if you were to have another son?"

"Oh! we're married now! There were two ceremonies. I believe the Dean knows quite as much about it as I do;—very likely more. What a rumpus there has been about a rickety brat who was bound to die."

"Am I to tell them downstairs?"

"Yes;—you might as well tell them. Wait till I'm gone. They'd say I'd concealed it if I didn't let them know, and I certainly shan't write. There's no Popenjoy now. If that young woman has a son he can't be Popenjoy as long as I live. I'll take care of myself. By George I will. Fancy, if the Dean had killed me. He'd have made his own daughter a Marchioness."

"But he'd have been hung."

"Then I wish he'd done it. I wonder how it would have gone. There was nobody there to see, nor to hear. Well;—I believe I'll think of going. There's a train at two. You'll let me have a carriage; won't you?"

"Certainly."

"Let me get out some back way, and don't say a word about this till I'm off. I wouldn't have them condoling with me, and rejoicing in their sleeves, for a thousand pounds. Tell Holdenough, or my sister;—that'll be enough. Good-bye. If you want ever to see me again, you must come to Como." Then Mr. De Baron took his leave, and the Marquis prepared for his departure.

As he was stepping into the carriage at a side door he was greeted by Mr. Groschut. "So your Lordship is leaving us," said the Chaplain. The Marquis looked at him, muttered something, and snarled as he hurried up the step of the carriage. "I'm sorry that we are to lose your Lordship so soon." Then there was another snarl. "I had one word I wanted to say."

"To me! What can you have to say to me?"

"If at any time I can do anything for your Lordship at Brotherton—"

"You can't do anything. Go on." The last direction was given to the coachman, and the carriage was driven off, leaving Mr. Groschut on the path.

Before lunch everybody in the house knew that poor little Popenjoy was dead, and that the Dean had, in fact, won the battle,—though not in the way that he had sought to win it. Lord Brotherton had, after a fashion, been popular at Rudham, but, nevertheless, it was felt by them all that Lady George was a much greater woman to-day than she had been yesterday. It was felt also that the Dean was in the ascendant. The Marquis had been quite agreeable, making love to the ladies, and fairly civil to the gentlemen,—excepting Mr. Groschut; but he certainly was not a man likely to live to eighty. He was married, and, as was generally understood, separated from his wife. They might all live to see Lady George Marchioness of Brotherton and a son of hers Lord Popenjoy.

"Dead!" said Lady Brabazon, when Lady Alice, with sad face, whispered to her the fatal news.

"He got a telegram this morning from Italy. Poor little boy."

"And what'll he do now;—the Marquis I mean?"

"I suppose he'll follow his wife," said Lady Alice.

"Was he much cut up?"

"I didn't see him. He merely sent me word by Mr. De Baron." Mr. De Baron afterwards assured Lady Brabazon that the poor father had been very much cut up. Great pity was expressed throughout the party, but there was not one there who would not now have been civil to poor Mary.

The Marquis had his flowers, and his fruit, and his French novels on his way up to town, and kept his sorrow, if he felt it, very much to himself. Soon after his arrival at Scumberg's, at which place they were obliged to take him in as he was still paying for his rooms, he made it known that he should start for Italy in a day or two. On that night and on the next he did not go out in his brougham, nor did he give any offence to Mrs. Walker. London was as empty as London ever is, and nobody came to see him. For two days he did not leave his room, the same room in which the Dean had nearly killed him, and received nobody but his tailor and his hair-dresser. I think that, in his way, he did grieve for the child who was gone, and who, had he lived, would have been the intended heir of his title and property. They must now all go from him to his enemies! And the things themselves were to himself of so very little value! Living alone at Scumberg's was not a pleasant life. Even going out in his brougham at nights was not very pleasant to him. He could do as he liked at Como, and people wouldn't grumble;—but what was there even at Como that he really liked to do? He had a half worn out taste for scenery which he had no longer energy to gratify by variation. It had been the resolution of his life to live without control, and now, at four and forty, he found that the life he had chosen was utterly without attraction. He had been quite in earnest in those regrets as to shooting, hunting, and the duties of an English country life. Though he was free from remorse, not believing in anything good, still he was open to a conviction that had he done what other people call good, he would have done better for himself. Something of envy stirred him as he read the records of a nobleman whose political life had left him no moment of leisure for his private affairs;— something of envy when he heard of another whose cattle were the fattest in the land. He was connected with Lord Grassangrains, and had always despised that well-known breeder of bullocks;—but he could understand now that Lord Grassangrains should wish to live, whereas life to him was almost unbearable. Lord Grassangrains probably had a good appetite.

On the last morning of his sojourn at Scumberg's he received two or three letters which he would willingly have avoided by running away had it been possible. The first he opened was from his old mother, who had not herself troubled him much with letters for some years past. It was as follows:—

"DEAREST BROTHERTON,—I have heard about poor Popenjoy, and I am so unhappy. Darling little fellow. We are all very wretched here, and I have nearly cried my eyes out. I hope you won't go away without seeing me. If you'll let me, I'll go up to London, though I haven't been there for I don't know how long. But perhaps you will come here to your own house. I do so wish you would.

"Your most affectionate mother,

"H. BROTHERTON.

"P.S.—Pray don't turn George out at the end of the month."

This he accepted without anger as being natural, but threw aside as being useless. Of course he would not answer it. They all knew that he never answered their letters. As to the final petition he had nothing to say to it.

The next was from Lord George, and shall also be given:—

"MY DEAR BROTHERTON,—I cannot let the tidings which I have just heard pass by without expressing my sympathy. I am very sorry indeed that you should have lost your son. I trust you will credit me for saying so much with absolute truth.

"Yours always,

"GEORGE GERMAIN."

"I don't believe a word of it," he said almost out loud. To his thinking it was almost impossible that what his brother said should be true. Why should he be sorry,—he that had done his utmost to prove that Popenjoy was not Popenjoy? He crunched the letter up and cast it on one side. Of course he would not answer that.

The third was from a new correspondent; and that also the reader shall see;—

"MY DEAR LORD MARQUIS,—Pray believe that had I known under what great affliction you were labouring when you left Rudham Park I should have been the last man in the world to intrude myself upon you. Pray believe me also when I say that I have heard of your great bereavement with sincere sympathy, and that I condole with you from the bottom of my heart. Pray remember, my dear Lord, that if you will turn aright for consolation you certainly will not turn in vain.

"Let me add, though this is hardly the proper moment for such allusion, that both his lordship the Bishop and myself were most indignant when we heard of the outrage committed upon you at your hotel. I make no secret of my opinion that the present Dean of Brotherton ought to be called upon by the great Council of the Nation to vacate his promotion. I wish that the bench of bishops had the power to take from him his frock.

"I have the honour to be,

"My Lord Marquis,

"With sentiments of most unfeigned respect,

"Your Lordship's most humble servant,

"JOSEPH GROSCHUT."

The Marquis smiled as he also threw this letter into the waste-paper basket, telling himself that birds of that feather very often did fall out with one another.

Chapter LIV.

Jack De Baron's Virtue.

We must now go back to Jack De Baron, who left Rudham
Park the same day as the Marquis,—having started before
the news of Lord Popenjoy's death had been brought down stairs
by Mr. De Baron. Being only Jack De Baron he had sent to
Brotherton for a fly, and in that conveyance had had himself
taken to the "Lion," arriving there three or four hours before the
time at which he purposed to leave the town. Indeed his
arrangements had intentionally been left so open that he might if
he liked remain the night,—or if he pleased, remain a week at
the "Lion." He thought it not improbable that the Dean might
ask him to dinner, and, if so, he certainly would dine with the
Dean.

He was very serious,—considering who he was, we may
almost say solemn, as he sat in the fly. It was the rule of his life
to cast all cares from him, and his grand principle to live from
hand to mouth. He was almost a philosopher in his
epicureanism, striving always that nothing should trouble him.
But now he had two great troubles, which he could not throw off
from him. In the first place, after having striven against it for the
last four or five years with singular success, he had in a moment

of weakness allowed himself to become engaged to Guss Mildmay. She had gone about it so subtlely that he had found himself manacled almost before he knew that the manacles were there. He had fallen into the trap of an hypothesis, and now felt that the preliminary conditions on which he had seemed to depend could never avail him. He did not mean to marry Guss Mildmay. He did not suppose that she thought he meant to marry her. He did not love her, and he did not believe very much in her love for him. But Guss Mildmay, having fought her battle in the world for many years with but indifferent success, now felt that her best chance lay in having a bond upon her old lover. He ought not to have gone to Rudham when he knew that she was to be there. He had told himself that before, but he had not liked to give up the only chance which had come in his way of being near Lady George since she had left London. And now he was an engaged man,—a position which had always been to him full of horrors. He had run his bark on to the rock, which it had been the whole study of his navigation to avoid. He had committed the one sin which he had always declared to himself that he never would commit. This made him unhappy.

And he was uneasy also,—almost unhappy,—respecting Lady George. People whom he knew to be bad had told him things respecting her which he certainly did not believe, but which he did not find it compatible with his usual condition of life altogether to disbelieve. If he had ever loved any woman he loved her. He certainly respected her as he had never respected any other young woman. He had found the pleasure to be derived from her society to be very different from that which had come from his friendship with others. With her he could be perfectly innocent, and at the same time completely happy. To dance with her, to ride with her, to walk with her, to sit with the privilege of looking at her, was joy of itself, and required nothing beyond. It was a delight to him to have any little thing to do for her. When his daily life was in any way joined with hers there was a brightness in it which he thoroughly enjoyed though he did not quite understand. When that affair of the dance came, in which Lord George had declared his jealousy, he had been in truth very unhappy because she was unhappy, and he had been thoroughly angry with the man, not because the man had interfered with his own pleasures, but because of the injury and the injustice done to the wife. He found himself wounded, really hurt, because she had been made subject to calumny. When he tried to analyse the feeling he could not understand it. It was so different from anything that had gone before! He was sure that she liked him, and yet there was a moment in which he thought that he would purposely keep out of her way for the future, lest he might be a trouble to her. He loved her so well that his love for a while almost made him unselfish.

And yet,—yet he might be mistaken about her. It had been the theory of his life that young married women become tired of their husbands, and one of his chief doctrines that no man should ever love in such a way as to believe in the woman he loves. After so many years, was he to give up his philosophy? Was he to allow the ground to be cut from under his feet by a young creature of twenty-one who had been brought up in a county town? Was he to run away because a husband had taken it into his head to be jealous? All the world had given him credit for his behaviour at the Kappa-kappa. He had gathered laurels,— very much because he was supposed to be the lady's lover. He had never boasted to others of the lady's favour; but he knew that she liked him, and he had told himself that he would be poor-spirited if he abandoned her.

He drove up to the "Lion" and ordered a room. He did not know whether he should want it, but he would at any rate bespeak it. And he ordered his dinner. Come what come might, he thought that he would dine and sleep at Brotherton that day. Finding himself so near to Lady George, he would not leave her quite at once. He asked at the inn whether the Dean was in Brotherton. Yes; the Dean was certainly at the deanery. He had been seen about in the city that morning. The inhabitants, when they talked about Brotherton, always called it the city. And were Lord George and Lady George at the deanery? In answer to this question, the landlady with something of a lengthened face declared that Lady George was with her papa, but that Lord George was at Manor Cross. Then Jack De Baron strolled out towards the Close.

It was a little after one when he found himself at the cathedral door, and thinking that the Dean and his daughter might be at lunch, he went into the building, so that he might get rid of half an hour. He had not often been in cathedrals of late years, and now looked about him with something of awe. He could remember that when he was a child he had been brought here to church, and as he stood in the choir with the obsequient verger at his elbow he recollected how he had got through the minutes of a long sermon,—a sermon that had seemed to be very long,—in planning the way in which, if left to himself, he would climb to the pinnacle which culminated over the bishop's seat, and thence make his way along the capitals and vantages of stonework, till he would ascend into the triforium and thus become lord and master of the old building. How much smaller his ambitions had become since then, and how much less manly. "Yes, sir; his Lordship is here every Sunday when he is at the palace," said the verger. "But his Lordship is ailing now."

"And the Dean?"

"The Dean always comes once a day to service when he is here; but the Dean has been much away of late. Since Miss Mary's marriage the Dean isn't in Brotherton as much as formerly."

"I know the Dean. I'm going to his house just now. They like him in Brotherton, I suppose?"

"That's according to their way of thinking, sir. We like him. I suppose you heard, sir, there was something of a row between him and Miss Mary's brother-in-law!" Jack said that he had heard of it. "There's them as say he was wrong."

"I say he was quite right."

"That's what we think, sir. It's got about that his Lordship said some bad word of Miss Mary. A father wasn't to stand that because he's a clergyman, was he, sir?"

"The Dean did just what you or I would do."

"That's just it, sir. That's what we all say. Thank you, sir. You won't see Prince Edward's monument, sir? Gentlemen always do go down to the crypt." Jack wouldn't see the monument to-day, and having paid his half-crown, was left to wander about alone through the aisles.

How would it have been with him if his life had been different; if he had become, perhaps, a clergyman and had married Mary Lovelace?—or if he had become anything but what he was with her for his wife? He knew that his life had been a failure, that the best of it was gone, and that even the best of it had been unsatisfactory. Many people liked him, but was there any one who loved him? In all the world there was but one person that he loved, and she was the wife of another man. Of one thing at this moment he was quite sure,—that he would never wound her ears by speaking of his love. Would it not be better that he should go away and see her no more? The very tone in which the verger had spoken of Miss Mary had thrown to the winds those doubts which had come from the teaching of Adelaide Houghton and Guss Mildmay. If she had been as they said, would even her father have felt for her as he did feel, and been carried away by his indignation at the sound of an evil word?

But he had asked after the Dean at the hotel, and had told the verger of his acquaintance, and had been seen by many in the town. He could not now leave the place without calling. So resolving he knocked at last at the deanery door, and was told that the Dean was at home. He asked for the Dean, and not for Lady George, and was shown into the library. In a minute the Dean was with him. "Come in and have some lunch," said the Dean. "We have this moment sat down. Mary will be delighted to see you,—and so am I." Of course he went in to lunch, and in a moment was shaking hands with Mary, who in truth was delighted to see him.

"You've come from Rudham?" asked the Dean.

"This moment."

"Have they heard the news there?"

"What news?"

"Lord Brotherton is there, is he not?"

"I think he left to-day. He was to do so. I heard no news." He looked across to Mary, and saw that her face was sad and solemn.

"The child that they called Lord Popenjoy is dead," said the Dean. He was neither sad nor solemn. He could not control the triumph of his voice as he told the news.

"Poor little boy!" said Mary.

"Dead!" exclaimed Jack.

"I've just had a telegram from my lawyer in London. Yes; he's out of the way. Poor little fellow! As sure as I sit here he was not Lord Popenjoy."

"I never understood anything about it," said Jack.

"But I did. Of course the matter is at rest now. I'm not the man to grudge any one what belongs to him; but I do not choose that any one belonging to me should be swindled. If she were to have a son now, he would be the heir."

"Oh, papa, do not talk in that way."

"Rights are rights, and the truth is the truth. Can any one wish that such a property and such a title should go to the child of an Italian woman whom no one has seen or knows?"

"Let it take its chance now, papa."

"Of course it must take its chance; but your chances must be protected."

"Papa, he was at any rate my nephew."

"I don't know that. In law, I believe, he was no such thing. But he has gone, and we need think of him no further." He was very triumphant. There was an air about him as though he had already won the great stake for which he had been playing.

But in the midst of it all he was very civil to Jack De Baron. "You will stay and dine with us to-day, Captain De Baron?"

"Oh, do," said Mary.

"We can give you a bed if you will sleep here."

"Thanks. My things are at the hotel, and I will not move them. I will come and dine if you'll have me."

"We shall be delighted. We can't make company of you, because no one is coming. I shouldn't wonder if Lord George rode over. He will if he hears of this. Of course he'll know to-morrow; but perhaps they will not have telegraphed to him. I should go out to Manor Cross, only I don't quite like to put my foot in that man's house." Jack could not but feel that the Dean treated him almost as though he were one of the family. "I rather think I shall ride out and risk it. You won't mind my leaving you?" Of course Jack declared that he would not for worlds be in the way. "Mary will play Badminton with you, if you like it. Perhaps you can get hold of Miss Pountner and Grey; and make up a game." Mr. Grey was one of the minor canons, and Miss Pountner was the canon's daughter.

"We shall do very well, papa. I'm not mad after Badminton, and I dare say we shall manage without Miss Pountner."

The Dean went off, and in spite of the feud did ride over to Manor Cross. His mind was so full of the child's death and of the all but certainty of coming glory which now awaited his daughter, that he could not keep himself quiet. It seemed to him that a just Providence had interfered to take that child away. And as the Marquis hated him, so did he hate the Marquis. He had been willing at first to fight the battle fairly without personal animosity. On the Marquis's first arrival he had offered him the right hand of fellowship. He remembered it all accurately,—how the Marquis had on that occasion ill-used and insulted him. No man knew better than the Dean when he was well-treated and when ill-treated. And then this lord had sent for him for the very purpose of injuring and wounding him through his daughter's name. His wrath on that occasion had not all expended itself in the blow. After that word had been spoken he was the man's enemy for ever. There could be no forgiveness. He could not find room in his heart for even a spark of pity because the man had lost an only child. Had not the man tried to do worse than kill his only child—his daughter? Now the pseudo-Popenjoy was dead, and the Dean was in a turmoil of triumph. It was essential to him that he should see his son-in-law. His son-in-law must be made to understand what it would be to be the father of the future Marquis of Brotherton.

"I think I'll just step across to the inn," said Jack, when the Dean had left them.

"And we'll have a game of croquet when you come back. I do like croquet, though papa laughs at me. I think I like all games. It is so nice to be doing something."

Jack sauntered back to the inn, chiefly that he might have a further opportunity of considering what he would say to her. And he did make up his mind. He would play croquet with all his might, and behave to her as though she were his dearest sister.

Chapter LV.

How Could He Help It?

When he returned she was out in the garden with her hat on and a mallet in her hand; but she was seated on one of a cluster of garden-chairs under a great cedar tree. "I think it's almost too hot to play," she said. It was an August afternoon, and the sun was very bright in the heavens. Jack was of course quite willing to sit under the cedar-tree instead of playing croquet. He was prepared to do whatever she wished. If he could only know what subjects she would prefer, he would talk about them and nothing else. "How do you think papa is looking?" she asked.

"He always looks well."

"Ah; he was made dreadfully unhappy by that affair up in London. He never would talk about it to me; but he was quite ill while he thought the Marquis was in danger."

"I don't believe the Marquis was much the worse for it."

"They said he was, and papa for some time could not get over it. Now he is elated. I wish he would not be so glad because that poor little boy has died."

"It makes a great difference to him, Lady George;—and to you."

"Of course it makes a difference, and of course I feel it. I am as anxious for my husband as any other woman. If it should come fairly, as it were by God's doing, I am not going to turn up my nose at it."

"Is not this fairly?"

"Oh yes. Papa did not make the little boy die, of course. But I don't think that people should long for things like this. If they can't keep from wishing them, they should keep their wishes to themselves. It is so like coveting other people's goods. Don't you think we ought to keep the commandments, Captain De Baron?"

"Certainly—if we can."

"Then we oughtn't to long for other people's titles."

"If I understand it, the Dean wanted to prevent somebody else from getting a title which wasn't his own. That wouldn't be breaking the commandment."

"Of course I am not finding fault with papa. He would not for worlds try to take anything that wasn't his,—or mine. But it's so sad about the little boy."

"I don't think the Marquis cared for him."

"Oh, he must have cared! His only child! And the poor mother;—think how she must feel."

"In spite of it all, I do think it's a very good thing that he's dead," said Jack, laughing.

"Then you ought to keep it to yourself, sir. It's a very horrid thing to say so. Wouldn't you like to smoke a cigar? You may, you know. Papa always smokes out here, because he says Mr. Groschut can't see him."

"Mr. Groschut is at Rudham," said Jack, as he took a cigar out of his case and lit it.

"At Rudham? What promotion!"

"He didn't seem to me to be a first-class sort of a fellow."

"Quite a last-class sort of fellow, if there is a last class. I'll tell you a secret, Captain De Baron. Mr. Groschut is my pet abomination. If I hate anybody, I hate him. I think I do really hate Mr. Groschut. I almost wish that they would make him bishop of some unhealthy place."

"So that he might go away and die?"

"If the mosquitoes would eat him day and night, that would be enough. Who else was there at Rudham?"

"Mrs. Montacute Jones."

"Dear Mrs. Jones. I do like Mrs. Jones."

"And Adelaide Houghton with her husband." Mary turned up her nose and made a grimace as the Houghtons were named. "You used to be very fond of Adelaide."

"Very fond is a long word. We were by way of being friends; but we are friends no longer."

"Tell me what she did to offend you, Lady George? I know there was something."

"You are her cousin. Of course I am not going to abuse her to you."

"She's not half so much my cousin as you are my friend,—if I may say so. What did she do or what did she say?"

"She painted her face."

"If you're going to quarrel, Lady George, with every woman in London who does that, you'll have a great many enemies."

"And the hair at the back of her head got bigger and bigger every month. Papa always quotes something about Dr. Fell when he's asked why he does not like anybody. She's Dr. Fell to me."

"I don't think she quite knows why you've cut her."

"I'm quite sure she does, Captain De Baron. She knows all about it. And now, if you please, we won't talk of her any more. Who else was there at Rudham?"

"All the old set. Aunt Ju and Guss."

"Then you were happy."

"Quite so. I believe that no one knows all about that better than you do."

"You ought to have been happy."

"Lady George, I thought you always told the truth."

"I try to; and I think you ought to have been happy. You don't mean to tell me that Miss Mildmay is nothing to you?"

"She is a very old friend."

"Ought she not to be more? Though of course I have no right to ask."

"You have a right if any one has. I haven't a friend in the world I would trust as I would you. No; she ought not to be more."

"Have you never given her a right to think that she would be more?"

He paused a moment or two before he answered. Much as he wished to trust her, anxious as he was that she should be his real friend he could hardly bring himself to tell her all that had taken place at Rudham Park during the last day or two. Up to that time he never had given Miss Mildmay any right. So, at least, he still assured himself. But now,—it certainly was different now. He desired of all things to be perfectly honest with Lady George,—to be even innocent in all that he said to her; but—just for this once—he was obliged to deviate into a lie. "Never!" he said.

"Of course it is not for me to enquire further."

"It is very hard to describe the way in which such an intimacy has come about. Guss Mildmay and I have been very much thrown together; but, even had she wished it, we never could have married. We have no means."

"And yet you live like rich people."

"We have no means because we have lived like rich people."

"You have never asked her to marry you?"

"Never."

"Nor made her think that you would ask her? That comes to the same thing, Captain De Baron."

"How am I to answer that? How am I to tell it all without seeming to boast. When it first came to pass that we knew ourselves well enough to admit of such a thing being said between us, I told her that marriage was impossible. Is not that enough?"

"I suppose so," said Lady George, who remembered well every word that Gus Mildmay had said to herself. "I don't know why I should enquire about it, only I thought—"

"I know what you thought."

"What did I think?"

"That I was a heartless scoundrel."

"No, never. If I had, I should not have,—have cared about it. Perhaps it has been unfortunate."

"Most unfortunate!" Then again there was a pause, during which he went on smoking while she played with her mallet. "I wish I could tell you everything about it;—only I can't. Did she ever speak to you?"

"Yes, once."

"And what did she say?"

"I cannot tell you that either."

"I have endeavoured to be honest; but sometimes it is so difficult. One wants sometimes to tell the whole truth, but it won't come out. I am engaged to her now."

"You are engaged to her!"

"And two days since I was as free as ever."

"Then I may congratulate you."

"No, no. It makes me miserable. I do not love her. There is one other person that I care for, and I never can care for any one else. There is one woman that I love, and I never really loved any one else."

"That is very sad, Captain De Baron."

"Is it not? I can never marry Miss Mildmay."

"And yet you have promised?"

"I have promised under certain circumstances which can never, never come about."

"Why did you promise if you do not love her?"

"Cannot you understand without my telling you? I cannot tell you that. I am sure you understand."

"I suppose I do. Poor Miss Mildmay!"

"And poor Jack De Baron!"

"Yes; poor Jack De Baron also! No man should talk to a girl of marrying her unless he loves her. It is different with a girl. She may come to love a man. She may love a man better than all the world, though she hardly knew him when she married him. If he is good to her, she will certainly do so. But if a man marries a woman without loving her, he will soon hate her."

"I shall never marry Miss Mildmay."

"And yet you have said you would?"

"I told you that I wanted to tell you everything. It is so pleasant to have some one to trust, even though I should be blamed as you are blaming me. It simply means that I can marry no one else."

"But you love some one?" She felt when she was asking the question that it was indiscreet. When the assertion was made she had not told herself that she was the woman. She had not thought it. For an instant she had tried to imagine who that other one could be. But yet, when the words were out of her mouth, she knew that they were indiscreet. Was she not indiscreet in holding any such conversation with a man who was not her brother or even her cousin? She wished that he were her cousin, so that she might become the legitimate depository of his secrets. Though she was scolding him for his misdoings, yet she hardly liked him the less for them. She thought that she did understand how it was, and she thought that the girl was more in fault than the man. It was not till the words had passed her mouth and the question had been asked that she felt the indiscretion. "But you love some one else?"

"Certainly I do; but I had not meant to speak about that."

"I will enquire into no secrets."

"Is that a secret? Can it be a secret? Do you not know that ever since I knew you I have had no pleasure but in being with you, and talking to you, and looking at you?"

"Captain De Baron!" As she spoke she rose from her seat as though she would at once leave him and go back into the house.

"You must hear me now. You must not go without hearing me. I will not say a word to offend you."

"You have offended me."

"How could I help it? What was I to do? What ought I to have said? Pray do not go, Lady George."

"I did not think you would have insulted me. I did trust you."

"You may trust me. On my honour as a gentleman, I will never say another word that you can take amiss. I wish I could tell you all my feelings. One cannot help one's love."

"A man may govern his words."

"As I trust in heaven, I had determined that I would never say a syllable to you that I might not have spoken to my sister. Have I asked you to love me? I have not thought it possible that you should do so. I know you to be too good. It has never come within my dreams."

"It is wicked to think of it."

"I have not thought of it. I will never think of it. You are like an angel to me. If I could write poetry, I should write about you. If ever I build castles in the air and think what I might have been if things had gone well with me, I try to fancy then that I might have had you for a wife. That is not wicked. That is not a crime. Can you be angry with me because, having got to know you as I do, I think you better, nicer, jollier, more beautiful than any one else? Have you never really loved a friend?"

"I love my husband with all my heart,—oh, better than all the world."

Jack did not quite understand this. His angel was an angel. He was sure of that. And he wished her to be still an angel. But he could not understand how any angel could passionately love Lord George Germain,—especially this angel who had been so cruelly treated by him. Had she loved him better than all the world when he walked her out of Mrs. Jones' drawing-room, reprimanding her before all the guests for her conduct in dancing the Kappa-kappa? But this was a matter not open to argument. "I may still be your friend?" he said.

"I think you had better not come again."

"Do not say that, Lady George. If I have done wrong, forgive me. I think you must admit that I could hardly help myself."

"Not help yourself!"

"Did I not tell you that I wanted you to know the whole truth? How could I make you understand about Miss Mildmay without telling it all? Say that you will forgive me."

"Say that it is not so, and then I will forgive you."

"No. It is so, and it must be so. It will remain so always, but yet you will surely forgive me, if I never speak of it again. You will forgive me and understand me, and when hereafter you see me as a middle-aged man about town, you will partly know why it is so. Oh dear; I forgot to tell you. We had another old friend of yours at Rudham,—a very particular friend." Of course she had forgiven him and now she was thankful to him for his sudden breach of the subject; but she was not herself strong enough immediately to turn to another matter. "Who do you think was there?"

"How can I tell?"

"The Baroness."

"No?"

"As large as life."

"Baroness Banmann at Mr. De Baron's."

"Yes;—Baroness Banmann. Aunt Julia had contrived to get permission to bring her, and the joke was that she did us all out of our money. She got a five-pound note from me."

"What a goose you were."

"And ten from Lord Brotherton! I think that was the greatest triumph. She was down on him without the slightest compunction. I never saw a man so shot in my life. He sent me to look for the money, and she never left me till I had got it for her."

"I thought Aunt Ju had had enough of her."

"I should think she has now. And we had Lord Giblet. Lord Giblet is to marry Miss Patmore Green after all."

"Poor Lord Giblet!"

"And poor Miss Patmore Green. I don't know which will have the worst of it. They can practice the Kappa-kappa together for consolation. It is all Mrs. Jones' doing, and she is determined that he shan't escape. I'm to go down to Killancodlem and help."

"Why should you have anything to do with it?"

"Very good shooting, and plenty to eat and drink,—and Giblet is a friend of mine; so I'm bound to lend a hand. And now, Lady George, I think I'll go to the hotel and be back to dinner. We are friends."

"Yes; if you promise not to offend me."

"I will never offend you. I will never say a word that all the world might not hear,—except this once,—to thank you." Then he seized her hand and kissed it. "You shall always be a sister to me," he said. "When I am in trouble I will come to you. Say that you will love me as a brother."

"I will always regard you as a friend."

"Regard is a cold word, but I will make the most of it. Here is your father."

At this moment they were coming from a side path on to the lawn, and as they did so the Dean appeared upon the terrace through the deanery room window. With the Dean was Lord George, and Mary, as soon as she saw him, rushed up to him and threw her arms round his neck. "Oh George, dear, dearest George, papa said that perhaps you would come. You are going to stay?"

"He will dine here," said the Dean.

"Only dine!"

"I cannot stay longer to-day," said Lord George, with his eye upon Captain De Baron. The Dean had told him that De Baron was there; but, still, when he saw that the man had been walking with his wife, a renewed uneasiness came upon him. It could not be right that the man from whose arms he had rescued her on the night of the ball should be left alone with her a whole afternoon in the Deanery Garden! She was thoughtless as a child;—but it seemed to him that the Dean was as thoughtless as his daughter. The Dean must know what people had said. The Dean had himself seen that horrid dance, with its results. The awful accusation made by the Marquis had been uttered in the Dean's ears. Because that had been wicked and devilishly false, the Dean's folly was not the less. Lord George embraced his wife, but she knew from the touch of his arm round her waist that there was something wrong with him.

The two men shook hands of course, and then De Baron went out, muttering something to the Dean as to his being back to dinner. "I can't say I like that young man," said Lord George.

"I like him very much," replied the Dean. "He is always good-humoured, and I think he's honest. I own to a predilection for happy people."

Mary was of course soon upstairs with her husband. "I thought you would come," she said, hanging on him.

"I did not like not to see you after the news. It is important. You must feel that."

"Poor little boy! Don't you grieve for them."

"Yes, I do. Brotherton has treated me very badly, but I do feel for him. I shall write to him and say so. But that will not alter the fact. Popenjoy is dead."

"No; it will not alter the fact." He was so solemn with her that she hardly knew how to talk to him.

"Popenjoy is dead,—if he was Popenjoy. I suppose he was; but that does not signify now."

"Not in the least I suppose."

"And if you have a son—"

"Oh, George?"

"He won't be Popenjoy yet."

"Or perhaps ever."

"Or perhaps ever;—but a time will probably come when he will be Popenjoy. We can't help thinking about it, you know."

"Of course not."

"I'm sure I don't want my brother to die."

"I am sure I don't."

"But the family has to be kept up. I do care about the family. They all think at Manor Cross that you should go over at once."

"Are you going to stay there, George. Of course I will go if you are going to stay there."

"They think you should come, though it were only for a few days."

"And then? Of course I will go, George, if you say so. I have had my visit with papa,—as much as I had a right to expect. And, oh George, I do so long to be with you again." Then she hung upon him and kissed him. It must have been impossible that he should be really jealous, though Captain De Baron had been there the whole day. Nor was he jealous, except with that Cæsarian jealousy lest she should be unfortunate enough to cause a whisper derogatory to his marital dignity.

The matter had been fully discussed at Manor Cross; and the Manor Cross conclave, meaning of course Lady Sarah, had thought that Mary should be brought to the house, if only for a day or two, if only that people in Brothershire might know that there had been no quarrel between her and her husband. That she should have visited her father might be considered as natural. It need not be accounted as quite unnatural that she should have done so without her husband. But now,—now it was imperative that Brothershire should know that the mother of the future Lord Popenjoy was on good terms with the family. "Of course her position is very much altered," Lady Susanna had said in private to Lady Amelia. The old Marchioness felt a real longing to see "dear Mary," and to ask becoming questions as to her condition. And it was quite understood that she was not to be required to make any cloaks or petticoats. The garments respecting which she must be solicitous for the next six months would, as the Marchioness felt, be of a very august nature. Oh, that the future baby might be born at Manor Cross! The Marchioness did not see why Lord George should leave the house at all. Brotherton couldn't know anything about it in Italy, and if George must go, Mary might surely be left there for the event. The Marchioness declared that she could die happy if she might see another Popenjoy born in the purple of Manor Cross.

"When am I to go?" asked Mary. She was sitting now close to him, and the question was asked with full delight.

"I do not know whether you can be ready to-morrow."

"Of course I can be ready to-morrow. Oh George, to be back with you! Even for ten days it seems to be a great happiness. But if you go, then of course you will take me with you." There was a reality about this which conquered him, even in spite of Captain De Baron, so that he came down to dinner in good-humour with the world.

Chapter LVI.

Sir Henry Said It Was The Only Thing.

The dinner at the deanery went off without much excitement. Captain De Baron would of course have preferred that Lord George should have remained at Manor Cross, but under no circumstances could he have had much more to say to the lady. They understood each other now. He was quite certain that any evil thing spoken of her had been sheer slander, and yet he had managed to tell her everything of himself without subjecting himself to her undying anger. When she left the drawing-room, the conversation turned again upon the great Popenjoy question, and from certain words which fell from the Dean, Jack was enabled to surmise that Lord George had reason to hope that an heir might be born to him. "He does not look as though he would live long himself," said the Dean, speaking of the Marquis.

"I trust he may with all my heart," said Lord George.

"That's another question," replied the Dean. "I only say that he doesn't look like it." Lord George went away early, and Jack De Baron thought it prudent to retire at the same time. "So you're going to-morrow, dear," said the Dean.

"Yes, papa. Is it not best?"

"Oh yes. Nothing could be worse than a prolonged separation. He means to be honest and good."

"He is honest and good, papa."

"You have had your triumph."

"I did not want to triumph;—not at least over him."

"After what had occurred it was necessary that you should have your own way in coming here. Otherwise he would have triumphed. He would have taken you away, and you and I would have been separated. Of course you are bound to obey him;—but there must be limits. He would have taken you away as though in disgrace, and that I could not stand. There will be an end of that now. God knows when I shall see you again, Mary."

"Why not, papa?"

"Because he hasn't got over his feeling against me. I don't think he ever gets over any feeling. Having no home of his own why does he not bring you here?"

"I don't think he likes the idea of being a burden to you."

"Exactly. He has not cordiality enough to feel that when two men are in a boat together, as he and I are because of you, all that feeling should go to the wind. He ought not to be more ashamed to sit at my table and drink of my cup than you are. If it were all well between us and he had the property, should I scruple to go and stay at Manor Cross."

"You would still have your own house to go back to."

"So will he,—after a while. But it can't be altered, dear, and God forbid that I should set you against him. He is not a rake nor a spendthrift, nor will he run after other women." Mary thought of Mrs. Houghton, but she held her tongue. "He is not a bad man and I think he loves you."

"I am sure he does."

"But I can't help feeling sad at parting with you. I suppose I shall at any rate be able to see you up in town next season." The Dean as he said this was almost weeping.

Mary, when she was alone in her room, of course thought much of Captain De Baron and his story. It was a pity,—a thousand pities,—that it should be so. It was to be regretted,—much regretted,—that he had been induced to tell his story. She was angry with herself because she had been indiscreet, and she was still angry,—a little angry with him,—because he had yielded to the temptation. But there had been something sweet in it. She was sorry, grieved in her heart of hearts that he should love her. She had never striven to gain his love. She had never even thought of it. It ought not to have been so. She should have thought of it; she should not have shown herself to be so pleased with his society. But yet,—yet it was sweet. Then there came upon her some memory of her old dreams, before she had been engaged to Lord George. She knew how vain had been those dreams, because she now loved Lord George with her whole heart; but yet she remembered them, and felt as though they had come true with a dreamy half truth. And she brought to mind all those flattering words with which he had spoken her praises,— how he had told her that she was an angel, too good and pure to be supposed capable of evil; how he had said that in his castles in the air he would still think of her as his wife. Surely a man may build what castles in the air he pleases, if he will only hold his tongue! She was quite sure that she did not love him, but she was sure also that his was the proper way of making love. And then she thought of Guss Mildmay. Could she not in pure charity do a good turn to that poor girl? Might she not tell Captain De Baron that it was his duty to marry her? And if he felt it to be his duty would he not do so? It may be doubted whether in these moments she did not think much better of Captain De Baron than that gentleman deserved.

On the next day the Manor Cross carriage came over for her. The Dean had offered to send her, but Lord George had explained that his mother was anxious that the carriage should come. There would be a cart for the luggage. As to Lady George herself there was a general feeling at Manor Cross that in the present circumstances the family carriage should bring her home. But it came empty. "God bless you, dearest," said the Dean as he put her into the vehicle.

"Good-bye, papa. I suppose you can come over and see me."

"I don't know that I can. I saw none of the ladies when I was there yesterday."

"I don't care a bit for the ladies. Where I go, papa, you can come. Of course George will see you, and you could ask for me." The Dean smiled, and kissed her again, and then she was gone.

She hardly knew what grand things were in store for her. She was still rebelling in her heart against skirts and petticoats, and resolving that she would not go to church twice on Sundays unless she liked it, when the carriage drove up to the door. They were all in the hall, all except the Marchioness. "We wouldn't go in," said Lady Amelia, "because we didn't like to fill the carriage."

"And George wanted us to send it early," said Lady Sarah, "before we had done our work." They all kissed her affectionately, and then she was again in her husband's arms. Mrs. Toff curtseyed to her most respectfully. Mary observed the curtsey and reminded herself at the moment that Mrs. Toff had never curtseyed to her before. Even the tall footman in knee-breeches stood back with a demeanour which had hitherto been vouchsafed only to the real ladies of the family. Who could tell how soon that wicked Marquis would die; and then,—then how great would not be the glory of the Dean's daughter! "Perhaps you won't mind coming up to mamma as soon as you have got your hat off," said Lady Susanna. "Mamma is so anxious to see you." Mary's hat was immediately off, and she declared herself ready to go to the Marchioness. "Mamma has had a great deal to trouble her since you were here," said Lady Susanna, as she led the way upstairs. "She has aged very much. You'll be kind to her, I know."

"Of course I'll be kind," said Mary; "I hope I never was unkind."

"She thinks so much of things now, and then she cries so often. We do all we can to prevent her from crying, because it does make her so weak. Beef-tea is best, we think; and then we try to get her to sleep a good deal. Mary has come, mamma. Here she is. The carriage has only just arrived." Mary followed Lady Susanna into the room, and the Marchioness was immediately immersed in a flood of tears.

"My darling!" she exclaimed; "my dearest, if anything can ever make me happy again it is that you should have come back to me." Mary kissed her mother-in-law and submitted to be kissed with a pretty grace, as though she and the old lady had always been the warmest, most affectionate friends. "Sit down, my love. I have had the easy chair brought there on purpose for you. Susanna, get her that footstool." Susanna, without moving a muscle of her face, brought the footstool. "Now sit down, and let me look at you. I don't think she's much changed." This was very distressing to poor Mary, who, with all her desire to oblige the Marchioness could not bring herself to sit down in the easy chair. "So that poor little boy has gone, my dear?"

"I was so sorry to hear it."

"Yes, of course. That was quite proper. When anybody dies we ought to be sorry for them. I'm sure I did all I could to make things comfortable for him. Didn't I, Susanna?"

"You were quite anxious about him, mamma."

"So I was,—quite anxious. I have no doubt his mother neglected him. I always thought that. But now there will be another, won't there?" This was a question which the mother expectant could not answer, and in order to get over the difficulty Susanna suggested that Mary should be allowed to go down to lunch.

"Certainly, my dear. In her condition she ought not to be kept waiting a minute. And mind, Susanna, she has bottled porter. I spoke about it before. She should have a pint at lunch and a pint at dinner."

"I can't drink porter," said Mary, in despair.

"My dear, you ought to; you ought indeed; you must. I remember as well as if it were yesterday Sir Henry telling me it was the only sure thing. That was before Popenjoy was born,—I mean Brotherton. I do so hope it will be a Popenjoy, my dear." This was the last word said to her as Mary was escaping from the room.

She was not expected to make cloaks and skirts, but she was obliged to fight against a worse servitude even than that. She almost longed for the cloaks and skirts when day after day she was entreated to take her place in the easy chair by the couch of the Marchioness. There was a cruelty in refusing, but in yielding there was a crushing misery. The Marchioness evidently thought that the future stability of the family depended on Mary's quiescence and capability for drinking beer. Very many lies were necessarily told her by all the family. She was made to believe that Mary never got up before eleven; and the doctor who came to see herself and to whose special care Mary was of course recommended, was induced to say that it was essential that Lady George should be in the open air three hours every day. "You know I'm not the least ill, mother," Mary said to her one day. Since these new hopes and the necessity for such hopes had come up the Marchioness had requested that she might be called mother by her daughter-in-law.

"No, my dear, not ill; but I remember as though it were yesterday what Sir Henry said to me when Popenjoy was going to be born. Of course he was Popenjoy when he was born. I don't think they've any physicians like Sir Henry now. I do hope it'll be a Popenjoy."

"But that can't be, mother. You are forgetting."

The old woman thought for a while, and then remembered the difficulty. "No, not quite at once." Then her mind wandered again. "But if this isn't a Popenjoy, my dear,—

and it's all in the hands of God,—then the next may be. My three first were all girls; and it was a great trouble; but Sir Henry said the next would be a Popenjoy; and so it was. I hope this will be a Popenjoy, because I might die before the next." When a week of all this had been endured Mary in her heart was glad that the sentence of expulsion from Manor Cross still stood against her husband, feeling that six months of reiterated longings for a Popenjoy would kill her and the possible Popenjoy also.

Then came the terrible question of an immediate residence. The month was nearly over, and Lord George had determined that he would go up to town for a few days when the time came. Mary begged to be taken with him, but to this he would not accede, alleging that his sojourn there would only be temporary, till something should be settled. "I am sure," said Mary, "your brother would dislike my being here worse than you." That might be true, but the edict, as it had been pronounced, had not been against her. The Marquis had simply ordered that in the event of Lord George remaining in the house, the house and park should be advertised for letting. "George, I think he must be mad," said Mary.

"He is sane enough to have the control of his own property."

"If it is let, why shouldn't you take it?"

"Where on earth should I get the money?"

"Couldn't we all do it among us?"

"He wouldn't let it to us; he will allow my mother and sisters to live here for nothing; and I don't think he has said anything to Mr. Knox about you. But I am to be banished."

"He must be mad."

"Mad or not, I must go."

"Do,—do let me go with you! Do go to the deanery. Papa will make it all square by coming up to us in London."

"Your father has a right to be in the house in London," said Lord George with a scowl.

When the month was over he did go up to town, and saw
Mr. Knox. Mr. Knox advised him to go back to Manor Cross,
declaring that he himself would take no further steps without
further orders. He had not had a line from the Marquis. He did
not even know where the Marquis was, supposing, however, that
he was in his house on the lake; but he did know that the
Marchioness was not with him, as separate application had been
made to him by her Ladyship for money. "I don't think I can do
it," said Lord George. Mr. Knox shrugged his shoulders, and
again said that he saw no objection. "I should be very slow in
advertising, you know," said Mr. Knox.

"But I don't think that I have a right to be in a man's
house without his leave. I don't think I am justified in staying
there against his will because he is my brother." Mr. Knox could
only shrug his shoulders.

He remained up in town doing nothing, doubtful as to
where he should go and whither he should take his wife, while
she was still at Manor Cross, absolutely in the purple, but still
not satisfied with her position. She was somewhat cheered at this
time by a highspirited letter from her friend Mrs. Jones, written
from Killancodlem.

"We are all here," said Mrs. Jones, "and we do so wish
you were with us. I have heard of your condition at last, and of
course it would not be fit that you should be amusing yourself
with wicked idle people like us, while all the future of all the
Germains is, so to say, in your keeping. How very opportune
that that poor boy should have gone just as the other is coming!
Mind that you are a good girl and take care of yourselves. I
daresay all the Germain ladies are looking after you day and
night, so that you can't misbehave very much. No more Kappa-
kappas for many a long day for you!

"We have got Lord Giblet here. It was such a task! I
thought cart-ropes wouldn't have brought him? Now he is as
happy as the day is long, and like a tame cat in my hands. I
really think he is very much in love with her, and she behaves

quite prettily. I took care that Green père should come down in the middle of it, and that clenched it. The lover didn't make the least fight when papa appeared, but submitted himself like a sheep to the shearers. I shouldn't have done it if I hadn't known that he wanted a wife and if I hadn't been sure that she would make a good one. There are some men who never really get on their legs till they're married, and never would get married without a little help. I'm sure he'll bless me, or would do, only he'll think after a bit that he did it all by himself.

"Our friend Jack is with us, behaving very well, but not quite like himself. There are two or three very pretty girls here, but he goes about among them quite like a steady old man. I got him to tell me that he'd seen you at Brotherton, and then he talked a deal of nonsense about the good you'd do when you were Marchioness. I don't see, my dear, why you should do more good than other people. I hope you'll be gracious to your old friends, and keep a good house, and give nice parties. Try and make other people happy. That's the goodness I believe in. I asked him why you were to be particularly good, and then he talked a deal more nonsense, which I need not repeat.

"I hear very queer accounts about the Marquis. He behaved himself at Rudham almost like anybody else, and walked into dinner like a Christian. They say that he is all alone in Italy, and that he won't see her. I fancy he was more hurt in that little affair than some people will allow. Whatever it was, it served him right. Of course I should be glad to see Lord George come to the throne. I always tell the truth, my dear, about these things. What is the use of lying. I shall be very glad to see Lord George a marquis,—and then your Popenjoy will be Popenjoy.

"You remember the Baroness,—your Baroness. Oh, the Baroness! She absolutely asked me to let her come to Killancodlem. 'But I hate disabilities and rights,' said I. She gave me to understand that that made no difference. Then I was obliged to tell her that I hadn't a bed left. Any little room would do for her. 'We haven't any little rooms at Killancodlem,' said I;—and then I left her.

"Good-bye. Mind you are good and take care of yourself; and, whatever you do, let Popenjoy have a royal godfather."

Then her father came over to see her. At this time Lord George was up in town, and when her father was announced she felt that there was no one to help her. If none of the ladies of the family would see her father she never would be gracious to them again. This was the turning-point. She could forgive them for the old quarrel. She could understand that they might have found themselves bound to take their elder brother's part at first. Then they had quarrelled with her, too. Now they had received her back into their favour. But she would have none of their favours, unless they would take her father with her.

She was sitting at the time in that odious arm-chair in the old lady's room; and when Mrs. Toff brought in word that the Dean was in the little drawing-room, Lady Susanna was also present. Mary jumped up immediately, and knew that she was blushing. "Oh! I must go down to papa," she said. And away she went.

The Dean was in one of his best humours, and was full of Brotherton news. Mr. Groschut had been appointed to the vicarage of Pugsty, and would leave Brotherton within a month.

"I suppose it's a good living."

"About £300 a year, I believe. He's been acting not quite on the square with a young lady, and the Bishop made him take it. It was that or nothing." The Dean was quite delighted; and when Mary told him something of her troubles,—how impossible she found it to drink bottled porter,—he laughed, and bade her be of good cheer, and told her that there were good days coming. They had been there for nearly an hour together, and Mary was becoming unhappy. If her father were allowed to go without some recognition from the family, she would never again be friends with those women. She was beginning to think that she never would be friends again with any of them, when the door opened, and Lady Sarah entered the room.

The greeting was very civil on both sides. Lady Sarah could, if she pleased, be gracious, though she was always a little grand; and the Dean was quite willing to be pleased, if only any effort was made to please him. Lady Sarah hoped that he would stay and dine. He would perhaps excuse the Marchioness, as she rarely now left her room. The Dean could not dine at Manor Cross on that day, and then Lady Sarah asked him to come on the Thursday following.

Chapter LVII.

Mr. Knox Hears Again From The Marquis.

"Do come, papa," said Mary, jumping up and putting her arm round her father's shoulders. She was more than willing to meet them all half-way. She would sit in the arm-chair all the morning and try to drink porter at lunch if they would receive her father graciously. Of course she was bound to her husband. She did not wish not to be bound to him. She was quite sure that she loved her husband with a perfect love. But her marriage happiness could not be complete unless her father was to make a part of the intimate home circle of her life. She was now so animated in her request to him, that her manner told all her little story,—not only to him, but to Lady Sarah also.

"I will say do come also," said Lady Sarah, smiling.

Mary looked up at her and saw the smile. "If he were your papa," she said, "you would be as anxious as I am." But she also smiled as she spoke.

"Even though he is not, I am anxious."

"Who could refuse when so entreated? Of course I shall be delighted to come," said the Dean. And so it was settled. Her father was to be again made welcome at Manor Cross, and Mary thought that she could now be happy.

"It was very good of you," she whispered to Lady Sarah, as soon as he had left them. "Of course I understand. I was very, very sorry that he and Lord Brotherton had quarrelled. I won't say anything now about anybody being wrong or anybody being right. But it would be dreadful to me if papa couldn't come to see me. I don't think you know what he is."

"I do know that you love him very dearly."

"Of course I do. There is nothing on earth he wouldn't do for me. He is always trying to make me happy. And he'd do just as much for George, if George would let him. You've been very good about it, and I love you for it." Lady Sarah was quite open to the charm of being loved. She did not talk much of such things, nor was it compatible with her nature to make many professions of affection. But it would be a happiness to her if this young sister-in-law, who would no doubt sooner or later be the female head of the house, could be taught to love her. So she kissed Mary, and then walked demurely away, conscious that any great display of feeling would be antagonistic to her principles.

During the hour that Mary had been closeted with her father there had been much difficulty among the ladies upstairs about the Dean. The suggestion that he should be asked to dine had of course come from Lady Sarah, and it fell like a little thunderbolt among them. In the first place, what would Brotherton say? Was it not an understood portion of the agreement under which they were allowed to live in the house, that the Dean should not be a guest there? Lady Susanna had even shuddered at his coming to call on his daughter, and they had all thought it to be improper when a short time since he had personally brought the news of Popenjoy's death to the house. And then there was their own resentment as to that affray at Scumberg's. They were probably inclined to agree with Lady Brabazon that Brotherton was not quite all that he should be; but still he was Brotherton, and the man who had nearly murdered him could not surely be a fit guest at Manor Cross. "I don't think we can do that, Sarah," Lady Susanna had said after a long silence. "Oh dear! that would be very dreadful!" the Marchioness had exclaimed. Lady Amelia had clasped her hands together and had trembled in every limb. But Lady Sarah, who never made any suggestion without deep thought, was always loth to abandon any that she had made. She clung to this with many arguments. Seeing how unreasonable Brotherton was, they could not feel themselves bound to obey him. As to the house, while their mother lived there it must be regarded as her house. It was out of the question that they should have their guests dictated to them by their brother. Perhaps the Dean was not all that a dean ought to be,—but then, who was perfect? George had married his daughter, and it could not be right to separate the daughter from the father. Then came the final, strong, clenching argument. Mary would certainly be disturbed in her mind if not allowed to see her father. Perfect tranquility for Mary was regarded as the chief ingredient in the cup of prosperity which, after many troubles, was now to be re-brewed for the Germain family. If she were not allowed to see her father, the coming Popenjoy would suffer for it. "You'd better let him come, Susanna," said the Marchioness through her tears. Susanna had looked as stern as an old sibyl. "I really think it will be best," said Lady Amelia. "It ought to be done," said Lady Sarah. "I suppose you had better go to him," said the Marchioness. "I could not see him; indeed I couldn't. But he won't want to see me." Lady Susanna did not yield, but Lady Sarah, as we know, went down on her mission of peace.

Mary, as soon as she was alone, sat herself down to write a letter to her husband. It was then Monday, and her father was to dine there on Thursday. The triumph would hardly be complete unless George would come home to receive him. Her letter was full of arguments, full of entreaties, and full of love. Surely he might come for one night, if he couldn't stay longer. It would be so much nicer for her father to have a gentleman there. Such an attention would please him so much! "I am sure he would go twice the distance if you were coming to his house," pleaded Mary.

Lord George came, and in a quiet way the dinner was a success. The Dean made himself very agreeable. The Marchioness did not appear, but her absence was attributed to the condition of her health. Lady Sarah, as the great promoter of the festival, was bound to be on her good behaviour, and Lady Amelia endeavoured to copy her elder sister. It was not to be expected that Lady Susanna should be cordially hospitable; but it was known that Lady Susanna was habitually silent in company. Mary could forgive her second sister-in-law's sullenness, understanding, as she did quite well, that she was at this moment triumphing over Lady Susanna. Mr. Groschut was not a favourite with any of the party at Manor Cross, and the Dean made himself pleasant by describing the nature of the late chaplain's promotion. "He begged the Bishop to let him off," said the Dean, "but his Lordship was peremptory. It was Pugsty or leave the diocese."

"What had he done, papa?" asked Mary.

"He had promised to marry Hawkins' daughter." Hawkins was the Brotherton bookseller on the Low Church side. "And then he denied the promise. Unfortunately he had written letters, and Hawkins took them to the Bishop. I should have thought Groschut would have been too sharp to write letters."

"But what was all that to the Bishop?" asked Lord George.

"The Bishop was, I think, just a little tired of him. The Bishop is old and meek, and Mr. Groschut thought that he could domineer. He did not quite know his man. The Bishop is old and meek, and would have borne much. When Mr. Groschut scolded him, I fancy that he said nothing. But he bided his time; and when Mr. Hawkins came, then there was a decision pronounced. It was Pugsty, or nothing."

"Is Pugsty very nasty, papa?"

"It isn't very nice, I fancy. It just borders on the Potteries, and the population is heavy. As he must marry the bookseller's daughter also, the union, I fear, won't be very grateful."

"I don't see why a bishop should send a bad man to any parish," suggested Lady Sarah.

"What is he to do with a Groschut, when he has unfortunately got hold of one? He couldn't be turned out to starve. The Bishop would never have been rid of him. A small living—some such thing as Pugsty—was almost a necessity."

"But the people," said Lady Sarah. "What is to become of the poor people?"

"Let us hope they may like him. At any rate, he will be better at Pugsty than at Brotherton." In this way the evening passed off; and when at ten o'clock the Dean took his departure, it was felt by every one except Lady Susanna that the proper thing had been done.

Lord George, having thus come back to Manor Cross, remained there. He was not altogether happy in his mind; but his banishment seemed to be so absurd a thing that he did not return to London. At Manor Cross there was something for him to do. In London there was nothing. And, after all, there was a question whether, as a pure matter of right, the Marquis had the power to pronounce such a sentence. Manor Cross no doubt belonged to him, but then so also did Cross Hall belong for the time to his mother; and he was receiving the rent of Cross Hall while his mother was living at Manor Cross. Lady Sarah was quite clear that for the present they were justified in regarding Manor Cross as belonging to them. "And who'll tell him when he's all the way out there?" asked Mary. "I never did hear of such a thing in all my life. What harm can you do to the house, George?"

So they went on in peace and quietness for the next three months, during which not a single word was heard from the Marquis. They did not even know where he was, and under the present circumstances did not care to ask any questions of Mr. Knox. Lord George had worn out his scruples, and was able to go about his old duties in his old fashion. The Dean had dined there once or twice, and Lord George on one occasion had consented to stay with his wife for a night or two at the deanery. Things seemed to have fallen back quietly into the old way,—as they were before the Marquis with his wife and child had come to disturb them. Of course there was a great difference in Mary's position. It was not only that she was about to become a mother, but that she would do so in a very peculiar manner. Had not the Marquis taken a wife to himself, there would always have been the probability that he would some day do so. Had there not been an Italian Marchioness and a little Italian Popenjoy, the ladies at Manor Cross would still have given him credit for presenting them with a future marchioness and a future Popenjoy at some future day. Now his turn had, as it were, gone. Another Popenjoy from that side was not to be expected. In consequence of all this Mary was very much exalted. They none of them now wished for another Popenjoy from the elder branch. All their hopes were centred in Mary. To Mary herself this importance had its drawbacks. There was the great porter question still unsettled. The arm-chair with the footstool still was there. And she did not like being told that a mile and a half on the sunny side of the trees was the daily amount of exercise which Sir Henry, nearly half a century ago, had prescribed for ladies in her condition. But she had her husband with her, and could, with him, be gently rebellious and affectionately disobedient. It is a great thing, at any rate, to be somebody. In her early married days she had felt herself to be snubbed as being merely the Dean's daughter. Her present troubles brought a certain balm with them. No one snubbed her now. If she had a mind for arrowroot, Mrs. Toff would make it herself and suggest a thimbleful of brandy in it with her most coaxing words. Cloaks and petticoats she never saw, and she was quite at liberty to stay away from afternoon church if she pleased.

It had been decided, after many discussions on the subject, that she and her husband should go up to town for a couple of months after Christmas, Lady Amelia going with them to look after the porter and arrowroot, and that in March she should be brought back to Manor Cross with a view to her confinement. This had not been conceded to her easily, but it had at last been conceded. She had learned in secret from her father that he would come up to town for a part of the time, and after that she never let the question rest till she had carried her point. The Marchioness had been obliged to confess that, in anticipation of her Popenjoy, Sir Henry had recommended a change from the country to town. She did not probably remember that Sir Henry had done so because she had been very cross at the idea of being kept running down to the country all through May. Mary pleaded that it was no use having a house if she were not allowed to see it, that all her things were in London, and at last declared that it would be very convenient to have the baby born in London. Then the Marchioness saw that a compromise was necessary. It was not to be endured that the future Popenjoy, the future Brotherton, should be born in a little house in Munster Court. With many misgivings it was at last arranged that Mary should go to London on the 18th of January, and be brought back on the 10th of March. After many consultations, computations, and calculations, it was considered that the baby would be born somewhere about the 1st of April.

It may be said that things at Manor Cross were quite in a halcyon condition, when suddenly a thunderbolt fell among them. Mr. Knox appeared one day at the house and showed to Lord George a letter from the Marquis. It was written with his usual contempt of all ordinary courtesy of correspondence, but with more than his usual bitterness. It declared the writer's opinion that his brother was a mean fellow, and deserving of no trust in that he had continued to live at the house after having been desired to leave it by its owner; and it went on to give peremptory orders to Mr. Knox to take steps for letting the house at once. This took place at the end of the first week in December. Then there was a postscript to the letter in which the Marquis suggested that Mr. Knox had better take a house for the Marchioness, and apply Mr. Price's rent in the payment for such house. "Of course you will consult my mother," said the postscript; "but it should not be anywhere near Brotherton."

There was an impudence as well as a cruelty about this which almost shook the belief which Lord George still held in the position of an elder brother. Mr. Knox was to take a house;—as though his mother and sisters had no rights, no freedom of their own! "Of course I will go," said he, almost pale with anger.

Then Mr. Knox explained his views. It was his intention to write back to the Marquis and to decline to execute the task imposed upon him. The care of the Marquis's property was no doubt his chief mainstay; but there were things, he said, which he could not do. Of course the Marquis would employ someone else, and he must look for his bread elsewhere. But he could not, he said, bring himself to take steps for the letting of Manor Cross as long as the Marchioness was living there.

Of course there was a terrible disturbance in the house. There arose a great question whether the old lady should or should not be told of this new trouble, and it was decided at last that she should for the present be kept in the dark. Mr. Knox was of opinion that the house never would be let, and that it would not be in his Lordship's power to turn them out without procuring for them the use of Cross Hall;—in which Mr. Price's newly married bride had made herself comfortable on a lease of three years. And he was also of opinion that the attempt made by the Marquis to banish his brother was a piece of monstrous tyranny to which no attention should be paid. This he said before all the younger ladies;—but to Lord George himself he said even more. He expressed a doubt whether the Marquis could be in his right mind, and added a whisper that the accounts of the

Marquis's health were very bad indeed. "Of course he could let the house?" asked Lord George.

"Yes;—if he can get anybody to let it for him, and anybody else to take it. But I don't think it ever will be let. He won't quite know what to do when he gets my letter. He can hardly change his agent without coming to London, and he won't like to do that in the winter. He'll write me a very savage letter, and then in a week or two I shall answer him. I don't think I'd disturb the Marchioness if I were you, my lord."

The Marchioness was not disturbed, but Lord George again went up to London, on this occasion occupying the house in Munster Court in solitude. His scruples were all renewed, and it was in vain that Lady Sarah repeated to him all Mr. Knox's arguments. He had been called a mean fellow, and the word rankled with him. He walked about alone thinking of the absolute obedience with which in early days he had complied with all the behests of his elder brother, and the perfect faith with which in latter days he had regarded that brother's interests. He went away swearing to himself that he would never again put his foot within the domain of Manor Cross as long as it was his brother's property. A day might come when he would return there; but Lord George was not a man to anticipate his own prosperity. Mary wished to accompany him; but this was not allowed. The Marchioness inquired a dozen times why he should go away; but there was no one who could tell her.

Chapter LVIII.

Mrs. Jones' Letter.

A few days before Christmas Mary received a long letter from her friend Mrs. Montacute Jones. At this time there was sad trouble again at Manor Cross. Lord George had been away for a fortnight, and no reason for his departure had as yet been given to the Marchioness. She had now become aware that he was not to be at home at Christmas, and she was full of doubt, full of surmises of her own. He must have quarrelled with his sisters! They all assured her that there hadn't been an unpleasant word between him and any one of them. Then he must have quarrelled with his wife! "Indeed, indeed he has not," said Mary. "He has never quarrelled with me and he never shall." Then why did he stay away? Business was nonsense. Why was he going to stay away during Christmas. Then it was necessary to tell the old lady a little fib. She was informed that Brotherton had specially desired him to leave the house. This certainly was a fib, as Brotherton's late order had been of a very different nature. "I hope he hasn't done anything to offend his brother again," said the Marchioness. "I wonder whether it's about Popenjoy!" In the midst of her troubles the poor old woman's wits were apt to wander.

Mary too had become rather cross, thinking that as her husband was up in town she should be allowed to be there too. But it had been conceded by her, and by her father on her behalf, that her town life was not to begin till after Christmas, and now she was unable to prevail. She and the family were in this uncomfortable condition when Mrs. Montacute Jones' letter came for her consolation. As it contained tidings, more or less accurate, concerning many persons named in this chronicle, it shall be given entire. Mrs. Montacute Jones was a great writer of letters, and she was wont to communicate many details among her friends and acquaintances respecting one another. It was one of the marvels of the day that Mrs. Jones should have so much information; and no one could say how or whence she got it.

"CURRY HALL, *December 12, 187—.*"

Curry Hall was the name of Mr. Jones' seat in Gloucestershire, whereas, as all the world knew, Killancodlem was supposed to belong to Mrs. Jones herself.

"DEAREST LADY GEORGE,—We have been here for the last six weeks, quite quiet. A great deal too quiet for me, but for the three or four winter months, I am obliged to give way a little to Mr. Jones. We have had the Mildmays here, because they didn't seem to have any other place to go to. But I barred the Baroness. I am told that she is now bringing an action against Aunt Ju, who unfortunately wrote the letter which induced the woman to come over from—wherever she came from. Poor Aunt Ju is in a terrible state, and wants her brother to buy the woman off,—which he will probably have to do. That's what comes, my dear, of meddling with disabilities. I know my own disabilities, but I never think of interfering with Providence. Mr. Jones was made a man, and I was made a woman. So I put up with it, and I hope you will do the same.

"Mr. and Mrs. Green are here also, and remain till Christmas when the Giblets are coming. It was the prettiest wedding in the world, and they have been half over Europe

since. I am told he's the happiest man in the world, and the
very best husband. Old Gossling didn't like it at all, but
every stick is entailed, and they say he's likely to have gout
in his stomach, so that everything will go pleasantly. Lord
Giblet himself is loud against his father, asking everybody
whether it was to be expected that in such a matter as that
he shouldn't follow his own inclination. I do hope he'll
show a little gratitude to me. But it's an ungrateful world,
and they'll probably both forget what I did for them.

"And now I want to ask you your opinion about
another friend. Don't you think that Jack had better settle
down with poor dear Guss? She's here, and upon my word I
think she's nearly broken-hearted. Of course you and I
know what Jack has been thinking of lately. But when a
child cries for the top brick of the chimney, it is better to let
him have some possible toy. You know what top brick he
has been crying for. But I'm sure you like him, and so do I,
and I think we might do something for him. Mr. Jones
would let them a nice little house a few miles from here at a
peppercorn rent; and I suppose old Mr. Mildmay could do
something. They are engaged after a fashion. She told me
all about it the other day. So I've asked him to come down
for Christmas, and have offered to put up his horses if he
wants to hunt.

"And now, my dear, I want to know what you have
heard about Lord Brotherton at Manor Cross. Of course we
all know the way he has behaved to Lord George. If I were
Lord George I should not pay the slightest attention to him.
But I'm told he is in a very low condition,—never sees
anybody except his courier, and never stirs out of the house.
Of course you know that he makes his wife an allowance,
and refuses to see her. From what I hear privately I really
do think that he'll not last long. What a blessing it would
be! That's plain speaking;—but it would be a blessing!
Some people manage to live so that everybody will be the
better for their dying. I should break my heart if anybody
wanted me to die.

"How grand it would be! The young and lovely
Marchioness of Brotherton! I'll be bound you think about it
less than anybody else, but it would be nice. I wonder
whether you'd cut a poor old woman like me, without a
handle to her name. And then it would be Popenjoy at once!
Only how the bonfires wouldn't burn if it should turn out to
be only a disability after all. But we should say, better luck
next time, and send you caudle cups by the dozen. Who

wouldn't send a caudle cup to a real young lovely live Marchioness? I'll be bound your father knows all about it, and has counted it all up a score of times. I suppose it's over £40,000 a year since they took to working the coal at Popenjoy, and whatever the present man has done he can't have clipped the property. He has never gambled, and never spent his income. Italian wives and that sort of thing don't cost so much money as they do in England.

"Pray write and tell me all about it. I shall be in town in February, and of course shall see you. I tell Mr. Jones that I can't stand Curry Hall for more than three months. He won't come to town till May, and perhaps when May comes he'll have forgotten all about it. He is very fond of sheep, but I don't think he cares for anything else, unless he has a slight taste for pigs.

"Your affectionate friend,

"G. MONTACUTE JONES."

There was much in this letter that astonished Mary, something that shocked her, but something also that pleased her. The young and lovely Marchioness of Brotherton! Where is the woman who would not like to be a young and lovely Marchioness, so that it had all been come by honestly, that the husband had been married as husbands ought to be married, and had not been caught like Lord Giblet; and she knew that her old friend,—her old friend whom she had not yet known for quite twelve months,—was only joking with her in that suggestion as to being cut. What a fate was this in store for her—if it really was in store—that so early in her life she should be called upon to fill so high a place. Then she made some resolutions in her mind that should it be so she would be humble and meek; and a further resolution that she would set her heart upon none of it till it was firmly her own.

But it shocked her that the Marquis should be so spoken of, especially that he should be so spoken of if he were really dying! Plain speaking! Yes, indeed. But such plain speaking was very terrible. This old woman could speak of another nobleman having gout in his stomach as though that were a thing really to be desired. And then that allusion to the Italian wife or wives! Poor Mary blushed as she thought of it.

But there was a paragraph in the letter which interested her as much as the tidings respecting Lord Brotherton. Could it be right that Jack De Baron should be made to marry Guss Mildmay? She thought not, for she knew that he did not love Guss Mildmay. That he should have wanted an impossible brick, whether the highest or lowest brick, was very sad. When children cry for impossible bricks they must of course be disappointed. But she hardly thought that this would be the proper cure for his disappointment. There had been a moment in which the same idea had suggested itself to her; but now since her friendship with Jack had been strengthened by his conduct in the deanery garden she thought that he might do better with himself than be made by Mrs. Jones to marry Guss Mildmay. Of course she could not interfere, but she hoped that something might prevent Jack De Baron from spending his Christmas at Curry Hall. She answered Mrs. Jones' letter very prettily. She trusted that Lord Giblet might be happy with his wife, even though his father should get well of the gout. She was very sorry to hear that Lord Brotherton was ill. Nothing was known about him at Manor Cross, except that he seemed to be very ill-natured to everybody. She was surprised that anybody should be so ill-natured as he was. If ever she should live to fill a high position she hoped she would be good-natured. She knew that the people she would like best would be those who had been kind to her, and nobody had been so kind as a certain lady named Mrs. Montacute Jones. Then she spoke of her coming trial. "Don't joke with me about it any more, there's a dear woman. They all flutter me here, talking of it always, though they mean to be kind. But it seems to me so serious. I wish that nobody would speak to me of it except George, and he seems to think nothing about it."

Then she came to the paragraph the necessity for writing which had made her answer Mrs. Jones' letter so speedily. "I don't think you ought to persuade anybody to marry anyone. It didn't much signify, perhaps, with Lord Giblet, as he isn't clever, and I daresay that Miss Green will suit him very well; but as a rule I think gentlemen should choose for themselves. In the case you speak of I don't think he cares for her, and then they would be unhappy." She would not for worlds have mentioned Captain De Baron's name; but she thought that Mrs. Jones would understand her.

Of course Mrs. Jones understood her,—had understood more than Mary had intended her to understand. Christmas was over and Mary was up in town when she received Mrs. Jones' rejoinder, but it may as well be given here. "The child who wanted the top brick is here, and I think will content himself with a very much less exalted morsel of the building. I am older than you, my dear, and know better. Our friend is a very good fellow in his way, but there is no reason why he should not bend his neck as well as another. To you no doubt he seems to have many graces. He has had the great grace of holding his tongue because he appreciated your character." Mary, as she read this, knew that even Mrs. Montacute Jones could be misinformed now and then. "But I do not know that he is in truth more gracious than others, and I think it quite as well that Miss Mildmay should have the reward of her constancy."

But this was after Christmas, and in the meantime other occurrences had taken place. On the 20th of December Lord George was informed by Mr. Knox that his brother, who was then at Naples, had been struck by paralysis, and at Mr. Knox's advice he started off for the southern capital of Italy. The journey was a great trouble to him, but this was a duty which he would under no circumstances neglect. The tidings were communicated to Manor Cross, and after due consultation, were conveyed by Lady Sarah to her mother. The poor old lady did not seem to be made very unhappy by them. "Of course I can't go to him," she said; "how could I do it?" When she was told that that was out of the question she subsided again into tranquility, merely seeming to think it necessary to pay increased attention to Mary; for she was still quite alive to the fact that all this greatly increased the chances that the baby would be Popenjoy; but even in this the poor old lady's mind wandered much, for every now and then she would speak of Popenjoy as though there were a living Popenjoy at the present moment.

Lord George hurried off to Naples, and found that his brother was living at a villa about eight miles from the town. He learned in the city, before he had made his visit, that the Marquis was better, having recovered his speech and apparently the use of his limbs. Still being at Naples he found himself bound to go out to the villa. He did so, and when he was there his brother refused to see him. He endeavoured to get what information he could from the doctor; but the doctor was an Italian, and Lord George could not understand him. As far as he could learn the doctor thought badly of the case; but for the present his patient had so far recovered as to know what he was about. Then Lord George hurried back to London, having had a most uncomfortable journey in the snow. Come what might he didn't think that he would ever again take the trouble to pay a visit to his brother. The whole time taken on his journey and for his sojourn in Naples was less than three weeks, and when he returned the New Year had commenced.

He went down to Brotherton to bring his wife up to London, but met her at the deanery, refusing to go to the house. When the Marchioness heard of this,—and it became impossible to keep it from her,—she declared that it was with herself that her son George must have quarrelled. Then it was necessary to tell her the whole truth, or nearly the whole. Brotherton had behaved so badly to his brother that Lord George had refused to enter even the park. The poor old woman was very wretched, feeling in some dim way that she was being robbed of both her sons. "I don't know what I've done," she said, "that everything should be like this. I'm sure I did all I could for them; but George never would behave properly to his elder brother, and I don't wonder that Brotherton feels it. Brotherton always had so much feeling. I don't know why George should be jealous because Popenjoy was born. Why shouldn't his elder brother have a son of his own like anybody else?" And yet whenever she saw Mary, which she did for two or three hours every day, she was quite alive to the coming interest. It was suggested to her that she should be driven into Brotherton, so that she might see George at the deanery; but her objection to go to the Dean's house was as strong as was that of Lord George to come to his brother's.

Mary was of course delighted when the hour of her escape came. It had seemed to her that there was especial cruelty in keeping her at Manor Cross while her husband was up in town. Her complaints on this head had of course been checked by her husband's unexpected journey to Naples, as to which she had hardly heard the full particulars till she found herself in the train with him. "After going all that way he wouldn't see you!"

"He neither would see me or send me any message."

"Then he must be a bad man."

"He has lived a life of self-indulgence till he doesn't know how to control a thought or a passion. It was something of that kind which was meant when we were told about the rich man and the eye of the needle."

"But you will be a rich man soon, George."

"Don't think of it, Mary; don't anticipate it. God knows I have never longed for it. Your father longs for it."

"Not for his own sake, George."

"He is wrong all the same. It will not make you happier,—nor me."

"But, George, when you thought that that little boy was not Popenjoy you were as anxious as papa to find it all out."

"Right should be done," said Lord George, after a pause. "Whether it be for weal or woe, justice should have its way. I never wished that the child should be other than what he was called; but when there seemed to be reason for doubt I thought that it should be proved."

"It will certainly come to you now, George, I suppose."

"Who can say? I might die to-night, and then Dick Germain, who is a sailor somewhere, would be the next Lord Brotherton."

"Don't talk like that, George."

"He would be if your child happened to be a girl. And Brotherton might live ever so long. I have been so harassed by it all that I am almost sick of the title and sick of the property. I never grudged him anything, and see how he has treated me." Then Mary was very gracious to him and tried to comfort him, and told him that fortune had at any rate given him a loving wife.

Chapter LIX.

Back In London.

Mary was fond of her house in Munster Court. It was her own; and her father and Miss Tallowax between them had enabled her to make it very pretty. The married woman who has not some pet lares of her own is but a poor woman. Mary worshipped her little household gods with a perfect religion, and was therefore happy in being among them again; but she was already beginning to feel that in a certain event she would be obliged to leave Munster Court. She knew that as Marchioness of Brotherton she would not be allowed to live there. There was a large brick house, with an unbroken row of six windows on the first-floor, in St. James' Square, which she already knew as the town house of the Marquis of Brotherton. It was, she thought, by far the most gloomy house in the whole square. It had been uninhabited for years, the present Marquis having neither resided there nor let it. Her husband had never spoken to her about the house, had never, as far as she could remember, been with her in St. James' Square. She had enquired about it of her father, and he had once taken her through the square, and had shown her the mansion. But that had been in the days of the former Popenjoy, when she, at any rate, had never thought that the dreary-looking mansion would make or mar her own comfort. Now there had arisen a question of a delicate nature on which she had said a word or two to her husband in her softest whisper. Might not certain changes be made in the house at Munster Court in reference to—well, to a nursery. A room to be baby's own she had called it. She had thus made herself understood, though she had not said the word which seemed to imply a plural number. "But you'll be down at Manor Cross," said Lord George.

"You don't mean to keep me there always."

"No, not always; but when you come back to London it may be to another house."

"You don't mean St. James' Square?" But that was just what he did mean. "I hope we shan't have to live in that prison."

"It's one of the best houses in London," said Lord George, with a certain amount of family pride. "It used to be, at least, before the rich tradesmen had built all those palaces at South Kensington."

"It's dreadfully dingy."

"Because it has not been painted lately. Brotherton has never done anything like anybody else."

"Couldn't we keep this and let that place?"

"Not very well. My father and grandfather, and great-grandfather lived there. I think we had better wait a bit and see." Then she felt sure that the glory was coming. Lord George would never have spoken of her living in St. James' Square had he not felt almost certain that it would soon come about.

Early in February her father came to town, and he was quite certain. "The poor wretch can't speak articulately," he said.

"Who says so, papa?"

"I have taken care to find out the truth. What a life! And what a death! He is there all alone. Nobody ever sees him but an Italian doctor. If it's a boy, my dear, he will be my lord as soon as he's born; or for the matter of that, if it's a girl she will be my lady."

"I wish it wasn't so."

"You must take it all as God sends it, Mary."

"They've talked about it till I'm sick of it," said Mary angrily. Then she checked herself and added—"I don't mean you, papa; but at Manor Cross they all flatter me now, because that poor man is dying. If you were me you wouldn't like that."

"You've got to bear it, my dear. It's the way of the world. People at the top of the tree are always flattered. You can't expect that Mary Lovelace and the Marchioness of Brotherton will be treated in the same way."

"Of course it made a difference when I was married."

"But suppose you had married a curate in the neighbourhood."

"I wish I had," said Mary wildly, "and that someone had given him the living of Pugsty." But it all tended in the same direction. She began to feel now that it must be, and must be soon. She would, she told herself, endeavour to do her duty; she would be loving to all who had been kind to her, and kind even to those who had been unkind. To all of them at Manor Cross she would be a real sister,—even to Lady Susanna whom certainly she had not latterly loved. She would forgive everybody,—except one. Adelaide Houghton she never could forgive, but Adelaide Houghton should be her only enemy. It did not occur to her that Jack De Baron had been very nearly as wicked as Adelaide Houghton. She certainly did not intend that Jack De Baron should be one of her enemies.

When she had been in London about a week or two Jack De Baron came to see her. She knew that he had spent his Christmas at Curry Hall, and she knew that Guss Mildmay had also been there. That Guss Mildmay should have accepted such an invitation was natural enough, but she thought that Jack had been very foolish. Why should he have gone to the house when he had known that the girl whom he had promised to marry, but whom he did not intend to marry, was there? And now what was to be the result? She did not think that she could ask him; but she was almost sure that he would tell her.

"I suppose you've been hunting?" she asked.

"Yes; they put up a couple of horses for me, or I couldn't have afforded it."

"She is so good-natured."

"Mrs. Jones! I should think she was; but I'm not quite sure that she intended to be very good-natured to me."

"Why not?" Mary, of course, understood it all; but she could not pretend to understand it, at any rate as yet.

"Oh, I don't know. It was all fair, and I won't complain. She had got Miss Green off her hands, and therefore she wanted something to do. I'm going to exchange, Lady George, into an Indian regiment."

"You're not in earnest."

"Quite in earnest. My wing will be at Aden, at the bottom of the Red Sea, for the next year or two. Aden, I'm told, is a charming place."

"I thought it was hot."

"I like hot places; and as I have got rather sick of society I shall do very well there, because there's none. A fellow can't spend any money, except in soda and brandy. I suppose I shall take to drink."

"Don't talk of yourself in that horrid way, Captain De Baron."

"It won't much matter to any one, for I don't suppose I shall ever come back again. There's a place called Perim, out in the middle of the sea, which will just suit me. They only send one officer there at a time, and there isn't another soul in the place."

"How dreadful!"

"I shall apply to be left there for five years. I shall get through all my troubles by that time."

"I am sure you won't go at all."

"Why not?"

"Because you have got so many friends here."

"Too many, Lady George. Of course you know what Mrs. Jones has been doing?"

"What has she been doing?"

"She tells you everything, I fancy. She has got it all cut and dry. I'm to be married next May, and am to spend the honeymoon at Curry Hall. Of course I'm to leave the army and put the value of my commission into the three per cents. Mr. Jones is to let me have a place called Clover Cottage, down in Gloucestershire, and, I believe, I'm to take a farm and be churchwarden of the parish. After paying my debts we shall have about two hundred a-year, which of course will be ample for Clover Cottage. I don't exactly see how I'm to spend my evenings, but I suppose that will come. It's either that or Perim. Which would you advise?"

"I don't know what I ought to say."

"Of course I might cut my throat."

"I wish you wouldn't talk in that way. If it's all a joke I'll take it as a joke."

"It's no joke at all; it's very serious. Mrs. Jones wants me to marry Guss Mildmay."

"And you are engaged to her?"

"Only on certain conditions,—which conditions are almost impossible."

"What did you say to—Miss Mildmay at Curry Hall?"

"I told her I should go to Perim."

"And what did she say?"

"Like a brick, she offered to go with me, just as the girl offered to eat the potato parings when the man said that there would not be potatoes enough for both. Girls always say that kind of thing, though, when they are taken at their words, they want bonnets and gloves and fur cloaks."

"And you are going to take her?"

"Not unless I decide upon Clover Cottage. No; if I do go to Perim I think that I shall manage to go alone."

"If you don't love her, Captain De Baron, don't marry her."

"There's Giblet doing very well, you know; and I calculate I could spend a good deal of my time at Curry Hall. Perhaps if we made ourselves useful, they would ask us to Killancodlem. I should manage to be a sort of factotum to old Jones. Don't you think it would suit me?"

"You can't be serious about it."

"Upon my soul, Lady George, I never was so serious in my life. Do you think that I mean nothing because I laugh at myself? You know I don't love her."

"Then say so, and have done with it."

"That is so easy to suggest, but so impossible to do. How is a man to tell a girl that he doesn't love her after such an acquaintance as I have had with Guss Mildmay? I have tried to do so, but I couldn't do it. There are men, I believe, hard enough even for that; and things are changed now, and the affectation of chivalry has gone bye. Women ask men to marry them, and the men laugh and refuse."

"Don't say that, Captain De Baron."

"I'm told that's the way the thing is done now; but I've no strength myself, and I'm not up to it. I'm not at all joking. I think I shall exchange and go away. I've brought my pigs to a bad market, but as far as I can see that is the best that is left for me." Mary could only say that his friends would be very—very sorry to lose him, but that in her opinion anything would be better than marrying a girl whom he did not love.

Courtesies at this time were showered upon Lady George from all sides. Old Lady Brabazon, to whom she had hardly spoken, wrote to her at great length. Mrs. Patmore Green came to her on purpose to talk about her daughter's marriage. "We are very much pleased of course," said Mrs. Green. "It was altogether a love affair, and the young people are so fond of each other! I do so hope you and she will be friends. Of course her position is not so brilliant as yours, but still it is very good. Poor dear Lord Gossling"—whom, by the bye, Mrs. Patmore Green had never seen—"is failing very much; he is a martyr to the gout, and then he is so imprudent."

Lady Mary smiled and was civil, but did not make any promise of peculiarly intimate friendship. Lady Selina Protest came to her with a long story of her wrongs, and a petition that she would take the Fleabody side in the coming contest. It was in vain that she declared that she had no opinion whatsoever as to the rights of women; a marchioness she was told would be bound to have opinions, or, at any rate, would be bound to subscribe.

But the courtesy which surprised and annoyed her most was a visit from Adelaide Houghton. She came up to London for a week about the end of February, and had the hardihood to present herself at the house in Munster Court. This was an insult which Mary had by no means expected; she had therefore failed to guard herself against it by any special instructions to her servant. And thus Mrs. Houghton, the woman who had written love-letters to her husband, was shown up into her drawing-room before she had the means of escaping. When the name was announced she felt that she was trembling. There came across her a feeling that she was utterly incapable of behaving properly in such an emergency. She knew that she blushed up to the roots of her hair. She got up from her seat as she heard the name announced, and then seated herself again before her visitor had entered the room. She did resolve that nothing on earth should induce her to shake hands with the woman. "My dear Lady George," said Mrs. Houghton, hurrying across the room, "I hope you will let me explain." She had half put out her hand, but had done so in a manner which allowed her to withdraw it without seeming to have had her overture refused.

"I do not know that there is anything to explain," said Mary.

"You will let me sit down?" Mary longed to refuse; but, not quite daring to do so, simply bowed,—upon which Mrs. Houghton did sit down. "You are very angry with me, it seems?"

"Well;—yes, I am."

"And yet what harm have I done you?"

"None in the least—none at all. I never thought that you could do me any harm."

"Is it wise, Lady George, to give importance to a little trifle?"

"I don't know what you call a trifle."

"I had known him before you did; and, though it had not suited me to become his wife, I had always liked him. Then the intimacy sprang up again; but what did it amount to? I believe you read some foolish letter?"

"I did read a letter, and I was perfectly sure that my husband had done nothing, I will not say to justify, but even to excuse the writing of it. I am quite aware, Mrs. Houghton, that it was all on one side."

"Did he say so?"

"You must excuse me if I decline altogether to tell you what he said."

"I am sure he did not say that. But what is the use of talking of it all. Is it necessary, Lady George, that you and I should quarrel about such a thing as that?"

"Quite necessary, Mrs. Houghton."

"Then you must be very fond of quarrelling."

"I never quarrelled with anybody else in my life."

"When you remember how near we are to each other in the country—. I will apologise if you wish it."

"I will remember nothing, and I want no apology. To tell you the truth, I really think that you ought not to have come here."

"It is childish, Lady George, to make so much of it."

"It may be nothing to you. It is a great deal to me. You must excuse me if I say that I really cannot talk to you any more." Then she got up and walked out of the room, leaving Mrs. Houghton among her treasures. In the dining-room she rang the bell and told the servant to open the door when the lady upstairs came down. After a very short pause, the lady upstairs did come down, and walked out to her carriage with an unabashed demeanour.

After much consideration Lady George determined that she must tell her husband what had occurred. She was aware that she had been very uncourteous, and was not sure whether in her anger she had not been carried further than became her. Nothing could, she thought, shake her in her determination to have no further friendly intercourse of any kind with the woman. Not even were her husband to ask her would that be possible. Such a request from him would be almost an insult to her. And no request from anyone else could have any strength, as no one else knew the circumstances of the case. It was not likely that he would have spoken of it, and of her own silence she was quite sure. But how had it come to pass that the woman had had the face to come to her? Could it be that Lord George had instigated her to do so? She never made enquiries of her husband as to where he went and whom he saw. For aught that she knew, he might be in Berkeley Square every day. Then she called to mind Mrs. Houghton's face, with the paint visible on it in the broad day, and her blackened eyebrows, and her great crested helmet of false hair nearly eighteen inches deep, and her affected voice and false manner,—and then she told herself that it was impossible that her husband should like such a creature.

"George," she said to him abruptly, as soon as he came home, "who do you think has been here? Mrs. Houghton has been here." Then came that old frown across his brow; but she did not know at first whether it was occasioned by anger against herself or against Mrs. Houghton. "Don't you think it was very unfortunate?"

"What did she say?"

"She wanted to be friends with me."

"And what did you say?"

"I was very rude to her. I told her that I would never have anything to do with her; and then I left the room, so that she had to get out of the house as she could. Was I not right? You don't want me to know her, do you?"

"Certainly not."

"And I was right."

"Quite right. She must be a very hardened woman."

"Oh George, dear George! You have made me so happy!" Then she jumped up and threw her arms round him. "I never doubted you for a moment—never, never; but I was afraid you might have thought—. I don't know what I was afraid of, but I was a fool. She is a nasty hardened creature, and I do hate her. Don't you see how she covers herself with paint?"

"I haven't seen her for the last three months."

Then she kissed him again and again, foolishly betraying her past fears. "I am almost sorry I bothered you by telling you, only I didn't like to say nothing about it. It might have come out, and you would have thought it odd. How a woman can be so nasty I cannot imagine. But I will never trouble you by talking of her again. Only I have told James that she is not to be let into the house."

Chapter LX.

The Last Of The Baroness.

At this time Dr. Olivia Q. Fleabody had become quite an institution in London. She had obtained full though by no means undisputed possession of the great hall in the Marylebone Road, and was undoubtedly for the moment the Queen of the Disabilities. She lectured twice a week to crowded benches. A seat on the platform on these occasions was considered by all high-minded women to be an honour, and the body of the building was always filled by strongly-visaged spinsters and mutinous wives, who twice a week were worked up by Dr. Fleabody to a full belief that a glorious era was at hand in which woman would be chosen by constituencies, would wag their heads in courts of law, would buy and sell in Capel Court, and have balances at their banker's. It was certainly the case that Dr. Fleabody had made proselytes by the hundred, and disturbed the happiness of many fathers of families.

It may easily be conceived that all this was gall and wormwood to the Baroness Banmann. The Baroness, on her arrival in London, had anticipated the success which this low-bred American female had achieved. It was not simply the honour of the thing,—which was very great and would have been very dear to the Baroness,—but the American Doctor was making a rapid fortune out of the proceeds of the hall. She had on one occasion threatened to strike lecturing unless she were allowed a certain very large percentage on the sum taken at the doors, and the stewards and directors of the Institute had found themselves compelled to give way to her demands. She had consequently lodged herself magnificently at the Langham Hotel, had set up her brougham, in which she always had herself driven to the Institute, and was asked out to dinner three or four times a week; whereas the Baroness was in a very poor condition. She had indeed succeeded in getting herself invited to Mr. De Baron's house, and from time to time raised a little money from those who were unfortunate enough to come in her way. But she was sensible of her own degradation, and at the same time quite assured that as a preacher on women's rights at large she could teach lessons infinitely superior to anything that had come from that impudent but imbecile American.

She had undoubtedly received overtures from the directors of the Institute of whom poor Aunt Ju had for the moment been the spokeswoman, and in these overtures it had been intimated to her that the directors would be happy to remunerate her for her trouble should the money collected at the hall enable them to do so. The Baroness believed that enormous sums had been received, and was loud in assuring all her friends that this popularity had in the first place been produced by her own exertions. At any rate, she was resolved to seek redress at law, and at last had been advised to proceed conjointly against Aunt Ju, Lady Selina Protest, and the bald-headed old gentleman. The business had now been brought into proper form, and the trial was to take place in March.

All this was the cause of much trouble to poor Mary, and of very great vexation to Lord George. When the feud was first becoming furious, an enormous advertisement was issued by Dr. Fleabody's friends, in which her cause was advocated and her claims recapitulated. And to this was appended a list of the nobility, gentry, and people of England who supported the Disabilities generally and her cause in particular. Among these names, which were very numerous, appeared that of Lady George Germain. This might probably have escaped both her notice and her husband's, had not the paper been sent to her, with usual friendly zeal, by old Lady Brabazon. "Oh George," she said, "look here. What right have they to say so? I never patronised anything. I went there once when I came to London first, because Miss Mildmay asked me."

"You should not have gone," said he.

"We have had all that before, and you need not scold me again. There couldn't be any great harm in going to hear a lecture." This occurred just previous to her going down to Manor Cross,—that journey which was to be made for so important an object.

Then Lord George did—just what he ought not to have done. He wrote an angry letter to Miss Fleabody, as he called her, complaining bitterly of the insertion of his wife's name. Dr. Fleabody was quite clever enough to make fresh capital out of this. She withdrew the name, explaining that she had been ordered to do so by the lady's husband, and implying that thereby additional evidence was supplied that the Disabilities of Women were absolutely crushing to the sex in England. Mary, when she saw this,—and the paper did not reach her till she was at Manor Cross,—was violent in her anxiety to write herself, in her own name, and disclaim all disabilities; but her husband by this time had been advised to have nothing further to do with Dr. Fleabody, and Mary was forced to keep her indignation to herself.

But worse than this followed the annoyance of the advertisement. A man came all the way down from London for the purpose of serving Lady George with a subpoena to give evidence at the trial on the part of the Baroness. Lord George was up in London at the time, never having entered the house at Manor Cross, or even the park, since his visit to Italy. The consternation of the ladies may be imagined. Poor Mary was certainly not in a condition to go into a court of law, and would be less so on the day fixed for the trial. And yet this awful document seemed to her and to her sisters-in-law to be so imperative as to admit of no escape. It was in vain that Lady Sarah, with considerable circumlocution, endeavoured to explain to the messenger the true state of the case. The man could simply say that he was only a messenger, and had now done his work. Looked at in any light, the thing was very terrible. Lord George might probably even yet be able to run away with her to some obscure corner of the continent in which messengers from the Queen's judges would not be able to find her; and she might perhaps bear the journey without injury. But then what would become of a baby—perhaps of a Popenjoy—so born? There were many who still thought that the Marquis would go before the baby came; and, in that case, the baby would at once be a Popenjoy. What a condition was this for a Marchioness to be in at the moment of the birth of her eldest child! "But I don't know anything about the nasty women!" said Mary, through her tears.

"It is such a pity that you should ever have gone," said Lady Susanna, shaking her head.

"It wasn't wicked to go," said Mary, "and I won't be scolded about it any more. You went to a lecture yourself when you were in town, and they might just as well have sent for you."

Lady Sarah promised her that she should not be scolded, and was very keen in thinking what steps had better be taken. Mary wished to run off to the deanery at once, but was told that she had better not do so till an answer had come to the letter which was of course written by that day's post to Lord George. There were still ten days to the trial, and twenty days, by computation, to the great event. There were, of course, various letters written to Lord George. Lady Sarah wrote very sensibly, suggesting that he should go to Mr. Stokes, the family lawyer. Lady Susanna was full of the original sin of that unfortunate visit to the Disabilities. She was, however, of opinion that if Mary was concealed in a certain room at Manor Cross, which might she thought be sufficiently warmed and ventilated for health, the judges of the Queen's Bench would never be able to find her. The baby in that case would have been born at Manor Cross, and posterity would know nothing about the room. Mary's letter was almost hysterically miserable. She knew nothing about the horrid people. What did they want her to say? All she had done was to go to a lecture, and to give the wicked woman a guinea. Wouldn't George come and take her away. She wouldn't care where she went. Nothing on earth should make her go up and stand before the judges. It was, she said, very cruel, and she did hope that George would come to her at once. If he didn't come she thought that she would die.

Nothing, of course, was said to the Marchioness, but it was found impossible to keep the matter from Mrs. Toff. Mrs. Toff was of opinion that the bit of paper should be burned, and that no further notice should be taken of the matter at all. "If they don't go they has to pay £10," said Mrs. Toff with great authority,—Mrs. Toff remembering that a brother of hers, who had "forgotten himself in liquor" at the Brotherton assizes, had been fined £10 for not answering to his name as a juryman. "And then they don't really have to pay it," said Mrs. Toff, who remembered also that the good-natured judge had not at last exacted the penalty. But Lady Sarah could not look at the matter in that light. She was sure that if a witness were really wanted, that witness could not escape by paying a fine.

The next morning there came a heartrending letter from Aunt Ju. She was very sorry that Lady George should have been so troubled;—but then let them think of her trouble, of her misery! She was quite sure that it would kill her,—and it would certainly ruin her. That odious Baroness had summoned everybody that had ever befriended her. Captain De Baron had been summoned, and the Marquis, and Mrs. Montacute Jones. And the whole expense, according to Aunt Ju, would fall upon her; for it seemed to be the opinion of the lawyers that she had hired the Baroness. Then she said some very severe things against the Disabilities generally. There was that woman Fleabody making a fortune in their hall, and would take none of this expense upon herself. She thought that such things should be left to men, who after all were not so mean as women;—so, at least, said Aunt Ju.

And then there was new cause for wonderment. Lord Brotherton had been summoned, and would Lord Brotherton come? They all believed that he was dying, and, if so, surely he could not be made to come. "But is it not horrible," said Lady Susanna, "that people of rank should be made subject to such an annoyance! If anybody can summon anybody, nobody can ever be sure of herself!"

On the next morning Lord George himself came down to Brotherton, and Mary with a carriage full of precautions, was sent into the deanery to meet him. The Marchioness discovered that the journey was to be made, and was full of misgivings and full of enquiries. In her present condition, the mother expectant ought not to be allowed to make any journey at all. The Marchioness remembered how Sir Henry had told her, before Popenjoy was born, that all carriage exercise was bad. And why should she go to the deanery? Who could say whether the Dean would let her come away again? What a feather it would be in the Dean's cap if the next Popenjoy were born at the deanery. It was explained to her that in no other way could she see her husband. Then the poor old woman was once more loud in denouncing the misconduct of her youngest son to the head of the family.

Mary made the journey in perfect safety, and then was able to tell her father the whole story. "I never heard of anything so absurd in my life," said the Dean.

"I suppose I must go, papa?"

"Not a yard."

"But won't they come and fetch me?"

"Fetch you? No."

"Does it mean nothing."

"Very little. They won't attempt to examine half the people they have summoned. That Baroness probably thinks that she will get money out of you. If the worst comes to the worst, you must send a medical certificate."

"Will that do?"

"Of course it will. When George is here we will get Dr. Loftly, and he will make it straight for us. You need not trouble yourself about it at all. Those women at Manor Cross are old enough to have known better."

Lord George came and was very angry. He quite agreed as to Dr. Loftly, who was sent for, and who did give a certificate,—and who took upon himself to assure Lady George that all the judges in the land could not enforce her attendance as long as she had that certificate in her hands. But Lord George was vexed beyond measure that his wife's name should have been called in question, and could not refrain himself from a cross word or two. "It was so imprudent your going to such a place!"

"Oh George, are we to have that all again?"

"Why shouldn't she have gone?" asked the Dean.

"Are you in favour of rights of women?"

"Not particularly;—though if there be any rights which they haven't got, I thoroughly wish that they might get them. I certainly don't believe in the Baroness Banmann, nor yet in Dr. Fleabody; but I don't think they could have been wrong in going in good company to hear what a crazy old woman might have to say."

"It was very foolish," said Lord George. "See what has come of it!"

"How could I tell, George? I thought you had promised that you wouldn't scold any more. Nasty fat old woman! I'm sure I didn't want to hear her." Then Lord George went back to town with the medical certificate in his pocket, and Mary, being in her present condition, afraid of the authorities, was unable to stay and be happy even for one evening with her father.

During the month the Disabilities created a considerable interest throughout London, of which Dr. Fleabody reaped the full advantage. The Baroness was so loud in her clamours that she forced the question of the Disabilities on the public mind generally, and the result was that the world flocked to the Institute. The Baroness, as she heard of this, became louder and louder. It was not this that she wanted. Those who wished to sympathise with her should send her money,—not go to the hall to hear that loud imbecile American female! The Baroness, when she desired to be-little the doctor, always called her a female. And the Baroness, though in truth she was not personally attractive, did contrive to surround herself with supporters, and in these days moved into comfortable lodgings in Wigmore Street. Very few were heard to speak in her favour, but they who contributed to the relief of her necessities were many. It was found to be almost impossible to escape from her without leaving some amount of money in her hands. And then, in a happy hour, she came at last across an old gentleman who did appreciate her and her wrongs. How it was that she got an introduction to Mr. Philogunac Coelebs was not, I think, ever known. It is not improbable that having heard of his soft heart, his peculiar propensities, and his wealth, she contrived to introduce herself. It was, however, suddenly understood that Mr. Philogunac Coelebs, who was a bachelor and very rich, had taken her by the hand, and intended to bear all the expenses of the trial. It was after the general intimation which had been made to the world in this matter that the summons for Lady Mary had been sent down to Manor Cross.

And now in these halcyon days of March the Baroness also had her brougham and was to be seen everywhere. How she did work! The attornies who had the case in hands, found themselves unable to secure themselves against her. She insisted on seeing the barristers, and absolutely did work her way into the chambers of that discreet junior Mr. Stuffenruff. She was full of her case, full of her coming triumph. She would teach women like Miss Julia Mildmay and Lady Selina Protest what it was to bamboozle a Baroness of the Holy Roman Empire! And as for the American female—.

"You'll put her pipe out," suggested Mr. Philogunac Coelebs, who was not superior to a mild joke.

"Stop her from piping altogether in dis contry," said the Baroness, who in the midst of her wrath and zeal and labour was superior to all jokes.

Two days before that fixed for the trial there fell a great blow upon those who were interested in the matter;—a blow that was heavy on Mr. Coelebs but heavier still on the attornies. The Baroness had taken herself off, and when enquiries were made it was found that she was at Madrid. Mr. Snape, one of the lawyers, was the person who first informed Mr. Coelebs, and did so in a manner which clearly implied that he expected Mr. Coelebs to pay the bill. Then Mr. Snape encountered a terrible disappointment, and Mr. Coelebs was driven to confess his own disgrace. He had, he said, never undertaken to pay the cost of the trial, but he had, unfortunately, given the lady a thousand pounds to enable her to pay the expenses herself. Mr. Snape, expostulated, and, later on, urged with much persistency, that Mr. Coelebs had more than once attended in person at the office of Messrs. Snape and Cashett. But in this matter the lawyers did not prevail. They had taken their orders from the lady, and must look to the lady for payment. They who best knew Mr. Philogunac Coelebs thought that he had escaped cheaply, as there had been many fears that he should make the Baroness altogether his own.

"I am so glad she has gone," said Mary, when she heard the story. "I should never have felt safe while that woman was in the country. I'm quite sure of one thing. I'll never have anything more to do with disabilities. George need not be afraid about that."

Chapter LXI.

The News Comes Home.

During those last days of the glory of the Baroness, when she was driving about London under the auspices of Philogunac Coelebs in her private brougham and talking to everyone of the certainty of her coming success, Lord George Germain was not in London either to hear or to see what was going on. He had gone again to Naples, having received a letter from the British Consul there telling him that his brother was certainly dying. The reader will understand that he must have been most unwilling to take this journey. He at first refused to do so, alleging that his brother's conduct to him had severed all ties between them; but at last he allowed himself to be persuaded by the joint efforts of Mr. Knox, Mr. Stokes, and Lady Sarah, who actually came up to London herself for the purpose of inducing him to take the journey. "He is not only your brother," said Lady Sarah, "but the head of your family as well. It is not for the honour of the family that he should pass away without having someone belonging to him at the last moment." When Lord George argued that he would in all probability be too late, Lady Sarah explained that the last moments of a Marquis of

Brotherton could not have come as long as his body was above ground.

So urged the poor man started again, and found his brother still alive, but senseless. This was towards the end of March, and it is hoped that the reader will remember the event which was to take place on the 1st of April. The coincidence of the two things added of course very greatly to his annoyance. Telegrams might come to him twice a-day, but no telegram could bring him back in a flash when the moment of peril should arrive, or enable him to enjoy the rapture of standing at his wife's bedside when that peril should be over. He felt as he went away from his brother's villa to the nearest hotel,—for he would not sleep nor eat in the villa,—that he was a man marked out for misfortune. When he returned to the villa on the next morning the Marquis of Brotherton was no more. His Lordship had died in the 44th year of his age, on the 30th March, 187—.

The Marquis of Brotherton was dead, and Lord George Germain was Marquis of Brotherton, and would be so called by all the world as soon as his brother was decently hidden under the ground. It concerns our story now to say that Mary Lovelace was Marchioness of Brotherton, and that the Dean of Brotherton was the father-in-law of a Marquis, and would, in all probability, be the progenitor of a long line of Marquises. Lord George, as soon as the event was known, caused telegrams to be sent to Mr. Knox, to Lady Sarah,—and to the Dean. He had hesitated about the last, but his better nature at last prevailed. He was well aware that no one was so anxious as the Dean, and though he disliked and condemned the Dean's anxiety, he remembered that the Dean had at any rate been a loving father to his wife, and a very liberal father-in-law.

Mr. Knox, when he received the news, went at once to Mr. Stokes, and the two gentlemen were not long in agreeing that a very troublesome and useless person had been removed out of the world. "Oh, yes; there's a will," said Mr. Stokes in answer to an enquiry from Mr. Knox, "made while he was in

London the other day, just before he started,—as bad a will as a man could make; but he couldn't do very much harm. Every acre was entailed."

"How about the house in town?" asked Mr. Knox.

"Entailed on the baby about to be born, if he happens to be a boy."

"He didn't spend his income?" suggested Mr. Knox.

"He muddled a lot of money away; but since the coal came up he couldn't spend it all, I should say."

"Who gets it?" asked Mr. Knox, laughing.

"We shall see that when the will is read," said the attorney with a smile.

The news was brought out to Lady Sarah as quick as the very wretched pony which served for the Brotherton telegraph express could bring it. The hour which was lost in getting the pony ready, perhaps, did not signify much. Lady Sarah, at the moment, was busy with her needle, and her sisters were with her. "What is it?" said Lady Susanna, jumping up. Lady Sarah, with cruel delay, kept the telegram for a moment in her hand. "Do open it," said Lady Amelia; "is it from George? Pray open it;—pray do!" Lady Sarah, feeling certain of the contents of the envelope, and knowing the importance of the news, slowly opened the cover. "It is all over," she said, "Poor Brotherton!" Lady Amelia burst into tears. "He was never so very unkind to me," said Lady Susanna, with her handkerchief up to her eyes. "I cannot say that he was good to me," said Lady Sarah, "but it may be that I was hard to him. May God Almighty forgive him all that he did amiss!"

Then there was a consultation held, and it was decided that Mary and the Marchioness must both be told at once. "Mamma will be dreadfully cut up," said Lady Susanna. Then Lady Amelia suggested that their mother's attention should be at once drawn off to Mary's condition, for the Marchioness at this time was much worried in her feelings about Mary,—as to whom it now seemed that some error must have been made. The calculations had not been altogether exact. So at least, judging from Mary's condition, they all now thought at Manor Cross. Mrs. Toff was quite sure, and the Marchioness was perplexed in her memory as to certain positive information which had been whispered into her ear by Sir Henry just before the birth of that unfortunate Popenjoy, who was now lying dead as Lord Brotherton at Naples.

The telegram had arrived in the afternoon at the hour in which Mary was accustomed to sit in the easy chair with the Marchioness. The penalty had now been reduced to an hour a day, and this, as it happened, was the hour. The Marchioness had been wandering a good deal in her mind. From time to time she expressed her opinion that Brotherton would get well and would come back; and she would then tell Mary how she ought to urge her husband to behave well to his elder brother, always asserting that George had been stiff-necked and perverse. But in the midst of all this she would refer every minute to Mary's coming baby as the coming Popenjoy—not a possible Popenjoy at some future time, but the immediate Popenjoy of the hour,—to be born a Popenjoy! Poor Mary, in answer to all this, would agree with everything. She never contradicted the old lady, but sat longing that the hour might come to an end.

Lady Sarah entered the room, followed by her two sisters. "Is there any news?" asked Mary.

"Has Brotherton come back?" demanded the Marchioness.

"Dear mamma!" said Lady Sarah;—and she went up and knelt down before her mother and took her hand.

"Where is he?" asked the Marchioness.

"Dear mamma! He has gone away,—beyond all trouble."

"Who has gone away?"

"Brotherton is—dead, mamma. This is a telegram from George." The old woman looked bewildered, as though she did not as yet quite comprehend what had been said to her. "You know," continued Lady Sarah, "that he was so ill that we all expected this."

"Expected what?"

"That my brother could not live."

"Where is George? What has George done? If George had gone to him—. Oh me! Dead! He is not dead! And what has become of the child?"

"You should think of Mary, mamma."

"My dear, of course I think of you. I am thinking of nothing else. I should say it would be Friday. Sarah,—you don't mean to say that Brotherton is—dead?" Lady Sarah merely pressed her mother's hand and looked into the old lady's face. "Why did not they let me go to him? And is Popenjoy dead also?"

"Dear mamma, don't you remember?" said Lady Susanna.

"Yes; I remember. George was determined it should be so. Ah me!—ah me! Why should I have lived to hear this!" After that it was in vain that they told her of Mary and of the baby that was about to be born. She wept herself into hysterics,—was taken away and put to bed; and then soon wept herself asleep.

Mary during all this had said not a word. She had felt that the moment of her exaltation,—the moment in which she had become the mistress of the house and of everything around it,—was not a time in which she could dare even to speak to the bereaved mother. But when the two younger sisters had gone away with the Marchioness, she asked after her husband. Then Lady Sarah showed her the telegram in which Lord George, after communicating the death of his brother, had simply said that he should himself return home as quickly as possible. "It has come very quick," said Lady Sarah.

"What has come!"

"Your position, Mary. I hope,—I hope you will bear it well."

"I hope so," said Mary, almost sullenly. But she was awestruck, and not sullen.

"It will all be yours now,—the rank, the wealth, the position, the power of spending money, and tribes of friends anxious to share your prosperity. Hitherto you have only seen the gloom of this place, which to you has of course been dull. Now it will be lighted up, and you can make it gay enough."

"This is not a time to think of gaiety," said Mary.

"Poor Brotherton was nothing to you. I do not think you ever saw him."

"Never."

"He was nothing to you. You cannot mourn."

"I do mourn. I wish he had lived. I wish the boy had lived. If you have thought that I wanted all this, you have done me wrong. I have wanted nothing but to have George to live with me. If anybody thinks that I married him because all this might come,—oh, they do not know me."

"I know you, Mary."

"Then you will not believe that."

"I do not believe it. I have never believed it. I know that you are good and disinterested and true of heart. I have loved you dearly and more dearly as I have seen you every day. But Mary, you are fond of what the world calls—pleasure."

"Yes," said Mary, after a pause, "I am fond of pleasure. Why not? I hope I am not fond of doing harm to anyone."

"If you will only remember how great are your duties. You may have children to whom you may do harm. You have a husband, who will now have many cares, and to whom much harm may be done. Among women you will be the head of a noble family, and may grace or disgrace them all by your conduct."

"I will never disgrace them," she said proudly.

"Not openly, not manifestly I am sure. Do you think that there are no temptations in your way?"

"Everybody has temptations."

"Who will have more than you? Have you thought that every tenant, every labourer on the estate will have a claim on you?"

"How can I have thought of anything yet?"

"Don't be angry with me, dear, if I bid you think of it. I think of it,—more I know than I ought to do. I have been so placed that I could do but little good and little harm to others than myself. The females of a family such as ours, unless they marry, are very insignificant in the world. You who but a few years ago were a little school girl in Brotherton have now been put over all our heads."

"I didn't want to be put over anybody's head."

"Fortune has done it for you, and your own attractions. But I was going to say that little as has been my power and low as is my condition, I have loved the family and striven to maintain its respectability. There is not, I think, a face on the estate I do not know. I shall have to go now and see them no more."

"Why should you go?"

"It will probably be proper. No married man likes to have his unmarried sisters in his house."

"I shall like you. You shall never go."

"Of course I shall go with mamma and the others. But I would have you sometimes think of me and those I have cared for, and I would have you bear in mind that the Marchioness of Brotherton should have more to do than to amuse herself."

Whatever assurances Mary might have made or have declined to make in answer to this were stopped by the entrance of a servant, who came to inform Lady George that her father was below. The Dean too had received his telegram, and had at once ridden over to greet the new Marchioness of Brotherton.

Of all those who first heard the news, the Dean's feelings were by far the strongest. It cannot be said of any of the Germains that there was sincere and abiding grief at the death of the late Marquis. The poor mother was in such a state, was mentally so weak, that she was in truth no longer capable of strong grief or strong joy. And the man had been, not only so bad but so injurious also, to all connected with him,—had contrived of late to make his whole family so uncomfortable,— that he had worn out even that enduring love which comes of custom. He had been a blister to them,—assuring them constantly that he would ever be a blister; and they could not weep in their hearts because the blister was removed. But neither did they rejoice. Mary, when, in her simple language, she had said that she did not want it, had spoken the plain truth. Munster Court, with her husband's love and the power to go to Mrs. Jones' parties, sufficed for her ambition. That her husband should be gentle with her, should caress her as well as love her, was all the world to her. She feared rather than coveted the title of Marchioness, and dreaded that gloomy house in the Square with all her heart. But to the Dean the triumph was a triumph indeed and the joy was a joy! He had set his heart upon it from the first moment in which Lord George had been spoken of as a suitor for his daughter's hand,—looking forward to it with the assured hope of a very sanguine man. The late Marquis had been much younger than he, but he calculated that his own life had been wholesome while that of the Marquis was the reverse. Then had come the tidings of the Marquis' marriage. That had been bad;—but he had again told himself how probable it was that the Marquis should have no son. And then the Lord had brought home a son. All suddenly there had come to him the tidings that a brat called Popenjoy,—a brat who in life would crush all his hopes,—was already in the house at Manor Cross! He would not for a moment believe in the brat. He would prove that the boy was not Popenjoy, though he should have to spend his last shilling in doing so. He had set his heart upon the prize, and he would allow nothing to stand in his way.

And now the prize had come before his daughter had been two years married, before the grandchild was born on whose head was to be accumulated all these honours! There was no longer any doubt. The Marquis was gone, and that false Popenjoy was gone; and his daughter was the wife of the reigning Lord, and the child,—his grandchild,—was about to be born. He was sure that the child would be a boy! But even were a girl the eldest, there would be time enough for boys after that. There surely would be a real Popenjoy before long.

And what was he to gain,—he himself? He often asked himself the question, but could always answer it satisfactorily. He had risen above his father's station by his own intellect and industry so high as to be able to exalt his daughter among the highest in the land. He could hardly have become a Marquis himself. That career could not have been open to him; but a sufficiency of the sweets of the peerage would be his own if he could see his daughter a Marchioness. And now that was her rank. Fate could not take it away from her. Though Lord George were to die to-morrow, she would still be a Marchioness, and the coming boy, his grandson, would be the Marquis. He himself was young for his age. He might yet live to hear his grandson make a speech in the House of Commons as Lord Popenjoy.

He had been out about the city and received the telegram at three o'clock. He felt at the moment intensely grateful to Lord George for having sent it;—as he would have been full of wrath had none been sent to him. There was no reference to "Poor Brotherton!" on his tongue; no reference to "Poor Brotherton!" in his heart. The man had grossly maligned his daughter to his own ears, had insulted him with bitter malignity, and was his enemy. He did not pretend to himself that he felt either sorrow or pity. The man had been a wretch and his enemy and was now dead; and he was thoroughly glad that the wretch was out of his way. "Marchioness of Brotherton!" he said to himself, as he rested for a few minutes alone in his study. He stood with his hands in his pockets, looking up at the ceiling, and realizing it all. Yes; all that was quite true which had been said to himself more than once. He had begun his life as a stable-boy. He could remember the time when his father touched his hat to everybody that came into the yard. Nevertheless he was Dean of Brotherton,—and so much a Dean as to have got the better of all enemies in the Close. And his daughter was Marchioness of Brotherton. She would be Mary to him, and would administer to his little comforts when men descended from the comrades of William the Conqueror would treat her with semi-regal respect. He told himself that he was sure of his daughter.

Then he ordered his horse, and started off to ride to Manor Cross. He did not doubt but that she knew it already, but still it was necessary that she should hear it from his lips and he from hers. As he rode proudly beneath the Manor Cross oaks he told himself again and again that they would all belong to his grandson.

When the Dean was announced Mary almost feared to see him,—or rather feared that expression of triumph which would certainly be made both by his words and manner. All that Lady Sarah had said had entered into her mind. There were duties incumbent on her which would be very heavy, for which she felt that she could hardly be fit,—and the first of these duties was to abstain from pride as to her own station in life. But her father she knew would be very proud, and would almost demand pride from her. She hurried down to him nevertheless. Were she ten times a Marchioness, next to her husband her care would be due to him. What daughter had ever been beloved more tenderly than she? Administer to him! Oh yes, she would do that as she had always done. She rushed into his arms in the little parlour and then burst into tears.

"My girl," he said, "I congratulate you."

"No;—no, no."

"Yes, yes, yes. Is it not better in all ways that it should be so? I do congratulate you. Hold up your head, dear, and bear it well."

"Oh, papa, I shall never bear it well."

"No woman that was ever born has, I believe, borne it better than you will. No woman was ever more fit to grace a high position. My own girl!"

"Yes, papa, your own girl. But I wish,—I wish—"

"All that I have wished has come about." She shuddered as she heard these words, remembering that two deaths had been necessary for this fruition of his desires. But he repeated his words. "All that I have wished has come about. And, Mary, let me tell you this;—you should in no wise be afraid of it, nor should you allow yourself to think of it as though there were anything to be regretted. Which do you believe would make the better peer; your husband or that man who has died?"

"Of course George is ten times the best."

"Otherwise he would be very bad. But no degree of comparison would express the difference. Your husband will add an honour to his rank." She took his hand and kissed it as he said this,—which certainly would not have been said had not that telegram come direct to the deanery. "And, looking to the future, which would probably make the better peer in coming years;— the child born of that man and woman, and bred by them as they would have bred it, or your child,—yours and your husband's? And here, in the country,—from which lord would the tenants receive the stricter justice, and the people the more enduring kindness? Don't you know that he disgraced his order, and that the woman was unfit to bear the name which rightly or wrongly she had assumed? You will be fit."

"No, papa."

"Excuse me, dear. I am praising myself rather than you when I say,—yes. But though I praise myself it is a matter as to which I have no shadow of doubt. There can be nothing to regret,—no cause for sorrow. With the inmates of this house custom demands the decency of outward mourning;—but there can be no grief of heart. The man was a wild beast, destroying everybody and everything that came near him. Only think how he treated your husband."

"He is dead, papa!"

"I thank God that he has gone. I cannot bring myself to lie about it. I hate such lying. To me it is unmanly. Grief or joy, regrets or satisfaction, when expressed, should always be true. It is a grand thing to rise in the world. The ambition to do so is the very salt of the earth. It is the parent of all enterprise, and the cause of all improvement. They who know no such ambition are savages and remain savage. As far as I can see, among us Englishmen such ambition is healthily and happily almost universal, and on that account we stand high among the citizens of the world. But, owing to false teaching, men are afraid to own aloud a truth which is known to their own hearts. I am not afraid to do so and I would not have you afraid. I am proud that by one step after another I have been able so to place you and so to form you that you should have been found worthy of rank much higher than my own. And I would have you proud also and equally ambitious for your child. Let him be the Duke of Brotherton. Let him be brought up to be one of England's statesmen, if God shall give him intellect for the work. Let him be seen with the George and Garter, and be known throughout Europe as one of England's worthiest worthies. Though not born as yet his career should already be a care to you. And that he may be great you should rejoice that you yourself are great already."

After that he went away, leaving messages for Lord George and the family. He bade her tell Lady Sarah that he would not intrude on the present occasion, but that he hoped to be allowed to see the ladies of the family very shortly after the funeral.

Poor Mary could not but be bewildered by the difference of the two lessons she had received on this the first day of her assured honours. And she was the more perplexed because both her instructors had appeared to her to be right in their teaching. The pagan exaltation of her father at the death of his enemy she could put on one side, excusing it by the remembrance of the terrible insult which she knew that he had received. But the upshot of his philosophy she did receive as true, and she declared to herself that she would harbour in her heart of hearts the lessons which he had given her as to her own child, lessons which must be noble as they tended to the well-being of the world at large. To make her child able to do good to others, to assist in making him able and anxious to do so,—to train him from the first in that way,—what wish could be more worthy of a mother than this? But yet the humility and homely carefulness inculcated by Lady Sarah,—was not that lesson also true? Assuredly yes! And yet how should she combine the two?

She was unaware that within herself there was a power, a certain intellectual alembic of which she was quite unconscious, by which she could distil the good of each, and quietly leave the residuum behind her as being of no moment.

Chapter LXII.

The Will.

Lord George came back to England as quick as the trains would carry him, and with him came the sad and mournful burden which had to be deposited in the vaults of the parish church at Manor Cross. There must be a decent tombstone now that the life was gone, with decent words upon it and a decent effigy,—even though there had been nothing decent in the man's life. The long line of past Marquises must be perpetuated, and Frederic Augustus, the tenth peer of the name, must be made to lie with the others. Lord George, therefore,—for he was still Lord George till after the funeral,—travelled with his sad burden, some deputy undertaker having special charge of it, and rested for a few hours in London. Mr. Knox met him in Mr. Stokes' chambers, and there he learned that his brother, who had made many wills in his time, had made one last will just before he left London, after his return from Rudham Park. Mr. Stokes took him aside and told him that he would find the will to be unfavourable. "I thought the property was entailed," said Lord George very calmly. Mr. Stokes assented, with many assurances as to the impregnability of the family acres and the family houses; but added that there was money, and that the furniture had belonged to the late Marquis to dispose of as he pleased. "It is a matter of no consequence," said Lord George,—whom the loss of the money and furniture did not in truth at all vex.

Early on the following morning he went down to Brotherton, leaving the undertakers to follow him as quickly as they might. He could enter the house now, and to him as he was driven home under the oaks no doubt there came some idea of his own possession of them. But the idea was much less vivid than the Dean's, and was chiefly confined to the recollection that no one could now turn him out of the home in which he had been born and in which his mother and sisters and wife were living. Had his elder brother been a man of whom he could have been proud, I almost think he would have been more contented as a younger brother. "It is over at last" were the first words he said to his wife, not finding it to be more important that his greatness was beginning than that his humiliation should be brought to an end.

The funeral took place with all the state that undertakers could give to it in a little village, but with no other honours. Lord George was the chief mourner and almost the only one. One or two neighbours came,—Mr. De Baron, from Rudham Park, and such of the farmers as had been long on the land, among them being Mr. Price. But there was one person among the number whom no one had expected. This was Jack De Baron. "He has been mentioned in the will," said Mr. Stokes very gravely to Lord George, "and perhaps you would not object to my asking him to be present." Lord George did not object, though certainly Captain De Baron was the last person whom he would have thought of asking to Manor Cross on any occasion. He was made welcome, however, with a grave courtesy.

"What on earth has brought you here?" said old Mr. De Baron to his cousin.

"Don't in the least know! Got a letter from a lawyer, saying I had better come. Thought everybody was to be here who had ever seen him."

"He hasn't left you money, Jack," said Mr. De Baron.

"What will you give for my chance?" said Jack. But Mr. De Baron, though he was much given to gambling speculations, did not on this occasion make an offer.

After the funeral, which was sadder even than funerals are in general though no tear was shed, the will was read in the library at Manor Cross, Lord George being present, together with Mr. Knox, Mr. Stokes and the two De Barons. The Dean might have wished to be there; but he had written early on that morning an affectionate letter to his son-in-law, excusing himself from being present at the funeral. "I think you know," he had said, "that I would do anything either to promote your welfare or to gratify your feelings, but there had unfortunately been that between me and the late Marquis which would make my attendance seem to be a mockery." He did not go near Manor Cross on that day; but no one knew better than he,—not even Mr. Knox himself, that the dead lord had possessed no power of alienating a stick or a brick upon the property. The will was very short, and the upshot of it was that every shilling of which the Marquis died possessed, together with his house at Como and the furniture contained in the three houses, was left to our old friend Jack De Baron. "I took the liberty," said Mr. Stokes, "to inform his lordship that should he die before his wife, his widow would be entitled to a third of his personal property. He replied that whatever his widow could claim by law, she could get without any act of his. I mention this, as Captain De Baron may perhaps be willing that the widow of the late Marquis may be at once regarded as possessed of a third of the property."

"Quite so," said Jack, who had suddenly become as solemn and funereal as Mr. Stokes himself. He was now engaged to Guss Mildmay with a vengeance!

When the solemnity of the meeting was over, Lord George,—or the Marquis, as he must now be called,— congratulated the young heir with exquisite grace. "I was so severed from my brother of late," he said, "that I had not known of the friendship."

"Never saw him in my life till I met him down at Rudham," said Jack. "I was civil to him there because he seemed to be ill. He sent me once to fetch a ten-pound note. I thought it odd, but I went. After that he seemed to take to me a good deal."

"He took to you to some purpose, Captain De Baron. As to me, I did not want it, and certainly should not have got it. You need not for a moment think that you are robbing us."

"That is so good of you!" said Jack, whose thoughts, however, were too full of Guss Mildmay to allow of any thorough enjoyment of his unexpected prosperity.

"Stokes says that after the widow is paid and the legacy duty there will be eight—and twenty—thousand pounds!" whispered Mr. De Baron to his relative. "By heavens! you are a lucky fellow."

"I am rather lucky."

"It will be fourteen hundred a year, if you only look out for a good investment. A man with ready money at his own disposal can always get five per cent, at least. I never heard of such a fluke in my life."

"It was a fluke, certainly."

"You'll marry now and settle down, I suppose?"

"I suppose I shall," said Jack. "One has to come to that kind of thing at last. I knew when I was going to Rudham that some d—— thing would come of it. Oh,—of course I'm awfully glad. It's sure to come sooner or later, and I suppose I've had my run. I've just seen Stokes, and he says I'm to go to him in about a month's time. I thought I should have got some of it to-morrow?"

"My dear fellow, I can let you have a couple of hundreds, if you want them," said Mr. De Baron, who had never hitherto been induced to advance a shilling when his young cousin had been needy.

Mr. Stokes, Mr. Knox, Mr. De Baron and the heir went away, leaving the family to adjust their own affairs in their new position. Then Mary received a third lecture as she sat leaning upon her husband's shoulder.

"At any rate, you won't have to go away any more," she had said to him. "You have been always away, for ever so long."

"It was you who would go to the deanery when you left London."

"I know that. Of course I wanted to see papa then. I don't want to talk about that any more. Only, you won't go away again?"

"When I do you shall go with me."

"That won't be going away. Going away is taking yourself off,—by yourself."

"Could I help it?"

"I don't know. I could have gone with you. But it's over now, isn't it?"

"I hope so."

"It shall be over. And when this other trouble is done,— you'll go to London then?"

"It will depend on your health, dear."

"I am very well. Why shouldn't I be well? When a month is over,—then you'll go."

"In two months, perhaps."

"That'll be the middle of June. I'm sure I shall be well in three weeks. And where shall we go? We'll go to Munster Court,—shan't we?"

"As soon as the house is ready in St. James' Square, we must go there."

"Oh! George,—I do so hate that house in St. James' Square. I shall never be happy there. It's like a prison."

Then he gave her his lecture. "My love, you should not talk of hating things that are necessary."

"But why is St. James' Square necessary?"

"Because it is the town residence belonging to the family. Munster Court was very well for us as we were before. Indeed, it was much too good, as I felt every hour that I was there. It was more than we could afford without drawing upon your father for assistance."

"But he likes being drawn upon," said Mary. "I don't think there is anything papa likes so much as to be drawn upon."

"That could make no difference to me, my dear. I don't think that as yet you understand money matters."

"I hope I never shall, then."

"I hope you will. It will be your duty to do so. But, as I was saying, the house at Munster Court will be unsuitable to you as Lady Brotherton." On hearing this Mary pouted and made a grimace. "There is a dignity to be borne which, though it may be onerous, must be supported."

"I hate dignity."

"You would not say that if you knew how it vexed me. Could I have chosen for myself personally, perhaps, neither would I have taken this position. I do not think that I am by nature ambitious. But a man is bound to do his duty in that position in which he finds himself placed,—and so is a woman."

"And it will be my duty to live in an ugly house?"

"Perhaps the house may be made less ugly; but to live in it will certainly be a part of your duty. And if you love me, Mary—"

"Do you want me to tell you whether I love you?"

"But, loving me as I know you do, I am sure you will not neglect your duty. Do not say again that you hate your dignity. You must never forget now that you are Marchioness of Brotherton."

"I never shall, George."

"That is right, my dear," he said, omitting to understand the little satire conveyed in her words. "It will come easy to you before long. But I would have all the world feel that you are the mistress of the rank to which you have been raised. Of course, it has been different hitherto," he said, endeavouring in his own mind to excuse the indiscretion of that Kappa-kappa. This lecture also she turned to wholesome food and digested, obtaining from it some strength and throwing off the bombast by which a weaker mind might have been inflated. She understood, at any rate, that St. James' Square must be her doom; but while acknowledging this to herself, she made a little resolution that a good deal would have to be done to the house before it was ready for her reception, and that the doing would require a considerable time.

When she heard the purport of the late lord's will she was much surprised,—more surprised, probably, than Jack himself. Why should a man who was so universally bad,—such a horror,—leave his money to one who was so—so—so good as Jack De Baron. The epithet came to her at last in preference to any other. And what would he do now? George had told her that the sum would be very large, and of course he could marry if he pleased. At any rate he would not go to Perim. The idea that he should go to Perim had made her uncomfortable. Perhaps he had better marry Guss Mildmay. She was not quite all that his wife should be; but he had said that he would do so in certain circumstances. Those circumstances had come round and it was right that he should keep his word. And yet it made her somewhat melancholy to think that he should marry Guss Mildmay.

Very shortly after this, and when she was becoming aware that the event which ought to have taken place on the 1st of April would not be much longer delayed, there came home to her various things containing lectures almost as severe, and perhaps more eloquent than those she had received from her sister, her father, and her husband. There was an infinity of clothes which someone had ordered for her, and on all the things which would bear a mark, there was a coronet. The coronets on the pocket handkerchiefs seemed to be without end. And there was funereal note-paper, on which the black edges were not more visible than the black coronets. And there came invoices to her from the tradesmen, addressed to the Marchioness of Brotherton. And then there came the first letter from her father with her rank and title on the envelope. At first she was almost afraid to open it.

Chapter LXIII.

Popenjoy Is Born—And Christened.

At last, not much above a week after the calculations, in all the glory of the purple of Manor Cross, the new Popenjoy was born. For it was a Popenjoy. The Fates, who had for some time past been unpropitious to the house of Brotherton, now smiled; and Fortune, who had been good to the Dean throughout, remained true to him also in this. The family had a new heir, a real Popenjoy; and the old Marchioness when the baby was shown to her for awhile forgot her sorrows and triumphed with the rest.

The Dean's anxiety had been so great that he had insisted on remaining at the house. It had been found impossible to refuse such a request made at such a time. And now, at last, the ladies at Manor Cross gradually forgave the Dean his offences. To the old dowager they did not mention his name, and she probably forgot his existence; but the Marquis appeared to live with him on terms of perfect friendship, and the sisters succumbed to the circumstances and allowed themselves to talk to him as though he were in truth the father of the reigning Marchioness.

It will be understood that for forty-eight hours before the birth of the child and for forty-eight hours afterwards all Manor Cross was moved in the matter, as though this were the first male child born into the world since the installation of some new golden age. It was a great thing that, after all the recent troubles, a Popenjoy,—a proper Popenjoy,—should be born at Manor Cross of English parents,—a healthy boy,—a bouncing little lord, as Mrs. Toff called him; and the event almost justified the prophetic spirit in which his grandmother spoke of this new advent. "Little angel!" she said. "I know he'll grow up to bring new honours to the family, and do as much for it as his great-grandfather." The great-grandfather spoken of had been an earl, great in borough-mongery, and had been made a marquis by Pitt on the score of his votes. "George," she went on to say, "I do hope there will be bells and bonfires, and that the tenants will be allowed to see him." There were bells and bonfires. But in these days tenants are perhaps busier men than formerly, and have less in them certainly of the spirit of heir-worship than their fathers. But Mr. Price, with his bride, did come down and see the baby; on which occasion the gallant husband bade his wife remember that although they had been married more than twelve months after Lord George, their baby would only be three months younger. Whereupon Mrs. Price boxed her husband's ears,—to the great delight of Mrs. Toff, who was dispensing sherry and cherry brandy in her own sitting-room.

The Dean's joy, though less ecstatic in its expression, was quite as deep and quite as triumphant as that of the Marchioness. When he was admitted for a moment to his daughter's bedside, the tears rolled down his face as he prayed for a blessing for her and her baby. Lady Sarah was in the room, and began to doubt whether she had read the man's character aright. There was an ineffable tenderness about him, a sweetness of manners, a low melody of voice, a gracious solemnity in which piety seemed to be mingled with his love and happiness! That he was an affectionate father had been always known; but now it had to be confessed that he bore himself as though he had sprung from some noble family or been the son and grandson of archbishops. How it would have been with him on such an occasion had his daughter married some vicar of Pugsty, as she had herself once suggested, Lady Sarah did not now stop to enquire. It was reasonable to Lady Sarah that the coming of a Popenjoy should be hailed with greater joy and receive a warmer welcome than the birth of any ordinary baby. "You have had a good deal to bear, Brotherton," he said, holding his noble son-in-law by the hand; "but I think that this will compensate for it all." The tears were still in his eyes, and they were true tears,—tears of most unaffected joy. He had seen the happy day; and as he told himself in words which would have been profane had they been absolutely uttered, he was now ready to die in peace. Not that he meant to die, or thought that he should die. That vision of young Popenjoy, bright as a star, beautiful as a young Apollo, with all the golden glories of the aristocracy upon his head, standing up in the House of Commons and speaking to the world at large with modest but assured eloquence, while he himself occupied some corner in the gallery, was still before his eyes.

After all, who shall say that the man was selfish? He was contented to shine with a reflected honour. Though he was wealthy, he never desired grand doings at the deanery. In his own habits he was simple. The happiness of his life had been to see his daughter happy. His very soul had smiled within him when she had smiled in his presence. But he had been subject to one weakness, which had marred a manliness which would otherwise have been great. He, who should have been proud of the lowliness of his birth, and have known that the brightest feather in his cap was the fact that having been humbly born he had made himself what he was,—he had never ceased to be ashamed of the stable-yard. And as he felt himself to be degraded by that from which he had sprung, so did he think that the only whitewash against such dirt was to be found in the aggrandisement of his daughter and the nobility of her children.

He had, perhaps, been happier than he deserved. He might have sold her to some lord who would have scorned her after a while and despised himself. As it was, the Marquis, who was his son-in-law, was a man whom upon the whole he could well trust. Lord George had indeed made one little error in regard to Mrs. Houghton; but that had passed away and would not probably be repeated.

Of all those closely concerned in the coming of Popenjoy the father seemed to bear the greatness of the occasion with the most modesty. When the Dean congratulated him he simply smiled and expressed a hope that Mary would do well in her troubles. Poor Mary's welfare had hitherto been almost lost in the solicitude for her son. "She can't but do well now," said the Dean, who of all men was the most sanguine. "She is thoroughly healthy, and nothing has been amiss."

"We must be very careful—that's all," said the Marquis. Hitherto he had not brought his tongue to speak of his son as Popenjoy, and did not do so for many a day to come. That an heir had been born was very well; but of late the name of Popenjoy had not been sweet to his ears.

Nothing had gone amiss, and nothing did go amiss. When it was decided that the young Marchioness was to nurse her own baby,—a matter which Mary took into her own hands with a very high tone,—the old Marchioness became again a little troublesome. She had her memories about it all in her own time; how she had not been able to do as Mary was doing. She remembered all that, and how unhappy it had made her; but she remembered also that, had she done so for Popenjoy, Sir Henry would have insisted on three pints of porter. Then Mary rebelled altogether, and talked of drinking nothing but tea,—and would not be brought to consent even to bitter beer without a great deal of trouble. But, through it all, the mother throve and the baby throve; and when the bonfires had been all burned and the bells had been all rung, and the child had been shown to such tenants and adherents and workmen as desired to see him, the family settled down to a feeling of permanent satisfaction.

And then came the christening. Now in spite of the permanent satisfaction there were troubles,—troubles of which the Marquis became conscious very soon, and which he was bound to communicate to his sister,—troubles of which the Dean was unfortunately cognisant, and of which he would speak and with which he would concern him,—much to the annoyance of the Marquis. The will which the late man had made was a serious temporary embarrassment. There was no money with which to do anything. The very bed on which the mother lay with her baby belonged to Jack De Baron. They were absolutely drinking Jack De Baron's port wine, and found, when the matter came to be considered, that they were making butter from Jack De Baron's cows. This could not be long endured. Jack, who was now bound to have a lawyer of his own, had very speedily signified his desire that the family should be put to no inconvenience, and had declared that any suggestion from the Marquis as to the house in town or that in the country would be a law to him. But it was necessary that everything should be valued at once, and either purchased or given up to be sold to those who would purchase it. There was, however, no money, and the Marquis who hated the idea of borrowing was told that he must go among the money-lenders. Then the Dean proposed that he and Miss Tallowax between them might be able to advance what was needed. The Marquis shook his head and said nothing. The proposition had been very distasteful to him.

Then there came another proposition. But it will be right in the first place to explain that the great question of godfather and godmother had received much attention. His Royal Highness the Duke of Windsor had signified through young Lord Brabazon that he would stand as one of the sponsors. The honour had been very great, and had of course been accepted at the moment. The Dean had hankered much after the office, but had abstained from asking with a feeling that should the request be refused a coolness would be engendered which he himself would be unable to repress. It would have filled him with delight to stand in his own cathedral as godfather to the little Popenjoy; but he abstained, and soon heard that the Duke of Dunstable, who was a distant cousin, was to be the colleague of His Royal Highness. He smiled and said nothing of himself,—but thought that his liberality might have been more liberally remembered.

Just at this time Miss Tallowax arrived at the deanery, and on the next morning the Dean came over to Manor Cross with a proposition from that lady. She would bestow twenty thousand pounds immediately upon Popenjoy, and place it for instant use in the father's hands, on condition that she might be allowed to stand as godmother!

"We could not consent to accept the money," said the Marquis very gravely.

"Why not? Mary is her nearest living relative in that generation. As a matter of course, she will leave her money to Mary or her children,—unless she be offended. Nothing is so common as for old people with liberal hearts to give away the money which they must soon leave behind them. A more generous creature than my old aunt doesn't live."

"Very generous; but I am afraid we cannot accept it."

"After all, it is only an empty honour. I would not ask it for myself because I knew how you might be situated. But I really think you might gratify the old lady. Twenty thousand pounds is an important sum, and would be so useful just at present!"

This was true, but the father at the moment declined. The Dean, however, who knew his man, determined that the money should not be lost, and communicated with Mr. Knox. Mr. Knox came down to Manor Cross and held a long consultation at which both the Dean and Lady Sarah were present. "Let it be granted," said the Dean, "that it is a foolish request; but are you justified in refusing twenty thousand pounds offered to Popenjoy?"

"Certainly," said Lady Sarah, "if the twenty thousand pounds is a bribe."

"But it is no bribe, Lady Sarah," said Mr. Knox. "It is not unreasonable that Miss Tallowax should give her money to her great-nephew, nor is it unreasonable that she should ask for this honour, seeing that she is the child's great-aunt." There was a strong opposition to Miss Tallowax's liberal offer,—but in the end it was accepted. The twenty thousand pounds was important, and, after all, the godmother could do no lasting injury to the child. Then it was discovered that the offer was clogged with a further stipulation. The boy must be christened Tallowax! To this father and mother and aunts all objected, swearing that they would not subject their young Popenjoy to so great an injury,— till it was ascertained that the old lady did not insist on Tallowax as a first name, or even as a second. It would suffice that Tallowax should be inserted among others. It was at last decided that the boy should be christened Frederic Augustus Tallowax. Thus he became Frederic Augustus Tallowax Germain,— commonly to be called, by the Queen's courtesy, Lord Popenjoy. The christening itself was not very august, as neither the Royal Duke nor his fellow attended in person. The Dean stood proxy for the one, and Canon Holdenough for the other.

Mary by this time was able to leave her room, and was urgent with her husband to take her up to London. Had she not been very good, and done all that she was told,—except in regard to the porter? And was it not manifest to everybody that she would be able to travel to St. Petersburg and back if such a journey were required? Her husband assured her that she would be knocked up before she got half-way. "But London isn't a tenth part of the distance," said Mary, with a woman's logic. Then it was settled that on May 20th she should be taken with her baby to Munster Court. The following are a few of the letters of congratulation which she received during the period of her convalescence.

"GROSVENOR PLACE.

"MY DEAR MARCHIONESS,—Of course I have heard all about you from time to time, and of course I have been delighted. In the first place, we none of us could grieve very much for that unfortunate brother of yours. Really it was so very much better for everybody that Lord George should have the title and property,—not to talk of all the advantage which the world expects from a young and fascinating Lady Brotherton. I am told that the scaffolding is already up in St. James' Square. I drove through the place the other day, and bethought myself how long it might be before I should receive the honour of a card telling me that on such and such a day the Marchioness of Brotherton would be at home. I should not suggest such a thing but for a dearly kind expression in your last letter.

"But the baby of course is the first object. Pray tell me what sort of a baby it is. Two arms and two legs, I know, for even a young Lord Popenjoy is not allowed to have more; but of his special graces you might send me a catalogue, if you have as yet been allowed pen and paper. I can believe that a good deal of mild tyranny would go on with those estimable sisters, and that Lord George would be anxious. I beg his pardon,—the Marquis. Don't you find this second change in your name very perplexing,—particularly in regard to your linen? All your nice wedding things will have become wrong so soon!

"And now I can impart a secret. There are promises of a little Giblet. Of course it is premature to speak with certainty; but why shouldn't there be a little Giblet as well as a little Popenjoy? Only it won't be a Giblet as long as dear old Lord Gossling can keep the gout out of his stomach. They say that in anger at his son's marriage he has forsworn champagne and confines himself to two bottles of claret a-day. But Giblet, who is the happiest young man of my acquaintance, says that his wife is worth it all.

"And so our friend the Captain is a millionaire! What will he do? Wasn't it an odd will? I couldn't be altogether sorry, for I have a little corner in my heart for the Captain, and would have left him something myself if I had anything to leave. I really think he had better marry his old love. I like justice, and that would be just. He would do it to-morrow if you told him. It might take me a month of hard work. How much is it he gets? I hear such various sums,—from a hundred thousand down to as many hundreds. Nevertheless, the will proves the man to have been mad,—as I always said he was.

"I suppose you'll come to Munster Court till the house in the square be finished. Or will you take some furnished place for a month or two? Munster Court is small; but it was very pretty, and I hope I may see it again.

"Kiss the little Popenjoy for me, and believe me to be,

"Dear Lady Brotherton,

"Your affectionate old friend,

"G. MONTACUTE JONES."

The next was from their friend the Captain himself.

"DEAR LADY BROTHERTON,—I hope it won't be wrong in me to congratulate you on the birth of your baby. I do so with all my heart. I hope that some day, when I am an old fogy, I may be allowed to know him and remind him that in old days I used to know his mother. I was down at Manor Cross the other day; but of course on such an occasion I could not see you. I was sent for because of that strange will; but it was more strange to me that I should so soon find myself in your house. It was not very bright on that occasion.

"I wonder who was surprised most by the will,— you or I?" Mary, when she read this, declared to herself that she ought not to have been surprised at all. How could anyone be surprised by what such a man as that might do?

"He had never seen me, as far as I know, till he met me at Rudham. I did not want his money,—though I was poor enough. I don't know what I shall do now; but I shan't go to Perim.

"Mrs. Jones says you will soon be in town. I hope I may be allowed to call.

"Believe me always,

"Most sincerely yours,

"JOHN DE BARON."

Both those letters gave her pleasure, and both she answered. To all Mrs. Jones' enquiries she gave very full replies, and enjoyed her jokes with her old friend. She hinted that she did not at all intend to hurry the men at St. James' Square, and that certainly she would be found in Munster Court till the men had completed their work. As to what their young friend would do with his money she could say nothing. She could not undertake the commission,—though perhaps that might be best,—and so on. Her note to Jack was very short. She thanked him heartily for his good wishes, and told him the day on which she would be in Munster Court. Then in a postscript she said that she was *"very, very glad"* that he had inherited the late lord's money.

The other letter offended her as much as those two had pleased her. It offended her so much that when she saw the handwriting she would not have read it but that curiosity forbade her to put it on one side. It was from Adelaide Houghton, and as she opened it there was a sparkle of anger in her eyes which perhaps none of her friends had ever seen there. This letter was as follows;—

"DEAR LADY BROTHERTON,—Will you not at length allow bygones to be bygones? What can a poor woman do more than beg pardon and promise never to be naughty again. Is it worth while that we who have known each other so long should quarrel about what really amounted to nothing? It was but a little foolish romance, the echo of a past feeling,—a folly if you will, but innocent. I own my fault and put on the sackcloth and ashes of confession, and, after that, surely you will give me absolution.

"And now, having made my apology, which I trust will be accepted, pray let me congratulate you on all your happiness. The death of your poor brother-in-law of course we have all expected. Mr. Houghton had heard a month before that it was impossible that he should live. Of course, we all feel that the property has fallen into much better hands. And I am so glad that you have a boy. Dear little Popenjoy! Do, do forgive me, so that I may have an opportunity of kissing him. I am, at any rate,

"Your affectionate old friend,

"ADELAIDE HOUGHTON."

Affectionate old friend! Serpent! Toad! Nasty degraded painted Jezebel! Forgive her! No,—never; not though she were on her knees! She was contemptible before, but doubly contemptible in that she could humble herself to make an apology so false, so feeble, and so fawning. It was thus that she regarded her correspondent's letter. Could any woman who knew that love-letters had been written to her husband by another woman forgive that other? We are all conscious of trespassers against ourselves whom we especially bar when we say our prayers. Forgive us our trespasses, as we forgive them who trespass against us,—excepting Jones who has committed the one sin that we will not forgive, that we ought not to forgive. Is there not that sin against the Holy Ghost to justify us? This was the sin that Mary could not forgive. The disgusting woman,—for to Mary the woman was now absolutely disgusting,—had attempted to take from her the heart of her husband! There was a good deal of evidence also against her husband, but that she had quite forgotten. She did not in the least believe that Adelaide was preferred to herself. Her husband had eyes, and could see,—a heart, and could feel,—an understanding, and could perceive. She was not in the least afraid as to her husband. But nothing on earth should induce her to forgive Mrs. Houghton. She thought for a moment whether it was worth her while to show the letter to the Marquis, and then tore it into fragments and threw the pieces away.

Chapter LXIV.

Conclusion.

It is now only necessary that we should collect together the few loose threads of our story which require to be tied lest the pieces should become unravelled in the wear. Of our hero, Lord Popenjoy, it need only be said that when we last heard of him he was a very healthy and rather mischievous boy of five years old, who tyrannised over his two little sisters,—the Lady Mary and the Lady Sarah. Those, however, who look most closely to his character think that they can see the germs of that future success which his grandfather so earnestly desires for him. His mother is quite sure that he will live to be Prime Minister, and has already begun to train him for that office. The house in Munster Court has of course been left, and the Marchioness was on one occasion roused into avowing that the family mansion is preferable. But then the family mansion has been so changed that no Germain of a former generation would know it. The old Dowager who still lives at Manor Cross has never seen the change, but Lady Sarah, who always spends a month or two in town, pretends to disbelieve that it is the same house. One of the events in Mary's life which astonishes her most is the perfect friendship which exists between her and her eldest sister-in-law.

She corresponds regularly with Lady Sarah, and is quite content to have her letters filled with the many ailments and scanty comforts of the poor people on the estate. Lady Sarah is more than content to be able to love the mother of the heir, and she does love her, and the boy too, with all her heart. Now that there is a Popenjoy,—a coming Brotherton, of whom she can be proud, she finds nothing in her own life with which she ought to quarrel. The Ladies Susanna and Amelia also come up to town every year, very greatly to their satisfaction, and are most devoted to the young Marchioness. But the one guest who is honoured above all others in St. James' Square, for whose comfort everything is made to give way, whom not to treat with loving respect is to secure a banishment from the house, whom all the servants are made to regard as a second master, is the Dean. His lines have certainly fallen to him in pleasant places. No woman in London is more courted and more popular than the Marchioness of Brotherton, and consequently the Dean spends his two months in London very comfortably. But perhaps the happiest period of his life is the return visit which his daughter always makes to him for a fortnight during the winter. At this period the Marquis will generally pass a couple of days at the deanery, but for the greater part of the time the father and daughter are alone together. Then he almost worships her. Up in London he allows himself to be worshipped with an exquisite grace. To Mrs. Houghton the Marchioness has never spoken, and on that subject she is inexorable. Friends have interceded, but such intercession has only made matters worse. Of what nature must the woman be who could speak to any friend of such an offence as she had committed? The Marchioness, in refusing to be reconciled, has never alluded to the cause of her anger, but has shown her anger plainly and has persistently refused to abandon it.

The Marquis has become a model member of the House of Lords. He is present at all their sittings, and is indefatigably patient on Committees,—but very rarely speaks. In this way he is gradually gaining weight in the country, and when his hair is quite grey and his step less firm than at present, he will be an authority in Parliament. He is also a pattern landlord, listening to all complaints, and endeavouring in everything to do justice between himself and those who are dependent on him. He is also a pattern father, expecting great things from Popenjoy, and resolving that the child shall be subjected to proper discipline as soon as he is transferred from feminine to virile teaching. In the meantime the Marchioness reigns supreme in the nursery,—as it is proper that she should do.

The husband now never feels himself called upon to remind his wife to support her dignity. Since the dancing of the Kappa-kappa she has never danced, except when on grand occasions she has walked through a quadrille with some selected partner of special rank; and this she does simply as a duty. Nevertheless, in society she is very gay and very joyous. But dancing has been a peril to her, and she avoids it altogether, pleading to such friends as Mrs. Jones that a woman with a lot of babies is out of place capering about a room. Mrs. Jones remembers the Kappa-kappa and says little or nothing on the subject, but she heartily dissents from her friend, and still hopes that there may be a good time coming. The Marquis remembers it all, too, and is thoroughly thankful to his wife, showing his gratitude every now and then by suggesting that Captain and Mrs. De Baron may be asked to dinner. He knows that there is much for which he has to be grateful. Though the name of Mrs. Houghton is never on his tongue, he has not forgotten the way in which he went astray in Berkeley Square,—nor the sweet reticence of his wife, who has never thrown his fault in his teeth since that day on which, at his bidding, she took the letter from his pocket and read it. No man in London is better satisfied with his wife than the Marquis, and perhaps no man in London has better cause to be satisfied.

Yes! Captain De Baron—and his wife—do occasionally dine together in St. James' Square. Whether it was that Mrs.

Montacute Jones was successful in her efforts, or that Guss was enabled to found arguments on Jack's wealth which Jack was unable to oppose, or that a sense of what was due to the lady prevailed with him at last, he did marry her about a twelvemonth after the reading of the will. When the Marchioness came to town,—before Popenjoy was born,—he called, and was allowed to see her. Nothing could be more respectful than was his demeanour then, nor than it had been ever since; and when he announced to his friend, as he did in person, that he was about to be married to Miss Mildmay, she congratulated him with warmth, not saying a word as to past occurrences. But she determined that she would ever be his friend, and for his sake she has become friendly also to his wife. She never really liked poor Guss,—nor perhaps does the Captain. But there have been no quarrels, at any rate, no public quarrels, and Jack has done his duty in a manner that rather surprised his old acquaintances. But he is a much altered man, and is growing fat, and has taken to playing whist at his club before dinner for shilling points. I have always thought that in his heart of hearts he regrets the legacy.

Whether to spite his son, or at the urgent entreaty of his wife and doctors, Lord Gossling has of late been so careful, that the gout has not had a chance of getting into his stomach. Lord Giblet professes himself to be perfectly satisfied with things as they are. He has already four children. He lives in a small house in Green Street, and is a member of the Entomological Society. He is so strict in his attendance that it is thought that he will some day be president. But the old lord does not like this turn in his son's life, and says that the family of De Geese must be going to the dogs when the heir has nothing better to do than to attend to insects.

Mrs. Montacute Jones gives as many parties as ever in Grosvenor Place, and is never so well pleased as when she can get the Marchioness of Brotherton to her house. She is still engaged in matrimonial pursuits, and is at the present moment full of an idea that the minister from Saxony, who is a fine old gentleman of sixty, but a bachelor, may be got to marry Lady Amelia Germain. Mary assures her that there isn't the least chance,—that Amelia would certainly not accept him,—and that an old German of sixty, used to diplomacy all his life, is the last man in the world to be led into difficulties. But Mrs. Jones never gives way in such matters, and has already made the plans for a campaign at Killancodlem next August.

I regret to state that Messrs. Snape and Cashett have persecuted the poor Baroness most cruelly. They have contrived to show that the lady has not only got into their debt, but has also swindled them,—swindled them according to law,—and consequently they have been able to set all the police of the continent on her track. She had no sooner shown her face back in Germany, than they were upon her. For a while she escaped, rushing from one country to another, but at last she was arrested on a platform in Oregon, and is soon about to stand her trial in an English Court. As a good deal of sympathy has been expressed in her favour, and as Mr. Philogunac Coelebs has taken upon himself the expense of her defence, it is confidently hoped in many quarters that no jury will convict her. In the meantime, Dr. Fleabody has, I am told, married a store-keeper in New York, and has settled down into a good mother of a family.

At Manor Cross during the greater portion of the year things go on very much as they used. The Marchioness is still living, and interests herself chiefly in the children of her daughter-in-law,—born, and to be born. But the great days of her life are those in which Popenjoy is brought to her. The young scapegrace will never stay above five minutes with his grandmother, but the old lady is sure that she is regarded by him with a love passing the love of children. At Christmas time, and for a week or two before, and a month or two afterwards, the house is full of company and bright with unaccustomed lights. Lady Sarah puts on her newest silk, and the Marchioness allows herself to be brought into the drawing-room after dinner. But at the end of February the young family flits to town, and then the Manor Cross is as Manor Cross so long has been.

Mr. Price still hunts, and is as popular in the country as ever. He often boasts that although he was married much after the Marquis, the youngest of his three children is older than Lady Mary. But when he does this at home, his ears are always boxed for him.

Of Mr. Groschut it is only necessary to say that he is still at Pugsty, vexing the souls of his parishioners by Sabbatical denunciations.

THE END.

Lightning Source UK Ltd.
Milton Keynes UK
UKOW051821300712

196800UK00001B/78/P